RALPH DARNELL

THE BARONET IS EXPLICIT.

RALPH DARNELL

MEADOWS TAYLOR

ISBN : 978-93-5324-601-3 (HB)

First Published, 1879

Published, 2020

Published by

Facsimile Publisher
12 Pragati Market
Ashok Vihar, Ph-2
Delhi-110052
E-mail: books@facsimilepublisher.com

Printed at: G. Print Process, Delhi.

Ralph Darnell

Author: Meadows Taylor

TO

MY DEAR FATHER,

WITH THE LOVE OF MY LIFE

I Dedicate

THIS VOLUME.

PREFACE.

When I wrote "Tara," it was to illustrate one of the events which had an important effect upon the history of India: the first blow against the dominant power of the Mahomedans, which was struck in 1657.

A hundred years later, on the 23d of June 1757, a blow still more momentous in character fell upon all native powers in India, Mahomedan and Mahratta alike, by the foundation of a Political authority which, heretofore insignificant, rose into immediate action after the battle of Plassey.

In this volume I have endeavoured to follow the events and actions of history; and to invest it with such English interest as was, in many instances, common to the period.

MEADOWS TAYLOR.

CONTENTS.

PART FIRST.

PART SECOND.

PART THIRD.

PART FOURTH.

PART FIFTH.

PART FIRST.

RALPH DARNELL.

CHAPTER I.

THE GOLDEN COCK, LOWER THAMES STREET.

It was a rough afternoon that of the 21st March 1755. True to its period, a blustering equinoctial gale had set in since morning, and was rapidly increasing. Clouds of dust in the then ill-swept streets of London swirled along with little intermission, enveloping horses, vehicles, and passengers in temporary obscurity; then passing on to meet wayfarers, caught them suddenly at the corners of sheltered streets, causing them to stagger, or clap their hands hastily upon the small three-cornered hats which sate lightly upon the wigs then worn by most of the liege subjects of His Most Gracious Majesty King George the Second. During the course of the morning, a few smartly-dressed and venturesome beaux had tried the Mall; and even a few of the ladies of the then "fast" species of our ancestresses had sallied forth, for the sky for a while was clear and bright; but the wind was too much for them. It blew in fierce gusts from the river down Birdcage Walk, and even the unavoidable precautions of gay bandanas tied round hats and wigs, or curls and toupees, had been frequently insufficient, and many an honest sixpence had been earned by gamins, porters, and chairmen, following and recovering lost possessions. Beaux and belles, with their own powder blown into their eyes, together with street dust; their mouths closed tightly, or tied up in mufflers; the hoops of the one, and the gay-laced coats and ruffles of the other, sorely discomposed by the storm; unable to flirt, or even in most cases to exchange more than the barest civilities, had already given up the fight, and left victory with the boisterous element. It was difficult, very difficult, for chairs to get about; extra porters were reaping a plentiful harvest by steadying those top-heavy vehicles; and as each passed, you might have seen that, whether gay lady powdered and frizzed after the wonderful fashion of the time, or gentleman of quality in lace or embroidered satin or velvet, bound to the rout, club-house, or coffee-tavern, the person within expressed anxiety at every succeeding blast; and you might have heard very often a faint shriek of alarm, as a fair inmate nervously clutched the tassels which hung at her sides. Hackney coaches seemed but little if anything better, for they swayed about on their long springs; and their drivers, half-blinded, and barely able to keep their lofty seats, seemed hardly to be trusted by the passengers within; for here and there a head might be seen to emerge suddenly from the window, to be as quickly withdrawn when there came up a fresh whirlwind, and its fellow-travellers urged the throwing up of the glass as rapidly as possible, and apparently yielded themselves to their fate.

It was, however, on the river that the gale was beginning to be felt most severely. Often during the morning, the skippers and mates of the vessels lying below London Bridge, by the Tower Wharf, and elsewhere, had looked up to the sky in their short, rapid deck-walk; and as they swung their arms with loud thuds against their sides, had said, "It will blow off; it's only a fresh breeze, after all." They are thankful, nevertheless, that they are not off Flamborough Head, or the Goodwin, pitching and labouring in the heavy seas. As the afternoon drew on, however, scraps of grey cloud came one by one out of the east, and hurried up the river, seeming to sweep past the cross of St. Paul's or touch the weathercocks on the church steeples. They might easily be counted at first, as they disappeared over Westminster Abbey and St. James's, and joined together beyond; but they increased so fast, that the sun, who had blinked from among them as long as he could see, gave up at last, and was hidden away altogether before he had set. As the sky grew thicker and the scud drove lower, many a watchful mate and skipper looked to his ship's tackle, and made everything as snug as he could. Topgallant masts were lowered, and their yards struck; topsail and lower yards were braced up sharp to the wind; the strong cables and hawsers by which vessels were moored in their places were carefully looked to, precautions to prevent chafing were taken as far as possible, and soft rope-fenders were thrown over the vessels' sides. Still the wind rose, and the scud flew faster overhead.

The wind was rising with the tide. As the sea-stream hurried up, it seemed impelled by the gale, which swept on in gusts, blackening the surface as the wind struck it, and often, indeed, scooping up and whisking away in spray whatever it could lay hold of; but there were no waves as yet. The current set upwards through London Bridge, and a few wherries, plied with lusty stroke, seemed to fly over the surface, and, as if endowed with life, to enjoy their rapid course westwards. Those coming down the river, however, grew fewer and fewer. It was next to impossible to meet both tide and wind, and, after struggling for a while, one by one the stout watermen, like the fashionables on the Mall, gave up the contest, landed their fares at the nearest steps, and made their boats fast for the night as best they could.

As it was no time for out-door amusement, or even safe passage through the streets—for here and there a slate, or tile, or chimney-pot came flying down through the air, and was smashed to pieces on the pavement, barely avoided in many instances by those on foot—so the taverns and coffee-houses were full of people. Some, driven into them by stress of weather, were taking temporary shelter; others had fairly settled down to a night of cards, dice, or drink, as it might be. East or west it was the same; and in the more fashionable resorts of St. James's, as in those of the city proper and its outskirts, the gay and dissolute of London gathered together. What matter if the houseless poor roamed about in rags and misery, and shivering sought what shelter they could find in by-lanes and under porches of great mansions or churches? what matter if, on the roaring sea, many a crew of hard-pressed seamen began to find sails blown from their bolt-ropes and grim death staring them in the face, and, with little hope of clawing off the dreaded lee-shore of eastern England, prayed their last prayer and commended their souls to God? I say none of these fierce and horrible strivings with the elements troubled the tavern-goers. Within were warmth and comfort; rich viands, generous wines, or strong spirits; and amusement and excitement blended together in bright contrast with the hideous riot without; and thus the gay world, flirting, playing, or drinking—in palace, mansion, or tavern—was happy after its fashion, and defied the storm.

Not far from London Bridge, in Lower Thames Street, on the right-hand side as you went eastwards, stood at that time an old tavern of high local repute, which, as its sign without informed the passenger, was "the Golden Cock." This building was long and low, being of one story only over the ground-floor. Above, three long projecting oriel windows in the centre, with others at the sides, marked the positions of the large apartment frequented by parties of the higher character of guests, and its smaller ones for possibly more select or private company; and the bright light which now streamed from all, and the dark forms which occasionally flitted before the latticed windows, showed them to be well filled as they were brightly lighted. To the street, the oblong windows of the lower story, of similar shape to those above, but guarded by grim iron stanchions, were also full of light; and the whole place looked so cheerful in comparison with the street, that many a chance passenger had entered in at the half-open door, which was sheltered by a deep projecting porch, instead of struggling more with the gale—and, according to his quality, and perhaps the length of his purse, either went up the broad black oak stairs which led to the upper rooms, or turned into the long low apartment to the left of the great hall. There a crowd of persons sat drinking ale or hot punch, and smoking vigorously; and from the room, as the door opened occasionally, a confused clamour of tongues, or a droning song or lusty chorus, and a cloud of tobacco-smoke, and reek of ale, and gin, and brandy-punch, escaped into the outer hall, till the door was shut again.

This hall was a large room, in fact, with benches all round, and opened into an apartment or deep bay towards the river, which in summer was a favourite resort of watermen and sailors. Above it was a similar projecting room, which formed a portion of the central apartment before alluded to, and from both of these there was an uninterrupted view of the river; and nothing could be pleasanter on a fine sunny day than to sit at the open windows of this room, watching the wherries, the ships, and the varying objects and changes of river life. On the right of the hall was the bar, now set out gaily with bright pewter pots, glasses, and a few silver flagons for the use of quality who would drink their mulled wine only out of precious metal. The place was brightly illuminated with strong oil lamps, whose light was reflected by sconces. A roaring wood-fire burned in a wide chimney; and through another door the large kitchen was discernible, glowing with brilliant tin and copper vessels, and with delf plates and dishes on its shelves. Here a long bright coal-fire glowing in the grate was covered with various pots and pans, stewing and bubbling, and partly screened by several active wenches with bare arms and short petticoats, whose principal employment at the present time seemed to be the frying of rashers of bacon and eggs—the hissing, crackling sound of which, and their appetising odour, came strongly into the hall.

It was said that this tavern was part of an old mansion which had stood in the time of the Plantagenets; and perhaps it did. Suits of mail and weapons might once have hung on the great hooks round the hall, and the benches and the wide fire-place have seen the rough merriment and watch and ward of the retainers of the house. The place was perhaps little altered from its original condition; and if well-worn flags in the hall, and the almost black colour of the staircase, with its heavy carved banisters, of the oak wainscot and the paneled ceiling, might be accepted as a proof of antiquity, there could be no doubt of that of the Golden Cock.

The doors and windows of the rooms looking upon the river had been carefully shut since the gale had risen; else, as you passed through the hall and bay beyond, you emerged upon a broad wooden terrace or stage, built upon piles, and protected by a stout rail towards the water. Here, on fine summer days or evenings, parties sat at small tables provided by the house, and smoked, drank, played, or ate as they had a mind to do; while wherries rocked and bobbed on the wavelets in the river, and a crowd of smart watermen, dressed in their best, took fares for a row up to Westminster or Chelsea, or down river to see the large East and West Indiamen at Blackwall, or for a ramble in beautiful Greenwich Park.

It will be allowed, then, that the Golden Cock had many advantages of position for the entertainment of its frequenters; and there was not the least doubt that its host, Mister John Wilkins, was master of his trade, and did not neglect his opportunities. He was bound to serve his guests with the best, and he did so. A useful good-natured wife overlooked the kitchen; and her store of receipts for all old-fashioned English dishes, and many French, were the envy of all tavern-keepers in London who knew of them. Nay, I have reason to believe that they formed the basis of that excellent book—"The Compleat Housewife, or Accomplish'd Gentlewoman's Companion, compiled by Mister E. Smith, and printed for J. & J. Pemberton at the Golden Buck, over against St. Dunstan's Church in Fleet Street, in 1736." The excellent preface to which sets forth, no doubt with Mistress Wilkins's entire concurrence, not only the profane but the religious and metaphysical view of the science of cookery; and how, "in the Infant Age of the World the Inhabitants contented themselves with the provisions of Nature? The Art of Cookery was unknown; Apples, Nuts, and Herbs were both Meat and Sauce, and Mankind stood in no need of additional Sauce, Ragoes, etc., but a good appetite." How, also, "when Man began to pass from a Vegetable to Animal Diet, and feed on Flesh, Fowls, and Fish, their Seasonings grew necessary; and probably Salt was the first Seasoning discovered, for of Salt we read Gen. xiv." And then how, "when Digestive Faculties became Weak and Impotent, the use of Soops and savory Messes began. So that Cookery began to be a Science, though Luxury had not brought it to the Height of an Art." Thus we also read that "Jacob made such palatable Pottage, that Esau purchased a Mess of it at the extravagant Price of his Birthright; and Isaac, before by his last Will and Testament he bequeathed his Blessing to his Son Esau, required him to make some savoury Meat, such as his Soul loved—*i.e.*, such as was relishable to his blunted Palate." I am afraid I cannot find time to follow the learned argument as to the identity of the first cook, therein set forth—whether it was Abraham, Esau, or Rebekah. This, it is pithily stated, is a question "too knotty for me to determine"—and no doubt it is so. I am convinced that Mrs. Wilkins had studied it profoundly, as she did the practice of her noble art. Was it not needful that she should be as much mistress of her peculiar department as her husband was of his? For the shipping was nigh at hand, and many foreign captains and their mates came to the

Golden Cock, and were glad indeed to eat "ragoo," "friccassee," "ollas," and other dainty messes savouring of their own countries; while there were many liquids, such as hot sack with cream, clary wine with spices, brandy-punch or brandy-butter, ale-flip, and the like, for rich and poor, which had raised the good dame's reputation to a high pitch; and those that drank them declared them to be incomparably the best in London city.

Perhaps, too, Mary and Susan, the two rosy-cheeked, bright-eyed, good-natured daughters of this worthy and loving pair, with their smart caps and bright-green stuff gowns turned out through their pocket-holes over their tiny hoops, the bright scarlet quilted linsey petticoat beneath, and we will not say how much of swelling calf and neat ankle showing above the natty high-heeled shoes, might be described as they sat in the bar overlooking the bar-maids, pot-boys, and serving-men. But I am afraid this might only lead me into a detail of the whole establishment, including Mrs. Sarah Baker the cook—irreverently called "Sallibaky," as invented by the French and Dutch captains; and Richard Wiggins, the head-waiter, who was called, in like manner, "Dickiwig"—both being well known to the frequenters of the Golden Cock, and thriving well upon the bounties paid for their particular and individual services. And, I think, as all this might prove wearisome, and we are only visitors, like all the other guests on the evening of the 21st March 1755, we had better not stay with the young women in the bar, lest we should be tempted to flirt with them—an amusement in which, by frequent practice, they are doubtless well exercised—but go up-stairs at once, and join the genteel company assembled there.

CHAPTER II.

COMPANIONS.

A BUSY and a noisy party filled the best apartment of the tavern. The room was low and broad, set out with tables round the sides, at which most of the company there were engaged with cards; or, with flagons or glasses before them, were drinking the many-titled potations which they ordered as fast as they could be brought by the ever active Richard and his mates. According as the guests were old customers or new-comers driven in by the storm, the cries of "Dickiwig" or more respectful "Richard" sounded from impatient thirsty throats on all sides, and the errands to be done for viands or for liquid compounds, were only equalled by the number of the guests and their requirements.

The room afforded evidence of the noble rank of its ancient proprietors. The walls were of polished oak wainscot, laid out in panels; the corners were finished in rich devices of flowers or scrolls of carved ornaments; and the ceiling, also divided into panels, had three divisions along its length, the centre of each being marked by a boss of carving similar to that on the corners of the panels, but richer and more elaborate. From the dark colour of the wood, the room might have had a gloomy aspect but for the brilliancy with which it was lighted. All round the walls, in the centres of each of the panels, were brass branches, holding polished silver or plated reflectors, which increased the light of the oil-lamps burning therein; and from the centre bosses of the ceiling depended brass chandeliers, holding in each twelve wax candles. The game, as old Wiggins used to say—he had picked up the saying from the French captains, who often came—"*was* worth the candles," and he would have nothing but the best wax tapers in his domain. So, with the wind roaring without, and now beating furiously against the long windows towards the river, the room had a peculiarly rich and comfortable appearance; and even those who had intended only to stay a while altered their minds, called for cards, and betook themselves to boston, piquet, or cribbage; or ordered supper and wine, and determined to make a snug night of it.

There might have been fifty people or more in the room. Here were groups of the foreign captains, who, overtaken by the storm, could not get back to their ships, French and Dutch together, men with dark, bronzed faces, ear-rings in their ears, and wearing costumes gay with lace and embroidery, or clad in the plain cloth and baggy breeches of Flanders and the Low Countries. Few, if any, of these mingled with the Englishmen present; they gathered together according to their nationalities, and carried on their conversation in their own tongues, playing at dominoes or cards, and apparently with no stakes on their games. The Englishmen present, however, were very different.

We see now in old portraits of the time, on the stage, in pictures, or at fancy balls where proper costume is a point critically observed, what the dress of our great-great-grandfathers was, and how richly and how becomingly it clothed their figures: satin and velvet in full dress, with a liberal use of costly lace and embroidery in silk, silver, or gold; cloth also, but never without gold or silver trimming on those who affected or indulged in fashionable costume. The high riding-boot, the neat long gaiter, or the bright silk stocking, fitted well with the short nether garment; while the waistcoat fell low over the hips, and was as resplendent as the genius of the tailor, or the pocket of the wearer, could contrive it to be. My own opinion is, also, that these garments were very comfortable. The sleeves were wide and loose, the waistcoat sat easily in its place, and the nether garments, however continued below, gave free scope to the limbs. For the trader or quiet merchant, the colour and fashion were as sober as he could desire; while for the gay man of fashion, what limit was there, except his purse, to the brilliancy of the costume, whether for day or night?

Not that there were any very memorable examples of this costume present on this evening; and the dress of the majority might have been called plain almost to soberness; but there were a few exceptions, and as they belong to characters which have to do with this history, I may briefly note them.

At a small table, not far from the roaring fire, which was liberally supplied with logs of wood, sat two men, more richly dressed than others present, who, by the attention paid to them by the head-waiter, were evidently persons of some consequence in his, and no doubt in their own, opinion. The younger of the two wore a light grey velvet suit, with bright steel buttons, which, as well as the richly-cut hilt of his sword, sparkled in the strong light. On the front and flaps of his waistcoat was a delicate embroidery of flowers in silk, and the dress jabôt or cravat, as well as the ruffles on his wrists and breast, were of the finest Flanders lace. He was evidently dressed for an evening party, and was not perhaps in the best of humours at being detained by the rough weather, into which he was in no trim to emerge from his present shelter.

He was eminently handsome. A fair fresh face, the colour of which was almost effeminate in its tone and bloom, with light wavy hair, a high white forehead, and large blue eyes, were the first features you noticed, and generally with a pleasurable impression: but just then, the eyes were redder than they need have been; the colour on the cheek was heightened, and had flushed up into the forehead; the brows were knit; and it was evident that the combined influences of a good deal of wine and some high play were making themselves felt. The other features were perhaps not remarkable or worth discussion, for there were weakness and sensuality about the small but pale-red lips, and irresolution in the shape of the chin, and white, soft, woman-like throat; and as he now sat, there was a reckless expression in the eyes which plainly betrayed a dissolute character. His figure left nothing to desire. It was tall, and to all appearance strong; and the very movements of the broad sloping shoulders and back, as he shifted his position occasionally with impatient gestures, showed him to be lithe and active.

In truth, there were few better figures, or more graceful young men in London, than George Elliot at twenty-four. He walked well, danced well, was master of his sword's use, and had already fought severals duels with credit. He had excellent taste in dress, and always made a conspicuous figure upon the public promenades; and because of all these outward evidences, and an independent position as to fortune, he was already well advanced in the favour of the gay ladies of the town, and into the rank of society which it was his highest ambition to attain. When he should become a member of White's or Arthur's, indeed, he considered he should take his proper place in the world's esteem and his own.

Before him sat John Forster, his companion, and, for the time, sworn friend, handsomely dressed in brown cloth, trimmed with gold lace. Not that the man was wealthy, or belonged to that higher class of gay folks to join which Elliot strove so hard; but he knew, or seemed to know, everybody, and partly by effrontery, partly because of his very determined manner, and indifference to all obstacles in the gratification of his own will, Forster had risen to the place he occupied and maintained. Older by several years than Elliot, but hardly yet thirty, John Forster was a man who at once attracted attention and puzzled a good deal. He was not handsome or noble-looking, or even dignified; but his face interested at once, nay, almost fascinated, especially the large brown eyes, which were soft or fiery as it might be, varying with every thought—now shadowed, by the long lashes, as with a woman's tenderness, or opened wide with a daring, flashing stare, which few cared to provoke or encounter. It seemed as if there were more than ordinary intelligence between those eyes and the mouth, for both varied together in intensity of expression which could not be controlled. His might have remained a gentle, loving, trustful, though passionate face under happy influences; but these were long past, and it was fast hardening into reckless vice under the combined influence of entire selfishness, the society which he frequented, and its pursuits. John Forster was shorter than George Elliot, and he appeared thinner; but the strength of the man was in reality much greater. In the muscular throat, the strong round chin, the low square forehead and high head, and the very slight projection of the under lip, which was only noticeable under strong excitement, there were evidences of strength of character as well as of body; and as the two men sat holding their cards, so that their loose cuffs fell back from their hands, the contrast of the nervous resolute grasp of the one with the comparative irresolution and dimpled softness of the other, was very remarkable. It was a critical period of the game too. Elliot, far ahead of his adversary in score, had backed himself heavily to win, but in this hand luck seemed to have changed.

CHAPTER III.

A LITTLE PLAY.

Both parties had counted up their cards, and begun to play. Forster exhibited irrepressible triumph, though when his companion occasionally spoke to him he replied from behind his hand, as if he feared to show the expression of his mouth. Elliot played very slowly, and with much thought—and he was by no means an indifferent player; but this was no common hand. Chance, or the coolest calculation, might save him from a capot; but he knew Forster would exert every ingenuity to mislead him, and there was a heavy stake on the game, more than he cared to lose. At last there remained but two cards in his hand, and one of these might win a trick and save him; which should he play? What card had Forster reserved? Perhaps, if he had shut his eyes and considered well, he might have saved the game; but it was already as good as lost. In Elliot's nerveless fingers the two cards were moved about irresolutely; then he closed his eyes and played one desperately.

"The wrong one, by G—— !" he exclaimed, throwing the other passionately on the table. "I thought it would be so. Thou hast the devil's luck to-night, Jack !"

"Nay," retorted the other, "if thou wilt be such a fool, Geordie, as to trust to luck when memory would have helped thee better, I have no more to say. It was no clean capot, only thou hast made it one; and but for this," and he held up the card, "as your score was at eighty-two, I had a poor chance."

"Well, so be it, Jack; and what's to pay? Let me see—I bet thee three to two on the rubber, and there is the score besides."

"In ponies, Geordie. Nay, thou wouldst have it so."

"Yes, by George, it is true; and here is only enough to pay the score on the table, and my purse is empty."

"I wish my I O U were as good as thine," returned his friend.

"Well, I suppose it must be so. Here, Dickiwig! a pen, ink, and paper—sharp, my lad; and a glass of brandy next, to wash down my ill luck. Come, Darnell," he continued, turning round to a young man sitting by the fire with a glass before him which was half full of steaming punch—"come, rouse thyself. Art asleep? It is thy turn now; here's Forster has won nigh a hundred of me, and I hope it will all get back to thee. Come, bring another chair, for there is no luck in this."

The person to whom Elliot spoke belonged to the small party which that night, as often before, had met at the Golden Cock to play. The youngest of the three, he was not more than twenty; and as he will have a good deal to do with this history, and may be briefly described, I will not now pass him by. A fresh-faced, curly-headed youth, who, you could not help thinking, would have been safer and better in other company. What hair there was on his face had been late in coming, and was as yet but down. Thick, wavy, dark-chestnut locks clustered over the brow and temples, and, uncut, curled over the ears and on the shoulders. The face was a good deal freckled, but not plain—quite the contrary; and though it was not that of a man of good blood, so to speak, in which respect those of Elliot and Forster were remarkable, it was one which many a woman would have looked on with favour, from its bold, manly, and usually good-natured expression. The mouth was small and well-cut, showing white even teeth: the eyes dark grey with black lashes, and sufficiently large to be capable of much affectionate expression, though liable to passion, which was evinced by the bold nose and open defiant nostril. In figure he was as tall as Elliot, and showed evidences of greater future strength, though certainly of less grace, than had been attained by that accomplished beau. Believing Ralph Darnell to be the heir of a north-country baronetcy and a large estate, his fellow-countrymen had taken him under their patronage, and were educating him in the accomplishments of the day, after their own particular fashion: while he, nothing loath, was by no means an indifferent pupil.

"Come!" cried Forster, theatrically. "Ralph Darnell! I dare thee! Sir Ralph Darnell, Baronet, of Melcepeth Castle to be. Gad! it has a sound of sea-waves in it, befitting the neighbourhood of Dunstanborough and Warkworth. I dare thee to battle! I have just capotted Geordie, and intend to capot thee! Awake, O sleeper! Thou art not drunk, surely?"

"Drunk!" retorted the young man, drinking off the remaining contents of his glass at a gulp—"no more drunk than you are. I thought you would never have done with that infernal rubber, and had wellnigh gone to sleep over my punch and the bright fire. Here, Dickiwig—fresh cards, old fellow, and a fresh jorum of punch."

"Indeed, Mr. Darnell," replied that worthy, as he brought the cards, "if you're going to play with Mr. Forster, you'd as well not have more punch; that's the second glass I've brought you, and you'll please to pay at the bar for what you had before."

"Mind your own business, you old fool," cried the young man, "and I'll mind mine. I want the punch, I say, and if you won't bring it, I'll go to the bar myself."

"Coming, sir!" was Dicky's answer, as, in reply to some real or fancied caller, he dashed away.

"But the punch," cried Darnell after him—"you old sinner—"

"Be quiet, Ralph," said Elliot. "I don't know that it is good for you, but as you will. I am going to change these gay garments of mine, and will tell Susan, your beloved, to send it to you; and I think I shall take a turn at hazard when I return."

"That means he'll flirt with her himself," said Forster; "but come, man—cut for deal, and let's begin. What shall it be?—guineas, and ten on the rubber?"

"Susan's a jade, and you may tell her so, Geordie, from me, and you're welcome to her—if—you can get her, which is more than I can; but then you're a beau, you know, and I'm hardly a 'blood.' Well, John! Oh ay! I got twenty yellow boys from old Sanders to-day, and there they lie against yours. And I've won the deal, huzza! Now for it."

They continued playing, and the luck had changed. Forster's face was no longer triumphant, but it changed very little with ill-fortune, the under lip only grew out, as it were, as the teeth were set and occasionally ground passionately, and the strong upper lip closed over it with a rigid pressure under a profane oath, which I cannot record. Indeed, in this respect, the conversation of these young men was ordinarily interlarded by explosive expressions, which our ancestresses used not to object to; and therefore the quiet form of speech I use to express what they said may appear strange and untrue to nature. But as I think that I could not safely record the conversation exactly as it was, without offence, it were therefore best modified.

"You will give me my revenge, Darnell," said Forster, with an attempt at gaiety, as the rubber ended, and he had lost heavily: "you're not going yet?"

"No, by George, not in this furious storm; and that's hail," he continued after a pause, as sheet after sheet was dashed against the shutters, and the blast fairly shook the old room, whistling through crevices in the panels. "No, I'll play as long as you like, and you may win all this back if you can. One, two, three—"

"I hate the chink of money. Ralph, let it alone, will you, and play," cried Forster, nervously.

"Ha, ha, ha! a good joke! Mayn't I count my coin? Come, I've only won six-and-twenty of thee after all; and here, Dicky, more drink's wanted—burnt sack this time."

"Indeed, Master Ralph," said Dickey, you shan't have it to-night; you'll never get home, and it's time you were there."

"Then I'll sleep here, you stingy old scoundrel. I'll sleep on the floor; it's as soft as a ship's plank—isn't it? No sack! Look, Dickiwig, here's the guinea for thee I've promised so long. Dost see it? Ay, but bring the sack, and then thou'lt get it; not before, old boy!"

"Well, Master Ralph, and if I have Mr. Darnell here to-morrow, asking why his nephew was drunk over-night, or Mr. Sanders, what's to be said?"

"D—n Mr. Sanders!" cried Ralph; "if ever you say a word to him about me, I'll break every bone in your skin, or to my uncle either. There, that's what you want, you old miserly rascal; there's your guinea," and he threw one to the old man. "Away now for the liquor! Tell Miss Susan to sweeten it with her sweet lips before she sends it up; and if it's weak, by Jove I'll make thee drink it thyself, at the point of my sword! Ha, ha, ha! I shall get my liquor now, I think, after the guinea—eh, Jack?"

"Come over here, Jack," cried Elliot, now advancing from the centre table, where they had seen him playing after his return; "leave that cursed piquet; they've got some hazard a-going here, and that's better. What a glum face, to be sure! and so thou'st been losing, Jack?"

"Only six-and-twenty to me, Geordie," said Darnell; "and thou wouldst say it was six-and-twenty drops of his life's-blood. Let him alone. Let him win it back as he grudges it. I'm not drunk, Geordie, not a bit; I can see the cards quite well, and if they will come points and quarts, don't blame me. 'Pon my life, I can't help it! I've played fair, indeed I have—and—I'm not—drunk! I'm—"

"Come away, Jack! I'll not let thee play another card with him —no, not one, by the Lord Harry!" cried Elliot, dragging Forster from his chair. "Nay, no need to look savage, man; you know I care nought for that. Can't we get him to my place some evening, and do what we like with him?" he whispered hurriedly. "Come away, I say, both of ye. Look what I've won from the sea-captain yonder, who is flourishing a bag of guineas as if they were half-pence."

"If—you'll give me another glass of hot sack, Geordie," said Darnell, steadying himself upon his chair, "I'll go with you—to the devil—old fellow—if you like. Here, Dickiwig!"

"Come away, I say, you fools, and curse the cards!" cried Elliot, seizing the packs and flinging them to the other end of the room; "and, you old sinner, Dicky, if you give Mr. Darnell another drop, I'll be the death of you! mind that. Come along boys."

Darnell rose and steadied himself as well as he could before he moved. He was not very tipsy after all, but in that state when he would have braved anything or done anything without a thought. "I'll give you your revenge any day—six-and-twenty, you know, Jack —that's all—and don't be angry now."

"What a fool you are to think me angry," said Forster between his teeth. "Lend me five pieces, and see if my luck turns against that sailor fellow."

"Five? nay, but here's ten," replied Darnell, gravely counting them on the palm of his hand, "and good luck to you with them."

"Seven's the main, gentlemen," cried the man of whom Elliot had told them. "Don't be afraid of the gold, or of me. Here it is, won on the coast of the Indies, gentlemen. Ah, you should see the soft Hindu girls there, and the palm trees, and hear tales of Mr. Clive's doings, and how he fights the blacks as I have. I'd a mind to have joined him, sirs—by the Lord Harry I had, with my ship's crew!"

The speaker was a dashing, bronzed young man, wearing richly-laced cloths, and a strong sword, half hanger, half rapier, by his side. His faced looked as though fierce suns had scorched it, and the hand in which he held a leather bag of coins was as dark as mahogany. "Should be glad to see you, gentlemen, on board the *Valiant* any time convenient," he continued; "got a comfortable cuddy there, and the best of grog, and these bones always ready. Seven's the main, gentlemen; who'll join?"

"I will for one," cried Darnell, throwing down a handful of pieces at once. Who's afraid? Come Jack, come Geordie, don't be afraid. I'm—I'm in luck, and I'm not drunk. Huzza for King George! and d—n—"

"Be quiet, you fool?" cried Forster; "you don't know who may be here; do you want a fight?"

"Anything for me! I'm not drunk!" hiccuped Ralph. "Huzza, I say, for King George, and damnation to all Pretenders! They're your friends, Jack, that you wince, aren't they?"

"By Jove! if you don't pick up your money I will," cried Elliot. "Look out—see what you've won."

"Huzza! double or quits, Captain? What do you say?" roared Darnell. "Here's thirty of 'em!"

"Done, sir," replied the other. "I don't think he's fit to play, though," he continued, apart to Elliot. "I'd have everything fair, gentlemen."

"Mind your game, sir," cried Elliot, haughtily; "we can look after our friend's play as well as our own. You've a heavy stake on that throw."

"Mind yours, sir," retorted the Captain; "I know well what I'm about. Any one backing the gentleman there? I'll take odds against him—two to one? three two five? name your sums, gentlemen. I've only brought a small bag to-night, but there's plenty more where that came from."

"I back him then, three to five," said Forster, sharply.

"That's right, my blood of bloods!" cried Ralph, slapping his thigh. "Who's afraid to-night? Gad, sir, we'll clean you out! and there, my hand that it'll be all fair! Drunk, sir? I'm not drunk!"

As Darnell spoke, and put out his hand to grasp the Captain's across the table, he felt his coat gently pulled behind. "What's that?" he cried sharply. "Let me go, Elliot; I will shake hands with him!"

"It's me," said a soft girlish voice behind him—"it's only me. Oh, come home, Mr. Ralph! Nanny's in a sore fright for you, and mother's ill, and I've run over the bridge with your cloak—come with me."

"I'faith, a brave little wench!" cried a dozen of voices round the table. "Who art thou, my darling?" coarsely added a man near, who put his arm round the girl. "Nay, but I'll have a kiss from thy sweet lips—by George, I will!"

As the girl struggled to free herself, Ralph Darnell struck the man heavily in the mouth with a back-handed blow, so that he staggered back. "Who dares touch her!" he exclaimed, haughtily, as if suddenly sobered; and drawing his sword with one hand, gathered the girl to him with the other, in spite of her frantic efforts to drag down the weapon.

The dice had been thrown, and Darnell had won. Elliot gathered up the stakes, and thrust them into Darnell's breeches pocket, just as the man who had been struck attacked him fiercely, and the swords crossed. "No brawling here, gentlemen!" cried Mr. Wilkins —"no brawling; ye can go into the streets for that; the Golden Cock is no place for Mohocks. Mr. Elliot, Mr. Forster, look to Mr. Darnell!"

Neither, however, nor the company present, had any mind to let the quarrel go on. The stranger was forthwith disarmed and dragged away; and Forster, wrenching Darnell's sword from him, thrust it into the scabbard, and he was hurried to the end of the room near the door.

"I am well known," cried Elliot to the Captain, as he returned to the table; "and Mr. Wilkins will answer for me. Let him go; you shall have your revenge to-morrow night; if you will come, we will bring our friend."

"Nay, 'twas but a trifle," replied the good-humoured fellow; "and one must lose and another win with the bones' rattle. I shall be happy to see you, sir, here or in the cabin of the *Valiant*, as you will. The ship is easily found; and I am Captain Abel Scrafton, at your service or your friend's, always."

Meanwhile Ralph Darnell had been hurried on by Mr. Wilkins, Dicky, and a posse of tapsters—some of whom had caught up stout sticks and flourished them over their heads—down the stairs, and into the hall, where he sat down doggedly on the flags, swearing frightful oaths, and declaring he would not stir till he had more drink. The girl was crying bitterly, but would not leave him; and now folded his thick cloak about him, buttoning it at the throat—an office in which Forster and the old waiter assisted—trying to raise Darnell to his feet.

"Susan, another flagon of sack, and a kiss from thee, my darling," hiccuped Ralph; "and I'll go, I'll go; I'm not drunk! and Sybil, wait! 'pon my soul, I'll go home quietly if I get it."

"Oh give it him, Mr. Wilkins," cried the girl, clasping her hands piteously; "give it him, else I shall never get him away, and they don't know I am out—indeed they don't—and I can't wait, sir; I will not leave him."

"Now, that's the last, Mr. Ralph, and it's only because you promised to go home that I give it you," said the host, gently. "Now, go—that's a good lad, and let's have no more of this nonsense."

"If that fellow had not insulted Sybil," cried Darnell, rising to his feet and steadying himself, as he received the small tankard, "I would not have hit him. Served him right; didn't I Jack? didn't I, Mr. Wilkins? Here's to your good healths, all round. Now, Sybil, your arm, my darling. It's a bad night, isn't it?"

"Never mind, Mr. Ralph, we have not far to go, and we'll soon be over the bridge," said the girl, who, not heeding the pitiless storm without, was only anxious to get Ralph away.

"Good night, then, Mr. Wilkins; good night, Jack; where's Geordy? Ah! I'm the better for that hot sack and the ginger. Bless thee, Susan! I blow a kiss to thee, my dear."

The damsel in the bar tossed her head scornfully as Ralph blew his parting benediction from the tips of his fingers, and the door being opened, admitted a furious blast of wind with snow, as he emerged from it staggering into the street.

"My mind misgives me about the lad, Jack," said Elliot good-naturedly, as he returned from the upper room; "we had better follow him and see him safe home."

"It will be a charitable act, gentlemen," added the host. "He has too much money about him to be alone so wild a night as this."

CHAPTER IV.

SAFE HOME.

I LEAVE it to scientific professors to define why, if a half tipsy man goes out suddenly into cold air, the inevitable result is that he advances a stage further in inebriety. No doubt this phenomenon is capable of a most easy-to-be-comprehended solution, but I have only to do with the fact; and though it is no doubt painful to have to exhibit a fine young fellow like Ralph Darnell in the condition he had attained after his steady potations of strong brandy-punch and burnt sack, I profess that this history has to deal with the truth, and that, whether the acts of those who have part in it be good or evil, they shall be faithfully set forth to the end.

For after all, my friend, this is the true aspect of all human nature—poor, imperfect, blind, striving, jostling human nature; and my opinion is, that you would no more believe all the characters I have to bring before you to be perfectly good, not though I painted them with the brightest colours and the softest moral brushes I could find, than you would believe them to be perfectly bad, even though I blackened them with all the sins named in the commination service. And while I shall have no occasion, I hope, to do either one or the other, you must be prepared, in the course of this history, to take the people who belong to it in general, and this very Ralph Darnell in particular, as you may find them.

Just now, as we see him, he is certainly in no very dignified condition; but we cannot help that. After passing out of the porch of the Golden Cock, above which that resplendent bird was swinging rapidly and creaking loudly in the blast, Ralph and Sybil fairly faced the snow and wind; and it was as much as the girl could do to steady her companion, even though the gale helped them occasionally, as the blasts came from the east down the street—and the snow, whirled round and round by the eddies among the houses, had settled into drifts which were deep enough to puzzle any one whose footing was not quite within his own control. Ralph, then, had fallen more than once into soft places, but he was in good humour, laughing heartily at his own erratic steps, and the girl, gaining confidence from his merriment, was leading him as well as she could onwards. Fortunately there was a good deal of light, not only from the effect of the moon, dark as the clouds were, but from the snow, which now lay thick on the ground.

It was, however, very different when they turned the corner of Thames Street, and emerged upon the bridge. There they had to encounter the full force of the storm, and for a while Darnell's spirits appeared to rise higher as he struggled against the furious wind and blinding snow. I am afraid no modern ears would like to hear of the scraps of vile, ribald songs he sang, of the volleys of profane oaths he fired against the tempest, or of the frantic manner in which he roared and howled more and more impotently as he struggled on. He had flung off Sybil more than once as she attempted to steady and guide him; and it was evident to the terrified girl that his intoxication was much increased, and increasing. What if he fell insensible! She could not stir him; he must be snowed up, and so perish. She had heard her mother and Nanny tell of travellers on northern moors overtaken by the snow, who had gone to sleep, and were found dead in the morning; and her terror increased. There was no one on the bridge, not even a watchman, and only a few street lamps, at great intervals, remained alight in the storm. What should she do if he fell, but watch by him like a dog? Ah! yes, she would be as faithful.

The bridge, too, was steep—steep, that is, for a tipsy man to ascend with such a storm raging; and Darnell's steps became so painfully erratic that Sybil no longer dared to touch him. His shouts and songs had gradually died away, and a change was coming over the young man, by no means uncommon in phases of such excitement. He was now sullen and silent, and Sybil feared these moods, which came over him sometimes even when there was no cause like the present. Suddenly, as he staggered more than usual, a blast from the river, fiercer than any they had met before, flung Darnell into a drift of snow, and he lay there without stirring.

It was what Sybil had feared, and she crept to him under shelter of the parapet; but he had raised himself up, and sat crying and sobbing in a maudling tone, which to her was far more painful than the previous ribaldry, and cursing all belonging to him; and, as it often happens, what is nearest the heart of any one so affected comes out first.

"Curse 'em, I say—curse them all," he whined, "for a pack of miserly scoundrels, who want—cheat me—cheat me. There's Uncle Geoffrey—Sir Geoffrey—and I'm Sir Ralph to be, by-and-by, if they'll let me; but no! they won't. I know they won't, else why was I sent to this infernal place? And they won't let me have my Constance—no, they won't; and I curse them all, and Uncle Roger, and Sanders, and—. O Constance! my darling, my darling," he continued, stretching out his arms and whimpering, "come here—come and get me out of this snow. I can't get up. O my darling! don't, don't leave me here." Then he howled more curses and profane oaths, and the gentle girl crept nigher and nigher to him in the snow-drift.

"Oh, Mr. Ralph, don't curse so," she said gently; "get up and come home with me. Lean on me; I'm quite strong, and we'll soon be there. It's only Sybil—your own Sybil—come."

"No, d—n you," roared the young savage; "get away! I hate you! I want Conny! Go and fetch her, you—. They've taken my Conny from me: they've sent me here, and won't let me see her, and I shall never go to Melcepeth any more—no, curse them—and you—everybody!—"

The girl had raised him up partially, and helped to get him on his feet, but this time he caught hold of her dress, shook her violently, and flung her from him with all his strength. It was well that the snow lay thickly on the pavement, else she had been terribly hurt. As it was, she was partially stunned; and he looked at her lying before him with a stupid wonderment which, for the moment, partially sobered him. As he rose and staggered back to the parapet, to which he clung moaning, his feet refused to obey him.

How the wind shrieked and the snow fell! To look towards the river was impossible. Darnell had faced the storm for a moment; and his small hat, over which one of the tapsters had kindly tied a handkerchief, had been wrenched instantly from his head, and blown away like a feather. Nothing could be seen of the water, or the ships, or the houses by the river-side—all was a confused cloud of battling, whirling, blinding snow-flakes: but the sounds were fearful. Far below, the tide was running out—and some of us may remember with what violence it used to pour through the old arches at ordinary times; but now the ebb-flood met the gale, and the furious waves dashed high against the bridge piers, or raged in a fearful turmoil in the centre of the river. From the shipping there was a hoarse and continuous roar of the wind through the rigging, which often rose into a wild howl as if of evil spirits riding on the storm. With it, a confused sound of plashing and rolling vessels mingled with heavy thuds of collision: and above all these, hoarse but constant cries of human voices came up fitfully. It could not be said whether they were orders on board the ships, shouts for help, or the death-shrieks of the crews of shattered and sinking vessels.

But of anything precise, Ralph Darnell was now unconscious. Just as he had steadied to advance, Sybil raised herself and looked round. Wiping the snow from her face, she saw Darnell; and, remembering his curses and despair, the first thought which occurred to her was that he would destroy himself in the river beneath.

"No! no! no! Ralph!" she shrieked, as she rose suddenly and staggered through the snow. "Help! help! Oh save him, save him!"

Her cry had been heard. She was clinging to him in her terror, as his two companions, who had followed on the track of his footsteps, came up.

"Ay, thou art a rare brave wench!" cried Elliot; "and hast not left him. But for thee, indeed, we had missed ye both, for we were on the other causeway. Hallo, Ralph! who is this fairy? A sweetheart of thine? Fie! man, she's but a child."

"Hie on home, lassie, and get into shelter," said Forster, good-naturedly. "We'll bring him to you safe. This is no place for the like of you."

"Please, sir," said Sybil, timidly, "I'm not his sweetheart—I'm only—"

"Never mind what thou art!" cried Elliot; "there's a smack of my ain county's 'burr' about thee; and thou'rt a brave lass. If I hadn't more sweethearts than I know what to do with already, thou shouldst be chief of mine. But there's Jack Forster—he wants one; and a canny lass frae the North will just— Bless me, she's gone!" he continued—"vanished, 'i faith! perhaps in the snow among Mother Bunch's feathers; an' wha kens, Johnnie Forster, but the deil's maybe sent ye a leman, my bonny lad—an' you've letten her gang. Did ye no see her broomstick?"

"Peace, with your ribald foolery, George," retorted the other; "and help me with this stupid ass. Darnell! do you know who we are?"

Ralph looked dreamily from one to the other, and dashed the snow from his eyes. "I know you," he hiccuped. "It's the sack, Geordie, that did it! One shouldn't mix—you know— I'm better now! Come along. Hurrah for King George, and d—n the Pretender! Tol de rol, de rol, de rol! Fol de rol de ray!"

There is nothing so efficient for the care of a tipsy man as two stout sober companions, one on each side. The sufferer may stumble, or stagger, or reel; but he must walk; and legs incapable of any independent action, obey the laws enforced upon them by those of others. Accordingly, though Ralph Darnell did huzza for the King once more, and d—n the Pretender—much to Elliot's amusement, who knew Forster to be one of the secret agents of a ruined house—and roar out scraps of ditties, he was forced along the bridge till the trio reached Tooley Street corner, where they stopped. They knew Darnell lodged somewhere in that vicinity—but where? And could he direct them now Sybil was gone?

Ralph, however, was now somewhat more sober, and knew his way perfectly. "Come on, boys!" he said, with tipsy gravity; "Mrs. Morton will be glad to see my friends; and I've got a glass of brandy apiece for ye. It is but a step;" and he moved forwards by himself.

"Let's see where he lives," said Forster; "we may need to know some day; and I should like to look at that little girl's face again, to know it better."

"I hope she may never see thine to know it better," rejoined Elliot, laughing. "If she ever do, so much the worse for her—that's all. I hope the old lady may give us the brandy too; we've got to face that bridge again, and a cordial will do us no harm."

And they followed close on Darnell's heels, lest he should fall again; but, partly by aid of the wall, and by considerably more command over his legs than before, the young man made his way forward very surely, and, turning into a small street apparently close to the river, as the dashing and gurgling of waves among the piles denoted, he stopped at the porch of an ancient house and knocked at the door, which was instantly opened by an elderly woman, carrying a candle, who held out her hand to Darnell.

"Tak' care, Master Rraafe," she said, in a broad Northumbrian accent; "tak' a grrip o' me, and haud fast doon the step; that's richt. Eh lad! but what hae ye been doin' wi' yoursel'! an' wha's them wi' ye? 'Deed, gentlemen," she continued, curtsying to Elliot and Forster, "ye've dune the daft lad a gude turn the nicht—A've heerd on it, of my young leddy; an' my mistress, that's Mistress Morton, ye ken, she's vary obligated t'ye."

"Don't prate, Nanny," said Ralph, who had steadied himself against the parlour door as she shut the outer one; "let us in here, and stir up the fire; they're not going yet. Come in, Geordie—come in, both of ye. It would be hard if a Darnell turned out an Elliot and a Forster in sic a nicht wi'out a tass o' brandy to help them hame; quick, Nanny! I'm not drunk now, ye auld fule! ha! ha! ha!—not now."

The fire was blazing up cheerily as the parlour door opened and they were shown in.

"You're welcome to my poor room, Geordie—not like yours exactly," continued Ralph; "but you've both done me a good turn to-night, and I'll drink your healths for it, I'm d—d if I don't. Now Nanny!"

"Ma mistress's compliments, surrs," said Nanny, bringing in a small tray with glasses, and a case-bottle in a filigree stand, "and she hopes ye'll tak' no harm o' the nicht; and she's thankfu' t'ye for your service, and hopes ye'll tak' a glass apiece, or mair if ye like the sperrit; but it's frae Melcepeth Castle, ye ken, so that's paid no king's duty. Ye'll be frae the North yersels, gentles. Forster an' Elliot they ca'd ye? eh sirs! but they're canny names, an' ye'll be of gude people, I'll warrant."

"We'll drink Mrs. Morton's good health," said Forster; "and if you'll tell her I am Mr. Forster of the Craig Peel, she'll know who I am; and this is Mr. Elliot, of Wooler Hall, and she'll know well of him too: we're friends of Mr. Darnell's."

Nanny curtsied low as each familiar name and place was mentioned, and, pouring out bumpers of spirit, handed them to the guests, as she set down the tray on the table near Ralph, who was looking from one to the other with tipsy gravity. As he saw the tray set down, however, and as Nanny was smoothing her apron prior to beginning a set speech, he suddenly poured out a quantity of the spirit into a large silver flagon which Nanny had brought with the glasses, and, with a wild hurrah to their health, drank it off at a draught, and fell heavily to the floor.

"Enough for to-night," exclaimed Forster, with a sneer; "keep him quiet, ma'am, and his head high, and let him lie there before the fire till he comes round. Take care of the money in his pockets—he has more than he needs, and," he added bitterly, "he won much of it from me, with his cursed good luck. But perhaps we could see the young lady again to say how much we admired her courage," he continued, "if we might be so honoured before we go."

"Miss Morton's wi' her mither, surrs," replied Nanny, with some dignity, and drawing up her tall slight figure; "an, she's no minded to see stranger gentry at this time o' nicht. A'll mind him mysel', surrs—a' ken weel what to dee. Ye'd as well go, surrs."

"Come away, Jack," cried Elliot, laughing, and pulling Forster to the door, "the old woman's more than a match for you. Eh, but that's good stuff! wadna ye gie us just anither tass o't, my darlin'?" he added in the broad dialect she was speaking in.

"Awa wi' ye, ye reivin' loons," cried the old woman, angrily—"awa wi' ye! a'll be glad when I've steekit the dure behint ye. There!" she exclaimed, when they had gone out, and she drew the heavy bolts and turned the key twice in the lock. "Elliots and Forsters were ever a dour set, and these are nae good, I reckin. Miss Sybil, they're baith gone; come doon and see till Mister Ralph; he's in a sair dwam; come doon, hinny, if yer mither's asleep."

"Thank God, Nanny," said Sybil, descending the stairs gently, with a candle in her hand. "I was sore afraid of those bold men, but the Lord has truly protected us this night."

"Ay, hinny darling, ye may say that indeed; but there's nae sleep for me the nicht; he'll be restless in his drink, an' need watchin'. Get thee to bed, childie, I'd be better wi'out thee, darlin'; drunken lads is no fit company for the likes of thee."

"Nay, Nanny, but I'll sit by you for a while and watch. I'll go by-and-by."

And the two sat down beside Ralph, while he groaned and moaned in his heavy sleep; and the storm raged still without, the river waves surging up against the piles, and the wind roaring its unearthly chorus in the ships' rigging.

"It's the first time he ever was like this, Nanny," said the gentle girl, as she smoothed the pillow beneath the sleeper's head, and covered him more carefully, while she prayed for him after her simple fashion, "May the Lord in His mercy grant it be the last!"

"Amen, amen, hinny; but men's dour folk, ma darlin,' and uz women has to bear wi' mony an evil time they bring on uz. Wae's me! but I've seen mony o' them; and this callant 'll be nae wiser, I reakon, in his young time, than his folk wuz before him. The Darnells wuz iver a wild race, and it's ill gettin' a tame bird oot o' a wild bird's nest. Eh! but thou'rt a brave lassie, ma pet. If iver a man's life was saved before, it was done by thee the nicht."

"God was good to me, Nanny," murmured Sybil, wiping away her tears.

CHAPTER V.

MORNING.

If the house where Mrs. Morton dwelt was not so imposing in its appearance as the Golden Cock nearly opposite, on the city side of the river, it was perhaps as old, and much in the same style. The ground floor had similar narrow oblong windows, and the story above the like projecting oriels, which, over some intermediate stairs and wharves, commanded a beautiful view of the river. Originally the house had been large; and, as with the Golden Cock, might have been the residence of a noble family in days gone by; but what remained of the original structure had been divided into several tenements, occupied by respectable, but comparatively poor families; and in one of these lived Mrs. Morton, her daughter Sybil, and her old servant, Nanny Keene, with Ralph Darnell as a regular boarder in the family.

Mrs Morton's story was a sad one. Her husband's family, and indeed her own, had been staunch Cavaliers, and adhered to the house of Stuart to the last. Others had fought in the civil wars, had risen and fallen with the times, and had finally settled down into recognition of, and adhesion to, the Hanoverian succession; but this Walter Morton's father could not do; and when he died, he left all his devotion, all his loyalty, all his energy and bravery, represented in his son. I am not, however, about to recapitulate old scenes in history, which are familiar to us under a thousand illustrations. We all know of the Pretender's campaign in 1745, and of its fatal termination. Colonel Morton was among the first to join the Prince Charles Edward, with a strong body of his tenantry and levies, and no more efficient troop of horse belonged to the *soi-disant* "Royal" army. To support these, and to aid the cause in general, Colonel Morton had not only raised money by mortgages on his estate, but had even pledged his plate, his wife's jewels and other valuables; and, in this respect, as in all others, there were few adherents of the Stuart cause who had shown more true devotion and disregard of personal interest. I feel certain, indeed, that, mercenary as were the motives of many of the Prince's friends, and deeply as they hoped for eventual personal aggrandisement by the success of his cause, no such motive had crossed the mind or tarnished the lustre of the character of Walter Morton. As with his father and his ancestors, so with him attachment to his Prince's cause was an article of faith, as earnest, and as devout, as his religious belief.

The story of the end is soon told. Colonel Walter Morton charged boldly, and shouted "victory," at Prestonpans; marched in triumph to Derby; and when Hawley's dragoons charged at Culloden, was knocked from his horse in a vain attempt to check them, stunned by the fall, and so taken prisoner. For the sake of a beloved wife and one darling daughter he would have been glad to live on; for the results of the campaign, the disunion of the leaders, and the irresolution of the Prince himself, had removed from his eyes many of the old veils of romantic devotion. But the Government of the day was not placable, and little mercy was shown to Charles Edward's adherents. From his well-known character, Colonel Morton expected no mercy, and received none; and being removed to London, was tried, condemned to death, and executed on Kennington Common with his companions.

You may read the terrible narrative anywhere in the history of the period, if you have a mind to do so. If you do, it will present to your imagination a fearful scene of human suffering and human revenge; and you will be thankful that times have changed, and that we are changed in them, I hope for the better. Whatever the provocation, England would not now endure the bloody, horrible executions of 1746; nor will Temple Bar ever again be garnished with that ghastly row of pale faces, blistering and rotting in the sun and wind, to which loyal London citizens, and many a fair dame of the period, then looked up with exultation.

Mrs. Morton had followed her husband faithfully to the last; had exerted what interest she had, personally or through others, with my Lord Chesterfield and Mr. Pelham, but to no purpose. Her dear husband had told her from the first it would be so; but she strove, nevertheless, as it behoved her to do, for it was hard to think that he, so glorious in his noble manhood, was to die at man's bidding, and leave her alone. She was an orphan, whom he had seen and had loved in the courtly society of St. Germains, and her family so completely died out, that her husband knew, and knew bitterly, there would be no one henceforth to protect her but the merciful Father into whose gracious care he fervently committed her.

I have said already there is no use raking up the past—else I might tell of the widow's frantic cries from her coach window on Kennington Common; of her prayers, even to the last, for rescue—for his life—which went by on the blustering wind unheeded, and were lost in the shouts of a crowd looking on traitors' deaths. Who heeded the misery of a traitor's wife, when huzzas for King George, and damnations to all Pretenders, rent the air? So she returned with her child to the city; and as all her husband's estate was confiscated, and she had no longer a roof to shelter her, she dismissed her servants, and henceforth lived in obscurity, on the comparative pittance which remained, guarded by the one faithful heart which, in all her direst agony, only clung more closely to her.

It was long, indeed, before she regained proper consciousness; and when any did return, that last frightful scene—the surging crowd; the tall gibbets beyond, rising grim and black out of the smoke of the fires by them; the Dutch dragoons, with their heavy brass caps; the halberdiers' pikes; and, above all, the huzzas, shricks, groans, and shouts of the multitude—fell upon her eyes and ears again, as though they were then present, and she relapsed. But the most terrible acuteness of misery can be blunted by time; and if in Mrs. Morton this proved a long process, it was only when the finer chords of her nature—relaxed by the daily cares and events of common existence—gave forth no painful responses.

It was well that a sum of money had been saved before the general wreck came on, and had been lodged with the great house of Roger Darnell and Company, of London, by Colonel Morton, in his wife's name, in case of accidents; for of this Mr. Darnell proved as faithful a steward as dear old Nanny Keene was a faithful servant. After many explorations, the old house near Tooley Stairs was found, and, as Nanny said, "was a bit cannie auld placie, where naebody wad care to speer after them; and though the watermen lads wuz whiles rough and drucken, yet she'd nae fear o' them, nor the mistress either, an' they were aye kind to the bit lassie."

If her mind were weakened considerably in some respect, Mrs. Morton had not forgotten her accomplishments. French she spoke like a native; she played prettily on the harpsichord; and a talent for embroidery, originally learned in France, was now a means of constant, and in many respects profitable, employment. By degrees all her little accomplishments had been imparted to Sybil. There was no need of any more formal instruction. The child had been docile and intelligent, and was now excelling her mother in many of these pretty arts, more especially in music and embroidery; and while they used the one for their pleasure and amusement, the latter was an occupation which could not now be interrupted without denial of many comforts. When also Mr. Darnell found it no longer convenient to have his nephew Ralph living in his house, he had taken a boat across the river, and paid Mrs. Morton a formal visit. The subject of her receiving the lad had been finally discussed, and being open to no objection, was gratefully accepted. There was a comfortable bedroom for him; and the sitting-room above stairs, which looked out on the river, as well as the small parlour below, were to be common to him as to them.

So Ralph Darnell had been living in the old house for five years, and had grown to be one of the family. He was an orphan, and his story will be told by-and-by; and while he had grown to look often upon Mrs. Morton as a mother (he had never known his own), Sybil was as a sister, and, after a fashion, a dear one. It was a convenient place for the young man to live in. The counting-house of Roger Darnell & Co. was in Lombard Street, and it was a pleasant row in the ferry-boat to the Tower Stairs on fine days, or an easy walk across the bridge, to his daily occupation, returning early to take Mrs. Morton and Sybil either for a row on the river, or a walk in the Temple Gardens or the country, which was soon reached in the direction of Newington, and too-well-remembered and fatal Kennington Common.

Yes, five years had passed pleasantly and peacefully in the house. Ralph had been as regular and orderly a lad as even the precise old Nanny Keene could desire, and he loved the old dame perhaps as much as Sybil did, which is saying a good deal. If Nanny scolded, he was penitent; if she praised him, he felt a greater pride in those few, simple, loving phrases, in the dear old Northumbrian dialect, than he did at the more elaborate speeches of Mrs. Morton. To the residence of Ralph Darnell beneath that roof, he owed whatever good principles and whatever religious feeling he ever displayed in after life; and Mrs. Morton was no niggard in her instructions, which he shared with Sybil. When he came home in the evenings—and merchants' offices closed then earlier than they do now—there were pleasant French and Italian exercises to do; a few stanzas of Dante, or a tale of Boccaccio to be read, for there was not much prudery in those times, and women read and heard innocently, what it would be an insult now even to repeat. Nor was music neglected. Ralph had developed a sweet manly voice, and it was the great delight of old Nanny to linger on the stairs by the sitting-room door, listening to some of those grand old Italian duets and trios, and oftentimes to passages from Mr. Handel's music, then growing into high repute, and rivalling, if not exceeding, that of the Italian masters.

Ah well, those were pleasant days! when there were no cares nor anxieties, and when passions had not been stirred which were slumbering unknown and unsuspected, growing in strength with age, to break out and distort what was otherwise fair to look at. As yet Mrs. Morton knew little, or comparatively little, of Ralph's wild doings. If she remarked he was not so regular as he used to be as a lad, and often came home at nights after she had retired to her room, were there not two apologists always ready in his defence?

"Wad ye hae the puir lad be always cooped up wi' twa auld wives and a bit lassie?" Nanny would say. "Eh, mum, but ye'd ne'er haud a Darnell that gate! Na! na! I'se seen mony siccan, and a'll see till him. Dinna ye speer too much at him; it'll do nae gude. Ye maunna check a het colt too sharp."

And there was truth in this homely advice of Nanny Keene's; nevertheless, she could not conceal from herself that Ralph's irregularities were increasing, and she and Sybil had had many an anxious conference about them, which had been productive of no very practical result. Now and then, for a week or even a month, Ralph would reform, and be once more what they were proud of. Then there would be fresh relapses. Is it not always so? *Facilis descensus Averni* is an ancient saying truly, now passed into a proverb; but I don't know that it is very easy in all cases, in spite of the old pagan's assertion. Then, as now, there were often sore struggles to regain lost footing, which sometimes succeeded; and as temptation must needs assail every son of Adam, it is well that some places are found on the slippery path where sorely tried souls can rest for a while, look round and think, and so, praying for safety, be helped up again.

Thus we have seen Ralph Darnell already slide down a long way. The path was very pleasant, and he was in good company too. He liked play, and was growing to like it still better, not for the sake of money, but for the excitement which accompanied it. He liked drink too. Most men of spirit drank heavily then, and to be drunk was a very venial sin indeed. Did not his most sacred majesty King George drink? Did not Sir Robert Walpole drink? Was there any one, in fact, who did not drink? And did our ancestresses think the worse of their brothers, lovers, and husbands if they drank? I fear not; and perhaps some of them even gloried in it. Above all, Ralph was getting into a set of his own: a right merry set of "hot bloods," not numerous but choice; such men as were his equals in birth and breeding, and who, having preceded him in the royal road of life, had experience to lead him on. No wonder he found it a pleasant one!

Very pleasant at the time; but afterwards? Well, I have heard it said, that the waking after a night such as Darnell had passed is not pleasant—quite the contrary; and so it proved in this case. As morning was breaking in grey streaks, and the few last patches of scud were flying lazily below the motionless clouds above, Ralph turned heavily on his pillow, yawned, stretched himself, and suddenly sat up. How the room seemed to reel! how ill he felt! how every bone ached! Where was he? On a floor somewhere, not certainly in his bed. What was that seated in the large arm-chair, with a red petticoat or cloak over it, and the feet set up on another, fast asleep? He looked again and saw it was old Nanny, and felt ashamed as most of the events of the evening flashed suddenly upon him. He remembered Sybil's calling to him in the tavern, and that he left it with her; but of what had passed afterwards, or how he got home, his memory was very confused. Had Elliot and Forster brought him home? Something hard pressed against his thigh as he turned round. Yes, it was money, a large sum, too—more than he knew of. "Nanny!" he cried softly, "dear Nanny!"

The old woman had too long attended sick-beds to be a hard sleeper; she opened her eyes at once, and looked down. "Master Rraafe, are ye wakin?" she said in a low tone, as if uncertain whether he had called or not.

He tried again to rise, but it was impossible; the heavy head sank down on the pillow, and he groaned aloud.

"Puir bairn! puir laddie!" she said, rising; "ye'll be no happy the morn; an' it's aye thatten wi' 'em. Dinna get up; lie there a bit, an' dinna stir for yer life. It's early yet, an' there's naebody movin'. Ma certie, but it was a wild nicht! let's see what it's like noo, and the daylight breakin'."

She went up into the sitting-room above and looked out on the river. The wind had quite fallen, and the dappled-grey sky was tinged with gold where the sun was now rising. The river had already calmed down, and the swell which broke lazily among the wooden piers, and rocked the ships and boats gently, was like the heaving of a child's breast with an occasional sigh and sob, after passion. Broken rigging and masts, however, showed what the force of the storm had been; but the seamen were already at work, damages would soon be repaired, and many wherries and other boats were busily plying to and fro among the shipping. It was a fair and beautiful sight; and the pure snow was lying upon the roofs of the houses and churches beyond the river, clear and bright in the sun's rays, which now broke out cheerily.

"It's the only thing for him noo," said the old dame to herself; "the only thing he'll care for; and maybe a het griddle cake and a bit of rede harrin' by-and-by, and a strong cup o' the green gunpouther tey;" and she opened the door of a cupboard in the corner of the room, and took out the flask which had been produced the night before. Holding it up to the light, "Eh my!" she exclaimed, "but it's nigh empty, and it was full! Wasn't I jist an auld fule for pittin' it nigh his hand? But there's enow for him the morn. It's a hair of the doggie that bit him that'll dee him service, an' nothin' else." And so saying she poured out a small glassful of spirits, and descended the stairs gently.

Ralph Darnell had risen from the floor and taken possession of the chair. A few embers of the fire were still alight, and he had stirred them into a blaze.

"An' sae ye're up, Master Ralph," said Nanny, kindly; "but did I no tell ye to lie quiet? Here, drink that, ma lad, and ye'll be the better o't. Aff wi' it at ance—it's no ony physic stuff!"

Ralph's hand trembled as he took the glass, but he drank off the contents, and felt revived. "O Nanny, darling!" he said, piteously, "what have I done? what have I done to be like this?"

Ah, what a face it was! So pale, so weak, so scared; the eyes so red and swollen: so different to that of the hale, ruddy, handsome youth, who had gone forth the evening before dressed in his smartest suit. "O Nanny, darling!" he cried again, "what have I done? You'll all hate me after this!"

Nanny brushed some hot tears from her eyes, and took the poor aching head to her bosom, where it lay helplessly, as she stroked the wan cheeks and smoothed down the rough curly hair. "A'll no greet," she said, "and a'll no be scoldin' ye neyther, ma bairnie, for that's nae gude, ye ken. Dinna dee the like again, Master Ralph, that's all old Nanny Keene asks o' ye. Ye will not? and ye'll promise me truly? The word of a Darnell's true before God and man, an' ye'll mind it, hinny. O ma bairn! but ye're safe hame, an' ye may e'en thank the Lord for it, as I do, and as sweet Miss Sybil did, when ye lay helpless in the snaa."

"Ah! she, too, saw me then. God bless her!" said the young man, fervently—"God bless her! But she'll never speak to me after this disgrace. And Mrs. Morton?"

"She was asleep, darlin', an' no sound of ye reached till her. I was watchin' her when Miss Sybil brought ye back, and the strange men wi' ye. But ye'll promise me—O Master Ralph! ye'll no deny me, nor her, what I axed o' ye!"

I will! I will, Nanny!" he said, hiding his face still deeper in the woman's breast. "May God help me! It was the first time, and it'll be the last. And she brought me home! O Sybil!"

Nanny sighed. Was this a promise to hold good? She had little hope of it in her heart, but she took what came, and treasured it up, praying that it might be true. "Ye're better noo," she said, "an' I'll believe be, Rreaafe Darrnell. It's no the likes o' me that suld be preachin' t'ye; and ye'll be none the better of an auld wife's foolin'. Get you to rest a while; I'll bring ye some het water, and ye'll soon be fit for wark again."

"But Sybil," said the young man,—"can I not see her?"

"Better not, ma pet—better not. When ye come hame the afternoon, the nicht's wark will be a' clean forgotten. Ye'll get across the river by the ferry, an' I'll have the het griddle cake, and a bit o' harrin', an' a cup o' the green gunpouther tey ready agin ye come doon; an' ye maunna be lang aboot reddin' yersel' up, ye ken. There, awa' wi' ye—that's a gude bairn."

CHAPTER VI.

ROGER DARNELL AND COMPANY.

THE counting-house of Roger Darnell and Company was situated, as I have before mentioned, in Lombard Street, precisely where the establishment of so great a merchant should have been. If there were no plate-glass windows, gay brass railings, or architectural decorations of the front in inconceivably magnificent Byzantine and other styles, such as we see prevalent at present in that and other parts of our most wonderful metropolis, there was at least a healthy, well-to-do look about the handsome red brick edifice, and its scrupulously clean bright windows, which imparted confidence as you entered it. In this respect there was a great and very pleasant contrast between it and other merchants' and brokers' offices in the vicinity, in which as much dirt outside and in, as much gloom and mystery as was consistent with any possible endurance, seemed to be affected, as proofs, perhaps, of wealth and devotion to trade.

Not such, however, in any shape or degree, was the house of Roger Darnell & Co. now, whatever it might have been before the days of good Queen Anne, when the old premises had been pulled down and rebuilt on a handsome scale by one of the best city architects of the period, for the residence, as well as the offices, of the then senior partner. We most of us know what good houses those were—how noble the broad staircases and halls, how richly ornamented the ceilings and cornices, how ample the dimensions of the rooms, and their quaintly decorated panels and lofty marble chimney-pieces. All through the reigns of the Queen and of the first George, Mr. Roger Darnell's predecessors had lived in this house, had entertained their friends there after a princely fashion, and had become in time magnates of the city where their wealth was gained, and to which their sympathies were confined. But though the upper portion was still well furnished, it did not suit the taste or the convenience of the present senior partner to reside there, and he had removed, on his marriage, to a handsome mansion of the same period in Bloomsbury. Not that Mr. Darnell, and still less his wife, affected the fashionable society of the higher gentry and aristocracy of the time, who were gradually progressing westward; but it was felt that a relief from City business, and in some respects a purer air, was desirable, and without going to any extreme, Bloomsbury afforded all that was desired. Many of Mr. Darnell's friends and contemporaries had already set up their Lares and Penates there; the neighbourhood was eminently respectable, in the highest sense of the word; and if the aristocracy and landed gentry of the realm gathered together in the western quarter of the metropolis, there was, in the Bloomsbury district, a genteel aristocracy of wealth which held its own defiantly, and was content therewith.

The upper portion of the house was not, however, deserted. When Mr. Sanders, the ostensible, head clerk and local manager, returned from Calcutta, where he had been for many years employed as a servant of the East India Company, and was, it was supposed, now the "Co." of the firm (though he was only advanced to the dignity of signing "per pro." for Roger Darnell and Compauy), he had arrived, as he went, a bachelor; and for the convenience of business, as well as on account of the high and well-earned regard in which he was held by Mr. Roger Darnell, was offered the use of the house, or such part of it as he needed. Here, then, Mr. Sanders ruled supreme. Two maiden sisters, whom his bounty had supported in his absence, lived with him and managed his household affairs with such admirable discretion and care, that it was assumed, and with good foundation, by those who knew them, that their brother would never need to marry, and the fact was that he never did.

How often, in the anxiety of business in India, in the half-mercantile half-political transactions of those days, in charge of up-country factories, making advances for silk, for saltpetre, sugar, or cotton, with the native merchants of Bengal, or negotiating with native princes, and in the lonely hours of endurance of sickness in a climate which had never suited him—had the thoughts of John Sanders turned wistfully and painfully to those two dear sisters, longing, and praying too, to be reunited with them. And when he could be spared—when, in fact, by the death of his predecessor in office, Roger Darnell had written that his experience, knowledge of the country, and of business in general, would be most valuable—how gladly and thankfully did John Sanders resign the service he had belonged to, and, investing all his savings in a last venture, had found it a profitable one, and so rejoined those whom he had left twenty years before.

They were changed, of course, those dear ones. Susan, the fair, merry, bright-eyed girl whom he had left just budding into womanhood; Mary, the elder, with her soft brown hair, now being streaked with grey, her gentle trusting face and loving eyes,—were changed into women of middle age, and yet not very much changed after all. They had watched, while they were permitted to watch, the declining years of a beloved mother, long spared to them; and they had laid her gently to rest in one of those quiet, still, beautiful city cemeteries with only one regret—that John was not with them to receive her last sigh of blessing for the care which he had guarded her from every discomfort. It was said that both sisters might have married, and that many a rich merchant or tradesman of consequence had wooed them, but in vain. Would they have been happier as wives and mothers, doing their parts in the world's work? I cannot tell. The natural yearnings of woman's inner life, which so few of us understand, may have existed for a while, and there may have been, for all any one knew, many a bitter struggle between duty and inclination to be overcome; but the sense of duty overbore all. Mother, dear mother, weakly as she was, could not be left; and, above all, there was such unbounded faith in, and love for, brother John, that, had there been no mother at all to absorb daily care, I think their absolute devotion to him alone would have borne them up. They were well repaid for it at last, and the yearnings for prattling children about their knees, or for the pride of independent establishments, had died out. Others of their schoolfellows or contemporaries had all these to their heart's desire, but they excited no envy. In their brother's safe return their fervent prayers had been answered, and daily, as I may say, these three persons seemed to grow more and more into each other.

Ah, how proud they were of brother John! Away in the East, in a land then unknown in any intelligible manner to English people, his letters, minute in detail as they used to be in his daily life, though very precious, were often quite incomprehensible. They only knew he had charge of vast responsibilities and of vast wealth, and was valued and trusted. But now they saw why this had been; they knew and felt, as a thing close to their hearts, that, as manager of Roger Darnell and Company's business, brother John was a great man. True faith ever exaggerates perhaps, and, I fear, more that of fond, devoted women, than of harder-minded men. "Mr. Darnell, indeed! he was very well; but what would he be, or have been, without John?"

"Had I remained in India," John had said to his sisters that morning at breakfast, "what might not I have been now? There's Drake—why, he was my junior by a long way, and Holwell, and Watts, and all the rest of them, second to me; and now Drake's head of the factory. And there are letters to-day from Wharton, by the *Valiant*, and he mentions—never mind, girls, you wouldn't understand it; but all I know is, that I might have been *now* head of the factory instead of Drake, and here I am, after all, only a clerk."

"What if you had been in your grave, brother John, with some of those wild Indians with scalps at their girdles dancing on it?" replied Mary, with a shudder. "You know you could never bear the heat; as it is, even here, on a warm day you are good for nothing."

"They would not have danced on it, Molly," he replied gravely; "and they don't carry scalps like the savages of the West, as I have often told you. Perhaps these simple people would have lighted a lamp every night there; and when the day came round on which they had laid me to rest, they would have hung garlands of flowers over me lovingly, or done something else equally foolish, as they have often done to those they loved, before now."

"No, no, John," both cried in a breath; "you are best here with us, you darling old brother; and what could Mr. Darnell do without you?"

But this, perhaps, is a digression altogether; for these worthy folks have little to do with our history, and might have been passed by altogether, but for their connection with the firm of Roger Darnell & Co.; and it will suffice to know that they exist, and that all investments in the house are secure so long as John Sanders is the manager; for he is certainly not the "Co."

For the "Co." was in Calcutta, and, after his fashion, very busy there. Presently we may even come to know him; but now I can only mention that one Henry Wharton was the mysterious person who figured as "Co." in the style and title of the London house, who, under cloak of his official situation as a servant of the Honourable East Indian Company, was in the habit of making large investments in silk, saltpetre, sugar, and the like, and transmitting them to the house of Roger Darnell & Company, and receiving and selling on mutual account hardware, broadcloth, and other English productions, which were readily negotiable with the native merchants of Bengal. The local official pay of Mr. Henry Wharton was not much above twenty pounds sterling per year, and how it was that he contrived to send to England some fifty thousand pounds' worth of goods every year, seems incomprehensible to us, though it was not in the least so either to Mr. Roger Darnell or John Sanders. One way or other, the goods came; and again, one way or other, a corresponding shipment was made against them; and so, on the whole, a very pretty trade resulted. Its generalities, Mr. Roger Darnell's very clear mercantile head could master; but the details, and the purchases from Juggut Seit, Omichund, and Ram Narrayun, or the bazaar or market prices, and the Exchange, were mysteries only known to, or capable of being checked by, John Sanders. Alone, Mr. Darnell would have been much at the mercy of his Indian agent; but no Bengal factor would have dared to venture an irregularity when his invoices, and bills of sale and purchase, were to be examined by "the manager."

So this morning, precisely as the office clock began to strike ten, Mr. John Sanders had opened the glazed door which led from the hall into that spacious apartment; and as the last stroke sounded through it, he had seated himself in a comfortable arm-chair at a table covered with green baize, as befitted the rank of "the manager," and looked around him.

"Mr. Darnell is not come yet, I think, Mr. Sims?" he said to a respectable, plainly-dressed clerk, who bowed humbly as he desposited a pile of rather yellow-looking letters before him.

"No, sir, not yet; it is hardly time."

"Is Mr. Ralph come?" he continued, brushing a very imaginary speck of dust from his elaborate and neatly-adjusted breast ruffles.

"No, sir," rejoined Mr. Sims, with somewhat of a sneer perceptible in his voice; "Mr. *Ralph* Darnell usually takes his time."

"Ah! it was a bad night—a great storm indeed, and part of the river is still too rough to cross. He will be walking round by the bridge. Let me know, Mr. Sims—ahem!—when he comes."

"Very good, sir;" and as Mr. Sims retreated to his desk, the manager applied himself to his task of opening and docqueting the several despatches which Mr. Roger Darnell had to read.

CHAPTER VII.

THE DARNELLS PAST AND PRESENT.

NOT many minutes afterwards, Mr. Roger Darnell entered the office, shook hands warmly with John Sanders, who rose to receive him, and passed on into his own sanctum, which, by a door near the large fireplace, communicated with the counting-house. Here he carefully hung up his laced hat, deposited a stick with an ivory handle in the corner, and a cloak, which the sharp morning air had rendered necessary. After this, he took off his high strong shoes, and gaiters, spread them before the fire, and put on a pair of warm fur slippers, which had been duly set out for him: at the same time seating himself and stretching out his hands and handsome legs, cased in ribbed woollen stockings, to be well warmed ere he should proceed to business. Mr. Darnell also removed the wig in which he had walked to the office, took another of a lighter fabric from a stand in a small cupboard, and, having perfectly aired it, put it deliberately on his head, looking at the same time into a mirror on the marble chimney-piece to see that it was quite straight, and smoothing down the ruffles on his breast, which had become slightly discomposed.

You will say, perhaps, that Mr. Roger Darnell was exceedingly particular, and took very good care of himself: and you are quite right. He did so in every respect, and had need to do so. Was he not the head of the great house of Roger Darnell & Co.? a director of the Honourable East India Company, and the brother of a baronet descended from one of the most ancient Saxon families of England?

Was he not also an alderman of the city of London, a member of the Honourable Company of Goldsmiths, and governor or director of I hardly know how many charitable institutions? Truly Mr. Roger Darnell had need to be careful of himself. Dear me, I dread to think what would have happened if, by any mischance or neglect of precaution, Mr. Darnell had then fallen ill and died! But as I cannot bring myself to anticipate anything so shocking, I will not attempt to portray what will eventually ensue, when he, like all others who have sat in the same chair, and who are looking at him from their canvases from all sides of the room, receives the awful message which they have heard in turn and answered.

If they could speak, all those predecessors would agree that their present representative was worthy of them, as well in professional reputation as in personal appearance. The Darnells were ever a handsome race. There was not one of the portraits round Roger Darnell then which did not show talent, high-breeding, and intellectual character which had elevated their mercantile pursuits. There they were, grave men in costly suits, from the time of Henry VIII. and Elizabeth—one painted by Holbein and one by Vandyke—down to the first George. One more too would be shortly there, for Mr. Roger, as befitted his position, was sitting to Mr. Reynolds for his portrait; and as it may be seen by the curious in the noble mansion of the Earl of Whinborough, in Midlandshire, I may be pardoned if I describe it briefly.

Mr. Reynolds had become Sir Joshua before he entirely finished this picture: on which, as the original interested him more than ordinarily, he had bestowed unusual pains, and hence its great value now. Was there a more beautiful specimen of the master in the Manchester Exhibition, or the noble collection of Sir Joshuas in 1862? I do not think there was, and I believe it to be priceless. Dr. Johnson had watched its progress on the easel, and had given his opinion freely as to the high intellectual character it demanded. "None of your turtle-eating, port-wine-drinking, guttling aldermen, sir," he had observed, "and I won't have you make it like one. That man ought to be Prime Minister of England, sir, and I wish he were. Look at his eyes, sir—look at his eyes."

Well, whether Dr. Johnson's, Mr. Boswell's, my Lord Chesterfield's, Sir Horace Walpole's, or any other individual or collective opinions of the time urged the painter to do his best, I know not; but this I do know, that I can never look at that face for any time uninterruptedly, but it seems to me to be alive. The deep, dark grey-blue eyes, with their long soft eyelashes, flash from under the strong black eyebrows, with no scowl of ambition or excitement of study, but with a keen healthy intelligence, worldly if you like, but most piercing; they verily look through you. If they were alive, you would feel them busy about any skeleton you had hidden away in your mental cupboard; and I can imagine how they may have looked a thousand times upon petitioners for advances, dishonest tradesmen, struggling merchants, or keen rivals in business, who had encountered them in that room. All the Darnells round you had fine eyes, black, brown, and grey; but there was not one pair to equal their descendant's. The forehead is high and broad, the complexion is bright and clear; and though the vivid carnations of the original painting have perhaps faded somewhat with time, they have been treated gently by the old destroyer, and are clear as skin itself. The lips are a little full, and the mouth and chin are perhaps somewhat sensual; no matter, they are firm, and yet have a very sweet expression—benevolent, one would rather call it—which you at once respect and honour involuntarily; and over it sits a grand nose, which you would swear projects from the canvas, so admirably is it drawn—a strong manly nose, with the thin, open, quivering Darnell nostril, the effect of which has been deftly given with pure scarlet in the shadow.

A glorious picture truly, and you feel perhaps, if the man there painted were great, this is greater. You do not care about the clothes, beautiful as they are. The satin is satin, the embroidery silk, the lace gold, and the figure—it is full length—standing at a table on which are some letters; and one dated Moorshedabad, July 4, 1757, and signed "Robert Clive," is shown as far as the date and signature of a dear friend. Ah! that is a wonderful letter too, for it tells how the battle of Plassey was won, and what marvel if Mr. Darnell asked Sir Joshua to put it where it is? You do not care for this letter, O casual spectator! as I do, who have to tell you about it, and even perhaps many have forgotten who Mr. Clive was; but you do care for the manner in which the man stands before you, so nervously, yet so firmly, as if with the will to stand and command, and never be displaced. Involuntarily you do him homage, and remember the head of the house of Roger Darnell & Co. as long as you live.

When Mr. Darnell was ready—after, as we have seen him, he had secured his person from all chances of damp—he tapped at the door, at the same time wheeling round his chair to his writing-table, which he unlocked, and the cover of which he turned over. Mr. Sanders knew the signal, and, gathering the bundles of letters together, took them in.

"Sit down, Mr. Sanders," said Mr. Darnell, rising, and courteously handing the manager a chair—"sit down. A rough night, sir, last night. I hope the *Valiant* took no harm; we have a good deal in her, I think. I hear there was some damage done on the river."

"Principally upon the small craft, sir—colliers and coasting smacks, and some were even sunk at their moorings; but the large vessels are all safe. I sent one of the porters to Blackwall early, and he has just returned to say the *Valiant* had not started a rope. The captain had gone ashore last evening, and could not get back; but the chief officer, Mr. Duggan, had her well in hand."

"As was certain, Mr. Sanders. Oh yes, Abel Scrafton would be after— No matter, sir; he is a good commander and a good fellow; and we've no occasion to mind what he does when he gets ashore after five months of the sea."

"None whatever, sir," replied Mr. Sanders, smiling; "and here are some of the letters and invoices. You must have received private letters from Deal direct—they were put ashore by the pilot-boat."

"Here they are," said Mr. Darnell, taking a bundle out of his pocket. "Wharton is as particular as usual in regard to purchases and sales; and, by the prices quoted, we shall do very well both here and there. Look over them at your leisure. Stay, there is one letter which will interest you more, perhaps, than it does me, for there is a good deal of political news in it. You can cast your eye over it while I examine the rates of silk and sugar. It appears to me that we shall do very well to sell all at once, Mr. Sanders, and realise. What do you think?"

Mr. Sanders did not immediately reply—the letter put into his hand had absorbed all his interest, and he read it to the end so attentively, that he did not notice how Mr. Darnell had several times looked up from his papers, and even said, "Well! what do you think?" more than once.

"I beg your pardon, sir," said Mr. Sanders at length, when he had finished all, and laid down the letter with a deep sigh—"I beg your pardon, but Mr. Wharton's news is most interesting; and, indeed, sir, for the time I seemed to be back once more in the old factory, hearing the old sounds, talking the old language, and looking on the broad river with the royal ensign flying from our grand ships over a crowd of native boats, which I used to think emblems of the difference between us and the people there. And the notices of all my old companions, too! I have no letter myself; perhaps you would let me have a copy of this, Mr. Darnell?"

"Certainly, Mr. Sanders, certainly; take it with you; I don't profess to understand it, and these are much more to my purpose. Ah yes! I remember; Wharton regrets you are not there instead of Mr. Drake. You would have been head of the factory, he says. Well, I don't know what that may be; but, for my own part, I would rather live in a snug house in Lombard Street, with two pleasant sisters and a troop of friends about me, than—"

"It means," broke in the manager, with enthusiasm, "that I, John Sanders, should be now the political chief of Bengal. That the native princes, the native bankers, the zemindars, even the Emperor of Delhi himself, would be suitors to me; and that I should be wielding a power of which even you, Mr. Darnell, director though you be, would have but a faint—a very faint—idea. And it means, too, that all this power is now in the hands of that drivelling coward Drake. But forgive me this earnestness, Mr. Darnell. It appears to me a very momentous period indeed—a crisis, as I may say. What will be done when Ali Verdy Khan dies? What terms will the factory get? What amount of nuzzurana—that is, fine—will they be obliged to pay—"

"Well, I daresay this is very interesting to you Indians," observed Mr. Darnell, interrupting him, "and I have no doubt we shall discuss it all very wisely in Council by-and-by, for all we cannot affect actual occurrences in Calcutta one way or other; but what I want to know is, shall we sell what the *Valiant* has brought, or not?"

"No, sir, not yet; not certainly the saltpetre or the sugar. A good deal will depend upon the succession in Bengal whether we get any more. In any case we can afford to wait; and we may soon have a war with France."

"We should gain cent. per cent., Mr. Sanders, now."

"We shall gain five hundred per cent., Mr. Darnell, if I am right."

"Well, I daresay you will be—you always are," said Mr. Darnell, laughing, "I never knew you wrong, by George!" and the keen eyes looked up and through his manager.

All he saw was clear and pure, person as well as heart. The first as nice in all respects as his own—the second perhaps purer, nay, a good deal purer; and the blue eyes met black ones as intelligent and apparently as fitted, if not for command, at least for counsel. Large black soft eyes, with at times a dreamy expression in them; but not often, though an occasional look of languor could not be mistaken. A colourless olive face, in which a blush like that of a girl showed itself beneath the skin sometimes, and instantly faded away. A thin straight nose, and a firm expression, but a most kindly one, about the mouth. Titian has painted some such faces, which we meet occasionally among our galleries; and he is the only man except Vandyke who ever could paint that clear yet sallow complexion. Mr. Sanders wore no wig; his strong iron-grey hair was enough; and it fell in waves and curls about his brow and neck, to the great pride of his sisters and his own comfort. In regard to wigs "he defied," he said, "the English fashions." For the rest, a tall thin figure, as tall as Mr. Darnell's, and much thinner—perhaps constitutionally, perhaps the effects of the Indian climate.

Mr. Sanders rose to go. "By-the-bye, sir," he said, "I wish you would speak to Mr. Ralph—he is not steady, I fear, at all, and sets a bad example in the office. He only just came in as I got up to come to you, and it was half-past ten by the clock. His looks, too, are not pleasant this morning."

"What! again, and so soon, Sanders? Well, send him to me," and Roger Darnell sighed. He loved Ralph, and he had no son of his own. Here was the last Darnell, it seemed, and he looked round the room. He was looking round the familiar pictures as Ralph entered.

No, as Mr. Sanders said, Ralph was not pleasant to look upon; and there was a sullen expression about his red swollen eyes which Mr. Darnell saw at a glance was only to be met with one course. Anger would not answer then—it would only aggravate.

"Ralph," said Mr. Darnell, kindly, putting out his hand, "I was just looking round at the old folks—they are so bright to-day from the snow on the roof beyond, and so beautiful, that I hardly heard you come in. Beautiful, are they not? look at the old Holbein yonder; and there, my namesake, Roger, the Vandyke; and your namesake by Heine."

"Beautiful indeed, sir," replied the young man, who did not see what was to follow, and whose heart was thumping almost loudly against his ribs.

"And I was thinking," continued Mr. Darnell, "that not one of them was unworthy, and that we can look back on them all to Queen Bess's time, ay, and beyond that, too, without a blush. Can we not? and hope that those to come, if there be any, will be like them? May we not, Ralph?" And as he spoke he turned his keen blue eyes straight upon the youth, and looked into him, as Ralph felt, into his very heart.

We know what he saw there, and it was not pleasant; but there was no deep vice as yet, only low habits, for which Roger Darnell thought he knew a reason, and cure might come. There was no occasion to speak; a kind look had been enough, and all the Darnells round the room were witness to it.

Ralph fell on his knees before his uncle. It was a common thing to do in those times: more respectful than the prodigal son nowadays is, who swaggers into the "governor's" room, and thinks "the governor awful slow." I say Ralph fell incontinently on his knees, and put up his clasped hands. He could not speak, and the tears had started from his eyes, and were rolling down his cheeks, as he was gasping with a choking ball in his throat. Oh, what would he not have given to lay his head on his uncle's breast, as he had laid it on Nanny Keene's, and sob out his penitence there and then!

"I know, Ralph—I know it all," said his uncle, kindly. "Bless the boy! don't choke; thine eyes tell tales enough. There now. I want no promises, and will take none. Make them to the Lord, not to me, and pray to be delivered from temptation, as I do every day of my life. Enough, Ralph!—get up, lad, and never forget that there was never a Darnell—not one of those yonder—that was not a gentleman. We have all of us gone through what you have, Ralph—may God forgive us: but no Darnell ever forgot he was a gentleman. Now, up with you; and if you have nothing particular to do, go to Mr. Sanders as you leave this, and tell him I wish you to copy Mr. Wharton's letter, that he took away with him. I give you this work in proof that my confidence in you is not weakened."

Ralph Darnell did not venture to speak; but he rose, and taking his uncle's hand, kissed it fervently, and turned away to the door. "I will do it carefully, uncle," he managed to utter, brushing away his tears as it closed after him.

Roger Darnell sighed. "Where will it all end," he said to himself, "and how? O Henry! O once dear brother! we have, indeed, an anxious care of what thou left us! but that shall not be neglected. And now for these invoices."

CHAPTER VIII.

AN INDIAN LETTER OF 1755.

MR. SANDERS felt what had happened. He was thankful there had been no violence between the two, such as had occurred before; but he thought for a moment Mr. Darnell might have been too indulgent. Would he have been less so? I think not.

"I am to copy a letter of Mr. Wharton's, which my uncle gave you just now," said Ralph; "may I have it?" The young man's eyes were wet with tears, and the wide nostril was scarlet and quivering; but there was a better expression on the face, and therewith Mr. Sanders was content.

"Here it is, Mr. Ralph," he said gently; "please be careful about the copying, for the letter is important. Bring it to me, with the copy, and we will compare the two."

And Ralph took the letter to his desk, not noticing any one, and set to work diligently. A great load of apprehension had been removed from him. "Yes," he said to himself, "they were gentlemen. I shall be a baronet some day, and I will be a gentleman too."

Perhaps Mr. Sims, the book-keeper, and others who had been speculating upon his disgrace, were disappointed; but they saw, plainly enough, that Ralph, smiling through his tears, was not; and so went on with their work as steadily and noiselessly as Ralph Darnell did.

Yes, to Ralph this was a curious letter, and in spite of his ignorance, interested him warmly. Who were these Eastern magnates of whom he read in Mr. Wharton's clear, clerk-like hand? What like the great country which they inhabited? Let me transcribe from the paper itself, now yellow, and the ink faded, some of what was written there. We have nothing to do with the mercantile portion of it, which was of temporary interest only to those immediately concerned; but the rest belonged to the time—to all time—and was full of momentous considerations, present and future.

"And now that I have finished with details of Purchases and "Sales," Mr. Wharton wrote, "it is necessary to inform you, "in some sort, as to our local Position, and of what is going "on about us, which causes me much anxious Thought, "which I doubt whether any of my colleagues do quite share "with me. It is reported that the Nabob, Ali Verdy Khan, "is growing to be more and more infirm, and very incapable "of Business. On the whole, I may say he hath been, and "still continues, a fair Friend to us. His loss, whenever "it may happen, will be one we shall have much reason to "deplore seriously; for I do not see, in the Heir to whom we "shall have to look, any good Hopes, nor any Hopes at all, of "that consideration which we have enjoyed, and which we "must strive hereafter to maintain. For, Sir, in this country, "among Gentoos and Moors—who look more to the effects of "physical than moral Power than you are accustomed to do "in a free country like England—'tis only by showing our-"selves prepared to resist and overcome any attempt at Oppres-"sion, that we can insure that Weight and Respect which are "the foundations of all Commercial transactions, with which "those of a Political Nation are inevitably involved. On this "point it appears to me a miserable Fatuity to risk anything; "and a very poor œconomy also, when the vast amount of "Trade and Capital vested in it, both public and private, is "considered. Should any reverse overtake us by any Native "combination, or sudden onslaught, the sacrifice of immediate "Advances and Investments, however great the loss would "prove, would be trifling in comparison of the difficulty of "regaining a lost Position—a position which, no one knows "better than our friend Mr. Sanders, it hath costs years of "pain and anxiety and a vast expenditure of Money, to main-"tain and raise to what it is.

"We know the Nabob's Armies to be very considerable, and he "hath some excellent Soldiers among them. He may have "from thirty to forty thousand men, with Artillery; while we, "to defend ourselves, have barely one hundred effective Euro- "peans. We have no hope of assistance from Madras or Bom- "bay, or from the Dutch—in short, of none, Sir; and this it "is that makes our native friends so apprehensive, and our "credit so low. These men, Sir, are as keen and careful in "their business as any merchants of London: and had we the "means of assuring them, and protecting them as well as our- "selves, there is no saying to what extent we might not extend "our authority in Bengal; yea even to the control of the "country itself.

"It is not too late to assist us, and, by a timeous display of Force, "to guard the Company's interests and our own. With a "strong Fort, and such extension of the present as would "afford us more accommodation, and with a respectable Army "of English Soldiers and Artillery, our position would be "strong and beyond any risk; and we could make our own "terms with the young Nabob. He is no valiant Hero, we "hear; and comparatively very little addition to our means "would deter him from any overt act against us. 'Tis not "that, as hath been the case at Madras, I would advise war "with the Nabob, or with any one. There, great Wars have "been undertaken with varying success. Mr. Clive, who is "now in England, will have related to you all particulars of "these great doings. I, a humble servant of the Company, "have no right to discuss the propriety or otherwise of the "Madras course of Policy—nor, indeed, that of Bombay. "Both Factories are in the neighbourhood of much more am- "bitious and unquiet folks than we are; and it hath been "necessary for them to defend themselves against Treachery: "and they have Forces enough for this. But we, dear Sir, "are very helpless; and we ought not, nor ought the Com- "pany, to trust to good appearances, which at any moment "may break down.

"And there is another great subject of disquiet to my mind, "and that of Mr. Holwell, and others, at this critical junc- "ture, which is, the French progress in the central part of "the Deccan, under Monsieur Bussy. 'Tis said openly at "Chaudernagore, by Natives of good repute, that the aim of "M. Bussy is to extirpate us from India; and, if he cannot "effect this in Madras or Bombay—which, thank God, are "too strong for him just now—that nothing will deter him "from an attack upon us in our weakest Settlement: and, "furthermore, that the young Nabob, who hateth us with a "bitter Hatred, hath already covenanted with the French for "assistance, which they will readily give. If, therefore, M. "Bussy can, by marching by the Sircars (for he hath already "the control of the whole of the Deccan Soubadar's Do-"minions, and possesses a large Army devoted to himself, "both of Frenchmen and of natives—Telingas they are called, "whom he hath trained and disciplined—with much heavy "Artillery), penetrate to Chandernagore, and join the young "Nabob—then, dear Sir, may God help us; for we have no "hope to resist this double combination, and no Means whatever. "We should, so far as I can see, be driven from the Country "ignominiously; and in this opinion not only does Mr. Hol-"well and all steady thinking men here concur, but our "Native Friends are perpetually warning us of it, and most "heartily marvelling at our Inaction. As I have said before, "Sir, Power can alone insure us respect, and the faithful "observance of all Treaties and Agreements. Without it, I "well believe them to be only so much waste Paper—nay, "worse, the very means of provocation for their annulment.

"*Most Private.* With these anxieties on general political "grounds, I am more beset by others of a local nature than I "can describe. Our chief here hath, I may say it to you, "neither Ability nor Firmness to guide our Ship into a safe "Haven if ever a Storm should arise, which may God avert. "Depend upon it, dear Sir, that I write the Truth, and the "Truth only; and hard as it may be to say anything deroga-"tory of my Superior, I cannot think it inconsistent with my "Duty to allude to this painful Subject. Sir, he hath no "Respect from us nor from the Natives; and I sadly fear—"and many share this fear with me and Mr. Holwell—that "he hath no Courage neither. Alas! that I should have to "say so of any Englishman; and alas! if ever it hath to be "put to the proof! If you could send us Mr. Clive, indeed, "Courage would at once be infused into every one; and "though he might come in a Military capacity, there is not "one of us who would not stick to him in case it were neces-"sary for him to assume the chief Authority.

"You may say we may still depend upon the Emperor of Delhi. "Alas, Sir, that great Empire is breaking up fast, and little "beyond very nominal Power remains to him. He could not "protect us against the Nabob, even did he desire to do so. "The Morattoes are pressing him hard. His own subjects "are everywhere rebellious and inconstant; his Viceroys and "Deputies are growing fast into independent Princes, and "the Morattoe kingdom is increasing. 'Twas only last year, "as you may have heard, that the old Emperor, who, for his "part, was well affected towards the English factories, was "taken by treachery to the Morattoes, and had his eyes "cruelly put out in their camp, and is now a prisoner. His "Successor is powerless to help himself—a mockery in truth "of an Emperor; from whom, or indeed from any other "Native Power, near or far away, it would be only a delusion "to hope.

"Now, dear Sir, if I have written in any despondent tone in "this most confidential Communication, I pray your Forgive-"ness; for indeed I cannot help doing so under the threaten-"ing circumstances of our Position; and, for the better com-"prehension of its details, I pray you also to lay it before our "excellent friend Mr. John Sanders, who, from his long resi-"dence here, and great Experience, hath Ability to give you "such explanation as may serve you in the Council-parlour "of the Directors. Were Mr. Sanders indeed here, we "should not need Mr. Clive. We deplore that his Health "would not allow him to remain, to be, as he would be now, "Chief of the Factory; for were he among us, we should "have no occasion to fear the treacherous wiles of the Moors "or the Morattoes, however we might be apprehensive of "their great Armies."

CHAPTER IX.

IMPROVEMENTS.

RALPH DARNELL'S penmanship was none of the most rapid; and in common with the political portion of the letter, there was a long detail of mercantile, official, and private transactions, which had also to be copied. Ralph had done it all in his best and clearest hand. He was very happy, and with a light heart no toil is irksome. It was nearly two o'clock when he had finished the whole, and he had not moved once from his seat. Just as he was about to conclude, a stout active young man of middle height, richly dressed in a military uniform, opened the office door, and crossing the room with a quick decided step, greeted Mr. Sanders kindly, and asked whether Mr. Darnell was to be seen; the reply was in the affirmative, and he passed on to the parlour; and while Ralph was showing his work to Mr. Sanders, and they were about to commence their comparison, the door opened, and Mr. Darnell requested the Indian letter might be sent to him.

"Let me take it, Mr. Sanders," said Ralph eagerly—"let me take it; I'm not afraid now, and my uncle will be glad to see that I have made clean work of what he bid me do."

"By all means, Ralph," replied the good-natured manager; "one of the gentlemen mentioned in that letter, Colonel Clive, is now with your uncle, and you may like to see him; go at once."

Ralph did not then understand the weight of that illustrious name, though the mention of him by Mr. Wharton had excited his curiosity; but as he entered the room it was impossible not to be struck with the soldierly aspect, the quick, penetrating glance, and energetic gestures of the man before him. How well Ralph remembered this meeting in after times! Perhaps he was not much struck with Mr. Clive's appearance because he knew nothing, so to speak, of his history or his achievements, beyond a very confused impression of battles in India; but he felt, as he entered with the papers, that, for a second time that day, he was being measured from head to foot, and looked through."

"No need to say who that is, Mr. Darnell," said Mr. Clive, laughing; "I'd swear he was one of your blood, if I had met him in Fort St. George; yet I did not know—"

"Not a son of mine, Colonel," replied the merchant, hastily—"a nephew. Ralph, I must present you to Colonel Clive, about whom you have read a little to-day, and of whom you will read a great deal more by-and-by."

"Glad to see you, sir," said Clive, cordially offering his hand. "I wish I could tempt a Darnell to join me in the East; but I suppose no scion of the great house would think it worth his while to become a poor soldier of fortune like me."

"Don't unsettle the lad's mind, Mr. Clive, I pray you," said Mr. Darnell, laughing. "We shall have him flying away with you to India; but look, here is the letter I told you of. You will read Ralph's fresh clear writing better perhaps than the original. Show Mr. Clive, Ralph, where the political portion begins—he won't care about our trade details—and wait till he has done."

Colonel Clive read with evident interest, and Mr. Darnell, as Ralph could see, watched him narrowly. His uncle's keen eyes were fixed upon the well-bronzed face of the soldier, and followed every change of his countenance. As the letter was finished, Clive rose, gave it to Ralph, and began to pace the room rapidly.

"Well," said Mr. Darnell, "what do you make of it all?"

"Make of it, Mr. Darnell? why, only this, that, by God, I will see it out with that d—d Frenchman yet, and you'll hear then who is best man in India, he or I. He's a very clever fellow, sir, and a good soldier, and I respect him for all he has done at Hyderabad; but there's no room for both of us in that country, and one, sir, will have to leave it. If I had a doubt on the subject of going soon, that letter has done more to clear it away than anything else I have heard or read."

"But about our Calcutta factory, Mr. Clive? shall we get any more sugar? and what of this young Nabob, sir?"

"Ask Mr. Sauders," replied Colonel Clive, with somewhat of a sneer. "What do I know about sugar and saltpetre? my hand has ever been more familiar with this, Mr. Darnell," and he touched his sword, "than with mercantile affairs. I do not think there is any immediate danger in Bengal, and if there should be, I will see to it when I get out. Sugar and silk, silk and sugar, and that's all you folks here care about; I can't account for it, Mr. Darnell. Have you no ambition? With all the old political organisation of that vast country breaking up—resolving itself into new forms, can't you—cannot England, strike in," he cried, as he paced to and fro more rapidly, "and establish a political power which should overwhelm every other? That Nawab, sir! why, he's only of yesterday! why should not we be there instead of him? Give me a couple of thousand Englishmen, Mr. Darnell, and let me march through India to Bengal; I will sweep away Bussy, clever as he is, and the Company—by God, sir!—shall rule in Bengal instead of the Nabob, and do as they please. But no, you cannot understand this here, Mr. Darnell—not yet, not yet; wait till I get there."

"I trust sincerely, Mr. Clive," said the merchant, gravely, "that you will become dispossessed of such wild, impracticable thoughts. What could we do with any territory? what do we want with Eastern politics? what does the crown want, sir? Have we not enough of anxiety already with America? No, sir! I shall grieve to see one whom I love and honour, betraying the trust we repose in him by wild ambition, which may only lure him on to destruction."

"You cannot understand the country, Mr. Darnell," replied Mr. Clive, "and we might only quarrel over what my poor thoughts lead me to express; but that we shall possess that country, Mr. Darnell—that we *must* inevitably possess it—I believe as firmly as that I am Robert Clive. I thank you for showing me that letter; it is most important to any one who can understand it."

"In confidence, Mr. Clive—in the utmost confidence that one man can show to another," said the merchant, decidedly.

"Certainly, Mr. Darnell—certainly; Robert Clive never yet forfeited any that was reposed in him, and I may live to repay this. Good morning, And you, young gentleman," he continued, turning to Ralph, "cannot you be tempted to follow a soldier's fortunes? There should be one Colonel Darnell to hang up among that goodly company. No? well, I don't blame you. If I had had wealthy uncles like you, and were heir to a baronetcy, instead of being the poor son of a poor lawyer, I should never have seen India. Now my fate is there, and I must follow it. Farewell, Mr. Darnell, I do but interrupt you; but I shall see you again before I leave England, and I shall be at the Council by-and-by, and you must wish me good luck."

"That I shall always do, Colonel Clive," returned Mr. Darnell, "from my heart; and you have but to command my best services. Don't let his offer tempt you, Ralph," he continued, as Ralph thought, gravely, after Mr. Clive left the room. "He is one of the finest fellows that ever served the King, but that is no country for a Darnell while we are here. I am quite satisfied with you, Ralph, to-day; you have copied this letter very neatly and carefully, and had better get home; I am going to the Council, at which there may be some anxious matters to discuss;" and as he turned to gather up his papers, Ralph bowed to him and left the parlour.

"My uncle has taken the letter, Mr. Sanders, but here is the copy; it is quite correct, for Colonel Clive has just read it all through."

"And what did he say? what did he say?" cried the manager, eagerly; "can you remember?"

"Very little indeed, sir," said Ralph, laughing; "he seemed to care more for the mention of Monsieur Bussy than about Bengal. He said you knew more of that country than he did."

"Just like him, Ralph," replied the manager; "he has been all his life as yet fighting with the French, and has thoughts just now for nothing else. But we shall see—we shall see. Now you may go; there is nothing else to do."

"Thank you, sir," replied the young man, "and good-day to you."

"You are going home, Ralph, I hope?" added Mr. Sanders, with some emphasis on "home."

"Yes, sir; I intend to go home."

It would have been well for Ralph if he had gone—if he had turned towards the river and taken the ferry-boat at the Tower Stairs; and for a moment, as he stood at the hall-door of the house, he was irresolute. In truth, the events of the past night were rapidly coming more clearly to his mind, and the money he had won was lying heavily in his pocket. He had not dared to count it, and he knew he had promised his revenge to the sailor captain. It would be an ungentlemanly thing to evade this, and Darnells should be gentlemen; had not his strict uncle said so? He would at least offer the captain his chance; and Gracechurch Street, too, would lead him home quicker than round by the Tower. If he met Elliot and Forster, well and good; he would take his chance of the result. Yes, it was the open and manly course to follow. Why should he sneak home with a pocket full of another man's money? So, he turned into Gracechurch Street, and walked rapidly towards the Golden Cock.

I am not going to moralise upon this act. I, too, as well as you who read this, well know what has befallen some of the best of *our* virtuous resolutions; and here I have to tell you of one by no means strong-minded, or as yet strongly grounded in *his*. Many a hard tussle, many a painful weary fall, has to be endured before they become able to compete with what they have to encounter in the fierce struggle of life; and many a slip on the road, which I have before noticed, to be regained, with cries and tears before God, ere the mental footing is firmer. Happy they who have had none of them; I say, very happy, and to be envied truly. But are there any? Well, Ralph Darnell was not at least one of them, and so he went on.

Nor had he to go far. As he neared Thames Street, the trio he almost looked for met him plump, and could not be avoided.

"Confound that counting-house of yours, Darnell," cried Elliot, cheerily; "we thought you had been shut up for good by that great uncle of yours for being a naughty boy last night, as we did not find you at the old place of tryste. Why, we have been there ever so long, and had wellnigh given you up."

"A good day to you, sir," said the Captain, raising his hat courteously, "and I hope you are none the worse of last night. Your friends have done me the honour to accept my invitation to take their dinner on board my ship, and I hope you will not object. We are not yet in harbour trim, sir, and things look rusty after a long voyage; but I have a fair cook, and for the rest will do my best, gentlemen, to entertain ye. I have a boat ready at the stairs here, and I will send another crew to see ye home. It is calm on the river, and a row down will be pleasant pastime for you landsmen."

Could Ralph refuse? The Captain's guineas were clinking in his pocket, as heavy there as they were on his mind. Before him was the bridge, and Nanny and Sybil would be looking for him, he knew, anxiously. Should he go on? What excuse could he make? Another time he could meet them--to-morrow. Could he say so?

Forster seemed to read his thoughts. "No time like the present, Ralph," he said, taking the young man by the arm. "Come along! we have enough to do to-morrow, Elliot and I, and we may not have another chance for a week. Come along," and—he went. The party passed through the Golden Cock, and by the wooden stairs was a smart eight-oared cutter lying. "Oars!" cried the coxswain, as he saw the party; and they were raised at once, as if by men-of-war's-men. "Now, men, let these gentlemen see how a *Valiant's* crew can row them down to the good old ship. Give way—with a will," cried Captain Scrafton, cheerily; and the boat shot down the noble river more rapidly than ever Ralph had been rowed before.

His care gone; and, with a perversity of judgment, he was now rejoicing in the idea of having done what it was incumbent on a gentleman and a Darnell to do. He only hoped he might lose, and so be rid of the captain's money, and of play for ever; and he was as joyous and cheerful at the thought of this as his companions had ever seen him.

And it was a pleasant dinner in the cuddy of that stately ship, where they had been welcomed with all the honours of the boatswain's pipe, a guard of marines with side-arms, and the officers in uniform. As the captain saluted them, and the quarter-deck, with a wave of his laced hat, the others followed his example, and looked around with admiration on the white deck, and polished brasses, and carved wood-work of the deep poop awning.

"You are welcome, gentlemen, to the Honourable East India Company's ship *Valiant;* not quite a frigate, sirs," said Captain Scrafton, looking proudly about him, "but a ship of which no officer of King George's navy need be ashamed."

It was a pleasant dinner, I say, with honest English fare. Many a strange and savoury Eastern condiment; pickles, and preserves of rich flavour too, were set before them; and the party did justice to the gallant captain's good cheer and generous wine, while they enjoyed his tales of sea life, of Indian experiences, and of the wars there, in which Englishmen were beginning to bear so proud a part. Of most of these Indian stories Colonel Clive was the hero; and as Ralph heard of Wandiwash, Arcot, and many another bloody fight, he began to understand what manner of man that was, of whom his uncle's kindred nature was so fond.

I will not go through the rest of the evening. Ralph had come there with two settled objects—one to lose his money if he could, the other to be sober like a gentleman; and he fulfilled both. Captain Scrafton did not press wine upon him, and he was for the time proof against the raillery of his companions. The captain, too, had his revenge, for Ralph not only lost all that he had won, but more to boot; for Elliot had pressed money upon him persistently; and while the play went on, could he withdraw with any spirit? He did not think so at any rate, and so played on. It was well that the party broke up early. Elliot and Forster had both other engagements for the night at the west end of the city, and must fulfil them; and the captain, after many hospitable protestations against it, ordered the cutter, and let them go. It was a calm, moonlight night, the water was smooth, and the men stretched to their oars, as they believed only Captain Scrafton's "Valiants" could do. As the clocks were striking ten, the cutter ran in among the wherries at Tooley Stairs, and, giving a crown to the coxswain, Ralph sprang ashore, and watched the boat in its course through the rapids under the bridge, dashing the spray from its bows in bright sparkles as it danced over the roaring ebb.

"An' what hae ye dun wi' a' them gouden guineas, Maister Rraafe?" asked Nancy Keene, as she lit a candle for him in the parlour. "Maybe ye ha' bin winnin' mair o' them?"

"Nay, Nanny dear; but I've lost them all to the man I won them from, and I'm glad of it—aren't you? Where's Sybil?"

"Deed an' she's gane to bed this lang time, Maister Rraafe. D'ye think she'd be stoppin' up for yow? An' sae they're gane? Deed, then, I'm glad o't, Maister Rraafe. What wad a Darnell, that's to be a barrinit, be doin' wi' ither folk's gowd in his pouch? Has they not enou' o' their ain? Deed, then, I'm jist glad, ma bairn, an' that's a' aboot it. Get to bed wi' ye—they're a' gane langsyne, an' when a've steekit the door, a'll follow ye. A' thank the Lord," continued Nanny to herself aloud, "there's nae ony sign o' drink on the lad. Eh my! but we bided his comin' wi' sair hearts—didn't we jist?"

It had been an anxious watch. Sybil and the old servant had listened for every footfall near the porch door for many an hour since early evening, vainly speculating upon the reasons of Ralph's absence, and dreading a recurrence of the scene of the previous night. Indeed, Nanny's reminiscences of tipsy men, and how the "drout o' the drink drav them agin an' agin to't," seemed to be the sole burden of her tale, till Sybil could bear it no longer, and had retreated to her room, whence, as Nanny opened the porch door, she listened with a throbbing heart; and as the old woman's soliloquy fell on her ear, she gently closed her door as Ralph steadily ascended the stairs, knelt down, and with a grateful heart blessed God that he was safe.

I fear Ralph Darnell's heart was not so grateful or so devout; and that as he lay down, his thoughts presented a very different aspect to Him who saw them, than did those of the gentle girl's. He had lost money, more than fifty pounds, and given Elliot an I O U for it. Where was he to get this sum? Well, Elliot said, "it might lie over till he was a baronet;" and had they not drunk his health with a hip-hip-hurrah, wild and earnest, and his speedy succession to the ancestral dignity of all the Darnells? Yes, he would be a baronet, but when? His Uncle Roger never mentioned the subject; Sir Geoffrey sent him an occasional blessing, and paid his quarterly allowance, which had been his father's, regularly. That was all. He would be of age in a few months; would he then be recognised and placed in his proper position? Proper? pshaw! Roger Darnell might yet have sons, and did not he come first after his brother?

All seemed dark here too—uncertain and undefined, as if some mystery hung over him which he could not penetrate. Who was Mr. Smithson, and who Miss Grover? Gradually, as sleep followed, the lines of thought in the young man's mind seemed to cross each other, and interweave like confused webs spinning around him. His Uncle Geoffrey and his Uncle Roger appeared to be at cross purposes with each other and with him; and along with them, the deeply bronzed and keen-eyed Colonel Clive, wearing an Eastern dress, was beckoning him on through hosts, countless and still increasing, of struggling, surging, turbaned men, while his mouth felt parched, and his brow was covered with sweat in the fierce turmoil. Then all this faded away, and there was with him a bright fair-haired girl by the wooded banks of a brawling northern river, with the trout rising in its pools, and a warm summer sun shining upon all.

"O Constance! my own, my darling, why was I sent away? I will come; I have not forgotten," the lips murmured; and if the young man could have been watched, it would have been seen how the knit brow, the clenched hand above the bed-clothes, and the uneasy restless postures, were changed for a soft sleep, while tears glistened on the eyelashes, and the name of Constance seemed to linger upon the smiling ruddy mouth.

CHAPTER X.

THE DARNELLS OF MELCEPETH.

Above the point where the present railway bridge crosses the deep bed of the Coquet river, in Northumberland, and from thence to the sea, there are few streams in England which surpass this in beauty of a striking and peculiar character. The banks are high and broken; there are lofty scaurs, and bold knolls and promontories, covered with luxuriant woods; and the river itself brawls over a rocky bed, or lies in still, deep pools speckled with foam and overhung with graceful foliage, where there appears scarcely any current at all. Such localities seem to have afforded favourite sites for the old local princes, or Saxon thanes; and examples of them still exist in the county, which are proud and precious memorials of the past.

Of such, the most remarkable, perhaps, is Mitford Castle, above Morpeth, in the lovely valley of the Wansbeck, a sister stream to the Coquet; for the site combines the utmost picturesque effect with natural strength at a period when artillery was unknown, and when bowmen, and rude engines for casting stones, could have had little effect upon defenders protected by those massive walls. For many a century, Mitford must have flourished defiant and uninjured; but its now shattered walls and keep evince the terrible power of a comparatively modern system of warfare. Centuries have passed since the artillery of an English king was planted against those stout defences and brought them low; and Time has perhaps done little more than hang his victorious banners of ivy and fern, woodbine and wild rose, over the ruins, till they have assumed their present graceful and romantic aspect. In other respects the place is little changed. The broad meadow round the castle foot is smooth and green, as when Norman and Saxon fought there, or tilted in manly sport. The beautiful Wansbeck babbles by, under the lofty scaurs festooned with hanging ivy; the rooks swing and caw in the great trees by the little church; and the Mitfords still possess those noble ancestral properties they have held round their castle for a thousand years—nay more, far back into the dim period of Saxon possession. But it has been otherwise with the Darnells.

I have no doubt, in old times, before the Conquest, that these Darnells and Mitfords were stanch friends or bitter enemies, as it behoved neighbours to be in rough old border society, and the various feuds and petty wars then occurring; and there can be no doubt that Melcepeth, like Mitford, was a place of strength and of war. Like it, also, the castle had suffered heavily, perhaps at the same period; but the destruction had either been more complete, or the place had been less cared for afterwards; for at the period of this history there was little of the ancient structure remaining, except a portion of the keep, and one tower, which had been incorporated with the more modern stables and farm-buildings. Part of the great hall was the present baronet's dog-kennel; the ancient buttery was the dairy; and, in like manner, some other portions remained, while all the stones of the rest had been used to build the present manor-house. I cannot say, either, that this was a noble or a capacious building. It had the look of being a temporary structure, and had, in fact, been built in the time of Elizabeth as one. Not, however, in the elaborate style of that period, or with the comfortable adaptation to improved domestic habits which was then progressing; but as a makeshift and in the prospect of an altogether new edifice, which had never been carried out. One possessor after another had left that work to his heir; no building fund, as I may call it, had been accumulated; and though the present baronet, Sir Geoffrey Darnell, having encountered much rough weather in the early portion of his life's voyage, had gained smooth water, he, too, did not seem inclined to launch again into new enterprises, and always said to his steward, as he looked up at the old place, "It will last my time, Smithson; anybody after me can do as they like with it."

And so, with a patch here, a new floor there, and general overlooking, the old castle, as it was still called, lasted very well.

There could be no doubt of the beauty of its situation. A little further back than the old castle—that had been perched upon a high scaur, with an almost precipitous face towards the river, which boiled and foamed at its foot in a rocky channel, here considerably narrowed—the present Melcepeth occupied a round knoll, sloping down from the fields above to a meadow by the river-side, now converted into a lawn. To the north and east, the high castle-crag protected the house from the bitter winter winds; and the hollow, as it were, in which the mansion lay, always presented a warm and cheerful aspect. I have often wondered why such a situation was neglected; but when the place was no longer wanted as a residence, the Earl of Whinborough's family having a palatial mansion in Midlandshire, and other noble houses on other family properties, it fell to ruin, was not worth repair, and being inconvertible into a farmhouse, was pulled down, and so has disappeared as completely as the Darnells have, who owned it, and as has been the fate of many another Saxon family as proud and as wealthy as they were.

But at the time of this history, the castle was in excellent order. Sir Geoffrey Darnell was not perhaps wealthy, so to speak, but he had an income quite equal to his position, drawn from prosperous estates in Durham and Yorkshire; and he always said that when a new place was necessary, it had far better be built in either of those pleasant counties, than in the locality in which the family possessed least land, and where they lived only in conceit of the "Saxon" Darnells. "If they had," Sir Geoffrey said, "like the Mitfords, indeed, all their lands about them, it would be a different matter truly; but, as it is, Smithson, *as it is*, I am not going to be such a fool as to burn my fingers with bricks and mortar. The place will last my time very well."

There was a good deal in that simple "as it is" of the baronet, which Mr. Smithson understood perfectly; and I owe it to the elucidation and comprehension of this history, to explain in some degree why the baronet had laid such particular emphasis on a repetition of those three little words; and I think, when my readers' eyes have glanced over what I have to write, that, in consideration of its details, I may be forgiven for an apparent digression.

There is no need for me to go into the past. Any curious person can, by paying a registrar's fee, know all about the family—whom they married, who were born, who died, and when—if the family-tree in the Heralds' College be consulted; but I don't know, after all, that any one would be much the wiser if they did this. There had been always a Darnell a baronet, since baronets began, and always a Darnell—brother, uncle, or cousin, or as it might be—at the head of the great firm in Lombard Street. Therefore we have only to do with the present, Sir Geoffrey and his belongings.

I must now mention that the family had always been loyal—most loyal, to their ancient princes; and that the Stuarts possessed their adhesion and support as heartily as those of any family in the land—so heartily, indeed, that Sir Geoffrey, then a young man of twenty-five, had joined Forster and the Earl of Derwentwater in 1715, and shared their fortunes, rough and fatal as they were to many. The youth only, perhaps, of Geoffrey Darnell had saved him from the fate of the chiefs of that unhappy rebellion. I do not think the Jacobite Northumberland baronet had many friends, or much interest at Court; but his life was spared when he was taken with others at Preston, and he was one of that sad company which, amidst thundering huzzas for King George, and uproarious demonstrations of London loyalty, suffered the indignity of being marched, bound and pinioned, through the streets, as a warning to future dabblers in treason and rebellion.

Geoffrey Darnell, as might be supposed, did not often visit the city after that. "He hated the d—d place," he said; and had no craving for town pleasures or occupations. In 1745, when his neighbour Morton, and many another too, joined Prince Charles Edward, Sir Geoffrey was not to be deluded. He had had enough of the first trial; he thought this would succeed no better: and though he gave what money he could spare secretly—through Morton—he personally kept entirely aloof. Sir Geoffrey had married, too, and his wife's pleadings accorded with his own thoughts. Morton had left as dear a home, as deeply loved a wife, and a child nearly the same age as his own, and what had been the result? Misery to all, and ruin past redemption. Sir Geoffrey Darnell, personally because of his disgrace, and hereditarily because of his family predilections, detested the house of Hanover; but saw it was no use contesting its power with any Jacobite means, and, as he escaped all accusation or suspicion in 1745, he was grateful that he had been able to resist so much temptation.

His first wife, Lady Jane, died in childbirth of her second child—a boy still-born. Had she lived, indeed, or had that infant lived, Sir Geoffrey's situation would have been very different to what it was at the present juncture. He grieved deeply for his wife, indeed for a time was inconsolable; but he was lonely, and he married, about five years after her death, a lady whom he loved as dearly, and who, with more grace, more accomplishments, and allied to greater families, promised to be a lifelong joy to him. But it was not fated to be so. Ah! it was a sad story—a sad tragedy, too. They were riding out one day; they had ridden to Mr. Smithson's farm, near Dunstanborough, and, on their return, Lady Honoria's horse had swerved at some object, as she cantered homewards, too heedlessly, by her husband. The spirited animal had then reared and become unmanageable; there was a heavy fall, and the poor lady never spoke more. This had happened in 1749. Sir Geoffrey did not marry again. He began to conceive that fate had set against the Darnells; and though many friends, and, most of all, his brother Roger, urged him to take a third wife, he would not hear of it, and the expectations of many a bright county damsel were sorely disappointed. Bessie Grover, his first wife's companion and schoolfellow, who had lived with her, and taken charge of her child after her death, was again invited; and, acting as governess to the little Constance, as well as housekeeper, she reigned, as much supreme as she desired to be, at Melcepeth.

The baronet had two brothers; one, Roger, we know already. He had been early sent to his uncle and godfather, Roger, after whom he had been named, and, being adopted by him, became, on his death, head of the house. There was little communication between these brothers. Roger Darnell the elder had no Jacobite sympathies, and he, as well as his nephew, had looked with shame upon Sir Geoffrey's march through London city, where their name stood so high. The only consolation was, that no one knew the sufferer, and the event soon died out of men's memories. As the brothers grew older, and Geoffrey never came to London, the connection grew even slighter, and was confined to interchanges of game from the north in the season (which, Roger complained, seldom reached him so as to be fit to eat), with a box of Indian (East or West) condiments or preserves, and tea, in return, such as money could not buy. There were letters of sincere condolence written on the deaths of both Ladies Darnell, and of congratulation when Roger married the daughter of a rich Virginia merchant and quondam planter, who, having sold his estate there, had again settled in London. When the Baronet had proposed that nephew Ralph should come to London, when he was falling into wild country ways, as his father had done, Roger had accepted the charge under some necessary reservations only known between the brothers; and the young Ralph had been sent about five years before—shortly, indeed, after the last Lady Darnell's sad death. Perhaps, had she lived, he would not have left Melcepeth; but, as we know, she had been early taken, and Ralph had lost in her the truest friend he ever possessed.

As it sometimes happens in families, the youngest born had been the father's favourite. Geoffrey held his own as heir; Roger was gone to London to his Uncle Roger; and Henry, a fair, beautiful child, remained to the old baronet Sir Henry, as his life faded away quietly enough. Geoffrey had gone to Oxford, and had worked his way through London society with the nominal profession of the law;

but Henry, whose mother died when he was young, was never sent away, not even to school. The curate of the village near, who acted as domestic chaplain at Melcepeth, and lived in the house, was the young Henry's tutor; and so he grew up, learning very little—for some of his letters that I know of are sadly illiterate, both as to spelling and composition—but the best rider, the best shot, the best tier of flies, and the best fisherman in all Coquetdale.

If that had been all, Henry Darnell might well have been alive at this period, and as prosperous in some honest calling as either of his brothers; but his Jacobite sympathies had prevented him joining the Hanoverian army; and his father had always said he would not part with Harry, and had allowed him a handsome income as he grew up—indeed, settled it upon him; and looked to his marrying a county beauty, and becoming a squire of the land. The issue, however, was not so. There was no one to check Henry Darnell; and his sporting friends were none of the cleanest handed, or most respectable. If there was good salmon-fishing by Warkworth, there were men there who followed the exciting trade of smuggling; and, among many more, Robert Smithson, the farmer and land-agent, was not idle. Was he not owner of three smart luggers, which, under pretence of herring-fishing, ran over to the Low Countries and brought tea and silks, tobacco and brandy? Many a pleasant trip had Henry Darnell taken in them, and many a keg of hollands had he assisted to run ashore among the caves and rocks under the gaunt walls of the old castle of Dunstanborough!

A wild, lawless life it was; against which the old baronet, Sir Harry, now reaping the fruits which his own course of conduct had rendered almost inevitable, often protested in vain. When at last he died, and Geoffrey succeeded, the brothers tried to live together for a while, but it would not answer: they quarrelled bitterly. The remonstrances Henry had endured from his father were inadmissible from his brother Geoffrey, and they separated in anger.

Henry's character declined after this rapidly. He went to reside in the fishing village at Warkworth, built a lugger for himself, and in fine weather ran across to the Low Countries or to Northern Germany so frequently, and stayed away so long, that it was often said he had married there. There was a daughter of Smithson's, however, who grew up to be very lovely, and was the belle of the fishing village and of the country-side. Her mother, a vain, foolish woman, doted upon this child, her only one, and lavished on her all the means and finery which could be procured by the skippers of her husband's luggers. Dutch ear-rings, and brooches, and chains of the purest gold; laces, silks and satins, which many a town lady would have envied, were made up for the beautiful child; and so what marvel that she grew out of her natural rank of life, and that, in spite of her broad Northumbrian dialect and utter want of the commonest education, her mother told her she "wad be a bonny leddy some day;" and she believed what she was told every day of her life.

At sixteen, Grace Smithson was truly lovely; and, till she opened her mouth, might have passed for a daughter of the highest house in the land. When she spoke, however, you knew what she was, and grieved that she had been spoiled. Henry Darnell had watched Grace grow up, and the fond mother encouraged the intimacy. "Why should her Gracie no marry a Darnell? Gin they had birth, Gracie was bonnie, and fit bride for a king—bless her! an' a gude lassie tae," said the mother. The result of all was, that one summer day the *Ariel* went out for "jist a bit sail roond the castle," as Mrs. Smithson told her husband when he came in and asked for Gracie, and Mr. Henry said "he'd not keep her oot long;" but they did not return at sunset—no, nor afterwards; and when the distracted parents looked into the girl's room, they found all her clothes had been removed, and that she had gone away from them deliberately. Grace did not return for nearly two years. Henry had taken her to Amsterdam, and there she had learned some accomplishments; and her native grace and beauty were developed by foreign culture. Her parents had forgiven her; and as she always told them in her letters she was lawfully married, they had believed her fully, and never—her mother at least—beyond the first miserable suspense, had had any doubt on the subject.

They returned, I say, in about two years, bringing with them an infant of a few months old; but Henry Darnell could not be persuaded to remain, nor indeed could Grace. Both had imbibed a liking for foreign society, where they had formed a position; and both felt they could obtain none at Warkworth. Sir Geoffrey Darnell had once received his brother, but had refused to receive Grace, and denied the legality of her marriage; and Henry, ever haughty and wilful, did not press proofs of it upon him. "So long as there is hope of a son being born to you or Roger," he had said, "I will be silent. When that no longer exists, I will defend my boy's rights." So the brothers parted in anger—never, as it proved, to meet again.

The object of Henry Darnell and Grace in coming to Warkworth had been to leave the boy with her mother; and for this Grace had pleaded very earnestly. "There was naebody like mither to rear the child; an' I dinna trust thae Dutch wives, nor their ways, wi' my ain bairn; and wha was to christen it? I dinna like them Dutch parsons wi' black cloaks, neyther—they're no canny," she had said in her own broad mother tongue; and Henry Darnell had consented. So the child was christened Ralph Darnell, and left with its grandparents; and the ill-fated pair sailed again in the *Ariel.* They were never heard of afterwards. John Robson, the skipper of Smithson's best lugger, cruised long off the Dogger Bank and round to Amsterdam, visiting all the ports, and even fishing villages, on the coast; and returned with only part of a broken stern-frame which had been thrown up, with "GRACE, OF W——," on it, in the gold letters which he knew Davie Smith, of his own village, who had painted the lugger's pretty cabin, had put on the vessel's stern while she lay there, to please "Miss Gracie." Wasn't it "her ain wee boatie?"

The first Lady Darnell knew the story, and believed in the marriage. She always told her husband that if he had received Henry kindly he would have told them all about it; but, under the circumstances, she did not marvel that Henry was intractable and defiant, and ought not to have been threatened. She had liked Henry in spite of his faults—as who indeed did not? and she grieved over his fate very sincerely. And I must do Sir Geoffrey the justice to say that he too sorrowed much. As the child grew up, a bold handsome boy, Lady Jane induced her husband to ask for it, and to rear it with their own girl. The boy had been christened Ralph Darnell; and whether legitimate or otherwise, was not to be left to the Smithsons, to be brought up among the rough farmer's children, fishermen, and smugglers of the little village by the sea. There had been no opposition on the part of Smithson or his wife—quite the contrary. They were wise enough to see that provision would be made for the boy; and the fond grandmother in her heart believed it possible that her darling Gracie's child might be yet Sir Ralph Darnell of Melcepeth Castle, and believed it the more firmly as time passed, and no heir to the baronetcy was born.

So the lad grew up, a strong, daring boy, and, in spite of many misgivings, Geoffrey Darnell loved him deeply. As time flew by, the good points of his brother's character returned upon him with greater force and frequency than his faults and follies; and could the stolen marriage, if there ever had been one, have been proved by any means, he would not have hesitated in formally acknowledging it. True, his brother Roger might have male children, and time could not be anticipated. There was no course open but to wait patiently. Meanwhile the boy grew and thrived well; like his father, a good fisherman, a bold rider, and with winning ways which none about him could resist. With Bessie Grover—his almost mother—as instructress, and occasional help from the parson, who, in succession to the former one, was domestic chaplain and curate, Ralph was fairly educated; learned rudiments, if no more, of Greek and Latin, and made progress in French and Italian, in both of which Bessie Grover was a proficient. In those respects he promised well;

but in spite of all precautions, the father's spirit seemed to be revived as he grew up, and the company of the fishermen—with whom Ralph fished every pool and run of the beautiful river, and was sometimes taken "a sail" in their fishing luggers, and from whom he heard many a thrilling tale of his father's wild exploits—of old Smithson, who had not abandoned his smuggling propensities, and of others even perhaps more objectionable, was gradually changing the lad's disposition to what his uncle well remembered of his father, and had so much cause to dread. Therefore the baronet and Bessie Grover had held many an anxious council on this subject, and they ended in the formal proposal, which we already know of, to Roger Darnell, that, to save the youth, he should be transferred at once to new scenes, and duties in a profession which would save him from farther risk of local contamination. Whereupon, Ralph had been sent to London to his Uncle Roger, when he was fifteen years old.

It was a hard parting on all sides. The boy was stupid with grief. As to Constance Darnell, his dear, beautiful, loving cousin—his playmate, his confidant, his ally in all his enterprises, troubles, and often disgraces; for whom he would dare anything or do anything; for whom he caught the finest trout in Coquet, and shot woodcocks when he was old enough to be trusted with a gun; the companion of all his rambles in the woods after birds' nests;—and had she not the most beautiful strings of eggs that could be collected?—ah! she was stupid too, and wept, as her nurse said, "her bit heart oot o' her." But the fiat had gone forth, and the boy went to the great city to grow into a man; clinging more and more fondly, under the effect of absence, to those home scenes in which his young life had opened, and to one object more dear to him, far as he was away from it, than all the world besides.

CHAPTER XI.

ROBERT SMITHSON'S VISIT.

Although Mr. Smithson and Sir Geoffrey Darnell had the peculiar relationship to each other which has been detailed in the last chapter, the subject of their mutual concern was rarely alluded to in any form between them. One of the first stipulations made by Sir Geoffrey, after he took Ralph to the capital, was to that effect. If his brother Henry had indeed openly and defiantly married Grace Smithson, as, being independent of his brothers, he had a perfect right to do if he pleased, there is little doubt that Sir Geoffrey would at once have discarded his steward for having lent himself to bring about a connection which his station in life did not warrant a thought of. But there was no question whatever, from the man's frenzy at the time, his deep vows of revenge on the seducer, which he had poured out to his master, as well as from the circumstance of the girl's flight, that neither her father nor her mother had known of her intention.

When that flight was discovered, however, and the bereft husband and wife were alone in the room whence their child had gone, her father's mind had misgiven him as to his wife's possible, nay probable, complicity; and the scene between them had been violent in the extreme. A woman who was serving in the dairy had seen Mrs. Smithson on her knees, in the middle of the floor, with her hands uplifted, and her husband, "the master," "wi' a meikle pistil, cock'd and set at her heed, and cryin' out, 'Did ye no know o't, ye daft, dooless womin? Can ye deny that ye sent them awa' owre the sea, d—n ye, ye dotin' auld ——?' an' the puir mistress's face as white as deeth, ye ken; an' only sayin', 'A' didn't, a' didn't, Rrobert; if ye kill me, a' didn't; she's gone and gane, and ne'er tou'd me a word o't.'" And this story had come round to the baronet, and he respected a grief which he himself shared, and of the truth of which he had no question.

I have said that Robert Smithson still continued to be the baronet's land agent and collector, as he was also farmer of a large farm near Dunstanborough. Smithson's father had been so before him; and one of the Darnell sources of revenue, belonging to feudal times, was the right of fishing the sea for a certain distance, collections of fish, whatever they might be, and, above all, salmon-nets. Not at that time indeed was salmon selling at half-a-crown a pound; but for all that, the revenue was considerable, and required looking after. This was spring time too; the clean fish were coming in fast, and money had been collected which Robert Smithson had to pay to the baronet.

It was on rare occasions that he told his wife he was going to Melcepeth—indeed he kept those visits from her as much as possible; for they only raised griefs long since dead and buried in the deep sea. It was this sorrow, combined with Ralph's absence, which had made poor Mrs. Smithson the wreck she was; for her whole soul had been centred in one object—her daughter while she lived, and upon the boy so long as he remained. True, she had let him go to Sir Geoffrey's; and as long as he was at Melcepeth, and she could see him occasionally, or the lad came down to the sea when the nets were to be drawn, or she herself was driven up by Robert in the light cart, she was content; but since he had gone to London she had become very restless, and could with difficulty be pacified. With her interest and her thoughts centred upon one object, from the time she awoke in early morning till she went to sleep, it is not strange if her naturally weak mind had become morbidly diseased; and the point now reached was, that her boy, "her ain Grace's bit bairnie, wad be speerritted away."

"Wha kens," she would whine to her husband as he smoked his last pipe before he went to bed—"wha kens, Rrobert, but he'll be speeritted awa' owre the sea, maybe to Virginny, where them wild Injins is that scalps folk; an' ye sit here quiet, as if there was nae manhood left in ye; an' nae wonder, for ye never cared for the bit lassie like mey—no, niver."

These garrulous groanings of his wife had little effect upon Smithson at the time; but, nevertheless, he too brooded over the past, after his own fashion, and saw no light in the future. Ralph was growing to be nearly of age—the baronet would never marry—Mr. Roger Darnell had no son. For his own part, he had faithfully kept the secret of his birth from Ralph; but why should it be kept? Was Sir Geoffrey going to acknowledge him or not? If not, why did he keep him at all? Better let the boy come back to Warkworth; he would be at least as independent as his father had been, for Henry Darnell's property was kept under strict trust; and if he were illegitimate, he had far better be told so, than be kept in an uncertain and anomalous position. Beyond being the son of Henry Darnell, Smithson doubted whether Ralph had ever been told anything further. He certainly did not know that he, Robert Smithson, and his wife Lucy were his grandparents.

Why, it is immaterial to detail. Smithson could not indeed have accounted for it himself, except that Johnnie Robson had run a new cargo during the night under the old castle walls, and as they met in the morning, there was a package of tea for the castle, and an anker of brandy; and talking together, some old allusions about Mr. Harry had come up, and Robson had asked about the "lad Raafe" kindly enough;—I say, why Smithson, as he put the fish-dues in his pocket on the 20th May 1755, should have said to himself, as he ground his teeth, "that he'd be shot if he didn't 'hev it oot' with the baronet about Raafe," I do not know—but so it was; and when Mrs. Smithson, who had seen her husband taking money out o' the "barrinit's" box, and heard him give orders for the gig, tottered to him on her weak limbs, and, putting her thin hand on his arm, looked up in his rough, weather-beaten face with wan, wasted features, and scared, hollow eyes, from which the tears were streaming, he was obliged to listen to her.

"Eh, Rrobbert," she said solemnly, "if ever ye loo'd yer puir Lucy, if ever ye loo'd that sweet darlin' that's lyin' under the sey, ye'll speyk to the barrinit aboot the lad the day—ye'll no come back an' tell me ye couldna speyk, ma man; if ye dee, a'll be deed afore the morn, Rrobbert, for a'm no strang, ye ken—no like what I was. 'Deed, a'd gae mysel' an' speyk till Mistress Grover if a' could, an' maybe she'll come an' sey me before the Lord takes mey. Ye'll tell her that, Rrobbert, frae mey; an' ye'll be true tae our puir sweet lassie—yer ain bit Gracie; for oh, Rrobbert, she was married as gude as a' wuz, and she always sed she had her marriage-lines safe at her breest, though she niver showed them me. Oh, Rrobbert, if ever ye loo'd the mither o' that sweet bairnie, ye'll no deny me the day what I'm asking o' ye?"

Smithson was startled by his wife's earnest, solemn manner, so unlike her habitual querulousness, and he put his arm round her tenderly, and looked at her till his own shaggy eyelashes glistened, and tears blurred his sight. How well he remembered her lovely youth and the little village by Mitford Castle where he had courted her, and wandered with her in the woods, or fished the Font and Wansbeck down to Morpeth Bridge, while she proudly carried his well-filled creel! Ah, yes! as he looked into the wasted light-blue eyes, still so tender, all the events of years rushed upon his memory in a flood, and he stooped down and kissed her brow tenderly. "A' had it in ma mind, Lucy," he said kindly, "to speak to the barrinit to-day, an' I'll no come hame empty-handed, ma lassie, mind that; an' if Mistress Grover 'll come to see ye, 'all bring her doon, or maybe she'll like the castle gig better. Dinna fash yersel', Lucy dear; a'll no be lang away. Come, get intil yere cheer, an' dinna greet. It's a' in the Lord's hands, an' He'll jist dee as He pleases—ye ken that weel."

And with these thoughts at his heart Smithson had driven up to the castle, had duly made over his freight to the butler in the stable-yard, and asked for Sir Geoffrey.

"'Deed, then, Mister Smithson," said Mr. Harbottle, the worthy old butler, "if I wuz you, surr, I'd gae back hame wi' mey, an' no see the barrinit the day. He's no canny, surr—he's no canny! mind that."

"An' what ails him, Mister Harbottle? Is't the goot agen?"

"Na, na, surr; no the goot. There wuz letters to-day frae brither Roger; an' as he redde ane o' 'em, the barrinit he gi'es a skiril, surr, ye'd ha' heer'd in the servants' haale, and a great 'Dammnation!' surr, between his teeth, as he threw the letter till Mistress Grover, that ye'd ha' thowt it was the big bull rroutin' in the meddy yonder; an' she winked at mey, an' I git oot o' the parler: an' a' I heer'd was, 'Curse Rra-a-ffe!' and that's a', surr?"

"I'm no feered o' him, Mr. Harbottle, an' I've gotten some fish-money to pay him, an' maybe that'll pit him in good humour. Whar is he?"

"Jist in the justice-room, Mr. Smithson, an' ye'll excuse ma goin' wi' ye. Ye can knock at the door, and if he won't let ye in, he'll d—n yer eyes, and ye can come awa' to mey; a'll have jist simthin' fur ye in my ain room—a'ready, surr."

Mr. Smithson took the package of tea, and well knew where he had to go, and what he was to see. He knocked at the door bravely, and the baronet knew the knock. "Come in," he shouted; "are ye afraid?"

"No, Sir Geoffrey," replied Smithson stoutly, "not of you, Sir Geoffrey; I was only puttin' doon ma hat in the haale. A gude mornin' till ye, surr, an' I hope ye're weel. A've brought ye some o' the fish-dues, an' there's a rare take of salmon in the castle pool; an' I'd like to see ye there wi' a rrod to-day, surr. There's some heavy fish lyin' there, surr.

"Curse the fish!" cried the baronet, testily—"curse the fish! What have ye brought? Let's see."

"Weel, surr, it's vary weel for the first o' the season. An' I've left a gude clean fish wi' Mister Harbottle; a' thowt ye'd like it, or Mistress Grover, or Miss Constance maybe; an' there's saxty-fowr guineas, Sir Geoffrey—a'll coont them, surr, if ye please;" and untying a leather bag, Smithson poured the contents out on the table.

The baronet began to count them, but it was easy for Smithson to see that the strong sinewy hand trembled mnch, and that his agitation could not be concealed. While he is counting them, let me tell what manner of man sat there.

Sir Geoffrey Darnell's white hair, and a beard which he had allowed to grow, equally white and curly, mingled together round a face which, as became a Darnell, was undeniably striking; but it was flushed and angry. A storm of passion seemed to be collected about the small, quivering mouth and nostril, and the deep-set blue eyes flashed beneath the shaggy white eyebrows. The baronet was a hale, strong man yet, and, from his great height and stalwart figure, was always remarkable. When he was in good humour—and I am bound to say his fits of passion were not frequent or lasting—the expression of his features was as sweet as it was dignified and manly; but passion sadly disfigures most faces: and here, certainly, there was no exception. Smithson, however, was too old a servant to care a rush for anger which he had endured many a time without flinching, and it suited the grim humour in which he had left his suffering wife, to meet whatever was to happen—calmly if he could—but at least to meet it; nor did he delay in his purpose.

"It's a' richt, Sir Geoffrey?" he asked respectfully; "it's a' richt, a' hope?"

"Yes, it's right enough, Smithson—quite right; but what the devil brought you here to-day? Why did *you* come to disturb me?"

"'Deed, surr, there was the money, ye ken, an' the tey there, an' an anker I've given till Mister Harbottle, and the fish for Mistress Grover, an'—an'—"

"Well, au'—an'—" cried the baronet, mocking him with a sneer; "somebody won't pay his rent, I suppose, or—"

"No, surr," returned Smithson, interrupting him, "it wasn't that; naebody's behint wi' rent, a' reckin; but mey and ma gude womin was talking o' Maister Rraafe the morn, an' we'd be thankful if ye'll tell uz what the lad's doin'."

"Ah! some of your old plots and contrivances up again, Robert Smithson?" retorted the baronet, grimly; "but I'm—" (I fear I cannot write all the baronet's peculiarly savage and offensive expletives, which the reader may fill in if he pleases, after the fashion of 1755) "if you or he, or your croaking old wife, get anything more out of me for him. There, if you want to know, read that; it came only this morning, and spoilt my breakfast—it did, by George!"

"'Deed, surr, an' it wad take mey a lang time to read quality writin'; but if you'd only say what—"

"There, take it to Mistress Grover, your friend and his," interrupted the baronet, with a sneer, "and she'll read it to you. Doing, sir? why, he's a disgrace to us, that's what he is; gambling and drinking, like his father, and going the same road to hell, sir. Is that enough for you, or—"

"If that's the case," said the steward, firmly but respectfully, I'm not tired of him, Sir Geoffrey, if you are, an' a'll see to the lad's richts when he needs them. You'd better give him up, sir, an no daum him, surr, like that, wha's yer ain blude, an' mine—"

"I thought so," said the baronet, throwing himself back in his chair, and striking the table so violently that many of the guineas leaped up and rolled in confusion to the floor—"I thought so. I was certain some more of your sneaking schemes were on your face when you came in. Well, sir, have you anything new to tell me of about that bastard?"

"Bastard in your thrrote! crruel man that ye are," retorted Smithson, starting to his feet. "Weel ye ken that lad's nae mair bastard than ye are yer ain sel', Sir Geoffrey Darnell. If I wuz yer equil, ye daur not say bastard to mey."

"I'll say it again in your teeth, Robert Smithson," cried the baronet, fiercely. "Bastard! there—d'ye hear?—bastard! That's what I call him; that's what I think him; and that's enough for you and the like of you. Prove he's not one, and I, Geoffrey Darnell, will do him and you justice; yes, before God and man, and a Darnell's word is true before both. But listen, Smithson; I'll have no scheming, no lawyer's work, for his 'richts,' as you call them; nothing less than good proof of that horrible marriage—d'ye hear me?—good proof, I say, that even my lawyers will admit. When you've got that, come to me; till then, if ever you mention that wretched lad's name to me, Smithson, it'll be the last word you'll ever speak to Geoffrey Darnell. Now, mind that, and be off with you; don't stand snivelling there."

Alas! there was no proof. How often had Robert Smithson gone to Lamberton Pike, where the marriage was said to have been performed by the pike-keeper, before whom many an honestly-living couple in the country had ascended "the steps o' grace," as the mock altar was called. How often had he heard his poor child declare with bitter sobs that it was "a' right; that she had the marriage-lines at her heart, only she had sworn to Harry never to show them to mortal man or woman—no, not even to her father and mother—till he bid her." How well he knew of weary pilgrimages to every church, small or great, lying near the sea, from Berwickmouth to Tynemouth Priory, over and over again; and searches of registers without a gleam of success. How much money had he not paid to a smart attorney of Newcastle to help him; and how honestly he had resisted the sore temptation which *had* been set before him, to have papers prepared which should defy scrutiny! How often had all this ground been gone over, and the conviction arisen that the girl had fallen, and had been carried off willingly; and if married at all, married away in Holland, by some outlandish Dutch parson who would never be discovered. Ah yes! and the marriage-lines were all the time, as he believed, lying against that true loving heart when it sank into the sea and beat no more! All this, I say, flashed upon Robert Smithson's heart as vividly as the sweet courtship of his wife had in the morning, and he hung his head; he had no strength to say more; the sad truth was too strong for him, and overmastered his passion.

"Eh, Sir Geoffrey, then she maun dee—ma puir Lucy!" he said, gasping as it were at every word; "ma puir Lucy!"

"Your poor Lucy," cried the baronet, rising kindly, all his passion gone, under the effect of non-resistance and his old servant's evident grief. "Your poor Lucy? What, Mrs. Smithson? God bless my soul, she's not ill! What on earth's the matter? Here, Grover, Mrs. Grover," he cried, opening the door, "come in, come in. Here's Smithson and I, like two fools as we are, have had a fight about the old matter: and there's poor old Mrs. Smithson dying—dying, by George! and there's something on her mind, I daresay, as she sent her husband to beset me on a subject on which he has held his tongue—yes, held his tongue, I must say, Mrs. Grover, for years—for years. Now go, put on your things directly, and get away to Warkworth. Let me know what she says before evening—before evening, ma'am, if you please. Now be off, Smithson, with her; don't mind what an old passionate fool like me said to you. What the devil, as I said at first, brought you here to-day, and be d—d to you?"

"'Deed, Sur Geoffrey, but ye flung hard words at mey and at Master Rraafe—hard words, barrinit; an' if I said onything, ye ken—"

"Never mind what you said. I daresay I deserved it all, and much more. Be off with you, and take Miss Constance with you, if you like."

"Oh, papa," cried that young lady, bursting into the room with a bright, joyous face, beaming with excitement, "Grover says—that's Mistress Grover, ye ken, papa," she continued, dropping a demure curtsy, "says she's goin' to Warkworth, and there's lots of fish there, and the nets'll be drawn, and if dear Rralph was here he'd catch me a salmon with his ain rrod. Oh, Mr. Smithson, do take me; I'll go wi' you, it's such a lovely day—"

"If Sur Geoffrey will let ye, Miss, we'll gang on before Mistress Grover. Ma mear'll beat the castle gig, an' we'll get the nets into the water as the tide's makin'."

"Oh, yes, I'll come, I'll come; mayn't I go, you dear old daddy—mayn't I go?"

"Be off, then, for a spoilt minx, as you are, and come home quietly with Grover. Now mind."

Away sprang the excited girl, her long curls flying behind her, up the stairs three at a bound, and away down the corridor.

Both men looked after her. "God bless her, the darling!" said Smithson devoutly,—"God bless her!"

"Amen, Robert, Amen! It must be true justice, ye see, to change her hopes and prospects in this world; but you and I have to do it Robert Smithson, if needs be, and there's my hand on it."

Smithson took his master's hand, kissed it reverently, and turned away. The baronet thought he heard a sob break from his steward as the door closed after him, and perhaps he did.

"Gad," he said to himself, as, having picked up his guineas, he locked them away in his escritoire, and once more sat down in his arm-chair, turning it to the fire, "I suppose that old woman has the marriage-lines after all; she was always a doting old fool, but the girl may have told her more than she told her father. Suppose she has, how it would clear up everything, and I could have the lad back, and the salmon up the river too! Gad, how he would enjoy a month's fishing! One thing, however, is certain, whether there is clue or not to the marriage, I must make my will; it's no use delaying that, with this gout flying about me; and what's more, I must go to London to get Peed to draw it up. What a fool I was to get angry! Oh, Henry, Henry! if— Well, nothing can be helped now, unless the old woman— I wonder what Grover will say to it all. Ah, here you are, Bessie! Well?"

"I came to ask, sir, whether you have any particular message to

Warkworth, for I must go. Conny and Mr. Smithson are off," said Mistress Grover.

"Yes, I have—don't be in a hurry—sit down there and listen for a minute, can't ye, and don't fidget."

Then Sir Geoffrey told Mrs. Grover what Smithson had said, and how he had called Ralph a bastard, and was sorry for it.

"Now, Bessie," he continued, "my opinion is, that that croaking old parrot has got those marriage-lines, or knows where they are; or at any rate there is something more than common in what brought Robert Smithson here to-day in that grim humour. So you'll just find it all out and come back to me. Don't waste your time with that mad child; she'll be leading you a dance after the nets, and is quite safe with old Smithson. That's all, and come back as sharp as possible, and get all you can out of the old woman."

"Gad," said the baronet to himself as he settled once more into his chair—"Gad, I wonder what Bessie'll find out—and what the old woman'll say about the will?"

CHAPTER XII.

BESSIE GROVER'S MISSION.

Bessie Grover belongs so essentially to this history, and the persons connected with it, by so many ties of interest, which began with her earliest life, and were never broken to its close, that I should be wanting to my readers if I did not make more particular mention of her than I have yet done. She had been Lady Jane Darnell's friend, and was an orphan. The same cause that had desolated so many Northumbrian hearths, and ruined so many families, had ruined hers also, for her father was killed in General Wills's attack on Preston, and her mother, after giving birth to Bessie, and struggling with her grief for a while, gave up the contest and died. Such bereavements, however, have often raised up kind friends, and Lady Jane Darnell's mother, Mrs. Craster, took the desolate child and brought her up with her own. When Lady Jane married, she begged of the baronet to let Bessie Grover come with her to Melcepeth. The old housekeeper was infirm, and had not Bessie kept the keys and the house-accounts at home? and could mother have done anything without her? was she not the most useful creature in the world, and knew everything? So Bessie Grover had taken her place at Melcepeth and never left it. She had many offers of marriage, for she had a little property of her own, enough for independence; and with a bright open face in her youth, a lithe, active figure, she attracted many admirers; but somhow or another she had preferred a single life, and a respectable position which involved exercise of all her useful accomplishments, to one which might prove uncertain.

We already know that she had lived with Lady Jane Darnell till her death, and till the baronet remarried; after that, there was no need of her services, and she went to reside with a friend in France, with a view, as she averred, of perfecting what accomplishments she possessed, and accepting teaching in families of the upper class, as a profession for her future life; but when the second Lady Darnell died, as we know, so sadly, and her sweet pet Constance, ay and the lad Ralph Darnell too, were more uncared for than they ought to be, and the baronet wrote to her to come, "for he could not get on without her," she went to him bravely, and did her duty.

I say she went bravely, because it required a strong will and self-reliance to place herself voluntarily in a position which must necessarily be unchanged for many years, and would expose her to some suspicion; but she loved the children dearly, and Sir Geoffrey also, after his own fashion, very truly. For a time county gossips sneered, and were even shy of her. She might be the baronet's mistress—what more likely? or she was scheming to be Lady Darnell the third, and had worked upon him so that he had fallen irretrievably into her hands. I daresay, after the fashion of that time, and of all time, there were enough virtuous folk to canvass the arrangement in every aspect, except, indeed, a charitable one; and Bessie Grover knew this perfectly well, and had prepared herself to meet it all. In the end, as she foresaw must be the case, she had triumphed. That she had not been tempted to become Lady Darnell would have been next to impossible; for in her, perhaps more than in either of his wives, were the comfortable and useful requisites of a wife combined, and the baronet had offered to share his life with her; but she had refused him, gently, yet firmly—had told Sir Geoffrey that on any recurrence of such a proposition she would have no resource but to leave the house instantly; and was troubled no more. Nay, it became an additional bond of obligation upon the baronet, that she had resisted the temptation he had set before her, to become Lady of Melcepeth.

How she loved the dear old place, she could hardly explain herself. It had grown to be part of her very being. Every stone of the shapeless castle mound, every portion of the old house, the gardens, the woods, the shrubberies, and the beautiful noisy river which held with her perpetual pleasant talk, as it roared, murmured, or babbled in turn—I say, all these were as much part of her life as the children and the baronet were of her daily care. So what marvel if she not only lived down all scandal or detraction, but rose immeasurably higher then she had dared to hope in local esteem? The servants—and representatives of generations passed through Melcepeth as if they had an hereditary right to be there—loved and respected her far more than they did Sir Geoffrey; and as to the poor folks about, in every village within a walk or a drive, I can only say that, like myself, they lacked words to tell of her good deeds. At first she was Miss Grover, and for many years she was so; but Bessie was now nearly forty years old, and she had assumed the honorary title of Mistress, as was needful by the advanced spinsters of 1755.

But in reality, Bessie Grover was not so old in appearance. Her figure was yet round and perfect, a little stouter perhaps than strict grace prescribed, but not more so than beauty admitted of. No one could have said that she was handsome; but the quick hazel eyes, well-cut though rather large mouth, perfect teeth, which she showed a good deal as she spoke or laughed, a bright fresh colour, which had been downy like a peach when she was young, but had now grown into more of a soft, rosy, apple tint, and, above all, a smooth open forehead, over which thick brown curls clustered naturally, assured even the most casual observer that no ordinary character was before him.

"Eh! but she's bonny—Bessie Grover is," was the enthusiastic cry of Mistress Darling, the old housekeeper, when any one asked her "what sorrt the mistress wuz." "She's bonnie in her face—and she's bonnie in her ways—an' she's bonnie a'thegither, is Bessie Grover," was the reply—and she was so indeed.

Bessie Grover was not sorry for the mission she had been despatched upon so hastily. The baronet was evidently anxious, and might have cause for it. There was a good deal to do at Warkworth, and at several villages on her route. Jane Tait, late a housemaid at Melcepeth, had lain in of her first child, and had sent a girl to say, "If ye please, ma'am, and if ye'd come and see the wee bairnie, Jane 'ud be thankfu'." So with flannel for one, tea for another, a pretty frock with real lace on it for Jane Tait's baby, and above all, some sack wine, such as Smithson could not buy, for the old lady, Bessie Grover's light conveyance was soon laden, and she followed Smithson and Constance as fast as the stately castle horse would condescend to drag so undignified a carriage as "the gig."

I hope most of my readers, or many of them, know the country through which Bessie Grover passed. If not, I advise them, in all kindness, to go and see what they will remember with pleasure through their lives. The road is, perhaps, little altered in direction, though it is improved in character; and it will lead them by the river sometimes, over knolls and promontories, through deep woods, with the stream flashing and foaming below, until it debouches upon a small estuary, on the high right bank of which are the noble Norman ruins of Warkworth Castle, and, looming in the distance, the tops of the old Saxon Castle of Dunstanborough, by the sea. Both so beautiful, so picturesque, that they will linger hours among their precincts. They will be taken to the lovely Hermitage, up Coquet, hidden in woods, the scene of one of the tenderest ballads in our language; or they will explore the rough cliffs, caves, and silver sands at Dunstanborough; or bask dreamily on the green-sward, looking up into the summer sky, in which soft clouds are floating, or away over the ocean, where there are ships sailing as lazily in the blue element below, as the clouds are in the blue above.

But Bessie Grover was not going to enjoy any of these pleasant sights. True, she could see the white flecked sky, see the hedges covered with sweet hawthorn bloom, and the fields now bright with young corn, daisies, and buttercups; and she could feel the soft south wind, laden with pleasant sea-odour, more and more as she drew nearer to the shore—and feel, too, as she always did, how thankful she should be, and was, that she was not indifferent to all these; but, as I tell you, she was not going on any holiday visits, and what she did see was a sad sight, one she little expected, and remembered for many a day afterwards.

Robert Smithson would fain have gone first to his house to see his wife, but Miss Constance would hear nothing of that, and a more imperious or pleasanter little tyrant never existed. Mr. Smithson had never attempted to oppose her in his life, and was not going to try now. "A' don't mind the barrinit one strraw," he would say; "but Miss Constance, she's gey wilfu', ye ken, and would the like o' mey say her no, surr?" So as he proposed to go home and "pit up the mear," she would not hear of it. "No, no, Mr. Smithson; ye'll be wanting the gig for a' the fish I'm going to catch, and to carry me back, so just get on at once. Mrs. Smithson won't run away, and Grover's coming to take care of her. Maybe they'll give us some tea by-and-by." And Robert Smithson turned away from his field gate, and went down to the village on the sea with his happy companion.

"Perhaps I'd better pit the horse up at the Arms, ma'am?" said William, one of the stable-boys who had driven Mistress Grover down, and who was longing to be at the shore among the fishermen.

"Yes," replied Mrs. Grover, "you had better do so, and see after Miss Constance—she may want you; and tell her I'll walk down to her by-and-by."

The lad touched his hat and whipped on the horse, which remembered there were good oats and sweet hay at the Darnell Arms, and went on merrily.

Bessie Grover tapped gently at the door of the farm-house, looking round her, also, to see if there was any one about, but saw nobody. Every one, she knew, would be at the net-drawing; and Mrs. Smithson was not so infirm but that she could help herself very well about the house; and so, having tapped again and received no answer, she entered without further ceremony. "Yes," she thought, as she saw Mrs. Smithson reclining in her chair, "the old lady's asleep, and it will be almost a pity to wake her. I'd better go down to the nets, and come up with Constance;" and she was about to turn back to the door, when a sound, as if of a heavy sigh, or groan, arrested her attention, and sent her with rapid steps to the old woman's side.

Mrs. Smithson was not asleep; her eyes were wide open, staring indeed, with a vacant, scared expression, so painful to see, that Bessie Grover, with a beating heart, shaded her own for a moment involuntarily. Was she dying? Had the spirit even passed in that sound that had stopped her? Bessie Grover was accustomed to sick-beds, and she put her fingers on Mrs. Smithson's wrist. Yes, there was a pulse, but a very feeble one; perhaps a word might rouse her.

"Mrs. Smithson, look up! Bessie Grover's come to see ye. How do you do? Won't you speak to me?"

The old woman raised her hand feebly, and passed it over her face, with a weary action. "It's nicht," she said; "pit mey till my bed, Rrobbert, and a'll get to sleep. It's a' dark noo."

"No indeed, Mrs. Smithson, it's a lovely day; and I don't see why you shouldn't have the curtains drawn and the sweet sunlight let in on you." To say the truth, Bessie Grover's heart was beating faster than ever; for as she drew the heavy curtain, and the sun streamed in on the figure before her, she saw little to assure her that life would long remain. But the sudden flash of light had roused Mrs. Smithson a good deal, and she shaded her eyes with her hand for a moment, though the next it dropped powerless into her lap. It was evident her visitor was not recognised.

"I'm Mistress Grover, Lucy!" she said kindly. "Don't you know me?"

"Wha ca'd me Lucy?" returned the woman, feebly. "A' don't mind wha it is. Grover? ay, that's Bessie Grover up at the castle—whar is she?"

"I'm here, Lucy—here; my hand's on your forehead now. What ails ye? tell me," said Bessie Grover, gently, as she smoothed down the white hair, and passed her soft dimpled hands over the wan cheeks.

"Whar's Rrobbert?"

"He's gone with Miss Constance, Lucy, to the nets—they're drawing them to-day. What can I do for you?" There was no reply, only a low moan occasionally, as if of heaving breath, which came with difficulty. "What can I do?" thought Bessie. "She is very ill, dying perhaps. I cannot leave her, and there is no one to send." Stay! she may be roused; and she poured out some wine from her bottle into a glass on the table near, and held it to Mrs. Smithson's lips; but she could not swallow.

"Tak' it away," she said hastily—"tak' it away; a'm past that noo. Bessie Grover, is't they?"

"Indeed, indeed it is. What ails ye, Lucy? speak to me," she cried earnestly.

"I'm jist bad," she replied faintly. . . . "Gracie, ma bairn, ma bairn, are ye nigh me, nigh me? nigher . . . nigher, ma sweet hinnie! O Gracie! dinna ye gae mair frae mey—nae mair—Harry and you, an' the bit laddie 'll no gae far frae mither ony mair, ye ken. . . . Yer puir auld . . . mither. O Gracie! whar are ye hidin', childie?" and she moved her hands restlessly before her.

Bessie Grover's tears were flowing fast, falling hot upon the woman's face and hands, in heavy drops. "I'm here, Lucy," she said in her ear—"Bessie Grover; don't ye know me?"

"Bessie Grover? ay, she knaa's a'! I tou'd her the childie wuz married, ye ken, an' the lines was at her heart, lyin' there in a silken bag. . . . I tou'd her a' that, Gracie, dear. . . . Come, show me the bag, darlin', an' a'll nivir tell nobody; a' winna, ma pet. . . . no naebody, not even him. . . . The lines, ye ken, darlin', the lines. . . . Wanna ye jist show the dear leddy yer lines, ma wee sweetie . . an' she'll kna' o' them for Rraafe's sake. . . . D'ye no hear me, bairnie? D'ye no listen to yer mither? . . . Ah, shame on ye for a fause licht ane that ye are, . . . goin' rampagin' ower the sea wi' a Darnell! . . . Shame on ye, to bring sorrow to ma heart! . . . Winna ye listen till mey? Oh, no, no!" she continued, excitedly, after a distressing pause. "Nay, but she's na fause—Rrobbert—dinna greet—dinna be anger't wi' the puir wee lassie—A'm no greetin' mysel' noo. She's married, man—married, a' tell ye—hear that? . . . An' the lines . . . is at her heart . . . in a silken bag . . . a rede silken bag, man—an' a' seed it . . . mysel', when . . ."

How awful it is to listen to words slowly dropping with many a gasp and sigh from dying lips, let those tell who have heard them. The weary spirit, seeing sights and hearing voices unknown to us, is trembling upon the shore of that illimitable ocean of which the vast heaving waves and impenetrable obscurity beat back our thoughts, and may pass its inscrutable barrier in a moment—nay, while we listen. The nearer the transition, the more awful are those expressions which hold the listeners' senses in thrall. Bessie Grover could hardly hold up the feeble head, so violently did her hands tremble, and she listened again to the fainter and fainter gasps, in which words were spoken that could not be heard intelligibly. Mrs. Smithson was long past help, but there was hope that her husband might come in to receive her last breath; and Bessie Grover's prayers were ascending to that merciful throne where none are cast out, more fervently than she herself perhaps knew of. She did not dare to withdraw her hand from Mrs. Smithson's neck, and, kneeling by her chair, felt that her head fell forward gently, and rested quietly on her own bosom. How long she knelt there she hardly knew; but there were again a few trembling words.

"Ah, hinnie, it's your ain saft . . breest. A' kna's it weel. . . The Lord be praised . . Gracie, darlin' . . An' its vary sweet, ma pet, . . for yer puir mither's head to go by-by—there. . . . D'ye mind, darlin'—ye'd use to go, by-by—an' it's langsyne—on my ain. Oh! the lines, bairnie; . . . Ye'll hae them safe, bairnie, an' Bessie Grover 'll maybe read them—maybe—maybe . . . Look!" she cried. starting up, as if with a new force and energy, and stretching out her arm—"Look, she's there! she's there! Rrobbert, she's yon' . . . an' the flowers, an' the glory . . . an' the glory . . . o' the Lord! Comin' . . . comin' . . . A'm comin' . . . Gracie. Look! . . . the glory—o' the Lord!"

It was ended, that strange weird passing of Life into Death. Where would the next words be spoken? In her child's arms, whom she saw brightly, with the glory of the Lord shining about her among the flowers of heaven, while the earthly eyes were blinded with the films of death? Who can tell? The weary head sank down once more upon that loving bosom, and rested there, and the arms fell heavily; but the divine light of life had gone from the eyes, the jaw had dropped, and all that remained of human emotion was the bright smile of triumph—the ineffable expression of yearning maternal love fulfilled, which lingered there. Bessie Grover put back the wasted frame into the chair, and covered the face reverently. She could do no more, and so waited—by the Dead.

From death to life, as from life to death, how startling! There were merry voices outside for a moment, and ere she could rise to check her, Constance Darnell burst into the room, crying joyously, and clapping her hands.

"O Grover! we have had such glorious fun! Such heaps of salmon were in the net, and they leaped in the sun like silver. Why didn't you come? Why—"

There was something in Bessie Grover's face which checked the girl instantly. "Is she ill?" she asked, pointing to the chair, and rushing into Bessie's arms. "I ought not to have made such a noise."

"She's dead, Conny," said Bessie Grover, gently; "she died, poor thing, in my arms. Where is Mr. Smithson?"

"He went round with the gig," said the terrified girl, he'll——"

As she spoke, he entered the room; and the expression of the faces that met him—the still figure in the chair—told at a glance what had happened.

"I sudna ha' leeft her the day," he said; "an' she's gane noo, ma puir Lucy, an' mey not wi' her. O Lucy, Lucy, but ye're wi' the puir bairn ye greeted sair for."

And the strong man knelt down by the chair reverently, and, bowing his head, wept bitterly. But the wasted mother, and the child that lay beneath the sea, were once more together.

"A'll no be lang ahint ye, Lucy dear," he murmured—"A'll no be lang!"

CHAPTER XIII.

RESOLUTIONS AND PREPARATIONS.

"God bless my soul!" (this was a favourite interjectional expletive of Sir Geoffrey's) "you don't mean to say so, Grover? Dead! and died in your arms? Bless my heart! why, we never even heard she was ill; and I was so savage with that poor fellow, too, this morning, God forgive me! And she said nothing about that matter?"

"Nothing, Sir Geoffrey; and what's more, she knew nothing about it either; she only knew that her child wore a silken bag at her heart, and that 'the lines,' as she called them, were in it, which she was not allowed to show; and Lucy died, poor thing, with this thought on her lips, and—and—"

"And what, Bessie?"

Bessie's eyes were full of tears, as she remembered the last glorious but awful words which had passed the dying woman's lips, and she continued with enthusiasm, "'the glory of the Lord,' which was said with her last breath, and I believe she saw it too—"

"I hope she did," returned the baronet reverently, taking off his hat. They were walking in the Pleasance, as it was called, full of wallflower and early stocks, whose fragrance filled the soft evening air, and were alone—"I hope she did; I hope we shall all see it. And there was no one with you?"

"No, Sir Geoffrey, no one; she had been more than an hour dead when Constance came in—I don't know indeed how long."

"And you were not frightened, Bessie, to be with her alone?"

"I, Sir Geoffrey?"

The baronet was silent for a while, and as he walked, struck the ground heavily with his stick. "Ay," he said, as if to himself, "there's one the less now that knows of that marriage—if it was one. That silken bag—ah! poor thing, poor thing—and that's at the bottom of the sea. You told Smithson, Bessie, what she said?"

"I did, sir, every word, and he asked me to write them down; and I shall do so when you let me go."

"By all means, Bessie—they will be a satisfaction to him; but I'll tell you what," and he stopped suddenly, and struck his stick so sharply into the gravel walk that the pebbles flew up on all sides, "I'm d—d if I wait another day about it; and mind you, none of your plaguy objections now—I'm no match for women, I know, and never was, least of all for you—I won't wait another day, mind that—"

"You are pleased to be complimentary this evening, Sir Geoffrey," returned Mrs. Grover, curtsying ironically; but may I ask what *it* means?"

"Didn't I tell you, Bessie? God bless my heart! No? it was after Smithson left, and as I was sitting by the fire—I remember now. *It*, why *it*, my dear, means that I'm going to London."

"I'm glad to hear you are, Sir Geoffrey—very glad," returned Mistress Grover quietly; "about Ralph, I suppose, and Mr. Roger's letter."

"Well, yes, that, and—'faith, Grover, I may as well out with it—I shall make my will, that's all. I don't think I'm going to die, Bessie, and I hope not; but I shall make my will all the same. Ralph's near twenty-one, my dear; and he must be put in his proper place one way or other before then. It's due to him, it's due to his poor father, and, above all, it's due to Conny. Don't you think so?"

"I have not a doubt—I never had one—on the subject, Sir Geoffrey; and I am thankful you have come to this determination without any influence of mine or others, and of your own accord."

"Well, Bessie, I have been thinking for a long time what was best to do," continued the baronet, "and I believe, after all, it was that foolish quarrel with Smithson this morning that brought me to a decision. Now, as you have no objection, we will go—and as soon after the funeral as possible. I can't see Smithson till after that, and shall tell him exactly what he has to expect. You see I can't take any steps about the matter myself, because that would only raise up the old scandal; but I shall tell Braithwaite, of Morpeth, what I want him to do. He's good enough for that: but the rest must be done—can be done—by Peed only, and Roger. There is a good deal depending on my will under these circumstances, and a clever London attorney is the only man to make it—don't you see?"

"I am quite of your opinion, Sir Geoffrey," answered Mistress Grover, "and there are many other reasons why a visit to London would be most agreeable: indeed, you would have had Constance and myself upon you about it soon, sir, whether or no."

"Then you too had been plotting, Bessie? Ah, you women! Always hankering after balls and routs and fine clothes, no matter how old you get! No? then what *had* you been thinking about?"

"Constance, sir. It's time she should see something of city manners and form her own. It won't do to coop her up in the country here, speaking with a broader burr every day in spite of me, and hoydening about with the keepers and grooms. It was only yesterday I found her playing a young salmon in the pool yonder; and if she'd had her way this morning, she'd have taken 'Rraafe's rrod,' as she ca'd it, and 'done fine at Wackworth.' Then my darling has the most delicious voice in the world, and should have lessons in the new Italian style; and it would be well if she spoke with a French and Italian teacher every day, and learned how to walk a minuet better than I can teach her. And, let me see, Sir Geoffrey—yes," continued the lady, with the utmost gravity, "there are, of course, new dresses, and new styles—new everything, in fact. Would you wish it otherwise for the heiress of Melcepeth as she comes out?"

"Quite enough, Mistress Grover: one never asks a woman for one plain reason for anything, but she flings twenty at one's head in return. I want simply to know about my will, and have a masked battery opened upon me, which I must charge and take if I can, as they did the French at Malplaquet, by George; and if this is not enough to make a man swear, I don't know what is. Don't *you* think so, you pert puss you?"

"What, daddy?" said Constance, who walked up demurely—she had hardly yet got over the shock of the morning. "What, daddy? Poor old Mrs. Smithson needn't make you swear; nor me! a've been dooin' nothin', daddy."

"A've been dooin' nothin', daddy, haven't I? Who caught the salmon there yesterday?" said her father, mocking her broad dialect good-naturedly—"a seven-pound clean fish, too, by Jupiter! Well, we must get rid of burr, and sammin, an' a'—and gae away—far away—to—to—Loondin."

"Oh, daddy, how can you torment one so!" cried Constance, flinging her arms round the old man's neck—"to London? Oh, Grover! to London? I shall go wild!"

"Yes, darling, to London. Your father and I have been talking over the matter, and find there is no time to be lost; and perhaps Miss Constance Darnell may be of the same opinion. But there is not the least occasion to 'go wild,' as you call it. You are quite wild enough already, and if we can tame you a little, we shall be very glad."

"Oh, auntie darling!" cried the girl (auntie, you must know, was her most solemn as well as most loving appellation for Mistress Grover). "I'll be so quiet, so good, you can't think. Dear papa, indeed I will," and she turned from one to the other demurely and pleadingly. "Only trust me—"

"We don't doubt you, my child," said the baronet, laughingly, "and you needn't be so very earnest. I don't doubt but you'll be as steady as Grover herself by-and-by; but as that, perhaps, is not saying much for you after all, I'd better get out of the way, and go and tell Harbottle. The coach and chaise may need some looking into. When will the funeral be—Saturday or Friday?"

"Friday, I think, Sir Geoffrey. Mr. Smithson said so," replied Mistress Grover.

"Good: then I can see him on Saturday, and we will be off, God willing, on Monday. There, now, who says Geoffrey Darnell can't make up his mind?" and he walked away cheerily, striking his stick into the gravel.

Shall I tell you of the beautiful Constance Darnell as she stood on those steps of the pleasure-terrace, with the ruddy glow of sunset shining on her fair face and among the bright golden threads of her hair? I am afraid you would only find what I wrote very common-place. Are there not golden-haired heroines in every novel and romance you take up? do not threads of gold run about among their glossy hair, and are not their rich tresses bathed in golden light if the sun, or silver light of the moon, be shining? Now, I don't pretend to be able to write any such florid descriptions, and none are necessary from me; for if you, reader—gentle or whatever you may chance to be—will only go to Granton Towers, the seat of the Right Honourable the Earl of Whinborough, in Midlandshire, you will see what the great Sir Joshua painted of Constance Darnell, and you can wonder at it as I have done. All the Darnell portraits are there now, and a very noble collection they are. Sir Geoffrey had to sit when he went to London—"it was a thing to do, by Jove, sir,"—and the grand old head is nobly represented; but for remark-able portraits I commend you to Roger Darnell's and Constance's, which, once seen, you will never forget.

I only say, that had you seen her standing there that soft spring evening with Mistress Grover, the gentle wind just stirring the heavy curls hanging about her sweet neck, and a light of fun, of love, of excitement, of anticipation combined, dancing in those great marvellous grey eyes; and had seen also that singularly perfect embodiment of the best Saxon grace and vigour which existed in her budding figure, you would have said Constance Darnell was one of the loveliest creatures you had ever beheld, and you would have been quite right. You would have remembered many women with more regular features—more noble, more classical, or what you please; but none more piquant or more expressive. Now, after this, go, I pray you, to Granton Towers, and look at the portrait which no one ever passed in 1862 without exclaiming involuntarily, "How delicious!" and you will know much more in five seconds than I could write you in five hours, even if you could read all my prosiness, which would be impossible. And yet Bessie Grover was quite right: the girl was naturally very graceful and very beautiful, but wanted those last touches of art which would perfect all; and which *she* could not put on, any more than Constance could have taught her to play a salmon or ride after her father's harriers as she did herself.

We don't want to know about the thousand plans which all seemed to be formed and dismissed in a moment, and which were chasing each other in and out of the girl's busy brain as fast as they could, and a great deal faster than was intelligible to Bessie Grover; but when Constance said, "And we shall have Ralph again; dear me! I wonder what he's like?" and sighed—Mistress Grover sighed too. If she had known how Constance had wished for the young man to help her when the salmon had well-nigh got the better of her the day before—how she often longed for her old playmate and dear cousin—she might have been even more anxious, for Ralph's future seemed very dark just then.

"Dear Ralph," said Constance, sighing again, "how much we shall have to tell him—sha'n't we, Grover? Now you're not to sigh, Bessie Grover, when I mention him—you're not, indeed. I won't have it. Ralph and I are very good friends, and I intend—I intend, you know, to quarrel with him just as much as ever. Oh, it will be such fun!"

Mistress Grover did not perhaps see this exactly; but she said nothing. What could she say, with many a sad thought and anticipation lying at her heart?

So the preparations went on. In his way, Sir Geoffrey Darnell had as much decision of character as his brother Roger; and had Mrs. Grover even opposed him, he would, in all probability, have become obstinate, as he very often did. But now, as I tell you, there was no occasion to be so; trunks were packed, servants prepared, plate put by, and domestic arrangements made for an absence of at least three months, perhaps more. The old coach was thoroughly inspected, and also a lighter carriage for the luggage. Harbottle, and the housekeeper, Mrs. Darling, would remain in charge; and the two footmen and two grooms were enough for town service, with two maids, one a London girl, a mantua-maker, whose delight at return to town was beyond all control, and Susan Robson, the daughter of John Robson, of Warkworth, who had always a daughter in service at the castle; and with these necessary preparations, everybody was as busy as they could be. There was, of course, the utmost speculation in the "servants' haale" as to the cause of a sudden movement the like of which only the oldest dependants could faintly remember; and Mr. Harbottle's confidences to Mistress Darling in the housekeeper's room were to this effect:—

"'Deed, mem, a' won't be certin, ye ken; but it's a' aboot Master Rraafe, ye ken, an' nathin' else, mem. 'Deed, an' the barrinit wuz jist awfu' wi' Rrobbert Smithson that day—jist awfu'. Ma lug was nigh the doore, mem, a' the while; an' the barrinit roared bastard, mem, bastard! jist awfu', ye ken, like the auld bull routin' at ane o' the wenches' rede peticotes, mem; jist that, ye mind, mem."

"An' is the lad nae better than—than—"

"A bastard, mem? Well, I canna sey, Mistress Darling, nor naebody can; an' that's jist a' aboot it, ye ken. There used to be a story aboot a loup owre Lamberton Pike, but a' dinna ken, ye sey."

Robert Smithson came, true to his word, on the day after the funeral—to which Bessie Grover had been driven in the best coach, and which all the castle servants had attended in their best liveries—to receive his last orders. It was evident that the stout old man had been much bowed by the heavy and unexpected stroke; but he had borne up bravely, and the respect shown to his Lucy, as well by the baronet as by the whole country-side, had been heartily felt and acknowledged. It was easy, however, for Sir Geoffrey to see the weight of care which lay at his steward's heart, and to understand why it lay there, and to endeavour to soothe it to the best of his power.

"It's no use, Robert Smithson," he said, as he held out his hand once more at the justice table, where the previous quarrel had taken place—"it's no use grieving, man. When I was in hot blood—in a d—d passion, by George—I held out this hand to you in good faith about that boy; and now I'm cool, and can see my way better, I give it you again. I thank the Lord I have no wish but to do right, Robert, though my duty to my child has the first place. See, here's the memorandum I've given to Braithwaite. He's to use it in concert with you, and I hope you'll go over to Morpeth to him; indeed, I told him you would. I've offered a reward of a hundred guineas to any one who will give true information about Harry's marriage, or produce registers; and I'll double that with pleasure. I know you'll not be idle yourself; and you can act with him, or apart, or both ways, just as you like, and may God speed you! But listen, there's the other side to look at, and we can't blink it. Bless my heart, no; for that dear child's sake, no! I shall put all before Mr. Peed as faithfully and unreservedly as if you were present; nay, you can come up to town, if you like, and act on his advice. I'm growing old, Robert; and your poor wife's sudden death is like a warning to us all to put our houses in order before the Lord, that nobody may suffer or be troubled after us with law and lawyers, and be d—d to the whole crew of them! So I shall go to Peed, and that long-headed brother of mine, and the will 'll be drawn up—"

"But not executed, Sir Geoffrey," interrupted Smithson, earnestly. "Oh, Sir Geoffrey, ye're vary kind; mair kind and mair true than the likes o' uz deserves; but don't execute it till ye sey mey. A'll dee a' I can dee, Sir Geoffrey, for my puir wee bairnie's sake; and I can dee nae mair, surr. What time will ye gi'e me, surr?"

"No, I will not execute it, Robert, till I see you—that is, unless I'm dying; and we are all in the Lord's hands. No, I will not execute it," said Sir Geoffrey, firmly, "till I see you, and there's my hand on it: you'll have two months from this, and if the marriage records can't be found at Lamberton Pike or anywhere else before then, you had as well give up the matter, and we'll see Ralph wants for nothing all his life, though he may not be master of Melcepeth. Now, go to Mistress Grover; see if she wishes anything done. Depend upon it, you could not have a better advocate than she is—no, not though you paid all the lawyers in Christendom."

Robert Smithson had heard his doom. He could say nothing. What was there to say? He rose, but he could not speak; he could only see dimly—for his eyes were blurred with a mist of tears—the baronet's tall figure before him, with the sun streaming upon it through the stained-glass window of the room, clothing it in a radiance of crimson, purple, and gold; and there was a swelling in his throat which, old as he was, denied utterance of many words.

"A'll dee it a', Sir Geoffrey," was all he could say, "an' may the Lord above help mey!"

"Amen!" replied the baronet, sadly, as the gaunt figure turned from him and left the room.

"He'll only give me tow months, ma'am," said Smithson to Bessie Grover, after he had told her what had passed; "could ye na get me a while mair?"

"He'll be just, Robert," she replied; "and you know it. The matter must be settled before Ralph comes of age, and there's little time to lose."

"A' dinna ken, ma'am—a' dinna ken. A'll dee ma best, an' nae man can dee mair; an' maybe the barrinit 'll let them pit in a bit word for what might—*what might*, ye ken—turn up true for the laddie. He'd be sorry to know that Rraafe was wrranged by no word at a'. But I daurna say this to Sir Geoffrey, Mistress Grover; he's owre kind and guid as it is—"

"I know he means to do that, Robert Smithson," replied Mistress Grover; "and I'll see that it is done."

"The Lord bless ye, Bessie Grover! the Lord bless ye for the truest heart that iver beat! A'll gae hame noo, ma'am, content. A've nae mair to say, nae mair, but to dee the Lord's will; an' I wish ye a safe journey, ma'am, an' safe back to Melcepeth."

END OF PART FIRST.

PART SECOND.

PART SECOND.

CHAPTER XIV.

STEADY, RALPH!

LEAVING Sir Geoffrey Darnell and his party to pursue their way to London by the slow stages, over the bad roads, and amidst the alarms of highwaymen, and other incidents and difficulties common to the time I write of—this history requires that I should return to London, and relate what progress Mr. Ralph Darnell was making in fashionable education, under his accomplished instructors Messieurs Elliot and Forster. Not indeed that I feel myself called upon to enter very much into detail on this subject; for it so happened that just about a year after the period we have reached, one Mr. Henry Warrington arrived from Virginia, with a handsome pocketful of money; and was taken in hand by my Lords Castlewood and March, and other noblemen and gentlemen who delighted in seeing a young fellow of spirit spend his fortune freely, and indeed in easing him of it themselves in as great a degree as they could contrive. We know, too, from the veracious and inimitably recorded history of that young gentleman—which hath been written by one who, alas! is gone to his everlasting rest, and the like of whom may never be seen again among us—how Mr. Warrington comported himself as a man of spirit and of fashion; how the great society at White's and Arthur's received him, and what it made of him: what horses and phaetons he possessed; what flirtations he and his black servant indulged in; and, in short, what the conclusion of his very pleasant career was. And having all this to instruct and amuse us—writ in imperishable characters which time will only strengthen—I feel that, putting all other considerations aside, it would be absolute temerity and profanation to attempt to detail Mr. Ralph Darnell's progress, even were that needful or possible.

But indeed it would be impossible, for many obvious reasons. Mr. Ralph was not in the same rank of life or station as that which Mr. Henry Warrington attained at once through his aristocratic family connections; nor were the means of that attainment by the other greatest road, money, at all abundant; nor were his companions acknowledged by my Lord March, or other persons of their station, at White's. It is true that Mr. George Elliot had attained to the dignity of a passing bow, or other acknowledgment, from several noble and fashionable persons of the town; and that he cherished hopes of reaching that sublime goal—the bow-window of White's—in process of time and by a liberal expenditure of his patrimony: but as yet he was as far from that triumphant and much-coveted consummation, as Mr. Ralph Darnell from the status at which Mr. Elliot and his friend Mr. Forster had arrived. Ralph, however, was daily receiving as much encouragement as he could hope for, and was as much content perhaps with that, in its degree, as his friends were with theirs; and he considered, whether with or without substantial grounds, that when that point in his career should be reached which should elevate him to the rank of acknowledged heir to the Darnell properties, though his actual possession of them might, in course of nature, be long delayed, he should, in point of fact, occupy a superior position to either of his friends, and his recognition by leaders of fashion might even be more certain.

I am bound, however, to state that, whether from pride, want of means, or from a certain cast of character in which good and evil strongly conflicted and combined, Ralph Darnell's progress was not altogether consistent, nor perhaps so hopeful as his friends desired. Mr. Elliot, on many occasions, offered him the use of his purse to some extent; and Mr. Forster, while he professed to appreciate the high sense of honour which restrained Ralph from availing himself of this privilege, had tendered—in an equally affectionate spirit—the offices of friendly and even benevolent persons who, for certain considerations, had no objection to anticipate the events of nature, and supply funds whereby ambitious youths might become possessed of means to compass their ends—those ends being secondary considerations altogether. Nevertheless, Ralph Darnell's principles were yet so far true to his family connection, that he would not be persuaded to drag down the proud Darnell name into the mire of post-obit bonds or other securities, which were described by Forster as mere matters of form; nor could he be persuaded to apply to either of his uncles for money, well knowing as he did, that he should take not only no benefit thereby, but very possibly the contrary. At this period, therefore, of his career, he had become an anomaly to his friends; and after several consultations in regard to his advancement, they had come to the conclusion that he was a great deal too careful, and had by far too great control over himself, to be brought under their influence as much as it behoved a follower of theirs should be. And yet it would not answer to pass him by altogether. By-and-by he would be a great man, one with whom acquaintance would be a thing of note; and thus they were content to let Ralph do very much as he pleased, and come and go as he liked.

The apparently steady conduct of the young man was subject of great delight to several persons of whom we know a little already. In the first place, to Mr. Sanders, who, having had but little real hope of Ralph's amendment, saw with pleasure his former regular attendance to business renewed; and had entrusted him, after his successful essay in Mr. Wharton's letter, with other documents of a private and confidential character. Ralph, too, on several occasions had been favoured by invitation to tea with the ladies above stairs; and while he told them of the country scenes and pastimes of the (to them) rude North, heard from Mr. Sanders, with as strange a fascination as he had listened to Captain Abel Scrafton—and I might say even greater—tales of Indian life—of the occupations of Englishmen in that far country; of hunting, such as could not even be imagined; and how, mounted on the Nabob's elephants, parties of the factors would kill tigers, wild boars, and buffaloes.

Ah! for all that he looked so demure and passionless as he sat at his desk day by day, Ralph felt that hot blood had once coursed through Mr. Sanders's veins, and that warfare with men had taken its place with warfare against wild beasts. Who were these men he spoke of?—Moors, Gentoos, Brahmins, with their hideous idols, glorious old poetry, and quaint sacred legends, of which Mr. Sanders—a studious man—possessed many specimens. Who were these Emperors, Nawabs, Rajahs, who ruled over cities larger and richer than London, and territories larger—far larger and more populous—than all Europe? Mr. Sanders delighted in instructing Ralph in these details. They brought old scenes to his memory, and political events which were daily becoming more interesting. Who in England knew or cared about them in comparison with their importance? and I suppose—even though Ralph had heard daily since his career in Roger Darnell and Company's office began, more or less about Indian sugar and silk—that he never would have cared to know where and by whom they were produced, but for these pleasant evenings at Mr. Sanders's.

I am bound to state also, that in a comparatively short period, the good sisters were able to bring Mrs. Morton more from her seclusion than she had ever ventured before since Colonel Morton's death. She had actually, on two occasions, crossed the river in a wherry, and ridden from the stairs in a coach to Lombard Street; and no harm had come of this. Sybil had become an object of the deepest interest to the Misses Sanders; and those good ladies had in turn, and almost with more difficulty than Mrs. Morton, ventured to Tooley Stairs, and to the old house. There they had heard those sweet voices sing Italian trios and duets, which they had believed impossible to English folk. They had heard Miss Sybil play selections from Mr. Handel's oratorios upon her harpsichord; and had they not eaten of dear Nanny Keene's hot griddle and other Northumberland cakes, and declared they could not be equalled in London?

So this kind of society—for Ralph Darnell had ordinarily no other —was for the time pleasanter than that of wild bloods, and the excitement of cards, in which he indulged only occasionally: and he was soothed by it. He was even beginning to persuade himself that he was feeling satisfaction in keeping his word to his Uncle Roger; and Uncle Roger was almost regretting that he had ever complained of the lad to Sir Geoffrey. You will think that Mr. Roger Darnell was unkind, inhospitable, neglectful, or what you please, in not inviting Ralph to dinner occasionally, or treating him as an uncle should treat a nephew who might come to be his heir. I am bound to say, that I think Mr. Roger Darnell would, in this respect—and except, indeed, that of the heirship—have done, as you, my good sir or madam, conceive you yourself would have done in this case; but there was a Mrs. Darnell, who, as I have said before, had been born in Virginia, and whose temper, I lament to state, had neither been improved by early colonial religious exercises, colonial habits of dealing with slaves, or subsequent education in England. I am afraid, also, that she looked upon Ralph as an interloper—as a something existent in the shape of a male heir to all the Darnells, the like of which had not been vouchsafed to her, and of the possible contingency of which she was beginning to have very serious misgivings.

To be sure she had heard, and her wise female friends—nay, even the celebrated physician, Doctor R——, had told her of certain cases, when, after many years of interval, sons and heirs had been born; and it was quite certain that in her private form of—but I have no business, perhaps, to touch upon so very private, delicate, and confidential a subject; nor to transcribe from the diaries upon which the facts of this history are related, what struggles this poor lady had with herself; nor how bitterly and unavailingly she recorded her disappointments. This, however, I may be allowed to state, that she hated Ralph with an unwarrantably jealous and very unrighteous hatred; that she rejoiced whenever she heard complaints of him; and rebelled, and grieved her husband, whenever—as was sometimes the case—Ralph came to eat a Sunday dinner at the mansion. On such occasions, not only was Mrs. Darnell severely and rigidly pious, as befitted a regular attendant at Mr. Whitfield's chapel in Tottenham Court Road; but painfully strict in regard to the dinner to be provided. I am not, indeed, quite sure that cabbage or potatoes were even boiled; but I am quite certain that there were no hot dishes of meat on the table: and Mrs. Darnell hated the periodical apology of Mr. Roger Darnell upon the subject to his nephew, which, as especially addressed to his wife, invariably ended by his emphatic declaration, that "if she prevented his having a good dinner, she could not help his having a good bottle of wine after it, nor his giving a share of it to Ralph."

I have no hesitation either in declaring, that Ralph's four cousins, Anne, Dorothy, Maria, and Rachel—of ages varying from seven upwards—were always taught by their mother, and by Mistress Higgins the housekeeper, and Mistress Lamb the head nurse, to uphold their mother's opinion that Ralph was no more than *a poor beggar*, whom the charity of the Darnells had supported; and cousins Anne, Maria, and Rachel openly professed this belief, and scorned Ralph accordingly. I do not think, however, that Dorothy—a dear, dimpled, rosy, cosy, merry damsel of fifteen—at all fell into the female faith of the family; and I fear she had undergone many a snubbing, not to say boxes on the ear, from her mother, and pinches from her sisters, for being defiant on the subject of cousin Ralph—speaking kindly to him, and declaring him the handsomest and dearest cousin in the world.

So you see Ralph Darnell was not without friends; and, to say the truth, the friends seemed far more powerful than the enemies; for, after all, what could one spiteful Mrs. Darnell and three cousins do against him? And he had another friend too, far more precious than any we have mentioned, had he but known of the fact; yes, Ralph was growing very dear to Sybil Morton—very dear indeed. I do not think she could have defined how dear he was to her, or how his image was growing to be part of herself—and his mind, so far as she could follow it, of her mind. This was no sudden love or fancy; it was the growth of years. It had been growing ever since he came to the house, and seemed to be increasing. I have heard of strange love of men by mere girls, not children, though a child's love is very touching in its unselfishness and purity; nor yet woman's, for with woman's love, passion must be developed; but that pure devotion which becomes absolute over all other feeling, and is undefinable, perhaps, because a new sense, as it were, only known to the possessor, is created, which cannot be shared by another; and were it known to the object, would be changed or altogether destroyed. Such a love is a treasure which the possessor secretes and guards more jealously than his hidden gold by a miser; a rich store of enjoyment—selfish, perhaps, for a time—which dare not be openly acknowledged.

Was Ralph Darnell worthy of such love? Well, something is known of him even by this time, and you can judge for yourself, O reader; but he is beside the question altogether. Sybil Morton knew no one else; and so Ralph Darnell had grown up with her to be an incarnation of manly power—of gentle protective attachment to her—of perfection in many accomplishments which they shared together; and thus to take a place which no brother could have supplied. Sybil's watch over Ralph was perfect. No matter if he were wrong, or wilful, as we know him to have been, or profligate, as he seemed sometimes to be becoming; no matter if her mother was grave and anxious, or Nanny Keene prophesied that "the Darnell bluid 'ud come oot some time;" "that it was ill gettin' a tame birrd oot o' a wild birrd's nest," and so on—Sybil Morton could see no fault in Ralph Darnell, and, as we know, had a thousand apologies always ready for any irregularity.

It would have pained her sorely—shocked her, indeed—if she could have fancied Ralph understood anything of this. It would have changed their positions utterly, and destroyed the romance of her faith. She was content to watch and believe, and had her reward in his kindness. He was kind, and true also, though his feelings to Sybil were of a very different character from hers to him. Something after her fashion to him, was his ideal in his cousin Constance. To Sybil would he speak of her: of their early days of companionship, of their adventures, mishaps, quarrels, and loves; and he believed that she encouraged him in persistence in this love. Ah! could she have told him that Constance was not—could never be—to him what she was—never so true, never so devoted—would he have believed this? I fear not: but she could not tell him, and so she had watched and loved, and loved and watched, through many a day, through many a night, gathering her comfort from kind words, from helpful companionship, and from hope, dim and blurred with a mist of uncertain futurity, but still hope. Could it last? Would he ever be to her what she was to him? Ah! what would she not do to prove this? More even than she had done when, perhaps, she had saved him that night in the snow. She often longed for something to occur in which she might be put to a higher test even than that; and the test came, too, sooner than she thought.

On the day I speak of—it was the quarter-day—Mr. Sanders called Ralph to him before the morning's tasks were appointed, and taking from his desk a private ledger, opened it at the letter D, and running his fingers down a column of names beginning with that letter, stopped at one, took the number of a page, and turned to it. The heading was plain enough: "Ralph Darnell, in account current with Roger Darnell & Co.;" and after a number of To's and By's, which were carefully gone over, the balance was a pleasant one for a young man to look at, and Mr. Sanders read it with some satisfaction. "Three hundred and twenty-four pounds, seven shillings, aud twopence!" he said. "Why, Ralph, you are growing quite a man of fortune. Now, by the last arrangement, you know, one hundred must be invested till you are of age, and a pretty little sum there is too, I can tell you; but of the balance you are master. What will you do with it?"

What would he do with it? There were many pleasant things in his mind in a moment to do with it. Elliot could be paid for one; his tailor for another; then he could take Nanny and Sybil into council, and lay out something upon a new carpet; perhaps exchange the old harpsichord for a better. Yes; he would take it all, and he said so, and gave some of the reasons.

Mr. Sanders sighed. "Well," he said, "I had rather you didn't, all your pleasant intentions to good Mrs. Morton notwithstanding. You had better leave half with me, Ralph, or more. You may want it when Sir Geoffrey comes."

"You shall keep the balance after you have given me the two hundred, Mr. Sanders; but indeed, indeed, sir," said the young man, laughing, "I'm sure about the rest. I shall have quite enough for my uncle's visit."

Mr. Sanders said no more, but gave the money. Like Mr. Darnell, he had grown to believe that the best way to treat Ralph was in confidence. He made the entry in the ledger, where it stood for many a day as a mark—a record, as it were, of a turning-point in a future eventful life—"25th May 1755—By cash, £200"—and having drawn a line with a ruler, the balance, £24, 7s. 2d., was entered below.

What should he do with it? The money seemed to burn in his pocket, worse than Captain Abel Scrafton's, and Ralph's plans were not difficult to make. He should find Elliot at home, no doubt, and would but change his dress and go to him before anything else was done. He could not go in his shabby office suit, and he might stroll down by St. Paul's into Fleet Street and the Strand, or even as far as Pall Mall or Bond Street, and find something—a fairing they called it in the north—for Sybil, and one for his dear Constance too—why not? she could not be changed! In short, he had delight in the possession of money, and the intention of laying it out well; and was in proportionably high spirits, taking an oar in the ferry-boat from the Tower to Tooley Stairs, and pulling with a hearty good will. Sybil and Nannie heard him open the front door, go up to his room, whence he presently emerged in one of his holiday suits of brown velvet and gold-lace, with a white satin waistcoat worked by Sybil, a handsome rapier by his side; his best wig, and a small fashionable laced hat on his head. He was undeniably handsome, and the women looked upon him with that foolish kind of pride-worship which women will always evince for those they love, and in which you, sir, or I, take a strange delight.

Yes, Ralph turned himself round as he was told to do; and Sybil brushed off an imaginary speck of dust, or a thread, or something, just, as it appeared, in order to touch him, apparently to satisfy herself that he was real; and then he took an ivory-headed cane from the corner, and lifting off his hat, saluted them with a grand bow, and a sweep of it, which had much grace and dignity.

"Very well, sir," said Mrs. Morton, who was lying on a sofa, looking out upon the river, by the open casement, for the sweet evening breeze was soft and pleasant—"very well indeed. Your bow reminds me of—"

"Never mind now, mother," said Sybil hastily, for she had good reason to dread her mother's reminiscences—"never mind. And pray, sir," she added with mock gravity, and curtsying profoundly, "for what fair lady is this display, so unusual?"

"Ye're no gaun to that fause loon Elliot the nicht, Master Rraafe," said old Nanny, interrupting Sybil. "'Deed yon Forster's a bit quiet, decent young man, a'm thinkin'; but that Elliot—ah, them Elliots wuz a'ways fause."

"Not the Forsters, Nanny," said the old lady, rebuking her solemnly—"not the Forsters; they died, but they were true."

"Indeed, mother," said Sybil peremptorily, "you are to look at Mr. Ralph, and not to talk of anybody else."

"And I think him a very handsome, gallant young gentleman, who will, I am sure, have many admirers as he walks down the Strand," said the old lady. "Good evening to you, sir; and we shall expect a relation of your adventures when you come home."

"And you shall have them, madam. I wish you a good afternoon, ladies;" and making them another sweeping salute, half in fun, half in earnest, Ralph left them.

"Tak' gude care, Maister Rraafe, darlin'," said old Nanny Keene to him as he went out; a'll be jist waitin' for ye afore ye come hame; but ye'll no be late, hinny?"

"Oh, no, Nanny, not late; I'll be home long before you are in bed. I must go to Elliot's, to pay him what I owe; an' that's like a true Darnell, ye ken, Nanny. I must be all clear before the baronet arrives."

"Na, na, he'll tak nae harm, wan't Maister Rraafe, Miss Sybil, an' ye'll ne'er hae nae mair pykin' o' him oot o' the sna' drift. We'll jist let the mistress gae to bed, hinny, an' we'll sit here, you and I, lookin' oot on the rriver. Eh, but it's sweet the nicht;—an' he was a brave-lookin' lad, tey—wasn't he jist? Maybe the liken o' him won't be in a' the haill Strand; and Sir Geoffrey 'll be jist prowd o' him—jist prowd, ye ken."

Sybil thought so, decidedly.

CHAPTER XV.

MR. ELLIOT'S SUPPER AND CONCERT.

Mr. Elliot's lodgings were in Norfolk Street, in the Strand, and being in the house nearest the river, there was a very pretty view thereof, as well as great convenience for going to the city, or to Westminster, by boat, then a favourite mode of conveyance. As Ralph issued forth from his house, his friends the watermen at Tooley Stairs crowded about him with offers of service, and he was finally dissuaded from undertaking the long walk by land. The day had been showery, and the streets were very muddy. It did not matter for the evening return: there would be a moon, and he could come home at night on foot or row back again as he pleased; but the wherry would take him, clean and fresh as he was, direct to Mr. Elliot's house, and afterwards he could walk on and execute his commissions. There is no doubt that Mr. Ralph, by this course, missed seeing many celebrities of the time—men in whom we even of this generation feel a strange delight and interest, stronger perhaps because we know more of them than we do of any others before or since. Men who lived much in coffee-houses and taverns, said smart things, and arranged to say them beforehand—shrewd, hard-witted, and hard-headed fellows, who knew their own value, and received it in the homage paid to them. But Mr. Ralph had no acquaintance with any of these. He was certainly not literary or critical, and assuredly was not learned in classical lore. I question whether he could have translated the first hundred lines of Virgil, although he had a pretty knowledge of Boccaccio, and even of Dante. This, however, he never paraded; I believe, indeed, in my heart, that the foolish youth would have denied such knowledge altogether, because it had originated with two girls, one of whom he loved, and the other was his daily companion and friend. What would Mr. Elliot or Mr. Forster have said to either? and how much banter would he, Ralph Darnell, not have had to endure, had it been surmised that he had ever studied with them!

No matter; the afternoon proved bright and warm, and hundreds of wherries were skimming the calm surface of the noble river, laden with many smartly-dressed parties enjoying the balmy air and pleasant companionship of those with them. Mr. Ralph's thoughts were quite sufficient for him. Was not Constance coming—should he not see that dear face again, and be greeted heartily by his old uncle and Mrs. Grover? Yes, all the world was bright to him that afternoon, and he made the best of it. Altering his destination slightly, he was set down at the stairs by Somerset House, and thence walked into the Strand. His tailor, Mr. Price, lived there, and would be glad to see him with money in his pocket, and all arrears wiped off; little, perhaps, after the fashion of tailors in general, expecting any such good fortune.

"And you'll have something new, Mr. Darnell?" said that worthy tradesman, with a profusion of bows—"something in the best style of the fashion? Here are a few of the last things I have made up; and that suit for my Lord March is just going home. No? too rich? Well, we can suit you better, perhaps, in a quieter pattern, though, with such a figure, Mr. Darnell, you can take your place among the best; and I hope you'll not forget me, sir, when you come to your property."

And Ralph made his choice of two new suits, one for the morning and one for the evening; and I believe, as he did so, that he had visions of many a walk on the Mall or at Ranelagh with his beautiful cousin, and many a happy evening at the theatre, concerts, or other entertainments. He told Mr. Price to dress him as a gentleman should be dressed, and there was no question of that great artist's taste and judgment.

The interview with his tailor had occupied more time than Ralph had imagined, there were so many pretty things to choose from. It was already too late to see after the carpet or the harpsichord; but he could buy something for Constance and Sybil, and, turning up the Strand in the direction of Essex Street, he entered a goldsmith's shop he well knew, and made his selections—a pretty gold chain and locket for Constance, and a brooch for Sybil. He was standing at the shop door, looking carelessly up and down the street, when Elliot and Forster, with three other well-dressed men, came up. Ralph would have greeted them as familiarly as usual, but to his surprise both merely raised their hats, and passed on.

What was the meaning of this? Was he to be thrown off altogether? Had he done anything to offend? The young man was generous, passionate also, it is true; but, as is most frequently the case with such characters, slow to take offence. One otherwise constituted, would most likely have turned back and resented the seeming coldness; but Ralph had a duty to fulfil, a payment of honour to make, and, allowing his friends to precede him a little, he followed them. He saw with satisfaction that they turned down Norfolk Street, and, continuing his pace more rapidly, he overtook them before they had entered the house. The three men who were with Elliot and Forster stared at him from head to foot. They were new to Ralph; and Elliot, again removing his hat, seemed in doubt as to what he should say or do, when Forster interfered.

"Gad," he said, "Darnell, you have been near us so little for a month past, that we concluded you had gone for good to Mr. Whitfield's connection, and that Mrs. Roger had taken you up at last. Indeed you made so very stiff a bow to Geordy, that we could think nothing else—could we Elliot?"

"I?" said Ralph; "I did not." . . .

"Never mind him," said Elliot, laughing; "it was only to tease you, Ralph. We thought your conscience would smite you when you saw old friends. Come in, man; you won't refuse a quiet supper, and it's all ready, or will be soon. Nay, I insist. Selwyn, let me introduce you to Mr. Ralph Darnell, one day to be Sir Ralph, Baronet. Wilson—Mr. Darnell. Come along; let us see what good things the gods have provided us with."

"A word with you, Elliot," said Ralph, drawing him back as the others entered the hall door, which was held open by a negro servant in a rich livery and a cauliflower wig. "I cannot stay; but I want you to take the money I owe you, which I have brought with me. If you'll bring the I O U I gave you, I will wait in the ante-room."

"Indeed, you shall do no such thing, Ralph Darnell. What, man," replied Elliot quickly, "after not showing us the light of your countenance for a week, you are going off unceremoniously! By Jove, the old woman in Bloomsbury must have done for you. Ha! ha! ha!—a good joke, and thou'rt turned Methody at last, with that solemn face of thine. Damme if I can believe it, however, Ralph. Not stay! and Peg Woffington and the little Signora Blandini and a lot more coming, and some of the Italian fiddlers and singers too. Nay, but thou art a singer—a classical singer, by Gad—and wilt delight in them. Not stay? By George, sir, I'll take no denial; and, what's more, I know that money is burning thy pocket, and it may burn there and be d—d, for not a stiver of it will I ever touch if thou dost not sup with us. Nay, not a word more"—for he saw Ralph about to speak—"we would think thou wert turned into Mister Sanders settling an account, or that Jew Levi taking up a bill, and waiting in the anteroom with it."

The good-humour of the young man was contagious, and there was nothing in Ralph's mind to jar with it. Was he not happy? He knew he was well dressed. He had money enough to give away ir needs be; but the play would be deep, and he dreaded that.

"I won't play," he said, "George, and there will be a good deal of it among your grand friends."

"Just as you please, Ralph; this is Liberty Hall to-night, and it would be uncivil in me to say to my guests, Play, when they didn't please, or, Don't play, when they did please—you can do just as you like."

"Then let's settle the private matter first; and, that off my mind, I'll try and make myself agreeable to the company," returned Ralph.

"By all means. Come to my bedroom; you may need to wash your hands, you know, and I'll go with you."

"What are you fellows chattering about?" said Forster, as they passed the drawing-room door. "Are you not going to tay, Darnell?"

"Certainly he is," replied Elliot; "I'll show him where to wash his hands, and we'll be down with you directly. Are any of them come?"

"Plenty. Be quick, Geordy—I'll do host till we see you."

It was a great relief to Ralph when the old I O U paper was in his hand, torn into one hundred fragments, and thrown into the fire-place. "The first and the last," he said to Elliot, and he looked as if he were in earnest.

Elliot sighed. "Ah, Ralph," he said, "I wish I had thy determination—I wish such papers were my first and my last; but I feel there'll be a plentiful crop of them before I've done. Come—Mistress Woffington will scold and pout if I delay, and there is a fair friend of hers too, whom I would not provoke."

Mistress Woffington, however, was as placable as she was well dressed and agreeable. It was no point of her character to quarrel with a gay gentleman who was going to give her a good supper, and entertain her with the best Italian music then procurable after it. She cast a favourable eye over the stalwart form and handsome face of young Darnell, and introduced him to her companion, with whom Ralph was soon on easy terms. Certainly Mistress Woffington, as she looked from one to the other, could hardly make up her mind as to which she would award the palm of manly beauty to. George Elliot was richly dressed and looking his best. He had improved in appearance since we saw him first at the Golden Cock. He was rising in the social scale. He would have several noblemen and some men of fashion there that night, men who had no objection in life to descend a step from their lofty pedestals to meet others striving thereto. Certainly George Elliot was rising—Mistress Woffington was perhaps falling; but still she was holding her own, and he must be a man of mark who could entertain her, or by whom she would submit to be entertained.

And George Elliot did his part of host to perfection. Calm, courteous, and well-bred, he took his place at the head of a table (Forster was at the bottom) on which gold and silver plate and bright crystal sparkled, and the most perfect French dishes of the period were provided. He looked—as he was—proud of the occasion and of his company. The guests were twelve only; and to make room for Ralph, Mr. Wilson had given up his place.

Ralph's companion was an Italian girl, not beautiful, but with one of the softest, richest voices he had ever heard. True, he could read Italian, but, except to a dear friend, he had not dared to speak it. What more likely mode, however, of trying his speech than with one who only spoke a few broken words of English? and once loosed, his tongue had occupation enough, and pleasant occupation too. The girl had found few with whom she could converse in her own language, and her remarks on England, on her receptions, on the people, and on music were racy and piquant. She soon gauged Ralph's musical knowledge, and claimed him as her most attentive listener to be. "I shall sing *to* the rest of the company; but *for* you, signor," she said as the ladies rose, "take care that you listen."

I daresay I need not record Ralph's gallant speeches on this occasion; no doubt they were tender, and that he put his hand to his heart exactly at the proper time. I say he was very happy. "What a fool I should have been," he thought, "if I had gone away! why, this music is worth all the rest, and I would not have missed it on any account;" so he joined heartily with his companions, and drank his Burgundy to the King's health with right good will: bearing the banter of Elliot, Forster, and Mr. Selwyn on his conquest of the Signorina, with great good-humour.

There were a few toasts only: our great-grandfathers could partake of no repast without toasts, and as there was much to do, the gentlemen soon broke up and rejoined the ladies in the drawing-room, where the company was assembling fast, and chairs were set for the music, and it was commenced without delay. A concerted piece of Mr. Handel's and one of Pescetti's overtures were played, then the Signorina was led forth gallantly by Elliot, and sang with a bewitching execution and grace the beautiful bravura, "Sventurata non ho pace," out of "Ezio" by Perez, with which Signora Mingotti was enchanting the town; and being heartily encored, followed it by the tender "Tu sai ch'io sono amanti," in which she cast very tender glances at Mr. Ralph, well knowing that he understood her—which few others there did—and of which he could not very well mistake the meaning; and the applause was again as rapturous as the rewards were substantial.

Mistress Woffington was fond of play—what actress, what lady, was not, in 1755? and the little Signorina seemed to have no objection either. She had sung several other songs, and there had been some concerted vocal pieces, also well performed; but the entertainments of the evening were by no means ended. Indeed 'twas even then early; Ralph's little friend would take no denial—who would speak to her if he went away? she could not pretend to talk that hard "Eenglis." He would not play? no? then he must bet on her, and give her all he won—she was sure to win—she never lost. These were easy terms, and Ralph won. He bet Mr.

Selwyn three to two in fives and won, and handed the stakes to the young lady.

"Won't you back me, Mr. Darnell?" cries Mistress Woffington from the end of the faro table—"won't you back me?"

Perhaps she was a little jealous of her Italian friend.

"Thank you, I am with the Signorina, and I am not going to desert her," returns Ralph, gallantly; "we're very lucky, madam, and I hope you're the same."

"That boy will make a fool of the girl," said Mistress Woffington, after awhile, with a vexed look, "and that won't do at all. Don't you see her eyes? they are as full of love of him as they can hold; can't you call off your dog, Mr. George? he sha'n't worry my pet—I won't have it."

"Let her alone, Peggy," said Mr. Elliot, calmly; "she knows very well what she's about; he's betting on her, and giving her all he wins. Capital, by Gad, and he's screwing that fellow Selwyn too, who always has a pocketful of cash, wherever he gets it. Again? there's no play like a woman's, after all."

"Double or quits, sir?" cried Selwyn, excitedly; "I've lost a cool fifty, by Jove, and here's another fifty upon it, and that's the last to-night."

"Shall I, carina?" whispered Ralph: "all or nothing, what say you?"

"Mio cara, all or nothing!" sighed the damsel: "with you—all or nothing."

"Damnation!" cried the man, "she's won again. Here, Forster, lend me a pony, will ye? I'm done for to-night, Elliot; there's plenty more where the last came from, by— !"

"Not a stiver, Albany," returned Elliot; "you might as well play against the fiend himself as that girl; who ever saw her lose? Away with you to-night; you'll do better another time. What have you won for her, Darnell?

"Only a hundred, George, from Mr. Selwyn, but there's plenty more beside his."

"By George, but she's got a heap before her, and we'll have to see her home some of us—what do you say? Will you come, Darnell? I suspect your company would be *very* pleasant."

The girl caught the meaning of the words, and said anxiously to Ralph in her own soft language, "You *must* see me home—you must come—you will not refuse? Come! I cannot go alone, not even with her."

Ralph did not—could not—refuse those pleading eyes and that soft Italian speech; he pressed her hand tenderly in acknowledgment: nor had he long to wait. The party was breaking up; boys with links, chairmen shouting, bawling, and jostling, were in the narrow street. Elliot and Forster, with Selwyn, had gallantly offered to escort Mistress Woffington to her house not far off, and the Signorina lived hard by, and so the party went on. Ralph took his post of honour, and I am sadly afraid he was thinking neither of Constance nor Sybil just then, but of a pair of soft dark eyes gleaming from the chair window, and a small jewelled hand which lay very temptingly on the open frame.

Suddenly, as they turned out of the Strand towards Covent Garden, several watchmen came flying down the street, springing their rattles.

"The Mohocks! Mohocks are out: turn your chairs, gentlemen—turn or they will be upon you," they cried and so ran on.

But it was too late to turn. Hard at the heels of the watchmen, followed a confused rabble of men; some carrying torches, and waving them in the air, some brandishing naked rapiers which flashed in the torchlight as they rushed wildly along, and all shouting damnation to Hanoverian rats and Tories, in one of the obscene Mohock "war-cries," as they were called, with which I refuse to defile these pages. Ralph, and the chair by which he was walking, were at once surrounded by the foremost, shouting, and dancing a mock Indian war-dance in wild and fanastic capers, occasionally too making lunges at him.

"Pink him! pink him! let daylight into him; d—n him, pink him! Let's see who's in the chair! Turn her out! pull out the strumpet!" shouted a dozen voices, while the girl within was shrieking piteously, and hiding her face with her hands.

Ralph had drawn his sword, and was trying, in good-humour, to induce the Mohocks to pass on, while he cried to the girl not to fear; but as he stood by the chair door, one fellow pricked him sharply in the leg, so that the blood spurted forth, and two others, closing rapidly on his guard, while a third pushed a half-extinguished torch into his face, prevented his defending himself as it behoved one of Mr. Sutton's favourite pupils to do. Ralph managed, however, to parry a few passes; but missing a return lunge at one, received a deep wound in his breast from another man, and after attempting to steady himself against the chair, fell senseless, and bathed in his blood, upon the pavement.

It was well for Ralph that his friends had held their ground, and saw him fall. Some watchmen had rallied by them, and the Mohocks were now charged in turn and chased down the Strand. The chairmen had returned, and there was no chance of further molestation. Elliot and Forster, with Mr. Selwyn, ran forward at once, and found the Italian girl vainly trying to raise Ralph and stanch his blood with her handkerchief as she was crying and sobbing bitterly over him. Perhaps it was well Ralph Darnell was as far past hearing what she said, as the men were from comprehending it; for the girl's heart had been touched deeply, and she was telling Ralph of this in her passionate Italian. Mistress Woffington too came up, and got out of her chair; and the group of richly-dressed men, with their drawn rapiers and lace—the jewels of the women, and their bright satin dresses—flashing in the torchlight, with what appeared to be Ralph's body only, before them, lying in a pool of his blood—formed a strange picture.

"He'll die, poor fellow," said Elliot, much shocked and sobered. "I fear that lunge went through him, Jack. But we can't leave our poor friend here, ladies, and you are near home; will you excuse us? Here are a dozen watchmen to guard you, and here's a guinea among them for beer. Don't think us ungallant, I pray, if we ask you to go with them."

Mistress Woffington saw the necessity of doing so at once. This was more than a stage adventure, and she kindly bade Elliot see to the wounded man; so the ladies' chairs were again taken up, though I believe truly that the little Italian would have rather gone with Ralph. Another chair was called, into which he was carefully put, and propped up, and the three friends, true to their word, saw him home. Nor indeed did they leave him till a surgeon—summoned hastily as they proceeded—had dressed the wound, and till Ralph a little revived, had pressed their hands in token of thanks and recognition—for he could not speak. I will indeed do Mr. Forster the justice to say that he offered to sit up with Ralph, and perhaps he had reasons of his own, which were not yet developed; but Nanny was peremptory. "She was used to see after wownded men," she said, "an' she didna care to have stranger folk in the hoos at siccan a time."

Would he live or die? I know not if there were others, but the prayers of one utterly distracted heart, which had been already anxious for many hours, went up all that night to a throne of mercy, incoherently perhaps—what matter?—as Sybil Morton sate till day-break by the sufferer, wiping the clammy sweat from his brow, and moistening his parched lips with the drink ordered by the doctor; hearing no comfort from old Nanny, nor heeding the terrified whining of her mother, who sat rocking herself to and fro like one distraught, till Nanny took her away and put her to bed.

"Ay, Miss Sybil," she said, when she returned to watch, and looked at Ralph's ghastly, pinched face, and heard his short gasps for breath —"ay, he's jist bad, but I ha'e seed waur nor that git ower it fine. Dinna greet, dinna greet ma bonnie pet; that'll no help you or him, ye ken."

I think if Sybil could have wept, it would have relieved the misery which had overwhelmed her, but her eyes were hot and dry, and her lips as parched as Ralph Darnell's.

CHAPTER XVI.

IN WHICH MISS CONSTANCE DARNELL'S POLITICAL OPINIONS ARE EVINCED.

"AND when did this happen, brother Roger?" said Sir Geoffrey Darnell, a few days after the occurrences recorded in the last chapter, when the baronet, having made his journey in safety, had arrived that morning at his brother's house, and being duly refreshed by a hearty breakfast, the ladies having retired, was enjoying a quiet chat with Roger upon family affairs, general and particular. "When did you say this happened?"

"Five days ago, Geoffrey. I did not know by which road you would come, and all I could do was to send a messenger to Barnet to wait for you."

"Ay, and a pretty to do we had, by George, sir! I thought Constance and that old goose Grover would have broken their hearts with crying, and I don't know, faith, which was worst of the two. The landlady and all the chambermaids were busy with hartshorn and burnt feathers, and all the waters in the doctor's shop, for a good hour or more before we could get on; but here we are at last, thank God! And so it happened five days ago, and he's no better, you say?"

"I fear not, brother; the surgeon finds the fever still high, and cannot lower it, though the lad hath been thrice blooded."

"God help him, Roger! why, 'tis enough to take all the blood out of his body: and he can't speak?"

"He could not when I saw him yesterday," replied his brother, "but the messenger reports him better to-day; less fever, he says, and pulse lower."

"Faith, the boy may be dying, Roger—dying, sir, who knows? and for my own part I won't delay. We can look at the rooms as we come back, and get into them to-night maybe."

"Nay, Geoffrey, not so soon surely. I plead only for a few days, and Mrs. Darnell—"

"If thou wert alone, Roger, I'd never leave thee, my lad, said the baronet, affectionately throwing his arm round the stout merchant's neck. "I'd stay here, and be thankful to look on that dear old face again. But it won't do, Roger—it won't, indeed. I'm d—d if I could bear a perpetual snubbing, or a virtuous frown from thy wife, if ever I rapped out an oath; and my temper is grown none of the softest with age. No, no, Roger; we haven't been in the house three hours, by George! but I've been taken to task a dozen times for swearing—for profanity—for— Well, never mind, Roger; thou'rt used to it, I suppose, and don't care; but we've got no Methodies yet in Melcepeth, and I don't see we're a bit less further from heaven, God forgive me! than our fathers were, who swore worse than we do —I do—I mean. No, no! I don't know how the women get on; Grover's sharp enough, and as for that saucebox Constance, there'd be fine doings shortly between her and that very prim daughter of yours, Anne, who echoes all her mother says. Don't be angry— Roger, don't be angry; I've not come to quarrel after a dozen years' absence; but we'd better be on safe ground."

Roger Darnell felt his brother was right, though he grudged his absence. He had taken a well-furnished house in Soho Square for him: not a very fashionable quarter perhaps, but more convenient, in many respects, than a location farther west. It would do for awhile, at any rate, and could be changed if needs be. "Well," he said at length, "as you please, and perhaps you're right; but you'll dine here, Geoffrey, and we'd as well take the chariot down to Mrs. Morton's till then; I own I'm quite as anxious about the lad as you are yourself"

"And about Peed, Roger?"

"We can call in Chancery Lane as we go, and he can come to the office in the morning to meet you—we shall be undisturbed there. I'll call for you and take you down after breakfast." And then the brothers fell to talking of old times, and people gone to their rest, and in that forgot Mrs. Darnell and her virtuous daughters—for the time.

The baronet had, however, been quite right in his determination. Miss Constance had already shocked the demure Miss Darnell by telling her of that salmon of which we know, and how "she'd ha' lost it, only Johnny Robson—that's Jenny Robson's brither, ye ken— got a grrip o' me round the waist, an' I held on, and the tackle was good," and so on. And when Anne asked and was told who Johnny Robson was, and heard he acted as a stable-helper, I'm afraid the eyebrows of mother and daughter were considerably more elevated, and their glances more significant, than was quite polite—as they looked, somewhat in wonderment and disdain, at the round beautiful waist about which Johnny Robson's arm had been thrown, and no doubt with envy at the glorious roses which the soft dimpled cheeks of the fresh country maiden displayed, in contrast with the faded looks of the town girl.

I think, too, that Mistress Grover and Constance were both of the same opinion when they compared notes above stairs in Grover's room, as they were unpacking some finery for dinner, for there was to be a party, they heard, in their honour. When Mistress Grover said, "No, Conny, it would never do; and your papa is quite right to go *at once;* we shall do *much* better by ourselves. I have not forgotten the town, and we can get about famously with the town coachman. Why, my dear, we should *never* see that dear Ranelagh, nor the Mall, nor the theatre. Bless me! what's the use of coming all this way if we're not to enjoy ourselves? And did you see what a verjuice look my lady put on when I asked her who were singing and playing? Ha! ha! ha! I'm like to split at the bare remembrance of it; but I *will* see that dear Woffington, and you shall see her too, in spite of Mrs. Darnell."

"And then about poor Ralph," whimpered Constance, wiping her eyes, which were as full, for the moment, of grief for him as of fun at Grover's descriptions. "She hadn't a good word for the poor fellow, and cousin Anne was worse. She told me that he was with—" but here, I think, a whisper began, which, being of a private and confidential nature, I have no right to record. "How I hated the chit," continued Constance, pouting. "I did hate her, and I do hate her, and I will hate her, for what she said; and I love Dorothy, who told me Ralph was the dearest, best, handsomest cousin she ever saw; and oh, Grover! I wish I could go and nurse him instead of that Sybil Morton, whom I shall hate, I know, if I think more of her. But daddy's gone to see him, dear old daddy! and he'll not preach like these Methodies, with their sour faces, when he comes back."

The brothers had gone to Mrs. Morton's, and both were shocked, sadly shocked, by what they saw. Poor Ralph was by no means out of danger; and repeated depletion had drawn every vestige of colour from his handsome face, except the red spot of fever which was burning his cheek. He was thin and gaunt, and moved restlessly about, throwing his hands here and there, and muttering in a low delirium. By his side, smoothing his pillow, giving him spoonfuls of barley-water, wiping his face with a soft cambric handkerchief, and doing the thousand careful offices which love suggests to a stricken sufferer, moved Sybil Morton, her sweet face full of misery, but bearing up to do her duty. Bravely? Well, as best she could in this sore trial. She was the only one Ralph knew, or would allow to touch him; and as the brothers came into the room, she held up her finger in warning that they were not to disturb him. Ralph appeared to have fallen asleep, and she was watching him with many a prayer, dear soul! that rest might come to that poor wasted body.

Presently he opened his eyes, and stared wildly at the baronet and Mr. Roger, but he did not appear to know either. Sybil, however, said gently to him, "They're your uncles, Mr. Ralph; won't you speak to them?"

But the great weary eyes closed again dreamily. "No, no," he murmured; "they'll let me die, Sybil—who cares for me?" and then thought wandered away to Constance, and to Elliot and Forster, and

Mr. Sanders; and they could distinguish nothing clearly but broken words, and so stood watching.

"I think it's the crisis the doctor spoke of, Mr. Darnell," said Sybil gently. "He does not know you; and if he did, he might be excited more than is good for him."

"We had better leave him, Geoffrey," said the merchant; "he is in the kindest hands; and may the Lord be merciful to him, poor lad!" and he drew his brother away gently.

Rough as the baronet was, the sad sight touched him deeply, and he wiped his eyes and blew his nose very audibly as he descended the stairs softly, and entered the drawing-room, where Mrs. Morton was reclining, as usual, on her sofa, propped up with pillows, looking out on the river.

"How do you find Ralph, Mr. Darnell?" she said, as he greeted her kindly.

Mr. Darnell shook his head. "You do not know my brother, Mrs. Morton; let me introduce Sir Geoffrey Darnell."

"I remember the name long ago—in the old times. Ah! they were different to these, Sir Geoffrey; but I bid you welcome to a lone widow's house, sir, if you'll accept a sad greeting—. If—" but the old lady could say no more; there was a flood of memories rushing into her heart, faster than she could bear them—of wild times full of hopes and excitement—of rumours of victory and defeat—and then of the last horrible scene. What marvel if a weak woman—physically and morally weak—broke down? Sir Geoffrey Darnell, far away in her own dear country, was endurable in thought; but present—he who had served with her husband and escaped—was to her a terrible reality. Yet she rallied.

"I'm very weak," she said feebly, "and you must forgive me, sirs. I'm not accustomed to see my friends now, as I used to be once, and I'm sorely troubled, too. Won't ye sit down, sirs?"

"Very much with my nephew Ralph, I'm afraid, madam," interrupted Sir Geoffrey, in the hope of changing the direction of her thoughts. "I'm afraid he's been an anxious care to you these many years: and I am sure we—that is, my brother and myself—have good reason to be grateful to you for your motherly care of him."

"Indeed, sir, I've done my best," returned Mrs. Morton, wiping her eyes. "I've had a great trial with him; and since he's fallen into bad company I've not known how to guide him. It's the Lord only, sir, that can do that, for I'm very helpless. But indeed, sir, I've always had prayers morning and night, and he often read them, and he's taken Sybil to church, too, every Sabbath; and Nanny has always given him his hot posset, or gruel, at nights, and his hot water to wash with when he needs it, and clean sheets twice a month; and he's had, gentlemen, whatever we've had—bite of our bite, and sup of our sup, like my own bairn. Indeed, sirs, if there was anything else I could have done—and he's well in French and Italian, Mr. Darnell, I venture to tell Sir Geoffrey; and he reads a play of Mr. Shakespeare's to us whiles of a night, and maybe a story out of Boccaccio. But oh, sirs! it's been all thrown away, and he's well-nigh graceless now;—to think, gentlemen, of his being drunk, and going with player-queens, the hussies! who're nae better—"

And here the poor lady broke down again. The recollection of all cares for the young man seemed as oppressive and affecting as her own sad history.

"And now he's come to blood," she continued; "blood, always blood, sirs, follows Hester Morton! And where will it end?"

"We will relieve you of Ralph if it pleases God to restore him, Mrs. Morton," said the baronet, kindly. "He'll want change of air in the north, and we can't spare him yet. We'll ever be grateful for what you have done, I'm sure."

'No, no, Sir Geoffrey!" cried the widow, excitedly; "no, no, it wasn't that. What should we do without Ralph, that's like a son to me? What would Sybil do, or Nanny? Who would read to me? who would sing to me? who would—"

"Well, well, Mrs. Morton, we will see by-and-by," said the baronet, cheerily; "there's no hurry in life about him. Damme! I like to hear a good word of the lad, too, and thank ye for it, ma'am—by George, I do!" and he held out his rough hand, which, shall I say it? the widow kissed reverently. "And now we'll leave you, madam, and I'll send the best doctor in London to Ralph to-night; yes, as soon as I can get speech of him—the very best doctor, ma'am, if I have to pay him a hundred guineas—a hundred guineas, ma'am—he shall have it, and double too, if he'll put that lad on his legs again!"

"It'll be the Lorrd's doin', surrs," said Nanny Keene, who had been standing reverently with her arms folded across her bosom; "the Lorrd's doin', an' no' man's, for he's jist bad the day ye ken, surrs, jist bad, an' luiks worrse. But Miss Sybil says he's gane to by-by, mem; a' jist ax'd at the dure, an' she's sittin' by him; an' a' thowt it 'id be jist like her, ye ken, surrs, if a'm richt—a' thowt maybe—she'd jist been askin' the Lorrd for him, an' maybe He'll gi'e him to herr, surrs. Whiles a' think sae mysel', an whiles no—"

"Amen," said the baronet, reverently. "It will be very hard for us, I see, to repay what you're all doing. But we may do something. Good day t'ye, ma'am, and I'll send the doctor—the best doctor, by Jove! to be had in London."

I am quite sure, when the baronet got home, and was questioned on the subject by Mistress Grover and Constance, that although he gave a doleful account of Ralph, he was not without hope; and it is also equally certain that he told them of Sybil's care and Mrs. Morton's love for him. How she had cried out, as if in pain, when he had alluded to Ralph's removal, and how she had told him she had brought him up; and I think, before the beautiful girl laid her head on her pillow that night, Constance too had asked God for her cousin's life; and that Bessie Grover, more coherently perhaps, and solemnly, had done the same. Gladly, too, would each or both have shared the watch of Sybil Morton, helped only by Nanny, but which both envied, for it was a happier one than any since the wound. Dr. —— had called, and had sent his chariot at once for Dr. ——, and the surgeon who had attended from the first was summoned, and there was a learned consultation in the parlour, which ended, I consider, satisfactorily; inasmuch as all agreed that while there was no discoverable mortal injury, nature was doing more for their patient than they could.

For Ralph slept, slept as if never to wake again, while the girl and the old servant watched, and listened to the now soft, regular breathing, and welcomed the easy postures.

"Eh, hinny, but we'll mak' him the rare caaves'-foot jelly that a' ken of, by-and-by; an' he'll be just strang and weel, and nae the worrse o't. Didnae a' tell ye at furrst that a' seyd far waur nor hey?" And for the first time since she had watched, Sybil Morton felt that Nanny was right.

I cannot say, while the afternoon passed, as we know, thankfully, if still anxiously, at Ralph's sick-bed, that it was spent pleasantly at the great dinner provided by Mrs. Darnell. That very good woman —for she felt herself good, was told she was good, and believed it religiously—that good woman, I say, though her goodness prevented hot meals on Sabbath-days, had not the least objection to them on week- —quite the contrary. She had as great pride in the wealth of her kitchen as she had in that of her priceless damask—always washed in the country; in her splendid plate, whereof, as behoved a Darnell, the dessert-service was of gold; in her glass and china; in the mahogany, which like a mirror, reflected the guests after dinner, in a sort of

"Double, swan and shadow"

fashion; in her splendid footmen, of whom Peter Grimes was upwards of six feet high, and would have been made a sergeant in his gracious Majesty's foot guards at once, had he ever been so rash as to enlist; and their gorgeous liveries of light-blue and gold lace, with crimson plush breeches, and crimson satin waistcoats to match; in her Turkey carpet, her rich curtains made of some rare Indian silk, the like of which *no one* had in London; and much more secret wealth in the house which I need not detail. I say she had as great pride in all these worldly vanities as she had in herself; and in saying that, I say all I can say, for she believed in herself and in them religiously. Religiously, because when she heard twice every Sunday, at Mr. Whitfield's chapel, in Tottenham Court Road, of the vanity of worldly possessions and of the world in general, she was also told of her own election to grace; and as all the good things she possessed had accompanied these, and she had never been without them, had she not a right to believe that because she was good she possessed them? I say, therefore, she believed religiously in this comfortable doctrine, and her worldly possessions were part of it. But to Mistress Grover and Constance, and even the baronet, these glories were oppressive: they had none such at Melcepeth. The gossip of the friends who came to dinner was not about vanities of fashionable life, or passing follies of the great city; but of chapel and parson doings, and, I am sorry to say, neighbours' affairs, and the characters of many "worldly" people. I regret also to state, that Mrs. Darnell confided confidently to one Lady Warrington, who was there, that Sir Geoffrey was a "worldly" man, "decidedly so, my dear;" and she feared for her dear niece, and that Mrs. Grover was ——. As to poor Ralph, "it would be a great mercy if he were taken before his sins were scarlet—indeed it would!" and much to the same effect, which was respectfully listened to by Miss Anne. But Grover, Constance, and Dorothy had got into a snug quiet corner; and the town cousin opened out her heart to the country one, and found sympathy therein. Finally, when Constance was asked by her aunt to sing, that saucy young lady, after pouting for a while, went to the harpsichord, and, after a lively prelude, sang with infinite spirit and piquancy a lilting border ballad, of rank Jacobite tendency, in which, I fear, the house of H-n-v-r did not shine brightly, though one Johnnie Forster and his P—e did, and this was the end of it—

"The Earl's died bravely in London toun,
An' his head glow'rs grim upon Temple Ba'a;
But mony a heart, as his blude ran doun,
Swore death to the Whigs; an he'll ding them a'a!—
Will the gallant Johnnie Forster!"

"Eh, hinnie! ye mauna sing them-like tunes in London city," said Roger Darnell, good-humouredly, in the old broad Northumbrian, which he had not forgotten, as he listened with a glow to which he had long been a stranger, and snapped his fingers in time to the lilt—"else ye'll ha'e King George an' a' his grrannadeers after ye, ma bairnie."

"'Deed then, uncle Roger, an' a'll jist dee as a' like, ye ken, an' daddy 'll no hinder mey. Wad ye care to heer anither, surr? I'se plenty mair," said the saucy young lady, replying in the same spirit and dialect, and putting up her rosy mouth to be kissed.

"How shocking! how forward! Indeed I cannot allow *this* to go on, Lady Warrington. I am so sorry that anything of the kind should have occurred in *my* house. Quite shocking, I declare, and I shall speak about it," said Mrs. Darnell, bridling.

"Indeed, mamma," began Miss Anne; but what she was going to say was lost in the somewhat unsteady approach of the baronet, in anticipation of which Lady Warrington put aside her hoop, while she cast some furious matrimonial glances at her husband, who followed in a like condition.

"So you've got Conny to sing, Mrs. Darnell, have you?" said Sir Geoffrey—"I hope, one of the old songs. Damme! madam, there was a spirit about them which we don't hear nowadays. What d'ye think, Lady Warrington? Here's your husband and I have had a glorious crack over old times; it makes one young again to think over them. Doesn't it, Miles?"

I don't think Sir Miles could speak very well; at any rate he did not try to do so before his wife; but he took Sir Geoffrey's hand and continued to shake it, while the baronet called lustily to his daughter.

"Give us that song about Johnnie Forster. Here's Mrs. Darnell and Lady Warrington dying to hear it, Conny." The baronet did not see Mistress Grover's admonitory nods and gestures, and it is well perhaps he did not hear Mrs. Darnell's interjections of scorn at his profanity. "Now then, get on, lassie."

"I ha'e just singit it, daddy," replied Constance, rising and coming forward, "an' uncle Roger told me I'd ha'e King George an' a' his grannadeers after me, daddy. An' what'll ye say to that, surr?" and the girl dropped a profound curtsy as her flashing eyes swept round the circle before her, wherein Lady Warrington and some other prim elderly ladies were holding their fans to their faces. "Ye're no' shamed o' me, daddy, are ye?"

"No, by G—d," cried the baronet, laughing; "I hope they liked it. But come, Sir Miles, shall we have a rubber at piquet? I'm for what you like to-night;" and he moved towards the card-table, which was set out with wax-lights in massive silver candlesticks.

"We only play for love, Sir Geoffrey Darnell, in *this* house," said the hostess, with much emphasis and a stately sweep past him.

"Love! Ha! ha!" cried the baronet. "Love! Ah! I've played too deeply, madam, for that in my life to risk any of what remains to me; but you may find others with a longer purse than I have, and I wish you luck, ma'am."

I suppose that others were in a like strait, or that love was too valuable a commodity to be risked in such pastimes; and I do not wonder that when the great Peter Grimes made a solemn announcement at the door that the chairs were ready, our country friends were right glad to hear it, and to get home to comfortable beds in Soho Square.

CHAPTER XVII.

"INSTRUCTIONS FOR A WILL."

"I THINK I understand the position perfectly, Sir Geoffrey," said Mr. Peed, who had attended the professional summons he had received from his eminent clients with a punctuality befitting the great legal firm of which he was the head. "Perfectly," he continued, brushing away some grains of rappee from his shirt ruffles, while he offered the gold snuff-box, which had a long inscription on the lid, to the baronet. "This young man may be, as we lawyers call it, 'nullius filius,' that is, nobody's son—ahem! in law only, of course—or he may be in the position possibly of prospective heir to the baronetcy and estates of Melcepeth Castle; all depends upon the production of certain 'marriage lines,' or certificates more properly, which, as you have reason to believe, were in the possession of Mrs. Henry Darnell, otherwise Grace Smithson, deceased, but which were lost with her."

"Exactly," said the baronet, "that's just it, and now I want you, Mr. Peed—"

"Your pardon, Sir Geoffrey; we must not be in a hurry. We must have counsel's opinion upon it. To my mind, sir, this is a most momentous case—truly a momentous case indeed; and we cannot be too careful. What would be said, Sir Geoffrey, in the profession—in the profession, sir—if through any overlookment the firm of Peed, Peed, & Brisbane made a mistake—a mistake which might involve future interests, and produce im—men—se litigation? It is dreadful to think of—to contemplate, my dear sir!"

"That's just it, Mr. Peed. I want to have no trouble after I'm gone, you know, and—"

"Of course, baronet," interrupted Mr. Peed—"of course. I see it all at a glance; and I think you will believe that I am equally anxious with yourself. Now in these cases I find the best, the only plan is, to take your written instructions for this will; which, if you will sign, will not be the will, sir, but a document which I can lay before counsel with confidence, and which will be considered far superior to any memoranda of my own."

"Write my own will, sir!" cried the baronet, aghast; all I ever wrote in my life were a few foolish love-letters, and an occasional line to my brother there. Bless my soul! write my own will!"

"Not at all, Sir Geoffrey," remarked Mr Peed, blandly—"not at all. All we shall require is your signature. The purport will be written for you."

"He is right, Geoffrey," said Mr. Darnell, "and he did precisely the same for me. True, I put in a sentence here and there, but then I'm used to writing, and you are not."

"Very good," said the baronet, resignedly, and with a sigh. "I daresay you're both right; and as I came to get the thing off my mind, it shall be done. Who's to write, Mr. Peed?"

"I thought he might be needed, Sir Geoffrey, so I've brought my clerk with me—my private and confidential clerk, Mr. Wilson."

"Why, it will be all over the town to-morrow," cried Sir Geoffrey, angrily. "No, no, Peed; if, if—"

"I assure you, Sir Geoffrey—if possible—*if possible*, Mr. Wilson is *more* to be depended upon than I am," cried Mr. Peed, waving his white hands eagerly. "It is his peculiar office to attend bedsides—deathbeds—very often, sir, I am sorry to say, to take down last wishes, when dying men, and women too, sir, can only perhaps speak a few words at a time, and he has them down at once. Never knew him make a mistake in my life, sir, by George!" cried the little lawyer, quite energetically; "and as for secrecy, Gog himself could no more speak to Magog about what he has heard, sir, than Wilson to his dearest friend, if he has one. Quite a rare talent has he, Sir Geoffrey, I assure you."

"I fully agree with Mr. Peed, brother," said Mr. Darnell; "Mr. Wilson has no doubt so many secrets to keep, that they are no more to him than—"

Mr. Darnell seemed at a loss for a simile, but his voice in council determined the baronet.

"Very well, gentlemen," he said, "have in Mr. Wilson, by all means;" and that functionary entered, carrying a green bag, carefully, as it behoved a solicitor's clerk to do, and bowed generally to the party.

"Sit down, Mr. Wilson," said Mr. Darnell; "we have a little work for you to do."

Mr. Wilson looked to his principal, but did not speak. "Instructions for a will," said Mr. Peed, and Mr. Wilson fumbled in his bag, took out a leather portfolio, which he unlocked, spread his paper, put a pen on it, drew an inkstand to him, and having written "Instructions for a will," as a heading, looked up.

"Now, Sir Geoffrey, please to say to my clerk just what you have said to me," said Mr. Peed; "Mr. Wilson is at your service."

Sir Geoffrey took a long breath, like a sigh, and drummed nervously on the table with his right hand; but at last his brother saw the strong fingers clench, the nostril quiver, and the upper lip close firmly, as he smote the table slightly, and began—

"I wish," Sir Geoffrey said, "in case of no direct male heir, after my brother, being in existence, that, on his death, the whole of my estate, lands, money, and whatever it may be, except Melcepeth itself, and the few acres about it, should pass to my daughter Constance, without reservation of any kind. My brother is rich enough, sir, not to want any of *my* money or *my* property; and if I die before him, and he inherits the baronetcy I hold, I mean that that succession should not affect the other Melcepeth estates, which are not entailed. He and I, Mr. Peed, have come to this conclusion long ago—have we not, Roger?"

Roger Darnell put out his hand and pressed his brother's. "Quite," he said; "go on."

"If it had pleased God to spare—" continued the baronet, with tremor in his voice; "never mind—I mean, if I had had an heir of my own, there would have been no trouble; but as it is, I have to mention that, after my brother Roger's death, supposing he should have no son, my brother Henry's son, Ralph Darnell, is to be considered.

"Now if this young man be legitimate—if the marriage of his father, Henry Darnell, with Grace Smithson, of Warkworth, can be proved legally now, or at any time henceforth, and after the manner required by the law—I will that he be considered heir to the baronetcy of Melcepeth after my brother, or his male heirs, and that with it he receive one-half of the property belonging to the estate—lands, money, or whatever it may be. There's no saying," continued Sir Geoffrey, after another pause, "how long this may remain unproved; and all I wish recorded is, that whenever he is proved legitimate, no matter after how many years, and whether my daughter be married or not, that then he shall receive what I will to him, and have no claim to anything more."

"That precludes claim for mesne profits, of course, Sir Geoffrey?" observed Mr. Peed.

"I don't know what that may be; and I hope I'm clear in what I say, sir. I don't want the lawyers, sir, to have a finger in this pie, Mr. Peed; and you must keep them out of it, if you please."

"Certainly, Sir Geoffrey, you are quite clear. Go on, sir."

"Meanwhile, and until his legitimacy is proved," continued the baronet, "Ralph Darnell will receive from my estate what was settled upon his father by my father, which is four hundred pounds per annum. After he comes of age, I wish to add a similar sum; and I will that the sum of eight hundred pounds per year, to continue for his life, be paid out of the Melcepeth property, in quarterly payments of two hundred pounds. It is distinctly to be understood that this additional payment is to continue for his life only. My father's bequest will not be interfered with; it is a charge on the property for ever.

"I don't think there is anything more; and you've got all that down, young man, I hope?"—Mr. Wilson bowed. "Stay, there's

Grover. Mistress Grover, sir, is to get from the estate one hundred and fifty pounds per year till she dies. I don't suppose she will ever marry; and if she does, by George! her husband will be the better of it, and Constance won't miss it. Now, Mr. Peed, will that do? I can settle about Smithson and the servants hereafter. That's what I've had on my mind for many a year; and, by Gad! sir, when it's all done, we'll have a jolly dinner at Arthur's. Can you think of anything else, Roger?"

"Nothing. If any point is not clear to the lawyers, you'll have to explain it, or they will— But I daresay Mr. Peed will do all that is necessary."

"Certainly," replied Mr. Peed. "*Our* Will will be a longer document than that, perhaps; but I don't know that it will be more explicit. The paper is ready, Mr. Wilson?"

Mr. Wilson's reply was by rising, putting his pen behind his ear, and taking the sheet to Mr. Peed, who, after an adjustment of spectacles, read out the writing. Nothing had been added, or taken away, or modified; as Sir Geoffrey had spoken, so Mr. Wilson had written.

"Sign, it, sir, if you please," said Mr. Peed, handing the sheet to the baronet.

"Ay, I may sign it safely indeed!" said Sir Geoffrey. "I could hardly have believed in such exactness;" and, taking the pen from Mr. Wilson, he wrote in a strong bold hand,

"GEOFFREY DARNELL, Baronet,

"of Melcepeth.

"My signature in good health, and perfectly understanding all that has been written here."

"Now you may go, Wilson. Go straight to the office and get a copy ready for Sergeants Green and Brown, who are retained specially."

"And when will the will be ready, Mr. Peed? Make haste with it, if you please."

"Ah, Sir Geoffrey! don't hurry us. You're not going to leave town to-morrow; and really the sergeants are so busy now that—that—"

"Well, Mr. Peed, I won't hurry you; but it must be executed before I leave London, for I intend to keep it at Melcepeth."

"Just as you wish, Sir Geoffrey; only all the old wills are safe in my office. But you say there is no trace of this marriage-paper—none? None at all?"

"None, Mr. Peed. I have just again offered two hundred pounds for the original registry; and Braithwaite, of Morpeth, will do his best, I doubt not, in the matter."

"A most respectable country attorney, Sir Geoffrey. And I have no more to say but to take my leave;" and Mr. Peed took his hat and cane, brushed the snuff from his ruffles, made a formal bow, and departed.

"Enough for to-day, Roger," said the baronet; "and may God grant I have done my duty by them all, as I hope to nswer for it—I trust I have. And Ralph's better to-day, you said?"

"He is much better, Geoffrey; the fever is gone, and there is only weakness. The messenger saw him, and spoke with him."

"Ay, when he's strong he shall know all about this, Roger." But the more Sir Geoffrey thought over the matter, the less he liked the idea of breaking to Ralph that he feared he was illegitimate. "Well, it's good news about the lad; and now let me have the coach home, unless you'll come too—it's early, and we're going for a walk on the Mall—won't you come, Roger?"

"I can't, Geoffrey. There are letters from India; and I've to attend the Council at one. I wish you a pleasant day. Is the coach ready, William?" he asked of a porter.

"It's at the door, sir, since you came," replied the man.

"Then I'm off!" said the baronet. "Good-bye for the present."

"Mr. Peed had some other city engagements, and did not immediately follow his clerk, who returned direct to the office in Chancery Lane. We have met Mr. Wilson before at Mr. George Elliot's; but he was not a prominent character there. Mr. Wilson was not a prominent character anywhere; but he was a peculiar one in many respects. I am not going to describe him further than that he had sharp, piercing black eyes, deep set in his head; thin eyebrows; a sallow, parchment-coloured face; thin pale lips, and a long hooked nose. You remembered the eyes and nose, but nothing more. His figure was lean and wiry, rather tall than otherwise, and he walked with a peculiar fast shuffle, acquired probably in the London streets. Mr. Wilson had a corner of the office to himself—a sort of bay window, or, in fact, a former turret, of which his den, as he called it, had been made. Of this he drew the heavy curtain—there was no door—and was quite private. He then proceeded to make two careful copies of the draft, one of which he put into a portfolio on which was MR. PEED in gilt letters. The other he again read over, and placed carefully into a soft black leather book, which he deposited in a mysterious deep pocket in the breast of his coat. Having accomplished this he leaned back in his chair, and began to think what was to be done; and his thoughts took the form which I shall now briefly follow.

"So that Ralph Darnell is not legitimate—*filius nullius*, as the governor would say. Of course he is. They've been twenty years trying to find out a certificate of marriage, and it can't be had—no, not even for the baronetcy and eight thousand a year. Forster and Elliot think he is legitimate—that is, they know nothing about it, and suppose he's all right. Elliot lent him some coin, I think, but it may not be much. Can anything be made out of the affair? Would the lad like certificates made up? John Wilson, I think, could make good ones that would defy all the proctors in Doctors' Commons. Perhaps—he, he! the boy may have scruples! Stay, Forster's a north-country man, and may know of this marriage. Henry Darnell and he may have done something together in the '45 affair, and I can trust *him*. Selwyn—d—n the fellow! why does he take so grand a name? would not his own plain Dicky Smith serve him? No, no, he is right, perhaps. Well, Selwyn, then, does many a job in *his* own line on the border, and he may be useful. But does the lad know anything of this will to be? Nothing more, I think, to be got out of him, therefore, than any one else. Let me see, a hundred or two for the facts would be little enough, and as many thousands if all came right in the end. Sir Ralph Darnell to be under a bond for two, nay, five thousand pounds—faith, it would be cheap—and his gratitude to John Wilson for ever secured, and a good connection, by George!"

"Mr. Wilson, have you the paper ready?" said Mr. Peed, putting his head into the den; "Sergeant Brown is here."

"Quite ready, sir; perhaps you'd just compare them before you take the documents?"

Yes, it was quite correct; when was Mr. Wilson ever careless?

CHAPTER XVIII.

RALPH DARNELL'S VISITORS.

It would not have been in accordance with Mr. Wilson's character if he had suffered any consideration to delay him from the execution of his new project; but some days elapsed before he was able to carry it into effect. Mr. Elliot was, perhaps, more intimate with Ralph Darnell than Forster was; but Elliot was not in Mr. Wilson's confidence, nor he in Mr. Elliot's, to the same extent as the other gentlemen with whom, to say the least of it, Mr. Wilson's relations were peculiar, and of high mutual interest and occasional profit. Mr. Elliot was not, in fact, in Mr. Wilson's power at all; and the others were so in many essential respects, though in different degrees. I think it would lead me into a considerable digression from the subject of this history, to which it is necessary to adhere very closely, if I were to enter upon Mr. Forster's antecedents and his curious relations with parties who, for divers cogent reasons, political and otherwise, found it safest to remain out of England and communicate with their friends and adherents in it. Vitality is not necessarily extinct in any national party because of one failure or many failures; and it becomes the interest, as it suits the love, or the prejudice, or devotion, or fanaticism of those concerned, to raise hopes and maintain them—to convey information and disseminate it; in short, to be active and pertinacious agents and intriguers. Now, we know that Mr. Forster's opinions were decidedly of a Jacobite tendency; and he, as well as some others, were still retainers of the house of Stuart. If the Prince himself, now poor, were fast sinking into contempt, there were adherents of his party who were rich—rich enough to make what disbursements were needful for information from secret agents, spies, or whatever they might be called—and of these John Forster was one.

By this connection he was enabled to keep up a respectable, not to say wealthy, appearance, and to enter into society in London which, under any other circumstances, would have been denied him. What he could glean there in regard to political events, changes of party, party politics, and the like, was duly written in cipher and transmitted through sure channels to the fountain-head; and it was astonishing how little real nourishment satisfied those concerned in such matters. Do we not see such parties even in present existence about ourselves? Fenians and Nationalists in Ireland; Orleanists, Bourbons, and Red-Republicans in France; Mazzinists in Italy; Wahabees in India; and I know not how many others, of all sorts, in every kingdom and nationality of the world? All these do not exist free of cost—by no means. There are heavy expenses attendant upon them, and collections are made which go into very unintelligible somebodies' pockets. It need not, therefore, be considered marvellous if, at a tavern then well known as the Cock in Cornhill, Jacobite gentlemen had their private meetings and councils, subscriptions and collections; and that Mr. Forster, of whose ability high opinion was entertained, held confidential and profitable occupation among them.

I am quite aware that Mr. Forster would have preferred exceedingly to write his own despatches in cipher, or even in plain English; but, unfortunately, he was unable to do so. His education had been none of the best in that lonely border Peel where his father had lived; and had it not been for the excellent assistant whom chance had thrown in his way in the person of Mr. John Wilson, I am of opinion that Mr. Forster's services would have been held of mean account. As it was, however, these men maintained their position after an ingenious and able manner, and shared the profits. Whatever news Forster picked up at coffee-houses, over card-tables, at the public promenades, or clubs, or wherever he went in society, he communicated to Wilson, who wrote it down ; or if there were nothing to be had, they taxed their invention to prepare the best dishes they could for every hungry anticipant. But, as I have already observed, our history has nothing to do with these transactions. They might have been called treason : and would, if discovered, have rendered these confederates liable to those ingenious horrible pains and penalties devised in the statute-book ; but they were pursued notwithstanding with a most pertinacious diligence.

In several awkward cases too, Mr. Wilson's legal experience had proved of the greatest use to Mr. Albany Selwyn, as he was known at his lodgings in Bury Court, St. Mary's Axe, where, at that time, there were many comfortable houses of some pretension. It was, in fact, a most respectable court, and quite above ordinary suspicion. Mr. Albany Selwyn professed to be a horse-merchant, and had a set of mews in a by-street at the back of the court, in which a number of stout horses, and some thorough-breds too, were always kept for sale, or for any service required of them. If Mr. Selwyn were absent occasionally for days together, it seemed the concern of no one. He was gone to buy horses, or to attend Doncaster, or Carlisle, or Chester races, or country markets; and when he returned, and kept a good deal of fine company, no one doubted his means or his hospitality; and, in fact, he was envied as doing a remarkably good business, as, indeed, was the truth. If it were a business which involved some risk, personal or otherwise, and an occasional hint from a Bow Street runner to "look out," why, it only made the profession more exciting and interesting, and involved the expenditure of some capital in properly-timed douceurs. But if I were to follow Mr. Richard Smith, *alias* Albany Selwyn, into any of his enterprises, I might have as much, or even more, to write, than I should have had of Mr. Forster's; and, as a consequence, I shall omit all such episodes which have no direct concern with Mr. Ralph Darnell or his affairs.

Now whether Mr. Forster were a partner with Mr. Selwyn in his professional dealings in horse-flesh, or only accompanied him occasionally in his country expeditions, or used Mr. Selwyn's horses in secret journeys which the CAUSE demanded, I do not pretend to say; but Mr. Wilson knew that both, having been temporarily absent, would be at Selwyn's in the morning to breakfast; and, indeed, as Mr. Forster's apartments were in the same court, nigh to Mr. Selwyn's, there was always a certainty of that mutual communication which was necessary, and insured Mr. Forster's presence at all times. To Bury Court, then, Mr. Wilson proceeded from his own lodgings, which were not very distant, and we may look in upon these gentlemen after they had finished a substantial and pleasant repast; and the lady who officiated as Mrs. Selwyn having retired, Mr. Wilson's announcement that he had something curious and amusing to communicate, was received with much satisfaction.

I think we need hardly go over the old ground; there was no question as to the instructions for the will, or Ralph Darnell's position, present and future, which to these far-sighted gentlemen seemed exceedingly clear. Forster was of opinion, from his northern experiences, that there had been no marriage at all. He had often heard, now that he remembered it, at Belford and Berwick, that Harry Darnell and Grace Smithson had "jist louped ower Lamberton Pike ane day," and sailed off in his lugger which lay off the coast; and Mr. Selwyn, in his cracks with buxom chambermaids in northern inns, had had Grace Smithson's example and sad fate often thrown in his teeth. The only question was, what was to be made out of it all?—whether the baronet should not be plied and threatened with anonymous letters, and so brought to terms, which would be well paid for? or whether Ralph were not the most proper engine to be put in motion? and after some discussion, and chiefly upon Mr. Wilson's legal view of the case, Ralph, though he had no money presently, except four hundred a year, and four hundred more to begin in three months or so, was evidently the most promising. Four hundred a year! how much might not be raised upon it! what funds there appeared for a grand suit! Mr. Wilson was not to be for ever bound to Peed, Peed, & Brisbane; and with a cause like Ralph's to begin with, his fortune was made. Mr. Wilson, I am sure, much coveted independent action; and Mr. Peed's house in Queen Square, where he had the honour of dining sometimes on Sundays, was just like what he hoped eventually to earn for himself.

Ralph Darnell having been selected as the fittest person to be approached, the three gentlemen agreed to meet at the Golden Cock at four o'clock that day, and a proviso was made, that if Mr. Selwyn did not arrive (he had some horses to show to gentlemen at the west end of town), the other two were not to wait for him. They knew that Ralph was convalescent, for Mr. Peed had mentioned what he had heard from the baronet the day before, that the wound was almost healed, and that only some weakness remained; in short, that in a few days more Ralph Darnell would be "about again" as usual.

It happened too, on this beautiful summer morning, that Sir Geoffrey had promised Mistress Grover and Constance a row on the river. The chariot was to take them from an early walk in the Mall to Chelsea, and thence they were to row down to the Tower, where it would meet them to take them home. Mrs. Morton's house lay in the way, and for the first time the ladies were to see Ralph. The baronet, I am glad to say, had paid the young man several kindly visits, and had become quite intimate with Mrs. Morton and Sybil; and especially so with old Nanny, who had already received several crowns from him, and was deeply impressed with his generosity, and the splendour of his majestic appearance.

"Ay! he's a trrue barrinit yon Surr Geoffrey," she would say to Sybil; "jist a gran' man, hinny. Ye'll no sey siccan like, except they're o' the Norrth blude, ye ken. Oh but he's the richt sort! An' he's gi'en mey anither crroon the day, tey."

I am glad also to be able to record, that one of the first acts of Mr. Ralph Darnell, when he was allowed to come down stairs, and lie in the sunshine at the window of the drawing-room, was to perform his promise (to himself) of renewing several articles of furniture therein; and if there were anything to be regretted in this act, it was the surreptitious manner in which the refit was made. For Nanny had been taken into Ralph's confidence; the money in Ralph's pockets had not been disturbed; and an upholsterer's man had been introduced into the house clandestinely by Nanny, who had taken the measure of the room for a new carpet, of a pretty pattern, from Kidderminster; a new sofa, of peculiarly comfortable construction, was to fit a certain place; and new curtains were to be hung round the windows, and a new arm-chair and footstool for Mrs. Morton. And one evening Nanny, after advising Mr. Ralph that all was ready, had said, in the most unconcerned manner, as she brought in the tea-tray—

"'Deed, Mrs. Morton, mem, an' ye'll not get up quite sae soon in the mornin,' nor you, Mister Ralph, if ye please. A'm goin' to shake the carpet an' the curtines, mem, an' if ye hear a bit knockin' an' hammerin', mem, ye'll know why is it, an' sae jist keep quite, mem, and you tey, Miss Sybil."

It was wonderful with what calmness Nanny told this deceptive tale; but it succeeded perfectly, and, indeed, the upholsterers worked so well, that by the usual breakfast-time they had completed everything, and the dear old room had a very smart look and pretty appearance. Perhaps the reader will imagine how Mrs. Morton was rejoiced by Ralph's kind contrivance, how Nanny enjoyed her share in the deception, and how Sybil, in her heart's joy to see Ralph, still pale and weak, but looking handsomer than ever—her own dear, kind, thoughtful Ralph—could have thrown her arms about him, and sobbed out her thankfulness to God and to him, on his shoulder. And when Mrs. Morton asked whether he was sure he could afford all this, he said he had enough still for a better harpsichord, and they should have that, too, when he could get out to choose it. I say, when all this was done, there might have been many to envy their quiet happiness.

Mrs. Morton was essentially a lady, and it gave her no apprehension to receive Sir Geoffrey and his daughter on a visit; but it would be idle in me to say that two others were not much disturbed. Ralph, lying at the window, for Mrs. Morton would have him lie there, had grown almost hectic again in anticipation of seeing Constance—his own Constance—to see whom once more ere he died had been his earnest prayer in his great weakness—and Grover, too! Ah! what springs of pleasant old memories were opening and flowing again as he lay there thinking. And Sybil, to see his dear cousin Constance, of whom she heard daily and hourly; for whom messages of such love, such devotion—messages from the very border of that dark inscrutable, illimitable sea of which Ralph had had a glance—to be delivered, by her, and her only, the hearing which had been like so many cruel, fierce, deliberate stabs with a sharp weapon into her very heart's core, that she could never deliver them—to see Constance, and meet after those many years, and to know then that she was only a mere spectator—she who had tended him so devotedly—who— But no matter, she would be only a spectator. She had no claim on him or on her—only on his gratitude, which she did not doubt, but none on his love. Poor Sybil! how often had she retired, in an agony she could ill conceal, to her own chamber that day! how often had tears rushed to her eyes, and blinded them! The boats were darting to and fro; the city lay beyond, all clad in the glorious splendour of that glowing summer sun, as she shared Ralph's watch for his cousin; and when Ralph suddenly cried out, as a large four-oared wherry shot the bridge gallantly, and swept round, with beautiful even strokes of the flashing oars, to Tooley Stairs, "Look, there they are, Sybil! O my Constance! my Constance!" Sybil could not contain herself, but laid down her head on the sofa-back, hid her face, and sobbed as if her heart would break. And when Ralph put up his hand, and stroked her soft brown hair, and told her pleasantly not to be a goose, she looked up and tried to smile, and I am afraid made but a poor hand of it; but when Ralph told her to stand by him, and let him lean on her shoulder as they entered, she did not go away.

Yes, they were a merry, happy party; no more of a cloud upon any one of the three who were coming than there was on the sun then blazing in the clear blue sky. And yet how often do we see the bluest, brightest skies overcast, or a cloud rise out of the horizon, which, no bigger than a man's hand, spreads over the heavens like a pall, and out of which comes crashing thunder and fierce red lightning almost ere they can be accounted for! Ralph was trembling much as he rose with Sybil's and Mrs. Morton's assistance, and steadied himself as well as he could on Sybil's shoulder; but his lips seemed dry and clammy, the fever spot again burned on his cheek, and he asked for the ptisan, which he sipped hastily. He heard the hall door open, a brief colloquy with Nanny, and a light step on the stair; and as Mrs. Morton opened the door, a beautiful apparition, as it seemed to him, to which he stretched out his arms, bounded in, crying, "Ralph, dear cousin Ralph!" and then stopped suddenly, as it were spell-bound, and hesitated. Ah! Ralph would fain have held her in his arms and pressed her again to his heart, where she had lain many a time; but it was not so. Constance only held out her hands before her, turned away her head, and burst into a passionate fit of weeping, throwing herself upon Mistress Grover's shoulder, and hiding her face in her handkerchief.

He did not seem to her to be Ralph at all. What she remembered was something quite different. A laughing, glorious cousin Ralph; a little fellow, though much bigger than she was herself, with fun dancing in the brightest of blue eyes; a face that she could take between her tiny hands, look at all over, and kiss in nice places where she pleased. What she saw was a tall gaunt figure; as tall as her father and nearly as square, with great dilated eyes, a quivering mouth and nostril, and utterly colourless except two bright spots on the cheeks, stretching out long arms, and crying in a broken voice, with tears rolling down the wan cheeks, "Constance! Constance! I'm Ralph," and then choking and putting its hand to its throat with an impatient gesture, as if to tear away the hysterical lump which gathered there.

"No, no, no," cried the sobbing girl; "it's not Ralph—not my Ralph! O Grover, not my Ralph!"

No; no more it was any longer.

"Don't be a goose, Conny," cried her father, patting her on the back—"don't be a little goose; and this, too, after all your fine speeches! Go to him, there's a darling; the poor fellow has been dying to see you. Confound it, don't be shy, now!"

I am afraid there was another goose present, and that was himself, for tears had started to the baronet's old eyes; and another, too, in the person of Mistress Grover, who was trying to console Constance. But poor Ralph could ill wait for her; trembling before he felt utterly helpless, and sank down on the sofa, burying his face in his hands. This action, utterly unpremeditated as it was, did more for him, perhaps, than the baronet's intervention; for seeing him fall, as it seemed, Constance darted to his side, and cried—it was only the truth—"Forgive me, Ralph; but you were so altered—so altered. Now look up, and I'll be Constance again."

Ah, never, I fear; never again as she was before, by sweet Coquet side, in the green woods of Melcepeth!

Nor did Mrs. Grover hesitate. She kissed Ralph fondly, and helped to lay him back on his cushions; then smoothed away the hair from his forehead, held her scent-bottle to his nose, and poured out her thanks that she had seen him again—that "he was her own dear boy; that they were all the same as ever, and he would soon be well again and among them." When Ralph dared to lift his eyes, he saw Constance's beautiful glowing face, all wet with tears, looking up to him as she knelt by him, and pleading to be forgiven. But she did not kiss him—she could not. He only took the hand she held out, and, pressing it between his own wasted fingers, laid it upon his heart; but he could not speak. I don't think that he drew any real comfort from this; but one who had tremblingly watched the scene, hanging back behind the curtain and the sofa, felt a throb of exultation, perhaps, at what she had witnessed, and thought, if the old cord were loosened, that— But I fear I could not tell what she thought, or what she hoped; all was too wild, too indefinite, to describe.

Sybil and Constance. They were together now, talking in the window, for Mistress Grover had much more to say to Ralph than Constance, and Constance held the girl's hand in hers, and after her fashion was pouring out grateful thanks for all her kindness. Sybil and Constance—a contrast indeed! The one dressed plainly, even sadly; and her sweet, calm face bearing those traces of watching which are so unmistakable. Her soft brown hair falling in long curls upon a neck as white as ivory, and her generally almost colourless face with a faint blush now, like that of a pink shell, upon the cheeks. The other richly dressed in the extreme of the prevailing fashion, her hair tied up and slightly powdered, with a dainty hat gay with feathers and lace upon it, her slip of French brocade over a bright quilted satin petticoat, her beautiful face radiant with smiles, and her bright eyes now flashing with excitement. Ah, it was a contrast indeed! but I think, of the two, that Mrs. Morton thought her own sweet Sybil the more beautiful.

"Please, mem," said Nanny Keene, who entered shortly afterwards, and when the first embarrassment was past, "there's Mr. Elliot just ca'd to ask after Mr. Raafe; an' he says p'raps you'd have nae objections if he'd be allood to pay his respects to the barrinit, an' see Mr. Raafe tey."

"Elliot? Elliot?" cried the baronet, hastily; "not young Elliot of Wooler Hall, surely?"

"'Deed, Surr Geoffrey," said Nanny, "an' I dinna ken, surr; but he's frae the north, a' knaas. Deil mend him for a graceless—" she added to herself; "only for him the laddie 'd a' been vary differt the day, a'm thinkin'."

"Mrs. Morton, by your leave I should like to see him; and maybe he would help to cheer this poor lad a bit. I have often wished to meet him."

"Any friend of Sir Geoffrey Darnell's is always welcome to my poor house," said Mrs. Morton, with dignity. "Show him up, Nanny."

And in a few moments Elliot entered—a striking figure, certainly, and now looking his very best. What clothes in town richer or in better taste than George Elliot's at all times? and to-day, in deep brown velvet and silver, with ample ruffles of lace, his naturally fine figure was set off to the greatest advantage. He made a courteous though stately salute to the baronet, a more graceful one to the ladies, each of its kind perfect, and then advancing took Ralph's hand kindly, indeed affectionately, for he felt deeply for him. It was evident that his visit helped Ralph, for he sat up, and the conversation became cheerful and general.

"I assure you, Sir Geoffrey," he said, speaking at last of the affair of the wound, "and you especially, ladies, that Mr. Ralph Darnell's conduct on that occasion was beyond all praise. But for him, those ruffianly Mohocks would have pulled that poor little singer out of her chair and robbed her; and we could have done nothing, for we had Mistress Woffington on our hands. It was all the work of a moment, ma'am," he continued to Mistress Grover, "and our poor friend was down before we could get to him. We would not have left thee, Ralph."

"Indeed it was to you, George, I owe my life; indeed, uncle, to him and Mr. Forster," said Ralph; "for if they had not bound up my wound as well as they could, I should have bled to death, I fancy, on the stones, to say nothing of getting home."

"I hear, too, Sir Geoffrey, that there is a report Ralph was not sober. This I deny upon my honour as a gentleman. He had drunk nothing, he would not play, and he was altogether as steady as I am now," said Elliot.

"I thank you heartily, Mr. Elliot, for your defence of Ralph," returned Sir Geoffrey. "I feel sure you are a good friend of his, and I shall be rejoiced to make your better acquaintance. Am I right in supposing you are the son of my old friend Edward Elliot of Wooler Hall?"

"I am indeed, sir—his only son. I have not been in the north to reside for several years, but I have often heard while I was a minor of Sir Geoffrey Darnell of Melcepeth."

"Let us shake hands on it, then," said the baronet, "and let me introduce you to Mistress Grover and to my daughter there. Constance—Mr. Elliot of Wooler Hall. And as we are going to the play to-night, shall be glad to see you there, Mr. Elliot, and to a quiet supper afterwards. And now let's be off, ladies; we have a good deal to do yet. Don't fret, Ralph, my boy; in a few days more you'll come with us to the play too—I'll be d—d if you sha'n't."

"I accept your invitation with gratitude, Sir Geoffrey, and will attend you down—"

"No, no! stay with Ralph," cried the baronet, as Elliot was

preparing to accompany them to the boat. "Cheer him up, sir, and bring us a good report of him; we can find our way very well."

Elliot had seen many beautiful women; he was in the habit of seeing every day all the town beauties on the Mall, at Ranelagh, at the play, and in private dramas; but he had never, he thought, seen anything like Constance—a flash of loveliness, indeed, unexpected, and therefore the more destructive. And Constance! she too had seen several noble gentlemen, and had been stared out of countenance by a great many since her arrival in London; but, in her eyes, this gay spark was the brightest of all. Well, they would meet again in the evening.

I don't think Ralph was a very cheerful companion, and Elliot, having some arrangements to make, left him shortly. I do not think either that Ralph liked the sudden acquaintance which had been struck up; but what could he do? So Elliot left, and he remained looking out of the window at the spot where he had seen the wherry and its gay freight disappear behind a ship lying off the Tower.

"Constance has grown very beautiful, Sybil," he said at length with a sigh to the girl who was sitting behind him looking out too—"did you think she would be so beautiful?"

"She is dazzling; I could hardly look at her, Ralph," replied Sybil, "and she appears so kind too—yes, she is very beautiful."

"She is very beautiful," he echoed. I doubt whether he thought she had been kind.

"There's Mr. Forster, and a Mr. Wilson I think he caad him, been asking after you, sur, when the barrinit wuz here; but when I tou'd 'em the ladies wuz wi' you, they said they'd maybe caale agin in the evening, or maybe to-morrow."

"What can they want?" thought Ralph. "I'm glad you sent them away, Nanny. All this is more than I can bear."

"A' think, Mr. Rraafe, you'd be better i' yer bed, surr."

"Let me alone, Nanny," he replied peevishly, and so sat, watching.

CHAPTER XIX.

A DINNER IN BLOOMSBURY SQUARE.

"My dear, it's all nonsense; we *must* ask my brother to a proper dinner—we've been quite uncivil to them, I declare," said Roger Darnell to his wife Anne one morning late in the month of June.

You will remember when the baronet arrived that he partook for the day only of his brother's hospitality; but since then, although Roger was constantly in Soho Square, and dined with his brother whenever he had a mind to do so, and Mrs. Darnell had paid a stately visit of ceremony to the Melcepeth ladies, no further intercourse had taken place; and if Mrs. Darnell had had her own way, I am of opinion that any further interchange of courtesies would have been out of the question. On the occasion above referred to, however, Mrs. Darnell observed certain hard lines growing about her husband's mouth, and her experience of these lines was, that he would have his own way. Perhaps there was a momentary struggle in Mrs. Darnell's mind as to whether she would submit before a battle or after one; but as a defeated army is ever in a worse plight than one which makes a judicious retreat and takes up a new position, so the army of Mrs. Darnell's thoughts decided on retirement, and the position taken up by them was this—"Well, if they are to come, they are to come; but if I do not make this dinner the last . . . I will do it upon *principle*, and for the sake of *example*," thought the lady; and I'm quite sure that she acted conscientiously, and according to the brightest lights she possessed.

"You know, Roger," she replied therefore, that I should be the last person in the world to grudge the hospitalities of *this* house to Sir Geoffrey; but—but—in short, my dear, he has many *peculiarities* which do not suit with my *principles*, and I cannot consent to violate those which I have adopted, and to which I believe I have had a special and merciful call."

"Well, well, Anne," said Mr. Darnell, we can't help my brother, you know. He means no harm, and hath the tenderest heart—"

"May the Lord turn it to good!" said the lady, piously casting up her eyes. "It was but yesterday that excellent man Mr. Fletcher said he was about to wait upon Sir Geoffrey, and in regard to the profane habit of swearing, to—"

"Ha! ha! Egad, Anne," cried Mr. Darnell laughing, "I'm afraid he would get more than he bargained for, and the reverend gentleman come out of the house faster than he went in. We have a north-country proverb, too, 'Keepin' ane's breath to cule ane's parridge.' But about the dinner. *My* guests are, my brother's party, and Ralph and Mr. Sanders; and you may fill up the rest as you please. Perhaps you had better leave out the Warringtons; I don't grudge Sir Miles the wine, but he and Geoffrey take more than you would like to see."

"I am quite prepared to endure any amount of offence, or indeed insult, from *your* relations, Mr. Darnell, if it is your wish," said the lady, bridling, "even to the singing of profane Jacobite songs by Miss Constance Darnell; but I cannot submit to allow a 'governess,' a mere companion or housekeeper, who appears to me to occupy a *very equivocal* position after all, to come here on an *equality* with Lady Warrington and other persons of *distinction* who may do me the honour of accepting my invitation; and as to Mr. Ralph Darnell—"

The hard lines about Mr. Roger's mouth grew together again, and he exclaimed, I am afraid, with a round oath which caused Mrs. Darnell to put her handkerchief to her eyes, that Ralph was his nephew, and he *should* come.

"He! a reprobate who had but just recovered from a wound received in defence of an actress!" cried the lady, virtuously—"he a fit associate for your *poor* daughters! I knew you would go very far, Mr. Darnell; I was prepared for it—but this—"

"Anne, I desire it shall be as I have said," interrupted Mr. Darnell; "when this lad is Sir Ralph Darnell of Melcepeth, Anne Darnell, and Anne Darnell's children, will not deny him, and need not do so now. If you don't like Mistress Grover, you need not ask her; but, please remember this—if Ralph is not properly asked—I mean properly *by you*, as mistress of my house, and his aunt—you and I shall quarrel about it; and I think, Anne, you know what that means."

So Mistress Darnell had again retreated to her former position, and the invitations were issued accordingly. None was sent to Mistress Grover, and Constance was up in arms on the subject; but Grover was a woman of the world, and quite understood why she was left out; and, from Constance's account of the affair, did not regret her absence at all.

Perhaps the solemnity of the whole transaction—the sour looks of all the prim ladies that could be collected, the several nonconformist divines that were specially invited, who drank their Oporto and Burgundy heavily, and conversed apart on spiritual subjects after dinner, while the ladies above stairs were occupied chiefly with accounts of their own and their children's "experiences," terrible stories of flirting maid-servants, and the latest chapel sermons—I say the studied lugubrity of the whole affair had attained the special point desired by Mrs. Darnell. It was a complete success. Her position had become impregnable, and some small assaults upon it, made by her husband and by Sir Geoffrey during dinner, fell flat to the ground, and a jolly oath was even impossible. No, there were no worldly people to assist them—not one. If even mention of town gaiety was made, or fashionable doings, the godly company fell silent at once, and looked at Mr. Darnell, or Sir Geoffrey, or Constance, as it might be, with hard stony eyes, and contumelious comportments, which I am bound to say routed the worldly enemy at once, and imparted a vast amount of highly refreshing spiritual triumph. As to Constance, the only refuge she had was with Dorothy when they went up-stairs; and when asked to sing, she gave the company the most doleful ditty she could remember, which commenced—

> "Hark ; now the solemn peal begins ;"

that is, the tolling for a funeral; and ended by a moral—

> "Virtue alone this peace bestows,
> And thus rewards the blest ;"

and as all present knew themselves to be essentially virtuous and blest to boot, this virtuous elegy was particularly acceptable. Nay, one Mistress Bennett then present, a comfortable motherly-looking woman, observed to Mrs. Darnell that she had formed *quite* a different opinion upon Miss Constance Darnell's behaviour since she heard it, and straightway went to the harpsichord and complimented that young lady upon her sweet voice.

And when the gentlemen came up-stairs, and Constance saw her father's rueful face, she was wellnigh laughing outright, and many a laugh indeed they had afterwards over all that had happened. As Constance was speaking to Dorothy in their own corner, and her father came up to ask her whether she was ready to go, Constance begged hard for him to ask Mrs. Darnell's permission for Dorothy to come to Soho Square for a day or two. I believe the baronet considered this a service of danger; but he stormed the enemy's entrenchment very gallantly, and I am inclined to think, from the little resistance made, had surprised it. I am even of opinion that this service quite raised the baronet's spirits; and the victory he gained, so easy that it had not needed a single expletive asseveration, made amends for the terrible ordeal he had undergone during the previous part of the evening.

"We want that dear little Dorothy of yours, madam, for a few days in Soho Square. I love the child, ma'am," he said, in a stout, cheery voice, "and Constance and she are fast friends; poor Conny has no friends of her own age, ma'am, and here is her own cousin, whom you will not deny us, I hope—eh, Roger?"

What could Mrs. Darnell say, when her husband, before all the company, actually took Dorothy's hand, put it into the baronet's, and said he might carry her off there and then? I consider Sir Geoffrey on that occasion to have evinced the highest valour and generalship, and to have turned the enemy's flank. What could she say or do? Snatch away Dorothy's hand from the polluted touch of a worldly uncle? It was impossible. I know that for that hesitation—which was the actual cause of Dorothy's seeing Ranelagh and the Mall, and, oh horror! the play, which events went far to produce utter eventual disruption between the families—Mrs. Darnell had to undergo some very sharp remonstrative discipline from her spiritual confessor the Reverend William Fletcher. But Dorothy nevertheless went, was carried off triumphantly to Soho Square that night in a chair, a handbox being sent with her. And I am quite sure if you and I, O reader, could have heard the florid descriptions of the "Darnellian banquet," as Miss Constance irreverently call'd it—of the parsons snuffling through their noses, clad in their black Geneva gowns and bands, and with the solemnest faces—of the prim ladies' scandal over their tea—of herself singing the doleful elegy, and the hypocritical manner in which she had drawled it to suit the company—and finally of aunt Anne being routed by the baronet, I think we should have laughed as heartily as Mistress Grover, who listened to the wild creature, and to Dorothy, whose tongue seemed to be wonderfully loosed.

"Eh, that I should ha' sung the elegy that gate, and keepit my face, Grover," cried Constance; "just listen—

'Hark! now the solemn peal begins;'

that's how I sung it;" and then she made a face, "and that's how I looked; and I made 'blest,' that's the end, ye ken, into four bars, and all breves too, my darling. Oh, it was beautiful—bee-you-tiful, and I'm sure that helped me to get Dorothy. And we'll have such fun, won't we, you darling cousin? and we'll see the Mall, and go to my milliner's and get ye a new hat, Dolly; and Ranelagh; and maybe Mr. Elliot 'll be there, and he'll tell us such dear *wicked* stories about the singers, and fiddlers, and the opera, and the play, and that bee-you-tiful Woffington that was nearly killed by the Mohocks, when Ralph got his wound, ye ken."

"And Ralph?" said Mistress Grover, who got in a word as best she could.

"Oh, he's vary weel, mem; he's jist mendin'," continued Constance, curtsying and imitating old Nanny Keene. "He's vary weel, ye ken, mem, the day. Only listen, Grover, he's not my Ralph now. He's a great solemn, stiff, stupid fellow, that I push about anywhere, and he'll go anywhere, like the old poodle Muff at home. Nay, I do think he'd sit on his hind legs for a bone if I told him, and never move a muscle of his grave face. I don't like it, Grover; I don't indeed. Sometimes I see him looking at me as if he wanted to eat me up, and I won't be ate up. What did he do at dinner? Why, ma'am, if you please, he ate his dinner off his poor little cousin's face, arms, body—all he could see, and he ate nothing else; and when the cloth was taken away, and there were two cousins, one before me on the table, he ate them both, and I do believe he grudged the decanters what they took of me on the table. No, I don't like it, and I won't have it, that's more; there isn't a bit of fun in him, and Dolly and I'll torment him to-morrow as sure as he comes. Why can't he be my old cousin Ralph who was at Melcepeth? I'm sure I'm Conny—I'm not changed like him."

Mistress Grover sighed; I do not think she knew why; it was better as it was. For Constance she had feared more than for Ralph, and now she feared more for Ralph than for Constance. I am afraid that dinner had been a very doleful one for the young man. He had been infected with the general lugubriousness. He could not talk with either of the persons between whom he sat—a parson on the right and a prim old lady on the left—upon any subject they broached. The opera, Mingotti's bravuras, or Mr. Handel's sacred music; Italian, French, pleasant books, or even Mister Shakespeare, one or two attempts he had made he had given up, as they were met by frowns. He had no appetite. If he looked at Constance, she turned away her head disdainfully, and the more he looked the more she turned away. After dinner he could not get near her, and all he could do was to shut her chair door as she left, kiss her hand, which she snatched away impatiently, and he saw her no more. His uncle would not have a chair, and they walked down to Soho Square together, and he was asked in, and Sir Geoffrey smoked a pipe, abused Mrs. Darnell, and swore all the oaths he had been balked of at dinner together, that he would never go again, about the same time that Mrs. Darnell was saying to her husband,

"I can't help if it were stupid, Roger: I'm sure the table was beautiful; and if—"

"Why did you ask such a set, Anne? All the old frumps you could collect, and all the parsons too, by George!"

"It is quite impossible, Mr. Darnell, to reconcile the world and our connection. If Sir Geoffrey had understood '*grace*,' he would have spent a delightful and comforting evening; but as we had no *profane* people he was dull. I cannot—no I can-not—Mr. Darnell, ask *profane* persons to this house, and deliberately violate the principles in which my children—"

"Well, well, go to sleep, Anne; I'm glad it's over. Geoffrey 'll quite understand why you don't want him, and won't cry, I daresay."

Just then, too, his pipe was finished, and Sir Geoffrey was tired and yawning, so Ralph bade him good night, and left Soho Square. He forgot to tip the footman who let him out, which was a mistake. A few shillings, crowns, and what not, judiciously disbursed, especially among one's own relations' servants, are true economy. Ralph had plenty of money in his pocket, and loose silver besides, but he thought the servant, a north-country lad, looked at him with a sneer, and he gave nothing, in which course he was wrong and mean.

Why did not his uncle speak to him about the birthday he had been promised to spend at Melcepeth? Why did Constance never talk of old times, or put him off when he began them? Why did Grover so look at him, and often sigh when she spoke to him? No, his uncle's visit as yet had been no pleasure. He had no heart to attend the young beauty to the Mall, to Ranelagh, to the opera, to concerts, though he went to all, whither she pleased; carried her fan or her scent-bottle or her prayer-book to church. Why should he have to listen to the undisguised admiration she excited? Twenty times a day his hand was on his sword at remarks he heard. He ground his teeth, and would have been pleased to fight it out to the death with all the impudent fops who noticed her. Why did she not object to all this, and take him away alone to some shady alley of Kensington Gardens, and dream away time as they used to do at Melcepeth, lying under great trees, or on the river bank, watching the trout rise when it was too hot to catch them, or the white clouds sailing lazily on the sky?

I fear all these thoughts were, to say the least, unsatisfactory, and produced a restlessness which might be attributed to recent illness by those who knew no other cause. But no, Ralph's recovery was rapid; he was nearly as strong as ever again, quite able to do his office work again, and he had been better there than where he was; but Mr. Darnell insisted he should have a holiday as long as the baronet remained, and go to Soho Square every day, and he had gone; yet he was beginning to doubt whether he has quite welcome or not. In short, though Ralph's body was in the main well, his mind was ill; and his sullen moody manner disquieted his friends at Tooley Stairs, if possible, more than his wounded body had done, and they had no remedy to offer. I don't think Ralph's walk home was at all a pleasant one that night; but he resisted every temptation by the way, and when he was admitted by Nanny she said,—

"There's been that Mr. Forster and Mr. Wilson speerin' after you again, Mr. Ralph, and they're but jist gane ower the watter; ye'll hae come by the bridge, a' reckin? They waited half-an-hour or mair for ye, surr, an' waz vara agreeable to the Mistress an' Miss Sybil; and Forster's just a canny man, sir, and played on the harpsichord, and singit bew-tiful, surr, amaist like yersel', surr."

"I wonder what they want, Nanny? I must go and see to-morrow."

"'Deed, surr, Mr. Wilson said it war vara particular, that's a'; canna ye gae till him to-morrow, an' ha' dune wi' him?"

I think if Ralph had done so it might have quickened the action of this story; but he had more Mall, more Ranelagh to do—and could he leave Constance to Elliot?

CHAPTER XX.

PROMENADE.

So it went on—Mall, Ranelagh, play, concert—play, Ranelagh, ball, dinner, opera, or whatever it might be—by day or by night. Ralph lived all day in Soho Square; he would have slept there had there been a bed to give him. Nanny let him out in the morning before breakfast, and in again late at night. He had suits of clothes in his uncle's dressing-room, and only returned home when an occasional afternoon change was needful. He never went to the office; never saw his uncle Roger or Mr. Sanders. He had plenty of money still remaining; for though his uncle Geoffrey played a quiet game at cribbage or piquet sometimes for sixpences—and he had even been with him several times to Arthur's, and had lost and won a few guineas to and from the noblemen and gentlemen there, to whom Sir Geoffrey introduced him as his nephew, and by whom he was treated with high consideration, and was even offered a nomination for the ballot—I think Ralph was too careful to play deeply before his uncle, or even at all. He had much and very commendable command over himself in this particular, as much as he had over his wine; and that, I believe, is saying a good deal for a young man of fashion of those days.

I am not sure, indeed, when he thought over them in after times, that Ralph did not think these visits to Arthur's and White's in company with his noble-looking old uncle—one of the stateliest men to be seen at either resort—as the very pleasantest of that period. He could remember with pride the distinction allotted to the baronet; the cordiality with which old friends met him; the offers to take him to the King's daily levee, and the hopes that all former matters would be forgotten and forgiven. But though the baronet said he had forgiven all, I fear he had not forgotten that horrible march through London pinioned like a felon, with a hideous crowd shouting after him and his companions, for he never could be persuaded to go. "I have no son to introduce," he would say with a sigh, "and an old Jacobite like me will soon be in his grave, at rest from all politics. Not that I wish the Hanover family ill; no, they've been true to our country, and may God bless 'em; but they don't want me, my Lord Chesterfield, and I'm better away."

"But your nephew, Sir Geoffrey—he ought to take his place among us," some noble lord would say.

"Ay, ay; well, by-and-by perhaps, my lord, but not now. There's quite time enough to think of that."

So it one day happened that, as usual, after breakfast, the baronet called Ralph from the drawing-room, and bid him come with him to Arthur's, to hear the news from America, which interested the town much more than that from the far-distant and obscure East Indies; and when Constance, who was in high spirits and good humour, had told him they would meet in the Mall by-and-by, and kissed the rosy tips of her fingers to him, with, as Ralph, poor fellow! thought, a more loving gesture than usual (for I must say that imperious young lady was often more capricious than I care to record), that he went with great cheerfulness with his uncle, entertaining him in their walk westwards with sprightly anecdotes and pleasant talk; and, well dressed as he was, causing the baronet to feel proud of him, both by the way and in the club, where many new acquaintances greeted him kindly, and noticed him, as it gratified his uncle to see him noticed. And when all this was over (there was no play so early, except among some old stagers), and they strolled past St. James's Palace, and into the Birdcage Walk, enjoying the bright sun, and the sight of so many parties of well-dressed people, and they had sauntered to and fro several times without meeting the ladies, at length they saw them advancing.

If there had been Mistress Grover and Constance only, as Ralph had expected, there would have been no cross in his lot that day. To have walked there, as he had hoped to do, with his beautiful cousin, and afterwards in the sweet cool gardens of Kensington, as had been arranged, would have been to him a deep, deep draught of joy, only to be equalled by Melcepeth; but it was not so to be. By Constance's side, dressed in a new and gorgeous suit of black velvet, walked George Elliot; and it was easy to be seen by all beholders that the young lady was quite content with her gay and handsome companion. She was looking her best, was Constance, in that beautiful dress of pink satin brocade, looped over a light violet-coloured quilted petticoat. The ribbons from her tiny hat were fluttering in the gentle summer breeze; and she carried her fan in the most coquettish and triumphant manner she could assume.

Fie on you, Miss Constance Darnell! You knew as well as I know who write it, that you were flirting outrageously with Mr. Elliot. You had begun to do so when he called in Soho Square, just as the coach had driven up. You had agreed to his offer of escort, as if two footmen behind, and the coachman on the box, were not enough; and you would not attend to Mistress Grover's sage counsel as to letting him find his way on foot; and after handing you and Grover into the vehicle, moreover, you had allowed him to enter it and seat himself before you, and devour all your inexpressibly enchanting charms, after a much more hungry fashion than poor Ralph had, during his lugubrious dinner at Mr. Roger Darnell's. You knew all this, and you knew, when Ralph and your father met you, that you gave only a little scornful toss of your beautiful head to your poor cousin, while you cried to your father, "Oh daddy! daddy! isn't this sweet? We have had such a de-li-ci-ous drive all round by the Bedford Gardens, and so here; and that's why we're late, daddy. And oh, sir! I hope you'll forgive me." And she dropped a solemn curtsy, which made her still more enchanting,

The baronet only saw his lovely child, only thought that, of all God's creatures, gay and noble as they were about him on every side, this was the gayest and loveliest. He did not think of Ralph—why should he?

"Ah, you sly puss!" he said; "so you have had your drive, and in honourable company too, by George! Glad to see ye, Mr. Elliot; hope you're well, and have had a pleasant jaunt." And the baronet turned round with his daughter.

"I have had the happiness of Miss Darnell's company, sir; and that is the most delightful in the world. Can I say more?" said Mr. Elliot, gallantly. And as he spoke he drew himself up proudly, and lifted his laced hat with an air and a look of such unmistakable triumph towards Ralph, that had the poor fellow dared, he would have drawn on him on the spot, and fought for his life.

I know that Mr. Elliot felt what Ralph was thinking of; he meant him to think it. He was no coward. There was not a cooler head or a steadier hand if needs be in London than George Elliot's; and neither had ever failed him. He knew that there was a beautiful girl and a large heiress to be won; and he had determined to go in and win. Why should he not? She appeared to notice no one else. He had seen a score of gay beaux fluttering about her in public places, and her acceptance of that general homage due to her beauty and her rank; but she had singled out nobody. He had the privilege of visiting at the house; he was of her own county, where his position was a high one. His father, Sir Geoffrey had said, was an old and dear friend; and he had a general invitation to Melcepeth if ever he came to the North. I am afraid Mr. Elliot did not think, in that moment of triumph, of the many bonds he had to redeem, or of the deep, very deep, inroad he had made upon his hereditary property; or of what he had paid as the price of the social distinction he had attained. Let him but win Constance Darnell and all this would disappear. It was the means, above all others, to a final end of present triumph; and, not yielding his place to Ralph, while her father took Mistress Grover, who fell back with Ralph behind, George Elliot walked on, majestically it might be said, dispensing many gracious bows and salutes to ladies of fashion and to companions, being, as he very well knew, the envied of all beholders.

And yet, even in that moment of triumph, there were certain memories rising up in Mr. Elliot's mind which he vainly tried to shut out, of another fair girl of whom we may come to know something after a time; with whom certain solemn vows had been already exchanged, which she, to her sad cost, poor soul! had once believed binding enough, and who was now far away in a strange distant land with no possibility of return to scare him from his purpose. Yes, that at least was secure! I trust that none of us, my friends, may have skeletons like this to hide away in our mental cupboards, out of sight of men perhaps, but, like evil familiars, terrifying us when we are alone, or rising up in hideous mockery in our moments of triumph or anticipation when we least expect them. Possibly, had Miss Constance been observing her gay companion more narrowly, she might have detected a sudden spasm as if of pain, a shudder such as we sometimes feel involuntarily and cannot account for; but it passed without notice. That was no time for Mr. Elliot to admit of doubt or hesitation in his pursuit; and the presence of his skeleton only perhaps urged him to be more reckless and defiant.

Mistress Grover saw Ralph's agony. How the strong young man trembled! how the drops of sweat stood out on his broad forehead! how firmly his white lips were compressed! "Ralph," she said, "she is very young, and all this is new to her. She will be wiser when we get back to Melcepeth."

Ralph could only take her kind hand, which she had placed on his arm, and wring it passionately. "I will be patient, dear auntie," he said; "but oh! this is hard to bear. It has been so from the first day. She is not what she was to me!"

"She loves you like a dear cousin that you are, Ralph," was the evasive reply. "But, indeed, you must be patient—very patient, and not tease her—"

"Patient!—not tease her! When did I ever tease her, auntie? Oh, do not say I am to be patient! Patient! and see that—look!"

Ah, yes! Miss Constance was enjoying homage. She felt every bow to her from gay gentlemen, every sweep of a laced hat, every inclination of Elliot's handsome head towards her, was real true homage, and she revelled in it. The world, the gay world of London, was at her feet, as was fitting for Constance Darnell, the heiress of Melcepeth; and her fond old father felt the same. On she paced, or rather seemed to glide. Even her carriage and height had increased in these few minutes!

"Look!" said Ralph, in a hoarse husky voice. "I can't bear it, auntie—I can't indeed!"

Constance had just tapped Mr. Elliot's arm with her fan, and was looking up to him with a saucy smile as she asked some question they could not hear. Her glorious eyes were full of soft expression—was it love? Even Grover thought it might be; and Ralph was sure.

"I will go home," he said, faintly; "this hot sun is too much for me." If Grover had not caught him, he would have fallen; and she called to the baronet, who, with Elliot, supported him.

I must say that Mr. George Elliot showed much kindly feeling on this occasion, and even offered to see Ralph home in a hackney coach, at which Mistress Grover marvelled. Yet Elliot was sincere. He would have gone to show his devotion to the baronet's nephew and to Constance's cousin. It was not, however, needed.

"The sun *is* too much for Ralph," said the baronet, kindly. "Here, James!" and he called to the coachman, "take Mr. Ralph at once to Soho Square, and come for us to Kensington Gardens. 'Tis nothing of a walk, Conny, through the park."

"Oh, nothing, daddy!" She would have walked miles and miles that day in her present humour, and in that company. "Mind you get well, Ralph, before we return. I've plenty of new music for you to try to-night," she continued, shaking her fan at him cheerily.

Ralph put out his hand. I think he had a wretched, ghastly face. "God bless you, Conny," he said, "for thinking of me;" and so got into the coach, fell back very faint, and was driven away. The place where he had been wounded hurt him; but his heart was hurting him even worse. "I will have it out with her," he said; "he or I, he or I—it must come to that, and the sooner the better;" and before the gay party arrived to dinner, he had time to make up his mind.

In this respect, like a true Darnell, he did not hesitate. As the carriage drove to the door, and the ladies were handed out, he saw with infinite satisfaction that Mr. Elliot raised his hat, made a graceful bow, and took the direction of Greek Street. So he should have Constance all to himself: and had she not promised to try some of Dr. Arne's duets with him? Those he had learned to sing with Sybil, he was to teach her; it would be a delicious evening, and he would have the field all to himself. The ladies went up to their rooms at once to dress for dinner, for it was close on the time, and did not come down till the baronet had told Ralph of their glorious walk, and the distinguished company he had seen. "Even his Majesty was at the promenade, and asked kindly after me. 'Gad, Ralph, after that we must go to see him, though 'tis against the grain, my boy."

Half-a-dozen times Ralph had begun "Uncle," but could not get in a word. The baronet was full of the promenade, and anecdotes of old people and old days, which meetings with his friends brought about. Constance was pleasant. She seemed very well satisfied with her day's performances; and evinced a pretty interest in Ralph's health, and joy to see him again "looking himself," after the faintness caused by the sun. "It must have been that hot sun, Ralph," she said—"not like Melcepeth, you know, where we could lie under the trees and listen to the river."

Ah, these cruel words, which brought a rush of blood to the poor fellow's cheeks, as he handed her down stairs to dinner! She had better not have said them, for they did but set his brain in a whirl; and he said and did such foolish, pleasant, happy things at dinner-time, that he not only set the baronet heartily laughing, but Miss Constance confided to Mistress Grover, when they retired to the drawing-room, that "Ralph, after all, was a dear fellow, and *so* handsome."

When the ladies had retired, and the butler had opened a bottle of rich Burgundy, in which the baronet delighted, and left the two together, and they had taken a couple of bumpers, one to the ladies and one to the baronet's favourite toast of "All absent friends," Ralph said hesitatingly again, "Uncle—"

"Well," said the baronet, "I mind me thou hast said 'Uncle' several times. What is it? Money short? Eh?"

"No, sir," said Ralph as steadily as he could; "not that; I've plenty of money, sir. It's—it's—it's about Conny, sir—about Constance. Oh, sir! oh, uncle Geoffrey, I love her—I do love her dearly."

"Well, I don't see why you shouldn't, Ralph; I'm sure she's very fond of you. She's always been fond of you since you were children together."

"But, sir," continued Ralph, blushing all over, "it's more than that, it's—"

"Phe-ew!" whistled the baronet. "God bless my heart and soul! Don't be a goose, Ralph!"

"Please sir, if you'd only let me ask her. I'd be quite content; I'd be very grateful to you, dear uncle."

"You? No, I'll be d—d if— Stay! Off with you; go up stairs at once, and I promise you I'll not interfere. I think I know what she'll say," he muttered to himself. "She's quite safe, and it's better done with. I'll keep to my bottle, Ralph; and there'll be a glass for you when you come back—wiser, too, I hope," he added, as Ralph closed the door.

It was impossible for Constance to look more charming than she did that evening. The windows were open, and the soft cool breeze rustled gently in the trees of the square. Constance was standing by the harpsichord. She had put on a silk dress of very light blue, over a white satin petticoat. The dress was cut low and square, and edged with pure white Mechlin lace; but it was difficult to say at a distance where the lace began, the skin on which it rested was so fair. Grover was not there: could anything be more fortunate? Ralph advanced to her with eager, rapid steps, holding out his hands, and his face all a-glow. She was not looking at him, but at the new music which she was turning over. "Oh, I am glad you've come," she said; "we shall have time to go over one or two of these before—" and then she started back.

Ralph had flung himself at her feet. "Uncle said I might speak to you," he cried, holding up his clasped hands; "and oh, Conny! Oh, dear, dearest Constance, I love you!—I love you more than I have words to tell! I have loved you all these long years, my own darling, and no one knew it; now I tell you, and oh, Constance, pity me, my darling; I cannot bear it."

It would be difficult for me to describe the scorn—the pitiless scorn with which Constance looked down upon her helpless, foolish cousin. "Get up, sir!" she cried—"get up this moment, and don't insult me! Who are you, sir, to ask me to love you that way? Get up, sir, this instant, or I shall be tempted to box your ears. Look, Grover!" she cried, her eyes flashing as that good lady entered—"look what my gentleman's sulks have come to! Take him away, or I shall faint—I really shall. Oh, Ralph, that you should have vexed me so! I thought you were changed, but not thus—not thus," and she burst into passionate tears.

"Constance, Constance, my own darling!" was all he could plead, as he caught at the skirt of her petticoat, "I'm not changed."

"Take him away, Grover!" she cried again, stamping her little foot impatiently—"can't he let me alone! I declare to you, sir," she continued, rallying, and wiping her eyes hastily, but with a sob in her throat, "if ever you dream of talking such nonsense to me again, I'll never speak to you—no, never—nor see you. You ought to be ashamed of yourself. Get up, I say, this moment, and sing these things if you like, but remember—"

"I will remember, cousin Constance," said Ralph, bitterly, getting up with a white scared face. Good-bye; I'd better go." And he turned away.

"What possessed you to do this foolishness? O Ralph, what have you done?" said Mistress Grover anxiously, with the tears starting from her eyes. She had followed him out of the room.

"I've done it now, auntie, and I'd better go away," he said sadly. "I could not bear delay, that's all;" and so he tore away from her, ran down stairs, snatched his hat from the peg in the hall, opened the door, and rushed out.

His uncle heard the hurried step in the hall, and the door open. He got to the window, threw up the sash, and bawled after Ralph, who was hurrying towards Greek Street, and I am afraid that the baronet's loud laugh (whom the Burgundy had much comforted) fell on the youth's ears very painfully; and more, that when Mr. Elliot came to escort the party to the play, Miss Constance received him more graciously than ever.

CHAPTER XXI.

TEMPTATIONS.

I FEAR I cannot expect any sympathy for Ralph Darnell in this misadventure, and I certainly cannot claim any for him. Why will people do things at times which ensure their failure, rather than wait till there is good ground for expecting success? I am afraid most of us have acted, at some crisis of our lives, very much as Ralph, poor foolish fellow, did, of which we have unpleasant reminiscences. If I had only waited till—or if—but these ifs are interminable, and will ever be found haunting us, more particularly in early morning, when we have had enough sleep, or, being restless, cannot get more; and, as the clock on the stair-head strikes four of a winter's morning, in they march, a ghostly company—skeletons of broken hopes, broken speculations, and often, I fear, broken loves too, and ties which seemed strong, but alas!—each of which is heralded by the same ghostly IF that no bedclothes will shut out, or sleep put away, and from which there is no present retreat—IFS that only the cheerful sun, and daily work or care, or loving hearts and merry voices still left to us, drive back into their secret hiding-places till—the next time.

Why, then, will people do stupid things at wrong times—things good in themselves, but which become stupid, as they see afterwards, by wrong judgment? Mr. Elliot would no more have risked his rising position with Constance Darnell when he came home with her from the play that night, and had a quiet supper in Soho Square, than he would have chopped off his own left hand with his own sword. But I cannot compare the tact of this gay gentleman of the world with the foolish fondness of his friend—for whose absurd proposal, however, I am making no extenuation.

It was still early, the sun was shining bright, and the streets were full of people; but I fancy that all this looked dark to that young man, who had thus run away—yes, run away. It is the truth, and no more or less. If he had returned to his uncle, and told him Conny was cruel, I think the jolly old baronet would have ordered in a fresh bottle of Burgundy, and sworn a dozen of round oaths, and told him to "never mind, he would do better another day," or that "there was as good fish still in the sea as ever came out of it." But here another IF comes to my mind, and I put it aside sadly; I have only to do with stern realities. What was Ralph to do? Go home and have Sybil guessing at the truth, or be sickened by good old Mrs. Morton's platitudes, or be put to bed by Nanny Keene?

It was too late to go to the office; Mr. Sanders and his sisters would be out on the river this glorious evening, perhaps on board the *Valiant* with Captain Scrafton, perhaps taking tea at Blackwall or Greenwich. Ralph looked in at the Cock, hoping Elliot might be there, that he might quarrel with him; or Forster, that he might send a challenge by him; or Captain Scrafton, that they might play —and Ralph would have played deep then in his reckless humour. But there was no one there he cared for, and his fair friend in the bar tossed her head scornfully enough as he wished her a stately good evening, and would not stay to flirt with her. I think, too, that old Dickiwig and Mistress Sarah Baker, as they spoke together of the young man's changed appearance, attributed it to the effect of disappointed love, "wich," as Mrs. Baker observed, "is the terriblest think for hany young man, and worse than poxes, and measles, and them things, which comes natural like."

What was Ralph to do? He was, in truth, sorely tormented by his thoughts, and sauntered up and down the bridge very listlessly and idly, now making one resolve, now another, and cursing his own folly and Constance's cruelty in a breath. As he did all this, he saw Mr. Wilson posting up the incline with his habitual shuffle, and his green bag hanging from his arm in a professional manner. He would rather not have been seen by Mr. Wilson, but there was no avoiding him, that ferret-eyed person having indeed observed the tall figure of the young man from some distance, and was hasting to it.

"Your servant, Mr. Darnell," he said, respectfully, taking off his hat; "very fortunate to meet you, sir. Forster and I have called frequently, but you were always out."

"I have been with—"

"Of course, sir, with Sir Geoffrey Darnell and his sweet daughter. The town speaks much of her as the beauty of the season, and I hear her health is already drunk at White's and Arthur's. She's a a toast, Mr. Darnell—a toast."

Ralph could have knocked Mr. Wilson down and stamped upon him for his profanation of Constance's name. He, a vile pettifogging lawyer's clerk, to presume even to mention her! But Wilson had no such reticence: she was to him what a thousand other beauties of the day were—to be seen, however unapproachable; and he continued,—

"So glad I've met you, sir, for Mr. Forster has sent me to you to say he leaves town to-night or early in the morning on particular business, and will not return for many days; and he would gladly speak with you on an important matter concerning yourself—very important, sir, I assure you. He and Mr. Selwyn will be at a late dinner, and would be glad to see you, Mr. Darnell, if you are disengaged."

Ralph had been asking himself, as we know, what he should do, and he caught at this offer eagerly. "I fear," he said, "Mr. Forster will have thought me very rude that I did not call upon him after he has been so good as come here; and on you, too, Mr. Wilson, but I have been so engaged."

"I can quite understand it, sir. Not that I mean anything disrespectful of Sir Geoffrey, heaven forbid! but, sir, I always pray deliverance from country cousins. Why, sir, when mine come, I can't call a moment my own, nor even my life, Mr. Darnell."

"And you called, Mr. Wilson?"

"We had one delightful evening, sir; I shall never forget it. Miss Sybil Morton sang de-liciously; and, indeed, Mr. Forster hath a pretty musical taste also, and their voices blended, Mr. Darnell—blended."

"I shall be happy to attend you, Mr. Wilson, and will follow you." I think even then Ralph, dressed in velvet and lace, revolted against walking with a lawyer's clerk, with a green bag on his arm, dressed in snuff-coloured cloth.

"By all means," said Wilson, and preceded him.

. . . .

"Will you take a glass of wine, Mr. Darnell?" said Mr. Selwyn shortly afterwards. "We can have some dinner up for you directly, if you like, but we have dined."

"Nothing, thank you," said Ralph, "I too have dined; but I will take some wine with pleasure."

"*I* don't think there's any after-dinner drink like Burgundy, Ralph," said Forster, "and Selwyn's is of the finest; but if you would prefer Bordeaux, there is some Haut Brion there, which is exquisite, and these hothouse peaches are delicious."

Ralph's mouth was parched, and the goblet—a richly chased silver goblet of Haut Brion, which a smart maid-servant had set before him—which he drained after eating a cool peach, was indeed delicious. He had drunk his host's health, and had been thanked for it; and his own was given in return, and for a time the conversation was pleasant enough; but it flagged at last. "We had better go up-stairs if you fellows have had enough wine," said Mr. Selwyn, who had had as much as he needed, and perhaps a little more. "It's all quiet yonder, and you can talk as you please."

"We have no secrets from you, Albany," said Forster, putting his arm round the other's neck, "so you need not be particular. After you, Mr. Darnell."

"If Mr. Elliot's rooms were handsomely furnished, these seemed more gaudily decorated, and more expensively. It was evident that neither pains nor money had been spared. "Pretty, ain't they, Ralph?" said Forster; "by George! when they're full of well-dressed men, and the handsomest women in London—the *handsomest*, you understand—I don't know anything like them. But there's nobody coming now, and he and I must start at midnight."

"What had you and Wilson to say to me, Forster?" asked Ralph. "I have many apologies for not coming to you, but, as I told Mr. Wilson, I have not been my own master lately."

"Ah! yes, that's just what I wanted to tell you about;" but in truth, now that he had Ralph before him, Forster's courage (moral I mean, not physical) fell considerably. Mr. Wilson's, however, rose; and it is often a curious study in psychology to note how one man possesses the one and not the other, and how perhaps rarely both are equally combined. I say, then, the spider came out of his hole, and began to spin his web after this fashion, for Mr. Wilson came to the point at once.

"We have come to certain knowledge of Sir Geoffrey Darnell's will," said Mr. Wilson, seeing Forster's hesitation, "and as it is of a peculiar character, and knowing Mr. Forster to be much interested in you, Mr. Darnell, as well indeed as our mutual friend, Mr. Selwyn, and I may add my poor self, we, I say—"

"Sir Geoffrey Darnell's, my uncle's will!" cried Ralph, starting. "What will? I never heard he had made one."

"You were not likely to hear, Mr. Darnell," continued Wilson, "considering its purport."

"What d'ye mean, sir,?" exclaimed Ralph, fiercely—he was now dangerous to meddle with.

"Now, Ralph, if you're going to get into a passion about it, I'll be shot if we tell you a word; only keep quiet, and we'll conceal nothing," said Mr. Forster.

"The best thing I can do, gentlemen," said Wilson, looking round, "the best thing—far better than speaking—is to give Mr. Darnell the 'Instructions,' and the signature to the paper will be more convincing than— I remember in the case Clibborn *v.* Clibborn—"

"Damnation, sir! give me the paper" roared Ralph, huskily.

"Here it is, Mr. Darnell, and with it Sergeant Green's opinion, which I have taken to-day for Mr. Peed, and about which I was delayed. But for this indeed I could only have shown you the copy. You recognise and admit the signature? He continued, smoothing out the paper upon a table and drawing a wax candle towards it.

There was no mistaking it—the bold

"GEOFFREY DARNELL, Baronet, of Melcepeth,"

and what followed it was clear as noonday.

"May I read it?" said Ralph, in whose grasp the paper was rustling from the tremor of his hands.

"Certainly, Mr. Darnell," said Wilson; "you will consider this communication, however, as strictly confidential.

"On your honour, Ralph, the honour of a Darnell," added Forster, eagerly. "I'm sure you would not betray us, who do this for your good only!"

"On my honour as a gentleman," he said firmly, and read on to the end, then began again, and read all through once more; and to their wonder, those who looked on saw the hand steady gradually as the brow knit, the lips closed hard, and only the hereditary mark of his race dilating. Here was danger to be met, and his strong courage rallied to the necessity. But I am afraid in those few minutes Ralph's heart hardened—hardened against his uncle, against the world, and even against life! If he could but die—die there as he stood in his strength! If the Mohock's thrust had but been through his heart! I think he shut his eyes, and passed his hand drearily over them, perhaps expecting the death he thought of. If Forster or Selwyn had then put a sword through him, he would not have winced. Pshaw! he was there to live, to fight his fight with life, to fight on to eternity. "Drink this, sir," said Selwyn, offering him a small glass of cordial; "you will need it. Ay, sir, that's a nasty paper, and many a man would have fainted at it; but you're among friends, Mr. Darnell, who are sorry for you, and you need fear nothing."

The rough sympathy of the man touched Ralph, and roused him from his dream. What a hideous thing he had to contemplate! What a terrible story to listen to! And why had they not told him of this long ago, when he was a child, and it would have entered softly into his mind, and grown up with him? Why had not Grover told him?—why not the baronet?—why not?— Yes, he saw it all now. Constance knew of it—even the footman who had grinned at him overnight knew of it—all London knew of it; and he, a shame and a deceit upon the earth, had been walking with his uncle as though he were his heir! Ah me! what a crowd of thoughts were now wildly rushing to and fro!

"It may not be, after all, so bad, sir, as it seems. You see the baronet is perfectly just," said Mr. Wilson, blandly. "I wrote that from his own dictation, word for word, and I never—never, sir, in all my experience, saw justice and truth more strongly stamped on a man's face. He has decided nothing, sir: the law, the law only can decide by-and-by; and he has left a door open. You, Mr. Darnell, are no less presumptive heir to Melcepeth now, if that marriage can be proved, than you were before; and I, sir, though it is a difficult case, would, were I you, bestir myself to prove my rights, and that without loss of time."

"You can't be indifferent, Ralph," said Mr. Forster, kindly; "this must needs upset you at first, but you'll acknowledge by-and-by that we should have done no friendly part by you if we had let this will hang over you; and if you will act on our advice—"

"What do you advise?" said Ralph, drearily and anxiously.

"Tell him, Wilson," said Forster. "You have all that lawyer gabble at your tongue's end better than either of us."

"Well, Mr. Darnell," said Wilson, "don't take my advice—but look here;" and he took from his pocket-book two slips of curious character, from which he read easily. "I just put a hypothetical case to Mr. Green, and his opinion I took down under the table as he spoke it. It was this, sir, 'That you can't stay the will; let it be executed—it can do no harm. There is no occasion to prove your birth till Roger Darnell's death, or until it is your turn to be baronet, and there is ample provision made for the son of a younger son. You have eight hundred a year secured on the estate.' My own opinion, however, is, Mr. Darnell, that after the will is executed it should be lost—yes, lost, sir—should become irrecoverable. I think your uncle made it under some misapprehension, and my experience of men leads me to say he would *not* renew it; and now do as you please, sir."

"And when we can help you in this matter, as I know we can," added Mr. Selwyn, looking to Forster, "we will. If I were you, nobody should keep that will but myself."

"I do not profess to understand you," said Ralph, drearily; "and perhaps you will excuse my staying longer."

"I have—ahem—a copy of Sir Geoffrey's instructions at Mr. Darnell's service, if he pleases to be secret," observed Mr. Wilson.

"I have already passed my honour," replied Ralph.

"Give him twenty guineas for it, Ralph," said Forster, "it's cheap; and if you haven't the money, I'll give it now—here it is," and he handed a note to Wilson.

"Come home with me, Forster, and I'll give it you. I'm not fit to be by myself," said the poor fellow, almost breaking down—and indeed he was not; and they left the place together.

CHAPTER XXII.

THE BARONET IS EXPLICIT.

Perhaps my readers, the ladies especially, would like to hear how Miss Constance Darnell, being filled with the satisfaction of having summarily disposed of one presumptuous lover that memorable afternoon, comported herself to the other at the play; but that would involve an episode which it is needless to relate. All I can say is, that Mr. George Elliot's tailor, who was a spectator with Mr. Elliot at Drury Lane of Mr. Garrick's celebrated representation of Hamlet, Prince of Denmark, beheld that terrible tragedy, varied by some very genteel comedy between the beautiful heiress and one of his most distinguished customers; and thereupon next day wished him, with respectful homage, joy of his conquest, for conquest it seemed to be. And when Mr. Elliot, having handed the Melcepeth party to their coach, summoned two linkmen, and offered personal escort from the playhouse to Soho Square, which was graciously declined, became aware that a beautiful little hand lay upon the coach-door, which could not help being noticed on account of its brilliant diamond hoop—an ancient Darnell heirloom—sparkling in the torchlight; and when, somehow or other (one never *can* account for these things properly), the linkboys were called to lead the way, and there was temporary darkness—he was permitted to press his lips to that beautiful hand—he dreamed of it all night, as, indeed, did somebody else, who, as Grover came into her room to kiss her darling the last thing, put her arms round that dear good lady's neck and sighed out of her rosy lips, "O auntie, I've been so happy! and I hope that silly Ralph 'll come to-morrow, won't he?"

I fear not, nor for many days either. That silly Ralph had become much worse than foolish, I believe. He did not forgive his cousin—he did not forgive his uncle—he brooded over his misery, and was truly more wretched that I can contrive words to tell of. His love, his deep affections, were pulling his thoughts one way, and his sense of shame and his wrongs another, and the combat was hard and grim. He had poured out all his woe to Sybil, and she had listened with a trembling vivid interest which, I fear, had no misery in it except for Ralph's suffering. "The farther from them—from Constance," she thought, O foolish child, "the nearer to me—to me, O gracious Father," she cried, on her knees and in her solitude. "If it may be in Thy mercy, what are they to him now? His shame—Oh it is no shame! and if any, may not I share it?" Alas, poor Sybil! I do not care to open out the secret pleadings of that precious loving heart, wherein was no thought of worldly vanities—no plays or dinners or promenades—nothing but pure holy thoughts and prayers, to which guardian angels listened. Enough that we know them to be there, far more surely than the sullen gloomy young man, who might, we think, have seen them had his heart and eyes not been blinded by his terrible passion, and that ever-present sense of his wrongs.

Nor would it help us much either were I to tell of how poor old Mr. Smithson, much broken in spirit and in body, came at the appointed time to London in a collier from Newcastle; sought the baronet in Soho Square; was long closeted with him and Mistress Grover in anxious despairing council, and, sobbing bitterly, bemoaned the dead and his fruitless search after those "lines" in the silken bag! How Mistress Grover read to him the baronet's last instructions for the will, and caused the dazed old man to comprehend that the door was not shut on Ralph, nor would be shut till Roger Darnell was no more; and how Ralph Darnell had been provided for meanwhile. I find all this too sad a story to write, for grief has had enough to do with us all not to provide images and thoughts in plenty to save me the record of these.

None of them knew that Ralph had been told of this will, but Mistress Grover suspected it, and told the baronet frankly what she thought of his delays and evasions. She spoke out stoutly on this subject before Mr. Smithson, who, when they asked him to stay, said he had taken his passage by another vessel that was to sail that night. "London was no place for him. What could he do with the lad? But he would see him then, and why didna the baronet speak wi' him himsel'?"

"Tell him from me, in all kindness," said Sir Geoffrey, "that if he'll come up to dinner this afternoon, and bear it like a good stout fellow, as he is, I'll see him clear of it all, and we'll be as good friends as ever; mind that, Smithson."

"Ay, Sir Geoffrey, a'll tell him a'. He's mair active nor mey, an' he'll dee the best for his puir mither's sake. Ma puir Gracie! O bairnie, bairnie! but yer mither's wi' ye noo, an' a'll be wi' ye baith soon. A'm gettin' vara helpless noo, mem."

And so he left them and went to Mrs. Morton's, where he resolved to wait if Ralph were not there. Nor was he. Ralph had gone to the office with as heavy a heart as usual. I am bound to say, however, he had not entirely neglected Soho Square in this interval; but he got very little comfort there. He was changed himself, and he fancied all of them changed too. It is not pleasant, to say the least of it, for a man to speak again to a woman who has refused his love; but Constance, in this case, was not wilful nor coquettish. She saw the poor fellow's wound was deep, and, I believe, in her heart would have given much to take him to Melcepeth, and to cure him after her own fashion, not with her love, as he wanted it, but with hers, as she wished to maintain it for a brother, and a very dear one too. When the old steward went out of the parlour, Mistress Grover waylaid him in the hall, and gave him a note to Ralph, begging him to come that day, telling him that Smithson would break something of importance to him, about which his uncle desired to speak with him; and Constance, who knew nothing about the secret, took Mistress Grover's pen and added "Come.—C. D.," and that, she thought, would surely bring the poor fellow. Mr. Elliot was not to be there, and they had no engagement: she would try and be as kind as she could to Ralph. "Indeed I will, auntie," she said, with the tears rising to her lovely soft eyes. There was no anger there now—only pity, much pity, for the distress she had caused.

Ralph well remembered the old stalwart form of Mr. Smithson, and was shocked at seeing him bowed and gaunt, and the silvery hair hanging loosely about the rough weather-beaten face. Mr. Smithson was in the parlour when he reached home, where he had been sitting very sadly. It was a hard task for him to break all that had to be told—to tell again a tale of mystery, perhaps of deceit and shame; but he had a duty to do, to his master, to his grandson, to those who he felt were looking down on him, and after a rough and incoherent fashion he prayed for help. He knelt down at the table when he was alone, and prayed, I say, for help, and was calmed by it—as who is not in his extremity? Nanny came to him now and then; and Sybil, too, asked if he would have any refreshment—her mother hoped he would take some; but he said he needed none, and it was the truth.

When Ralph arrived, sooner than was expected, and the grandfather and grandson knew each other for the first time as such; and Ralph fell on his neck and wept—wept bitter, passionate tears—I fear he did not pray, for his heart was then very hard. What have I now to tell of this old, old story, which had begun at Warkworth with Ralph's father, Henry Darnell, and Grace Smithson, and now for the present ended? I could only say the same things again and again, and they are not worth repeating. Mr. Smithson said he was sure there had been a marriage, and a true one. His darling Gracie, "yer ain dear mither, lad, was no licht o' love—nae graceless, but pure as the snaw, though a wee wilfu' because of her beauty, like Miss Constance yonder, an' there's nae gude frettin' an' haverin' aboot it, sur. Yer uncle's a just man, an' he'll see justice done, an' a'm content to watch the Lord's will in it. An' when ye come up to Melcepeth we'll ha'e anither search: an', till then, keep a brave heart, my bairnie. It's yer mither's eyes that's lookin' at me as I say it; an' here's a bit letter from Mistress Grover, ye ken, an' ya'll go and dine there, Ralphie, like a dear laddie."

I think there would have been a passionate refusal if Ralph had not seen the "Come.—C. D.," which disarmed evil thought for the present, and softened his pride. Yes, he would go. He could not persuade his grandfather to stay: his vessel would be loosed with the tide. And when Ralph and he walked down to Tooley Stairs, the old man took a boat, directed the waterman where to go, and so was rowed into the stream. Ralph took another and was rowed to Hungerford Stairs, whence he walked to Soho Square, and arrived in time for the afternoon dinner.

I am quite sure that Constance was as good as her word. She could not divine why Grover had tears in her eyes, or why her father, with evident constraint at his heart, had put on an affected and forced hilarity. "They will settle it all after dinner over their wine," thought Constance: and so they did, after a fashion which will be recorded—"and then Ralph 'll come up, and we'll try those duets."

I don't think, either, that they were much better at dinner. Constance did her best, and was ready to cry at her ill success. Her father, she saw, drank more wine than usual, and perhaps Ralph did the same; still he was respectful and courteous, and promised to sing with her by-and-by. Could he refuse? Ah, no! of all there, to her he was most softened then; and she felt it, and rejoiced thankfully that it was so, and they would soon be better friends than ever.

Perhaps Mistress Grover was afraid to leave the gentlemen to themselves. She had a dread, almost presentiment, of mischief; but she could not delay, and with an injunction not to sit long over their wine, Sir Geoffrey and Ralph were left alone.

Why, of all topics, the baronet should almost immediately have selected Mr. Elliot, I do not know. *In vino veritas*, perhaps; and the baronet was drinking bumper after bumper of Burgundy and a toast with each.

"I'll give you another toast, Ralph, my boy," quoth he; "let's stand to it, for it's of as good a fellow as ever walked London, and as handsome and gallant, by ——!" and he filled his glass and stood up. "Here's to George Elliot of Wooler Hall, the noble son of a noble father, and success to him."

Ralph, who had risen, put down his glass, and folded his arms stiffly.

"You won't drink it, Ralph? What d'ye mean, sir?" It was an insult then not to drink to a toast proposed. "Is your uncle's toast not good enough for you? Drink it. What! are you jealous? Ha, ha, ha! jealous! Bless my heart, what a joke!"

"It's no joke, uncle," said Ralph, who was quivering with suppressed rage—"it's no joke, sir. I consider George Elliot, though I have the *honour* to know him, to be a spendthrift, a rake, and a common gambler, and, though he passes fair with you, to have one of the worst reputations in town; and I warn you of him; and I won't drink his health. I grieve to see him here, sir."

"On Conny's account, I suppose Ralph," the baronet returned, ironically. "Curse it, man, don't be a fool. If she won't have you, she may take anybody else, I suppose, without *your* saying nay to it. If George is wild, he's no worse than I have been, and a hundred others—*gentlemen*, sir! Here's another bumper to his health;" and he refilled his glass and drank it off at a gulp.

"I have said what I mean, uncle, and we'd better go up-stairs," returned Ralph. "I'll not drink George Elliot's health."

"No, I'll be d—d if you go yet! I've promised Grover to tell you all there is to tell about my will; and now it's in my mouth.

You know your mother's marriage has never been proved; and though you may not be a bastard" (the baronet had had too much wine to be particular as to what he said, or the words he used), "yet if you are one, why, you'll be provided for. Grover knows all about it, sir; and she'll show you the paper, which is with Peed & Peed. And now it's out, will you shake hands over the matter, and drink George Elliot's health?"

"What!—what did you say, uncle?—a—what?" cried Ralph, rising, and holding by the table, he shook so—"a what?"

"Don't threaten me, sir!" roared the baronet furiously—"don't threaten me, looking as you do, and clenching your fist! What did I say? Bastard!—yes, sir. Harry's bastard! and I'll say it to your teeth! Can you prove you're not one?"

"Uncle," said Ralph, calmly but determinedly; "uncle, take care what you're saying. Bastard!"

"I don't care!—I don't care a d—n, sir! I'm only saying the truth; and if you don't like it, by ——! you'd better go— I say be off, sir! I'm not to be bullied and insulted at my own table. Are you a gentleman, sir, as to what you say about George Elliot? It's a lie, sir!—a damned lie! and you know it!"

"Uncle!" cried Ralph; it was all he could say, as he moved towards him. I believe the poor fellow would even then have thrown himself at the old man's feet; but the action was mistaken.

"Damme, sir, keep your distance!" thundered the baronet, drawing his sword. Leave the room, sir, this instant, or, by ——"

I may not repeat the old man's torrent of oaths and curses, as, holding by the table with one hand, he held his naked sword before him with the other. It was a piteous sight, and I would rather not have writ what has been needful to tell; but Mistress Grover, who, anticipating mischief, had kept the drawing-room door ajar, now rushed down stairs, followed by Constance, and several of the men-servants, who also heard the oaths and shouts of the baronet—for they were little else—entered the door at the same moment. Her first care was for Ralph, whom she dragged away to the door; while Constance in vain tried to soothe her father.

"Go, go, Ralph!" cried Mistress Grover in her misery. "You don't know what he is when he is in this condition. Go!"

"But, dear auntie—" implored Ralph.

"No, no; not now! he will be sorry for it afterwards. Go, I beseech you, now! I'll see to him."

She had dragged him to the hall door; and the Northumberland footman held it open, with Ralph's hat in his hand, which he offered. He took it. He could not speak a word. As he went out, the door closed sharply; but the window opened, and the baronet, who had thrown up the sash violently, was standing there with his naked sword and a flushed face, foaming at the mouth—bawling "bastard," and "coward," and "damned cur," with terrible oaths and execrations: and Constance pulling him back, and the butler trying to put down the sash—were the last things Ralph saw and heard, as, with a dizzy brain and reeling steps, he dashed into the fast-darkening streets.

"A' telled ye sae," said the Melccpeth footman when he returned to the kitchen—"a' telled ye sae. They a'ways sed his mither loup'd ower the Pike o' Lamberton and gaed away ower the sey wi' Henry Darnell. An' it's come trow, ye ken; an' he's no't but a bastard after a', surrs!"

CHAPTER XXIII.

IN WHICH SEVERAL IMPORTANT MATTERS ARE DETAILED.

There is little interesting to be related of any of the persons with whom we have lately been in company for several weeks, except indeed, perhaps, of Miss Constance Darnell, who not only permitted, but encouraged Mr. George Elliot's attentions; and perhaps this young lady's general progress had been considerably accelerated by her visit to London. The recent outbreak of Sir Geoffrey against Ralph was not followed, as in the case of that with Mr. Smithson, by placability. In many respects the baronet, like others of his period who lived for the greater part of their lives in the country, was narrow-minded, and, though generous and liberal in the main, obstinate to a fault; and we have seen several sad specimens of his passion. In regard to Ralph, Mistress Grover pleaded very hard with him, as did also Constance, who, as the cause of this terrible war, was much grieved thereby; but they could not move the old man. And on one occasion when they had combined and thought they were gaining an advantage, he burst out again into such furious oaths and execrations that the women were frightened, and believed him when he declared, if Ralph went down on his knees before him he would only kick him off. "A lad," he said, "whom I, believing him to be a bastard, brought up in all love and affection, as you know, Grover, to turn on me at my own table, insult me by not drinking my own toast, and clench his fist at me afterwards! No, no. And, if you please, Mistress Grover, I beg you will not mention him again to me, or I may forget myself to you, which would grieve me; and all because he was fool enough to look up to Conny. Jealous, by Jove! and of Elliot too."

It is as equally certain that Ralph would no more have gone down on his knees to his uncle, than he would have done or said any other apologetic action or word. I can find no other phrase to express his state of mind than that it was sullen and revengeful, and perhaps vindictive also. He went moodily to his work, did it with more assiduity than he had ever done before; and neither Mr. Sanders nor his uncle Roger, in pity to the young man, alluded to the quarrel in Soho Square. Of this transaction Sir Geoffrey had given his own account to his brother, and had been believed; but Sir Geoffrey had not told all. What Roger Darnell most regretted was, that the doubtful position the young man occupied had not been sooner explained to him; but that could not be helped now: and over their wine, while Sir Geoffrey was for the time perfectly calm in speaking of Ralph, he told Roger that he could never see him again, and hoped the lad had enough Darnell spirit in him to take his own course in life. "We had better try and get him a pair of colours, I think, Roger," he said, "and we have interest enough for that." But Roger had no desire to see Ralph abandon Lombard Street; and, legitimate or the contrary, he might make a good merchant in time.

"*I* will take care of him, Geoffrey," he said; "and if he won't take your new allowance, he has what belonged to his father, and some thousands saved out of the yearly payments, of which he does not know: and he will do very well. I will see that he does so, and you may be reconciled to him by-and-by;" and hearing this, Sir Geoffrey had only shrugged his shoulders. Roger Darnell had seen his brother through many quarrels and misapprehensions, but never knew him to be in a humour like this.

There were two persons, however, to whom Ralph's disgrace was acceptable, though in different degrees. Mr. Elliot had no dislike to him, or cause of dislike—perhaps, indeed, quite the contrary; but he heard from the servants in Soho Square, to whom his largesses were liberal and manifold, that there had been a terrible quarrel about Miss Constance, and the baronet had called Ralph a bastard, loud enough "for the whole square to hear;" and after a few days, Mr. Elliot saw that Ralph came no more. I have before praised Mr. Elliot's tact and judgment. He did not press matters at all. He saw the family had been disturbed, and that they would not go out; but he was sure that calm must ensue, when his boat could glide gently into those pleasant waters. In this respect Mr. Elliot displayed a knowledge of human nature beyond his years, for which he was to be honoured. He bided his time, and when he felt there could be no risk, he went one day to Sir Geoffrey, told him openly how he adored Constance; was bid to go in and win if he could, and he did win.

Mistress Grover, dear soul, saw that Constance was beginning to fret about the matter; she had taken the fever kindly, but no crisis having occurred, she had become restless and ill at ease. So one delightful evening, as they all three sat at the open window looking out on the trees in the square, when Mistress Grover suddenly remembered she had not left out tea and chocolate (Mr. Roger Darnell was below with the baronet), she left them; and Mr. Elliot instinctively considered his time was come, and was not safely to be deferred, and so, dropping quietly on one knee, he—

Well, he asked Constance Darnell to marry him, and vowed he would be faithful to death to her; that is the plain English of the matter. I read constantly the most eloquent proposals, written in the most plaintive, elegant, flowing, romantic periods that it is possible to compose; and—I daresay I am very hard-hearted—I don't believe a word of them. I don't believe that any man ever proposed to any woman he loved in such set phrases; and I hope, if any one ever did such a thing, that he was refused outright. As a consequence, I do not see why any such pathetic proposals should be composed and printed; and that is the reason I do not write George Elliot's here. I believe he now sincerely loved Constance Darnell, and I am quite sure she loved him too, and acknowledged she did. So there were two very happy people sitting in the balcony when Grover came back, who told her—only what she expected—all about it; and when the baronet came up stairs (he had not had too much wine) and was told also, he cried out, I think from his heart,—

"God bless my heart and soul! I am glad of it, George, my boy. But for all that, I sha'n't let you marry her till she has completed her eighteenth year, so don't expect it."

While this effect of Ralph's disgrace had ensued to those I have mentioned—to Mrs. Roger Darnell that event was positively cheering and refreshing. She gloried in her prescience. She had prophesied a hundred times that she *knew* that "unfortunate" young man would become an affliction to his guardians; and I am afraid she quoted, as I should consider profanely, a part of the Second Commandment, which need not be repeated here, and rejoiced over it. In telling all she had heard to Lady Warrington, who professed herself seriously shocked at the bare idea of Ralph's condition, Mrs. Darnell said decidedly,—

"And, my dear, *I* believe him, after that treatment of his uncle, capable of anything; I believe he would not hesitate at—at—murder. My husband scoffs at me when I declare Ralph Darnell should be discharged from his counting-house; but he is obstinate. As to this young man's coming here any more—he never came with *my* consent."

But we may well spare continuance of these remarks, which were not pleasant ones; and at which poor dear Dorothy, who had much regard, perhaps something more, in her heart for cousin Ralph, went up to her room and cried ever so bitterly—cried till her mother boxed her ears, and set her a whole collect, epistle and gospel, as well as two psalms of a penitential nature, to learn by heart. But we must pursue the thread of this history, as more important than the doings of Mrs. Roger.

The day the baronet was to execute the will, which Peed, Peed, & Brisbane had prepared, after necessary consultation with eminent counsel learned in such affairs, and in the draft of which every chance of a flaw had been avoided, he was to come to the office for the purpose; and Mr. Roger Darnell having informed Ralph of the fact, sounded him as to any possibility of reconciliation with his brother.

"It's very unfortunate, Ralph," he said, kindly, "that there was concealment about this; but it was not my affair. Your uncle has not been to London since your father died, which is twenty years, and we had grown far apart till he sent you down to me; but as we can't recall the past, we must only make the best we can of the future. I should like you both to be on the old terms, and I consider both of you wrong—both: and you, as the youngest, ought to give way."

"And beg his pardon dutifully," said Ralph, with a sneer ill concealed, "for being insulted, blackguarded, and turned out of the house, because I— No, uncle," he continued, after a gulp and a pause; "if I am not legitimate it is no fault of mine, and I can follow my own road in life, and fear no one. I can love whom I please, and honour whom I please—and you, sir, ever first. I do not consider that I am under any obligation to my uncle Geoffrey; and I protest, sir, openly with all my heart, before you and Mr. Sanders, as I would before all the world, against the execution of this will, because it contains a record of what I am not proved to be. Why was there any mention of me at all? Why—"

"It is too late, Ralph," said Mr. Roger, kindly. "I am no lawyer, and Peed has taken the first advice in London, on which this will is drawn up. Peed will be here before your uncle, and, if you like, you can read it."

"Read the record, before witnesses too, of my own shame, uncle!" cried Ralph, passionately. "Do you forget that I am a Darnell—your brother's son—and that *you* have taught me to be a gentleman? No, sir, I had better go home; I would rather not see my uncle."

"I do not know, Ralph," replied Mr. Darnell, looking round upon all the Darnells about him. "Nothing of this kind ever occurred before among us, and I believe—that is, I think—I hope—that your uncle, if he saw you, might even now be deterred from his purpose."

"I am afraid not, sir," said Ralph, firmly; "no Darnell that you have ever told me of was vacillating. I am not afraid of my uncle—I have no reason to be so; and I will wait, as you request me, till he comes. If then—"

"Say no more, Ralph; I'm sick of it all," replied Mr. Darnell. "I'll stand by you whatever happens, and I can say no more. How do you do, Mr. Peed?" he continued, as that prim gentleman entered the parlour. "Sit down. I suppose you are all ready."

"Thank you, we are *quite* ready. Mr. Wilson has the documents in his bag, and I suppose Sir Geoffrey will not be long absent now," said Mr. Peed, as he pulled out his watch; "it's nearly two o'clock."

Ralph had no further business in the parlour, and, taking some papers his uncle handed to him, he left the room. Wilson was sitting in the office with a heavy green bag between his legs, which he slapped significantly. "It'll be done," he said, in a whisper, "and they'll expect you to-night at the old place."

Ralph made no reply, but went to his desk. I do not think he was conscious of what he looked over. More letters from Mr. Wharton, more invoices, more accounts of sales and purchases in Calcutta. He seemed to be in a dream, a hideous dream, which it is idle to follow. A seal was to be set on his shame, and witnessed too, perhaps by some of the clerks in the office; even Mr. Sanders, who as yet knew only of Constance's refusal of him, might know this family secret; and who at Peed's did not already?"

Ralph heard his uncle's coach drive up shortly afterwards, and saw him come in at the door, cross the office, and enter the parlour. His uncle saw him too, and made no sign—nay, he turned away his head, and the expression of his face was obstinate and defiant. Mr. Wilson was summoned and went in, so also did Mr. Sanders, and Ralph supposed the business had begun. The door had not closed entirely after Mr. Sanders. Ralph's desk was not far from it, and he listened, with his heart beating against the wood so violently that he could scarcely breathe. Mr. Peed spread out the parchments upon the table, and Ralph heard the rustling distinctly. "Would Sir Geoffrey Darnell wish to hear the paper again?" Mr. Peed asked; "Mr. Wilson would read it, and the witnesses should know the contents of what they signed." And it was read. What the party severally thought of those documents it is immaterial to conjecture. It is probable the opinions were of a varied character; but the reading was soon finished. Ralph could only hear a word here and there, for Mr. Wilson read in a lawyer's-clerk kind of professional gabble, without stops or pauses, which was inaudible except as a general murmur; and when that had ceased, Sir Geoffrey had to sign.

"Before you write your name to that paper, think again, Geoffrey, what you are doing," said Roger Darnell firmly. "I myself don't see the least need for it, nor for any mention of Ralph."

"I differ from you entirely; I think there *is* need," replied the baronet, doggedly; "and I *quite* know what I am doing. I came to London specially to do this, and, by George, I will do it! I'll finish it. If I had been wrong, all the lawyers in London, and Peed here would have told me so; but they think I'm right, and I think I'm right myself. And what's more, considering what Ralph Darnell is, and what he's done to me, I'm sure I've behaved very handsomely to him—much more so than he'd any right to expect."

"I think the terms used, brother," returned Mr. Darnell, "are particularly and needlessly offensive, and I would not, for poor Harry's sake, have had his son's name mentioned in the way it is."

"My dear sir," cried Mr. Peed—"in law, my *dear* sir, we are obliged to use the plainest and most distinct—the most, in fact, unequivocal terms—"

"I'll tell you what, and once for all, Roger," exclaimed the baronet, raising his voice, and interrupting Mr. Peed, "if you don't like to witness it, somebody else will; there are plenty of clerks in the office. But I'll have the will as it is, and in nowise altered. If that fellow is a bastard, as I told him to his teeth already he is, and believe him to be, it's no business of mine, and *I* can't make him anything else, nor you either! And I can't and won't have any interest of Conny's risked by delay. When I am gone, and Constance is Mrs. Elliot, as she will be, please God, the value of this will and that bastard's pretensions will be set at rest. Now I've come to do, and not to talk—it's too late for that; and I hope these gentlemen will bear me witness that I sign these papers in perfect knowledge of their contents, and consenting thereto with a calm mind."

Then Ralph heard only the scratching of his uncle's pen as he wrote the words we have before seen, in bold steady characters, where he was directed. Whether his uncle Roger signed as a witness he did not know; then, perhaps, it would have been of no comfort to him to understand that he did so. Mr. Wilson and Mr. Sanders were sufficient for all legal purposes, and Mr. Darnell objected to Ralph's secret being known to other clerks in the office.

Two expressions only of all those his uncle spoke, appeared to ring in Ralph's ears: "bastard," and "Constance is Mrs. Elliot." For a while he stood irresolute where he was; his uncle might perhaps say something kind as he passed out, and to this last hope the poor fellow clung in spite of his misery. Sir Geoffrey did not delay. He had come to do an act—a great act of his life—and he had done it. There was little more said by anyone. The brothers shook hands, as Ralph saw when the door opened.

"We shall leave town after an early breakfast to-morrow; everything's packed up, Roger, and Elliot's to follow us as soon as he can," said the barouet. "The ladies have gone to see Mrs. Darnell, but

I'm going there to pick them up. I only wish we were safe home again," and so he came out.

It must have been Ralph's white scared face and staring eyes that then attracted the baronet's special notice; and Ralph could not help looking at him, for there was a kind of fascination in the fearless dogged bearing of the old man, of which you may see the foundation in Sir Joshua's striking picture.

"Don't stare at me so, sir!" he cried, stopping and striking his stick upon the floor; "don't stare at me,—d'ye hear? Go in there and see what I have done for you," and he pointed with his cane to the parlour door; "and remember it's the last I wish to know of you, whatever you may be. If ever you cross my path again I'll kick you out of it—I will, by G— !—d'ye hear?"

"Geoffrey, Geoffrey! Here, in my office and before all my clerks; for shame, sir!" exclaimed Mr. Darnell.

"I don't care if it were before the King," replied the baronet, fiercely turning round on his brother; "I'll be stared at by ne'er an impudent bastard in England. Insulted! and here too; this might at least have been prevented, Roger. I wish you a good morning, brother;" and he took off his hat, and made a stately sweep with it, departing into the hall by the door which the porter was holding open.

"Ralph, Ralph, what have you done or said?" asked Mr. Darnell, anxiously; "I would not have had this happen here for a thousand pounds."

"He said nothing, Mr. Darnell, I assure you," replied Mr. Sanders. "Let me explain;" and they returned into the parlour and shut the door.

When they came out again to seek Ralph, for Mr. Darnell had been satisfied that no offence had been given or intended, the young man was gone; a clerk said he had taken his hat and hastily walked out after Sir Geoffrey's coach drove away.

"It has been a trying scene for the poor lad to-day," said Mr. Darnell, kindly, "and he will be the better of a quiet evening at home. And I will make amends to him for this, Mr Sanders; if one uncle has thrown him off, another will take his place, for he is the last male Darnell that remains to us, my friend: alas! the last."

CHAPTER XXIV.

BURY COURT, AND OTHER MATTERS RELATING TO THIS HISTORY.

We have not to go back very far, when I remind the reader of a visit Ralph Darnell paid to Messrs. Forster and Selwyn in Bury

Court, St. Mary Axe, when he became acquainted with the family secret now divulged. Mr. Forster, as they walked home together to Mrs. Morton's that night, professed a more kindly interest in Ralph than he had ever done before; and he related all that Mr. Wilson had explained to him in regard to the legal nature of the will, and Ralph's position: and their collective opinion that that document ought not to be permitted to exist. Mr. Forster did not state clearly by what process the will could be obtained or destroyed. If it were to be left at Peed's, it might be lost, as papers could be occasionally; but if Sir Geoffrey took it with him, some other course would have to be adopted. Ralph was in no condition to argue the matter that night, but he was grateful to Mr. Forster for his interest. And when they arrived at Mrs. Morton's, and, as it happened, were let in by Sybil, Mr. Forster asked kindly after her mother, and, his voice being heard, was invited to the parlour, where Mrs. Morton was sitting.

It may be in the reader's memory that on one occasion Mr. Forster, with Mr. Wilson, had spent an evening with Mrs. Morton—and very agreeably, too. Mr. Forster knew poor Mrs. Morton's antecedents perfectly; and though allusions to old times distressed her at first very much, yet Forster found that her interest in them, and in the present position and circumstances of the Prince, and others connected with him, were still very great. On this point, therefore, Mr. Forster had been, to a certain extent, communicative, and had risen to a high rank in the old lady's estimation. She well knew the family of which he was the last representative. She had often been at the old border peel, and had seen his mother, and even remembered Mr. Forster's sisters—who were both now in the Benedictine convent at Paris—when they were children. The Forsters were never rich, but they were of an old family in Northumberland; and when Mr. Forster told her that the peel still remained, with some farm folk in it—that reduced fortunes and his business compelled him to live in London—she was by no means surprised. Old Nanny, too, had much respect for Mr. Forster; and had received graciously a crown or two, which had been judiciously disbursed while Ralph lay so ill.

Sybil, however, had been disturbed by Mr. Forster. She had sung with him a duet of Dr. Arne's, which she had learned with Ralph, and Forster sang well. He had been in Italy, and told her of music which would suit her, and had even sent her some; but though she could make no positive objection to him, she shrank intuitively from contact with him. His looks were bold and licentious, and his manner was neither courtly like Elliot's, nor frank like Ralph's, but more that of a hard man of the world—and John Forster was a hard man indeed. On this night, therefore, when her mother had called graciously to Mr. Forster, Sybil could not shut the door in his face, as she would like to have done; and though he did not stay, the delight of looking, even for a short time, upon her sweet face was an intense gratification, a craving for which was growing upon him very rapidly. If he had had suspicions that Sybil cared for Ralph Darnell more than she even dared to think, that short visit would have proved it beyond a doubt. He saw how the sweet girl's countenance changed; how her eyes followed him restlessly; how she was conscious that some evil had befallen him: but he rejoiced to observe that from Ralph there was no return. He answered her questions indifferently; sat silently in a dark corner of the room; and as Forster took his leave, he saw that Ralph wished Mrs. Morton good-night, and went up-stairs. So far, then, the field was open, and he had hope; and were Ralph out of the way (for he dreaded his fearless character), there was good ground to think he might succeed, although much might have to be done. I am afraid that Mr. Forster had discovered the utter weakness of that little garrison, and assured himself that if the one defender could be withdrawn, there was no one else who could fill his place.

Although Mr. Wilson and Mr. Selwyn had experience of human nature after their several capacities—the one as an attorney's clerk, and the other as, we will say as before, a horse-dealer—yet their knowledge was not such as could be brought to bear upon Ralph Darnell. Any deliberate roguery which Mr. Wilson could have proposed, or any coarse suggestion of Mr. Selwyn's, would have opened Ralph's eyes to the true character of these confederates, and he would have escaped out of their hands. Mr. Forster's talents lay, however, mainly in his ability to read men's thoughts, and to act upon their passions; and to this end he had kept down his companions, and had opposed repeated invitations to Ralph. Ralph had come several times of his own accord to Bury Court, in the interval, to ask news of Wilson, who had prohibited his calling at the "Peed's" office; and whatever there was to tell, Ralph heard from Wilson himself, or from Forster. Thus the progress of the draft, of counsel's opinion, of the engrossing, and the day of signature and execution, were duly made known to him; and without pressing their advice, all Ralph heard was but a reiteration of what had been told him at first. These men professed indifference to whatever Ralph might decide, but they were not the less sure of their game. And when Ralph, with the same wild face which had attracted his uncle Geoffrey's notice at the office, made his appearance presently at Bury Court, they knew for certain that he had, at last, voluntarily thrown himself into their power.

Ralph meanwhile had done a good deal. He had gone to Mrs. Morton's; he had told them he was to accompany his grandfather, and packed up a small valise, containing a change of clothes. He then took a boat and went down among the colliers. There was no vessel to sail for three days; but he paid for a berth in one to sail on Thursday, and this was Monday. Then he returned home, leaving his valise on board the vessel, and spoke kindly to them all; and though he purposed never to return, said he should soon be back, and they were not to fret about him. It was very hard to see their tearful faces, and the look of misery upon Sybil's. He had never seen the like of it before, and thought upon it many a sad day after. When he was going, he bade Nanny put away his dress clothes in his trunk, for they would have to follow by sea, and his uncle would forward them to him. And when he had made over his little stock of trinkets to Sybil to keep, kissed Mrs. Morton, and held Sybil in his arms, trembling and sobbing, full of terrible fears which gave her deadly pain to conceal, and so left them; and Sybil threw herself on Nanny's breast, and moaned there, "that he would never come back—never, never!—that she was sure there was evil hanging over him, which he would not tell them of"—I say, while Nanny and she sat at the window nearly all that night, shivering in their horrible apprehension, and could get no rest—the misery of that fond heart of Sybil's is quite beyond my power to describe; and even prayer—her habitual refuge—seemed denied her.

Afterwards, and when the wherry in which Ralph crossed the river turned among the shipping, and he saw the old window no more, he began to know what he had to do. Whether he received the will or not, he could at least get to Newcastle, and to his grandfather. There, one more long search for the certificate of his mother's marriage, and if unsuccessful, the world was before him. East or west, what signified; or those foreign armies in which men won distinction or died. And was there not Colonel Clive? Even in Holland, his grandfather, he remembered, had connections; and one used to India merchant's work in London, would be sure of employment in Amsterdam.

So, as I have said, when Ralph came to Bury Court that summer evening, those there knew he was in their hands, and that the recklessness writ on his face had a source very deep in his worst passions.

Perhaps, now that he was come to them, one of the men, Forster, would rather have avoided a hurried ending to the affair; but Mr. Selwyn was not to be balked of a profitable professional undertaking, and his plans were already complete.

"A sharp ride, this fine summer night, would be delightful," he said. "A pleasant day in the country to-morrow, and a pleasant fright to the ladies in the evening. Why, a journey anywhere was worth nothing without an alarm of highwaymen; and this would be such fun. He and Forster would perform the rôle of highwaymen to perfection; and I, Albany Selwyn, like Claude Duval, shall be proud to dance a measure with the beautiful Constance Darnell, the toast of London! And then consider, Mr. Ralph, the happiness of making a gallant, beautiful speech, and dismissing the party on their way—nay, escorting them, if they so wished—in their own proper character." And when Ralph observed gravely that his uncle was the last man to try a joke upon, and would shoot one of them to a certainty, and if they had nothing more feasible to propose than this, they had better let him go, Mr. Selwyn laughed, and declared "he for one should run away if the baronet looked wicked; and if Ralph did not like the engagement, he could stay there and wait their return. They had promised to get him the papers, and—he should have them!"

They had been at supper all this time, and Ralph's mood of mind, desperate and reckless from the first, had become vindictive under the wine he drank. "He would take the paper from his uncle, which he had no right to keep—tear it into a thousand pieces before his eyes and his faithless cousin's—tell Mistress Grover why he had done this, and return to London. They might follow him if they chose, do whatever they pleased, he should not care; whatever they did could not affect his future life." There was very little sophistry in Ralph's thoughs when the wine began its mischief. He only saw certain means to an end, in which two intimate friends would help him as in a frolic. These were lawless times, too, when desperate men did desperate deeds, and "A 29" was unknown; when people who suffered, very often took the law into their own hands, and did as they pleased with it; and when might, to a certain, and very great degree, was right. As to Selwyn's ideas of making Constance —Pshaw! he was a wild rake certainly, but he was a gentleman, and Forster eminently one.

While these thoughts ran through Ralph's heart, I think, had he known that a certain company of gentlemen who habitually frequented his Majesty's high-road to York by night—marked down likely prey in London—at the extremities—or whatever they might be; who had been balked of Sir Geoffrey Darnell as he came up from the north, but were determined that family plate, and jewels of Darnell fame, should not be spared as they went back—had already made preparations for the baronet's reception after he should pass Barnet, I think, nay, I am sure, that Ralph would have shuddered at the precipice he so nearly approached; and would have ridden after his uncle, thrown himself in his way, and earned his gratitude and his own pardon by declaring his danger. This was not, however, to be. A grim, furious fate was on his track, driving him on under the horrible memories of insults and wrongs. Bastard! bastard! rang in his ears. Selwyn knew him to be one, so did Forster; so did that horrible Wilson, at whom his blood crept in his veins. Coward? No! he was at least no coward. They should not do for him what he could do for himself. If his uncle drew a pistol and shot him, what matter? there would be enough life left to explain, and he could die peacefully and happily with Constance and Grover by his side, and his uncle's once kind voice ringing in his ears!

I daresay it was some such reverie as this into which Ralph had fallen, when Forster cried cheerily to him,

"What a brown study thou art fallen into, Don Ralpho! Awake, most illustrious cabalero! and to horse, if thou'rt coming at all. If not, there's Wilson, and wine as much as needs be, for we'll have enough to do, and must away—away—away!"

Ralph rose, and held out his hand. "I was only thinking," he said.

"Pshaw!" cried his friend, "a fico for thoughts. Come, there is riding gear in the stables, and the gallant steeds are ready. No pistols? Well, nor need of them; but take a good whip. There are those on the road might take advantage of thee."

Mr. Wilson sat for awhile over the good claret and a plate of nectarines, which were delicious; and was he not a privileged guest? His thoughts were of a varied nature, and this was the cast of them, as he rose with a satisfied countenance.

"No harm will come of this—no natural harm; and more will be paid for what John Wilson can tell, after it is over, than before; and, besides, there is no time now to prevent anything. Selwyn has a good job in hand, and Satan is helping them all on kindly. Ha! ha! ha!—kindly—kindly!"

CHAPTER XXV.

THE JOURNEY AT NIGHT, AND WHAT CAME OF IT.

When Sir Geoffrey Darnell and the ladies arrived at Barnet, late in the evening of the following day, the footman had been sent on to order rooms for the party at the Red Lion Inn, met the coach at the entrance of the little town, and communicated the unpleasant, but in those days perhaps not very uncommon intelligence, that every room was full, and that he had been equally unsuccessful at other hostelries in the place. "The landlord of the Red Lion," he said, "had sent a servant with him a' rroond the toon, but there was na' a place to be had for love or money." The consequence of this communication was, that the baronet arrived at the posting-house in very bad humour indeed.

Beginning any long journey, even in these days of perfection of locomotion, involves, very often, trials of temper. There is the last hurried packing to do, when clothes will not fit into the trunk, and the trunk lid will not shut down, nor the key turn. There is the dread of being late for the train, and after all there is something forgotten perhaps; and yet, once the last shriek of the engine is heard, the certainty of progression is so entire and consoling, that most minor miseries are altogether forgotten. The trials of our great-grandfathers, however, must have been much more hard to endure, and Sir Geoffrey had had enough of them. The servants, I am afraid, were not quite sober, for there had been a good many very moist leave-takings, and the trunks were ill-packed. The light spring-cart which had accompanied them from the north was found to be unsafe; and the heavy baggage was to be forwarded by a collier brig to Newcastle, in charge of one of the men. The ostler and the maid-servant were to sit on the box; and a new mantua-maker—a smart young London damsel, highly recommended by the milliner—was to sit inside with the ladies. Fortunately, the coach was very large and roomy, and held six without hoops; so that there was a comfortable corner for each, and this ought to have satisfied the baronet; but he was not in good humour.

The last settling of accounts had been one heavy trial. Not that the baronet troubled himself about details—Mistress Grover managed all these; but when she added up the list in her private memorandum-book, and told Sir Geoffrey that she should require a thousand pounds to see them clear and to pay them home, I should not like to write the expletives by which he signified his astonishment of this reckless extravagance, and swore against the vanity of women and their milliners' extortions. "Had he not already twice paid the woman, by George, and here was the new account worse than any previous one!" Perhaps Mrs. Grover had been foolish in allowing her beautiful pet to order what she liked; and Madame Chevri, in her admiration for Miss Darnell, had almost daily brought the *sweetest* brocades of Lyons, the richest velvets of Genoa, and lace of Mechlin and Brussels, for her inspection, which was irresistible. Then jewellers' bills for resetting diamonds, and Sir Geoffrey's own tailor's bill for dress suits, and one for Ralph, with liveries for the servants, were no trifle. In short, Sir Geoffrey had had to pay for this visit to London very much more than he anticipated, and the last straw had nearly broken the camel's back.

Therefore, when the bowing landlord met the coach at the door of the inn at Barnet, and made a thousand apologies for being full—so full that he had only his own parlour behind the bar to offer to his guests, if they would please to take some refreshment, and had begged of my Lady Beaumanoir to allow the ladies the use of her room while they stayed—so full that he had never remembered a day like it. There was the Duke and Duchess of Beaumanoir going back to Eastshire, and Sir John Ribston and his family from Yorkshire, and—." There was no use swearing, or being violent, and Sir Geoffrey gave in.

The four horses that had brought Sir John Ribston's carriage were to return; and the landlord recommended two fresh ones, as the road was heavy, and there was a good deal of luggage. At the next stage, the landlord said, there was an excellent, quiet country inn; and he had taken the liberty of sending a message by the guard of the stage-coach, that he should send on Sir Geoffrey Darnell's party, for whom rooms were to be kept ready. And with the prospect of a quiet night's rest in a quiet place, instead of the disturbance which would ensue from travellers arriving and departing at all hours of the night, Sir Geoffrey and the ladies were glad to escape from the combined odours of fried bacon, roast mutton, stale ale, and tobacco-smoke, which pervaded the landlord's own parlour behind the bar, and to breathe the sweet evening air.

Not, however, that it was cool. The heat all day had been exceedingly great, and as they entered Barnet there was a huge pile of cloud stationary, and with white round tops like a cauliflower, to the westward, about which, in the twilight, they could see some faint lightning playing. There was not a breath of wind; and the scent from the woodbine and white lilies, stocks and gilliflowers in the inn garden, loaded the air heavily. As he bade them good-night, and wished them a safe journey, the landlord looked up and "thought there would be a shower, but it would be pleasant, and lay the dust. As to the roads—why, a girl might travel them alone at midnight, and Sir Geoffrey might save himself the trouble of opening his pistol-case. Why, they would be at ——— by eleven o'clock, or even sooner, and the boys would drive fast," as, indeed, they promised to do.

So the party passed on, and Sir Geoffrey, soothed by his dinner and the excellent pint of wine the landlord had given him, fell asleep and snored audibly; the mantua-maker did the same, and Constance and Mistress Grover alone remained awake. I do not think they were very communicative either. Mistress Grover had bad thoughts at her heart about poor Ralph; and, indeed, she was very sore about him. Perhaps in that quiet corner she found a relief when her tears fell hot and fast on her hands, as she thought of old times and the boy's early days, and put up a prayer that all might come right again.

I have no doubt, on the contrary, that Mistress Constance's thoughts were as pleasant as Grover's were melancholy. There were many bright spots upon her memory. That first evening on the balcony, and many such afterwards. Many delightful rambles in the quietest nooks of Kensington Gardens; many plays, much Ranelagh, and—she was not ashamed of them—many sweet kisses too from her handsome lover. Was she not only seventeen?—and I question much whether those delicious tokens of love are ever enjoyed more rapturously than at that romantic and credulous age. Ah, when he came up to Melcepeth—

Suddenly there was a bright flash which woke the milliner, and caused her to scream, and revealed the inside of the vehicle and its crimson damask lining perfectly; then a clap of thunder, and then a deluge of rain, a flood which made the road to seethe, as it were, with large bubbles, and for the time to cover it with water. Through all this the baronet slept and snored peacefully, and Constance and Mistress Grover kept the mantua-maker quiet. Neither of them was afraid of thunder or lightning; and, indeed, after the first clap, there was no more but some muttering growls far distant. As long as it was dry, the coach had got on very well with its six horses: but as the road became wet, the progress was not rapid, and as the rain fell faster, was little better than a walk. Mistress Grover heard Richard, the footman on the box, calling to the driver to get on; and being assured that "t'skoy war breekin yon', and they'd git on preasantly; t' 'orses wasn't freesh—they wasn't—but they'd do the stage."

Presently there was a terrible jolt, which flung the baronet forward into Mistress Grover's lap, with an exclamation of—"God bless my heart! what's happened?"

What, indeed, had happened? The fore wheel of the carriage had sunk into a hole up to the axle, and the hind wheel was little better. The horses refused draught, and the carriage leaned over so much that an upset appeared imminent. Mr. Macadam had not been born in those days, and His Majesty's high-roads were in a very different condition then to what they are now. The footman Richard had scrambled down from the box, and opened the door; the post-boys were employed in mutual recriminations, attended by hideous oaths, at having fallen into a hole, which had been visible while the road was dry, but which was now a puddle like any other; but it was too late to help what had happened, and the baronet was consoled with assurances that when the "'osses 'ad rested a bit, they'd pull out the coach sure-ly."

The rain had cleared off, and the stars shone out brightly. There was quite light enough to see all round the puddle, and even the road beyond; and the baronet was urging another good pull together, and promising a guinea to drink his health, when he heard the plash of horse's feet among the water in the road, and a smothered sound as if others were advancing on the turf by the wayside; and as he looked through the mist which was rapidly rising after the rain, his view being limited by the glare of the lamps, he was hardly aware that the party was close at hand, before he saw the boy on the leaders dragged from his saddle, a man with a pistol threatening the second postilion, and himself and the carriage surrounded by others.

True to his professions, Mr. Selwyn had dismounted while a confederate opened the farther carriage door; and was in the act of making the politest speech he could invent to the ladies, begging them to dismount, that the carriage might be righted, when Constance, who did not know at first the nature of Mr. Selwyn's address, and could not see her father, heard distinctly the clash of swords, a few deep curses from the baronet, and confused cries from the footman, the maid, and the drivers—and she leaped out past Mr. Selwyn, followed by Mistress Grover; while the mantua-maker, dragged into the puddle from the other door of the coach, was screaming wildly.

Now, while Mr. Selwyn held his brief parley with the ladies, Mr. Forster and another man had an equally brief one with Sir Geoffrey. The baronet had drawn his sword, which (why he could never account for, except that, being in the coach, it got between his legs as he stepped out) he had in his hand, and swore lustily "that he wasn't afraid of e'er a highwayman in England, and that he'd pink one of them if they did not clear off;" and forthwith attacked Mr. Forster, whose companion, having knocked down the footman, had joined Mr. Selwyn. Just at this moment then, and as Mr. Forster, hampered by his horse, which shied at the clash of the swords, was defending himself very feebly against Sir Geoffrey's impetuous attack, his foot slipped; and, unable to parry a thrust of the baronet's, found himself sharply wounded in the sword-arm. It is probable Mr. Forster did not intend mischief, but when he saw by the light of one of the coach-lamps that Sir Geoffrey was drawing back his arm for another thrust which could not be avoided, he drew a pocket-pistol from the breast of his coat, and fired it at his antagonist; and the baronet, staggering back, threw up his hands with a loud cry and fell into the arms of his daughter, now close behind him, with Mistress Grover following her.

All this happened in much less time, I believe, than I have needed to write it; and Mr. Selwyn and his companions were ransacking the pockets of the coach as fast as they could, when the sound of the shot and the cry sorely disturbed their proceedings. The shout or groan of a wounded man is unmistakable; and Mr. Selwyn, though no soldier, had heard many such. Who had fallen? Whoever it might be, the event was very serious and embarrassing, and he turned directly to see after it. Mr. Forster was standing by his horse holding his arm, and crying out for help. He had perhaps narrowly escaped with his life, for the baronet's rapier, grazing his breast, had passed through the fleshy part of his arm, which was bleeding profusely. It was, however, promptly tied up with a handkerchief; and, mounting their horses, the party galloped off by the way they had come. To say the truth, Mr. Selwyn believed the baronet to be dead; for, as he rode away, he saw him lying against the bank, and the poor ladies sobbing and wringing their hands over him, and the servant shrieking on the box.

There was no time, however, to wait, and Mr. Selwyn's curses against Forster's precipitancy were neither few nor mild; nor, indeed, were they much modified even by that gentleman's declaration, that he should have been a dead man in another moment if he had not used his pistol in self-defence. There was, however, no time to bandy words: Mr. Forster was already somewhat faint with loss of blood, and they must regain the hamlet whence they had started, and where a small tavern had been the rendezvous, in order to get some cordial and bind up the wound safely; so the party rode on at a rapid pace.

It will have been seen that, after all, Ralph Darnell had had no personal connection with this misadventure, and it is necessary to explain why he had none. Mr. Selwyn was, like other great commanders, very strict in what he termed the discipline of his profession. In any actual affair of this kind, none but the boldest and most skilful of his associates ever took a share in the work itself. Any blunder by a new hand, any hot-headed violence, would, he knew, ruin the best enterprise ever planned. Robbery on the highway was not very much thought about by the magistrates, but murder was quite another thing, and brought out Bow Street runners and other very inconvenient myrmidons of the law. Now, Ralph Darnell was in a state of progressive excitement, which his friends saw was nearly at its culminating point. Were he allowed to approach the baronet, not only Mr. Selwyn, but Forster was certain he could not be restrained; and he would assuredly do or say something by which he would be recognised and success prevented.

The confederates had ridden up a shady road which led from the hamlet to the highway, and joined it where some large oak-trees, meeting above, cast the mouth of the lane into perfect darkness. It was here that the party had agreed to wait for the coach, and dash out upon it as it passed. Perhaps Mr. Selwyn's ears were keener than the others', and he had heard the rumbling of the carriage stop; for he suddenly turned to Ralph and said, in a tone of command which was unpleasant—

"You will remain here, Mr. Darnell, till we return; we must reconnoitre the road;" and as Ralph resented what appeared to him a rough speech, Mr. Selwyn said a few words in the flash language of the time, and pressed on, while two of the men remained, and, each seizing a rein, drew their pistols, and advised Ralph to be quiet.

I do not mean this to be any excuse for Ralph Darnell. Had the coach come up to the end of the lane, he would, had he been permitted, have demanded what he had come for, and attempted to take it by force; but this would have been impossible under any circumstances, and Mr. Selwyn's rules of procedure, which have been partially explained, had already provided, in the two men who became Ralph's surly companions, an effectual preventive of any such course of action. As they stood there, however, listening eagerly, the dull sound of a distant clamour, and afterwards of the pistol-shot, broke the stillness of the summer night, and were followed by piercing shrieks: then Ralph suddenly drove the spurs into his horse, struck down the arm of one of the men who raised his pistol as if to fire, and dashed into the high-road.

It was not a quarter of a mile from the lane to the scene of the encounter; and about half-way Ralph met the party, and pulled up. How had he escaped from the men? that was Mr. Selwyn's first thought; a second, to turn Ralph.

"Come," he cried—"come with us, for your life—for your life, Mr. Darnell, or you'll be taken. Here's Forster badly wounded. Come; your uncle's past help, I fear, and it's no use going there;" and Mr. Selwyn tried to catch the reins of Ralph's horse, but this the young man avoided, and, dashing past the party, rode on at speed. All he heard was "London, the old place," and in a few moments more he was near the coach. It had been set up by the postboys, and was standing in the middle of the road, in a dim mist from the horses and the ground combined, through which one of the lamps shone feebly, while the other revealed a group on the bank by the hedge, which, horror-stricken, he instantly recoguised.

It was his uncle, lying pale and death-like, supported against the bank, with Constance's arm under his head, his silvery beard, and white satin waistcoat and ruffles, dabbled with blood. Over him stooped Mistress Grover, tearing away the shirt, and striving to stanch the blood with her handkerchief, the London girl and the servants standing apart, wringing their hands, and sobbing.

The misery of those dear faces, so white, so absorbed in their terror—the figure lying there, which, as he then thought, would never move more—it had every appearance of death—all this Ralph's eye took in at a glance; and perhaps he would have obeyed the suggestion of his instinct to go to them—never to leave them, whatever might happen—but for the footman Richard, who, having a loaded pistol in his hand, was standing by, and seeing a masked horseman appear suddenly before him, cried out,—

"Eh, leddies, bit they're come agin!" and fired the pistol at Ralph without further parley.

Ralph heard the ball whizz by his head, turned, and rode away at his utmost speed. He had not the courage to look on him in death, of whose murder he believed himself to be the cause.

CHAPTER XXVI.

SUSPENSE.

INSTEAD of following Ralph Darnell over fields and hedges in his wild ride that night, till he had struck another road to London, and reached the stables behind Bury Court by early morning; or instead of detailing, or attempting to do so, his frantic accusations of murder against Forster and Selwyn, or his fruitless and almost insane ravings, which the latter could not pacify—and Mr. Forster was too weak and peevish to attempt justification of his conduct; instead, also, of relating how Ralph received that fatal will from Mr. Selwyn, which had been the cause of all this misfortune, tore it in pieces fiercely, and watched them shrivel and blacken in the fire, crushing them down with his boot till they were consumed to a cinder: or of repeating Mr. Selwyn's injunctions to get out of the way, as he himself intended to do, till all this was blown over;—we had, I think, in preference, better see after Sir Geoffrey Darnell, whom we left lying under the hedge on the wet grass, and the horror-stricken ladies sobbing over him.

It was some time before the baronet could speak at all; and his first faint cry was for water, which he drank greedily. Then Mistress Grover found a bottle of his drops in the carriage-pocket, a dose of which revived him so much that, to his daughter's and her own great joy and thankfulness, he was able to sit up, and, though very weak and confused, to bid them be comforted, for "he did not feel dying, or anything like it; and though the fellow's ball was in him somewhere, he was pretty sure he had done for *him* at any rate," and wanted to know what had become of his body. But this excited talk was, as may be supposed, attended with reaction; and presently he fainted again, and was revived with difficulty. And when the coach had been turned round—for it was a much less distance back to Barnet than to the stage where they had intended to rest—and Sir Geoffrey had been carried to it by Richard, the maid-servant, and one of the postilions, assisted by the ladies, and placed in as easy a position as possible, and the coach was set in motion—it was clear to Mrs. Grover that he could not bear the jolting; and accordingly it went at a foot-pace, while Richard, taking one of the leaders, rode off at a gallop to Barnet, as well to give the alarm as to procure a chair or a litter, or some easier conveyance.

I daresay the consternation at the Red Lion, on Richard's arrival in the dead of night, can also better be imagined than described; but the worthy landlord was not slack in his duty. A chair which belonged to the establishment, with four stout men, was despatched at a run. Mr. Burgess, the surgeon of the town, was called up, and also departed on horseback forthwith. One of the guests in the inn at once gave up his bed for the sufferer; and I am bound to record that her Grace the Duchess, and various other ladies of distinction, who were staying in the house that night, dressed themselves in wrappers, and were prepared to render such assistance as they could to Mistress Grover and Constance on their arrival, and displayed the utmost interest in, and sympathy for, the baronet's misfortune.

And oh the joy, the unspeakable thankfulness which followed Mr. Burgess's first operation after the baronet had been laid gently in his bed, in the speedy extraction of the ball! That eminent country practitioner had galloped on to meet the coach, and had stopped it till the chair came up. His presence was at once an assurance and comfort to the poor ladies; and he was assisted by them in placing Sir Geoffrey in an easy position upon the seat. Sir Geoffrey was quite conscious, and would have thanked him, but was not permitted to speak; while Mr. Burgess examined the wound there and then, and saw it was not mortal, though severe. He found also, to his inexpressible comfort, that he had not to do with foolish hysterical women, but with two persons who, though suffering extreme anguish, were helpful and collected. Perhaps the young mantua-maker was the most difficult to manage. She had fainted at the sight of Sir Geoffrey's blood, which indeed had run out over his clothes in a great stream. Mrs. Grover, who had brought her to, had almost lost patience with her; and perhaps a downright good scolding from the doctor, who declared he would put her out of the coach there and then to be carried of by the highwaymen, if she were not quiet, induced that young lady to keep to her own corner, and snivel into her pocket-handkerchief. Altogether, Mr. Burgess, by comporting himself in a cheerful, hopeful manner, instilled a good deal of courage into the ladies' minds; and had the opportunity, which he did not neglect, of paying them some pretty professional compliments. When he had seen the baronet undressed and laid at ease on a bed, and begged to be excused for a few moments, the doctor hurried home, summoned his assistant, who brought the necessary instruments; and when in another marvellously short space of time he took to Constance and Mrs. Grover, upon a silver salver, a very small pistol-bullet, which, as he assured them, had not penetrated very deeply, having been deadened by the stiff buckram padding of the baronet's coat—it is impossible to conceive two more thankful hearts than those which, kneeling by the old man's bedside, poured out their gratitude for his safety, and sat watching by turns till the day broke.

There were offers in profusion of service. His Grace of Beaumanoir "would leave servants if need be." He had had the honour of meeting Sir Geoffrey Darnell only a few days ago at Arthur's. How shocking this was: What were the magistrates about that the roads were not better looked to at night! If he had only been going to London, indeed, he would have taken any message, and "'pon his soul" would ride back, if—. This, however was unnecessary—a stout, active young man, who was, he said, a commercial traveller, and who was about to depart on horseback when the party arrived, told the landlord he knew Mr. Roger Darnell, and would be soonest with him; and this being communicated to Mrs. Grover, she gave a short note to be delivered to him, and requested the young man to assure Mr. Darnell that, for the present, there was no danger. The consequence of this was, that Mr. Roger, with the same eminent surgeon who had attended Ralph, arrived that afternoon in a post-chaise and four, and found everything progressing satisfactorily. Mr. Burgess's speedy and skilful operation was the theme of much professional congratulation by Mr. ——, which I may spare my readers; and his assurances that, if Sir Geoffrey were kept perfectly quiet and all excitement were avoided, the baronet might even be able to travel again in a few days, removed all apprehension from the ladies' hearts. There was no need, he thought, for him to come again! He had—as they might have—perfect confidence in Mr. Burgess's skill and care.

While Constance, with tearful eyes and a grateful heart, was accepting Dr. ——'s comfort, and her dear old father was looking at her, not being allowed to utter a word, with a soft, placid, thankful smile, which bespoke his comparative freedom from pain, and pressing her hand now and then lovingly—Mr. Roger Darnell and Mrs. Grover were holding a very anxious conversation in that lady's bedroom, where she had taken him to be secure from interruption, and of which she had bolted the door.

Who could have done this? That was the point under discussion; and Mr. Roger being a city magistrate, and accustomed to investigations of all kinds, was taking down memoranda in his notebook of points which he intended to submit to a celebrated Bow Street runner of the time. As soon, indeed, as he had seen his brother was safe, Mr. Darnell had taken a horse, and, with the landlord, had driven to the scene of the night's adventure. Magistrates of the neighbourhood had been there before them, and the fresh traces of horses' feet were visible enough in the half-dried mud, and on the turf by the roadside, from the place of the attack—where there was blood still on the grass and on the bank—to the mouth of the lane. It was evident the gang had come up and gone back by the lane; but no one at the hamlet, about a mile off, had heard of any mounted party.

Mr. Darnell had made memoranda of all this. Now, what had been stolen? But little indeed. Mrs. Grover's own purse and her watch had been given up; but she had notes in an inner pocket. Constance had no money, and had not been molested. The girl had given her ear-rings, a brooch, and her purse. What parcels there were in the coach were gone; her writing-case and the baronet's great leather pocket-book, with a bundle of all the papers that had come from Peed's; and when Mr. Darnell heard this, I am afraid he declared that, "'pon his soul, he was glad to hear of it, and wished the thieves joy of them." "There were some bank-bills in Sir Geoffrey's book for some hundreds, perhaps, but nothing more," Mrs. Grover said, and her catalogue was ended. No, she could not swear to anybody. The man who opened the door was tall, and well dressed in a dark suit, with lace, and had a very pleasant, gentlemanly address; but crape was pulled over his face. The other was a common ruffian, who swore fearful oaths, and frightened Rose, that was the mantua-maker, out of her wits when he dragged her from the coach into the puddle.

Mr. Roger sat for a good while biting his pen, and jotting down what he remembered, and said nothing; and Mrs. Grover was about to get up and return to Constance, when he continued,—"Do you know, Bessie, that Ralph has been unaccountably absent since yesterday; I cannot trace him. Geoffrey was very hard on him again in my office, and he left it suddenly. I went to Mrs. Morton's afterwards, ostensibly to see her, as she is ill, poor soul! and was told by Sybil, whose face was as full of misery as I ever saw anybody's, that Ralph had come, packed up a valise of clothes, and said he had told them I should send for the rest. And, indeed, I cannot get that sad, sad face, and the despairing cry of 'Oh, Mr. Darnell, shall we ever see him again?' out of my mind. I'll tell you what, Bessie, my heart misgives me about the boy; and especially as that will's gone. You are sure he was not there disguised? Don't blink the matter now, for it will remain for ever between you and me."

At first the scarlet flush which rushed over Mrs. Grover's face and neck looked like consciousness, and Mr. Darnell leaned forward anxiously to hear confirmation of what he expected; but it was caused by the suddenness and nature of the supposition, and she denied the imputation earnestly. "Ralph? No! no Ralph was there; she should have known him at once. The man whom the baronet had wounded was as much shorter than Ralph, as he who had opened the door was taller, and there were only two others, perhaps three; and I will never believe," continued the lady, stoutly —"never, Mr. Darnell, that, foolish as that lad may be, he had anything to do with this. But oh, Mr. Roger!" she continued, after a pause, and with another great flush of crimson over her handsome face—"suppose if it were he! what a blow to the family. My poor Conny—my darling—how would you bear it?"

"She's not fond of him, Bessie?" asked Mr. Darnell, anxiously.

"No, no—not as a lover," she replied; "but the old sisterly love is stronger than ever, since that sad day in Soho Square. Mr. Elliot is much attached to him—sincerely so I believe; and I am quite certain Conny will allow her father no rest till they are all together again at Melcepeth, or wherever it may be."

"Amen to that, I say with all my heart," said Mr. Darnell, gravely; "and if those fellows have pitched my brother's will into a pond, I'm sure *I* wouldn't fish it out. I wish I were as easy about Ralph as I am about that infernal paper. I could have kicked Peed, and that snivelling clerk of his, out of my office, as they brought it. But it's no use talking—we must be doing, Bessie; and the first thing I do in the morning will be to trace this lad—ay, if I have even to pay a runner fifty guineas for it. Can he have gone to Warkworth?"

"My opinion, Mr. Darnell, is that he has gone there, and will be found with Mr. Smithson, whom he saw in London; and if I were you, I should look among the Newcastle ships."

"Has Geoffrey—has my brother spoken of him at all?" asked the merchant.

"Not yet," replied Mistress Grover; "but I think there is a good deal on his mind; and I heard him muttering in his sleep, before the coach was stopped last night."

"Come to him, then, Bessie. I should be glad if he did say something kind, that I could repeat to Ralph." And they went to the baronet's room.

They found Constance alone with her father, and as Mistress Grover opened the door gently, the girl held up her hand warningly. The baronet appeared to be asleep, and they waited a while in silence. Presently he opened his eyes, and seeing Mr. Darnell sitting on a stool by his bedside, put out his hand.

"I'm weak, Roger," he said, feebly; "and the getting out of that bullet was painful enough; but I thank God it was got out. I can't speak much, but I'll be better soon, and I know I'm in good hands—in the Lord's good hands," he continued, piously looking up. "And I've been doing some hard things lately, Roger—may He forgive me; and if Ralph were here now, I'd beg his pardon—I would, by George, as I do yours, brother;" and the old man pressed Roger Darnell's hand affectionately. "Tell him so—will ye?"

"You must not agitate yourself, brother," replied Mr. Darnell; "and you must not talk. Keep him quiet between ye, and I will do all I can," he continued to the ladies. "I shall be out again in a day or so, and hope to find you much better, Geoffrey. No, you could not be in better hands, and I'm quite easy about you."

Very soon after that, Mr. Darnell and the doctor were again on their way to London, and arrived there before any one was stirring in the merchant's mansion.

"Please, sir," said the sleepy footman, Grimes, who let him in, and attended him to his room, "this 'ere note was left for you last night by a boy, who said there was no answer. Mrs. Darnell and the young ladies were gone to bed, and I was jist a-lockin' hup when the lad came to the door."

"That will do, Grimes. Get me a cup of chocolate as soon as you can. I shall lie down here on the sofa till you're all up."

Mr. Darnell opened the note, which was written evidently in a disguised hand, and looked over the page for the signature; but there was none, except "A Friend of Roger Darnell & Company;" and he read as follows:—

"Mr. DARNELL: Sir,—The person who takes the liberty to pen these few lines to you, knows a good deal about the Gentlemen who does little jobs on the road for themselves and *their Friends.* He could tell you who attacked your Brother the night before last, *and all about it;* and if it's worth your while to know, you'll have to pay five hundred Pounds for it, sir, and it's worth your while to pay more.

"Now, sir, if you'll come to the Temple Gardens at half-past seven to-morrow evening, without anybody with you, and walk on the Terrace, you'll be met by one who'll be true to you, and give you every Information. There are people who will watch you; and if anybody else is seen with you, you'll not be spoken to, and you'll never know more than you do now; and I remain your Obedient Servant to command,

"A FRIEND OF ROGER DARNELL & COMPANY.

"LONDON, *the* 16*th August* 1755."

"Yes, I will go, whoever you are, my friend, and in good faith too," said the merchant to himself, as he lay down on the sofa, and shut his eyes. "After all, the Bow Street people would run up nearly as long a bill, what with journeys and so forth, and this will take me direct to the point, I think, though it loses more time than I can well spare.

"Thank you, Grimes," he continued, as the footman entered with a tray. "This is very nice; you may go to bed again, if you like. I wish to be quiet for a while." Whether Grimes did so or not is perhaps immaterial; but when Mr. Darnell had taken his hot chocolate and eaten several pieces of crisp thin toast, he felt refreshed, lay down, and slept soundly till the bells in the house and a general bestirring of servants awoke him, when he went up to his dressing-room and to his wife.

CHAPTER XXVII.

IN WHICH EVERYBODY IS VERY BUSY.

If Sir Geoffrey Darnell and his brother could have formed the least idea that when the little colloquy about Ralph, which I have recorded, was going on, their nephew was at that moment in the stable-yard, listening to a group of ostlers and idlers of all kinds, who, on occasions like this, thronged that public place of resort, and were discussing the attack and the probability of Mr. —— or Mr. ——, who did things on the road, being concerned in it—I am quite sure that all that hath to be recorded in this history would never have happened. In his mood of penitence, the good old baronet's heart was full of forgiveness. He would have taken the boy to his arms and bid him be comforted—nay, he had inwardly determined, when Ralph did arrive, and he supposed he would come, to give him "that d—d will," which he still supposed safe, and see him put it into the fire with his own hands; but they did not know it then, nor indeed for many a day afterwards. Ralph had not delayed in London. As Mr. Selwyn observed, that was no place for him; and when Ralph's anguish had fairly overcome him, he not only generously offered another horse, but told him of a small inn in a back street at Barnet which he frequented himself, and where, if he told the ostler that it was Mr. Richard Smith's property, the animal would be well cared for. More than this, he insisted that Ralph should eat a broiled steak, for he was fasting; and, above all, do nothing in a hurry. He comforted Ralph, moreover, by supposing, perhaps without much ground for it, that "that footy little tool of Forster's wouldn't kill a sparrow, and he needn't fret about his uncle." Mr. Selwyn also evinced some practical knowledge of human nature when he observed that Ralph might have an opportunity of "making it up." "He was not known nor suspected. He could account for his absence from town if he were asked about it; and neither he, Mr. Selwyn, nor his men, nor Forster, would peach on him about the will."

Perhaps Ralph *was* comforted in some degree; but if not to any very great extent, it was certain that no vindictive or passionate feeling remained. All he could see or remember was his dear old uncle lying under the hedge, the lamp shining dimly over him, and Constance and Bessie Grover beside him. Oh! if that shot had not been fired by Richard, a moment more would have seen him at their side, at their feet, and he would— No matter now.

When I say that no excitement such as had lately beset the young man remained, and that his only thought was with and for his uncle, it is not to be wondered at if all fatigue was forgotten, and that he was on his road to Barnet once more, as fast as a good horse could carry him. By the way, and when, to relieve his horse, Ralph was walking on foot up a hill, Mr. Roger Darnell's chaise had overtaken him; the postboys were urging on their horses, and his uncle and Dr. —— were leaning back in the corners of the carriage. They did not notice him, for he was on the further side of his horse, and the chaise passed him with the horses at a gallop; but he felt, under the sight of the doctor's anxious face, that there must be danger, and he mounted again, and kept them in sight to the end. The small inn he sought was easily found, and Mr. Richard Smith's horse duly put up.

"There'll be no danger, sir," said the ostler, quietly; "and if so be as you's come out to see arter what's a-goin' on, go to the Red Lion at once; but they do say there, sir, as how the barrinit's not much hurt arter all, and Dr. Burgess 'as got the bullet out of him all right."

What blessed news was this! what a load of apprehension was taken off that poor, sad heart by the homely speech of the ostler at the Bull! And when Ralph went to the tap of the Red Lion, which was at the back of that extensive hostelry, and asked for bread and cheese and a glass of ale, how heartily he ate it in comparison with Mr. Selwyn's juicy steak and chocolate in the morning, which had nearly choked him! It is on this account that I ventured to write, in the opening of this chapter, that, had the company on the quality side of the house known who was then at the other, there would have been a joyful meeting indeed, and everything would have been forgiven, if not forgotten. Ralph, as he lingered over his lunch in a quiet parlour off the taproom, heard various chambermaids who came to the bar declare, that the great London doctor had said there was no danger; that *their* Dr. Burgess had done quite right—bless him! that there was no need for *him* to stay, and he was going back to town as soon as they'd had some dinner. Moreover, that the dear, sweet, lovely young lady—who was all over her father's blood when she came in, and sludge and dirt—was dressed up and looking "so bee-yue-ty-ful as never was," and had been seen "a laughin' with her aunt," as Mistress Grover was supposed to be, perhaps because Constance had addressed her as auntie. When, therefore, Ralph heard all this, he felt, as it were, new life and new resolution. If his uncle had been dying, he would have entreated to be admitted—he would have given himself up there and then. If he had been dead—and he shuddered at the bare thought of such a catastrophe—he would have gone to the nearest magistrate and confessed himself guilty. But now he was free—free once more to go away, to be never again seen by any one till he could establish himself as a member of the Darnell family in his proper place.

He would not, he could not, meet them now; his pride had risen again as his passion had calmed down, and overcame him. He thought of the indignity of appearing in the light of a bastard before Constance and Mistress Grover, and of the almost certainty that with his freedom from danger the baronet's aversion to him remained. The assurance, too, that Mr. Elliot's suit was accepted and acceptable, returned on him in full force. What had he to do there—what was he to them? They had not even bid him good-bye! And so, with the fear of danger removed from Mr. Ralph's heart, I find that pride went in and dwelt there; and all the kind thoughts of his old uncle above stairs—of his dear cousin, who would most likely have thrown herself on his neck, and cried out all her wilfulness there—and of his almost mother, Bessie Grover, were in vain. Ralph had heard more good news than he had ever hoped to hear; and when his horse was fit to travel, and the landlady of the Bull gave him a comfortable dinner, and he had sent the ostler again, who returned with the same good accounts—he paid his reckoning, and rode quietly back to town.

Mr. Selwyn was glad to see Ralph after his journey—glad to see him in good spirits—glad, and indeed inexpressibly relieved, to hear that the baronet's wound was not dangerous; and so also we may believe was Mr. Forster, whose anticipations of the result of his pistol-shot had been very much the contrary. The prospect of having a search made for them on a charge of murder by an energetic man like Roger Darnell, was extremely disagreeable, to say the least of it, to these gentlemen; and the day had been passed in contrivances for escape, or at least for a temporary seclusion from active life. Such seclusion was part of the professional tactics of Mr. Selwyn, and he was seldom at a loss to effect them; but this time, it promised to be more complete and lasting than usual, and the relief from any such urgent necessity was most acceptable. They warned Ralph, however, of the need of some caution; and when he unfolded his plans of going to the north by a collier, and of not returning to London at all, they were cordially approved of.

When, therefore, Mr. Wilson arrived (he was in the habit of looking in now and then) at Bury Court, he informed Ralph and his friends that he had persuaded the landlord of the Cock to take Mr. Darnell in for a few days, and a quiet room had been provided for him. Mr. Wilson said indeed quite cheerfully, that old Dickiwig had confided to him that he felt "quite like a father for the young man, and that no bailiff in London would ever think of looking for him at the Cock;" and so it seemed that the worthy old waiter and the landlord, Mr. Wilkins, had been led to believe that Ralph's troubles were of a pecuniary nature which, from sundry experiences, was likely to be the case. Whereupon Mr. Wilkins had also declared "he might live there free, and welcome, as long as he had need; he had seen plenty of Mr. Darnell's money, and knew the colour of it."

To prevent any chance of being recognised, therefore, Mr. Wilson proposed going there in a hackney-coach; and as soon as it was come, he was kind enough to accompany Ralph in his drive, and to see him safely put up in a very comfortable bed-chamber, to which he was taken by the private door of the house, and carefully attended to, not only by Dickiwig himself, but by Mistress Sarah Baker, who, though much concerned at Ralph's position, bid him be of good cheer, "as she know'd of a many young gentlemen who'd been in trouble for a time, and had come all right at last."

We may presume, therefore, that Mr. Ralph was altogether better off than he had expected to be; and that though he cast many a wistful look to the old house across the river, and could even see Sybil sitting at the open window as the evening closed in, yet he did not attempt to go there. He was indeed very weary: body and mind had been kept on a stretch of excitement and exertion for the past two days, to which he was an utter stranger; and when, after a delicious supper of sweetbreads done by Mistress Sarah Baker with her own skilful hands, and served by the old waiter, he went to bed—Ralph slept most soundly.

It was not so comfortable a day, perhaps, with Mr. Roger Darnell. In the first place, his wife, when he went up-stairs to dress, heard with an undisguisable look of vexation and dismay that Sir Geoffrey Darnell was in no danger, and would be quite recovered in a few days. Since the arrival of the news of the attack upon the baronet, and the kindly commercial traveller's fears that, from all he could hear, he for one did not believe in a chance of Sir Geoffrey's life, Mrs. Darnell had been in a fever of excitement. She could do nothing in the house; she had gone round to several of her acquaintances in her coach; and one and all, more particularly perhaps my Lady Warrington, had congratulated her upon being speedily—and very speedily—Lady Darnell. We need not trouble ourselves about the details of those visits. *De mortuis*, etc., is an old adage, but it was not followed in this instance. To be sure, Sir Geoffrey was not dead yet; and though the old proverb applies to the dead, I cannot remember one of similar import to the living. If, therefore, Mrs. Darnell transgressed in one way, she was safe as to the other; and it is on this account that I forbear to record her own opinions and those of her *dearest* friends, "as to what an im-mense relief Sir Geoffrey's death would be to all concerned. He was a brute; he swore profane oaths; he was a rank Jacobin, and taught his daughter, who was going to marry one of the greatest rakes and profligates in London, to be as bad as himself—a little pert, stuck-up minx, who would come to no good. Not like darling Anne, who, *my dear*, was quite shocked by her cousin's levity, who took Dorothy to the play, and *quite* corrupted her morals."

I should not advance this history one step if I recorded a whole chapter of these visits; and my readers, who are entirely in my confidence, know very well already Mrs. Darnell's opinion of the baronet, and the baronet's of her, and that there was not *much* love lost between them. It will be the easier, therefore, for them to comprehend why Mrs. Darnell felt the pangs of disappointment come thickly upon her, as Mr. Darnell, with his face covered with lather, cried from his dressing-room—

"Oh, he's much better, Anne, thank God! and Burgess, the doctor there, says he'll soon be on his legs again. As to——, he told me, as we came home, that he needn't have gone up at all."

I am afraid, though Mrs. Darnell was in the habit of thanking God frequently, especially for her own state of "grace," that she did not join in her husband's thanksgiving; and indeed Mr. Darnell, when he had dressed himself, went down humbly on his knees before his Maker, and strove to say all he felt, and— But I have no business to follow him in these sacred moments. I may however mention, that when he had told his wife what I have written, he heard several sobs, and lovingly shut the door. He did not wish to be a spy upon a weak woman's infirmity; but he guessed the reason of it perfectly; and when Dorothy hung about him after breakfast, and he told her and the younger children of what he had seen at Barnet (Anne had gone away with her mother), the whole of them had a good cry over the relation, and were thankful, the darlings, that dear cousin Conny had not been harmed.

Mr. Darnell was restless in his office that day. He had sent for Captain Abel Scrafton, who was to sail to-morrow, and told him he might have a particular service for him to do before he left, and he was at any rate to bring up a large cutter, with a strong crew, to the Tower Stairs. He should like, perhaps, just to see the good ship before she sailed—she was then lying off Greenwich—and bid good-bye to the people, and wish them a pleasant voyage; to which order the gallant captain promised strict obedience. He had owned his rise in the world entirely to Mr. Darnell; and as he said, sailor fashion, "would go to the devil for him any day if he needed."

Then Mr. Darnell went down in the afternoon to the waterside, and took a boat to Tooley Stairs, and sat a good while with Mrs. Morton. Sybil was gone out with Nanny on a message, as the old lady said, which was no less than taking some embroidery to the tailor's, and getting paid for it. They talked of Ralph, of course; and the widow was comforted by being assured that the allowance for him would not cease during his temporary absence. Mrs. Morton guessed he had gone to the North with the baronet; and with, I must acknowledge, a very shameless hypocrisy, Mr. Darnell pretended to agree with her. When would Mr. Ralph's clothes be wanted? Nanny and Sybil had packed them all up, and the trunks were corded. Well—Mr. Darnell didn't know; perhaps to-morrow. They were to be delivered to his special order; and then he took his leave.

Thence (how idle and curious he was, to be sure, that day) he told the waterman, who knew him perfectly, to row down to the colliers. His nephew had, he thought, taken his passage on board a brig to sail soon. Now, as it happened, this very man, Frank Joliffe, was a great ally of Ralph's, and had taken him to the collier, where, as we know, he went with his valise; and as the wherry shot down the stream, the man pulled to the gangway of the *Mary* of Shields, on the shrouds of which was a board, with a chalk writing, that all "pasengers is to be on bord at seven o'clock to-morrow afternoon." Mr. Darnell went on board, looked at the berth and the valise, and took it away, as more things had to be put into it, and he would tell his nephew to be in time to-morrow. He even partook of a glass of rum and a biscuit, which the skipper offered him, refusing wine. Perhaps Mr. Darnell required a little stimulus for what he had farther to do.

When this was over, Mr. Darnell was rowed up to the Temple Stairs, where he left the valise in the boat, and ordered the waterman to wait. He then went into the Temple Gardens, and sat down on a bench there, looking at the stirring scene before him, and trying to shut out the thought of what was, in any case, a very disagreeable duty. I think he was hesitating whether he should prosecute or not; whether he should run down, as he could run down, the clever gang who had done this deed; but, indeed, it does not very much signify, for a man like Roger Darnell does not act so much upon previous plans, as upon conviction of necessity.

Mr. Darnell had arranged his visit to the gardens, so as to be in advance of the hour fixed by his anonymous correspondent; but the time passed very slowly. He walked down to the stairs again, and Joliffe touched his hat. "Not yet," he said; "I expect a friend, and am waiting for him." Then he came back, sat down, got up and walked about. Yes, Roger Darnell was more anxious than ever, more fidgety perhaps. The clocks chimed the half-hour, but still there was no one he could see likely to be the person who sought him. A nursery-maid with some children taking an evening walk, some quiet people reading on the benches—the usual saunterers, in fact, of the locality; and an old man who might be a Jew, who wore a long tunic, had a white beard, and limped, with a square-headed ebony stick to support him. This person, after several turns on the terrace, came and sat down on the bench, and, taking out a book, began to read, very unconcernedly. But Mr. Darnell had not long to wait. "I think," said the man in a strong Jewish accent, "dat I 'as de pleashure to shpeak wid Mr. Darnell?"

"I am Mr. Darnell—Roger Darnell, at your service," said the merchant decidedly.

"Glad to 'ear it, sir, wery glad, becaush I is friend, yes, goot friend, to Roger Darnell & Company. You are de mosh honourable man in London city, and a've troosted you to come here."

"What the devil have you to say to me? be brief," said Mr. Darnell, quickly. "Do you know what you risk in speaking to me at all?"

"I kno's, I kno's, very vell," was the reply—"I kno's vho did *dat* biznis. The old Jew kno's many a ting like *dat*, an' no fear for nobody. If you give me de monish, de faive hoondert pound, Mr. Darnell, I tell you troot, an' no more."

"I have the money here," said Mr. Darnell, showing his pocket-book; "but what security have I that you will tell me everything?"

"Holy Mosesh!" cried the man, tink of dat! I poor, lame, old Jew, here alone vit you, Mr. Darnell. I am best securitiss mysel—I cannot rone away, sir! You can call de porters, sir, and de vachmen. Oh, Mr. Darnell, you do not see dat! Ha, ha, ha!"

The absurdity of the lame old Jew being able to escape from him, seemed to assure Mr. Darnell.

"Good," he said; "take the money," and he counted the money upon the seat. "No fear," he added, "of them passing, with Roger Darnell & Company on the back."

"Dhey's quite good, sir, and mosh obleege," said the man, folding them up, and putting them into a greasy pocket-book. "And now, sir, to proove I'm honest Jew, here's four bills for fifty each, vhich vas in your brother's book; they's no use to my people, so they've sent them back."

"'Pon my soul, a very honest business! You steal two hundred and get five; I wish I could do such profitable trade, Abraham," cried Mr. Darnell, who began to think he had only one of the common receivers of stolen goods to deal with. "But stay; what of your promise to tell who did this?"

"If Roger Darnell vill give his vord of honour to me, Reuben Levi—his vord of honour, as Darnell, an' gentilman, and vill promise to do no prosecute, I vill tell him everyting—who did it, and who didn't."

Perhaps Mr. Darnell blushed as he gave it—the honour of a Darnell on such a bargain! but there was a craving at his heart to know the truth about Ralph, a truth which alone could determine their future positions. He gave his hand therefore, though he shrank almost at the cold clammy touch that met it.

"I tink Mr. Darnell kno's wery vell," said the man, with a sly wink, "but I vill tell the troot. Mr. Ralph Darnell had it done, but he did not do it himself;" and the man gave a succinct relation of all that had happened.

"Damnation!" cried Mr. Darnell, "this is worse and worse. Was he a coward?"

"No, no! no coward, sir. He vould have gone and taken de will from his oncle, you kno's; but dey did not let him, sir, as I tell you. Mr. Ralph—they not trust, sir."

"Who?"

"Oh, I need not maind tell you, sir; on honour, you know. Vy, dat Dicky Smeet, an'—an'—an' their men, you know, sir. They didn't let him do nothin', sir—only do themselves and sends you two hundert pound, sir, vit compliments too, and von't do so no more!"

"Then they know you make this communication, you rascal!" cried Mr. Darnell.

"Quiet, Mr. Darnell—quiet, sir. On honour, sir, you remember? Ha, ha! No, sir, they don't kno' at all. They only give old Reuben these bills to sell, an' he can't sell 'em except to Roger Darnell & Company, coot merchants, sir," he continued, getting up, and limping off. "Coot merchants, and do wery coot business. They get true information—dat's tree hundert, and deir own bills two hundert, and dey give me five hundert; now I give two hundert to Dicky Smeet for bills, and keep tree hundert for commission. How mosh per shent, Mr. Darnell? How mosh per shent? Coot evenin', sir. I mosh respect Mr. Roger Darnell."

Mr. Darnell looked after the man savagely. If he had only not pledged his honour! But it was too late, and what remained to be done must be done. There could be no vacillation now—least of all with Roger Darnell.

CHAPTER XXVIII.

AND WHAT CAME OF IT.

It was not extraordinary that Ralph Darnell saw from his chamber window the figure of Sybil Morton sitting at the open casement across the river as the evening closed in. Of course he could distinguish no features; even the figure was indistinct at that distance; but there it was without doubt. If Ralph could have seen that dear face, he would have been shocked at the misery expressed in it, and perhaps have understood more of what was lying at Sybil's heart than he had ever done before, even in the worst period of his wound. So long as Ralph was present, Sybil's love found vent in a thousand little unobtrusive services for him—in anticipating his wishes, in watching him, in speaking or in listening to him. He was there, her own glorious incarnation of manhood. A foolish, passionate, and sometimes not very well-behaved young gentleman, as we know him; but in Sybil's sight, brave, handsome, accomplished, and manly, with a quick, but sweet and generous disposition. Had he ever said an unkind word to her? Had he ever been impatient with her errands or messages or escorts, or their quiet studies, in which he learned latterly much faster than she? Ah no! And when in that terrible fever after the wound, and weakness almost to death, he had been peevish with old Nanny, and impatient with Mrs. Morton, who was ever too talkative and fussy—who to him was like Sybil? She felt that there was no one. She knew he would take neither food nor medicine from other hands, and night and day, with but short intervals, she was at her post by his bedside, working at her embroidery frame, reading to him when he was able to listen, or playing an occasional game of chess or piquet.

After his fashion, Ralph was very grateful for all this; and had his heart been free, only one result could have followed; but the reader knows already how Ralph was enamoured of his lovely cousin—how that dazzling beauty, which already had subdued the hearts of half the beaux of London, had so absorbed his that he had no thought for anything else. There is no need to repeat this, for it has already indeed combined with other affairs to lead to a serious catastrophe.

But since Ralph knew, and knew for certain, from Mistress Grover, that Constance never had, and never could have, anything but a sisterly love for him—his thoughts had turned a great deal more than before to Sybil Morton. He wanted sympathy, and he had found none except his dear old "auntie's," and that only partially. In her rough way old Nanny had, to be sure, told him "he'd better ha'e luiked afore he'd leep'd; and, puir dear laddie, he'd had a sair faa'." And he had also been petted after her fashion, and told that the "onely body beside hersel' that pitied him or cared for him, was darlin' Miss Sybil, bless her! and she'd been greetin' sair about the quarel wi' the barrinit. Ay," she said, "an' Mrs. Morton didna wonder that the barrinit had been angert, for she know'd mair than she'd like to tell; an' it was jist like the mad boy, first comin' hame tipsy, then gettin' wownded, and noo quarrellin' wi' his kind uncle." But this homely talk did not satisfy him; Ralph Darnell did not expect sympathy from Mrs. Morton, and looking all round his very narrow world of acquaintance, he saw none to be had from any one except those two, Bessie Grover and his dear Sybil, and most from Sybil.

To go to Bessie was impossible—to write to her equally so for the present. There was a great deal of stern duty to be done, of diligent search to be made, before he could approach her or his uncle Geoffrey with any hope of success. When one's heart is sore with grief or misfortune that has passed over, sympathy is perhaps most longed for and most needed. If danger or misery be impending, there is no room in the mind for sympathy; there is impatience of it; the mind is knit to bear whatever trial is to come; and that resolution does not brook disturbance. When there is reaction, however, the case is very different. We then cling to whatever is offered, and are calmed and soothed by it. This operation was not, however, altogether of a healthy character in Ralph Darnell's mind; and as he lay awake next morning early, with the bright summer sun streaming through the chinks in his shutters, watching idly the streams of motes which whirled, tossed, sparkled, and glistened in fantastic play, his thoughts went back over the last few months, and reviewed its incidents; and as is the case with most of us perhaps, he saw among them much of his own doing that he did not approve of, and could not justify. It was a dreamy state perhaps—the consciousness of rest after physical weariness, combined with active mental employment, leading only to unpleasant results. If he had but a friend, one friend near him to whom he could tell everything, and hear a few soothing words in reply—one friend!

There was indeed one near, very near to him, had he known then where to turn; but I am compelled to record that, in all his troubles, Ralph had never yet thought of Him save in a very casual way.

While he was ill of his wound, the family prayers, when he could hear them, had been read at his bedside; and perhaps he had heard Mrs. Morton's dreary, monotonous whining perusal of them, as well as some of Sybil's "chapters," with impatience. He had grown to dread Sundays, which denied him even a game of chess or backgammon or piquet with Sybil; and after his recovery, and thanks were offered in the parish church by Mrs. Morton's desire, I regret to state that he heard them with a kind of thankfulness that it was "all over at last." But if his heart was hard, or, more correctly perhaps, indifferent, in this respect, it was soft enough in others. It was as sensible of very much foolishness enacted, as it had been on other occasions already related in this history, and needed sympathy. Yes, he would go to Sybil; she at least would understand him. He must see them all again before he left that night, and the sooner he went the better.

It was difficult, however, for Ralph to escape the strict, though kindly meant espionage, that had been set over him. Mr. Wilkins had ordered him to keep in-doors. He would not have him "arrested" there on any consideration, and Ralph had yielded to Mr. Wilson's suggestion of maintaining an innocent deception. His egress was therefore opposed; and it was only by the application of a smart *douceur* to Dickiwig, who protested he thought a little fresh air would do the young man good, that he was allowed to hail a boat and row across to the old house. As the boat approached the stairs, he saw Sybil at her accustomed place. He had watched her as he neared his destination, and had seen her looking over the river vacantly, then bending down to her work, then raising her head again, and again looking out. His old signal was a wave of his hat; and when he was near enough to be seen, he gave it, and saw the girl start up, put her hand suddenly to her side as if a sharp pain had struck her, and then sit down again. Was she ill? Poor Sybil! Mrs. Morton was not there. Was she ill? He was not long in suspense: and Nanny's cheery welcome rang in his ears for many a day afterwards.

"Eh, laddie, but ye're welcome back. Whar ha'e ye gane thae days, an' ne'er sed a word to nane o' us? Eh, but puir Miss Sybil yon's been greetin' her eyes oot, jest haven't she? and speirin' at a' the wherries in the river, ye ken, an' nowt I could sey till her wad she mind. Ye maun ha'e ane o' yer auld cracks wi' her, an' comfort her, and set her richt agen, puir lassie! Eh, Mr. Rraafe, when you're gane, she's no hersel' at aalle."

Nanny had poured out her heart, or what was lying closest at it, as Ralph entered the door.

"And Mrs. Morton, Nanny?" he asked.

"Well, Mr. Rraafe, she's no that weel that aa'd be glad to tell ye of. She's weak, surr, the day, an' she's no up—dozin' maybe, for she didna sleep weel a' the nicht, an' she's had some brroth. They're vara gude, Mr. Rraafe; wadna ye like a sup o' some yersel'? Aa'll bring them up presently, an' ye'll like yer bit crack wi' Miss Sybil furrst."

Ralph went up the old stairs. I think he hesitated as he knocked gently at the door, and heard the low musical "Come in" from Sybil. Ralph noticed she did not open it herself, as she had used to do once, and drag him in, with a pleasant chiding if he were late. Ah me! was she changing too? Not so to him; but the figure at the window, which looked taller and more womanly than he had ever thought it before, seemed to hesitate, to totter a little, and, as he stepped forward briskly and held out his arms, to fall very helplessly into them, then recovering, to withdraw itself suddenly and hang back, while the pale face and neck flushed with a bright colour, which faded instantly.

"You are ill, dear Sybil," said Ralph, kindly, very kindly, for he could not mistake the happiness, the relief, he saw expressed in Sybil's face; "you have been ill?"

"I am quite well again," she said—"quite well; only your sudden departure and absence made us all very anxious, and I watched for you, Ralph, oh so wearily! My mother, too, is weak; and this, with you away, made me very very foolish and miserable, I believe. But now I am quite well, Ralph—am I not?"

That dear face! how beautiful it was as it looked up, with tears glistening on the cheeks, hastily wiped off, and lingering in the eyes, through which a bright gleam of joy was beaming! No need to answer Sybil's question; her glowing face was the reply—glowing as she looked into the great earnest eyes that met hers, and—was she wrong?—answered them. I do not think Ralph Darnell had ever thought of her beauty before, though he was proud of her; but he felt prouder than ever now, and "his own dear Sybil was so glad to see him."

"Yes," he repeated, "you are my own dear Sybil, and I tell you everything. What a fool I've been, and how badly they've used me! I've no one now, Sybil, dear," he continued, with a tremulous, faltering voice, "to tell it all to, but you; and I don't care if you—if you—scold, only don't hate me for being—for being— Oh, don't be ashamed of me, Sybil, as everybody is, else I shall leave you too with them all, and run away. I'd better be dead, Sybbie—better be dead. No one would miss me but you."

Ralph was sobbing now, and holding out his hands to her. All that reaction which had been going on since his first relief at Barnet, had come to a crisis. Perhaps he mistook Sybil when she turned away her head and was not able to look at the young man's flushed quivering features, and the hot tears streaming out of his eyes.

"Yes, every one's ashamed of me, Sybil," he continued, as she did not speak. "I'm—I'm—I'm—only a poor devil of a—a—bastard," he cried, with a great gulp. "I haven't a right to speak even to you—even to you. Oh my darling—O Sybbie, Sybbie, don't hate me! It's—not—it's not my fault, indeed—indeed it is not;" and he threw himself on his knees at her side, buried his face in her dress, and cried piteously, and as if his heart would break, "It's not my fault—it's not my fault."

No sympathy? If tears falling as fast as his own were proof of it; if her hand, now resting on his strong curly hair, now roving absently among it with loving touch; if the gentle cries of "No, no, Ralph, I'll never leave you—never, never, till I die. Don't fret; they will be kind—even your dear cousin—by-and-by,"—he need have been well assured.

I think perhaps it was this allusion to Constance that roused him, for he looked up with a scared, changed face. "Why did you mention *her*, Sybbie?" he said—it was his pet name for her. "Don't you know—"

"I know all," she replied, hastily; "she told me herself, when I went to see her in Soho Square before they left—she was your own dear dear sister; and she took me up to her room, and we talked about our old days, and she said you were to keep all she had given you, even the last ring as well, and she'd soon have you up to Melcepeth—and I do love her so, Ralph!"

I say I think this roused and relieved him; because, after Sybil had done speaking, he got up, sat down on the sofa by her, put his arm round her after his old loving brotherly fashion, with a great sigh, and told her what had happened at the office about the will, and what he intended to do; first, to go to the north, and then to act as circumstances might require. Thank God, he was at least indepeudent, and, once of age, was his own master!

All this required a long time, how long he cared and knew not. It was perfect confidence, not love, between them, and that knew no restraint. Ralph only concealed from her the attack on his uncle; he dare not tell that; and Sybil believed the baronet was far on his way to Melcepeth. How she cautioned him to be careful in future to cease persecuting Constance, who thought it hard he should do so; and how many promises were made by him of speedy return, and at least of communication with her—need not be told.

Even Nanny was satisfied, and said he might go, and ought to go, "for his ain sake, and his mither's sake," and Ralph took the "het brose" she had brought, and found *them* as good as ever. No, he would not stay longer. He was afraid to meet his uncle, who might come unawares. They had told him of Mr. Darnell's visit the day before, and he must leave by the collier that afternoon. He had slept at the Cock, and should wait there. Mrs. Morton he only saw for a few minutes; she was weak and peevish that day, and could not be brought to understand why it was necessary he should go at all. He might do as he chose, it was no use her speaking to him.

It was hard for Sybil to let him go, hard for Ralph to leave her—very hard; but the confidence between them had given both courage and comfort. Sybil could see nothing dark in the future, and Ralph at least felt he had the will to do and suffer; that boyhood, and perhaps dependence, were gone, and life with independent action, was about to begin.

"One kiss," he said, "Sybil—one only; nay, the last, for how long, perhaps?"

Ay, for how long? She yielded shyly to him, but very confidently. She kissed him as she would have kissed a brother; but she had to put down rebellious thoughts before she did so. On her fair brow, on her eyes, on her lips, she felt him kiss her tenderly and lovingly.

"May God keep you, my darling!" he said; "the only true friend I have on earth will not forget me."

And so they parted, and she watched Joliffe row him across the river; and the man came back and said he had sent his dear love to them all.

For the rest of the day Ralph kept quiet. He was well cared for, we have eaten in strange places, with strange relish, all our lives. I have myself a vivid recollection of a certain roasted fowl, eaten on the bank of the broad Godavery river, opposite to Nandair, and of a breakfast of fried pancakes and eggs at Ghenneh, on the Nile, cooked by an itinerant breakfast monger, a stout Egyptian woman clad in a blue shift, with a pleasant tattooed face, who fed my child with dainty bits with her own greasy fingers. So Ralph Darnell remembered his dinner of soles and veal cutlets—which Dickiwig told him Mistress Baker had cooked with her own hands—and about half-past six, he had paid his reckoning, which Mr. Wilkins was very loath to accept; had a pleasant flirtation with the smart young ladies in the bar, had interchanged a good deal of good-humoured "chaff," as it would now be called, with Mistress Sarah Baker in the kitchen, chucked the pretty chambermaid under the chin, and said he'd bring a sweetheart for her, only she'd got so many already that he'd be in the way—in short, feeling pleasant, Ralph had comported himself in as pleasant and affable a manner as could be, and so came out from the wooden terrace to call a boat to take him to the *Mary* of Shields, which lay ready to sail with the turn of the tide, while the soft summer wind was blowing down the river, ready to fill her topsails when they should be sheeted home.

As Ralph stepped out of a side door, he saw Captain Abel Scrafton of the *Valiant* standing near the bay window; and his handsome boat, with its eight oars, ready to fall, rocking at the stairs. Mr. Ralph saluted the captain in the same pleasant style he had bidden good-bye within. "When was he going to sail? This evening? Indeed! Well, he would have, he hoped, a safe and pleasant voyage."

The gallant captain returned Mr. Ralph's good wishes. "He had just come to clear off scores," he said, "and was going now to the ship direct. Would Mr. Darnell like a row down this fine evening? Mr. Roger Darnell had been over the ship that day, and he had just landed him at the Tower Stairs; and a noble gentleman, indeed, he was. Should they not drink his health? No? Well, then, when they returned from the voyage they would have a jolly carouse once more at the old place;" and so chatting pleasantly, they descended the stairs together. Ralph had hailed a wherry, and it drew up within an oar's length of the *Valiant's* boat.

"You can step across my cutter," said Captain Scrafton, politely. "Come, sir, and we'll get out of your way."

Ralph did not hesitate. He followed the captain, who stood in the stern-sheets to shake hands with him as he passed; and, as he grasped the hand held out to him, felt himself tripped up, heard the captain's sharp cry of "Oars!" and in an instant was held down, and a strong tarpaulin fastened over him. "Give way, men, for your lives!" called out Captain Scrafton; and before Ralph could recover from his amazement, the cutter had dashed into the stream, and was sped past boats, and ships, and city, with a swiftness which only the *Valiant's* picked boat's crew could have accomplished.

Ralph struggled hard, and tried to cry out, but it was of no avail —Captain Scrafton was inexorable; and a rough noisy chorus, sung heartily by the men, effectually prevented any of his cries being heard. When they reached the ship, a chair was lowered, into which Ralph, despite his resistance, was easily fastened, with a ship's flag and a boat-cloak tied over him. A shrill whistle, and the chair was hoisted over the ship's side; whence the captain and several others took it up, carried it into a cabin on the poop, locked the door, and Ralph was left to unfasten himself as best he could. When he had done so, he heard the jolly chorus which accompanied the heaving of the anchor, the orders of Captain Scrafton to "sheet home the top-sails," and the ripple of the waves against the gallant ship, as she bounded onwards under all sail towards the sea. Nor for many hours, nor until he was weary with fruitless endeavours to force the door, or the port in the cabin, did Captain Scrafton visit him, and then they were far out at sea, and the good ship *Valiant* was rolling deeply in the Channel waves.

CHAPTER XXIX.

OUTWARD BOUND.

MY readers will most probably have accounted for this event already. Mr. Darnell had no doubt whatever of the mysterious communication made to him in the Temple, for which, indeed, by Ralph's absence and other concurring testimony, he had been prepared. Ralph had not been at the office, nor at Mrs. Morton's; and why should he be at the Cock except for concealment? That he was there, Mr. Darnell had confirmed by Jenkins, the porter in his office, who had been sent to find out. One of the chambermaids there was a sweetheart of Mr. Jenkins's, and confided to him that "them bailiffs was a'ter Mister Ralph, and missis 'ad 'id 'im away quiet, for a day or two." No doubt Mary thought the secret quite safe with Mr. Jenkins, who only told it to Mr. Darnell, as he entered the office punctually at his usual hour of ten o'clock.

That was to be a busy day with the merchant. When Captain Scrafton made his appearance in Lombard Street at noon exactly, as he had been desired to do, and was sent into the parlour for instructions, Mr. Darnell at once opened his purpose to the commander, who, without scruple, entered cordially into his patron's views; nor was he squeamish on the project, or at all in dread of the law. I do not believe it possible for any one to make such a proposal to any captain in these days; and I look upon abductions of young gentlemen or young ladies in smuggling luggers, in yachts, or steam vessels, as stated sometimes in modern romances, to be sheer impossibilities; and therefore, that the kingdom of romance has lost one of its very valuable adjuncts of action in this respect. But in the days I write of, the sudden transmission of an obnoxious relative to his Majesty's plantations in Virginia, or to a friend in Calcutta, Madras, or Bombay, was by no means uncommon; attracted no particular attention if known; and indeed, in most cases, was considered a meritorious action; giving a young scapegrace nephew or cousin, or "*filius nullius*," a chance in life, which could not be had in England.

Mr. Darnell's project, which was a very simple one, was readily understood and carried out. Captain Abel Scrafton perfectly agreed with him that Ralph could not remain in England after what had happened. "Not i'faith, that I think him so much to blame; but I had rather he had gone up to his uncle and demanded those papers, even if he'd had to stand a shot for it," said Mr. Darnell; "but as it is, he can't remain here. Bless my heart! what would be said 'on 'Change' if it were ever known?"

So the matter was all settled in a few minutes; and as they passed out of the office, Mr. Darnell said to Mr. Sanders, in a sadly hypocritical manner, I fear, that he was just going to see all right on board, and if Ralph came in, that he was to wait, as there was something particular for him to do; and Mr. Sanders, and some others, wished Captain Scrafton a pleasant voyage, and he and Mr. Darnell went out towards the captain's boat at the Tower Stairs. Mr. Darnell knew of Ralph's clothes at Mrs. Morton's; but these would not last the voyage, and Captain Scrafton knew exactly where to get others. Close to the Minories was his own provider of such necessaries; and in a marvellous short space of time, two large chests were packed, directed, and despatched to the *Valiant* by a two-oared wherry. Free of this necessary work, Mr. Darnell went to Mrs. Morton's, and Ralph's trunks there were carried off by two of the *Valiant's* men. The simple women had no suspicion, and Mr. Darnell said no more than the truth, when he said they would be sent at once on board ship. Sybil asked timidly, when Ralph would return; and Mr. Darnell replied, he "could not tell her; it might be a good while—it depended on so many things," &c.

Ralph had not left the house half-an-hour, indeed, when this happened; and if he had been looking out sharply, he might perhaps have seen the *Valiant's* boat dash in among the wherries at Tooley Stairs; but if he had, I think he would only have hidden himself the closer. The last thing Mr. Darnell did before he bade the captain good-bye and a safe voyage, was to deliver to him a packet of letters, tied up as a parcel, and addressed to Mr. Ralph Darnell, per *Valiant;* and as he did so, he could hardly tell him, in a choking voice, to take care of the lad, for he was the only Darnell left, and that he was as fond of him as if he were his own son. "But after *that*, Captain Scrafton—*after that*, I could not have kept him here even were he my own son. By-and-by it may be different; but at present, he is safest and best out of the way;" and the captain thought so too.

It was this packet of papers which Captain Scrafton took to Ralph when he heard all quiet in the cabin. Landsmen who go to sea immediately upon a good dinner, such as Ralph had partaken of, very frequently find it disagree with them: and our hero was no exception in this respect. As the *Valiant* got further out of the river, she began to display the lively character of her nature; and, under a heavy press of sail, was, to the captain's great delight, passing ship after ship, "overhauling them," as he remarked to his chief mate, to whom he was telling, in confidence, what had happened. Perhaps the worthy captain was enjoying too deeply the pleasant rolling of his gallant ship, and the setting of stunsel after stunsel in that glorious summer night, to attend to his passenger; but it was time he should do so, and, saying he would go and have "a jaw with him before he turned in," Captain Scrafton went to the cabin, which he unlocked, and entered with a hearty greeting and question to Ralph, of "how he was getting on?"

Perhaps, if Ralph had been at that moment possessed of his usual vigour and strength, he might, as he had sworn he would, as long as he could stand, have fallen foul of the captain, and assaulted him; but Ralph was very miserable, very wretched indeed. He was in the agonies of sea-sickness, which were severe; and if Captain Scrafton had ordered him there and then to be thrown overboard as a nuisance to all concerned in him, I do not know that the poor fellow would have objected in the least, but on the contrary would have felt positively thankful.

The captain's cheery question was, therefore, only answered by a groan. Ralph could not lift his head from the berth where he had laid it, except to see the cabin turned upside down, Captain Scrafton swaying about on his sea legs, and everything in a state of distortion, which aggravated his malady. The captain was a kind host, however; the steward was summoned, and a boy introduced, who was ordered to see after Ralph, and to stay in the cabin. By all these combined, too, he was undressed, and made as comfortable as could be; and the captain, having administered a glass of "stiff hot grog," left the sufferer, telling him "he hoped he'd be all right presently. There was a jumble of a sea, to be sure, but the ship would be easier next morning, when they would be on the long waves of the ocean; and whenever he could, he'd better open his uncle's packet, and read what was written there. As for himself, he'd only obeyed orders; and after all, they'd have a pleasant voyage, depend upon it."

So Ralph lay there, not daring to lift his head or to speak a word, but grasping the packet of letters. His thoughts were not very clear certainly; but it was evident his uncle knew what he had done, or this step would not have been taken. The extreme wretchedness brought on by his malady, combined with his mental condition, was not enviable; and if he wept a good deal that night, it was no more than what might be expected. It is probable, indeed, that he sobbed himself to sleep; for, when he awoke at a late hour the next day, he was considerably better and calmer; and could speak to Captain Scrafton, who came constantly to see "how he was getting on," and who informed him, with great satisfaction, "that the ship had beaten everything, and had a glorious breeze on her quarter. Would he like to get up? Perhaps he had better not till to-morrow. He must take something to eat, however; and it would be as well, as soon as he could, to look at the papers, which would be a relief to his mind."

It hardly needed the captain's opinion to induce Ralph to do so. As he opened the packet, he found several letters to Mr. Wharton; one to Mr. Drake, the chief of the Calcutta Factory; one to Mr. J. Z. Holwell; one to Robert Clive, Esq., colonel, etc., "to be delivered in case of necessity;" and one to himself. This he opened without further delay, and it ran as follows :—

"LONDON, *the 17th August* 1755.

"NEPHEW RALPH,—If your own heart does not tell you why you are now on the way to Calcutta, it would be little need in my writing this. I know what you have done; but no one else does, and for the honour of our family, I shall keep your secret inviolate. When opportunity offers, I shall acquaint your uncle Geoffrey with the step I have taken; and whether he approves of it or not, will be a matter of perfect indifference to me. I have acted solely upon my own judgment, as the uncle to whom you are confided; and I consider that I have in this measure set you forward in life in a position in which you may rise to honour, and return to England with wealth. If you will look upon my act in this light, you will agree with me, and respect my motives. I have, indeed, had your going to the East Indies for a long time in my thoughts, and but for the uncertainty in which you have lived, should have put my design in execution: but I wished you to gain experience in my office, and to understand what you will have eventually to do there. Large interests will be entrusted to you; and I am quite assured that the honour and integrity of a Darnell will be proved in your conduct. I do not consider, however, that your bearing your family name would be safe or expedient; and I have introduced you to Mr. Wharton, and other gentlemen, as Mr. Smithson, a young man in whom I have an interest; and you will please to adopt this name—your mother's—on your arrival in India.

"During your minority, a considerable sum has accumulated in my hands, of which, as you will be of age on the 25th of September proximo, you are entitled to the use. Enclosed is the account-current; and you will observe that the total to your credit is now £5286, 13s. 4d. This I advise you to employ in the Company's investments; and your interests here will be carefully attended to by myself and Mr. Sanders. I do not doubt you, nephew Ralph; but when I say that your bills on me for only two thousand pounds sterling will be honoured, you will understand that I wish to put you to the proof, rather than that I mistrust you, and I expect you will employ your funds carefully.

"Your interest in your father's property amounts to about four hundred pounds per annum, which will suffice for a respectable maintenance in Calcutta. In the letter which I forward by you, Mr. Wharton hath directions to pay you one hundred pounds on your arrival; and to arrange with you such monthly or quarterly payments as you may need there.

"You will find all your clothes on board, and an outfit for the voyage provided. If you have no money with you, Captain Scrafton will supply you with what you may wish as far as twenty pounds. All expenses of your voyage will be defrayed from your own funds, except that of your passage-money, which I, as 'twas against your will, have paid myself. And now, nephew Ralph, I make no professions, as you know. I believe you to have courage and ability, and 'twas time you began life. I am not over sanguine either, for I know how weak you are; but I can see, under common care and honesty, a fine career open to you, and I wish you heartily success. I think you will remember that here, *as you are supposed to be*, you could have taken no position. There, even were it known, such a matter would not affect you. I shall write to you frequently, and you may believe your interests quite safe in my hands. Should the papers we all desire to see be discovered, your return home would be requisite, and no one would welcome you with more sincere joy than your uncle, ROGER DARNELL.

"*P.S.*—I have just heard that your uncle Geoffrey continues to improve. He hath no fever, and is pronounced out of danger, which it will be a comfort to you to know. I may also mention, that when I last saw him, he had desired to be forgiven by you in the matter of what passed at the office, and I trust that the feeling cannot fail to be mutual."

A new life! That life, which he understood daily from Mr. Sanders's descriptions and Mr. Wharton's letters, he was to become a part of. That life which Mr. Robert Clive, as he scanned him from head to foot in the office parlour, asked him to adopt; that which had begun so strangely, and so abruptly. Ralph could not doubt his uncle Roger. The letter was precise, but not upbraiding. His uncle knew the miserable error he had committed, and left the redemption of it to his own exertions in life, and his own honour. He had placed him in an independent position, and expected him to maintain it. I think if this letter had been other than it was, Ralph Darnell would have sunk in the turmoil in which he had become engulfed. As it was, he kissed it tenderly, put it to his heart, and vowed, even in his present weakness and prostration, to strike out manfully, and, as became a Darnell, to strive in life as became a gentleman. And when Captain Scrafton came next time into the cabin to ask Ralph "how he got on," the expression on the face he saw was not moody and morose, but bright, and full of hope.

And it was a pleasant voyage, and for those times a very speedy one. "We shall get in by Christmas Day, and have a jolly dinner in the old Factory hall," Captain Scrafton would say; and he was correct. They had rough and smooth weather by turns; but the captain was an able navigator, and on the 18th December, just four months after they saw the English coast disappear beneath the horizon, a few tall palm-trees, a low-lying shore fringed with jungle and mangroves, appeared above it, and from a strange craft a native pilot came on board, who spoke an almost unintelligible jabber of English combined with his own tongue, which Captain Scrafton appeared to understand perfectly. Then, aided by the tide, the good ship swept up the broad river, past towns, villages, temples, and mosques, rice-fields and jungles, till the masts of English ships, the walls of a low fort, and a confused mass of white houses beyond, at the head of a noble reach of the Hoogly, showed Ralph Darnell the end of his voyage. A new life indeed had opened upon him, with a hearty welcome from Mr. Wharton, and all who came to hear the last news from Home by the good ship *Valiant*. As the fort guns saluted her, she replied to them, the anchor dropped, and the vessel swung round to the tide which had brought her up.

I have had nothing to tell of incidents on the voyage. I do not indeed find there was anything particular to mention—nothing certainly that is worth record in this history; but in Ralph's own mind there arose gradully a change, and for the better in all respects. At first, despite the kind tone of his uncle's letter, he was often disposed to be rebellious, and to resent what had been done. He mourned after Sybil too, more perhaps than any previous intercourse with her seemed to warrant; and thoughts of the last scene with her, what he might have told her but refrained, were often too vivid to be denied. Images also of old scenes also at Melcepeth, and of his beautiful cousin, Constance, and her last message by Sybil, were not unfrequent; in short, there was a mingling of sweet and bitter memories which induced reflection, and tended in the main to healthy reaction despite his natural weakness and vacillation.

Perhaps it would serve no purpose were I to describe these, or quote passages from Ralph's diary. We have already record of some resolutions broken and of others maintained; but his experiences of life were limited as yet by a very narrow bound, and before that could be enlarged, his strife in the world's fight must begin and be carried on. It would be too much, therefore, to expect that one thus inexperienced should make any definite resolves in respect to a future so dim and so indefinite as that which awaited him, or that if he made any they should be worth recording.

END OF PART SECOND.

PART THIRD.

PART THIRD.

CHAPTER XXX.

RETROSPECT.

LET us go back a hundred years. In "Tara," where I recorded of 1657 those fierce struggles between the Hindus and the Mahomedans in the Dekhan, when Sivaji Rajah destroyed the army of Beejapoor at his fortress capital of Pertabghur, when Tara was led forth to burn by the beautiful river-bank at Waee, the Mahomedan empire was nearly at the zenith of its power; and except the Dekhan and south of India, all else of the vast continent owned its sway. After that, subverting in succession, and annihilating as independent kingdoms, Ahmednugger, Golconda, and Beejapoor in the Dekhan, the Mogul Emperor Aurungzeeb became supreme; and the imperial Mahomedan standard floated from west to east, from north to south, of India, unchallenged.

I am not writing history; and my readers will not care for instruction here which they can obtain better and in every completeness from those records of vivid romance—the histories of the period; but some connection with the past is, I have thought, necessary, and therefore I may hope to be forgiven if I briefly, very briefly, attempt to supply it. This short chapter will, therefore, have nothing to do with my tale, and may be passed over if my readers please; but there may be some of them, perhaps, who desire to remember how this interval from 1657 to 1757 was filled up; and who, bearing a few prominent details in their minds, will be able to understand the position of political parties in India at the period of Ralph Darnell's arrival in it, and the Nawab Suraj-oo-Doulah's accession to his father's power, better than without them.

It was a magnificent empire truly, that of the Mogul; but it was superficial. Looking into the core of it when at its brightest, we find a rottenness which was fast infecting the whole mass. The vast intellect, and extraordinary centralising administrative ability of Aurungzeeb, held the various portions together so long as his mind had power, and his body physical energy, for the vast task; but as these gradually failed, as he himself gradually descended into his quiet grave at Roza, and when the nine shillings (four and a half rupees) which he had earned by making caps had been expended upon his funeral, and the eighty pounds ten shillings (eight hundred and five rupees) he had also earned by writing copies of the Koran, had been given away in charity, men began to estimate how loosely the reins of the Imperial Government had been held—how speedily all those who had assisted to carry it on would strike out for themselves—and how easily they would attain their objects.

India had been parcelled out into vice-royalties; and when the sovereign who controlled them died, he left no one, with a pretence of power, to fill his place. His sons disputed the succession; and each striving for mastery, disappeared in the course of a few years, leaving a dismembered empire and independent princes, where there had been unity and able and zealous servants. There was still a nominal court at Delhi; but in 1756 only a few mean provinces around the capital remained to the Royal family, and the rest, Bengal, Oude, Central India, Goozerat, the Punjab, the Dekhan, and the Carnatic, had passed away to servants of the State, or to Mahrattas; and Nadir Shah, in 1739, while he dealt the death-blow to the Imperial Government, annexed all the provinces which lay west of the Indus to his own kingdom.

In 1657 the destruction of the army of Afzool Khan, as I recorded in "Tara," had laid the foundation of the Mahratta kingdom, which, even more than the treachery of dependents, was the deepest and most virulent canker at the heart of the Mahomedan empire. Gradually, in the Rajah Sivaji's reign, the predatory power evoked by him had attained a mighty consistence which could not be repelled, and yet was so intangible that it could not be grasped. If the Mahomedans were anywhere weak, Sivaji was defiant and insulting, and destroyed them; if they were strong, he crouched for his spring till they were off their guard; or by fomenting jealousies between the Mogul and the Mahomedan kingdoms of the Dekhan so long as the latter lasted, appeared now as the ally of one, now of the other—professing allegiance to all, but giving none to any.

He died; and there were men found among these rude Hindu landholders, farmers, shepherds, and mountaineers who, with their astute Brahmin advisers, were able to direct national councils and lead armies. With the English at Bombay they negotiated and traded; while the fierce Mahratta legions, vast hordes of horse and foot, poured forth over all India in numbers which it is now surprising to contemplate, and with a celerity, alacrity, and vigour, before which the already effete Mahomedans made but a feeble resistance, and in many localities altogether disappeared. Far away from their native Dekhan, into the Punjab, into the Carnatic, into Bengal and beyond Delhi, these armies went their annual rounds of devastation and plunder. The Mahomedans, distracted and divided, alike by situation as by local interest, saw province after province wrested from them, or burdens alike extortionate and exhaustive laid upon their independent principalities, and levied with a terrible exactitude; and their last humiliation by the Mahratta victory at Kurdlah in the Dekhan, over the Nizam, was only prevented from being converted into that universal Hindu sovereignity of India, which had been the object and aim of Sivaji Rajah, by the rise of a power which, no bigger than a man's hand, had risen out of the sea, and in the course of another century has subverted both, and overshadowed all. That power was our own, and it is with its first rise to political existence and territorial possession that I have now to do, as I had with that first struggle of the Mahrattas a hundred years before, which I tried to describe in "Tara."

The history of Bengal is no more than a chapter in the history of the dismemberment of the Mogul empire, or in the decay of all Mahomedan empires which have hitherto existed—of able generals or astute administrators, appointed as viceroys of provinces, taking advantage of weakness, assuming independence, and maintaining it hereditarily.

In the year 1702, the son of a poor Dekhan Brahmin, who had been forcibly converted to Mahomedanism, and had risen to distinction by his abilities, was sent to govern Bengal; and by a singular display of energy and talent, not only consolidated his position, but maintained it against all intrigues at the capital. We read how pertinaciously he opposed the settlement of Europeans in Bengal, especially the English; and, but for a fortuitous circumstance, would have succeeded. The Emperor, from whom the English had sought protection against this viceroy of Bengal, fell ill of a disease which baffled the royal physicians; the surgeon of the embassy then at Delhi, Mr. Hamilton, was called in, and under his care the royal patient recovered. He might have made his own terms for personal reward; but, following the example of Mr. Boughton nearly a hundred years before, and with true patriotism, he merged them into the interests of his country, and new deeds were executed under the Imperial seal, which the Bengal viceroy dare not disobey, and under which the factories in Bengal were established on a surer basis than ever. This viceroy's family did not maintain the power of its founder, though there were two successions in it; and in 1740 Ali Verdy Khan, the viceroy of Behar, a neighbouring province, who had earned distinction by his repulse of the Mahrattas, became ruler of Bengal, and continued to be so, as I have recorded, till the 9th April 1756, when he died, virtually if not actually, independent; and the prospect of any revival of imperial power at Delhi was a remote, and, indeed, impossible contingency.

What a romance is the early history of the merchant English in Bengal!—their struggles with imperial power, with local viceroys and delegates; their missions, their bribes, their intrigues, their defiance, and—their perseverance. Other European colonists were there—Dutch, Danish, Netherland, and French; but none established confidence among the people like the English, and with none was there so rapid and so lucrative a trade carried on. When we read that in the Mahratta invasion, driven back by Ali Verdy Khan, a sum of two and a half millions sterling (two and a half crores of rupees) had been extorted from the banking-house of Juggut-Seit at Moorshedabad alone by the Mahratta general, what ideas does this one act of spoliation convey to us of the local wealth of the native Bengal traders! I have, however, no concern with these old histories, in which all who read them will find sober truth far more wonderful than any fiction. I have only to do with the period I have already denoted—the rise of the English out of their heretofore capacity of merchants and the foundation of their political power.

To imagine, however, that up to this period the English had established no political status in India, would be wrong. In Bombay and Surat their influence had long been felt; and they had made treaties with Sivaji. In Madras they had begun wars, because the French, desiring to establish their own commercial power throughout the south of India, had fought against them, and at first overcome them. Afterwards, and even while the parent nations were at peace, Frenchmen and Englishmen were arrayed against each other, with varying results, in the cause of local native princes. In the Dekhan, at the court of the Nizam, Monsieur Bussy had established an authority, and possessed armies which, ostensibly belonging to the prince, were intended to be the instruments of a far wider national influence. Except in the Dekhan, the English had not only maintained their position, but had established a reputation as gallant soldiers which rivalled, if it did not surpass, that of the French, in the estimation of the people of India. It was that increasing French influence in regard to which the English Governments of 1755, and subsequently, were so jealous; that which Mr. Clive was burning to overthrow when he was in England in that year, and when, as we already know, he had prayed to be entrusted with a force with which he could meet Monsieur Bussy in the Dekhan, and prove who should be master there. All this was to come afterwards, as we know; but of the two, the French then were the popular favourites, and in Bengal were, perhaps, superior in power to the English.

Such, then, is a mere sketch of the political position of India in

1756. The Mahomedans without an imperial government except in name, and its viceroys become independent, employing their local revenues for their own aggrandisement, without any common purpose or national interest. The Mahrattas, still extending their conquests, but respecting the English, and perhaps the French, with neither of whom they had come into collision—being, in all respects, the greatest native power in India. The English and French, struggling slowly into political existence; but neither, except the ground on which their forts stood, or little beyond them, possessing any territorial authority. In Bengal, Ali Verdy Khan was dead; his son, Suraj-oo-Doulah, had succeeded to his wealth and power; and the Council of Calcutta, having given the protection of the English flag to a wealthy fugitive, were, with an army of less than two hundred Englishmen, deliberately defying a vindictive, passionate prince, who could bring against them fifty thousand good soldiers. Since a handful of French infantry under Labourdonnais had defeated in the open field the whole native army of the Carnatic, the fame of Europeans as soldiers had spread rapidly through India; and it has often resulted since, that mere odds have had very little to do with Indian victories. For all this, it is not difficult to understand why the young Nawab of Bengal, in the first flush of his power, should have despised the English at Calcutta: or why their many native friends, marvelling at their unaccountable temerity, should have deplored an issue with the Nawab which, to their perception, could only end in ignominious discomfiture and ruin.

CHAPTER XXXI.

SOZUN.

On the evening of a day in March 1747, the sun, which had been blazing all the afternoon upon an arid plain in the north-west of India, was now a blood-red orb slowly descending below the horizon, where a dim grey and a dull red haze were struggling for mastery. Above, was a glory of crimson and orange clouds floating in a sea of soft purple, which faded away by pink and greenish tints into the fast deepening blue of the heavens. Here and there were a few stunted bushes and thin scraggy trees almost leafless, and there was no sign of human habitation for many miles around. Upon some open spots, where the hard earth seemed to have denied the possibility of vegetation, as well as among the thorny bushes, lay many inanimate forms of men and horses, gashed with horrible sabre-cuts, or pierced with spear or shot wounds, in all possible distortions of agony, or quiet sleep in death. Great vultures were already stalking to and fro with noiseless steps and hungry glistening eyes, while others were wheeling in the air, or alighting with a loud rustle of their heavy wings. From among the low brush-wood, now and then the sharp muzzles, keen eyes, and fox-like heads of jackals peered cautiously; and, as if impatient of delay, one or two would occasionally sally out, look around, and retire again with a sharp bark or howl, as if to advise further caution—or a snarling hyena, with his striped coat, would chase one of them for a short distance, and then stopped to sniff at a carcass lying before him. For an instant, the sun's rays flashed out of a rent in the haze upon this scene with a glare as red as the blood shed there that day, which, in broad, blackening patches, had sunk into the thirsty earth. There would be a horrible banquet that night upon men and horses, and presently the moon would rise, and shine softly and peacefully, over all.

There had been a battle there that day. Ahmed Shah Abdalli of Candahar had invaded India at the head of a horde of his Affghan subjects, and had carried fire and sword through the Punjab; but had been met at Sirhind by an army of the old Mogul chivalry from Delhi, and overthrown, and, with his people, had fled westwards.

But there were two human beings alive near the spot I mention. One was a broad-chested, strong featured, stalwart Affghan, with a curly brown beard and blue eyes, who that morning, ruddy with the glow of health and excitement, had ridden with his troop of comrades in the confident hope of victory, which should lead him with the rest to the imperial city, the goal of many an Affghan freebooter's desires. He was now lying there with a gurgling in his throat, and his dim eyes already glazing in death that would soon come. He had done his work in that day's fight manfully, and had slain several of his assailants, whose bodies lay not far off; but a chance shot had killed his gallant horse, and as they fell together, a broken limb rendered him powerless to rise, and in the end, an arrow, shot by a Rajpoot bowman, had wounded him mortally. It had seemed a cowardly shot; for as the gallant fellow, little caring for himself, lay by his dead horse, he had protected with his broad shield a slight girlish form which crouched beneath it, and defended her and himself with his broad heavy sabre. Many comrades passed him by unheeded in the last charge as the victorious Mogul cavalry careered onwards, and the Affghans fled, till the last fatal shot came and left him as he was, helpless and dying.

By his side now knelt a girl of singular appearance, and even beauty, who strove to raise the drooping head and lay it on her shoulder—strove to moisten the parched white lips from the gourd which was slung at the horse's saddle-bow, and to rouse the dying man; but in vain. His mouth refused the water which he had drunk greedily at first, his lips uttered inarticulate sounds, and his breath came only by feeble gasps. He was bleeding inwardly, and to death; and the fatal barb, of which he had broken the shaft in his first agony, lay rankling near his heart. Suddenly, as the sun's red glare shone out into his dim eyes, and they gleamed with a last look of intelligence upon the girl's face, a faint smile trembled upon his features, and passed away into the majesty of death.

"Father! father!" she had said in her rough guttural Pushtoo tongue. "Father, look up! one word, but one! Ai Alla kureem! but one!" Alas! that faint dim flicker of life had been but as transient as the sun's rays which then passed from the earth, and left her —with the ravening creatures around her—alone!

Alone indeed! and it was a sad story, but a very simple one, soon told. When the Affghan forces were collected by Ahmed Shah, men had flocked to his standard from all parts of his dominions. A foray into India, with Delhi to be gained, was a national honour which every warrior burned to share. Sikunder Khan had little to keep him in his mountain home of Istaliff. Two sons had died, like others, in local quarrels, fierce and bloody, and his wife too, had died after them. There remained only Sozun, his daughter; and when the arms were being cleaned and sharpened, and the good horse shod for the long marches, the girl had looked wistfully at these preparations, bowed herself before her rough father, and said, "Thou wilt not leave me alone, father? I will ride with thee!" So, up to that day, the hardy girl had ridden beside him through many a weary march, through many a grim fight: doing her simple offices of cooking, and laying out the saddle-cloths when they were to rest, spreading garments over spears tied together to keep off the dew, and sleeping beside him as peacefully as she ever did in their mountain home. There was many a brave clansman in that flying rout who, if he had known her desolation, would have turned to bring her away; but in the clamour and confusion of the Mogul charge, Sikunder Khan's fate had been unnoticed, and the wild conflict had whirled fiercely along over many a mile, and would not cease till night fell upon it.

Alone indeed! With death in the battle-field, or among their own glorious mountains, the girl had long been familiar. Of the ghastly forms lying around her she was in no terror, nor at first had she any clear perception of her position. But the night was falling fast; a chill wind began to sweep over the desolate plain, and to sigh among the brakes, mingling with the horrid cries about her. Several times creatures she could dimly see, came about her with flapping wings, or stealthy steps and savage snarls; and she had then snatched up her father's sword, unfastened his shield, and held it over him as he had held it over her. Often and often, so long as there was any light, she had peered into his eyes and spoken to him—perhaps he was asleep! The misery that he was dead had hardly come into her heart yet, but it could not long be repelled. As she listened with her ear to his breast, there was at last no breathing; and as the moon rose and shed its first pallid gleam over the scene, it lit upon a pale ghastly face, the expression of which could not be mistaken, and the girl cast herself upon the body with a piercing scream of agony which could not be repressed.

How long she remained there she knew not; but was roused by a rough pull at her arms, and a feeling as if she were rudely flung aside, and she started to her feet in terror. Four men and two women were before her, and one of the men seized her arms, while another bound a part of a turban about her, pinioning them close to her body. The women were rifling her father, and two men were loosening the saddle upon the dead horse.

"Rip open the lining," cried one of the women; "those plundering rascals carry all their gold there. Who is that you've got there, Mullik? a boy? Give him the knife. What use is he to you? Be quick?"

The girl heard one of the men mutter a savage oath as he drew a knife from his girdle, which flashed in the moonlight, and saw it raised to strike her. She shut her eyes, and did not shrink from the blow; death would be welcome, and she did not fear it.

"Ha! ha! ha!" laughed the man, coarsely. "Come hither, Jumna; 'tis a girl I should have slain but for good mother moon yonder. Come and see."

"A girl?" cried both the women, leaving their hideous work; "what in the name of the fiend hath brought her here? Who art thou? Speak!" exclaimed one of them in her own Pushtoo tongue; "and where hast thou come from?"

The familiar language, perhaps, more than the question, roused the girl; but all she could answer was, "My father!—oh father!" and strove again to cast herself upon his body.

"He's dead, my lily," said one of the women, in a somewhat kinder voice—"he's dead, and with the blessed Lord and the Prophet now. He'll never help thee more, nor thou him; and only for us, the wolves and the jackals and the vultures would have had a tender meal to-night off thee. Thank the Prophet, who hath sent thee friends. We will take care of thee, child. Thou shalt be a daughter to me, and I will teach thee all the charms and the tricks."

"Who are you?" asked the girl, trembling. "I am Sozun."

"We? Well, men call us by many names—what signifies? and we dance, and sing, and sell charms. I'm too old for that now; but I have three daughters who do all they're taught, and thou shalt be one too, Sozun."

"She's not twelve years old," said the other woman, holding the girl's face up to the moonlight. "Allah! what eyes! what a colour! She's worth thousands."

"And here's a stout pony, sister," said one of the men, coming up, leading a strong, active "yaboo." "He wouldn't leave the bush yonder where he had been tied, though he broke the rein. Perhaps it's hers, and it will do to carry her."

Her dear old Môtee knew his mistress as he was led up, and with a low whinny put his nose to her breast and rubbed it against her. When her father fell, Sozun had thrown herself from his back and run to his side; but the pony had never stirred. Afterwards she had tied him to a bush; and except that he had kicked viciously at every beast that came and sniffed at him, he had not stirred. The turmoil of the fight had swept by him, but he was unnoticed.

There was short parley about Sozun. They would not trust her arms at liberty, though they loosened their bonds. "Remove them, my child? Aha! as if I had not been at Candahar and Ghuzni, and knew how women ride there! No, no; be quiet, and we will take care of thee."

Helpless, confused, moaning in her bitter misery, little caring what became of her, Sozun, the Affghan soldier's child, was led away on her pony to a new life, which was destined to be an eventful one.

I do not think it would answer our purpose to follow it. She was then little more than eleven years old, but her figure was tall, strong, and well formed, and her face gave promise of beauty. Her eyes were glorious—great brown flashing eyes, with long sweeping eyelashes, which seemed almost coarse. Her teeth were white and very even, and sparkled in her dewy ruddy mouth as she spoke, literally like rows of pearls. To those Indian gypsies she appeared very fair; and indeed, though her neck and arms were embrowned by constant exposure, her skin, where it had remained covered, was white and soft.

In the whirl of a camp life, in the excitement of change of place, with new and gay associates, Sozun at last forgot the misery of that night, though the ghastly dead face of her father, the beasts of prey howling around her, and their screams and shrieks as they fought over the dead carcasses—long, very long, haunted her in many a frightful dream. When she was a year older, she was taken to Delhi, and sold to the proprietress of a company of dancing-girls, to be taught her profession, begun rudely by the gypsy women in their camp. One of the crones who had found her, Jumna, had adopted Sozun as a daughter; and, though capricious in her disposition, was in the main kind. Other girls, slaves like herself, Sozun saw beaten frequently, and made to do the most menial offices in the rude tent camps of the gypsy tribes; but she was always protected, and cared for tenderly enough. She was taught to believe in her destiny; and her horoscope, cast after the fashion of gypsies in all parts of the earth, indicated such an elevation in life that she was in a manner venerated. The old woman had travelled to Bokhara, to Samarcand, and to every part of India, and knew her captive's value, the greater if the girl could be taught to know it herself; but Sozun could not be adopted into the tribe—she could only remain a slave like others, and be used for the worst of purposes.

"I love thee, my lily," the old woman would say—"I love thee as my life; but thou'rt too good for us, Sozun, and I will sell thee to the Padishah's dancers when we go to Delhi for a thousand rupees. Thou wilt become very beautiful, and thy star already shineth out of thy fair forehead like a queen's, as thou wilt be."

"Like a queen's, as thou wilt be," seemed to find an echo presently in the girl's heart; and when the dead was forgotten, and the old mountain home and her playfellows at Istaliff had faded dimly away into the past—love of fine clothes, of jewels with which she was decked, of desire to excel in the accomplishments of her profession, soon followed, and then Jumna, as I have said, sold her at Delhi, and parted from her sadly.

"I have got a good price for thee, my lily," she said one day, "and thou must go. Chunda Kour has promised to be good to thee, and make thee a queen. She is in love with thee; and many a one will love thee as thou growest older. Come, my child, dress thyself in thy best clothes, for they are bought with thee, and I will come often to see thee!"

A new life again, a grand house to live in, in the Chandnee Chowk of Delhi, and an imperial establishment of palankeens, elephants, and luxuries. The mountain home, the white dead face, the rough camp-life of the gypsies, went further and further away. All her young companions laid plots for future distinction—what they would do, what lovers they would have, whom they would win, what jewels, what silks, what shawls they would possess; and she did the same. With this, Sozun learned all the art of her trade quickly and gracefully, for she enjoyed it. No positions, no graces of dancing were too difficult. Her teachers were proud of her; and, as her voice grew strong and sweet, she loved to sing. She had not forgotten some of the plaintive ballads of her own country, and, as a child, had played on the lute like other girls; and these old songs, though they sometimes made her heart ache, had a strange charm for her hearers. No music was too difficult to be overcome, and the singers of the Emperor's own chamber had pleasure in teaching the Affghan girl what they would have denied to others.

She made her début, as we should call it, at a public durbar in the palace at Selim Ghur, and was enveloped in costly shawls, her lap filled with gold pieces, and a title, which she bore ever afterwards, bestowed upon her, with a daily allowance from the imperial treasury. As she grew up, she became beautiful—certainly very beautiful—especially her figure, which was superb. Her Affghan origin gave her height and carriage beyond any of her associates. Her fresh colour, and healthy ruddy complexion, made her everywhere remarkable, and she felt a corresponding ambition growing upon her.

Love! ah no!—love could find no place in such a heart; and, when it did come, it was not akin to what we know of.

Chunda Kour knew her slave's value. From Delhi to Lucknow, at festivals, marriages, the durbars of princes, the merrymakings of rich bankers, even the sacred festivals of Hindu gods, and the anniversaries of Mahomedan saints, the Affghan girl danced and sang, and the gold of enraptured thousands was poured at her feet. Even the aged Ali Verdy Khan, the Nawab of Bengal, when Sozun arrived at Moorshedabad, thought no durbar complete without her; and when his favourite son, Suraj-oo-Doulah, besought him, besought his mother, to plead that Sozun might be presented to him, the girl felt her destiny was accomplished, and consented. The price demanded for her was paid, and she passed into the harem of the young prince, to be—as the gipsy astrologer had foretold—a queen? no; except in wealth and power, she could not be that, for a lawful wife was there before her; but when, on the 9th day of April 1756, the brave old Tartar viceroy breathed his last, and Sozun was among the ladies of his family who wailed loudly for him, while the priests were chanting the last services over his body, she seemed to be on the threshold of the fulfilment of her desire.

CHAPTER XXXII.

THE NAWAB AND HIS SLAVE.

> "He loved her with all love, except the love
> Of men and women when they love the best."
>
> TENNYSON.

"ART thou content now, my soul? or is there any desire at thy heart which I can fulfil? If there be, tell me. If it be on the world's face, it shall be got for thee. I would not see one frown on thy brow, or hear a sigh from thy heart, Sozun, and that thou well knowest. But I am weary now, and thou must sing to me—weary of all my court, of never-ending advice and counsel, of my mother's vain grief, of my friends and of my enemies, of all but thee, my life

—my soul—for thou art ever fresh, ever beautiful! Sing to me, sweet one, one of those old mountain songs of thine, soft and low, for my brain is dizzy." It was the Nawab who was speaking to his slave, Sozun.

"So soon weary, my lord," said the girl, "and thy power but just begun? Were I like thee I would not be weary: Hast thou not a kingdom, a brave army, wealth, and all newly come to thee? Wherefore, then, art thou weary?"

"Nay, nay, Sozun, no sage advice from thee," he replied. "Thou art my refuge from all this, which hath made my head throb and my heart sick. Sing to me, then, my soul, while I listen and forget."

The girl took up a small battered lute, tuned it, and began one of those old mountain airs in her own mother tongue, which still lingered in her memory. Years ago she had sung this to her mother, to her father in the camp by night, and to rough men who gathered round their little tent of spears and horsecloths. The lute was her own, which, part of the gypsy's plunder of her dead father, she had begged for, and kept ever since. She was changed now, but the song was not changed, nor the old memories which came thick upon her as she looked upon her master, whom the soft low song had lulled to slumber. Was she happy? All she had dreamed of as belonging to wealth and power was in her grasp already, for the last obstacle to the complete possession of them had departed with the old Nawab. Was she happy with it all? I think not then, with those old memories, dim and faded as they were, but sweeter and more precious nevertheless, lying at her heart.

Suraj-oo-Doulah was asleep. "For this," said the girl, scornfully, as she cast her eyes over the recumbent figure—"for this I am what I am, and but a slave after all. Better free, even at the old trade, and the praise of thousands ringing in my ears and swelling my heart; and, better than all, dead—and yet not so. Can I not rule that thing, and make him serve my will?"

She put down the instrument with a heavy sigh, opened the carved window-screen gently, and looked out of the balcony. It was high above the ground, and from it she saw the broad river, with a few boats sailing lazily with the stream, which glittered in the heat. Beyond, a fair level country, dotted with villages and corn-fields, and groves of trees with heavy foliage, out of which white tops of Hindu temples with gilded spires sparkled in the sun; while all the scene trembled, as it were, under the vivid heat, fading away into a dim blue distance. No sounds broke the stillness, except the distant low of cattle bathing in the stream—the shrill whistling cry of kites which sailed and wheeled in the air, and the hum of flies as they whirled in a dizzy round about the window. Below, a company of gay horsemen and some foot-soldiers were leaving the outer court of the palace, and the town seemed asleep in the blaze of light which fell upon it, for about the streets no one was stirring.

On this day, the first great durbar assembly of the young prince had been held. It had been the first public declaration of his accession; and after the reception of all his courtiers, the leaders of his troops, his ministers of state, and the leading bankers and merchants of his own city, and the English factory at Cossim Bazar, it was perhaps not strange that the young Nawab was weary.

She to whom he had spoken, however, was not so, and her thoughts were very busy. Gradually she had come to understand the nature of the man to whom her destiny had linked her; and the more she knew of it the more deeply she resolved that it should not overcome her. It would be strange, perhaps, were anything of love combined with this. Of all the cautions she had received from her instructress, the most constant was, that she must shut her heart to love. She had to gain honour in her art, to gain wealth and power, but must harden her heart against all else; and hitherto these mercenary teachings had been followed with a hardness in execution which had excited Chunda Kour's perfect admiration. She had no rule of life but her own, and its precepts were hereditary. Other women might marry, might have children to love them, might love themselves; but one like her, a Tuwäif, never! To do so would be to sacrifice all, present and to come.

I say the more Sozun thought upon the figure before her, the more rapidly all the old life memories faded out of her heart, and the rules, the hard rules of the new, entered it and abode grimly there; while the tears which had fallen fast from her eyes as she sang, dried on her flushed cheek as the hot air played upon it, and did not refresh her. The lute was still in her hand, and for a moment she was tempted to fling it away. "Thou wouldst be dashed to pieces, poor thing," she said to it, "but I could not forget thee. With thee I am as I am, and till I die thou shalt not leave me." The only bond of tenderness which linked her to the past, and to the good feelings of her nature, seemed to be that poor battered instrument; all else was hard and defiant now, as she had striven to make it.

Still he slept. That weary youth, with whom her destinies were linked, lay calmly before her. She knew him to be in her power. She believed, and believed truly, that of all about him—kindred, slaves, ministers, and creatures of his power—she alone was beloved. If in such a mind any love could exist, she had awakened and possessed it. She knew his heart to be cruel, rapacious, vindictive, insolent, and tyrannical. A coward, a profligate, and a traitor, she could not conceal from herself that he might some day turn on her unexpectedly, and destroy her as he had destroyed others. The girl even shuddered at the idea for an instant; but the next, had closed her teeth fiercely under the influence of the passionate thoughts which flashed through her brain. No; whatever he was—hated, despised, dreaded—the Nawab Suraj-oo-Doulah was at least hers; and with this assurance, a feeling of tenderness she had never before experienced—a fascination, as it were, she could not resist—had arisen slowly but surely, and was growing on her in spite of her precautions. It would be strange and unnatural, indeed, if any human mind could exist without the germ of such feeling, which time and opportunity might call into action.

"Tell me," she said, when he awoke at length, and stretched himself, holding out his arms as if to caress her—"tell me, my lord, what happened to-day in the durbar? Thou art my debtor for that sweet sleep, and to this old lute for playing thee to rest, and I ask payment."

"I will tell thee, Sozun," he said, as she seated herself by him, and his hand passed fondly over her fair cheek, "though thou wilt hardly care for our state doings and quarrels. Dost thou care, my soul?"

"My lord's friends are my friends, and his enemies are my enemies," she replied, as her bosom heaved. "If his slave's counsel is but that of a woman, it is at least sincere and true, and may be useful, my—"

"Nay, enough, Sozun," he replied, putting his hand on her mouth. "Who doubts thee, my pearl? Not I, by the Prophet. Thou shalt know all, and welcome. Listen. There was a servant of my father's who held a high place, and collected and embezzled much of the revenue. He died. His son has left his post with all his wealth, and has taken refuge in the Feringi fort at Calcutta, and defies me. What wouldst thou do?"

"Do?" cried the girl, her eyes flashing—"do? Thou, the Nawab of Bengal, whose bread they eat, under the shadow of whose splendour these Feringis live! and thou askest me? Do? I will tell thee. Give me thy army. I, Sozun, thy slave and a woman, will lead it to Calcutta—raze every stone of this Kaffir fort to the ground—and bring away that vile thief in defiance of them. Who are they that have eaten this abomination?"

"They are rich merchants, who bring hither stores of English goods—Kaffirs, and utter abominations to the faith of Islam; and I hate them, Sozun—I hate them because they do not fear me. One came to-day to the durbar from the Bazaar. It was he, I know well, who sent on that thief and traitor; and he behaved insolently before every one present. He looked round with an air of defiance, as though he were the Nawab, and I the Kaffir merchant, crouching at his feet."

"I would have had him seized and put in irons," cried the girl.

"I would rather have hanged him in the market-place, or tied him to the foot of an elephant, to have his Kaffir soul trampled out of him," he replied, savagely; "but their time is not come yet.

"Why not, my lord?" she asked; "are men afraid of these Feringis?"

He laughed bitterly. "My father was, but I am not, Sozun; I do not fear them," he said. "Men say they have received more guns from their ships, and have strengthened their fort. No, I fear them not; but, strange to say, my mother loves them! She sent for me to-day, and besought me not to quarrel with them. They were under the Emperor's protection, she said, and my father's, and she would not have the old agreements broken. I was angry with her, and I swore on the Koran which lay by her, that I would have revenge for their insulting defiance, and left her. I have written once more to Drake, who is in Calcutta, and if he gives up this thief Kissun-das, he is safe for the present; if not—Allah! he will rue it."

"Thou wilt take me with thee to see the English Kaffirs and their ships, and the English shops! Ha, ha!" she cried, clapping her hands; "and thou shalt have thy revenge on all."

"Yes, I will have it, Sozun," he muttered through his teeth, "if I hang those cursed Feringis, every one of them, upon their own walls; and thou shalt see it, too. I swear to thee."

"And what of her, my lord?" said the girl, almost with hesitation, after a silence which he did not care to interrupt.

"Curse her!" said the Nawab, rising, and striking the cushion on which he was lying; "why did they ever marry me to her—a poor puling thing, who hates me, and whom I hate as I hate the Feringis. What of her? She is safe from thee, my rose—safe for many a day to come, I hope, and she may rot where she is, in the vault below. Thou mayest go, if thou dost not believe me, and look at her. If she die soon, there will be one the less for thee to fret about."

"I do not fret about her, my lord," she replied, scornfully; "I hate her as thou dost, as I would hate anything that came between thee and me. Ah, thou lovedst her once, they tell me."

"Till I saw thee, Sozun? Never! But let that pass. What more have I to tell thee? A thousand things that vex me—of treachery, of plots, of intrigues. I know not yet whom to trust or whom to fear; but time will show all. There are French Feringis and English Feringis, who thirst for each other's blood, and if the French will join me, they might have the English Fort; but they dare not, for there is peace between their nations. I dread Meer Jaffier, with his smooth tongue and hollow heart, and he is too powerful for me to lay hands upon. I dread the bankers and their intrigues. I dread—"

"Thou shalt fear nothing," cried the girl, warmly—"no, not the fiend himself—while I am with thee, my lord. Strike boldly down all that oppose thee. If these English Feringis are strong, strike them down first, that men may tremble and obey. My lord is young in power yet, and needs to prove it. You said she was in the vault below: let me but see her there, and I am content till I see Calcutta blazing, and my lord victorious."

"Go, then," he replied. "Nasir will take thee;" and he clapped his hands.

One of the eunuchs without entered, and put up his hands, listening.

"Take him with thee," said the Nawab; "he will show thee the place. The way is private."

Sozun followed the man, and they descended by a private stair, which, long as she had been in the palace, she had never remarked before. When they reached the foundation vaults, the man stopped before a door on which was a heavy padlock, unlocked it, and pushed it open. Except by a narrow loophole, above which some green leaves were waving, there was no other light. The place had a damp, dank smell; but it was swept, and on a pallet in a corner lay a slight figure, which rose as Sozun entered, and, drawing her white muslin scarf over her face more closely, asked in a gentle, girlish voice, "Who art thou? and why art thou come here?"

"Look at me," said Sozun, advancing close to her. "Thou hast heard of me, lady, enough I daresay. Thou art Suraj-oo-Doulah's wife; and I— No matter, I am Sozun, his slave. Ah, he did not tell me how beautiful thou art! Dost thou know that I hate thee, O Begum!"

"I am very helpless," was the reply, "and wish to die. Why does he not kill me? O Allah! just and merciful, wilt thou behold such tyranny! Even as thou wilt, as thou wilt, O Lord!" and she sat down sobbing.

"He is mine, lady," resumed Sozun, in a hard voice—"mine, and cannot be thine. There is no peace between us, and if thou wert dead it would be well, or if I were dead it would be well."

"Hast thou no pity in thy heart? Why does he not let me go?" she returned.

"Pity, lady? None for thee, as thou hast none for me. No, thou canst not go hence; it would not be seemly."

"I would not harm thee—I never harmed thee," she replied, gently. "Let me go. What have I done to thee?"

"You would, you would!" cried Sozun, passionately. "You would drive me forth, you would trample on me if you dared, you would urge him to destroy me, as you have done before, and you know it, lady! It is my time now—why should I have pity? Have Affghans ever pity? I have none."

"If I could only die," said the lady, sighing dreamily, "there would be peace and rest. I have no friend but thee, O Lord!—none but thee!"

"Ameen," returned Sozun, bitterly—"ameen! May the good God and the Prophet hear thee!"

They were both silent. The lady was sitting upon the edge of her pallet, covering her face with her muslin scarf, and sobbing piteously. The other, standing over her triumphant; a gorgeous shawl of Benares tissue, crimson and gold, floating around her head and person, beneath which a petticoat of cloth-of-gold swept to the floor. Had the lady looked up, she would have seen her own jewels displayed upon the dancer's arms and hands, and one priceless diamond which, in the light which fell on them from the loop-hole, flashed as the girl's bosom heaved under her excitement.

"Dost thou see these?" she cried, waving her hands and arms, on which the jewels sparkled. "Dost thou know them? They were thine lady, and are now mine. Enough; I have seen thee, and will remember and dread thy beauty; and thou wilt not forget Sozun, the Affghan slave."

With these cruel words she turned, and when the door closed, and the clash of her anklets grew fainter and fainter, the lady bowed herself to the ground, and thanked God for the departure of her cruel enemy.

"I have seen her, my lord," said Sozun to the Nawab, when she returned to him, "and I have seen enough. Though didst not tell me she was so lovely. By Allah! thou wert a fool to take me instead of her."

"And thou a fool to say so, Sozun," he replied, sharply; "but we need not quarrel. Is she safe, and art thou content?"

"Is she fed, my lord?"

"Surely," was the reply. "Thou wouldst not have me do murder, Sozun? and for thee?"

The girl laughed scornfully. "No," she replied, "not on her, It will be my care to feed her daintily, that she may live, and that I. Sozun, may look on her as I wish. Yes, she is safe, and I will keep her so, even from thee, my lord—even from thee. I have taken the key. I am more to be trusted with it than Nasir perhaps."

"Thou art a devil!" cried the young man, starting to his feet, "but so beautiful that I dare not harm thee."

"Ah, my lord," she replied, caressing him, "if I am as precious to thee as thou sayest I am, I need to protect myself for my lord's sake. Thy wife is a royal lady, and I am only a poor Affghan soldier's child. She hath friends, but I have none save myself—and thee."

CHAPTER XXXIII.

THE DURBAR AND THE DERWESH.

Some weeks had elasped, but the young Nawab had as yet shown no sign of offensive operations against the English. A trustworthy envoy had been despatched to Calcutta in disguise, bearing a letter to the chief of the English Factory, expressing anger at the increase of fortifications, and demanding in very peremptory terms the surrender of the vassal and servant who had taken refuge there. This emissary had not been fortunate. He had found the Factory officials alarmed and cautious, and he was not only denied admittance to the fort, but, being dismissed beyond its boundaries as a spy, in an ignominious manner, had returned to his master, not only full of revengeful determination in regard to his own injuries, but as a very firebrand to the train already prepared to explode; for his tale fell upon willing ears. The Nawab had listened to it with a triumph he could ill conceal, and there were few present in that evening council in the palace who ventured to cross the young man's vindictive temper, or to point out the ultimate danger of the now meditated enterprise.

Perhaps indeed few, if any, could see its existence. The force of the English in Calcutta was accurately known, and seemed utterly insignificant. Each selfish in regard to individual ends and interests, it was not probable that any coalition of the European Factories would take place; and the Nawab knew for certain that, although the French would not openly break with him and espouse the cause of the English, they would greatly rejoice at their discomfiture. The French congratulations upon his accession had been peculiarly acceptable and submissive; and though he had received like courtesies from the English, the tone of independence which was perceptible in their letters had appeared to him, and to his councillors, little less than offensive arrogance. His own mind had been made up long ago; but to Sozun, the action she longed to see him engaged in had been delayed almost past endurance.

At home there were no enemies who showed themselves. Those who had supported other pretensions, or were supposed to do so, had been dealt with summarily and vindictively; but I need not detail any of these events. What the native historians of his own period as well as ours have depicted, Suraj-oo-Doulah had proved himself to be; and for recent, as well as former acts, many among his own people were already weary of him, though where relief could come from was not perceptible. Time was, when the outcry of the people of a Mogul province found hearing in the imperial court at Delhi; but that was past listening now: or when commanders of imperial armies, serving in provinces, preserved the honour of the empire untarnished; but the armies of the Nawab held no allegiance to Delhi; they were in his own pay, and he believed them devoted to his interests. He had bestowed large largesses upon them out of his father's treasures, and every officer supposed to be unsound had been dismissed or removed. Upon those who were about him, then, the young man had strong reliance; and it was with a company of them, and of his ordinary courtiers and officials, that he had heard that afternoon the story of his agent's disgrace, and of the implied insult to himself.

"We are fallen somewhat low, my friends," said the Nawab, looking round the apartment as the relation was concluded, "when we hear that a few Kaffir Feringis have defied our power, and have sent back our messenger with a blackened face! It seems to them, perhaps, that the glory and valour of the men of Islam has departed; and the swords which were red one day, that some here remember, in the blood of those infidel Mahrattas, are now washed in rose-water, sheathed, and laid by. What think ye, my friends? Is our cup full enough, or are we to have more abomination poured into it? Speak, Moulvee Sahib! you are the elder here, and have the experience of two generations. Nay, friends, be silent," he continued, as many cried out passionately; "let the holy man speak, that we may hear words of wisdom and inspiration."

Moulvee Wullee-oo-Deen was the chief priest of the great mosque at Moorshedabad; and, as his office required of him, was not only learned in all ceremonials and observances, but an intense and furious bigot, especially famous for sermons against Christians. Hindus, truly, were abominable infidels; but Christians were worse. Had they not impiously and defiantly broken the covenant which the Lord made with Abraham? They were uncircumcised dogs: and in his virulent attacks upon them, this breach of covenant was always his strong point of argument. The Moslem priest was a small, thin, sallow-faced man, with a large aquiline nose, a retreating chin, and a straggling beard, the hairs of which might be counted. His upper teeth were large and projecting, and his scraggy lean throat, barely concealed by a thin beard, seemed composed of bones and sinews only, with a few thick veins spreading over them, which swelled out, as did those in his forehead, when he began to speak and grew excited. But the Moulvee was already boiling over, and his sense of etiquette alone had prevented him interrupting the Nawab in the ironical speech he had just made.

"My lord! my lord!" he cried, "let the vengeance of Alla descend upon them! How often have I raised this feeble voice in vain against these detestable Feringis! First, there was one ship and a few merchants, and one nation; now there are three nations, and the ships come in fleets, like the flocks of birds at harvest time.

I have no new words to speak. To my lord's honoured father, to the lady mother, my speech hath been ever the same. Curse them! I have cried as I do now—curse them!" he continued, raising his shrill voice to a scream—"curse them, drive them into the sea, and let my land be delivered from them for ever!"

"Ameen! ameen!" rose in a low murmur round the room, as those present twisted their moustaches, and grasped the hilts of their swords.

"What say the stars, my friend? How are these infidels' horoscopes and our own at present? Hast thou proved this, O Moulvee?" asked the Nawab.

"My lord," cried the priest, "I have no knowledge of this art; I only know what is written in the blessed Koran—"

"I know it too, Moulvee Sahib. May the grace of God be on the writer; but I would fain know how the planets point in this matter. Such art is beneath your holiness, that I know; but there may be those known to you who can assist us by it."

"What need of the stars, my lord?" said a burly Tartar officer, who sat near. "These are the best stars we can follow, which each of us bears by his side," and he held up his sword.

The Moulvee turned on the speaker a scornful look as he replied, "We have holy warrant for astrology, sir, and you are ignorant to despise it."

"I don't know that we looked after the stars when Ali Verdy Khan told us to tighten our waistbands before we rode through those Kaffir Mahrattas," retorted the Tartar, angrily; "and if we had waited for them, they might have been long of coming. So may these stars of the accursed Feringis, who have thrown dirt on our beards. May their fathers burn in hell for it!"

"Peace!" cried the Nawab, interposing; when we know what our holy friend can tell us, we shall be the more sure; and thou, Moulvee Sahib, must see to it forthwith."

"I think," replied the priest, "that this need not long be delayed. In the cloisters of the mosque a wise man hath resided for some days past, who hath wonderful power, my lord—wonderful! Mashalla, it is great! and he has bestowed amulets on the poor, which heal sickness as by a miracle. In your servant's family a case occurred but yesterday, in which the malice of many devils was frustrated; and yet the patient had long suffered. The Durwesh hath visited Beejapoor, and the shrine of Sofee Surmust, and that of the blessed Geesoo Duraz, at Gulbergah; and, in short, my lord, he is an apostle of charity, but he is rough and free-spoken. Will your Highness submit this matter to him? I know no other so worthy or so wise."

"Inshalla!" cried the Nawab, whose well-known superstition was at once strongly excited—"Inshalla! How say you, my friends?"

When an Eastern ruler makes a proposition, there are few perhaps in his council hardy enough to oppose it; and except the old Tartar soldier, and some Hindus present, there were none certainly there who did not desire to see the Nawab's intention forthwith carried out. One, however, honoured and trusted perhaps beyond the rest—a secretary who had risen to distinction under the Nawab's father—was sitting behind the prince, and putting a handkerchief to his mouth, leant forward and whispered caution.

"This is no matter for public assembly, my Prince," he said. "Dismiss those that are here, and see to this matter in private. What if the result be unfavourable?"

Suraj-oo-Doulah laughed scornfully. He was in a reckless, defiant humour, and it was not safe to cross his purpose. "If any one but thee, Anwar Ali," he replied, "had said that, he should have had his tongue cut out. Be silent, and do not lose your respect. Beware, I say!" and as the man shrank back terrified and trembling, silence fell upon the courtiers, which was only broken by the Nawab himself. "Send for the man," he said—"for this holy fakeer from Beejapoor, who is thy friend, Moulvee Sahib. Let him be brought forthwith."

"God forbid!" returned the priest, lifting his joined hands. "He is no *friend* of mine, only a poor disciple, my Prince, to whom I have imparted some mysteries of revelation. A rough fellow, my lord, and unlearned in all science, except that of his art. They say," he added in a low tone, "he was once an infidel Brahmin, but hath been converted to the faith."

"Enough!" cried the Nawab; "where are the players? we have had sufficient of this Feringi council. Let us see the Kaffirs themselves. Let them enter—they will make some fun for us."

As he spoke, four men, dressed ludicrously in English costume of the period, and with whitened faces, preceded by others bearing a table and four chairs, with some glasses and a bottle, entered the hall: and having made their obeisance, seated themselves on the chairs, and, pretending to drink, made show of draining glass after glass, till the bottle was finished, and was replaced by another.

"Mercy of the Prophet! exclaimed the Nawab, "no one speaks."

"May it please your Highness," said another man, advancing, who acted as spokesman for the players, "these Kaffirs never speak till the wine begins to get into their brains. If your Majesty will only wait."

It was impossible to maintain gravity, and the Nawab and his courtiers burst into peals of laughter. The men, beginning to sway about in their chairs, as bottle after bottle was brought and supposed to be finished, held out their glasses to each other, clinked them together, and apparently tossed off the contents. One after another, too, dipped his head under the table, and raised it up with his face changed from white to scarlet, and drank more furiously than before.

At last one rose, and, steadying himself by the table, bawled out, "De King—hip! hip! hooray!"—and the three others, also rising—echoed, "De King—hip! hip! hooray!" and sat down again. No sooner had this been done than the first once more rose, and cried, "De Coompani—hip! hip! hooray!" and was answered as before by a cry of, "De Coompani—hip! hip! hooray!" After that, each man in quick succession bawled out other toasts, and filled his glass, while all together began to jabber an utterly unintelligible gibberish, in which a few coarse English words and oaths were intermingled. Presently, too, one of the players pretended to quarrel with another, and was pulled back by a third; and songs which had little tune, but of which the purport could not be mistaken, were howled independently, till the clamour and riot became indescribable, and the scene ended by one after another of the men tumbling from his chair to the ground.

"Protection of God!" cried the Nawab, holding his sides, "is this the truth? The Feringis at Cossim Bazar are not like this."

"May I be your sacrifice?" cried the spokesman, in an attitude of supplication, "your slaves have seen them all like this at Calcutta. There is no lie in it; and the next act is their dance, which is better still. Will my lord see it?"

"The Fakeer is present," said an attendant, "and salutes my Prince."

Suraj-oo-Doulah looked up as a remarkable figure advanced through the court, and stood before him without salutation.

"Salute the Nawab! salute the King!" cried many voices, but the man looked round him disdainfully, and said in a commanding voice, "I never salute any but God,"—then turning to the mummers, part of whose performance he had unwillingly witnessed, he cried,—"Begone, ye shameless, thus to defile God's image! I have seen the durbars of kings and princes of the faith from Constantinople to Delhi, but never, O Nawab, did I behold so shameless a scene as this. What dost thou require of me? Speak!" and the Fakeer drew himself up proudly, and looked around him.

A tall, gaunt figure, with matted hair twisted round his head; a long grey beard, partly turned over his ears; naked to the waist, with every bone of his attenuated body starting out under the skin in painful relief; a long purple and white cotton waist-cloth descending to his ankles, and a soft leopard skin depending from his shoulders. The Nawab had rarely beheld so weird a figure, and started at the abrupt and defiant address.

"Thou mightest use civil speech, friend," he said haughtily.

"Nay, my lord," whispered the priest, "a holy man, and rough of speech, as I said; to be pardoned, therefore, as it is his custom. He knows no master but God."

"Tell him what I want," replied the Nawab in a surly tone, "and let him depart in the devil's name, as soon as he has answered."

"Come hither, friend," said the priest, blandly, "and sit down here by me," and the Moulvee sidled away a little. "His Highness hath need of thy art, and would know how the holy mysteries of thy science explain the planets in conjunction on the—on the—" and he looked to the Nawab, uncertain whether he should tell what had passed.

"My army is going to Calcutta," said the Nawab, "and I would know the result. Dost thou fear to speak?"

"Fear!" cried the man—"only slaves fear. I am the slave of God and the Prophet, and I fear not man. I will tell thee, but I will not sit in this assembly.

For a few minutes the Fakeer was silent as if in prayer. He then took some silver tablets from his girdle and consulted them.

"Speak quickly," cried the Nawab, "and the less of thy mummery the better."

"Listen," said the Fakeer, solemnly. "The conjunction of planets is good. For a year there is no change, and there will be victory to thee, O Nawab!"

"Victory!" echoed the Prince. "Do you hear?—Victory!" and the words were taken up by all around, till the court resounded with the cry of "Futteh-i-Nubbee! victory to the Prophet!"

"Wouldst thou know more, Prince? It is not good what thy destiny reveals to me."

"I fear not," was the hard reply; "but if thou liest, by Alla, thou hadst better never have seen me."

"O Prince! a holy man, a holy man! His speech is privileged," interposed the Moulvee, with a deprecatory gesture.

"Be silent," said the Fakeer. "If thou wilt hear, listen to what I see in the future—defeat, misery, and to thy enemies triumph."

"A lie! a lie!" shouted the Nawab; "beat him on the mouth with a shoe."

"I fear thee not," continued the man, "raving as thou art like a madman. God hears thee, impious man, and will smite thee. Beware of these Feringis, I say, and harm them not. They are true, they are charitable. When I lay sick to death at Bombay, they put me into their hospital; they fed and clothed me, and I love them. They are just and true, I say, and I honour them, and do not forget them. Enough! If they have to suffer, they have to suffer. Ameen, ameen, and the grace of God be on them!"

"And the curse of the Shaitan be on thee, O foul-tongued Derwesh!" cried the Nawab, savagely, with an obscene oath. "Thou hast not forgotten them? Ah, well, nor thou shalt not forget me. Ahmed!—some of ye, cut off his ears—there, before me as he stands."

Before the Fakeer could resist—before he could speak—he was pinioned, dragged back a few paces, and mutilated with a sharp knife. Bleeding and faint, he was buffeted into the outer court, and thence pushed into the street, followed by mocking shouts.

"Ya, Alla!" he cried, lifting his hands—red with his own blood which had streamed over his body—to the sky. "O thou just God! wilt thou not avenge this? Enough for me that it is thy will!"

That night the Fakeer disappeared from the mosque, and was no more seen; but we may meet him again.

"And now, my friends," said the Nawab, when the ears of the Fakeer had been displayed to him, "we would be at rest. Be ready with your troops for to-morrow. Inshalla! we will plunder the English shops at Cossim Bazar, and there will be rare booty for all."

"What was the disturbance in the durbar, my lord?" asked Sozun, with a scared face, when the Nawab joined her in the zenana shortly afterwards.

"A mad Fakeer was insolent to me, and I had his ears cut off: wouldst thou like to see them? Take care I do not the same to thee some day," was the brutal reply. "Sing to me, Sozun; my spirit is disturbed to-night, and thou alone canst quiet it. Sing, dost thou hear? Art thou like him, insolent?"

The girl took her little lute, and sang: but there was no heart in her sad song that night; it had gone far away among the blue Affghan mountains, and would not return. "Ah me, alas!" she sighed, and burst into tears, as her master tossed restlessly on the bed where he had flung himself.

CHAPTER XXXIV.

THE FACTORY, CALCUTTA, 1756.

WHILE these scenes were passing at Moorshedabad, we may well believe that the gentlemen of the Calcutta Factory were not without serious apprehension. When Ralph Darnell landed, indeed, there was no suspicion of probable interruption to the general prosperity. Ali Verdy Khan was alive, and his life promised to be a long one. If a few of the most experienced men then feared, when the time did come, that a new succession to the throne of Ali Verdy Khan, for it was little else, would bring fresh demands and disturb existing rights—there were others who, despising such counsels, anticipated even greater extension of privileges, which as yet had experienced no serious interruption. Trade was very active and very prosperous;

and society was in accordance with its prosperity, free and reckless, not to say licentious and immoral. Ralph, as yet, had done no more than every fashionable man in London daily practised; but though by no means squeamish, he found, in the English society of Calcutta, harder drinking, coarser swearing, and deeper play than he had been accustomed to, and a general tone of profligacy which belonged, as it were, to a lower grade of society altogether. I am by no means desirous of claiming any remarkable amount of virtue for Ralph Darnell, or, as we must henceforth call him, Ralph Smithson, at this period of his life; but the old injunction of his uncle, that there never had been a Darnell that was not a gentleman, came more and more vividly to his remembrance as he witnessed, and often had to share, the orgies which were enacted, if not in the official Factory hall, at least in the private houses of the members and officers of the Factory. We should gain little, I think, by records of these doings, or of the men who passed their time in the society of Mahomedan dancing-women, or their native mistresses. Money was abundant, and was freely squandered upon these parasites. It did not signify much whether a man's nominal pay were twenty pounds a year or a hundred. All lived at the rate of thousands, and bought and sold their own investments with a boldness which Ralph gradually grew to comprehend, and in which he largely shared himself.

He had been received by Mr. Wharton with great kindness and hospitality. The worthy Captain Scrafton, and the chief officer of the *Valiant*, the only persons to whom his real name and history were known, had kept his secret; and to Mr. Wharton the young well-mannered Englishman Ralph Smithson, in whom Mr. Darnell "had an interest," and who came to Calcutta so well provided with money, was very welcome; while his frank manners and cheerful disposition soon rendered him a very general favourite.

Ralph had stared about him in wonderment at the first official dinner on New-Year's Day 1766, in the great Factory hall, where all the members of the service dined together off good old English fare of roast beef and plum-pudding, mingled with hot curries and dishes pertaining to the country, and after dinner the hookas of the guests were brought in, and with their long and richly ornamented shanks, and gold and silver mouthpieces and "chillams," deposited behind their chairs by well-dressed servants, and a general gurgling and bubbling began, and toasts were drunk in the Company's rare old Madeira—"The King," "The Honourable East India Company," and the like—at the hottest hour of the day, and the guests departed afterwards to don cooler garments and finish the evening with gambling and profligate riot,—if Ralph at first, as I say, wondered at all this, he very soon grew to be accustomed to it. One great trial and danger of his life had passed away, and his spirits were hopeful and elastic. It was strange, perhaps, to Mr. Wharton, and far stranger to young men of his own age, to see Ralph careful and prudent, and on this account he was not so popular among his young friends there as he might otherwise have been.

Perhaps Ralph's induction into gay life in England proved to be now of service to him. I am decidedly of opinion that it did; for it too often happens that those youths, sent direct from home influences and the strictest previous guidance into strange society, no sooner find themselves free from restraint, than they plunge more madly than others into excesses of all kinds. Hot, dissipated youths, who drank arrack-punch every night, gambled, and did other naughty things which I need not detail—feared, while they respected or disliked, as it might be, the young Englishman who declined to join their excesses, and, holding himself aloof from intimacy, was only courteous and kind to all.

It may hardly be supposed either that Ralph took the place he did without opposition, or that he had no enemies. Every society, in particular one which is necessarily limited, and composed of very heterogeneous materials, has its bullies, and that of Calcutta was no exception. When rough invitations were declined civilly, or refused peremptorily, taunts had followed, and insults. We have had already some specimens of Mr. Ralph's temper, and can understand that such were resented. Duels generally ended these quarrels, and gentlemen fought with their small swords as others did in England. As there "a man of spirit" had to fight before he was known to be one, so more especially in Calcutta; and our friend had already had two affairs, in both of which he had disarmed his antagonist, who, in fact, were weak and unskilful opponents of the stout Northumbrian gentleman. Ever since he could hold a rapier, his old uncle Geoffrey had taught him the use of one; and the baronet was beginning to say "Ralph was growing too much for him," when he was sent to London. There too, as a pupil of Mr. Sutton, Ralph had not neglected his opportunities; and his style of attack and defence was, as may be supposed, infinitely superior to that of the Calcutta gentlemen. His easy conquests of those by whom he had been challenged, therefore, rendered others careful. Ralph would allow no liberties to be taken with him, and every one came to know this in course of time.

Up to the period we are arrived at, Ralph had remained with Mr. Wharton as his guest. Mr. Wharton would not hear of his living in the chambers of the Factory, and presently grew so attached to him that what had been intended by Ralph as a temporary sojourn only, had now been protracted for several months, and was likely to be continued. There were two other alternatives—the one, to build a small thatched cottage or bungalow for himself; the other, to board with one of the chief clerks of the Factory who acted as book-keeper, and who lived in the native town, but at no very great distance from the fort. It was not uncommon to see two or more youths living together apart from the Factory; and any escape from the confinement of the fort was most desirable; but the style of such living did not suit Ralph—it was generally the precursor of those native attachments from which few were then free, and these in Ralph's eyes had no charm. As yet his mind was full of his sweet cousin Constance; and poor Sybil—ah, poor Sybil! does she ever think of me? he would ask himself sometimes, and so dream away his thoughts.

No doubt, Don Gomez da Silviera, the book-keeper, could have made him very comfortable; and the "Don Sahib," as all styled him, had taken unusual notice of Ralph. Soon after he began to attend the office of the Factory, the Don found Ralph to be a good man of business, who required no teaching; who, in fact, could teach many things himself. The Don called himself a Portuguese nobleman, and possessed a strange character of combined subservience and pride. When his noble ancestor might have come from his native Portugal to Bengal, and begun the black degenerate race of which the Don was the present representative, it is impossible to say; equally as impossible to account for the Portuguese of Bengal being, as they most frequently are, blacker than any natives. So it was in Don Gomez da Silviera's case; the Don was jealous of his pure descent from the "Don Gomez da Silviera" ancestor, and kept a family tree to prove it, and ancient Portuguese histories in which the Silvieras were mentioned as the companions and ministers of royalty. The Don was, therefore, an educated man in his degree; but his acquaintance with English literature was confined to the spelling-book of Mr. Mavor and the dictionary, and had resulted in the oddest collection of English words that could well be conceived. They were fine and high-sounding, but, as he spoke them, what meaning he intended to convey by them was generally very mysterious to the hearers, and could only have been intelligible to himself by his own thoughts. The Don's wife, Donna Luisa, was a fat worthy woman, who spoke no English, and there were two daughters and two sons; the latter working as copying clerks in the Factory, and the girls growing up at home as black as their parents, but in intense admiration of the fair, rosy-cheeked Englishman, whom they saw occasionally.

Don Gomez da Silviera had purposed to take Ralph as a boarder. He had a garden-house—that is, a house in a campao or compound, or enclosed space laid out as a garden—with a detached bungalow, all which Mr. Smithson might have to himself; and Ralph had seen that it was very comfortable. When he proposed to move from Mr. Wharton's house, however, there was such an outcry of opposition that he was forced to abandon the scheme altogether—nobody would hear of it. Mr. Wharton ridiculed the idea of a covenanted servant—for Ralph's papers had followed him—living with a mere clerk. Such a thing had never before been heard of. Mr. Wharton's children—he had three, two girls and a boy, whose mother was a native—burst out sobbing, and clung about him crying, scolding, and coaxing by turns, and most of all Mr. Wharton's wife's silent reproaches were hardest to resist.

Mr. Wharton had written to Mr. Darnell that he had lately married, and Julia Wharton had not been a wife for a year when Ralph arrived. One of the first parties in which the ladies and gentlemen of the Factory assembled together after Ralph's arrival, was to celebrate their wedding-day; and a merry one it was, after Calcutta fashion, in the cold weather. There had been jolly country-dances and reels, with here and there a minuet; and Julia Wharton had not forgotten, never would forget, one that she danced with the handsome fresh-coloured youth, dressed in the best fashion of London, and alike by his grace and manner putting to shame those whom she had assembled; nor could she forget, either, the walk afterwards through the garden, decked out with Chinese lanterns and Bengal lamps, and a glorious moon shining over all, and over the broad calm river with the ships and native boats lying there reflected in it. She had not forgotten that night, and her own heart was sorely stirred; but as yet Ralph Smithson was only her guest, a courteous and pleasant one, whom she could not part with to go to Don Gomez da Silviera and his dusky daughters.

Julia Wharton was no beauty perhaps, but she was a fresh English girl, with saucy blue eyes, a nose somewhat turned up, reddish auburn hair, a bright rosy mouth, pearly teeth, and a cheek like a peach, which even Calcutta had not yet blanched. She was very fair, with a plump figure and tiny waist, and knew how to dress herself so as to display her charms to the best advantage. Of education she had had little enough; but she could play on the harpsichord and guitar, and sing, rather theatrically perhaps, with a good voice. There were many speculations at Calcutta as to what Miss —— had been before she came out there; but whether true or false, we have no concern with them. Young women, as well as young men, were occasionally sent to India for indiscretions in those days. She had been received by friends to whom she had been sent out; and she was in the eyes of the gentlemen of Calcutta a dazzling beauty, so there was much competition for her hand; and finally, after a very short courtship, Mr. Wharton, one of the oldest, and certainly the richest of the society, offered to settle a lac of rupees upon her, presented her with a gorgeous necklace of pearls, and having promised to put away her native predecessor, married her. This was what the girl had been sent to India for, and she had done it, as every one told her, to the best advantage. Did she think so herself? I think not; but what had been done could not be undone, and I am afraid that her predecessor and Ralph Smithson together, gave her more uneasiness than I need account for.

CHAPTER XXXV.

DISQUIET.

TROUBLES were coming fast upon that small English settlement; and as the days passed drearily, the rumours which were hourly arriving in Calcutta were confirmed by news of overt acts on the part of the young Nawab, or Subah, as he was generally denominated, for which we have already accounted. I do not think it necessary to detail the native political events at Moorshedabad; but I may mention that, on the ostensible pretence of coercing a refractory vassal, the Subah had ordered his army to march, and had accompanied it. He did not, however, proceed to the first declared destination of his forces; but turned suddenly on the English Factory at Cossim Bazar, twenty miles below his capital, and invested the place; making prisoners of the few English gentlemen there, and appropriating all the spoils. Here was the first victory gained, and a bloodless one too, for there were no local means of resisting an attack by fifty thousand men. The poor gentlemen had written to Calcutta in their sore strait for help; but there was none to be had, and none could have reached them in time to prevent what, indeed, was not to be averted.

After that, deprecatory letters to the young Subah were written from Calcutta, with grave remonstrances and remindings of ancient friendship and of the imperial deeds and grants of Delhi; but to very little purpose, except to confirm the Nawab's idea, that the English were, after all, helpless beggars, and thus make him resolve once for all that their ancient arrogance was to be humbled to the dust. It was in vain that the kind old Begum, the Nawab's mother —always friendly to Englishmen—besought her son not to molest them. "She would become peacemaker," she said, "and restore the former good understanding." All she could effect, however, was to save the lives of the gentlemen who had given themselves up, trusting to her son's honour, and to preserve them, in some measure, from ill-usage and indignity.

Thais was urging on her royal lover, and his good mother's warnings were cast to the winds. Perhaps, indeed, he needed little urging. Cruel and vindictive by nature, as he had ever been, he could ill brook opposition at any time. Now the councils of the Affghan girl accorded with his own. Her fierce, passionate nature was developing itself, and his own had blended with it to ensure the rejection of any peaceful advice. Advocacy of the English cause had been interdicted; and whosoever had dared to offer any, might well have said his last prayer, and made himself ready for death or mutilation, as he proposed it.

Under these circumstances, what booted the English letters of remonstrance, the reiterations of no offence being intended, or the denial of new fortifications? Offence had been given; some new defences, under the apprehension of French attacks, had undoubtedly been constructed. The old system of bribery of officers to propose deprecatory offerings to their masters, which had often succeeded in the days of the empire, was now hopeless. No one would dare to propose what might result in instant death, or disgrace.

And all this having happened, the council that sat in Calcutta Factory on the 7th day of June 1756 were left in no doubt whatever as to what awaited them, when they heard direct from the Cossim Bazar Factory of what had been done there on the 2d of that month, and that the Subah's army had, for the most part, marched for Calcutta itself, under his own personal command. The bloodless victory which I have recorded had but whetted the young ruler's appetite, and, had there been no other reason, very shame at delay would have urged him on.

"Thou wilt be less than a man," had the Affgan girl said, "if this be abandoned. Thy people will spit at thee, and the children will cry coward in the streets. None of thy slaves in the durbar dare tell thee this, but I fear not. If I cannot live for my own honour, I can live for thine."

Perhaps such vehement adjuration was not needed; for the Nawab only laughed at his beautiful slave's enthusiasm, as he bid her be content, for she should see the English ships and the English treasury ere the month had passed, and she believed him now.

I have no need, then, to say that the council which sat in Calcutta that 7th of June was an anxious one. It was the end of the hot weather, and before the rain should fall the heat would be greater and greater. Those were not days of comfort in India: we Englishmen had not come to know how to live. In Calcutta, as everywhere else, it was for the most part a short life and a merry one. There were no good houses, no palaces as there are now. Some English-looking warehouses, a factory-hall and close chambers for the public servants, a barrack for the soldiers within the fort, and a few garden-houses without, where the air was fresher and cooler, with a church, completed "the Factory." There were few means of keeping but the heat, and little mitigation of it when it came into the houses, as it did fiercely on that 7th of June, when the English gentlemen sat in the great hall wiping their faces, and being fanned by their native servants.

What could they do? There were only a hundred and seventy-four soldiers there, many of whom were sick in hospital, and some weak convalescents. There were crews of ships to be sure, but these would be wanted on board. There was a large area to defend, and if the enemy were not checked at once, there was little hope of saving the settlement. There was great stress laid on this by the most experienced, and not without reason: for if the Subah once began to negotiate, they might hope to gain terms—hard enough perhaps—but still terms after all. What, however, if he refused all negotiation, as he had hitherto done?

There was certainly no aid to be had—neither the French nor the Dutch would, if they could, aid them: as one gentleman of the period has quaintly recorded, "The French gasconaded." They offered shelter, if the English chose to leave all and come up the river to them. I believe that the French gentlemen at Chandernagore felt very easy at the prospect of their English guests; and, as war was expected shortly, had little hope of seeing their invitation accepted. Leave Calcutta? Leave the Honourable East India Company's goods and chattels? their homes and their fort? There were the ships anchored before the Fort; and, if they pleased, if the worst came to the worst, nothing would be simpler than to get on board them and sail away as they had come: but what would they say in England?

The question has often been asked, and answered, for the most part, in the same way. I do not believe that all were brave in Calcutta that day—there were more despairing hearts there than it was pleasant to think about; but there were enough brave men to determine to fight the place to the last in any extremity, and these were the majority, as they always will be wherever Englishmen are gathered together with any great national honour or stake to be defended, whether on the land or on the sea. So when the military gentlemen had gone over their musters again, and calculated their means of defence, they called to the butler for a bottle or two of the prime old Madeira, and drank, with a cheer which made the roof ring, to the "Long life of the Company, and damnation to all Moors!" and felt their hearts stronger within them when they had done it.

When Mr. Wharton and Ralph Smithson walked up to the garden-house that hot evening, some of the preparations were in progress, some militia were being drilled, and Don Gomez, as the captain of a company, saluted them on the esplanade with a gravity worthy of a Silviera.

"Dis dam sulphurity night, gen'lemen," he said; "I'se too much countervaluated to obligatory dreel dese men; dey won't do regularity exercisements, nohow at all proper, because affrightenation in deir bellies, sir; 'cause of Nawab Sahib, dat is Subah we calls 'im, comin' with two lacs of armamentation, sir; so dey say in Bazar, sir—'pon my honour, sir, by George!"

"Pooh, pooh! Don, don't be frightened," said Mr. Wharton, laughing; "two lacs is a great many, that's two hundred thousand, you know. God bless me! enough to eat us all up, and we're not come to that yet. Now, you sirs, attention! Let me see what you're made of."

"Me frightened! Oh no, sir—not Don Gomez da Silviera. Me Portugueze, sir, service of Honourable Company, and Leften' in Calcutta Militia. No gentlemen terrified at all of dam' black Moors; w'en dey comes, sir, we gives 'em won wolly, and den dey alls runs away, sir, by George!—and w'en de incurvation of the flightiness happen, den we runs a'ter them, sir. I tell my men all dis, Mr. Smithson, but dey all indetermined to make warfare, dey says."

"Hallo! mutiny, Don? This will not do at all. What did they say?"

"Dey says, indexically, as I may say, sir, dat dey's no fi'tin' men, sir. Got childer, sir, an' women, an' all's got indexterity to never do no dreel. By George! Mr. Wharton, sir, dey's dam' coward, dat's what dey is; an' I can't make 'em magniloquent nohow; try all afternoon, sir, 'pon my honour, by George!"

"Well, drill them as well as you can, Don," said Mr. Wharton, good-humouredly; "if they won't fight, they'll do to stand on the rampart, and make the Fort look full of men, which it isn't, more's the pity. Good evening to you, Don Gomez; we may hear better news to-morrow."

"Good evening, gentlemen," returned the little Don, with a wave of his laced hat which would not have disgraced Birdcage Walk—"good evening. Now, 'tention men! Dere's Mr. Drake and Captain Minchin comin' up, and if dey sees you with dat longanimity of physionomities, I tink will scratch your backs, an' be dam'd to you, or put in black hole, 'pon honour, by George! dey will! So look out, you fellows. 'Tention! Shoulder armmes! Now, see you make present proper to Mr. Drake."

Leaving the Don and his company to be inspected, I shall follow Mr. Wharton to his pretty house, where he was expected anxiously. Evening was closing in as the gentlemen, after their usual stroll on the Mall by the river-side, went on to the gate, where a native soldier stood on guard, the barrel of his bright matchlock glinting in the setting sun as it shone across the broad river in a rich yellow light, flooding the air with golden radiance, and resting upon the vanes of the ships, the gilt pinnacles of Hindu temples in glowing sparkles; while, on the cavalier of the Fort, the old British flag clung heavily to the staff. As the sun dipped behind the trees on the western bank, a puff of smoke from a bastion was followed by the sharp report of a gun, and the fort-flag and the ensigns of the ships were hauled down, as the drums and fifes in the Fort played off the retreat. It was too hot to stroll farther, and Mr. Wharton was weary with his work of that day. As his children ran to meet him with a merry greeting in their native Hindustani, he put them aside; and as his wife came forward, he said, "I must have some rest, Julia; Smithson will tell you all about it; my head aches, darling, and I will lie down till supper is ready; sit outside—there will be a breeze from the river by-and-by, and it will be cooler."

CHAPTER XXXVI.

PERRIN'S REDOUBT, JUNE 16, 1756.

THERE is little time in the evening gloaming between light and darkness in Calcutta, and gradually, but swiftly, the objects on the further bank of the great river faded away. The broad stream itself seemed to mingle with the sky, and the gloom of night fell upon the little garden and shrubbery in front of the house which sloped down to the water's edge. Boats with lanterns twinkling from the tops of their high sterns were flitting to and fro mysteriously on the glassy surface like so many *ignes fatui*, becoming dimmer and dimmer amidst the mist which was slowly rising from the water. The fireflies innumerable came out and whirled among the trees; the crickets and frogs by the river-side kept up an incessant concert; within the house, where the candles were lighted, the air seemed full of insects flying about the flame, scorching their wings and falling on the tablecloth. That was no place to sit with comfort, and Mrs. Wharton and her companion were better without. Occasionally, the sound of shrill native music came up on the air from the town, where lights were sparkling in the distance: else all was still, and the merry laugh of the children at play in an inner room was hardly an interruption to a silence which was growing very oppressive to both. All that happened in the council was generally known to Ralph Smithson. He had told Mrs. Wharton as much of it as he could without causing her extreme alarm, and after that they were silent.

It was impossible for each not to be busy with their own thoughts; it was equally impossible to shut out the conviction of danger. There were those among the reckless who met it with defiance, or sought temporary oblivion in strong drink; and there were others, too, who looked upon the crisis with a higher fortitude and resignation.

"And there is no hope of bringing the Subah to terms, Mr. Smithson? Has everything been tried?" asked the lady, at length.

"I believe so," was the reply. "I am too young in rank to be admitted to the council; but Mr. Wharton told me as we walked from the Fort that he feared the Subah was implacable. There are a thousand reports, madam, flying about; but what I have heard from good authority—in fact, from Omichund, whom they have detained in the Fort—is, that the Nawab has a new favourite, and she urges him on to the sack of our poor Fort. This doth not appear openly, but all the people seem to know it, and these native bankers have always good intelligence. I have little hope, madam, if there is such an influence at work, that we can counteract it."

"Oh, Mr. Smithson, how wicked they are!" broke out Mrs. Wharton, "these shameless creatures. You will hardly believe what I have to endure even as I am. I do not understand a word of what is said to me even by those children; but they know I am not their mother, and—and—indeed, Mr. Smithson, I cannot bear it—I cannot indeed. Oh, if I had known in time, this would never have been; I would have died sooner—I would die now if I could. Look," she continued, repressing a great sob—"look into the parlour, you will not find him there; he is gone to her: he often goes now— Oh that I should have to bear this, and for a black woman too! Is it fair, Mr. Smithson, after all his promises? Is it honourable?"

Mrs. Wharton need not have feared her husband's honesty if she had known what then was passing between him and the mother of his children. What have we to do with the past, or with the connections which were matters of ordinary daily life in those days in India? There are some even now that say we are none the better there that they do not exist; and that in losing them we loosed one of the surest ties which bound us to the country and the people. Nay, the subject is gravely treated of in serious histories. I only say Mr. Wharton, when he married his wife, was faithful to her, as a true English gentleman should be; but he had not lost his respect, perhaps his love, for one who had loved and had been faithful to him for many a year. She had been put away. It was only what she had foreseen must ensue sooner or later; but her tie to Mr. Wharton, that of her three children, could not be altogether broken, and while he remained in India she had only implored to stay near them, that she might sometimes see them. I say, then, if Julia Wharton could have seen her husband, as ill thoughts of him flashed through her mind, and jealousy was possessing her, she would have seen no wrong that night.

He was telling a graceful native lady of middle age, who was weeping bitterly, that he believed his time had come; that he had a presentiment he should not survive the coming struggle, and had made provision for her; that, in case the Fort was attacked, she must protect her children, and was explaining to her how she was to obtain the large sum he had settled upon her, the interest of which would be paid to her by the agent of the great native banker, Juggut Seit. All this Mr. Wharton told to his wife afterwards when it was too late. Where he erred was in not doing this sooner, so as to have saved mutual misery in those sad sad days of trial.

Ralph Smithson got up and looked into the centre hall. Mr. Wharton was not there. The bedchamber was beyond, open to the verandah, and a lamp burning in it. The large bed, with its blue gauze musquito-curtains, was not occupied, nor was a sofa at its foot.

"Where is your master?" he asked of a servant who came to him.

"He is gone to the Begum Sahib's," said the man in a low whisper; "but the Madam Sahib must not know this."

Ralph Smithson returned to his chair. All that he could say was, Mr. Wharton had gone out, and would soon be back.

"I knew it!" cried his wife, with a burst of passionate weeping. "I told you where he had gone. He loves her more than me, and I will not bear it, Mr. Smithson—I cannot—I, an Englishwoman, to submit to this insult! Have you no sympathy with this misery? Oh! Ralph Smithson," she continued, flinging herself upon her knees before him, "you can save me from this. You can—you can." She could not speak for the hysterical sobbing which possessed her.

"Mrs. Wharton—Julia—rise, I pray you," said the young man earnestly. "Indeed you must. I will speak to your husband—"

"No, no, no!" she exclaimed, rising and sobbing still, "not to him—not to him. If I am mad—if I am beside myself with this misery—you alone know it. I have no one, not a friend in all the world, Ralph—not one—not one but you. Those I had all forsook me when—when—they sent me out here. I thought him true, and that he would help a poor child like me, and he promised me. But he is like the rest, and I cannot bear it—indeed I cannot. Only do you be true to me, and in all the misery we may have to endure, I will not give way if I am near you. Will you pity me?"

It was no easy matter to resist that pleading face, and the hands held out to him. Ralph Smithson had no hard heart, as we know. He had no higher motive on which to fall back for help, perhaps, except that feeling of a gentleman which had held him up; but he was no profligate seducer to take advantage of a jealous woman's weakness. "I do pity you," he said, taking her hands kindly in his and kissing them, "and I will be true to you, so long as I can help you or myself—I will indeed."

"Enough," said the lady. "I think I could endure any misery were I with any one to share it with me. But he must not see these tears, Ralph. I am a weak girl before you, but to him I have not yielded yet. Sit still—I will be back presently."

"Where is Julia?" asked Mr. Wharton, as he came round the end of the house. "I thought I heard her."

"She was here, sir, till this moment, and said she would be back directly."

Mr. Wharton sat down and sighed. "I will tell you, Ralph, some day, what I have been doing, and I'm glad it's done. The time may come to us all when we will need mutual confidence and support, and sooner than we think, perhaps. All I want you to promise me is, that if anything happens to me, you will see after her—after Julia—to the last. I was too old for her, Ralph, and I ought not—I ought not—"

Mr. Wharton did not finish the sentence, for he heard his wife's step in the verandah. "Promise me," he said in a low tone, putting out his hand.

"I do, sir, as you wish," replied the young man, taking it, "and with all my heart. I only hope that there may be no need."

Mr. Wharton could only press the hand he held, for the servant announced that supper was ready, so they went in together; and we may well believe that while the meal lasted, there was restraint upon all.

A few, very few days more, and it was evident that outlying houses could not be maintained, and they were abandoned one by one with sad hearts. The military officers of the settlement held daily consultations, and to the best of their judgment posts were arranged with a few guns on each, which, though they might afford means of a temporary check to the Subah's forces, were of too slight a nature to maintain defence against the odds they would have to meet when the real attack came. There was no news of any halt, even for refreshment, of the native forces. Day after day they were reported a march nearer; and this unusual vigour in the Nawab's proceedings presented a strange and alarming contrast to the usual marching of native armies. At the rate at which progress was reported, the enemy must reach Calcutta on the 17th or 18th of June at furthest; but on the 16th, about noon, there was no longer any doubt, for the drums and horns of the native forces were heard distinctly to the northward, as well as a few cannon-shots, which might be signals; and those posted in a redoubt called Perrin's, which commanded the northern entrance road to Calcutta, saw the first masses of cavalry debouch from among the heavy groves of trees which had concealed them, and for a moment halt irresolutely, while some of the foremost pointed to the British Fort.

There were a few English soldiers and sailors in that slight entrenchment; a few Portuguese and English artillerymen, and some native soldiers with matchlocks. Ralph Smithson was not in the military service, but he had volunteered to do his best, as did most of the others; and as that redoubt was the post of honour for the present, he had asked to serve there, and his companionship was gladly accepted by the officer in command of it. At anchor in the river, within musket-shot of the shore, was one of the Indiamen, the *Prince George*, the fire of whose guns would protect the flank of the post, and prevent its being turned. The earthwork was slight, but it was sufficient for protection and defence; and those who now garrisoned it had stout hearts. The day was insufferably hot, and light fleecy clouds sailed hither and thither in the upper air, dispersing, gathering, and changing perpetually, but without affording any shade. There had been no rain as yet, and that day the sun had blazed with a sweltering heat, from which even the natives shrank, as, with their heads tied up in heavy cloths, they crouched under the shade of the rampart, or clustered under that of a tree which overshadowed the redoubt, and spoke in low tones among themselves. Thus, from early morning till past noon, the advance of the enemy had been patiently awaited.

"The Moors! there they are!" exclaimed a burly sailor, who, with several others, had been lounging over the parapet. "Gentlemen, the enemy!"

The officers, too, had been lounging on the grass, in a temporary shed, and under what other shade they could find—chatting with each other, as men will do, cheerfully and gaily, when danger is imminent; and they started to their feet and hurried to their posts. The guns were already loaded with grape and round-shot, and matches were lighted.

"Steady, men!" cried the captain cheerily; "no firing without orders. Our shot must not be the first, the President says. Let's see what those fellows are going to do before we fire."

The horsemen had halted, and some could be seen unslinging their matchlocks, while others careered about, wheeling and turning their horses, while their naked swords flashed brightly in the sun.

"Very pretty, Mr. Smithson, is it not? I should not mind sending a round-shot among these rascals if they'd only fire," said Captain Brown, who commanded.

But there was a long pause, till a party of footmen, with a green standard and a small drum beaten quickly by a drummer, arrived and took post under some trees near the horsemen. Something more was evidently expected. Nor had they to wait long. Presently the heads of several elephants were seen over the bushes, and then a drove of white bullocks, dragging a gun which was pushed on by the elephants.

"That means mischief, Smithson," said a companion; "we shall hear its bark by-and-by. What a fool Brown is to wait! damme! I'd have a shot into it before they could unlimber."

"Are you ready with that gun, Mr. Scott?" cried the captain to an officer of the *Prince George*, who was on duty there with two boats' crews; cover that gun there, but don't fire till you get the word."

"I am laying her myself, sir," was the reply, "and I'll watch your signal, never fear. That's a small piece, and they won't like the long nine when it gets among them, I think, my lads. Steady now, and slew to the right, Jacobs. That's it—look out! they've lighted their match!"

There was a puff of smoke and a dull report in the heavy, heated air, and a shot passed high over the redoubt, roaring as it went.

"God save King George! Hurray!" cried the captain, waving his hat; "Three cheers, men!" and they were heartily given, while the officer at the gun touched his hat. "She's ready, sir," he said, "and I can see their gun now."

"Fire, then, Mr. Scott, in the King's name!" and as he spoke Captain Brown saw the aim had been perfect. Splinters of the weak native gun-carriage flew about, and the gun itself seemed to subside into a heap on the ground. "Now, the other, Mr. Scott! That's capital, by George!" he exclaimed. "I suspect they don't like cannister, gentlemen. Look!"

Fifty heads were above the rampart looking anxiously at the scene before them. Before the round-shot had been fired, a crowd of the native soldiery had collected about their gun, and into this mass the cannister of the nine-pounder descended with terrible effect, and a dozen or more men lay prostrate, some writhing, others still in death.

"Let's dash among them," cried Ralph Smithson, waving his cutlass. "Now's our time, sir."

"Not yet, Mr. Smithson—not yet," said the captain calmly. "For heaven's sake, sir, be cool. We'll do our best, but we can't risk this post."

He was right: the force of the attack had not yet come, for in a few minutes more they saw several other guns dragged into position, and prepared for action.

"By George! there's a woman among them!" cried the captain, who was looking through a ship's-glass. "What can she be doing there? Don't throw away a shot, Mr. Scott, and wait for my word. She's there—there on that elephant with the silk howda. Look out!"

The next discharges from the native guns were no better aimed than the first. The shot sang harmlessly over the English fort, and was replied to by so sharp a fire from the two guns, that the adverse artillery was dragged back among the bushes, while the place they had stood on was pretty thickly covered by the dead.

"A little nearer, and we'd have done for more of the d—d niggers," said the naval officer, wiping the sweat and powder from his face. "It's too far for the grape, Captain Brown."

"Wait," was the reply. "I see a body of new people forming in a mass behind the trees. Steady, men! Here they come, by George! If the ship only sees them!"

As he spoke, a mass, rather than a column of footmen, with drawn sabres glittering in the sun, and broad black shields across their bodies, advanced at a run; a man bearing a green standard, and another beating a small drum, preceding them.

"Let them come on, Mr. Scott—nearer, nearer!" cried the captain, who was standing bareheaded. "Now!"

The guns were fired almost simultaneously, and within perfect range this time, for the grape mowed lines through the mass, but did not stop it. At the same moment, a broadside from the ships took the column in flank, and did more havoc. This had not been foreseen by the enemy; and after an unsteady pause they broke and fled, a volley from the English muskets following them. Again Ralph Smithson and some of the men would have pursued, but were kept back.

"We have not done with them yet, I think," said Captain Brown. "They think they'll carry this post; but, by George! gentlemen, if you're all of my mind, they'll only get to Calcutta by this road over our bodies. Steady, men! and wait; when it's time I'll lead you. Does that satisfy you?"

The enemy were now more careful, and shifted their position more to the left, while a heavier column of attack was being formed; and a battery of rockets was opened upon the post, which, however, did no great harm. Every now and then plunging shots from the ship swept through the trees, but did not stop their advancing preparations.

"She's there again, sir," cried Ralph Smithson, who had borrowed the glass. "I see her plainly—a fair red-cheeked girl, richly dressed. What can she be? There's no English woman among them surely?"

No, it was no English woman; but the Affghan girl Sozun, who, unable to contain her excitement, had been in the front on an elephant when the unlooked-for obstacle in the road appeared. It was she who was appealing to the Rohillas of the Nawab's force to prove themselves men—to bring her the heads of the English Kaffirs, promising a shield full of rupees for every one. She was speaking to them in her own fierce Pushtoo, and reminding them of home, and what would be said there, as the English captain was reminding his men too; of dear old England.

So an hour or more passed, and a sputtering fire of matchlocks was kept up from the brushwood and hedges in front, which was galling, because they had a longer range than the clumsy English musket, and by it a few men were wounded and four killed.

"Ye'll be frae the North, surr, a'm thinkin'?" said a tall seaman, with greyish hair and a weather-beaten face, who belonged to the *Prince George*, touching his hat to Ralph Smithson. "A've heerd the burr a bit, surr, frae ye, and it's aye like music to mey."

"I am," he replied. "Why do you ask?" The North! ah, dear old Melcepeth! what a flood of recollections flashed through Ralph's mind at the simple question!

"Weel, surr, a' made bow'd t' speak t' ye, fur there's na tellin' wha'll be alive an' wha'll be deed the day; but if anything happens to mey, ye ken, a'd like to think what a' have wad be sent hame to my folk, surr. A'm John Drever, surr, frae Berwick, an' a countryman—"

"Look out, Mr. Scott!" was the captain's cry again. "By George! a gallant set of fellows they are! Ready there with the guns!"

"I'll see to it," cried Ralph to the seaman. "There's no time now for talking."

Little time indeed; for it was a heavy column that was advancing—perhaps a thousand men. The cries and shouts of the first party were changed for a rough chorus of some mountain war-song; the faces of those that came on were as fair as the English faces in the redoubt, and they wore a sort of uniform dress of blue cotton.

"Fire!" cried Captain Brown, standing on the parapet, while balls whistled round him like hail.

The aim was the same, the result was the same: a lane of maimed and wounded; but the fair-faced men's song did not cease, and the column surged on with increased speed. It was well that the commander of the *Prince George* had been watching carefully what was going on. With springs on the cables, he had warped the ship nearer to the shore, and so that her broadside commanded the green space before the redoubt, and at this moment a full broadside of grape and round shot struck the Rohilla column on its flank, while Mr. Scott's guns again vomited their deadly contents almost in their faces.

About fifty of the enemy still dashed on, and attempted to scale the breastwork, but were met by the English boarding-pikes and bayonets, and fiercely thrust back. They were all of that column which came to close quarters; the rest turned and fled, and Captain Brown, with a ringing cheer, leaped from the parapet, followed by Smithson and fifty others, in hot pursuit.

Ralph Smithson's powerful arm told well in the hand-to-hand *melée* which followed, and it was not a bloodless one. First in the pursuit, he had soon overtaken the hindmost of the retreating foes, and dashed among them with all the energy and passion of his race—the Darnell blood was fairly up, and he felt, for the first time, the uncontrollable excitement of actual battle. It might have fared ill with him, however, that day but for Drever the sailor, who was close at his heels.

"Hae a care, surr," cried the man, striking down a thick-bearded fellow with his cutlass—"ha'e a care. Thrree to ane. D—n ye for cowards!"

Three men had turned, and with all their force attacked Smithson; but it was for a moment only, as he parried the cuts made at him and fell back, for the seaman had rushed in, and others followed, and there was soon an end to the encounter.

"You're wounded, surr," cried the seaman. "A' hope it's no bad, an' a've jist gotten a clink mysel'."

Ralph Smithson had not felt the cut in his excitement: but there was a slash through his coat on the left arm, and his blood was flowing freely. It was not the first time he had seen it. Then he was sick to death, lying in a London street—now, had it not been that Captain Brown ordered them back, he would have gone on with the pursuit, little heeding his wound, perhaps beyond the bounds of prudence.

So they all returned to the redoubt, and shook hands over the affair, as stout Englishmen should do. There were a few wounds among the party hastily tied up, and four gone to their rest who could be ill spared; and with a can of grog all round, they waited for what should come next; but the "Moors" had had enough. There was an attempt made to form up more men, but a shot or two dispersed them, and presently the Englishmen heard the deep drums of the Subah's forces beating far away to their right, the sound growing more and more distant among the trees; and the fair face on the elephant was seen no more.

Nor were they long in suspense as to future plans, for a messenger arrived shortly afterwards with a written order for the post to withdraw to the Fort, the enemy having appeared in its vicinity, and every man being needed for its defence; and as the evening was drawing in, the garrison of "Perrin's Redoubt" was safe within the walls of Fort William, telling their tale to eager listeners, and receiving the congratulations they had so well earned.

CHAPTER XXXVII.

BESIEGED.

In spite of his wound, which, though slight, was painful, and irritated by the great heat, Ralph Smithson had fought through the whole of the 18th of June in a battery which, as belonging to the outer defences of the Fort, was one of the most important of those positions. He had never left this post night or day, so he had little idea what was doing in the Fort, and little inclination to be amidst the wrangling and coufusion which prevailed. He had seen nothing of Mr. and Mrs. Wharton, who, he knew, were there now; and their house was a post which, as long as it could be maintained, strengthened the line of defences to the south-east. There had come a hurried note from Mr. Wharton, bidding him take care of himself; that his wife was safe; and they hoped, God willing, to see him again. But there were reports brought up to the post by men from the Factory—reliefs when they could be sent, or parties with supplies of ammunition—that matters looked bad there, and the gentlemen had decided upon retreat to the ships in case they were pressed by the enemy, and some women and children had even been sent on board.

There was no time, however, to think of such matters. Early on the 18th, as the mist which had been lying dank and chill on the low grounds rose under the gleams of the sun, it was easy to be seen that, though the previous day had been one of comparative quiet, the Nawab's officers had not been idle. On every house from whose terraced roof part of the entrenched lines could be commanded, strong parties of matchlock-men had been posted during the night behind screens made of cotton bags, grain baskets, or such other contrivances for protection as could most readily be arranged; while in others, loopholes had been pierced with crowbars through the parapets of the terraces, and marksmen lying safely behind them could fire leisurely upon those who manned the guns at the posts, and pick off any who moved about or showed themselves at all so fast, that the officers in command were forced to keep their men under cover, and to await attack, rather than seek to anticipate it.

Nor was this confined to the outposts only. Many of these matchlock pickets commanded the Fort itself, outside as well as in; and though there was shelter enough for the garrison, the guns could not be worked except at great disadvantage, and the losses everywhere were constant and severe. It was no part of the enemy's tactics to come to close quarters with the defenders of the outposts, else, during that day, the whole of the outer lines might have been stormed; the result of one attack at the redoubt had been enough to prove the mettle of Englishmen. Now, beleaguered as it was, the whole of the English garrison had, it seemed, no chance of escape. It would be an affair of time only, that complete humiliation of the English which he had decreed; and till they were brought bound before him, asking pardon humbly, Suraj-oo-Doulah's revenge would be incomplete.

From early morning, in an upper room of a good native house, from whence, though out of range of musketry, the progress of the conflict could be watched, the young Nawab had sat at an open window with little intermission till noon. It was remarked by the English that there was a sudden cessation of firing then for about two hours for which they could not account, and in regard to which there were many speculations. The enemy might be eating, or some other movement was being arranged; perhaps a general charge on all the outlying positions. It was not so, however. The Nawab had kept up his attention as long as he could, but there was no perceptible progress; and the puffs of smoke, and dull reports of cannon, varied by the sputtering rattle of matchlocks and muskets, became so monotonous, that he had directed the firing to cease while he rested, lay down on a bedding, and slept heavily.

But Sozun, who was by him, driving away the flies with a light fan of feathers, was not sleepy. She sat at the open window, still looking out on the plain, and on the Fort of the mysterious people of whom she had so often heard. There were their ships which had come over the ocean in voyages of many months, with their white awnings glistening in the sun, and the red English ensigns flying from their mizen-peaks. There were a few small posts on the plain, defying the whole Moslem army as the redoubt had done—where even her own countrymen had been beaten back, and her promises of shields full of rupees for every infidel head, had failed to bring one. What were these Feringis who fought so boldly, and dared to defy the hosts before them? She could only see a few men in red coats and black caps moving about the outworks. She had watched more than one drop suddenly at a gun, as it was loaded and fired by a few, and a sharp storm of matchlock balls whistled about them, and sent them again under cover. Now, as the Nawab slept, and the silence was almost oppressive, she could see those in the nearest post (it was Ralph Smithson's) come out and look about them; peer over the parapet of their fascine battery, and look up to the houses from whence the matchlock firing had been incessant—wondering, no doubt, as well they might, why it had ceased. Well! she should see them nearer soon—those fair-haired ruddy Englishmen would all be captive! And their women? Were there any there among them, beautiful as houris—as angels of Paradise—as she had heard fairer than herself? What if he should see any and take them, and cast her out, or send her to the vaults below the palace, where there were others she knew of, like the Begum, who might never see the open light of heaven again? For this there was at least a remedy; and while she shuddered at a possible alternative, he who might occasion it lay in his heavy sleep prostrate before her, as he had lain often before. Oh for a free life! This was but that of a slave!—caressed and indulged, truly, but to an Affghan girl a very hateful one!

Hateful indeed! What had her own countrymen cried to her when she strove to urge them on to the attack two days before? "Hide your face, shameless one. We need no courtesan to tell us what to do. Hide your face, and begone from among honourable soldiers. Was ever an Affghan woman like you, O daughter of shame!" Ah, yes! they would not heed her protestations, or her frantic, passionate cries. They bade her begone, and one had lifted his matchlock to his shoulder, as he swore a shocking oath in her own tongue, which had terrified the driver of her elephant, who had turned the noble beast and hurried her away. Had she forgotten this? What to her were the cries, the fawnings of adulation, which attended her every movement abroad, from the servile courtiers and Bengalee officers whom she despised?

In many a fight worse than that had she ridden with her brave father, and had no terror of sharp swords or matchlock balls. What she saw now, seemed but child's play to those fierce conflicts, and to the sweeping charges of the chivalry of Delhi, as they burst through the Affghan squadrons and left her father dying in her arms on the bloody field of Sirhind! Had he but lived, she would now have been a wife in some quiet nook of the glorious valleys of Istaliff. There might have been children at her knee, and the rough choruses of her people ringing in her ears, instead of a life of shame. "Begone, O shameless one!" they had cried—"hide thy face from honest men!" And yet she might redeem the past. There were women in her country who, clad in coarse garments, went about singing the name of Allah, or in waste places ministered to the wants of faint and weary travellers—women who had changed their life of sin, to one of good works in the love of God and the Prophet—women who were honoured while they lived, and had shrines by lone waysides raised to their memories after death. If she lived—if she lived—this might be; but for the present there could be no change—she could not fly—she must endure. And these, and a thousand whirling thoughts, went through the girl's mind as her master slept.

"Is the Fort taken? are the Feringis here?" he cried at last, starting up from his sleep. "I hear no firing. Sozun, thou hast been looking on—how is it? Have they surrendered?"

"Surrendered!" she repeated, bitterly. "No; the English, they say, never surrender. My lord slept, and there could be no noise permitted—so they told me."

"The fools!" he cried—"as if I could not sleep soundly with the roar of cannon in my ears! The fools! and they have lost hours. Ho! Ahmed! Nasir! tell them I am awake, and look on at the war."

I think the Affghan girl, with shame lying deep at her heart, which her lord knew not of, would have gone forth there and then to her own countrymen if she had dared, and humbled herself before them, asking them to let her share their fate. She had been sorely tempted to do this many a time since she had heard their cries of shame; but she would have thus exposed them to fearful risk, and herself to destruction. Yet there was many a tale and legend she knew, in which women of her own mountains had cheered men on to victory with shrill cries, and had even led them sword in hand—which were sung round rude fireplaces when the snow fell, or at the house-mill in the early morning, when meal was ground for the day's cakes. Her lord was impatient for victory. If she died among her people, it would not be in shame; and as the firing recommenced suddenly, and she saw the red-coated Englishmen, who had been lounging about or lying on the grass, start to their feet and hurry to their posts—the desire to be with her countrymen in the hottest of the fray became more and more uncontrollable.

"There is nothing done, Sozun," cried the Nawab at length, as he rose and seated himself at the lattice, watching, as before, the interminable puffs of smoke, and listening to the patter of musketry. "Not even thy people, who boast they are the Feringis' masters, dare to venture out sword in hand against those few feeble Kaffirs. I tell thee, girl, there are not a hundred able men among them. See, here is the list, sent me from their Fort this morning; and yet no one dares—no one dares," he cried loudly and bitterly, "to go upon them."

"I dare, my lord," she said firmly, rising from her seat near the next window—"I dare! Will my lord let me lead my people?"

"They are cowards! they would leave thee dead on yonder plain. My rose," he returned, "I could not spare thee. What tales have I not heard of Rohilla prowess, and that their plan of war was to charge sword in hand up to guns and slay the gunners! Look! there are but two guns in yonder post, behind some faggots which a boy might jump over, and not twenty men to defend them. And there is Noor Khan with five hundred of thy people firing volleys of shot at them and killing none. Oh, shame, shame! they to call themselves men!"

"It is true, my lord—most true. I have watched this all day, and now am ready. My lord must let me go to my people; a woman's cry may shame them to victory. I am a soldier's child. Oh, my lord, do not refuse this! If I die, who will mourn? What I can do, will be but a poor return for all my lord's kindness and love."

The Nawab looked at her from head to foot with a strange puzzled expression. Such a request to come from a woman! What woman did he know—had ever known—that would dare to make it? Had ever such been before? There were a few dim Persian legends of woman's bravery and devotion which he remembered, and did not the noble wife of Humayoon the Emperor share her husband's battles and his camp life? Had not Chand Beebee of Ahmednugger fought on the breach of her own citadel hand to hand with the Mogul chivalry, and driven them back?

"By Alla! Sozun, thou mayst be right," he exclaimed; "but would I exchange that Fort and all its wealth for thee?"

"If so poor a thing as I," she said, "could win it for thee, my lord, and die on the rampart yonder, my death would be welcome. My people would then sing of me in the old home, that she who had lived in dishonour had redeemed herself, and was slain in fight. My lord, my lord! if thou hadst only heard their words of reproach, which still ring in my ears, which haunt me night and day—night and day—for the memory of which I cannot sleep—thou wouldst let me go, else—I shall die in my shame. If thou wilt, I may do this. If I win that place for thee, Sozun will be a thousand times dearer—if I die, a thousand, fairer than I, are to be bought as thou needst them. Let me go! It is my destiny—thine and mine are the same. Day by day I have had the book of the stars read, since that Derwesh told it to thee, and the planets do not change. The star of my lord's victory is shining above his head and over mine. My lord, I beseech thee, let me go."

The young man seemed to catch up some of the enthusiasm of his beautiful slave, and he clapped his hands, and cried to the attendants, who answered. "Let Noor Khan be called," he said.

Noor Khan was the commander of the Affghans in the Nawab's army. He was in a house hard by, directing a heavy matchlock fire upon the redoubt in which Ralph Smithson was posted, and admiring, with a grim satisfaction, the obdurate tenacity with which the few Englishmen left there were now serving their guns, now firing from their heavy muskets, when the Nawab's messenger reached him, and he was soon in the presence.

"He is as my father," Sozun had said to the Nawab, "and I will not withdraw."

"Hear what the lady has to say to thee, Noor Khan," he said, "and be kind to her. If it is to be, it is to be."

The Affghan looked grimly at the richly-dressed girl before him, and said, in the broken patois of the country he knew,

"Men who look on the like of these are but zenana soldiers, my lord. Pardon me; it is shameful!"

"She is of thy country, Noor Khan."

"She had better have died on the field of Sirhind," said the man, "where her father died, than live thus. I know her. If we dared, we would put her to death, as we do such in our country."

"Do not speak, my lord," cried the girl, her breast heaving: "Let me—he will not refuse me." And then, in a passionate flood of her own native tongue, she told her shame; her desire of death in dishonour, or life in honour; and begged, as she cast herself before the old soldier, that her prayer might not be rejected.

"Art thou content, O my king?" said Noor Khan, when he had heard all. "If she lives, I will take her inside yonder fort to-morrow; if she dies she will be at rest, and it will be well—she will have redeemed her shame."

I do not profess to say that the young Bengal nobleman at all understood or appreciated the wild sense of honour which the girl had inherited from her race. But he knew that Sozun, having once formed the determination, would not cease to beseech or taunt him. Perhaps—I will not avouch it—he was weary already of the wild Affghan girl whom no menance could terrify, and at whose hands, if he provoked her, he was as likely to meet death as she at his. He had been accustomed to other tempers—to women whom he could kick, or strike, or abuse, or insult at his pleasure. No doubt she was a restraint upon him, which he had never known before, and of which he was often impatient. It was only the girl's extraordinary beauty, and the fascination which she exerted upon him, that had held him faithful, or tolerant of her so long. Above all, to his superstitious mind there seemed to have entered a conviction that his destiny was in truth linked with hers; and that as she had brought him good fortune, it would continue.

"She is my pledge with thee, Khan," he replied, "and my honour is in thy hands. See what trust I place in thee! Thou art not the Noor Khan I know, if one of these Kaffirs escape thee."

As he spoke, he had pointed towards the plain, and an exclamation of surprise escaped him. "What are they doing?" he cried.

Noor Khan looked out upon the plain, over which the last rays of the sun before it set were streaming, upon a few parties of English soldiers here and there dragging a gun; carrying dead and wounded in blankets; some hobbling along weary and faint, holding by a comrade's shoulder; while others, covering their retreat, fired from time to time in answer to the shot which fell thicker and faster around them. All this was quite visible to those who looked on from that window—the green plain, the red coats on it, the small sad processions, and the little puffs of smoke from the muskets and matchlocks, fired as if by children in play. Beyond, the old Fort, and the vessels behind it; the evening breeze now and then floated out the English flag, which was flying there in defiance of the hosts which beleaguered it, and flights of great storks and crows were going to their roosting places.

"Too late!" cried Noor Khan. "While I have been prating here, they have escaped me. My lord, let me go! If thou art coming, girl, be quick; but not as thou art," and he turned to where she had been standing.

Sozun, however, had quitted the room; but as the old soldier was leading his men into the battery which Ralph Smithson had just left, a boyish figure, dressed in the blue tunic of his people, lightly armed, and with a rich handkerchief tied round the turban and mouth—overtook him, and, touching his arm, made a respectful salute; then dropping beside him, took up the hoarse war-chorus which the men were singing, as they went on at a swinging trot. Ah! it was like the dear old time when she was by her father; and the girl's heart bounded within her with a sense of freedom and exultation to which she had long been a stranger. There and then, had they gone across that green plain into the mouths of the English cannon, Sozun would have led them in a delirium of excitement which she could not repress—as she leaped high to the burden of the rude war-song, and waved her sword and clashed her shield with her countrymen. But for the present the Affghans' advance was soon checked, and night fell upon the scene of conflict.

CHAPTER XXXVIII.

RECONCILIATION.

Just then Ralph Smithson was entering the gate of Fort William with his men, weary, faint, and sick at heart, as well from his painful wound and hard day's fighting in the sun, as from the order to retreat, and to leave spiked the heavy gun, which could not be carried away. The dead, however, had been brought, and the wounded, and such ammunition as remained. The enemy had only got one gun, spiked, and that would at least be useless. Instead of finding an orderly garrison, and the usually grave quiet of the Fort, his ears were assailed with a clamour, and his eyes fell upon a scene of confusion, which he little expected there. An order had already been given for the women to be sent on board ship, and the boats lying at the landing-place were taking in cargoes of trunks and boxes, and terrified weeping women and children. In place of an embarkation with proper order, every one was clamouring for places as though all chance of escape was already cut off. Shrillest were the cries of the Portuguese women and children, which mingled with the hoarse oaths of English seamen and native boatmen; and it was in vain that some of the officers appeared to be endeavouring to persuade the terror-stricken people that the enemy were still far from the gates. Several boatloads of helpless persons had already been upset from the crowding in them, and the people rescued with difficulty from the stream—nay, some had even been swept away; but this did not deter the rest, and it was only when the last boatload had gone, and the water-gate was shut, that, for the night at least, confusion was stayed.

Sick, then, with heat and pain, and faint with hunger, as he might well be, for a little hard ship-biscuit and some cold ship's beef had been his only food for two days, it was with a sense of comfort, and enjoyment of safety, that Ralph Smithson sat down that night to the only comfortable meal he had eaten for several days. A plentiful cool bath had refreshed him; the surgeon had dressed his wound with a cooling plaster; the kind thoughtfulness of Mr. Wharton and his native servant had provided him with a clean suit of clothes; and if any of my readers can remember having been in Ralph Smithson's straits in India, and to have undergone cleansing and refreshing as he had done, they will acknowledge with me that, during a meal so comfortable, all previous hardship would be forgotten. After his experience of an open post, a blazing sun over him by day, and chill dank dews by night, with a rain of shot perpetually pelting into it, and an enemy shouting defiance with every volley—the quiet of the Fort, the apparent security of the walls and gates, the heavy cannon on the bastions, and the cessation from firing on the part of the enemy as the evening closed in—conveyed an assurance to his mind which, though it raised his own spirits, did not apparently affect those about him, and the Factory hall was dull indeed that night.

Supper was one of the pleasantest of the Factory public meals, at all times; a substantial hearty repast, wherein savoury curries, fresh mango, and bhilsa fish almost alive from the river, and Patna, or other up-country beef and mutton, smoked on the board; and such tea from China, such coffee from Mocha or Java, as money could not purchase in England—with old Madeira and punch—were freely spread out at that liberal and hospitable board. Sometimes the English ladies of the Factory spent the evening there; and not unfrequently there was a country-dance, or a minuet or cotillon, by way of wind-up among the younger folk, while the elders had their whist or picquet, or boston, or cribbage, and played pretty deeply too. It was not here that the coarse profligacy of the settlement was to be seen. That lay at no great distance perhaps, but apart, in the private bachelor houses, in purlieus of the native city and elsewhere, where we need not seek it.

But that night the meal was eaten almost in silence, and quickly removed. The old khansaman, or butler, saw his English masters were in no good humour, and that it would be safe to get out of their way as speedily as possible; and afterwards, instead of the pleasant card-parties, men gathered into knots and spoke little above their breath. There were some who, like Ralph Smithson, had had a post to defend, and who had much to tell of what had happened there. There were some still buoyant and defiant; not boasting, as Englishmen seldom do among themselves, but saying to their own hearts, and perhaps asseverating it with an oath, that they'd fight the old Fort to the last shot before they'd give it up to the Subah, or any d—d Nabob in the country.

And there was a group gathered round an elderly native, sitting very much as if he were extremely uncomfortable in a chair, with his naked legs tucked up in it, and his knees projecting for want of room—a man with a thin bony face, and small twinkling eyes, who had a hooked nose, which projected over his short upper lip and thin moustache; else close shaven, with a muslin skull-cap on his head, and a broad yellow mark of Hindu caste upon his forehead. This was Omichund, the great Hindu banker, who had been seized on suspicion of intrigue, and detained in the Fort, whom the President would not release; and who, very friendly to his rich English constituents himself, was professing his willingness to go and do what he could; but at the same time expressing honestly his opinion that he feared that matters had gone too far for adjustment, except by unconditional submission.

Omichund well knew the young Nawab's implacable disposition. A thousand stories of it, which concerned natives alone, were current among them. Men—the public—for there is a native public there, as we ourselves know *now*—knew how the ears of the Derwesh had been cut off in open durbar, because he had spoken a word in favour of the English; they knew that the Nawab had witnessed a special play in which Englishmen had been personated by the vilest of buffoons; and the astute Hindu banker judged badly of the chances of the English after this. But he had been honourable; he had paid every farthing of the heavy bills of exchange drawn upon him by the house of Juggut Seit, which were, in fact, the realisations of balances by the English Factory agent at Moorshedabad. He had done all this, but neither the Nawab's good mother, who had written to Omichund to do what he could for her English friends, nor Juggut Seit himself, powerful as he was, could turn the young Nawab from his purpose before he marched for Calcutta; and it was not likely that he, Omichund, could do anything either, now he had arrived there. He had no need to go, he said—they need not send him away. The Nawab would not hurt him, and if the Fort were soon taken, his mediation might be of use.

If the Fort were taken! Then it might be; the old banker thought it might be. I think many others that night thought the same, because the ammunition had been inspected that day, and the disgraceful neglect of years had come to light. Men's hearts sank within them when they found the fuzes of bombs green and mouldy, and their contents wet with the damp of the magazine; where also they found round-shot and grape hardly enough for three days' defence, and the powder so damp that it hissed long before it exploded. Under all these circumstances I do not marvel that the gentlemen of the Calcutta Factory spent an unpleasant evening; or that the minds of many, ordinarily cheerful, were filled with undefinable but miserable forebodings. It had not come home to those gentlemen yet, that Calcutta was unsafe; that the host thundering at their doors was in earnest. Such a thing had not happened since good old Job Charnock's time, and why should it be now? Here was only a weak sensual youth, whom anybody could turn round his finger—even his women and his eunuch—so they had been told, and so believed; but they forgot that, very often, these weak sensual youths are the strongest in obstinacy of profligate indulgence, and the hardest to be turned from their revengeful purposes.

Ralph Smithson had exchanged a few words only with Mr. Wharton since his return from the outpost, but he knew where he should find him. A bastion on the river face was a favourite resort of the Whartons, as it was of others—a place where people met in the evening, where chairs were set and gossip went on while the fresh air came up from the water, and the great stream, hurrying to the sea, sent up its indefinable murmur of small breaking wavelets and the rushing of the water amidst posts and tall sedges: a place where many a love-scene, honest and dishonest, had been played out, and where many a sadly heaved sigh had been sent over the great ocean to which the river was ever hastening; Ralph Smithson was sure they would be found there. And how had it fared with them? Had Julia Wharton's jealousy increased, or had her husband, at last, given her his confidence?

When Ralph Smithson had gone out to Perrin's Redoubt, to face what might be death, he had deliberately made his will. He could have no claim to his father's allowance from the estate, for that must lapse, with his life, to the baronet or Constance. There was no need, therefore, to say anything about it; but the property of which he was the owner he had a right to dispose of as he pleased; and he had willed half of it to Mr. Smithson, of Warkworth, in usufruct for his life, and the other half to Mistress Sybil Morton, with the reversion of what would come from his grandfather to the same person. He had not forgotten dear old Nanny either, and she had a share too. So it will be seen that, while this will secured all he had to those he best loved, there was no clue in it to what he was that could be understood by Mr. Wharton or the other gentlemen who witnessed it. The venture he had sent home would, he knew, prove very profitable; and Mr. Darnell held the rest of his property and would account for it.

When this was accomplished, Ralph Smithson felt that he had done his duty, and was the better for it. He had written, too, to his uncles; to the baronet praying his forgiveness, and to be remembered by him and Constance kindly; and to Roger Darnell very warmly, and out of the fulness of his heart; a few lines to Sybil also: and so was prepared to live or die as his Lord willed.

These papers he had made up into a packet and given to Mr. Wharton in his wife's presence, and had said, with a manly tear in his eyes, that if he lived he would hope to be of use to them, and if not, they should not forget him; and he took Mr. Wharton aside, and conjured him to do the same as he had done. In this time of common danger, there should be perfect confidence, and Ralph reminded him of the little scene outside the bungalow, when Mr. Wharton had promised to tell him all some day. Now he was anxious to know whether that had been done or no, and it was with a swelling heart, and a gush of thankfulness, that, as he ascended the steps of the rampart, he saw the bastion empty, except of two figures, whom he knew to be his friends.

They were standing with their backs to him, looking over the great river, shimmering in a faint moonlight. Mr. Wharton's arm was about his wife's small waist, and her head was lying on his shoulder quietly, with her hand in his. They were not speaking; but the figures had an expression of confidence and love in their position which Ralph Smithson had never seen before, and he thanked God for it. It was evident Mr. Wharton had done his duty.

"Ah! is it you, Ralph?" said Mr. Wharton, cheerily, turning as he heard the step. "You have found us out, and Julia has been so anxious to see you. How's your arm, since the doctor dressed it?"

"Thank God, you are safe, Mr. Smithson," cried Mrs. Wharton, turning to him; "you are welcome back—oh, so welcome!"

"And I trust you got the clean clothes, Ralph. I gave them to the servant," continued her husband. "Julia had them tied up carefully. There were all you wanted, I hope?"

"All, sir; and I feel so fresh and happy after that horrible post.

I don't think we could have held it all night, and we were right to withdraw, though we did leave a gun behind."

"And we are glad to be here too, Mr. Smithson, for we could not have remained in the dear old house; but we have done the best for our property," added Mrs. Wharton.

"All yours, and the papers, are safe on board the *Daddaley* yonder," continued Mr. Wharton, "and under the especial care of the captain—so we shall find them when we get on board—that is, if we have to go. I am quite prepared for *that*, Ralph, for you would have been as disgusted as myself at what has passed here. The President has written once more to the Nawab, through the Armenians, but I very much question whether it is of any use."

"Then we should retreat, you think, sir? It's an ugly word, Mr. Wharton."

"Well," replied Mr. Wharton, "Job Charnock, who was a wise man in his generation, once left the Factory, and came back in better plight, and so may we. However, there's no use speculating; to-morrow or next day we shall know all, and meanwhile we shall do our best, I daresay. And now I have some good news for you. I have followed your advice, and feel as if I were a far happier bridegroom than I was when I married Julia."

"And I, Mr. Smithson," said his wife, "have to thank you for this. I am sure I have, sir," she added quite gaily, and with some of her usual sprightly manner. "I feel as if the Moors yonder had brought me a treasure, and I'm so happy—oh, so happy! We sat on the other side of the walls, John and I, all the afternoon, after the firing began again, and watched you. John sheltered me behind some cotton bales; and we watched you coming in from the redoubt, and I prayed you might come safely, and so did he; and I thank God that you are here with us again."

"Ah yes!" said Mr. Wharton, "it was all over before we left the bungalow. I told her everything, and *she* came at Julia's request, and—and—no matter now, Ralph, it is happily over, and the children are safest with *her*."

"And he forgave me all my waywardness and foolish jealousy, Ralph. Oh, it was so good of him, wasn't it?"

I don't think Ralph Smithson could say much in reply—perhaps his heart was too full. Had he not known what it was to be jealous, and what had come of it? He could only take their hands and press them together in both his own, and they all sat down, and, without speaking much, looked out on the great river and its current, running swiftly to the sea.

CHAPTER XXXIX.

EVENING, JUNE 19, 1756.

I OFTEN think, as I write these pages, of other very sore straits into which our countrymen have fallen in that distant Indian land; and it is a strange but awful lesson in human bravery, endurance, and ghastly suffering, to compare what happened in Fort William on the next day, Saturday, the 19th of June 1756, with the occurrences of the same day a hundred years later, in the saddest of all memorials in India—the barrack entrenchment at Cawnpore. But there is hardly a parallel.

In the one, as many Englishmen as there were in Calcutta, beneath a fiercer and more burning sun, without cover save a slight breastwork, were fighting day and night, without relief and without rest, with a few poor field-pieces, and some light guns, fowling-pieces, and rifles, against a more cruel enemy than Suraj-oo-Doulah's Rohillas—cowards and traitors who dare not show themselves in fair fight, but skulked behind the buildings which screened their heavy guns, whose fire ceased not day or night. Those few English soldiers, railway constructors, shopkeepers, and clerks, were defending frail roofless buildings, riddled with heavy shot and shell; and a motley assemblage of helpless women and children were sitting within them in groups, huddled upon the bare floors, grown careless of the cannon-shot which whistled over them, or crashed through the tottering walls, or of shells which often burst among them—envying the happy fate of any whom they struck, or of others who, in disease or very weakness, sank gently to their eternal rest.

We who live in the happy homes of England, secure and peaceful, can have but a very faint idea of so terrible a reality; of its aggravation by lack of food and of water—of the scorching sun by day and chill dews by night—of the dawn and the sunset following each other without a change in that fearful strife—each day succeeding the last only to differ from it in intensity and augmentation of suffering—of the conviction that there was no retreat, and no alternative but to fight on to the last and die, if happily death might come fighting, and not by foul treachery. We know how all that ended; and pray God in His mercy that His glorious host of heaven may never witness the like again.

It was not thus in Fort William on the day of which I write. The morning broke calm and beautiful, and the fresh breeze curled the great river, and blew out the red English flags defiantly before the Indian host. The Fort was still secure. There was no slight parapet, as at Cawnpore, with scores of yawning breaches; but a strong fort wall and shelter enough. There was no artillery used against it which could breach such a wall, and there were no bomb-shells to descend from above, and, bursting, scatter their horrible fragments far and wide. There were ships lying in the stream, on board of which most of the helpless women and children had already gone, and more were following. From them at least there would be no hindrance, no unmanning of brave hearts by contemplation of their sufferings; and yet we know by the sad record of history, and by the testimony of men who shared and survived that trial, that—it is hard to write it—there was panic, and its inevitable accompaniment, cowardice. "Oh for Mr. Clive!" had been the cry of many a brave sorrowing heart, as boatload after boatload of men and officers who, having the responsibility of the defence, were now terror-stricken—abandoning the Fort, and flying shamefully to the ships.

"As soon," writes one of the officers, "as it was known that the Governor had left the Factory, the gate towards the river was immediately locked to prevent further desertion, and the general voice of the garrison called for Mr. Howell to take the charge of the defence upon him;" and, like a gallant Englishman as he was, he thenceforth did his best. There were no craven hearts in the Fort now, and there were no means of retreat; no boat, English or native, approached the doomed Fort. The English ships had dropped down the stream, but not to any distance; they could see among them the signals which Mr. Howell made for them to come up again to their anchorage, or to send boats for the garrison, but nothing stirred. As the tide turned, and the south wind blew gently from the sea, the garrison looked for a moment for one ship, one sloop, one pinnace, to come up and help them in their great need, but none came. I can believe this to have been no little aggravation of their misery—one which, amidst all their horrible varieties of suffering, the Cawnpore people were at least spared.

There, no hope of succour had ever existed; for it was soon known that those at Lucknow, from whence help alone could come, were in as great strait as themselves; and so, in the grim, calm energy of despair, they fought on. But here, in Fort William, their very friends had deserted the garrison, and had grown callous to what they might suffer, so their own more precious selves were safe. I feel that this must have been a most frightful aggravation of suffering, because a wound in the tenderest part of all true Englishmen's hearts—national honour. "What would they say in England if we were to give up these shattered walls now we hold them?" said the brave fellows at Cawnpore, at Lucknow, and Arrah, as others had once said at Jellalabad, when mighty Indian hosts were encamped against them. At least we who live on know what they have said, and will ever say—and hope, that the poor fellows who were taken away, have heard from awful lips that, like gallant British men—they did their duty.

And those in Fort William were minded now to do it too. They had still one hope, in the good ship *Prince George*, which lay above at the redoubt, and was ordered down. I believe that worthy Captain Hague, if he could, would have come down in the teeth of the enemy's shot; and as he weighed anchor, and sailed slowly under his topsails, there was many an eager eye looking to his manœuvres, and many a beating heart expecting him; and it must have been a sore pang to the brave fellow when, as we read, "his ship was run on a shoal, either by the 'Pilate's' treachery or want of skill, and his good ship stuck fast, never to be moved again." And so the last hope of the Fort garrison was blasted, and with many a heavy sigh, perhaps, but with clenched teeth and grim, defiant hearts, they set themselves—to do their duty.

And bravely, too, while they could, they did it, as history tells us, and as we can well believe. As the morning advanced, the Nawab's army closed rapidly round the Fort; the firing was heavy and constant, and their approaches grew nearer and nearer. The church without the walls, the offices and warehouses, were carried one by one, while the defenders plied their musketry and cannon, and sheltered themselves as well as they could with parapets of cotton bales, and packages of stout Yorkshire broadcloths. Many were killed, and many were sorely hurt: but the evening came, and with it the rest which night gave—for the young Nawab slept, and it was death to disturb his slumbers.

All that day had the Affghan girl urged on her people, and well had they answered her call. She had seemed to them to bear a charmed life; and superstition, as well as admiration of her bravery—it might have been called desperation—had already won for her the fame she had coveted. They had told her she would be sung of in the bazaars of Cabool, in the mountains of Istaliff, in the royal fort of Ghuzni. They—those wild, rude fellows—had bowed themselves before her, and touched reverently her hands and her feet. Where she led they would follow; and among them, some of the burliest and bravest had formed themselves into a bodyguard, and placed their shields before her when the English balls came hottest. She had won her fame, even did she survive; but I think the girl, in the fierce enthusiasm of her nature, rather longed for death, that she might live for ever in her people's memories.

So, too, fighting on the north-west bastion, all that day, were Ralph Smithson and Mr. Wharton. The few men that could be spared to them were weary and sick, some wounded too, and some fell occasionally; but none left the post alive, and Julia Wharton, utterly refusing shelter within the buildings, shared the danger with them. Perhaps this one day, of all that siege, might be likened in some wise to the corresponding day of June in the Cawnpore entrenchment—and yet hardly. Great as was this peril and misery, there was still the hope that ships might come up, or that the garrison might be able to hold out. There was not the weariness of fruitless fighting which was falling on the others; or that dull, leaden despair which contemplated grimly the few sacks of meal left, the empty provision-tins, and the gaunt, sun-scorched faces of hollow-eyed women and children.

So one more night of rest from shot ensued, and yet less peace than before. Though the Nawab slept, and scarce a shot was fired, the enemy were not idle. As the night advanced, fires broke out in various houses beyond the walls. Mr. Wharton's had been safe up to this time, and they had watched, with a curious interest, the proceedings of the first body of native soldiers which took possession of it. Would it be destroyed? They were not long in doubt. As they sat there on the floor of the bastion, behind their cotton bales, eating what their native servants had been able to cook for them, and truly enjoying the repast more heartily perhaps than they had done many a costly dinner—a sudden glare fell upon the little group which told its own tale, and a fierce roaring and crackling of the dry thatch and bamboos quickly completed the ruin. So on, through the night—the marine-yard, with all its stores of timber, tar, and pitch—many houses—the church—burst one by one into flames, and lit up, with a frightful glare, the Fort, the white houses of Calcutta, the trees and the river, and rested far away on the masts and sails of the faithless English ships, which lay in safety. I do not think the thoughts of those who were in them could have been enviable that night, and, though death in all its most horrible forms was before them, those in the Fort were perhaps the happier.

I daresay many a last strange tale or wish was told by English soldiers, one to another, that night, in their last watch, while the glare of conflagration around them lighted up every nook and corner of the Fort, and vast forked tongues of flame darted to the sky, sending up showers of lighted embers and brilliant sparks; but I have no concern with them. It was impossible to sleep, and our friends sat together on the bastion, where Mr. Wharton and Ralph Smithson had to watch by turns until the morning. They had nothing new to tell—nothing new to request—all that was needed had been already arranged. In a quiet bivouac or picket, with the soft stars twinkling in a dewy sky, the men might have told each other of their lives; but this was not a time for such confidences. It signified very little, death seemed so near, what had passed beforehand, and their thoughts were involuntarily solemn; and when Julia Wharton took from her pocket her small prayer-book, and began to read in her sweet voice, by the light of the glare beyond the walls, the Psalms for the evening of the nineteenth day of the month—many of the soldiers gathered round and listened bareheaded, and devoutly, to what I hope we all remember, while the girl's voice grew stronger as she proceeded—

"O sing unto the Lord a new song, for He hath done marvellous things. With His own right hand, and with His holy arm, hath He gotten us the victory."

Ah yes! Even in that sore strait they hoped and prayed for it, and reverently commended themselves to Him in whose hands the issues lay. And we know that all those in Cawnpore, daily and nightly, did the same.

CHAPTER XL.

THE STORM, AND WHO SURVIVED IT.

DAWN broke again, and the horrid stifling smell of burnt houses, the smoke of still blazing timber, had taken the place of the sweet dewy morning breath which ought to have been there. In place of trim garden-houses and the quiet of the English settlement, there were groups of smoking ruins and hosts of the native army, and roughly-constructed batteries, armed with cannon ready for the day's work. As the drums and fifes of the Portuguese musicians of the Fort beat off a quavering "reveillé," they were answered by defiant blasts of shrill native pipes and horns and the deep bass drums of the Nawab's nobut.

It was a Sabbath dawn. Far away in their dear England the church-bells on the bright summer day would ring out mellow chimes of invitation to prayer, and the soft south-west wind would bear them over fragrant bean-fields, over meadows strewn with sweet fresh hay, through avenues of lime-trees full of the murmur of bees, loading itself with perfume till it could carry no more. There, many a homely, bright-dressed group would wander leisurely by field-paths, and through green shady lanes, to hear the Sabbath service. Children would gather bright wild-flowers by hedgerows, and ancient men and dames would sit by cottage-doors basking in the warm sun, and looking on at harmless play. There, too, Coquet would be in its beauty, fretting over many a mossy rock and stone with a plashing murmur, or gliding through deep brown pools overhung by dipping woods, with the trout leaping in them. In many a house of God the holy message of peace and good-will towards men would be read, and many a choir raise melodious hymns and psalms to the glory of the Most High.

But this Sabbath day, the 20th June 1756, was to be very different to those who remained in Fort William. As the day broke, those who had been able to snatch a few hours' sleep hurried again to their posts, and joined their comrades who had been watching. Behind their little barricade of cotton bales, our friends and a few soldiers were assembled; and as soon as she could see, they all heard, reverently, the sweet voice of Julia Wharton read out the psalms for the day. Who does not remember them, and that sad, pitiful, cry for help?—

"Hear my prayer, O Lord, and let my crying come unto Thee!

"Hide not Thy face from me in the time of my trouble; incline Thine ear unto me when I call; O hear me, and that right soon."

Passing into the exultant song—

"Praise the Lord, O my soul! And all that is within me, praise His holy name!

"Praise the Lord, O my soul! O Lord my God, Thou art become exceeding glorious!"

While they listened, the enemy were gathering quickly in every post, which became thick with turbaned heads; and as daylight advanced, and the sun rose through the eastern mist and clouds, a fire more rapid and more deadly than any the English garrison had yet experienced, burst upon them on every side—from cannon, from wall-pieces, and from matchlocks it poured thick and fast—and a heavy column of men were soon seen forming towards the north-west bastion, with the evident intention of storming it.

Snatching a few hasty mouthfuls of food such as they could get, Mr. Wharton and Ralph Smithson hurried to the point of danger, and, with such of their men as could be assembled there, strove to check the progress of a body of blue-coated assailants who, with an energy and bravery they had not yet seen attempted, charged up to the foot of the works and attempted to scale them. It was here that Ralph Smithson noticed a slight active figure foremost in every charge, shouting the war-cry of those people, urging them forward, and using passionate gestures of reproach and entreaty as time after time they were hurled back by discharges of grape and musketry, and by bayonets and boarding-pikes, wherever escalade was attempted. They marvelled who this could be, so young and so fair: for the ruddy features could be easily seen, and looked almost English.

"Before he sleeps—before he sleeps at noon," had that Affghan girl cried to her countrymen, and so had led charge after charge in the name of Allah and the Prophet. But noon came, and the mysterious silence which they had always noticed at this hour fell again upon the native host, and once more there was to be temporary rest for all while the Nawab slept.

It was but a faint hope; but men in such straits will cling to any, while it was evident to all that another attack made with such resolution could not be withstood; so Mr. Howell requested the banker Omichund again to write to the Nawab's minister, and as the messenger with the letter was allowed to pass, there was hope for a while.

But not for long, though the cessation of firing had been of greater duration than usual. The letter had reached its destination; but with such a prize almost within his grasp, the Nawab was little likely to abandon his determination of revenge. Many a brave Moslem soldier had been shot down; the priest of the mosque, aided by other priests, had been busy all the day preaching a holy war against the infidels, and the army burned to revenge those who had already fallen. Above all, Sozun had sent message after message to her lord to encourage his obstinacy of purpose, and his belief in her destiny now surpassed all other motives for persistence.

There was no answer, therefore; and presently, as they watched the enemy, the preparations of several heavy storming parties could be easily seen, and the already exhausted garrison viewed them with a grim dismay. Before those thousands thirsting for their blood, without the possibility of defending or even watching the whole of the walls, there was no hope, and yet surrender was not yet spoken of among them. Even at that late hour, had the recreants in the ships below riding safely at their anchors—witnessing the strife, yet giving no aid—moved up a few vessels, the Fort might have been saved; but Mr. Howell, as he went to the south-east bastion to judge whether he were justified, under the circumstances, in prolonging the defence, saw no movement among them; not a boat was lowered, nor was one near by which any message might be sent, while the enemy were crowding up the defences in numbers which he had no hope of resisting. It was then that, seizing a flag, he waved it as one of truce; but the only reply was a volley of shot, and fiercer and hoarser cries from the men below. Then, on each other's shoulders—by ladders, clinging to pieces of broken walls—the Moslem soldiers gained the rampart, and, as he yielded his sword to a native officer, Mr. Holwell found himself a captive, while the few soldiers who still resisted died at their posts.

It was just before this that the Nawab's Rohillas, before whom ran and leaped the same youthful active figure which had been seen in the morning, came on in serried array, and at a rapid trot, holding their shields before their bodies to turn the English bullets, and reached the foot of the north-west bastion. There were fewer there now to receive them than before. Many of the militia—who, despite the Don's predictions, had fought well—now cowed and terrified, were sheltering themselves below. A few English soldiers, Mr. Wharton, Ralph Smithson, and the Don prepared to do what men could; and behind a screen of cotton bales Julia Wharton was loading muskets, and handing them to be fired. I do not think any of them spoke; death seemed very near now, but amidst that fierce strife it was little thought of. As the Rohillas climbed up, hewing fiercely at pikes and bayonets with their broad sabres and sharp battle-axes, Ralph was at last face to face with the person he had so often watched; that fair glowing face with its flashing eyes and a sword between its set teeth, the slight womanish hands clutching at the broken masonry, with a pile of dead beneath—was being raised up and covered with their shields. The Englishman's and the Affghan girl's eyes met for a moment as Ralph Smithson raised his cutlas for a blow which must have cloven her head to the teeth; but he could not strike.

"It is a woman!" he cried, as he dropped his sword point. "God help me, I cannot strike her!" The next moment he heard a sharp scream from Julia Wharton, and rushed to the spot. A glance told the story—her husband lay writhing in mortal pain. She was striving to raise his head, and as she heard his faint cry for water, to pour some into his mouth.

Ralph Smithson laid down his bloody weapon, useless now, for the Rohillas had crowded up the wall, and were spreading themselves on every side, as he reached his friends—all but Sozun and an old officer, who were arrested by the group before them.

"Strike him not!" she cried to some of her men, who had lifted their swords to cut down Smithson as he knelt over Mr. Wharton.

"He has killed our brethren. We have marked him these two days," shouted some of them, savagely.

"He is mine!" she said. "Away with ye to plunder!" and Smithson and Mrs. Wharton were saved.

Ralph heeded not the action, or thought of the blood-stained weapons lifted over him. There lay one he loved gasping out a last few trembling words, and amidst the din of strife he was listening with intense eagerness.

"I'm going . . . Julia—fast now. . . . It's very dark, darling. Where, where . . . are you? Where's Ralph? . . . Don't, don't forget . . . mother—mother . . ."

A last great sob, a quick convulsion, and Henry Wharton, like many another, had gone to his rest, with his mother's name last on his lips, spoken as it had been in days of childhood long gone by. The convulsion left no painful trace—there was a sweet smile of triumph on his sallow wasted face, a flush of almost bright colour upon his cheek; but the blue eye was set in death, and a great majesty of expression was settling upon the strong handsome features.

"Oh, Ralph, he is not dead! Lift him up," she said, faintly.

"He is gone, Julia—gone for ever to his rest."

She threw herself upon the body with a passionate wailing cry.

To have him snatched away in death, whom she had only begun to love within these last three weary days!—he, too, who had been spared through all previous danger. It was too quick a revulsion, and she had fainted.

"Raise her up, sir," said Sozun, who, fascinated by the scene of grief, so natural—so terrible—had remained. "Raise her up—I can protect her, and Affghans do not war against women or helpless men."

"Art thou a woman?" said Ralph Smithson.

"No matter," said the girl, "what I am. Raise her up, and give her some water, else she will die."

Between them, they raised Julia Wharton, and Sozun filled an earthen cup from a pitcher which stood there. "Drink," she said, as the Englishwoman's bosom heaved, and she sighed—"drink, and rouse thyself. He is dead—what canst thou do for him? Dost thou understand me?"

"I do," said Ralph Smithson. "Who art thou?"

"I told thee, Feringi, it does not matter; she is my care, and I can protect ye both. Take her up, and follow me. I hear the Nawab's procession. He is coming."

The sun was setting, and a blaze of light shone upon the bastion, the blood-stained breastwork of cotton bales, and the white upturned face of him who lay at rest there. Perhaps the Affghan girl remembered the white face of her dead father as the sun had gleamed upon it that evening on the field of Sirhind, for it was like an act of veneration, when she went, touched lightly the eyes and the lips of the dead, and then her own heart and forehead. "The peace and blessing of God be upon him—he has died a soldier's death," she said gently, and turned away. "Come, sir, if thou canst carry her—she is safe nowhere but with me. I am a woman, and can protect her and thee. Art thou her brother? Oh, she is very beautiful!"

"I was his friend in life," Ralph Smithson replied to the girl—"no more. She was his wife. Julia, we must go. I dare not leave you. Come; I will see to him afterwards. Come, this person will help us; she is a woman, and will save you from violence."

"O Ralph," cried the sobbing girl, falling upon his shoulder, "I have none left but you—no one. O my God! no one but you; do not leave me now."

So they descended the steps of the bastion, as the Nawab's palankeen was set down in the area of the Fort, and a concourse of people had crowded about it. "He must not see her," said the girl quickly; "it will be her death, or worse. Can you not conceal her, till I can make her safe? Thou canst understand me?"

"Perfectly," said Ralph, in good Hindustani. He had soon learned the colloquial dialect. "Is there danger?"

"I tell you, sir," she said, "upon a woman's honour, and I swear to you by my dead father, if he sees her she will be seized for his zenana, and then—God help her!"

"Who art thou?" cried Smithson quickly.

"I am his slave and his mistress," she replied; "do as I bid ye, else she is lost."

"She is right, Julia," said Smithson; "come here, it's the last place they'll seek you in—the black hole. It's dark there, and you will not be seen. Crouch down by the window, and I will come for you as soon as I can."

"Yes, she will be safe there," said Sozun. "Keep quiet, lady, and for your life's sake do not show yourself."

There was a group round the Nawab's palankeen, in which he was sitting speaking to Mr. Holwell, whom he was questioning as to the amount of treasure in the Factory. Men were loosing Mr. Holwell's hands which were tied, and he was telling the young prince that there was not much money in the treasury. Whatever there was should be looked after. There was no violence offered to Mr. Holwell; and others who were looking on augured well from that. The Affghan girl went and stood behind the Nawab's palankeen, and, except her countrymen, no one there knew her. The Nawab was inquiring who had climbed into the Fort first, and was holding in his hand a heavy gold necklace to bestow upon the person. Several soldiers had stepped forward, among them the officer to whom Mr. Holwell had given up his sword, and who appealed to that gentleman for corroboration of what he said.

"Nawab Sahib," said Mr. Holwell, "if I may speak, this man was the first beside me; but it was not till I saw the bastion beyond me full of Rohillas that I surrendered. One of them was the first."

"Let me speak, Nawab Sahib," said Ralph Smithson, stepping forward. "The first upon my post was a mere youth; I could have slain him, but he looked so like a woman that I could not strike."

"I am here, my lord," whispered the girl, bending down to him, "but take no notice of me for your honour's sake. Enough, that I have done what I needed."

"Nay, thou hast earned it, darling," whispered the young man, throwing the jewel about her neck, "and wilt not refuse it; now begone, I will follow directly. Come hither Noor Khan," he continued to the chief of the Rohillas—"well hast thou earned this, as well by thy bravery as," he whispered, as he tied a gorgeous ornament of rubies and emeralds into the old Affghan's turban, "by thy care of her; nor shall your men be forgotten."

Sozun waited to see the decoration bestowed upon her countryman; and was satisfied, when the old officer's eyes met her own, that he was content now. She had redeemed much, but not all. Could she but save that fair Englishwoman! Ah, should he but see her! It was hopeless to attempt it then, and till to-morrow they would be all safe; and, giving a sign to one of the eunuchs, she stepped into a litter, and was carried rapidly away.

There was little more to be done that evening. The Nawab's heart was following his slave. How beautiful had she looked with the flush of victory on her face. Again and again the Fort was searched, and plunderers and Portuguese driven out. The Nawab's seal was put on the treasury; "he would come," he said, "and count the money in the morning." Then guards were set, and there was quiet. The English gentlemen and soldiers, many of them wounded, were sitting about the courts in groups, speculating as to where they would be put for the night. That was the barrack square, close and hot enough; and many, faint and weary, were lying down. The barrack-rooms were at least open and airy, and the platform where the men slept especially so. Perhaps they would get something to eat; and the quiet, the relief from constant excitement of battle, had already sent some to sleep, and relieved the rest from all immediate apprehension.

Then, as the time for prayer came, the Nawab and all his people prepared for it, and carpets or scarfs were spread to kneel upon. There was no minaret; but a muezzin ascended a terrace hard by, and began to chant the Azan—"Prayer is better than sleep, O ye faithful! Prayer is better than sleep. God is victorious, God is victorious!"—and the cry, "Ulla hu Akbar," was taken up by a thousand hoarse voices. Thus, as the chronicle hath it, "the Moors sang a great psalm for their victory, and the Nawab with them." True, indeed, was the prophecy of the Derwesh, "There would be victory."

A few more directions as to the safe custody of the prisoners; a few last orders to the governor nominated in regard to the treasury, that it was not to be opened till he came in the morning; a few assurances to Mr. Holwell that he would be well taken care of; and the English captives saw the Nawab's palankeen taken up, and attended by his courtiers and soldiery, set out for the town; and they heard the matchlock shots and the great drums which accompanied his progress, till the sound grew fainter and fainter with the distance, and so ceased. It was almost dark now, and men with torches ran hither and thither exploring the Fort, for a safe place into which to put the captives. At last one cried, "There is the prison, it will hold them all."

Ralph Smithson had taken Mrs. Wharton a jar of water, and she was drinking it eagerly and thankfully, and put it down carelessly by the window. "It is so hot and close here," she said, "may I not come out, Ralph? they are all gone."

"Not yet," he replied. "After the Nawab is gone I will seek a safe place for you," and he went out again into the court. Some of his friends were sitting sadly, weary and sick with the day's fighting, and their losses; others were chatting together cheerfully. "The Nawab had been kind, and to-morrow the ships would be up again." "If John Company had to pay a swinging ransom, what matter? he was rich enough." Some of the soldiers, English and Dutch, had got to the arrack stores, and were roaring in drunken mirth, while others were trying to keep them quiet. Gradually all saw the soldiers of the Nawab close round them and drive them forward, while men stood at the prison door with torches to light them in. Ralph Smithson sprang forward to get Julia Wharton out of a place which he knew would not be fit for her, but he was too late. Those after him—some laughing, some shrieking in drunken madness, some protesting—came on in a dense mass, blocking up the doorway, while blows and pricks of swords and spears from behind urged on the rest. Then closer and closer the mass within pressed together and occupied all the standing room, till the last man was thrust in, and the door was shut and locked.

CHAPTER XLI.

THE BLACK HOLE—SUNDAY NIGHT, JUNE 20, 1756.

It did not need many moments to reveal to the prisoners the frightful situation in which they had been placed. It was indeed impossible for any one to move now, so closely was the mass wedged together; and had it been standing in the open air, the weakest must have inevitably fallen and been trampled down to death. This was a room but eighteen feet square, and into it one hundred and forty-five people had been crammed. On three sides there was a dead wall of brick without any aperture, which indeed formed part of the Fort. In the fourth side, which opened to the barrack courtyard, were two windows which had iron bars, and by these, whatever air could reach the interior found entrance; but what was it in comparison with the frightful need? "This is for life or death, Julia," whispered Ralph Smithson to the terrified woman, who had seen the throng troop by her with frantic cries and gestures. "Kneel down, keep your face to the bars, I will stand over you while I have life and strength! and I will yield to no other. Here, Mr. Holwell, there is room by us; come quick, and stay by me; you are weak, and I am strong."

"You are wounded, Mr. Smithson, and need a better place than I," replied the brave, generous man; "I shall do very well; we have others to look to, and must not forsake them."

There was little spoken, as men took the places in which they were to live or die that night.

"Eh, Captain Smithson!" said a rough but weak voice behind him, "ye'll no forget Drever, surr; that's the man fraa Berrik, ye ken; a'm vara weak, surr, an' if ye'll let me pit ma heed a'tween yer legs, surr, a'll no disturb ye, surr; a'll be vara patien'. Eh, captin, but it's vara terrible a' this; the Lord be gude to uz."

"Be quiet, then," said Ralph Smithson; "lie still, and take care of yourself—I cannot help you."

"It hardly matters, surr, if a' live or dee, it's jist the Lorrd's will; but if a'm deed in the mornin', jist send aale I ha' aboot me to ma folk at Berrik; there's a wee bit goud I've gotten, an'—"

"Don't talk," cried Ralph, sternly; "keep still, I'll see to you, if we're alive."

Julia Wharton dared not speak. She knelt there between Ralph Smithson's strong arms and knees, safe from any crush from without, her white face pressed against the bars, breathing, but almost unconscious then. Every now and then she heard a cheering word from her protector; and Mr. Holwell, and others standing and kneeling by her, tried to soothe her as best they could. Occasionally, when the pressure was heaviest, Ralph Smithson passed his arm round her waist, and held her up for a little to breathe more freely; and once, when those without had brought a torch to the window, he saw her turn round her head and smile at him. I think, if she had dared to speak, it would have been some passionate avowal of gratitude for his care. But she was better silent.

There were men who, in that awful time, comported themselves with fortitude and resignation only known to Him to whom their spirits had gone before morning dawned; and there were others as brave who were spared; but among all that hideous mass of suffering, there was perhaps no calmer heart than Julia Wharton's. To live or to die, who could tell? and she waited patiently for the issue. For a time the mass stood up quietly and patiently, and an order to strip off their upper garments was obeyed by most. Then they tried to sit down and get up at word of command; but this soon became impossible, for many who sat down could rise no more, and fell under foot to die; and the heat and stench were momentarily increasing, and becoming intolerable even to those in the foremost ranks. Who can tell of what passed further back? Even those who came out alive the next morning, and have left their records for us to read, could only guess. To look back into that thick darkness was impossible, for the steam of men's bodies increased the gloom; and when a torch was held up to the window by those outside, all that could be seen was a dim surging mass of naked men—English, Dutch, Portuguese, and natives—rising, falling, climbing on each other's slippery shoulders, only to drop between and be at once trodden to death.

Out of that horrible, seething mass came cries of "Water, water! open the door!" intermingled with prayers, wild and incoherent ravings, the shrieks of drunken men, to whom their intoxication gave temporary energy—fearful oaths and curses in English and Dutch—in a Babel of languages—and among them the groans and sobs of the dying.

So passed one hour—two hours—and many were already dead, and more were dying. There was now greater space within, but existence was more difficult and impossible every moment. Some gave up the struggle at the windows for air, and wandered over the dead, lying down in corners; and, if they had sense or consciousness, breathing a last prayer, and so dying. Was there no pity among their guards? At first, under the heartless intoxication of victory, the native soldiers crowded round the windows, and looked through them by the light of torches, jeering in horrid exultation, and mocking the shrieks and turmoil within; while the heat, the glare, and the smoke and smell of burning oil aggravated the general suffering. Even these hard men could not long bear this sight, and turned from it with horrible loathing. Water! water!—would no one bring any to the dying, for the sake of the Lord Jesus and his mother Mary?

They brought it at last plentifully, and dashed it in the faces of those who clung to the bars, while hats were held out from inside, and filled from the cool waterskins, and so passed on behind. Some fainting wretches got a little, but most was spilled in the frightful struggles for it; and after a time came no more.

"A thousand rupees to any one who will open the door and let us out," cried Mr. Holwell. "Ye all know me. I will answer with my life to the Nawab. We cannot escape—we will be quiet outside; and many are already dead. Oh! by your mothers, by your children, by the Prophet, do not look on at suffering like this, and deny us mercy!"

"Let them fire on us, Mr. Holwell," shouted many a voice; "better we should be shot down and put out of our misery than endure this."

Ah yes! it would have been better—an easier death than that horrible choking for lack of air; but no one fired.

"We dare not let you out," said a native officer, who had been roused by the tumult, and who came to see what it was; "but I will go and see what can be done."

It was but a mockery of hope. Again and again the man sent his dread message that all the Feringis would be dead ere morning if they were not liberated; but to no purpose.

"Two thousand—anything—ten thousand!" again besought Mr. Holwell, Ralph Smithson, and others who could speak the native language. "Go to the Nawab. He did not desire this; and ye will have to answer for it."

"We dare not wake him, gentlemen," said another superior officer, who had a compassionate face; "we dare not indeed."

Wake him! who dare do so now? In a luxurious apartment, on the softest of cushions, the windows open to admit the night wind, Suraj-oo-Doulah slept tranquilly, and his lovely slave, Sozun, restless and wakeful, now sat leaning out of the lattice, now with stealthy step moved near her lord, and gently fanned him. All her excitement was gone; there was only one thought at her heart—that if the lovely Englishwoman were but seen, her reign was over. Yet she must be seen. Her lord would waken early, and the prisoners would be called before him. She must appear with the rest—and then?

Could nothing be done? It is a desperate resolution. Could she go? The clothes she had worn were in the next room. She could but attempt it, and die if she failed—

But even this was impossible. As she went out of her lord's chamber, and drew the curtain which separated it from a corridor without, she saw a group of the eunuchs sitting there awake, their swords drawn and resting on their knees, who looked up at her with their bleared, red eyes. They at least were watchful and faithful.

"What is it, lady?" said one, rising. "It is but just midnight, and you are awake. Can we get anything, or call the women-servants?"

"Nothing, Nasir," said the girl. "My lord is resting quietly; but I am anxious, and could not sleep."

"Anxious!" said the man, respectfully; "we are all here—there is no fear. Go and rest yourself, lady."

Should she tell him? He was one she trusted more than the others, and it was her only hope. If she could but get the English woman into her own keeping, she would answer for the rest.

"Listen," she said, beckoning him to her, and speaking in a low tone. "There is an Englishwoman among those prisoners; take a palankeen and go for her. I would not have her escape in the morning—she is so beautiful. Go!—here is my lord's ring. Bring her here by the back way, and let me know when she arrives. She will need clothes and—and—no matter. Bring her hither, and to me."

"On my head and eyes!" said the man, whispering, "I will do it." And so he left her.

Sozun returned to the window and looked out. A heavy sultry

night it was, without a star visible, and a dull, oppressive weight seemed to hang in the air. All about was still; but over the plain before the Fort troops of jackals began to scream their midnight cry, and their unearthly howling seemed to be taken up from all sides by packs fighting over the dead. She drew the muslin scarf about her more closely, shuddered, and still watched. She saw torches moving over the plain, and a heavy litter borne rapidly along by men, and presently the torchlight gleamed upon the Fort wall and gate, and disappeared within it. Would she come? The girl's heart beat fast, as she strained her eyes to pierce the gloom of night; but there were no torches, nor any sign of movement over the black plain; and so she sat watching till the fresher air of morning warned her that daybreak was nigh. Then she sadly gave up hope, and went and lay down beside him whom she had often dreaded, and never more than then.

I do not say that Ralph Smithson never moved from his first position. It was nearly impossible to maintain it at all times; and nothing but his strong bony frame and great muscular power enabled him to remain where he was, and to repel the surging masses of men which assailed him from behind, climbing on his shoulders, and striving to drag his hands from the bars, to which he held with an almost iron grasp. Again and again he had fiercely and desperately struck down the poor wretches who thus assailed him. There was little pity between man and man that night. Often had he thought, if Julia Wharton died, he would go back among the crowd and die too. But she lived, and she was his—for that night at least. The poor seaman, Drever, too, held fast, and every now and then spoke cheerily.

"Eh! dinna ye let go, Captin Smithson, else we'll a' be deed men. An' the leddy, surr—my! but she's a brave lassie—an' the drooth's sair. Ye'll keep a brave heart, my leddy!"

"Julia, do you hear what he says?—that brave fellow behind you? Keep a stout heart. If we die, we shall but follow him," said Smithson, cheerily.

"I will, Ralph, I will. I do not fear so long as you are by. This water that you brought me so kindly, with God's help is keeping me alive. I dip my handkerchief in it, and suck it. Will you have some?"

"I will not take a drop, Julia. I have had plenty from the window, and Mr. Holwell says our shirt sleeves are the best. Mine are wet enough."

"How quiet they are!" she said after a long silence; there are few speaking now behind us."

Few indeed! He only dreaded that she might look back and see the ghastly heaps there, for a torch before them shed a lurid light into the room, and revealed all its horrors; but he did not allow her to turn her head. "Yes," he said, "they are quiet, but do not speak —it will increase your thirst."

"If the leddy'd like some of the Psaalms, Captin Smithson? Mither used to sing them, and a'll try if they'll come till mey. It's better than this dead silence. Eh, but it's vara awfu', surr! Ye wadna mind, mem?" and he began in a low quavering voice, weak from suffering—

"Since I have placed my trrust in God,
A rrefuge aaways nigh,
Why should I like a tim'rous burrd
To distant mountains fly?'

Eh, Mr. Smithson, but if the bonny Cheviots was nigh us, an' we could get a brreath o' the pure air, surr, an' a smell o' the brright bonnie heather, instead o' this horrid stench—or maybe the fresh rroar o' Coquet or Wansbeck, surr, an' no thae skirrls an' grroans o' dyin' crreatures, surr, we'd be happy! Ye'll mind thae rrivers? Eh me! eh me! but a'll niver see them nae mair—but it's the Lord's will, surr! . . . Ay, mem," he continued after a while, "that's the eleventh Psaalm, ye ken, an' a mind mair o't—

'Behold, the wicked bend their bow,
And ready bend their darrt;
Lurrking in ambush to destrroy——'

. . . A' mind nae mair, my leddy, an' a' canna sing—a'm too drey, mem, an' a sair dwam's comin' ower me—"

"Here, take this handkerchief and suck it," said Mrs. Wharton in a low voice. "Give it back to me—I've more here for you."

"God's blessing on ye, my leddy, but you've the noblest hearrt I ever seed in a womin. A' know'd anither ance. Ah! but she was a bewty too, like yersel', mem. But this is nae place for tellin' o' storeies, mem—"

"Don't talk, Drever," cried Ralph Smithson, sternly. "You'll die of thirst if you do."

"'Deed, then, a'm reddy to dee, surr, if it's the gude Lord's will, an' a'll no talk nae mair. Only if I could mind anither hymn or psaalm. Listen! wha's that?"

It was a hollow voice at the far end of the room, and it cried with a great moan—

"When the Lord turneth again the captivity of Sion, then were we like them that dream."

The words had an awful unearthly sound as they came from among the heaps of dead, and silence fell upon all. After a pause, as if striving to recollect, it said again, in a louder and more hollow tone—

"Turn our captivity, O Lord, as the rivers in the south. . . . They that sow in tears shall reap in joy. . . . . He that now goeth on his way weeping, and beareth forth good seed, shall doubtless come again with joy, and bring his sheaves with him."

Then there was a brief muttering of prayer, which died away into a hollow broken murmur, and again silence fell upon all. One more of that ghastly company had passed to his eternal rest; and there were some of the survivors who, like Ralph Smithson, never forgot those last solemn words of hope and trust, and felt even in that hour of horrible trial as though the peace of God were coming upon them.

CHAPTER XLII.

RELEASED.

So they remained enduring, and speaking little now. Except an occasional moan, the sufferers were quiet. It was past midnight when a messenger came to the bars of the window.

"There's a woman among you!" cried a shrill voice. "This is no place for her; she is to go to the Nawab's. Come out!"

Ralph Smithson instantly remembered the warning words of the Affghan girl; but Julia did not at first understand that the message brought regarded her.

"Let her go, Smithson," said Mr. Holwell; "she will be well cared for; we cannot save her. Mrs. Wharton, go—save your life—we shall all die before morning."

"Oh no, no, no!" she cried—"oh no, no! Kill me here—I am ready to die; but do not send me away! It would be horrible! Ralph! Mr. Smithson! I will not leave you—indeed I will not!"

She had struggled to her feet, and beheld, by the torchlight which streamed in, what Ralph had hitherto kept from her sight. Strong and resolute as she was, the sickening reality was more than she could bear, and she fainted.

"She is dead," he said to the man. "You have killed her! Look!"

The eunuch shrugged his shoulders. "Open the door," he cried, "and let her out; she will recover in the air."

But it could not be opened. The few chinks in it, and the openings underneath and beside the door-posts, had been so many air-holes, and men had fought for these, and died there in a heap; now no one could stir the door within or without.

Presently Mrs. Wharton revived. There was now water in plenty, and Ralph Smithson poured some into her mouth and upon her face. The soldiers without were trying to open the door, and did not perceive that the lady had rallied.

"Keep close down, Julia," he whispered; "hide yourself if you can under me. Drever, look to the lady if you are able."

"I will, Ralph—I will do all you tell me," she said, faintly. "But do not give me to them—oh, promise you will not! I had better die than that. How many are dead, and yet my worthless life is spared!"

She said this in broken sentences, and he could not reply. His assuring arm round her waist, as he held her up with his still great strength, was proof enough that he would be true to her.

If she can't be got out," said Nasir, to one of the native officers present, "she can't run away. Perhaps she is dead; are there many dead? I must wait till dawn."

"All," replied the man, with a sigh—"all except those round the windows. I wish it were daylight."

There were more than he who wished for daylight. Of those at that window, Mr. Holwell among the rest, some left it frequently, and wandered back into the room to die. Those who lived, struggled to their old places, and, with another terrible fight for air, lived on. But Ralph Smithson never quitted his hold on the bars. His left arm was much swelled, his wound had become exquisitely painful, and his right arm and hand, his legs and back, were bruised in every part. He was often faint and sick; but still the true endurance of his Darnell blood, and his awakening hope in an Almighty Providence, kept him up amidst that ghastly company. He had had much communing with himself that night; and felt, if he were spared, he might do better things hereafter, and be thankful if his life were saved.

At last the morning broke, and a Moslim priest, ascending the rampart above them, chanted the Azan, and its close—"Ulla hu Akbar! Ulla hu Akbar!"—God is victorious!—with more than usual solemnity and energy. Then the captives knew that their time had come either for deliverance or death. The fresher morning air had already revived some who could stand nearest the bars, and behind there was space enough now. Presently a message was brought from the Nawab that Mr. Holwell should come to him, and in no anxiety; but the door could not be opened, nor was it till after a weary labour, by the already exhausted survivors, that its ghastly obstruction could be cleared away. Then twenty-two men and one woman, weak, pallid, utterly exhausted in mind and body, staggered forth into the open air, and sat down helplessly—some weeping, some sobbing hysterically, some praying and thanking God aloud, and others, not seeming to comprehend that they were in existence, tottering here and there, buffeted by the rough soldiers.

"You are to come to the Nawab, Holwell Sahib," said a native officer he knew, who took him kindly by the arm and led him on—"you and the next to you in rank. Come, sirs, and fear not. The Nawab is sorry for all this, and will be kind to you."

No time was allowed for parley. There were some litters ready, and the poor gentlemen bareheaded, and burning with the fever produced by the sudden reaction to life, were hurried away at once. No one seemed to care for the sick.

Ralph Smithson had supported Mrs. Wharton out of the prison, and had seated her in a chair on the shady side of the court. He thought Drever, the sailor, whom he had seen as the dead were dragged away from the door, had showed signs of life, and he returned to carry him out if he were alive. Just then the eunuch Nasir, who had remained on the watch, and had carefully scanned every figure as it passed out of the prison door, had the litter brought up, and ere she was aware of his purpose, Julia Wharton found herself lifted by several stout men into the palankeen; then the doors were shut to, and a cloth fastened round them, and, followed by Nasir and a guard of soldiers, it was borne forward at the utmost speed of the bearers.

Ralph Smithson, as he came forth carrying the almost insensible sailor, saw the litter and the soldiers turning out of the barrack-yard, but hardly noticed it further, and for the time the poor fellow he had brought out received all the care he could afford. But this was not needed when he was rapidly reviving and could sit up. Then Smithson turned to the place where he had left Julia Wharton, but she was gone. "She will have gone to him," he thought, and went towards the steps which led to the bastion where Mr. Wharton had died.

"You cannot pass up here, Sahib," cried a sturdy native soldier, presenting his piece.

"Did a woman go up?" asked Smithson, hastily.

"A woman? No; there was one taken away in a palankeen by the eunuchs from the chair yonder—was that she whom you seek? They were the Nawab's people, and could not be stopped."

Ralph Smithson turned away, sick at heart. "Would that she had died in my arms!" he said, bitterly. "Would to God she had died rather than live a future life of shame! Was nothing possible to rescue her?"

Mr. Holwell and several other gentlemen had been taken away, and did not return. The sun was already high. Ralph felt very faint and weak, and sat down in hopeless exhaustion of mind and body. It was not that he loved the woman whom he had protected through that fearful night, but the thought of her probable future fate was very shocking. Could nothing be done, even to ascertain it? Rousing himself again from the strange chill languor that seemed to be rapidly spreading over him, he addressed himself to a group of the Nawab's officers who were present, and by them his worst fears were confirmed. "One of the Prince's most confidential eunuchs had come with special orders at night," they said, "and had just taken away the English lady; by this time she would be in the royal harem, and who dare follow her? No, they could give no help, no counsel. He was free to do as he pleased; but to approach the Nawab at all in his present humour, least of all in regard to Mrs. Wharton, would be madness." He felt this to be true, and again sat down in despair, sick and giddy, as he had never felt before.

A friendly touch on his shoulder caused him to look up. It was the Don, who, with other Portuguese, as the Nawab entered the fort the evening before, had escaped to his home, little thinking how the night would be spent by his masters, or what he should find in the morning. The little Don's face was wet with tears, and he could scarce speak from convulsive sobbing.

"Come, Mr. Smithson," said the little man, as Ralph looked up at him with a gaunt face and hollow eyes. "Come, sir—my house. . . . You ver ill, sir—come. Will die if stay here. All go w'ere dey like now; and dey take away poor Mr. Holwell and some more gentilmen. Oh dear! Oh dear! What for not take you, sir? I tank Almighty benefactions for you, sir; an' I got all Honorable Company's books safe, sir—lock up; and here de key all safe, sir, 'pon my honor. Come, sir, no good stay here. Dese dam Moor bury poor Mr. Wharton with dead men, sir, in night. *Requiescat in pace*," he continued, pausing and looking up reverently—"Amen; and I will get masses said, sir—by my Padre Sahib—Catolik Church, sir; never mind orthodoxation of comprehendings, Mr. Smithson—all quite good, sir, 'pon my honor! Come 'way, sir; I fritin to see debelopments of corpses out of dat dam Black Hole. Let 'em go into big pit, sir. Ugh! bah! Come 'way, Mr. Smithson, you very ill. I see you shiver, an' you gettin' fever. Dona Luisa glad to see you—'cuse me, but we's humblest people, sir, only truthfulnest of Honorable Company servants—and—King George. You not trust me, Mr. Smithson? I got all books safe, by George!—no lie, sir, 'pon my honor! Come, sir, I insist—you gettin' worse every minit. If you lie down now you never get up. Here, Cassim, help up your master," he continued, decisively, in Hindustani, to Ralph's native servant, who had just entered the court; and between them they dragged Smithson to his feet, and led him away.

In truth, the Don's long speech could hardly be followed by the young man. He felt he was growing worse every moment; and as it is recorded in history that many of the survivors of the Black Hole died of a putrid fever afterwards, I think he would have shared their fate, but for the skill and kind care of those who tended him. He could never remember perfectly how he got to Don Gomez's house, nor what befell him there; but when consciousness, accompanied by almost a child's weakness, returned to him, he found himself in the small bungalow which had been offered to him at first in the Don's garden—the cool wind playing over him and rustling in the trees above—unable to rise from his bed indeed; but, as the worthy Don and a Portuguese doctor informed him with thankful tears in their eyes, safe and convalescent. Then, too, he heard gradually that the Nawab had already left Calcutta, taking with him as prisoners Mr. Holwell and the other gentlemen; but of Mrs. Wharton's fate no traces had been discoverable.

CHAPTER XLIII.

SOZUN'S PLOT.

In her terrible impatience, the interval between the despatch of the eunuch and the last sight of the little procession as it passed into the Fort gate, was hardly endurable by Sozun, as she sat at the window watching. How long would it take to secure the Englishwoman and bring her forth?—had she escaped?—was she with the rest of the prisoners, who were, she had heard, locked up for the night, or was she with other women, hiding where she could? If she could be brought away at night, she might be hidden and saved; but once seen by day, there was no hope—she was far too beautiful to escape *his* notice. And at the remembrance of the misery of the English girl's face, bending over her dead husband, the best portion of Sozun's nature was touched to the quick—an honourable wife, she thought, who had loved him who lay there white and still in death. Had they children? If so, where were they? She had seen none. Hidden away, perhaps, out of the battle. So, chasing each other, as it were, thoughts of the scene on the bastion, and of her warning to Ralph Smithson, came thick and fast into her mind; and still she watched.

Who was he? She had not forgotten the stern, excited face and flashing eyes which met hers as she was being lifted over the dead up to the bastion he was defending, nor her thrill of expected death as the young man's bloody sword was raised above her head for a moment and then dropped. He had said something in English—what was it? Did he then know her to be a woman? or was it the

English girl's cry which had stayed his hand? How grand he had looked as her countrymen had crowded round him, and he held them at bay by the dead Englishman till she bade them begone. She had never seen one like him. Beside him, what was the miserable being lying there—tossing in an uneasy sleep—muttering words she could not distinguish? She crept near him to listen; but he was at rest again, and sleeping heavily, and having trimmed the lamp, she returned to the window.

She was weary with the day's work and the fierce excitement; but no sleep came to her heavy eyes. Though her limbs ached, she scarcely stretched them out to rest. Without she could see nothing but the dark plain, the river glimmering faintly beyond it, and the mass of the Fort and ruined warehouses, from among which dull fires gleamed, and light wreaths of smoke from smouldering embers rose occasionally into the air. Far away to the west, lightning was flickering among the clouds on the horizon; and she watched it vacantly, now brightly flashing, now glowing with a dull coppery gleam, and disappearing altogether. There was perfect stillness over all, except now and then the faint, distant cry of a sentinel, or the beat of a hollow-sounding drum and blast of a shrill horn, where a new watch was being set.

Still the eunuch did not return; and to her perception the danger had much increased. What if the woman were dead? Did Englishwomen, like other infidels she had heard tales of, sacrifice themselves to their husband's memory? Had she escaped to the ships, and Nasir feared to return without her? If she came, what was to be done? Where could she be lodged in safety, away from the Nawab? Would Nasir be faithful? and if not—? She had no attendant on on whom she could depend for aid. There were crowds about her, but they were the Nawab's creatures—not one of them would dare to brave his anger, with the memories of many a tortured, mutilated wretch vividly in their remembrance. No, there was no help there; whatever was to be done she must do herself. The palankeen, whenever it did come, must be brought into the inner court of the house where they were staying. It was true she had told Nasir to await her orders, and he might be obedient; but it was a fearful risk, nevertheless.

Then her memory went back to the young Englishman. She shut her eyes and thought of him—so beautiful and yet so terrible. She thought of him, too, as he might be—tender and gracious; as she had seen him when he spoke to the woman, full of pity, with tears flowing from her eyes as he comforted her and led her away. Would she have gone like her? Ah yes! They said—even her own people said—he was a hero, and no one would have harmed him.

A strange watch indeed, and with stranger thoughts for company.

Where had they not wandered in those weary hours, back from childhood, from the deadly field of Sirhind, through a life of false triumph and of shame—down to this? Was it enough to have lived for? A life without a tie, a life without love such as she had dreamed of in spite of evil influences! Yet one of splendour and of power such as she had hardly dared to imagine! She could not retract now—she durst not. Among her people she had won honour, but her shame remained—could she leave that, hang grave-clothes about her neck, and go forth a humble devotee of God? It was the only alternative she knew of, but one she dared not attempt. Would the Nawab let her go? Never with life; to be detected in flight would be attended with mutilation or death. But she was yet secure; and as she turned to her lord's couch, memories of kindness, of many a fond caress, of the only love he had given to any one, came back upon her heart, and for the time softened it. "He might wrong me, he might even strike me," she said; "but I could bear it: I could not leave him but for God's service, and I am not fit for that yet. So long as it may be my destiny I will live with him—or die, true even in death. See, he calls me, and I was in his thoughts as he in mine."

"Sozun, Sozun!" It was a moaning, plaintive cry in his sleep, and she went again to his side. "Sozun! ah, girl, do not leave me! I have only you—only you," and he stretched out his arms, while she saw by the dim lamp that his face was sorely troubled.

"It is some uneasy dream," she thought; "I had best wake him. "I am here, my lord," she said, gently taking his hand; "Sozun is here; why didst thou call? I have not left thee."

The Nawab started up and pushed away her hand apparently in terror. "Where am I?" he cried; "that Derwesh! save me from him; oh save me, Sozun!" and as he hid his face in her lap, she felt that he trembled.

"My lord, my lord! Let me take the evil off thee: what was the dream?" she said, soothing him. "There was no Derwesh near thee—there is no one but me. I could not sleep, and was watching thee, my lord. It is but a dream—let it pass."

"His eyes, his eyes! Oh, Sozun! they gleamed at me, as they did once in life. That dream! Ah! girl, that would frighten thee—even thee. Yes, let it pass. Is there yet much of the night?"

"I think not," she said; "the dawn is almost breaking. Wilt thou sleep again?"

"No," he said, "not now. I should dream again of him, perhaps. Sit by me, and tell me of the fight."

"Thou hast won Calcutta," she said; "is not that enough? For no one yet dared to attack the Feringis but thee. Did not the Derwesh—did I not tell thee, thou wouldst be victorious?"

"But for thee, my life, I should have lost it. Now, what my

father dared not do, I have done. But for thee, I should have been like him, afraid of a few white faces and a few guns. Now these Feringis fear me, and, Inshalla! they shall do so hereafter. I promised thee the plunder of Calcutta Fort, and thou hast won it, girl; and while I dispose of these Feringis, who have so long defied me, thou canst go there and do thy will."

"Be as merciful, my lord," she said pleadingly, "as thou hast been victorious; they cannot hurt thee now. Be merciful, for Sozun's sake."

"I will," he replied; "but the Priest thirsts for their blood, the blood of the Kafirs who deny the Prophet, and he hath inflamed men's minds."

"The blood shed yesterday was enough surely to satisfy him, my Prince?"

"I fear not, Sozun; but I will not yield. Ah! there is dawn, and the music begins. Get thee to sleep for a while—thou art weary, and thine eyes are heavy. I shall not see thee all day, my life; but in the evening thou shalt sing me to sleep;" and he passed out of the chamber to his attendants.

It was like a reprieve to Sozun to hear this: she would then be alone, and there was a better chance of success than she had dared to hope for. Sleep was out of the question, for her faculties were more than ever excited. Would the Englishwoman be brought? When she came could she understand her, and if not, what should she do? There were servants in Calcutta who spoke English—could one be sent for? Ah! why was she delayed?

Sozun seated herself again at the window. The morning breeze blew fresh and cool then, driving before it the heavy mist which had rested on the river in that close sultry night, and she watched the sails of boats gliding to and fro on the river. People were thronging toward the Fort, and some of the burned buildings were still smoking. Presently she saw the Nawab's retinue assemble below, and it was shortly in motion towards his tents, which were pitched in the camp. No one moved from the Fort as yet; but after a time some soldiers issued from the gate, then a few mean litters and men on foot, and she watched their progress to the camp; presently, too, a royal palankeen—she well knew its scarlet cloth covering—and Nasir mounted on his piebald palfrey urging on the bearers behind.

"It is she—it is she!" the girl exclaimed, clasping her hands; "and he is true." Ere many minutes had elapsed, footsteps were heard on the private stair which opened into an adjoining room, and she went to receive her strange visitor.

"She is here, lady," said Nasir, who first entered; but she has come out of the mouth of death, and is in sore plight. They all died last night but her and a few others—but she may be saved. Look!"

It was indeed as he had said. Julia Wharton—clothes wet, torn, and dirty, her hair dishevelled, her face haggard, and her eyes swollen with weeping and misery—the lovely Englishwoman Sozun had seen the evening before, could hardly have been recognised. "Thou art welcome, sister," she said, as Julia Wharton, weeping and trembling with terror, sank down before her, and was raised with cheering words of genuine compassion. "What can I do for thee? Dost thou understand me?" But the lady could not reply; in her terror and misery she was as one distraught.

"Some one must be brought who can speak her strange tongue. Canst thou get such a one, Nasir?"

"I will try," he said, "but it is dangerous. What wilt thou do with her, lady? Is she for him?—thy gift to him?"

"No, no!" she returned fiercely, stamping her foot. "Why do you ask?"

"I beg pardon," replied the man humbly; "I will seek for an ayah," and he left them together.

As he passed out there was a woman sitting alone by the steps of the house, weeping bitterly. "Who art thou?" he asked.

"I am Missy Baba's servant," she said, "and she has been taken here. Oh, sir, let me go to her; I have followed her."

"How lucky," thought the eunuch. "Come with me," he said; "she is safe;" and they returned through the private court.

"Missy—oh, Missy Baba!" cried the faithful creature, as she entered the room, and cast herself at the feet of her mistress; "come 'way—come my house; you no to stop here; dis no good place; come, I take you—come," and she tried to drag Mrs. Wharton to her feet.

"Let her alone," said Sozun; "she hath hardly sense to hear thee. Peace! ye are with a friend; speak to her, for she doth not understand me, and tell her not to be afraid."

CHAPTER XLIV.

JULIA'S CHANCE.

"MISSY not know Anna?" cried the woman. "Oh, look up, and no fear for any ting; dis lady kind lady, an' Anna come to help. Oh, Missis safe; and, I tank God, no dead in Black Hole."

Julia Wharton's great blue eyes opened, and she looked up. It was the only act of consciousness she had evinced since her entrance. With whom was she? Who were the man and woman—that

English girl in disguise, as she had thought Sozun? Where was she? She tried to speak, but all that Anna could understand was, "Water."

"Water—she wants water, lady," said Anna, anxiously. "Ah, lady, my mistress was in the prison all night, and hundreds died around her. She will be better presently; pardon her."

"And her husband was killed beside her," added Sozun. "I saw him lying dead on the bastion: would she had died too! Art thou a Moslimin?"

"Oh no!" cried the woman. "I am a Christian, Portuguese, and her servant. They told me she was in the Nawab's palankeen, and I followed it."

"It does not matter, if thou canst be faithful," replied Sozun. "Take of this water freely; there are no distinctions in such grief. Drink, lady."

"O Missy, drink some cool water, you will be better soon, and safe; dis lady goot lady, but I was afraid at first," said the servant.

"Who is she, and where am I?" asked Julia Wharton, after an eager drink.

"Me not know," replied Anna, but me here wit you, dat's 'nough. Now lie down, Missy—poor Missy—but will be well presently;" and raising her mistress she supported her to a carpet which was spread near them; while Sozun fetched pillows, which she arranged carefully under the poor aching head.

"Be quiet now, lady," said Anna in a whisper; "she may sleep;" and they sat down silently beside her.

Julia Wharton was weary, even to death she thought. Her senses were confused and stunned; she could remember nothing but portions of the fearful night she had passed, and shut her eyes shuddering, as the cries and groans of the dying seemed to fill her ears.

"Ah, you not tremble so, Missy—me wit you? Anna not go 'way now, never no more;" and she took her mistress's head on her bosom, and put away the dishevelled hair, while Sozun chafed her hands. Presently they saw a faint colour come into the wan cheeks; and as the girl grew calmer, tears welled from her eyes. "Do not leave me, Anna," she said softly; "they are all gone but you—all dead!—all dead!"

"Me never leave poor Missy Baba no more," said the woman, herself bursting into tears—"never no more. Now, go to sleep, that's a dear lady, me watchin' by missis;" and she began to sing a low crooning lullaby of the country, such as is sung to children. Gradually they saw the eyelids drooping more heavily, and the fair girl's countenance relax from the expression of terror; and they sat and watched her silently. The frame was utterly worn out, and kind nature was applying the only remedy for its restoration.

"Couldst thou conceal her—hide her away?" asked Sozun, after a while in a low whisper. "Dost thou wish to save her?"

"From what?" answered the woman. "You are kind, why should she fear? She is not a man that the Nawab should desire her blood. Has he not destroyed them all?"

"It is because she is a woman that I fear for her," returned Sozun. "It is because she is beautiful that I have had her brought to me. Who dare conceal her but me? Were he to know of this, dost thou think my life or her honour would be safe? Canst thou understand what I have dared—to—save her?"

"Who art thou, lady?" asked the servant, tremblingly. "His wife?"

"Ah, no," she said, "I am not his wife: and if she remained he would hate me, and forsake me for her. Look! her beauty is returning. Why did she not die?"

True, it was returning, for her sleep was peaceful and refreshing. As they looked upon the girl, there was a soft smile upon her mouth; the rosy lips were partly open, and disclosed the pearly teeth, and the cheek was flushed with the beautiful colour habitual to it, even in India.

"Look!" continued Sozun, "is she not beautiful? Such may be the houris of Paradise they tell of, but not women amongst us. Dost thou comprehend now what I fear?"

The servant's mind was a poor one, blunted perhaps by service and a rough striving life; but it was a woman's, and could comprehend jealousy and its accompanying dread and terror, which, in the fair face of Sozun, were fast increasing.

"I understand," she replied; "thou art not her enemy, lady?"

"If I were," returned Sozun, "I would take my lord by the hand and bring him to look on her. Even thus—as she lies, weary and faint—she is more lovely than he had ever dreamed of; and what would she be were she attired as I am? Ah, no—she or I—she or I: and I would save her."

"An English woman would not be the wife of the Emperor of Delhi," said the servant, proudly. "Why do you fear for her?"

"I fear thou, too, art a fool," returned Sozun, quickly. "His wife! No, but worse; the slave of his honour, to be cast away to perish when he was weary of her. Dost thou not understand? If thou canst not, wilt thou make her do so?"

"Where could I take her?" said the woman, drearily, passing her hand across her eyes; "who could now protect her? Even Don Gomez dare not, and the Nawab would hear of her, and hang him. Oh, lady, why was she brought at all?"

"That she might be saved," was the reply. "None but I could save her, or can save her. If thou hast any wits thou wilt not fail me. Think again; the Nawab will not stay many days—any hut, any cabin—what matter? If she once knows her own danger, she will save herself, or die. Does she fear death more than dishonour?"

"I cannot tell," said the woman, despairingly. "When she wakes we must tell her. There is one—yes, one—the Begum, who might—"

"What Begum? Tell me, quick!—I can send for her."

"No, no, lady, she would not come; she is hiding herself, but I know where. She lived with her husband, with Missy's husband, many years, and his children are with her."

"I bless thee, O Allah Kureem! that there is hope. She would not refuse her?"

"No, I think not now. Before the Fort was attacked they met, and fell on each other's necks. I could take Missy there at night if you would give her clothes."

"Surely, surely. Ya Allah, I vow thanksgivings to thee at every shrine. Yes, till night. Before then she shall be bathed and refreshed, she shall eat, and be strong. Oh that it were night! Till then — be thou but merciful, O Lord! See, the door there is fastened; no one can enter. I shall order water for the bath, which is beyond, and I shall tell them I bathe in private to-day. Yes, it will do," continued the girl to herself, quickly; "there is no fear; and when my food comes, she can eat of it with me. Fear not to be alone, I will soon rejoin thee." Would Nasir be faithful? That was her only dread now.

He met her at the anteroom-door of the Nawab's chamber. "I have been watching," he said, "and no one suspects as yet. But if he discover this lady, we must both die. Why didst thou risk it? Had I but known thy intention, I would not have gone for the woman—no, even for thee; why not give the Feringi to him?"

"There is no fear," she replied, with all the calmness she could command, but she well knew the truth of his word, and trembled—was it worth the risk after all? Might not she trust her lord, and send the English girl there and then into the street? Give her to him? Ah, no! The sharp old pang of jealousy once more shot through her heart, as she stood irresolute for a moment; and she who had not feared death as the Englishman's sword quivered over her head, did not fear it now. "She or I," she muttered—"she or I."

"As you will, lady," continued the man; "what will be, will be. Thou hast not eaten yet?"

"Tell them to make the bath ready, and to send little Janum to me; she will do what I need, Nasir. If there be danger, tell me of it, and keep watch."

"It is too late," said the man moodily to himself as he bowed and left her—"too late."

All day the house had been still, and Julia Wharton slept on her heavy sleep. When she woke, her eyes first fell upon Anna, who had never left her. A moment afterwards, as all the events of the night rushed upon her memory, she flung her arms round her servant in a paroxysm of terror. "Come away," she cried—"come away, Anna; why do we stay here?"

"Ah Missy!" said the woman, "where you go now? Got no house, no Fort, no nothin'; where you go, my darlin'? best to stay here till night, then go 'way to Begum Sahib; she will keep you safe."

Perhaps it was then only that her utter desolation was understood. Last night, even in the fearful death-prison, Ralph Smithson's stout arm was about her; and there were Mr. Holwell and other friends near; why was she not with them? "Where are the gentlemen?" she asked.

"I tell by-and-by every ting. Missy now bathe and eat something, then will be more stronger. I get clean clothes, native clothes missis wear, cause nobody not find out missis."

"Who was with me at first, Anna?" she continued. "I think I saw some European woman disguised in native clothes; but, indeed, I was very confused."

"Ah, she good lady dat! she send missis away to-night, den bad Nawab not get her."

"The Nawab! then I am in his power," she gasped. "O Anna, I remember now how they seized me, and carried me here when I had fainted."

"Lady will tell all when come; now be quiet an' wait. Me not dare go out, but missis get bath and eat; then get plenty strong, and night-time dey send away safe; missis understand?—safe to Begum Sahib."

I do not think Julia Wharton could then comprehend the danger of her position. She thought some compassionate native lady might have protected her, and she understood that she must go out at night to be safe. She was no coward; and if there was ever a moment of her life in which all her presence of mind was needed it was this. It was clear to her that she was alone, and that none of her English friends were near; but those who lived through the night must be alive, and if she could get to the Begum she would soon find means to communicate with them. With this thought her spirit rose, and she prayed fervently for help.

"I will do what you wish," she said; "and oh, Anna! how can I repay what you are doing—what you have done for me?"

"Missis, never mind dat," said the woman joyfully. "I very glad to help my darlin' Missy Baba. Now we take off dem dirty clothes, an' make pretty Mussulmani girl of my lady. Den rest quiet all day; and I pray good Virgin Mary she keep you safe. Dere's no helpin' w'at's been done neider. Dat's God's will, an' holy Virgin."

Sozun was right. It would have been little use overwhelming an already scared and nearly unconscious woman with a prospect of imminent danger; but when she herself and Anna, aided by the little slave, had bathed the fair stranger, Sozun's exclamations at her beauty could hardly be restrained. When all the dishevelled hair had been combed out and braided; when, refreshed more than she could have thought possible, she was dressed in a plain suit of Sozun's travelling clothes—the metamorphosis from the haggard draggled woman who had been brought in the morning, to the lovely being who sat before her, blushing at the strange attire in which she found herself dressed, was more wonderful than Sozun could have imagined. She pressed her guest to eat, and Julia Wharton was strengthened by what she took. She had only one object now—to escape thence; and though it was no easy matter for Anna to interpret the rapid impetuous speech of the Affghan girl, Julia soon comprehended what she had to do, and the reason why it should be done.

CHAPTER XLV.

HOPELESS.

I QUESTION which of the two women was the bravest—the Affghan who had gone to battle in a fierce desire of winning back the honour among her people which her evil life had forfeited—or the English girl who, with a calm brow and now serene beauty, heard what her fate might be, and in the purity of her faith looked up to Him to whose protecting care she committed herself. Sozun had expected tears, wailings, helplessness—which might mar her project altogether, or increase the difficulty of its execution. Instead of this, she saw a girl, hardly older than herself, who had already endured horrors such as she could not imagine—a stranger in a foreign land, far away from her people—undismayed, trusting in God, and prepared to do her best in whatever might follow. "Ah, yes!" she thought, "such are the mothers of those men whom we have feared; such was the mother of him who spared me! What marvel if, hereafter, they be our conquerors!"

From time to time Sozun had anxiously sent for news of the Nawab; and it promised well for the success of her enterprise that there were messages in reply from him that he was delayed—that he might be late—that it might even be night before he returned. The English gentlemen had to be examined as to their treasures; the agents of Jugget Seit, Omichund, and other bankers, as to the moneys lodged with them; the amount of advances made for purchases; and the stocks of goods in hand. Weary, unrefreshed, stunned by the calamity which had fallen on them, Mr. Holwell and his fellow-captives yet bore themselves stoutly that day; and the abuse and execrations of the Nawab, on his disappointment at not finding the treasure-hoards he had expected, were bravely endured. But I have no concern with them; nor can I follow them in their wretched captivity and distress afterwards, when they were taken up to Moorshedabad in an open boat, their bodies covered with boils and ulcers—the effect of the poisonous miasma of that horrible night in the prison—nor relate how at last they were released, and rejoined their countrymen in safety, after all their perils.

Nasir had not relaxed in his vigilance. In his heart he had disapproved of the child Janum having been admitted, yet he dared not cross the humour of the Nawab's favourite. He had now left his post, and had been able to lock up the door of the small court by which the Englishwoman had entered, and thus to prevent intrusion there; still it was almost impossible to believe that she could be long concealed. His fellow-servants were in their usual places: but some were in attendance on the Nawab, and brought occasional messages from him to Sozun. These were sometimes delivered by Nasir himself, sometimes by others; in short, there was a perpetual going to and fro, which could not be prevented. It was next to impossible, also, to keep the ordinary women-servants out of the private apartments without exciting suspicion, and he had several times, with dread at his heart, observed them whispering together, especially as the afternoon advanced; and once or twice, Chandbee, the head of the female attendants, tried the padlock of the closed door, wondered why it was shut, declared she must break it open if the key were not found, and was promised by Nasir as often that he would look for it.

Now the little Janum, who was a child of six or thereabouts, though passionately devoted to her kind mistress, whose pet she was, was also the general pet and plaything of the eunuchs on guard, and in particular of one of them, Juma, a negro of gigantic stature, a good-natured fellow, who was an especial favourite of his master's; and as the three women were speaking in the inner chamber, Janum had been bid to carry out the plates from which Julia Wharton and Anna had eaten, with injunctions to set them down and speak to no one. Probably, had she seen nobody she would have done her errand faithfully, though the longing to tell of the beautiful Englishwoman was burning at her heart; but as she went out, Juma, who was sitting, his sword across his knees, as usual in the corridor, caught her, and held her fast.

"Let me go, let me go!" she cried; "I cannot stay."

"No; I have caught you," he said playfully; "and till you tell me what the lady is doing, I won't let you go."

"She is tired with yesterday's fighting, and is asleep," said the child.

"Ah, Janum, that's a lie! Who ate all the pilao and the kabobs that I brought up?" said the man, laughing.

"Let me go!" cried the child.

"Who ate the kabobs, I say?" continued the man, again lifting her up, dishes and all, into the air. "Tell me, and I'll set you down."

"I won't tell you, Juma."

"Tell me," he persisted, "and I'll give you such good julaybees."

"I won't—let me go."

"Very well; then I won't let you go."

"Will you promise not to tell any one, if I tell you? Nasir would kill me if he knew, and so would mother."

"I will;" and he set her down.

"Swear on my neck, Juma."

He put his hand on her neck, with mock gravity. "I swear," he said.

"Oh, she is so beautiful!" whispered the child.

"She—who?"

"The Feringi; and we took off all her dirty clothes, and oh! she was as white as milk all over, and—"

"Ph-e-w!" whistled the negro to himself; "what strange creatures these women are! Here is one, a prime favourite, thinking to gain more favour by bringing in another. But it doesn't answer, and they don't see it. A Feringi, too! Perhaps if I were—"

"And the julaybees, Juma?" cried the child, stroking his cheek.

"I will go and get them from the shop close by, my darling. When I knock, come out again, and thou shalt have them," he said; and the child vanished.

Juma was not a bright character, but he was as faithful as a dog to his master. "She wants to surprise him," he said, "but I'll give him the first news. If the Feringi hath bathed and eaten, she is quite ready. I can but go and see. I am on my way to the durbar with a message," he said, as he passed out; "one of you must take my place," and he went on.

The durbar tents were full of people. All the state officers were there; and several of the English gentlemen were sitting in a corner on the ground, haggard, dirty, and weary. The native bankers of the city were huddled in groups near them, with dread plainly impressed on their countenances. There were several Persian writers busily making up an account, and a heap of money lying upon the carpet.

"It is impossible," cried the Nawab, angrily. "Fifty thousand rupees only! Am I a child to believe that you great Feringi merchants traded upon fifty thousand rupees? Beware, I say, lest I put you to the torture."

"Your Highness can do as you please," said one of the Englishmen, rising; "there is no more, and the Persian cash-book of yesterday proves it," and he sat down again.

What did Juma care for the cash-book? He took his place behind the Nawab's seat, and, watching an opportunity, bent down and whispered a few words in his ear.

The assembly saw the Nawab start, but were too polite to notice it, and after a moment he resumed his questions.

But it was clear to those who knew him best that he was now uneasy, and men in whispers asked why he should be so. It was already dusk in the tent, for the evening was cloudy, and threatened rain. The scribes, writing on their knees, shifted their positions to get more light, and one even asked for a lamp. The Nawab would perhaps have continued his work; he was by no means satisfied with what he had done; he was baffled altogether in his spoil; he had expected millions, and after all there were but a few thousands. But who was this Feringi woman, so beautiful, for Juma's description was an exaggeration of what he had heard from the child? On the one hand was the craving for gold, on the other a fast arising lust; and such men as he obey the stronger passion. "Put the Feringis in irons, and take them to camp," he cried. "We will hear more to-morrow. The durbar is closed."

"Durbar burkhast! Durbar burkhast!" roared the silver macemen. "Depart! depart!"

"Quick!" cried the Nawab, as he entered his palankeen—"quick to the house!" and he leaned back, smiling at the anticipation of what he should find ready for him.

The room where the women sat was already gloomy, and it seemed as though night were closing in. "It will soon be dark, lady," said Sozun, who had been looking out from time to time, "and the Nawab will stay till past the evening prayer. She is not afraid?" she asked of the servant.

"Missy Baba, my lady, has no fear," was the reply. "May we go?"

"What does she say, Anna? may we go?" asked Julia Wharton, rising.

"Nearly time to go, mem; when man come, then go. Missy not be 'fraid, I go with her."

A few minutes after, Sozun went to the door of the small

staircase; a man's footsteps were ascending it, and she stood there trembling.

"Lady, it is I," said Nasir, in a low voice. "Here is a blanket for her; come—there is no one without."

"Now we go, Missy, darlin'," cried Anna, joyfully. "Come along, an' I take you safe to Begum Sahib."

Mrs. Wharton stretched out her hand to Sozun, who took it and kissed it reverently. "May Allah be kind to thee," she said; "do not forget me when you are happy in your dear country."

Julia did not understand the words, but the action could not be mistaken. She put her arms round the girl's neck and kissed her.

"Come, come quickly!" cried the eunuch. "Why do you delay?"

So they went on, and Sozun followed them, weeping. It was a short stair, which ended in a small court, and Nasir led them into it. But they were too late. As he opened the door which led into the street, and they stepped out, there was a sudden blaze of torches, and the Nawab, hurrying on on foot to the private entrance, saw the group before him pause irresolutely; then he cried to Juma and others with him, "Seize them instantly. Who come out of my zenana disguised and muffled? Nasir, who are these?"

An instant more, and the coverings were torn from the now shrieking women, and the bright torchlight revealed the English girl's fair face and white arms, as she waved them wildly in the air struggling with Juma, who took her up like a child and carried her in.

"She would have escaped," cried the Nawab, foaming with rage, "and thou, Nasir, aiding her. Hew him down!"

"Spare me, O Prince!" exclaimed the man, frantically, falling at his feet. "Oh, have pity! it was not I—not I!"

"It was my order!" cried Sozun, who had turned when she heard the shrieks. "It was mine only; he is beneath thy notice. I, Sozun, would have sent her away. What is she, a poor Feringi woman, to thee?"

A fearful execration burst from the Nawab as he drew a dagger from his girdle and aimed a furious blow at her. The girl evaded it, but did not quail; she feared death too little.

"Strike," she cried, "if thou darest, one whose only crime is loving thee!"

The Nawab's uplifted arm fell to his side. "Thou art a witch,' he said, gloomily; "and I am captive in thy devilish arts. Bind her!" he cried, to other eunuchs, whom the disturbance had collected. "Put her in irons, and take her away to Moorshedabad. Now, now! she is in thy charge, Roostum," he continued, to one of the men, "and thy life shall answer for her. Listen," he added rapidly, in a whisper—"let her lie with the Begum in the vault;" and he passed on up the narrow staircase, where Juma," bearing the shrieking English girl, had already gone, driving Anna before him.

"Come, lady," said the eunuch to Sozun, as he dashed tears from his eyes—"come; it is thy destiny, and thou knowest we dare not delay."

"Yes, it is my destiny," she said, calmly, "and thy will, O Allah!" and she bowed her head and followed them out.

CHAPTER XLVI.

A LETTER FROM ENGLAND.

I DO not think that the details of a recovery from a severe illness present any matters for particular record in this history; and it is probable that the worthy Don's magniloquence, and the wonderful English addresses which he composed for Mr. Smithson, might be wearying to our readers. Nor perhaps would they care to know how Mr. Smithson comported himself to Doñas Caterina and Maria in their kind attendance upon him; nor how the worthy Doña Luisa hoped perhaps for a while that Catherina's budding charms might make a due impression on the handsome Englishman, and was sharply reproved by her husband for her foolishness. As to Maria, she was yet a child, and there was no danger for her; but I question very much whether she ever forgot those delicious days with the sufferer, when as yet too weak to do anything for himself. She was his devoted attendant, and was repaid by what she most craved for—details of English life, to which she would listen for hours. I say, then, let all this pass—we have no need to record it; and after some days' weakness, as we know, a strong constitution threw off the languor of fever, and grew to be vigorous as ever. Then Ralph Smithson and the Don held consultations as to the best way of getting to the ships, and found there was but little difficulty. The English gentlemen had had too many native friends to be without means of helping themselves; and though they were no longer masters of Calcutta, any who remained there were not ill used or distressed once the Nawab's forces marched on their return. Although Ralph Smithson was not then aware of the exact nature of Julia Wharton's fate, and only heard it long afterwards in a manner we shall come to understand ourselves, yet he made all the endeavour in his power to ascertain the truth; and, indeed, it was generally known that the lady who was found alive on the morning of the 21st June had been taken by the Nawab to Moorshedabad as one of his mistresses; and we can easily believe that out of his seraglio very little information that could be relied upon ever transpired. There she might live or die, and nothing more be heard of her.

It may be recorded also that the little Whartons came often, and when he was able to walk there, Ralph Smithson went to the house, and conversed with their mother, who sat behind a screen. She was of respectable people, and did not want for native friends; but there was much to do in regard to Mr. Wharton's property and the funds settled on herself and her children, and I need hardly mention that Ralph, as one of the executors, promised his hearty assistance when the Factory should be reinstated.

There was no one, except perhaps the Nawab himself, deluded by his flatterers and courtiers, who did not believe in the speedy restoration of the English. Already there were parties earnestly at work in their favour. The great Hindu bankers knew the value of their presence, and that the country itself would languish without the trade they followed. Even the Dutch and French trembled in their factories; and thought if the stout English could not beat back the Nawab, how easily they, in their turn, might be overwhelmed; and now, therefore, their mistrust of him increased. It is true that M. Law sent expresses to M. Bussy that the English influence in Calcutta and in Bengal was for the present destroyed, and urged him to press on to join the Nawab and strengthen him for good; but the monsoon had set in—for months to come the country would be impassable by any regular army—and nothing could be effected.

Don Gomez was no indifferent observer of events. "Wen you ready help yourselves, Mister Smithson," he said, as he bid his guest farewell, "den plenty people's ready help you; dat's my opinion. An' you come soon too, sir, if God will, an' blessed Virgin; an' all the books safe, sir, an' I got key too. Honorable Company not lose one cowry of advance, sir, 'pon my honor. You tell dat, please, Mister Drake, an' be d—d to him. Good-bye, Mr. Smithson, an' wish you well sincerity, sir, an' soon come back; den we have intensification of jollification in Factory, and drink de King's health and Honorable Company, by George!"

This was said in the little cabin of a budgerow, at a village somewhat below the Fort. The head boatman was an old friend of Mr. Smithson's, and had promised to take him safe to the ships, and he did so. All there had heard of his illness, for they kept up a constant communication with Juggut Seit's house, Omichund, and other bankers, and that he was safe with Don Gomez; and as his boat next day ran alongside the *Daddaley*, then lying with the fleet at Fultah, and many of the old familiar faces looked over the ship's side, I am quite sure that Ralph Smithson's heart was grateful at the wonderful preservation he had experienced.

There was much to do: a committee sat upon Mr. Wharton's effects, and his will was opened. Provision had been made for the Begum and his children very munificently, and the latter were to be sent to England by-and-by; but excepting some legacies to friends, his wife Julia was made residuary legatee over and above all that had already been settled upon her. Nothing, however, could be done in that matter, and it was a sad subject altogether. Several ships were expected, and they dropped in one by one from England. Ralph Smithson had hoped to receive letters by every ship for several months past; but, though there were kind messages to him from Mr. Darnell, none had arrived. It was not probable, he thought, that his uncle or Mr. Sanders would write to him direct till they had heard news of his arrival in India. A year had not elapsed since he left them, and he might not hear for six months more; but to his great joy the ship that reached them late in July, brought a packet addressed to Mr. Wharton, and enclosed in it were two letters, one from Mr. Darnell and one from Mr. Sanders; and being in India ourselves at present, we may like to hear what has been doing in the dear old country since we left it in Ralph Smithson's company. It was evident that though the letter had been begun on Christmas Eve, it had not been finished for some time afterwards.

"*Private.* LOMBARD STREET, *Christmas Eve*, 1755.

"DEAR NEPHEW,—It would be hard, for all that is past, if I didn't remember you at this season; and as I cannot be here to-morrow, I will begin, and trust it may find you as well as it leaves me. I cannot expect to hear of you for several months to come; and though I have sent messages to you, which I trust have been delivered, I have delayed to write, for in truth there was little to tell you of that you would care to hear. I will, however, begin at the period which followed your departure, and bring it up to the last date I can detain the letter, but not to-day. This is only to say, I do not forget you; and Dolly and I, whatever madam and the rest may do, will drink your health to-morrow in the Company's Madeira, and wish you a merrier Christmas than we have ourselves. I doubt not, also, they will drink your health at Melcepeth; for I am rejoiced to tell you your uncle hath quite forgiven you now. When you were fairly at sea, and past recall, I went to him and told him what I had done, and why; and at first he was sore wroth with me, and swore at me bad enough; but the doctor came in and stopped him, and presently he got calm, and we talked it over, and he was brought round to my opinion. Mistress Grover and I had much ado, however, to set him right. He would have not only forgiven thee, but had thee to Melcepeth again; and swore he deserved his wound for his hard-heartedness. What if thou *wast* lawful heir of Melcepeth, after all, how should he forgive himself? But enow of this—enow to satisfy thee that thou art forgiven—the best news I can give thee on the eve of that day when He was born, who will, as we hope, forgive us our sins.

. . . .

"It is well known to you that I have never interfered with your uncle's plans for Constance; and I had no mind to be, as I may say, a spy upon Mr. Elliot, nor to find out what he had, or what he hadn't, as Grover would have had me to. I told her she might even find out for herself; but it seems there was no long doubt on the matter. Although most of the people to whom he owed money were willing enow to let my gentleman follow the rich heiress, yet one of them clapt him into a sponging-house, and kept him there; and how-ever Peed came to know of it I can't find out, but he wrote to the baronet, telling him what had happened, and why; and this set my brother inquiring of Braithwaite, and other Alnwick and Wooler attorneys, and all came out—viz., that he had made ducks and drakes of a pretty property, and there was no recovery or chance thereof; and when my gentleman made his appearance at Melcepeth, I dare-say the baronet was cool to him, and Mistress Grover too, whatever sweet Mistress Constance might have been; and the end of all was, that the gentlemen quarrelled over their wine, and Elliot got his *congé* faster than he expected. Peed is delighted at his good work, and saith, moreover, that there is more to be found out, and, as usual, a woman's at the bottom of it all. He talks mysteriously about some one privately married to this spark, or seduced, and gone to the East Indies. Have you ever heard aught of him or her among your folks there? Well, we have no business with him or her; only, you will be glad to hear, though he was an old friend of thine, that Mistress Constance is well shut of him. Grover hath written me pages of her grief; but the lass, I warrant, hath sound sense under all, and the hint of the other woman hath, I fancy, quite cured her.

. . . .

"You will grieve to hear that poor Mrs. Morton is much declined in health, and Sybil hath but small hopes of her now. One Mr. Forster, also an old friend of yours, I think, hath been courting Miss Morton, and her mother and Nanny Keene advise her to take him; but she won't listen to them, which I consider foolish, because Mrs. Morton's little annuity dies with her, and, in event of her death I don't know what is to become of Sybil. They have no friends or relatives that I can discover; but God tempers the wind to the shorn lamb; and though, according to my poor judgment, I tried to per-suade the girl to settle herself honourably, and satisfy her mother's anxieties, I could make no impression on her; and faith, she fell into such a passion of weeping that I was thankful to get away, and have heard no more since.

"*Feb.* 26, 1756.

"I have writ you a business letter separate, and you will get more advice about your investments from Mr. Sanders. I see he is not easy about political matters, especially if we have war again with the French; but I confess I have no such anxieties as he hath, nor, indeed, doth any one here believe in what I call this croaking. And now I have writ enough. I am longing to hear from you, dear nephew; for whatever hath passed, you are the same as ever to your affectionate uncle, ROGER DARNELL."

Perhaps I need not record the mingled feelings of joy and anxiety with which Ralph Smithson again and again read this letter. My readers who know his antecedents will be able to follow them very easily. Constance was free again, and Sybil, poor dear Sybil, in trouble; but she would be firm against Forster, and even if Mrs. Morton died, his uncles would not forget her, and he would send her ample funds as soon as he could. No, he had no fear of her. Then he was forgiven, freely and amply, and his dear old uncle loved him still. Ah! on that burning July day, with the sweltering heat beating through the ship's awnings, his thoughts were far away in the Melcepeth woods, and Constance—still his own Constance—free from Elliot's wiles, beside him. No wonder, I think, if hot tears—tears of mingled thankfulness and regret—were fast falling upon the paper before him. Was Elliot then married?—and who could the woman be who was in India? Pshaw! It would be an idle task, indeed, to trace any of Elliot's amours; and, thank God! his dear cousin was safe from him.

Upon the contents of the despatches which had reached the fleet by the ship that morning, an anxious council had since been sitting in the cuddy of the *Daddaley*. I need not trouble my readers with any detail of its deliberations. But when Ralph Smithson was summoned to it, and told by Mr. Drake that the council, in the fullest reliance upon his ability and judgment, had resolved to send him to Madras—to represent there the affairs of the settlement, and to give all the information necessary for the assemblage of a powerful armament—to Mr. Clive and Admiral Watson, the young man's heart fairly bounded within him, and the honourable mission was indeed joyfully accepted.

END OF PART THIRD.

PART FOURTH.

PART FOURTH.

CHAPTER XLVII.

COLONEL CLIVE AT MADRAS.

If I am asked why I have given no account of the English society at Fultah, where the ships had lain at anchor ever since their retreat from Calcutta in June, up to the period of the stirring events which closed the year 1756, and with which the year 1757 opened, I reply that there was not only little to record, but that what there was would not probably elevate our countrymen in the opinion of readers of this history. I am not of opinion that it was either particularly sober or moral, or in the least degree intellectual; while of its political inability, my Lord Clive's records furnish ample proof. In books of the period we find occasional narratives, and from other sources, pictures of Calcutta society before and after the tragedy of the Black Hole, which are sufficiently entertaining; and though, to my knowledge, no one has written a particular detail of the events in the fleet at Fultah, yet from what had occurred previously, we can pretty well imagine that the habits of the Calcutta gentlemen had not altered, or perhaps improved; and that in their dreary sojourn on board the ships, being seldom able to venture ashore, they followed, perhaps with the greater avidity, their former occupations of drinking and play. Nor will I dare to allege that all were in this category; for there were no doubt some thoughtful, studious, sober, and religious characters among them, who kept mainly to themselves, and were little able to influence others of contrary dispositions. All, or most, had been ruined by the destruction of their property in Calcutta, and would have, as they thought, to begin their struggle with life again. They were, therefore, greedy and importunate; and though some were resigned and hopeful, I can imagine that the majority were reckless and discontented, burning with revenge against the author of their calamities, though helpless, for the present, to do aught to achieve it—and plunging into such dissipation as they could contrive, to pass the time and dispel painful thoughts. I consider these ample grounds for refusing to enter into details which may be better imagined than described—of weary days of heat and discomfort on board crowded and inconvenient ships; of quarrels and reconciliations, of bitter party spirit, and mutual contempt, if not actual abhorrence; and of not, perhaps, unfrequent insults one to another, to which their situation alone prevented fatal catastrophes.

But in one respect the desires of the society were unanimous, and their eager expectancy of relief never dormant. There were some, perhaps, who despaired of the assistance which they had solicited from Madras—of the possibility of assembling there an armament which would be sufficient to force a passage up the river, disperse the several garrisons left by the Nawab, and re-establish the Factory, or even of maintaining their position at Fultah till succour could arrive; but these, perhaps, were the minority, and there was one man whose name began to be a rallying-point with all—one whose tried bravery, great experience, and undaunted spirit, could alone of all in India, they thought, retrieve the past. They knew Colonel Clive was at his post as Governor of the small settlement of St. David; and, believing that he would eagerly accept the command of the military forces, they trusted that local questions of precedence or party spirit would not defraud them of their champion.

And they were right in the main, though the delays and deliberations of the Madras Council, in weighing the claims of the several parties for employment on this service, which lasted for two months, had as well-nigh exhausted the patience of the society on board the ships, as it had the supplies on which they were dependent. I may say also, that it had almost exhausted the patience of Colonel Clive himself, and of our friend Mr. Ralph Smithson, who, having presented his credentials at Madras, after he landed from the vessel which brought him down there, became for a time an object of great interest and admiration to the general society of the settlement. One who had fought through the attack on Calcutta, who had survived the horrors of the Black Hole, and who, with every advantage of person, was intelligent, modest, and unassuming—was, of all others, the person to make the deepest impression upon those upon whom the selection of the new commander depended.

The despatches themselves were urgent and even despairing requisitions. Men who have suffered almost to the extinction of hope, cannot often, collectively, easily arouse themselves to effective action; but Ralph Smithson had not suffered the depression which the Calcutta Council expressed. He had to make no apology for the desertion of his post, and he was ready to risk his life in its recovery. His local experience and knowledge were very valuable, and his comparative youth and recent admission to the service proved to be no obstacle to his being admitted to the assemblies of Council. He had, almost at once, begged to be allowed to visit Colonel Clive at Fort St. David, being assured, from what he remembered of him in the parlour in Lombard Street, not only of a kind reception, but of infecting him with his own enthusiasm. Colonel Clive had, however, been summoned from his post, and lost no time in obeying the order. He had heard, by the official communication, that one Mr. Ralph Smithson, a junior officer in the service, had been sent to Madras with the despatches from the Calcutta fleet, and though curious to hear, from one who had been engaged in them, an account of the recent transactions there, the mere name, as we may imagine, excited no kind of interest.

But when Ralph Smithson—having ascertained the probable hour of Colonel Clive's arrival at Madras, and the house where he was to put up being nigh to that in which he was a guest—went thither and claimed a private audience, the astonishment of the Colonel may be better imagined than described, when the youth to whom he had been introduced a year before as Ralph Darnell, entered the room and respectfully tendered his salutation.

"Mr. Smithson!" exclaimed the Colonel, looking at the card which the native attendant had taken in, and then at Ralph—"Smithson? God bless me! I never forget faces. I have seen you before, surely, and if ever there was a Darnell countenance on earth, it is yours. Who are you?"

"I am indeed, sir, Ralph Darnell—the lad whom you saw in the parlour of the office in Lombard Street—the lad you asked to accompany you to India, and said there should be 'one Colonel Darnell at least among the merchants. Ah, sir! much has happened since then—much, very much; my name even is changed, and I have to explain this to you if you will kindly listen to me; but we must not be interrupted."

"Sit down—sit down," said the Colonel, kindly. "Let no one in till I give permission," he said to the native attendant. "I have private business with this gentleman."

"And your uncle, Mr. Darnell—he is well, I hope?"

"I received a letter from him just before I left Fultah, sir, which I will show you by-and-by," said Ralph.

"God bless me!" continued Colonel Clive, "I can hardly believe my eyes that I see you here. Yes, the same fresh colour, the same quivering mouth and nostril. I well remember you, young gentleman; I thought there was some good stuff in you then, and I am seldom wrong in my judgments. Improved, too, by Jove! since then; more manly, and a good deal of sadness in your face. What has happened you? Nay, be assured, and speak to me as you would to a dear friend—to your uncle, Mr. Darnell, if he were here. There is no man on earth I love more dearly, sir, than Roger Darnell."

I think this speech gave more assurance than he would otherwise have possessed to the young man, for the quivering mouth and nostril which the Colonel had observed, were the results of more inward emotion than Ralph could easily suppress, and he had well-nigh broken down altogether; but under the Colonel's kind manners and genuine expressions of regard, Ralph began his story, and without the suppression of any fact, or attempt at extenuation of his own conduct, told it all—yes, humiliating as much of it was, told it all; and Colonel Clive felt, as he once more looked through the young man, that there had been no reservation, while in the letters that Ralph handed for his perusal, there was ample proof of his forgiveness by both his uncles. "I can say no more, sir," said Ralph, as the Colonel handed him back the letters; "you see how it is, and why I am no longer Ralph Darnell, the boy you knew in Lombard Street, but Ralph Smithson, at your service, sir, entirely, and longing to serve under you, if you will take me now as I am—disgraced, but forgiven."

"By Jove! as strange a history as ever I heard," said the Colonel. "Most of us here who leave England to cut out our way in life, have strange histories that are told only on deathbeds, for last instructions, or when a man is gasping out his soul with a bullet hole in his breast; but here you and I sit with no such pressure upon either of us, and you honour me with this confidence! I respect it, Mr. Smithson; you shall be Ralph Darnell no longer, nor till, as may be, I have to salute you as Sir Ralph Darnell of Melcepeth. For the present, you are better as you are; and if you will accept Robert Clive for your friend, and help him with your services, by G—, sir, you shall never have reason to regret it."

Ralph Smithson took the hand frankly held out to him, and kissed it fervently. I think the foolish fellow would even have dropped on his knees, as he did to his uncle, on an occasion that we may remember, but he was prevented; and I do not know that the Colonel thought the worse of the young man for the action, nor for his wet cheeks, which were glistening with fast falling tears. At last he had found a friend, and like the shadow of a great rock in a weary land, he felt he could shelter himself there.

"And now, Mr. Smithson," said the Colonel, "tell me about this Calcutta business; but you are not in the army—perhaps you did not see much of it?"

"I am not in the army, certainly," he replied; "but I fought at Perrin's Redoubt; I commanded a battery in the siege; and I was one of the last on the walls when the Fort was stormed."

"And you escaped, Ralph?"

"Not entirely, sir. I had a sharp wound on my arm, and some other hurts; but they are well long since," he added, modestly.

"And you were in the Black Hole and escaped?"

"I was, sir."

"By Jove, a hero already! Why, at your age, I hadn't done half as much myself; I congratulate you, sir. Now for some details: I have a plan of the Fort here; will you explain it, and what was done for the defence?—though, indeed, little could be done with such a place as that."

I think Ralph Smithson must have acquitted himself well under the professional examination which followed, for the Colonel encouraged him from time to time, asked his opinion of the native troops, and agreed with his young friend that, with the exception of the Rohillas who stormed the Fort, the rest were very cowardly. In short, the frankness and good sense with which the Colonel's questions were answered, and the evident local knowledge which Ralph Smithson possessed, contributed to raise him very considerably in Colonel Clive's opinion.

"You have told all this to the Council, I presume, Mr. Smithson?" he asked.

"No one ever asked me half as much as you have, sir," was the reply, "and I only answered immaterial questions."

"Then come to the Council with me to-day, and they shall see the stuff you are made of—good Darnell stuff, and no doubt about it; just what I expected."

"Ah, sir," cried Smithson, entreatingly, "do not forget the new name; my uncle is so well known that—"

"No fear of me, Ralph Smithson," replied the Colonel, laughing; "I will respect your secret and your confidence."

"The Council is waiting, sir; they have sent twice, but master say not open door," cried a servant without.

"Quite right, Ramasamy—let them wait. I'll lay my life, Smithson, that those old fogies don't settle anything for the next two months, and after all won't desire to send me; but I'll go, one way or other, by G—!" he cried, excitedly; "Robert Clive has work cut out for him there that no one else can do, or I'm much mistaken. Yes, Mister Bussy, they wouldn't let me have a slap at you in the Dekhan, but, by George! Ralph, we'll be before him in Bengal, and turn those cursed Frenchmen out."

Colonel Clive was right: the Council at Madras, as I have already recorded, with grave history to support me, wasted two precious months in preliminary discussions, and appointed him with independent power after all. I think if Ralph Smithson would, he might have received a military commission; but this he refused; as he was, he would continue to be—an independent volunteer, attached, with one Mr. Warren Hastings, to Colonel Clive only, to render such aid as he could afford.

So finally, on the 16th of October, a gallant fleet of ten ships sailed from the Madras roads; and after a weary passage, beating against the north-east monsoon which had now set in, and delayed their arrival more than a month, the expectants at Fultah, on the 20th December, as they still looked seaward with weary eyes often cheated by sails on the river's horizon, saw at last the square top-sails of His Gracious Majesty's men-of-war, which, as they reached the roads, joined the long-stationary fleet decked with flags as became the occasion, and with their yards manned. The salutes fired then, and answered by the Admiral's ship, were, I think, the most memorable and joyous that have ever since perhaps been fired on the waters of the sacred river.

Then too, news spread far and fast, that a fleet of huge Feringi ships of war, each carrying a hundred guns or more, had come to the rescue of Calcutta; and the native commander of the Fort there, as every other local officer of the province, despatched expresses to Moorshedabad to the same effect, that they were ready to die in the Nawab's service, but, if he desired to preserve his conquest, he must return to Calcutta with his whole army. Letters for the Prince himself, which were written from the English fleet, following the news report—(though the native commandant of Calcutta dared not forward them to his master)—proved plainly enough that a new vigour had been infused into the English councils, of which he had no experience, for the language was not that of abject suppliants for favour, but of haughty conquerors. Colonel Clive had not a thousand English soldiers with him; yet he was thinking it possible to rout the Nawab's army of 50,000 men should it appear against him, and was determined to exact retribution to the uttermost from a cruel enemy who, in his moment of triumph, had shown no mercy.

CHAPTER XLVIII.

COLONEL CLIVE AT CALCUTTA.

Nor did the leaders of the expedition await replies to these communications. During his varied service in the peninsula of India, Colonel Clive had already gained much experience of a political character, and much practical knowledge of the *morale* of Indian soldiery. He knew better than any one else present the necessity for immediate and decisive action, and what effect a few hard blows struck rapidly in succession would have upon native enemies, and native friends too. Calcutta must be regained before any political negotiation could ensue; and, though two of the ships had not yet arrived, and many men and *matériel* of war were in them that could be ill spared, yet there was sufficient force present to overcome all obstacles between the rendezvous of the fleet and Calcutta. In these respects there seemed no difficulties that could not be overcome.

But it was by no means so easy a task to reconcile opinions of parties into which men fell almost immediately; and, after the habit of Calcutta, the gentlemen of the fleet and army, with the civilians of Bengal, took up different sides, and began to be jealous of each other. Colonel Clive represented the political and military interests of the Company. Admiral Watson, and the officers of the Royal army, deluded by fantastic conceptions of huge amounts of prize-money, and unlimited exercise of authority, conceived the Colonel to be a common enemy, and held their own against him; while the gentlemen of the Factory, jealous of both, kept themselves aloof, or sided with one or other, their own private quarrels and jealousies being ever predominant. No wonder I find Colonel Clive writing to his wife and to his friends, that "he wished he had never come to Bengal at all." No wonder that, as he expressed himself to Ralph Smithson, "he was already sick of the whole thing, and it might go to the devil for all he cared about it." It was well he did care, and, after a time, viewed with contempt the strivings for shares of prize-money which was yet "in the clouds," or for petty commands which were yet to be detailed; and it seems to me it was only the stubborn resolution of the man that prevented those disasters which would have blighted the character of the expedition, and rallied the sinking spirits of the Nawab's commanders. To have remained at Fultah would have been to ensure the effects he dreaded. His own determination was never relaxed by any consideration; and we can now estimate the real value of the service done by Clive, when, in the midst of these petty jealousies, strivings, heartburnings, and opposition, he suffered no personal vexation or interest to disturb his purpose. So, in the first engagements with the enemy, when, after a weary march, for which there was no occasion, and surprised by a heavy body of troops from Calcutta, the detachment which had attacked a small fort fell into confusion, Clive went ashore, rallied the panic-stricken men, and led them to victory after his old fashion; and having gained their confidence, and that of the Royal officers present, he perhaps cared very little about the rest. With him, too, were some of his own Madras Sepoys—men who had fought with him at Wandiwash and Arcot—men who held all Bengalese in supreme contempt, and the gallant little fellows were ready to follow their Colonel anywhere.

When Manikchund, the Governor of Calcutta, brought down two thousand picked men to oppose the Feringis on this occasion, and boasted of the heads he would take back to make a pile of before the Fort-gate against the Nawab's coming, he little expected to be met with a ringing cheer from the 39th, the "Primus in Indis," and the Madras Sepoys, as the Colonel led them on; and so fell back in utter confusion, and fled away. He could not save the Fort, and the impression caused by his precipitate flight was that the English ships contained thousands of men; and it was certain that the reports of the people of the country, which flew faster than the fugitives, fearfully exaggerated all realities.

As to the Fort, broadsides from English men-of-war, which had never before been fired in those waters, were very terrible in the sight of people who had hitherto seen no ships but the peaceful merchant vessels of the Company on their trading voyages; and as ship after ship of the Royal squadron let go her anchor before the little fort of Budge-Budge, and, as the sails were being furled aloft, let fly broadside after broadside against its walls, sending stones, bricks, and mud parapets flying about the ears of the garrison, it is no wonder perhaps, that, when night fell, the terrified survivors of the day crept quietly out of the place, and made the best of their way northwards.

The voyage up the broad Hoogly was indeed more like a triumphant naval procession than a warlike armament; and the fleet of Royal ships, followed by the transports, all with flags flying and drums beating at quarters, the red uniforms of the soldiery in the waists, and the gay laced coats of the officers glancing from the poops, must have appeared to the wonder-struck Hindus who lined the banks as incarnations of supernatural power, whose might was to be deprecated rather than opposed: and indeed resistance there was none. The movements of the fleet depended mainly upon the tide, and it swept on day after day majestically under easy sail, passing towns and villages, mosques and temples, rice-fields, groves, and jungle, in stately array.

A strange contrast was it in Ralph Smithson's mind with his lonely sail up the river in the dear old *Valiant*, when all with which he was now familiar was new to him. Then he was an unknown and untried youth, whose highest ambition was to be a merchant; now, he had already achieved some military distinction. He was looked up to by many of His Majesty's officers with respect, which was increased and increasing by his position with Colonel Clive. One who had borne himself right gallantly in the affairs before Calcutta, and who, as all allowed, had been one of the last to quit the walls of the Fort in the attack upon it—who had evinced the highest spirit at Budge-Budge, and who was not a "country officer" —had already taken his place among the best of the Royal officers present, and needed no further introduction to their exclusive society; and many a man envied, while they all heartily congratulated him on, the distinction he had gained. We must remember how young he still was; but he had nevertheless reached that age when decisive steps in life can best be taken and pursued with ardour and enthusiasm. What were the desk, the huge wearisome ledgers, the interminable columns of rupees, annas, and pie to be added and checked, or the voluminous invoices and accounts of sales and stock, now to him?

"I began with them myself, Ralph," said the Colonel, as they interchanged hearty greetings on the 1st January 1757, and wished each other many happy years, "and have forsaken them for what you see me—a poor man, where others have made their fortunes, and gone home to enjoy them. But there's no glory in that. Come with me, and whatever honour I can win, you shall have your share of. I cannot indeed spare you, Ralph; and I intend to write to that grave old uncle of yours about the colonelship I talked to him of, and he will come round to my way of thinking—see if he don't. No, Ralph; 1756 sees the end of your attempt at being a merchant, and 1757 begins it as a soldier, and in this no one shall gainsay me."

It needed little persuasion to turn the young man; and if anything were needed, some gallant fellows serving with the 39th, Coote, Rumbold, and others, seconded the Colonel heartily, for there is an entry in R. S.'s journal of how his health was drunk with a hearty cheer among the many toasts given at the New Year's dinner on board the flagship; but that "whatever his ultimate decision might be, he was in no mind to accept a commission for the present, or to surrender the liberty he enjoyed as a volunteer."

Manikchund did not attempt to defend Calcutta; and as a few broadsides rattled over the old walls next day, and were feebly answered by the native garrison, and Colonel Clive, with some of his well-tried Sepoys, landed, and opened fire from another quarter, the garrison hung out a white flag, and surrendered the place. Then boats from the squadron soon took off enough men to receive possession of it, and the British ensign once more blew out proudly from the old flagstaff. History relates what took place on this occasion, and how Colonel Clive was denied admittance at first; and being afterwards, as he considered, in command, the fiery old Admiral threatened to open fire on him if he did not evacuate the place; and this and many other such instances of mutual defiance and jealousy cause us now to wonder how anything was brought to a successful issue under these melancholy bickerings.

Next day, however, Mr. Watson was pleased to acknowledge the Colonel's authority, and withdraw his objections as to the command of the Fort; but though this dispute was past, I consider that

Colonel Clive must have felt himself otherwise upon a seat of thorns. The gentlemen of the Factory had by no means attained their whole object in being restored to their Fort. The authority they had possessed was now in the hands of another who cared very little about those former positions which the gentlemen had not had the courage to defend, nor for their perpetual whine about losses and ruin. At the same time, as representatives of the civil interests of the Company, it was impossible for the haughty Colonel to ignore them altogether; and perforce he was obliged to listen to much he would rather not hear, and to do much that he did not like. I do not by any means feel myself bound to enter upon any details of these transactions. They have as little to do with the scope of this history as those of the Fultah society; and though I might write perhaps tolerably correct pictures of this period, I am not of opinion that my readers would care to have their time occupied by what Mr. Drake said, or Mr. Holwell, or any of the gentlemen then busy quarrelling among themselves—with Colonel Clive—or with the Admiral.

And I have the less to say to these matters, because, as we know, Ralph Smithson's one friend was dead, and it does not appear that he had ever cared much about any one else. There was no trace of Mr. Wharton's grave now discernible—none by which any particular pit among those dug on the 20th and 21st June could be recognised. The pretty bungalow was a mass of shapeless, scorched walls, and the garden where he used to walk with Julia, a tangled mass of weeds—the walls broken down, and the walks and shrubberies torn up by shot, and broken and destroyed by diggings for trenches. I think, had both been present to welcome him, Ralph Smithson might have stayed with them; but he foresaw no prospect of pleasurable residence there among the rest. He was already a stout partisan of Mr. Clive's, and his sympathies were with the army and the distinction that was to be won.

For in their private conversations Mr. Clive was beginning to shadow forth the beginning of the end. Baffled in England, when troops were denied him for driving Bussy from the Dekhan, he had accepted a minor position at Madras; but the spirit had chafed within him at inaction there, and was little likely to be still, now that there was opportunity of effecting in Bengal what had hitherto been the dream of his life. He had been brought up at Madras in active operations against the French. He had witnessed their successful striving for political power. He was aware that if Bussy could join Law at Pondicherry, and so reinforce the Nawab, their combined forces might even prove too much for his own armament, powerful as it was: and he hated them nationally and politically, as a thorough Englishman of the time hated a Frenchman, and with all the additional virus of the experience heretofore gained.

Probably the gentlemen of the Factory desired nothing more than a resumption of their old occupations; and it was with a feeling of pride absolutely glowing in his black face that our friend Don Gomez da Silviera met his masters in the hall of the Factory, the day after the Fort was taken, and delivered to them the keys of the private safe, which contained the records of the settlement, and the invaluable books on which the recoveries of advances and debts for goods sold were dependent; and under the congratulations of native merchants and bankers, no doubt sincere in many instances, the work of the Factory began again. Had not enough been done? Was it wise and politic to provoke the Nawab further? Could anything more be effected except the recovery of losses? Colonel Clive was, however, of opinion that his work had only begun, and was little likely to be turned from his purpose by timid counsels, which had only the recovery of these losses for their foundation. The troops required supplies which Calcutta could ill afford, and the g[illegible]ion of Hoogly was boastful and defiant—but not for long. T[illegible] city was stormed and sacked in a few days more, its garrison dispersed, and the native defenders of the province existed no longer. Then also, by a strange chance, news of the declaration of war between England and France reached Bengal, and was received with an interest which I can feebly portray. My reader may imagine Colonel Clive's exultation at an event by which his own aspirations were no longer fettered, and the amazement of the Calcutta gentlemen at this new complication of affairs. But there were others who listened to these tidings, which poured fast, one upon another, into the Prince's durbar at Moorshedabad; and we had better, perhaps, after having been so long tarrying with our own countrymen, inquire how they affected him, and others concerned about him.

CHAPTER XLIX.

THE NAWAB'S TROUBLES.

THE place is the same as that in which, we may remember, when, in his fit of fury, Suraj-oo-Doulah had caused the Derwesh to be mutilated, and where the cries of terrible vengeance against the English had resounded through the lofty hall of audience. Since then, Calcutta had been taken, and for six months the conquest had been undisturbed even by a rumour. The ships of the English lay at the mouth of the river, but attempted no return, and the bankers, who had been their fast friends in spite of their misfortunes, had almost begun to fear that they were gone for ever, and that the transactions with them, which had been the source of steady and increasing gain for many a year, were never to be renewed. Reports from the Nawab's district-collectors and other fiscal agents began to come in fast, that the revenue was languishing for want of support by the English trade, and unless the Prince himself would direct large advances to be made to supply the want of English capital, the cultivation must still further languish.

Under these circumstances, the late victorious expedition seemed likely not only to prove barren of results, but to induce a general discontent which had not been foreseen. In place of untold wealth in the Factory, the Nawab had only found a paltry sum, as we know, and the piles of broadcloth and calico, of hardware and general English goods, were useless to transport, and as useless for sale. The Nawab's commander, Manikchund, could not represent the English gentlemen, and Omichund and Jugget Seit and other Calcutta merchants declined transactions in general or particular with him. They were afraid to buy the plunder of the English. "Who knows?" the people said; "they may come back, and then?" The Calcutta bankers had agents too at Madras, and these wrote in their own cipher—an enigmatical language which it is difficult to imitate—that an armament was being prepared there, in which great war-ships would take a part, and many white soldiers would be sent; again that the ships had sailed. So each after his own fashion had expected the English; and those who had gained their bread by them, or under whose protection they flourished and grew rich, offered many a sacrifice to propitiate the gods, and many a vow of feeding Brahmins, and of giving largesse to the poor, and thought their prayers answered when Calcutta was taken, and the English expedition to Hoogly returned triumphant.

From the first day on which the Nawab—sitting there among his parasites and courtiers, seeing for the hundreth time the horrible scene of the Black Hole enacted before him, and the struggling, writhing Feringis climbing upon each other's backs fighting for water, shrieking, blaspheming, praying, and seeming to die in horrible contortions at the window-bars—heard the news of the arrival of the King's fleet at Fultah, laughed in drunken merriment, and, mocking the power of his enemies, told those around him that he had it from his friends the French, that there were not ten thousand soldiers in all England, and that not a man dared be sent, because the French with a mighty army were about to invade the country of their mutual enemy and destroy them all—from that day forward, I say, letters came rapidly in succession; and the royal news-writers attached to the military posts seemed to vie with each other as to who should most forcibly describe in flowing Persian the vast naval armament—the thousands of its guns—their terrible fire—and the drunken ferocity of Feringi soldiers—as excuses for cowardice; and thus the events we already know of had been listened to with increasing rage and gloom. It was in vain that minstrels sang or women danced—it was in vain that coarse buffoons played their most outrageous and indecent acts, or that astrologers consulted the stars, and gave forth their dubious responses; and when, on the evening I speak of, a messenger rushed breathless into the hall, and, untying his turban, gave to an attendant the despatch he had brought by express—the assembly present knew, as the Nawab read the paper himself, and his countenance assumed a savage expression, that some calamitous news had reached him; and all waited in apprehension, not unmingled with terror, for the result.

The letter was brief enough. Hoogly had been stormed and taken, thousands of true believers had suffered martyrdom, and the Feringis had sacked the town, carrying away lacs of treasure and property. Would not the Nawab send an army to save the country and his faithful people, and drive the accursed English back to their ships? Unless he did so, the English army would march on, and there was no one to oppose it.

I think that, as the Nawab at last read aloud the letter he had already twice perused, and laughed a hollow laugh, in which he vainly tried to disguise his own vexation, a strange dread and fear fell upon all who, craning over each other's necks, heard the fresh news. It had been utterly incomprehensible how the few Englishmen they remembered, the peaceful, patient merchants, could be transformed suddenly into revengeful victorious warriors; but there was no doubt in the last news. They had not halted at Calcutta: they were carrying, as was then believed, fort after fort, and city after city, and could not be stayed: so all who listened remembered the fearful act for which retribution was now being exacted: and what would satisfy it?

Who dare offer advice? Not one, I believe, of that company of holiday courtiers dared to have uttered a sound, for fear truly had fallen upon their hearts—or worse than fear, treachery, was taking up its abode there. In their master's present humour, who dare speak?

The Nawab glanced round on the dismayed countenances, and saw no comfort. I will not look into his own heart, for there is nothing pleasant there, nothing hopeful—only much hate, and desire of bloody extermination. "Does no one speak?" he cried at length. "Cowards and faithless as ye all are, does no one speak a word of comfort to your Prince?" but still the silence continued, and its effect, so rare and continuous, was almost awful.

"Nawab," at last cried the grim old Affghan chief whom we may remember, who rose and drew up his tall figure, now clad in a loose suit of chain-mail, with a proud gesture,—"Nawab, when Calcutta was stormed, who did it? When the Feringis fell in scores, who slew them? Hast thou forgotten, or is it with thee as with many another, that brave deeds are forgotten, and swords may rust in their scabbards when present danger is past? See, mine is as bright as ever!" and as he spoke he drew it flashing from its scabbard; "but it would be dim again in Feringi blood if thy heart is enough of a man's to lead us on. As thou art, a woman were better—not one who has lost his manhood in company with a Feringi wanton!"

It was well that the fiery old man was surrounded by a strong body of his clan, or perhaps he would never have left that assembly alive. If Eastern princes have for the most part to listen to empty platitudes or gross flatteries, there are occasions on which disagreeable truths are spoken in more than ordinarily forcible language, and this was one of them.

"Treachery, treachery! He has insulted the Prince! hew him down!" cried a hundred voices, mingled with obscene oaths, and many a weapon was unsheathed; but the old warrior stood erect and firm; and his clansmen, rising and throwing their shields before him, presented a phalanx before which the courtiers and eunuchs quailed. There were matchlockmen on guard at the entrance, who rushed into the court with lighted matches; but on whom were they to fire? friends and foes were intermingled, and inseparable.

"Peace!" cried the Nawab, who had risen as the door to his private apartments was opened, and the eunuch Juma tried to urge him into it—"peace! put down thy sword, Noor Khan; this is no place for wild brawling."

"We can slay him as he goes out, my Prince," whispered Juma, "if thou wilt come away."

But Suraj-oo-Doulah did not fear him then; he had no personal fear—he was too strongly guarded. "Peace," he cried, shaking off the negro. "Noor Khan, listen! when I send for thee, wilt thou come?—as a friend and a trusted and honoured servant, wilt thou come?"

"Send one known to thee and me for my safe-conduct," he said, "and I will come; not else, my lord," cried the old man—"not else. Death, no servant of Allah fears, and of my life thou hast ever been master; but of my honour I am my own guardian. I salute you, Prince, and pray permission to depart."

"Thou hast it—go," said the Nawab, "and be ready when I send for thee," and he passed into the private rooms. "Where is she?" he asked of Juma, now an especial favourite.

"Within," was the reply; "but wilt thou have his head to-night? Speak the word, and I will bring it thee."

"I will tell thee presently."

"He insulted thee, my Prince," persisted the negro, doggedly, "and should die that others may fear."

Die! How many had died? How many had suffered torture and mutilation for alleged treachery, in caprice, or in mad drunken revels? How many more would die? and yet was he safe? Yes; no insult that had ever been offered him was like that, rankling deep down in his heart. Send her! send Sozun! Was she not in irons in the vault? and yet, if he did not, Noor Khan would not trust him; the Rohillas in his force would be in mutiny by the morning, and who could quell them? If they pleased, they might depose him, tie him to the foot of an elephant, and— I think it was these thoughts which passed like quick flashes through Suraj-oo-Doulah's heart, as he stood irresolute for an instant in the chamber, which caused him to shudder as if a cold blast had struck him, and which were terrible to endure. I question whether he had any one to whom he could turn now.

"Shall I send for Mohun Lall?" asked the negro; "his counsel may be better than your slave's."

"Get thee to hell! and Mohun Lall too," cried the Nawab, striking him. "Blood! yes, more blood, he would say, as thou dost—butcher as thou art."

"I could kill Noor Khan as I would a sheep," said the giant; "why should my lord be angry with me?"

"But thou couldst not kill all his people, Juma; and if they will not fight for me, the Feringi will kill me," returned the Nawab. "No; bring her to me—her the singer. It must be," he muttered, "else—"

"Ah yes, I understand now," returned the man; "give me thy seal-ring. And if she will not come?"

"You carried a shrieking woman once up a staircase," said the Nawab, bitterly, "and can do it again."

"On my head and eyes be it," replied the eunuch—"I will not fail. When?"

"As soon as possible," was the reply. "I fear not that she should see her," and he passed in. Anna was sitting at the door, and rose respectfully. She was necessary to the Nawab, and he had loaded her with gifts. To her the months that had passed had been as pleasant as any she could remember of her long life. She had, after her Portuguese Eastern fashion, accommodated herself to the strict seclusion of the zenana, and she knew that intrigue or correspondence without could end only in death; so she had submitted to her fate. Had her mistress done the same?

It would have been impossible, and unnatural. The English girl was not pure, but her impurity was as virgin snow before him into whose power her wayward fate had thrown her. She had lived—

that was enough. She had sighed and prayed for death, but it did not come; and helpless, very helpless, she had resigned herself to her fate. At first she had fallen into the same raving fever which attacked so many others after the night of the 20th June, and had recovered from it worn and wasted, and with her beauty gone; and for a long time, Anna, who never left her, thought she would not recover; but even that fatal gift had returned, and remained in some sort. There were gardens in which she could walk, and in which she spent most of her time; but her mind was, I think, growing into a kind of numb vacancy of submission, rather than conscious endurance of her condition.

"Where is your mistress, the lady?" asked the Nawab.

"Within, reading her book, my lord," was the reply.

"She is ever reading, and never speaks to me," he said, almost sadly. "Dost thou know aught in which I could gratify her?"

"My lord will pardon his slave. She frets after her people night and day, and weeps. If she could hear of them, she would be thankful," replied the woman.

"I have just received news of them," he said bitterly; "come and tell her."

Reading! Ah yes; in the pocket of the dress which Anna had brought away, was the little prayer-book, out of which she had read the psalms on that eve of massacre which we may remember, and she had kept it lovingly ever since. The Nawab respected it as containing the words of Jesus of Nazareth, reverenced even by the most bigoted of his priests—the only book, she had; read sometimes in vague dreaminess, sometimes in bitter but unavailing grief, sometimes in humble faith. He had asked Julia Wharton to become a Mahomedan; but she had fallen into such deep misery at the thought, that even he relented, and had troubled her no more. The last words of the poor soldier, ejaculated so awfully in the prison, had not been forgotten. She had searched for them and found them, and had read the verses with streaming eyes and a contrite heart. A Magdalen, praying and weeping once, had found mercy before the Lord of life, and the blessed book told her it was denied to none. So, as He who had sent the trial knew best, she had lived, and prayed after a simple fashion of her own, which, unknown before, had grown up in her heart.

Memories! oh, many, many! Very hard to endure at first, but growing blunted by constant recurrence, and only occasionally causing misery. Even Anna forbore to speak of past times, and avoided all allusion to them, for it was on recurrence to these subjects that her poor mistress's spirit utterly refused comfort, and, recovering after a while, grew again to be dull and dead. But this scene could not be avoided.

"O dear, Missis," cried the servant as she entered the room suddenly, followed by the Nawab; "my lord got news for you."

"What news?" replied Julia sadly, putting down her book and not noticing his entrance.

"He tell hisself," she said, "and I tell my lady." And the conversation continued through the interpreter.

"Your people are in Calcutta once more, lady," said the Nawab, seating himself on his usual pile of cushions.

"And you have returned it to them? O sir! is this true?" she cried, looking up with a sudden rush of colour to her cheek, and a flash of intelligence in her eyes which he had never seen before.

"They have taken it and slain my people," he said, with an impatient gesture; "and it is too late now, for there is once more blood between us. But could it have gained me thy love, lady, I had offered it to thee long ago. Now it is too late."

She was silent.

"Thou dost not care to hear of their victory over their enemy?"

Ah, poor bleeding heart, it was throbbing fast now! Her own people—Ralph Smithson—would she ever be given up to them? Should she see him once more? She could hide herself away somewhere in her own land, and this hideous life would be a thing of the past. What a flood of thought rushed into her memory in an instant! "Send me to them, O Prince! send me to them?" she said in the broken Hindi she had learned; "what am I to thee, or thou to me?" And she clasped her hands convulsively, and fell on her knees before him, sobbing piteously.

"Send thee to them, lady!" he cried, savagely; "to them? Never! Let it not come into thy dreams that I ever spared an enemy! They shall die as others died; or I must die, and thou with me! Kaffirs! I hate them to death, and beyond death to hell. Take her away, Anna—she is mad. Take her away, lest I destroy her for the beauty which unmans me. Protection of God! I was told in my own durbar to-day that I had lost my manhood for a Feringi wanton! Am I to endure insult for her? Begone! take her away, for I am wellnigh mad myself to-night!—Who is there?"

As he spoke, Juma's burly form emerged from the stairhead, which opened into the chamber, and, advancing with little ceremony, he set down in the midst of them a woman he had thrown across his shoulders. Irons on her legs clanked as the feet reached the ground, and the figure sank down, as in a heap.

"Slave! thou hast not slain her?" cried the Nawab eagerly,

"No, no, she's well enough; she would talk, and this was the shortest way to manage such a girl," cried Juma, wiping his forehead, and departing as he had come.

Julia Wharton's memory had not failed her, and as the figure raised its head and looked round dreamily, the features of the Affghan girl were fully revealed by the lamp-light. "Save me! oh, send me to my people!" was all she could cry in her terrible sobbing, as she bent forward to the prostrate figure.

But she was not heeded. Sozun seemed awaking from a stupor. She was changed—much changed. The once ruddy cheek was white and wan, the large brown eyes seemed increased in size, and had a vacant expression, as she looked round her for a moment and shut them again; her once glorious figure was wasted, and her round white arms grown thin and gaunt.

"Strike! kill me at once—with one blow!" she said, rising to her knees, as she repeated the belief of her creed. "Strike! I am ready —now—now—why dost thou not strike?" She evidently expected death.

"It is thus brave men die," said the Nawab, with a sigh—"without a tremor; and she is as brave. Look up, Sozun; thou art a fool, as thou ever wast," he continued half kindly; "look up, O my darling! and fear not."

The girl did look up, and Julia Wharton never forgot the glance of scorn and defiance with which the bold eyes of the Affghan met those of the man in whose hands both their destinies seemed placed.

"Why dost thou not kill me?" she said; "what hast thou to do with me? Is not the Feringi enough? Art thou afraid?"

"Silence!" hissed the Nawab between his teeth, as he caught her arm; "do not provoke me to kill thee to-night, for truly devils have possession of me, and I burn as with fire—the fire of that Feringi witch. Away with ye!" he cried to Anna; "take her away! I would be alone. Begone!"

"Come away, lady," whispered the servant hurriedly, dragging Julia to her feet. "I not like him to-night 't all; he mad or drunk. Come away to your own room, an' lock the door."

And so they escaped.

CHAPTER L.

SOZUN AND HER PEOPLE.

"SHE is gone, Sozun; look up once more as thou used to look on one who hath done thee wrong. I have none but thee now—none but thee!"

"Thou wouldst not kill me; why didst thou not strike as I knelt? Where is the slave who brought me? The bitterness of death was past then. Ah, my lord!"

But not now: some renewed desire of life had come upon the girl, as she sank down covering her face with her hands, with a choking at her throat, over which her slender fingers moved nervously. The bitterness, the excitement of near death, as it had seemed to her, had passed away with the broken sentences she had gasped forth.

"Here is water! drink, O my beloved! and once more speak to me," said the Nawab; and he filled a silver cup from a water jar and held it to her lips.

Sozun drank slowly, for the oppression at her throat seemed that of death; and unable to sit up, she sank down again, after a few attempts to swallow, in utter prostration.

Suraj-oo-Doulah was touched. If he had ever loved a being on earth it was this girl—so fascinating to him in her beauty and so indomitable in her spirit; and yet what a wreck he had made of it all!

"I have killed her!—she is dead!" he cried, frantically, dashing his turban to the ground. "Ho, Juma! Juma!"

But there was no reply. Juma, as he thought, when he left the chamber, had best let the tiger and tigress, as he called them in his mind, fight out their quarrel together. His master's fancies were naught to him—was he not the Nawab, and could not he do as he pleased with his women? No, Juma had retreated to his guard-room for the present.

Some water poured hurriedly into her mouth and upon her face, roused Sozun; and, supporting herself upon her hand, she looked up. The Nawab's arms were around her; and a look of concern, alarm, and grief on his face, such as was new to her, touched her heart in spite of the wrongs she had endured from him.

"I have no one but thee, Sozun," he said—"none but thee, O my beloved! Canst thou forgive my madness? I have been mad, Sozun—bewitched; the sorcery of the Feringis is upon me; but I fear them not if thou art true. Thy destiny and mine are one—was it not thus said, and was it not proved?"

She sighed dreamily; and as she moved, the irons on her legs clanked.

"They have been there for six months," she said, pointing to them, "and have eaten into my heart. I am no longer Sozun, but a thing of the past—dead to all life, though I cannot die. Why didst thou not slay me?—it would have been so merciful!"

I think if ever Suraj-oo-Doulah felt shame, it was when the girl pointed to the irons on her legs and said they had eaten into her heart. How those weary six months had passed, who could tell but herself? With what paroxysms of fierce anger at first, of revengeful threats, of dull despair. Like her fellow-captive, she had been put away in that vault out of sight of man, to live or to die as it might please Allah; but unlike her in all respects, save that they were women.

At first the ravings of the Affghan girl shocked and terrified the unfortunate Begum; but we have already seen that Sozun could be kind and generous. There was no detested rivalry now: only alike for each, a pallet-bed, coarse clothes, and a dreary fate. Feeling the wrong of which she had been the instrument to an unoffending fellow-woman, Sozun could not resist the influence of the gentle resignation and the loving companionship of her once-fancied rival; and, bowing herself at last before her, besought her forgiveness, and vowed to her truth and service such as she could render. This summons at last, she thought, was the punishment of her life—first dishonour, then triumph, then destruction. There remained but death to end all, and the Affghan dancer would be forgotten, as a hundred others before her.

Six months had the iron eaten into her heart. Did her country-men know of her disgrace and her condition? I think if they had known they would have pulled down the palace stone by stone till they found her, and who would have dared to oppose them? But the secrets of that zenana were as the secrets of the grave. Rumour had it that the singer was not in favour, and those of her people who had believed in her promises to lead an honourable life now shrugged their shoulders and said, with a sneer, that "when her time came she would be in favour again."

Was it so? As the arms which had once been to her most dear were around her, and the voice tender and passionate by turns, as it used to be, sounded in her ears, was there no temptation to yield to old feelings? She had not been woman if there were not—she had not been the true loving woman she was at heart, if she were not ready to forgive the injury he had done her. In her old spirit she would have defied him—in her broken weakness the desire for revenge had died away. If he would only let her go. She had vowed her vow to the Lord's service, and would go forth to fulfil it.

"So long!" said the Nawab, "and I did not think of thee: O my beloved, wilt thou forgive? Put thy hand on my head," he sobbed—"on my head, and forgive me for what thou hast endured, and thou mayst lead me where thou wilt. I was mad, Sozun—oh, I was mad!"

"I forgive. Ah, my lord, let the good Allah forgive us all, for we have sinned before Him. I forgive? nay, if thou wouldst have thy slave say it, she will do so heartily. Let but these instruments of disgrace be removed, ere I am fit to touch thy head."

"Nay, but for once, Sozun, before I call."

"As thou wilt," she said; and, laying her hand upon his head lightly, withdrew it instantly. "Thou art forgiven of me," she continued—"may Allah forgive thee too."

Juma had resumed his post, and, entering as the Nawab called, stood with his hands folded.

"Canst thou remove these things, Juma?"

"A woman could do it," he said, bending down to the girl as the Nawab turned away from the sight, and breaking the rivets with a wrench from his powerful fingers—"a woman could do it. Thy people are uneasy," he whispered to Sozun—"beware!" and so went out.

They were once more alone. "Come to me, Sozun," said the Nawab. "Art thou content now?"

But she was silent. She had covered her face with her hands, and was sobbing silently.

"Why dost thou doubt me, beloved?" he cried, putting his arm round her. "I am not changed; and she, thy rival, is gone."

"Pardon thy slave," she said, coldly, withdrawing herself; "and respect my vow to God, made when I was naught to thee."

"What vow, Sozun? Art thou, too, distraught? Have I to win thy love again as before? What dost thou want? Thy rival is gone, and thou art here—what more? Jewels, clothes, wealth—thou hast them all!"

"Look on me, my lord," she cried; "look on these wan features, on this poor wasted body. Enough! what has been, has been; for, before Allah and the Prophet, I have vowed that man's love can never exist within me again. Ameen! and Ameen! I will serve thee to death as thy slave; but as—"

"Say it not—say it not, oh cruel!" cried the Nawab, putting his hand before her mouth. "May God and the Prophet forgive thee for frightening me. Ah, yes! thou art jealous still. She may not remain here; and she hath bewitched me. Ho, Juma!"

"Begone!" said Sozun to the negro, with some of her old spirit—"thou art not wanted. What wouldst thou have done, O my lord, with one so helpless as she? Art thou afraid of her? Swear to me that thou will respect her henceforth, and Sozun will be true to thee."

"I swear," he said, taking up his Koran and kissing it—"I swear henceforth she will not be molested. Art thou content now?"

"To serve thee and love thee; but not as of old," she continued—"that were sin. Enough that thou hast been generous."

Long did he plead earnestly, and, as it seemed even to her, truly; but we know enough of this girl's spirit to feel that the vow she had made could not be broken. Once more, as she strove to reason with her lord, the old beauty came into her face, and the cheeks glowed, as she spoke in the figurative and seemingly inspired strain of a devotee. It was in vain that he laid treasures, lands, estates, power, at her feet—that he bowed himself down and grovelled before her. He could not change her. He might send her back to the cell—that would be welcome; but unhallowed love, now, could not be. He had heard of such devotees; but was one so young, so glorious in her beauty, to be surrendered?

So in these struggles, pleadings, and often threats, on the one hand, and the calmness of despair and fervour on the other, hours passed. Suraj-oo-Doulah told her of the English advance, and as again and again she had begged to lead her own people to victory, he as often led her back to the subject on which she was inflexible. Revenge and pity influenced him by turns; and had not the old tenderness restrained him, I believe that that night Sozun had never passed through greater trial or danger. Often had his hand been upon his dagger-hilt—often it was half-drawn from its sheath to strike her down as she refused, and even defied, his solicitations. In her present spirit, dare he send her to Noor Khan? It seemed impossible. The old man had forgotten perhaps; but it was not so.

Midnight had passed, and the many noises without, in the palace, in the streets of the town, on the river, had all ceased—except the varied tones of their own voices, there was no other sound. Often, indeed, long and painful silences had fallen on both, hard to be broken. The usual music had played off the midnight watch; and when the noise of drums and cymbals, faintly repeated in the guard-houses of the town, had ceased, there was silence again, more profound and more striking. All at once there arose a confused murmur in the courtyard below, a shuffling of feet as though of men in motion, a hurrying too and fro, and the eunuch Juma, accompanied by several others, came suddenly in.

"The Rohillas are in motion," cried the slave; they are assembling and mean evil. They have taken possession of the bazaar, and are lining the houses with matchlockmen."

"I promised that I would send thee for Noor Khan's safe-conduct to me," said the Nawab to Sozun, "and he thinks himself forgotten. Thou must go, beloved, else there may be mischief."

"Does he know of these?" she asked, pointing to the marks which the rings had worn on her fair skin.

"I dare not tell him," was the reply. "He insulted me in the durbar to-day; he said before all that I had wasted my manhood on a Feringi wanton; and he believes that if I do not satisfy him, I shall revenge myself."

"It was but the truth, my lord," cried the girl frankly, "and he has saved thee. Let me go—yes, weak as I am, I can go to him. He will trust me; but can I trust thee to bear with his rough speech and bitter humour?"

"Bring him hither, and thou shalt see."

"And my lord will be saved. I know their humour, my Prince; and once more Sozun can save thy honour and her own. Bismilla! I am ready," she cried, rising with a strength and enthusiasm to which she had long been a stranger; and passing out, she snatched a blanket from an attendant, and hurried rapidly on. None opposed her; and as she proceeded, she saw a dense column of her countrymen assembled at the end of the broad street which led up to the palace court—their lighted matches glowing in the darkness, and their drum beginning to beat, and she ran with all the speed she was capable of exerting. As she reached the column it was in movement, and the old war-cry, to which she had leaped and bounded as she led her countrymen to the storm of the English Fort, was once more raised.

"Hold!" she cried in her own rough mountain tongue. "I am Sozun. Where art thou, O my father?"

"I am here, daughter," answered the strong voice of the old warrior. "Why art thou come?

"He has sent me to thee," she said. "Come and save him."

"Away with her! away with the harlot!" cried a hundred strong voices, which drowned her entreaties; and as she passed from man to man, kissing their hands and beseeching them with passionate gestures, she was thrown off rudely by all. "Slay her! slay the harlot who would betray her father," cried a powerful voice; "why should Affghans be dishonoured in her?" and a man rushed forward with his heavy sword uplifted, and would have cut her down had not his arm been arrested.

"Peace!" cried their old leader; "if she is true, she shall live—if she be false, let her die. Where hast thou been, daughter, since thou wast with us in Calcutta?" he continued briefly. "Speak truly, for thou dost not fear death."

"I have not been with him, O my father," she said humbly; "I was in the dungeon of the palace."

"It is a lie—a lie!" cried those around her; "let her be slain!"

"Peace!" said the old man calmly. "Canst thou prove this, Sozun?"

"He will tell you if you ask him," she said; "and look—here are the marks of the irons."

Some men blew their matches, and held them down where she pointed, and they were satisfied. The broad blackened rings round her ankles, which showed scars of sores, were unmistakable.

"I was released this night," she said, "and have come to ye, my brothers; and I have a vow to God and the Prophet to lead the life of a dervish henceforth. Slay me if ye will; but I have told ye the truth."

Then a hoarse murmur of approbation rose, and all who were near the girl kissed her hands reverently: while the man who, in his fierce enthusiasm, would have struck her down, prostrated himself before her, and would not rise. "Aman! Aman!" he cried, "be merciful!"

He had been one of the foremost in the storming of Calcutta, and had helped her up to the bastion.

"Thou art forgiven, Ahmed Khan," she said, "if a girl's forgiveness avails thee aught. Go—Sozun has not forgotten. And now, my father, come ; I have promised him to bring thee, and there is no danger."

Then broke out passionate entreaties from his clansmen, who hung around him. They would not let him go alone—all must accompany him. But Noor Khan would not listen. Had he not promised to go if Sozun were sent?—and she was here. She took him by the hand, and led him on unresistingly.

"I am here, Nawab," said the old man as he entered the private room. "What wouldst thou with me?" The bright lamp-light glanced from the chain-mail and steel helmet and gauntlets which the chief wore; his heavy sabre, with its richly inlaid handle, was in his hand. Juma the negro, who stood behind his master, thought, perhaps, that it was not so easy to slay him as a sheep.

"We are friends, Noor Khan," said the Nawab. "Thou hast nothing to complain of—hast thou?"

"Nothing," said the chief, "but an idle life. I would rouse my lord to action, and Affghan's have no such dainty words for thee as these traitor Bengalees. The Feringis are taking thy country—wilt thou not strike a blow for it? Awake, my lord! there are a thousand of my people without, who took Calcutta once, and will take it again. Be not afraid; she is hostage for us. Speak but a few words to them, and Noor Khan will answer for every man."

"I dare not face them," said the Nawab ; "if they knew—"

"I have told them all, my lord," said Sozun, rising—she had sunk down, weak and exhausted ; "my father knows all, and has again saved me from death."

"Poor child!—poor child!" said the Khan, stroking her head kindly; "henceforth devoted to God, who would harm thee? Yes, my lord, she will be safe with us. Come, speak to them from the window—come, delay may be unwise, and my people are not safe in delays ; tell them they will march to-morrow for Calcutta, and they will be satisfied. Come—listen ; they are impatient children, whom a kind word satisfies."

The eunuch advanced, and threw open the casement. The courtyard now blazed with torches, and the barrels of a thousand matchlocks glinted in the bright light, as men surged forward with a strange clamour, shouting; but all were silent when their leader and the Nawab appeared, and a few words, which told them they would march next day, as the advanced guard of the army, were answered by the same rude shouts and cries.

"Take them away, Khan Sahib," said the Nawab; "I like them not in their present humour, and I am weary, and would sleep."

"Let us depart, Sozun," said the old man. "Come, this is no place for thee," he added, in their own tongue; "I much mistrust yonder savage. Come, else the Prince is not safe—they would not go hence without thee or me."

"What dost thou say to her?" cried the Nawab, suspiciously.

"That she is safest with me, and my lord without her," he replied, respectfully but firmly. "Those without would not leave her with thee now, and I would not answer for them if we were delayed. Go thou before, Sozun; I will follow thee."

"I shall not see thee again, Sozun," said the Nawab, sadly. "Is it thus thou leavest me—alone!"

Sozun thought she saw tears upon his face glistening in the torch-light, and it might have been so; the tone of his voice, too, touched her, but there could be no hesitation now. "My lord will see his poor slave often," she said, humbly bowing herself to the ground; "she cannot forget—many benefits. She will be with her father and the Lord; but whenever there may be a service done in truth and faith for her Prince, Sozun will not fail, even to death."

"Let me drive my dagger through his back," whispered the giant, "now, as he goes down the stair. That he should take her away, even from thy presence, O my lord!"

"No, no, let them go," was the reply; "I dare not now, they would tear me in pieces—listen!"

The hoarse roar of the men below had arisen again as they welcomed their chief and the girl he led by the hand; and, placing them in the midst, they moved on singing the war-cry, which, with the hollow tramp of a thousand feet through the streets at that hour, sounded wild and strange in the ears of peaceful citizens, and gradually died away in the distance. There was a report next day that during the night the Affghans had mutinied for pay; and when the treasury was opened early, and the troops, receiving heavy donations, began to march southwards, it was known that the second campaign against the English had begun.

"Thou wilt remain here, Juma," said the Nawab, as his slave fell to rubbing his feet as he lay down to rest. It was then that their most confidential communications were interchanged.

"What have I to do, my lord?"

"I had thought of taking the lady with me," he replied, "but she is better here; when I am gone, do thou lead her below—she is safest there."

"Good, my lord. What more? my Prince will be fortunate, and capture others!"

"If I am, Juma," he cried, rising up, and striking the pillow savagely, "it is not Feringis, curse them all! that I shall bring back, but that girl from her clansmen. Let them but perish under the

Feringi fire; and were she a thousand times a devotee, she shall be mine again."

"Can my lord trust her with him?" asked the eunuch, with a sneer.

"To death—to death!" he cried; "the truest heart that ever beat for me; but I was mad, and have lost her, and am alone, for how long—O Allah! how long?" and so, raving and dozing in uneasy sleep by turns, the Nawab lay, and the negro watched.

CHAPTER LI.

THE NAWAB'S SECOND VISIT TO THE GENTLEMEN OF CALCUTTA.

Although the events of history cannot strictly be followed in this narrative, it is necessary to allude to them occasionally, so as to give, if no more, at least an outline of the motives which influenced the several parties now contending for mastery in Bengal—the English, the French, and the Nawab. The English movements we have already followed. They had regained and locally re-established their former position, and several communications had already passed between them and Suraj-oo-Doulah; but these had led to no result. The tone of the English letters had been haughty and defiant, and the Nawab was little inclined to submit to the terms demanded. His honour, and the desire of his troops to be led against the English invaders, which was daily more and more excited by the Mahomedan preachers, hardly left him an alternative between accepting the demands of the foreigners and the submitting to an unconditional admission of his inferiority to exact better; and it has been related how, under the exasperation of the last news he had received, his hurried march to Calcutta began. He relied upon the assistance of the French, and urged M. Law to join him with his forces, and to make common cause against a mutual enemy; for the news of the opening of war between the European powers soon reached him. He found the French, however, cautious and timid. M. Bussy was in no condition to march across India to the aid of his countrymen in Bengal as quickly as would be necessary to throw an overwhelming force into the scale against the English; and of themselves, the French could not defend their settlement and at the same time join the Nawab with men sufficient to make any impression. Feeling their weakness, therefore, they proffered a neutrality with the English, and negotiations to this end were set on foot: while at the same time, though he entertained the propositions until his way should appear clearer, Colonel Clive renewed his proposals to the Nawab, in the hope, perhaps, of gaining time or staying his march altogether. The Nawab's army was reported to be fifty thousand men—the flower of his troops, confident of victory, and excited to the highest degree; and when the returns of the English troops were taken, the means of meeting any such force in the field, or of even transporting supplies or *matériel* of war away from the ships, seemed absolutely wanting. It is no wonder, therefore, that with doubtful neutrality on the one hand, which in the event of any reverse would inevitably be changed to open war against him, and the march of a powerful army on the other, Colonel Clive should have made one more proposal for peace, and offered such terms to the Nawab as might prove acceptable.

He was not long, however, in suspense; Suraj-oo-Doulah was in no mood to listen to proposals which, modified as they were, still presented many points of humiliation. Colonel Clive's messengers were dismissed angrily, and the native army marched on unopposed, and without delays reached Calcutta on the 3d of February. The English flag was flying over the Old Fort, which was not changed; but the noble ships lying quietly at their anchorage, with double tiers of guns projecting from their sides; the white tents of, as it appeared, a considerable army, and the new fortifications, were very different objects from the few merchant ships which had dropped away from the Fort before, and the miserable garrison of weak Europeans and Portuguese which had in vain striven to defend it. The army, however, had suffered no check, and the defiant attitude of the English only excited them the more as they pressed into the suburbs of Calcutta, and with more than ordinary military skill took up positions by which all supplies to the English would be intercepted; and when in the afternoon a deputation from the gentlemen of the Factory waited upon the Nawab with remonstrances, and requests to withdraw, they met with a haughty refusal, and returned.

I can believe, when they came back and told of the heavy artillery they had seen—of the immense bodies of well-armed men, horse and foot, and the general splendour of the camp—of the demeanour of the Nawab, and his uncivil dismissal of them, that many hearts failed, and would have accepted any terms upon which the settlement might hope for future peace; but there was fortunately one mind present which not only comprehended the nature of the crisis, bnt the only way to meet it, and his decision was prompt. Hitherto, when danger was afar off, and was even exaggerated by distance, Clive had hesitated to thrust himself into contact with a remote and difficult contingency; but with that danger doubtful no longer, and present at his very door, the indomitable spirit of the man rose with the emergency. The Admiral, for the time sinking consideration of all the old vexatious questions between them, gave such aid as he could afford with a true sailor's energy ; and the naval contingent of six hundred gallant tars which that night assembled on the plain without the Fort, was a very substantial proof of it.

If we have lost sight of Mr. Smithson for some time, it is not because that young gentleman had grown idle, or had relapsed into the dull plodding life of the Factory ; on the contrary, he found his new position full of absorbing interest, and the affectionate confidence of Mr. Clive increasing daily : for there was no one to whom he opened his views so unreservedly as to Ralph—no one with whom he cared to discuss the tangled maze of political intrigue now existent, better than with the clear-headed, resolute, young Northumbrian gentleman. In him he found a spirit congenial to his own—as ardent and as brave. It was surprising, perhaps, to find how rapidly Ralph Smithson's mind had expanded under the excitement of the period—how readily and astutely it grappled with the difficulties of the momentous questions then pending, and how deep was his sympathy with his leader and friend upon the embarrassing claims upon his services ; while, on the one hand, the attitude of Monsieur Bussy, alike menacing Bengal and Madras, and ready to strike in either direction, caused Madras to be anxious for his return ; and on the other, the helplessness of the Bengal Council, with Mr. Drake at its head, rendered such a measure impossible till the interests of the English nation in Bengal should be confirmed beyond any possibility of future disturbance. When, therefore, the envoys returned from the Nawab's durbar on that memorable evening of the 3d February 1757, and Ralph Smithson heard with enthusiasm, common to all who were to take a part in it, that the native camp was to be attacked that night, he rejoiced that one more opportunity would be afforded him for earning the distinction he had more than ever grown to covet. Heretofore, what he had done, what he had been able to do, had been more the result of accident than design ; but that was all changed. He had no military rank, it was true ; but a volunteer such as he was, was too valuable to be overlooked, and his request to be actively employed met with an instant and flattering acceptance.

"Of course, my dear boy—of course. You didn't think I should leave you out, did you ?" said Mr. Clive, as the various officers to be engaged had received their instructions, and had left him to make the necessary preparations. "You know the ground, Ralph ?"

"Every yard of it, sir, for miles round the town. I can lead the column anywhere you please. I have not been idle all day, and have been watching the enemy as their troops took up positions, and thought them secure ones."

"And you have seen their guns, Ralph—what are they?"

"I know where they are to a yard, sir; but what they are I cannot tell you. They seem, however, to be a strong battery, with some heavy pieces."

"Then you must take us at once upon them. If we can spike the whole of them—and we must do it—there is no fear for the rest. A native army which has lost its guns is at best a disorderly rabble. But do you know the troops? Are there any of your blue-coated friends among them?"

"They are with the guns, sir; and they are the only fellows you need care about," was the reply. "They will fight, too, if they are led as they were before by that girl."

"What girl, Ralph? What! A woman in the enemy's camp?"

"I don't know, sir. There are curious stories abroad about her. Some say she's a favourite of the Nawab's, whom he sends on any desperate service because of some prophecy about her that she is to take Calcutta; others that she is a prophetess of the tribe—Affghans, sir, they call them, or Rohillas—who leads them with a marvellous bravery. Once—"

"Once, Ralph? Speak out, man. Why do you hesitate?"

"It does not matter now, sir," he replied; "but I have seen her as I never wish to see her again, brave as she was, and I hope I may not meet her to-night, that's all."

I think it crossed Colonel Clive's mind for a moment that his young friend might have been beguiled into some strange love affair with the native prophetess, or whatever she might be; but it was dismissed in a moment. There was no tender expression on Ralph Smithson's face; on the contrary, a knitting of the brow and a quivering of the nostril and lip, which told of other scenes than love.

"I will tell you, sir, perhaps, some day how it was," continued Ralph, after a pause; "I never hear of her that I do not associate that poor creature Julia Wharton with her; and I am certain if ever we hear aught of *her*, it will be through this girl. I should not have thought of her, but my servant, who is an excellent spy, hath been through the camp all day, and told me he was sure he had seen the girl among the Rohillas, crying to them wildly, pointing to the Fort, and beating her breast."

"Phe-e-ew," whistled the Colonel; "then we shall have those fellows at us first, and so much the better. If they are the stay of the Nawab's army, the more they are cut up the better. Now I remember, the worst charges I have ever seen by Indian soldiers, have been when some mad or drunken fakeer led them on shouting an incantation, or whatever it might be; and I had to kill such a fellow once myself on the breach at Arcot. Bah! A devil, sir, by

Jove! But a girl? well, I only hope I may not come across her, that's all—nor you either."

"I hope not, sir. Now, if you will tell me what to do, I will go and see after the men."

"Nothing but what I told you, Ralph: lead us right at the guns; we shall catch the fellows asleep, I daresay; if not, we must make the best of it. Just before we start, I shall call for volunteers of both the services for you; I daresay you will have a hundred, and well do I know 'Ralph Darnell' will not disappoint me. Go, get some sleep yourself. If you are ready by three in the morning it will do. I shall turn in myself, for people's heads and bodies can't be too fresh for such matters. Is there anything I can do, Ralph, in case—?"

"No, sir, nothing; all my papers are in my desk, and those affairs were arranged long ago."

"So much the better—I am glad to hear it," was the reply, and for the time they parted.

Ralph Smithson could not, however, sleep. Suppose the Affghan girl were to urge her clansmen to attempt a night attack—it was said to be a favourite mode of Rohilla warfare—and lead the men, as she had done before, with reckless bravery, much confusion might be the result. His servant met him at his tent, and pressed him to take rest, but he would not. "Come with me, Cassim," he said; "we will go forward and see if all be quiet. And you saw her in the camp?"

"I am sure it was she," he said—"the same face, fair and ruddy—I could not mistake it. She is a fakeer, sir, now; for I saw a green turban on her head, and a green dress, and strings of beads about her neck. She was standing on a gun-carriage, preaching in the Rohilla tongue to her people, and though I could not understand a word, I could see what she meant; and when she had done, the men gathered wildly about her and kissed her feet."

Strange and mysterious creature, thought Ralph Smithson, as the old scene came back on his memory: the wild fight, her attitude over the dead, her evident anxiety in regard to the concealment of Julia Wharton, and her disappearance behind the Nawab's palankeen—who and what could she be? The customs of natives of India were little known at that period, and the wildest stories of magic and paganism were readily believed. Could she be one of these strange magicians? He sat down on his camp-chair outside the tent, and, as he lit a pipe, fell to thinking. "Cassim," he cried at length, "couldst thou lead me to the place now?"

Cassim was a wiry little Madras Mussulman, who had been taken into Ralph Smithson's service before he went to Madras, and had returned thence with him. Very different in character was he from the timid, lazy, Bengali servants who attended the Factory. Half servant, half soldier, had he not been too short altogether, he would now have been bearing a musket among Colonel Clive's Sepoys, in whose regiment he had been born. He looked at his master from head to foot, as if to see whether he were sober or not.

"Do you wish it, sir? there may be danger," he said.

"Not if we are careful, I think. Come, perhaps I know the way myself, but we had best be sure."

"Tie this scarf round your head, and throw my black blanket over your head, sir, and there will be no danger; but as you are, with that hat, we should be known. Let me tie it."

Cassim's waistband became an excellent turban, and the black blanket covered as much of Ralph Smithson's figure as was needful. "That is good, sir," said Cassim; "no one could know you in the dark, only you are so tall and I so little. Come, we shall see some fun perhaps, and if we have to fight, I can use a sword as well as you."

So they went on. There was no moon, but the stars shone very bright and clear, and their light sufficed to show the ground clearly, which was wet with the heavy dew. The night was very cold, almost frosty, and in the native camps men had lighted fires, the smoke of which hung low in the air, and was bright from the blaze beneath them. It seemed like a canopy of cloud stretching in a semi-circle round the back of the city, and marked the place where the Nawab's troops rested. Cassim led on without speaking a word, past some purlieus of the native town, where nothing was stirring but dogs and jackals prowling about. On the side of the British camp all was still; a lantern here and there tied in a ship's rigging, or a lamp in the stern of a native boat, was the only sign of life. In the native camp there was an endless drumming and blowing of horns and trumpets; but this ceased suddenly, and all was quiet.

"The Nawab is gone to sleep," said Cassim—"tired, perhaps. I know the way to his tent, too, sir."

"Don't talk," replied his master. "Get on fast—it is farther than I thought."

"We can get round the corner right upon them presently," said the servant, "if you like to be near them."

"As near as you can," was the reply in a whisper; and as Cassim began to crawl on his hands and knees through some low bushes, Ralph Smithson did the same. It was not unlike some of the old night-work at Melcepeth, long ago! And as they reached the edge of the fringe of bushes, the whole scene before them was strikingly beautiful.

Stretched over the flat plain, here and there broken by date-palms and bushes, were the innumerable tents of the host. Some, large pavilions, enclosed in outer walls of cotton canvas; others of more humble pretensions, which sheltered a few soldiers; while a few spears, or poles, or matchlocks tied together, and a sheet or carpet thrown over them, protected the sleepers from the heavy dew. Here and there were groups of elephants snorting and blowing as they munched the succulent bulrushes cut for them during the day or threw trunkfuls of water over their backs; gentle tinklings of camel bells, and an occasional hoarse low of draught oxen, mingled with other sounds, the hum of voices, and the thousand undistinguishable murmurs of an immense mass of people: but it was on the scene immediately in their front, and hardly fifty yards distant, that the attention of Ralph Smithson was instantly riveted.

Before him were the heavy guns and their clumsy carriages and tumbrils, ranged in a long row, apparently ready for action; a slight trench had been begun before them, but discontinued; the white oxen which had dragged them, and some elephants, were tethered in the rear, and little screens of carpets and sheets had been made over the guns to shelter men who slept beneath them. Before the battery were a number of the Affghans sitting round a huge fire, which sent up crackling flames as dry thorns were thrown on it, and one of the men was singing in a strong rough voice, while another beat a small hand-drum in time with the song. Presently it ceased, and there was a hurried consultation among them, and some laughter, and several of the men went away; while more faggots were thrown on the fire, and a merry blaze went high into the air, lighting up every bronzed bearded face, and sparkling on helmet and matchlock. Then those who had gone returned, leading a slight figure in a green-coloured tunic and turban, and a heavy necklace of wooden beads about its shoulders, holding a small lute in its hands. Those about the fire made way for it respectfully, some stooping down to touch its feet, while others spread a saddle-cloth or carpet to which it was led. There was no doubt now, for the firelight was full and clear, and the Affghan girl was before him. She struck a few notes as a prelude, and one of the richest female voices to which he had ever listened, began to sing a low but plaintive ditty, which had an inexpressible charm; some of her audience wept, and some flung their arms wildly about. When she changed the melody to what seemed a song of war, the excitement was irrepressible—naked swords flashed in the light, and some of the men rose, clashed their shields, and made fierce gyrations, as if fighting. Then, as a softer strain followed, the wild listeners sank down, hung their heads, and seemed to weep.

"Come, sir, we are too long here," said Cassim,—"Come away."

Ralph Smithson could have sat there for hours, but delay was impossible; never afterwards did he forget the mellow voice, the wild melodies of that strange music, which, with the tinkling of the little lute, grew fainter and fainter as he retraced his steps. Yes, he could now lead on his volunteers without fail: but who was she?

Ah! he would soon know.

CHAPTER LII.

ITS RESULT—FEBRUARY 3, 1757.

THE noise in the native camp gradually died away, and the bright line of smoke canopy which had hung low over it, had altogether paled, or was mingling with the heavy grey fog which, as the night advanced, rose from the river and spread over the plain and town; now and then, whenever dry thorns and faggots were thrown upon watchfires, a light glimmered in the sky for a brief space, and again faded into gloom; but these were few, and the quiet which prevailed proved that, for the most part, the Nawab's great army slept.

Forty thousand stout soldiers, not wanting in individual courage, and of such temper as those of whom the victorious native armies of England have since been made, and have proved invincible among their countrymen—well provided with artillery, well paid, well fed, well armed, after their own fashion, with sabre and shield, matchlock and spear, deadly weapons in stout hands; horse and foot, there were they, forty thousand men: while advancing on this perilous enterprise against them were not more than a thousand English soldiers and sailors, with a few others to carry powder and ball, and drag field-pieces, for carriages there were none—slender means, one would think, to win a victory. And yet I believe that, from the gallant gentleman who, as the night was advancing to its close, dressed himself carefully, then knelt down and prayed God to help the cause of his country—committing also one very dear to His care—to the meanest soldier or sailor among whom he went from rank to rank, saying a few cheering words, there was not one then present who did not believe himself to be a host, and looked upon the work to be done as a mere morning's amusement. I do not think that one feeling of the risk of failure ever entered the mind of any one; and yet, if there had been a check, Messieurs the French at Chandernagore would have been ready enough to give up their proffered neutrality; and between them and the Nawab's army, Mr. Clive might have fared badly enough.

But Mr. Clive had no such apprehension; and when he went with Ralph Smithson, Major Kilpatrick, Mr. Coote, Mr. Rumbold, and other officers, to the head of the column, warned the men against straggling, and then called out in a cheery voice, "Volunteers for an advanced guard!" I think the whole column was stirred, and would have rushed towards him, had not stern discipline forbidden any such movement. As it was, of soldiers and sailors, nearly a hundred men had recovered arms, and, under officers of their own services, were given over to Ralph Smithson to lead; and with a muffled but hearty cheer, the intrepid band set out.

The fog had now thickened much, and, besides being dank and wet, had settled down low to the earth, and but little could be seen of anything around. The men's voices even were muffled by it, and indeed few cared to speak with a mighty combat before them, to which they were fast advancing, and absolute silence had been enjoined on all. So there was only heard the tramp of the men, the faint rumbling of the gun wheels, as the sailors, holding the drag-ropes, pulled them along, and low whisperings here and there between comrades. Had not, perhaps, the faithful little Cassim, now accoutred for fight with a sword and shield, stridden by his master, even Ralph Smithson might have been puzzled to lead the column as he had desired; but Cassim's instinct and keen perception of the localities proved of eminent use; and as the dawn was breaking, and objects began to be seen looming large and indistinct in the thick haze, the column reached the bushes whence, only a few hours before, Ralph Smithson and his companion had looked upon the scene which has already been described. As it proved afterwards, it was not the point desired by Mr. Clive, but there was no hesitation now.

"This is the place, sir," said Ralph Smithson, in a whisper; "there are the guns—we have them, for no one stirs." Indeed there was a quiet stillness then all over the camp, and except a few indistinct murmurs, there were no signs of the vast host before them.

"Spike every gun, my men!" cried Mr. Clive; "and now, On, gentlemen! charge in the King's name! Hurrah!" Then the force sprang on with a ringing cheer, and the grim work of death began. The foremost files of the 39th were among the Rohillas ere the sleeping forms could well arouse themselves, or comprehend what had occurred; and though many fell by bayonet and cutlass, yet others rallied; and their old chief's voice, and one which thrilled through Ralph Smithson's heart, as he pressed on striking down those who opposed him, were clearly heard above the din and clamour which now arose on all sides. If he could only capture her! But little could be distinguished; and now, increased by the smoke of the Nawab's guns, which were being wildly fired, the fog seemed to grow thicker and thicker. Again and again was the woman's shrill cry heard, and as Ralph Smithson, followed by a party of men, dashed after it among the guns, hewing down the artillerymen and spiking the pieces, he felt, from whom he could not see, a rain of heavy blows descend on his ill-protected head and shoulders, and at the same time a sharp stinging pain in his leg, and, staggering on a few paces, he fell to the earth insensible.

Ralph Smithson's fall had not been noticed; for the little Cassim, missing him in the *mêlée*, had attached himself to Colonel Clive, and as the first obstacle was passed, he cried in English which could be well understood, "I know Nawab's tent—come on—come on!" and so the column, dealing death as it went, and producing the wildest confusion, whirled onwards.

For some time—how long he knew not, but it was now broad daylight, and the sun's pale beams were struggling through the mist—Ralph Smithson's swoon continued. When he became conscious, and tried to raise himself up, his head was dizzy and confused, and his face covered with blood; and when he strove to move his wounded leg and arm, which were exquisitely painful, he utterly failed to rise, and again fell back. "Oh for a cup of water!" he thought, and could have cried out, but who could have heard around him? The silence was almost that of death, and except an occasional groan from a dying soldier, there was no sign of life. The oxen had broken their tethers and had scampered off, elephants had disappeared, and there was nothing left but the black guns, through which wreaths of heavy mist were sweeping before the slight morning breeze, and the dead lying among them, as it seemed to be, in heaps; blue-coated men, with faces almost as fair as the English soldiers and sailors who had died with them. Away in the distance, the clamour of war, the roar of men's voices, musketry, and occasional cannon-shots, were heard confusedly. "They have left me to die," groaned the poor fellow in his misery. "Oh that I were with them! Oh that some one might return to help me!" but indeed he was conscious of very little, and, exhausted by loss of blood and the pain of his wounds, he sank back again into insensibility.

When he woke, it was from excess of pain. He felt some rough hands dragging him by the hurt arm from under the gun-wheel, against which he had fallen, and, as a momentary consciousness returned, it was only, as he thought, to breathe an incoherent prayer ere he died. Several of the Rohillas were standing over him, and one of them had raised a long, dull, keen-edged knife to despatch him; but ere it could be used, he heard the shrill scream of a woman, who bounded to his side, and, seizing the arm of the man who held the knife, wrested it from him, and flung it away.

"It is he!" she cried—"the Feringi who spared me; I knew he was here, and ye shall none of ye harm him. He is mine!" and she sat down by Ralph Smithson and strove to raise his head, at the same time pouring some water from a long-necked gourd into his mouth, and wiping away the blood about his eyes with her scarf.

"He shall not live!" cried another of the men, advancing with a fierce gesture; "the Feringis have slain hundreds of our brothers, and he must die. Away with ye, Sozun! this is no place for the like of thee. Go!—leave men to men."

"I go not, Ahmed," she said, calmly; "I owe this poor life to him, as thou knowest. Dost thou not remember the youth? Look! He spared us both."

"By Allah and the Prophet! it's the same," exclaimed the man. "Yes, he spared thee, and he should be a brother to us. Stay, some of you, and help," he cried aloud. Other men were now crowding up, and those of their comrades who still breathed were being rapidly carried off by twos and threes together, and thus several men came to the place.

"Dost thou understand me well?" asked Sozun of Ralph; "fear not, thou art with friends, and art safe. O Allah, most merciful! can I repay that debt? Drink more water, sir; there—plenty—as much as thou canst; or hast thou any of the Feringi wine with thee?"

Ralph remembered his flask full of generous Madeira, which Cassim had filled, and insisted on his putting in his pocket. "It is here," he said, faintly, and Sozun took it out, and held it to his lips. How grateful it was! How that first mouthful seemed to send the blood once more coursing through his veins. He tried even to sit up, but Sozun would not permit him.

"Shabash!" cried the Rohilla—"well done!—that's what makes the Feringis so valiant: now, lady, lift him up; let me carry him."

"Not so," said the girl—"make a litter for him; he is very badly hurt."

In a few moments two loading-rods were fastened to the ends of a coarse black blanket, and Ahmed and others advanced to take him up. It was in vain that Ralph tried to resist, and appealed to his protectress; she would not hear him.

"You would have died in an hour, when the sun came upon your head; be thankful to God who sent me to your aid, as I am that I found you. You are safe with us, O Feringi, and Noor Khan will be a father to you, as he is to me. Take him up," she continued to the men, "and do not shake him as ye go."

Her orders were instantly obeyed. Utterly helpless as he was, Ralph was in no condition to resist, and felt himself carried at a swift pace through the almost deserted camp, the fair Affghan girl walking and running by his side, cheering him with friendly assurances.

All this time Mr. Clive had fought his way through the camp. The fog had misled him; and, as it cleared away, he found himself opposed to a fresh body of the Rohillas, and men of Oude and Behar, and for a time the fight was doubtful. How Mr. Clive himself escaped that day he knew not; but, though losing two guns, and upwards of two hundred of his small force, he had attained his object. The Nawab himself was soon in precipitate flight; and his army, lacking spirit to turn on the little English battalion, hurried after him, so Calcutta was once more free! But Ralph Smithson, with many another brave fellow, was missing; and though the whole plain, the place of the first charge, the track across the camp, and wherever the fighting had been sharpest, were thoroughly searched by parties who went for the dead, and by the distracted Cassim, no trace could be found of his body. It seemed little likely that one Englishman would be carried off, when so many wounded men had been unmolested. "My poor Ralph," thought the colonel, "now all your life's trouble is ended, and at last there's no heir to Melcepeth Castle, or to the bank. Ah! they will grieve bitterly and unavailingly now, but none more keenly than I—not one. What can I write to Roger Darnell? Well, thank God! I can say that Ralph died, as I hope to die, doing his duty."

I may here remark, and with great truth, that the loss of the poor fellow was deeply felt by all his friends; and it was noticed that, for many days, Mr. Clive was moody and restless, refusing society, and sending men and spies in every possible direction in hope of news of his young friend; but none came. And if any ship had been going to England, he would have written to Roger Darnell that his nephew had died in the fight of the 3d February.

But we know very well that Ralph was not dead, though sorely hurt—very sorely indeed. When the men set him down, he had a very confused notion of where he was; but under the care applied to him, he was soon partially relieved. The place he had been taken to was a village a few miles from Calcutta, which formed one of the new outposts of the Nawab's army, held by the Rohillas. For shelter, there was a shed near a Mahomedan cemetery, overshadowed by a huge banian-tree, in which, upon a village bed covered by a soft mattress, and over him a padded quilt, he rested easily. Old Noor Khan, and those who remained of the clan, had assembled by evening, and Ralph was an object of great curiosity and interest to them all. Among men used to a warlike life, the dressing of wounds was an easy task; and there was a native surgeon attached to them who took Ralph in hand, cut a bullet out of his left leg, which had not gone quite through, sewed up a heavy sabre wound in his neck and shoulder, fomented the bruises on his head, and set his right arm, which had been fractured. Ralph remembered how he had been suddenly beset by several men, and beaten down; and it seemed only wonderful how he had escaped with life.

Day and night the girl watched by him, or only left him for her place to be taken by one of the men. She rarely spoke to him, and allowed none to do so. Perhaps for a time he was delirious, for he was conscious of much fever; but the cooling drinks given to him, and skilful treatment, could not fail of acting upon a constitution naturally hardy and vigorous. With the English camp it was impossible to communicate. He passed for an Affghan; for his English clothes were removed, and the blue dress of the tribe was given to him. When the Nawab's camp moved on, he was carried in a litter, and he supposed he should be taken to the capital. He had no power to write. Peace, they told him, was concluded; the English were to return to Cossim Bazar; Mr. Watts was to be re-established as agent, and if he arrived there, a return to the fleet could be easily managed. Under these circumstances, therefore, we may believe that Ralph Smithson gave himself up to the luxury of getting well; and it would have been unnatural if the affectionate care of the strange and beautiful Affghan girl had not been returned with an increasing interest.

For many days she would not allow him to speak; but when the fever was past—when, lifted from his bed, he was allowed to recline on soft cushions, and could even sit up—the girl sang to him, amused him with tales, and though he could not frequently follow all her rapid speech, ordinary conversation was easily understood and replied to. From time to time Ralph strove to lead her to speak of Julia Wharton, but the topic was evaded when others were present, or only the general report, that she had been carried away, admitted.

One day, however, they were alone. His bed had been laid under the shadow of a mango-tree, in a grove where the men were encamped, and in the heat of noon all were asleep. Sozun had been singing one of her low crooning songs to her little lute, and he had been listening dreamily, but could not sleep. I believe little was wanting then for Ralph Smithson to have told the girl he loved her, and to have asked her to share his life. Many an Englishman had done the same, and lived happily; and who at home cared for him now? Perhaps, as he gazed at her, when the tender blue Darnell eyes filled with tears, and love was playing in them, she understood him.

"Ah no!" she said, laying her hand upon his heart calmly, and even solemnly. "I am thy sister, sir, now, and I have many brethren since I made my vow, and put on these holy garments. Thou art one too, and every needy, wounded creature of God whom Sozun can succour. To this, sir, I have vowed my life before the Lord. So it is merciful not to tempt one whose love is dead. I think I see thy heart, loving and generous; but, brother, it cannot be. Mine hath been a hard, shameless life; and such as thou shouldst mate with must be pure as snow. Even she, the English lady, hath endured misery, and would turn from thee with shame as I do. Listen, I could not tell thee before, but no one is near us now, and I will tell my own story and hers, whom I tried to save and failed." And it was with a vivid interest that he followed her strange narrative of Julia Wharton's fate.

"Cannot we save her, Sozun," he asked, when he heard all, "when we arrive there, and I am strong and well?"

"I fear not," replied Sozun. "Had Nasir been at his post, we might have depended upon him; but he, too, is in irons, and there is no hope of him. When thy people make another treaty, let them demand her, and hide her shame; but even in this there must be care. Thou dost not know him, sir; he might tell Juma to kill her rather than give her up. But what is her life to thee? Didst thou love her? She is very beautiful.

"Never, but as a sister," he answered, "whom I would rescue from shame and misery."

"Yes, hereafter thou mayst save her, but not now. Meanwhile she is well, with one of the most precious of God's creatures, the Begum, whom she will grow to love, and who will care more for the poor Feringi woman than she did for me, her enemy. And yet," she continued, with enthusiasm, "when he put me in irons, and sent me to share her lonely life, I was a shameless wanton with a hardened heart, and now I bless Allah that he hath permitted one such as I to do his service. Ah, sir, such a one as that angel should be thy wife—so pure, so beautiful, and so gentle. Listen! that coward Prince's good destiny was but for a year; the Derwesh said so by the planets, and he was right. Now men begin to say that the destiny of your people will follow his without a check, and that of all Hind ye will be the kings. His power is already on the wane. Many are discontented. Even my own people talk of a service without honour, and would go elsewhere. Wait till the year of the Derwesh is past, and she may be thine. I, Sozun, would give her to thee. Dost thou believe in the planets—in destiny?"

"No," replied Ralph, smiling; "our people think prophecies by the stars foolishness; but they believe in the will of God, and that is why I am here."

"It is the same—the same!" cried the girl, wildly, clapping her hands; "I could tell thee—but not yet—not yet! Wait, and thou wilt believe, even as I do, when the end comes."

CHAPTER LIII.

FREE!

But notwithstanding all Sozun's care, and that of the rough but affectionate people among whom he was, Ralph's recovery was but slow. His arm long continued stiff and numb, and his leg did not heal so kindly as the Indian doctor had hoped; nor was it till, of its own accord, a piece of the woollen cloth of his gaiter came out, that there were favourable symptoms. The Rohillas seemed to be moved from place to place about the country, and never to the capital. They did not appear contented, and often spoke among themselves of leaving the Nawab's service, and joining the Emperor, whose servants they properly were. Noor Khan, the chief, had been to Moorshedabad, and had returned ill-satisfied. Although the Rohillas had saved the army when Clive attacked it, no honour had been offered to him; and he could see that the Nawab had never forgiven the free speech of the night we may remember, nor the protection of Sozun, of whom, had it not been for her countrymen, whom he dare not attack, he would ere this have obtained forcible possession. Living as he was among natives entirely, and treated as an honoured guest with confidence, it was impossible but that Ralph should become aware of much that was passing; and he did not perhaps think it extraordinary when Noor Khan, the doctor, and several others were sitting round him one day, Sozun being absent, that the Nawab's conduct was much discussed, and his treachery, cruelty, and incapacity freely commented upon. It is quite certain that Ralph Smithson made no secret of his opinion, nor of that of Colonel Clive. He had seen enough of diplomatic passages to feel assured that there was mutual suspicion between the parties, and that each was preparing, when it was possible, to break through all engagements and strive for the mastery. The Nawab, they said, was grown gloomy and intractable; all his true friends were falling away from him. His mother used her entreaties in vain that he should make friends of his father's friends, and not waste their goodwill in intrigues with other powers, which were sure of detection. There was not a night now that he was not taken out of the durbar intoxicated. At Calcutta some of the Portuguese and Armenian merchants had supplied him with strong sweet wine, which he drank to excess. Even his eunuchs and servants were growing very fearful of him, and were flogged, put in irons, or tortured, in every variety of caprice, or fury of passion.

Very often, when they were together, Ralph strove to lead Sozun to the subject of the Nawab, but in vain. She had been his slave, was still his slave, and her life was his sacrifice, she would say. She might be able to help him even now if he would respect her vow; but it was evident she dared not trust him, and seeing that she only wept when he was mentioned, Ralph ceased to urge her on the subject. But, knowing how valuable information would be to Mr. Clive, he encouraged talk by others, and, to say the truth, heard a good deal of the general discontent, of the possibility of revolution, but above all, of the strange new prophecy about the English, of which he was often told. The people among whom he was, were, if anything, because more ignorant, more superstitious than others. Yet there were some who read the Koran, and one in particular, whom men consulted for lucky days, who performed priestly offices, and marshalled them at prayers. He had heard of the astrological combinations, and, after his rude fashion, tested them himself, and told Ralph they all believed the Feringis would be kings soon; and indeed everywhere the hundred years to come of Feringi rule were ringing through the land.

Once, too, Sozun accompanied the chief to the capital. "He will die," she said. "My master must die when his time comes, but I will see him before then. I cannot help him; his fate is in the Lord's hands; but I can at least see him and kiss his feet. Let me go," she said to Ralph, who in vain tried to dissuade her; "I am in no danger with my people, and I will bring thee news of Julia." It was an easy name to pronounce, and Sozun had learned it—and she went.

She was long away—more than a month, and Ralph Smithson had passed a weary time without her. He was now recovering fast; the wounds were healing kindly, and his strength was recovering in spite of the hot weather; but it was a dreary time nevertheless, and he sadly missed the pleasant companionship, the unceasing, untiring attendance, and the bright beauty of the girl. There was no strain on his mind when she was with him; and the perpetual and gentle ministering to his wants, without effort or officious zeal—the almost instinctive anticipation of every wish—had been hard to part with, and was gratefully remembered; and when he saw her dear bright face again, he was overjoyed and thankful.

She had much to tell him, for she had seen Julia. In one of the moments of the Nawab's caprice, Nasir, the eunuch, often threatened with death, had been released, and in his stead Juma was imprisoned. She had made herself known to Nasir, and, having disguised herself, had been taken to the underground apartments, and had seen Julia,

"They are happy," she said, "she and my beloved mistress. Julia is very pale, like a lily, for no sun reaches her, and but little light; yet she is cool there this hot weather, and reads her book, in which are the words of the holy Jesus. Look, she wrote a verse which I have kept as a talisman. I shall ever keep it, and here it is; tell me what it means. She could not translate it, nor could Anna."

Ralph Smithson opened the paper wonderingly. It was a fly-leaf torn from her prayer-book, and the writing was stiff and cramped, but here is what was written :—

"They that sow in tears shall reap in joy. He that now goeth on his way weeping, and beareth good seed, shall doubtless come again with joy."

"She said you would not have forgotten the verses. What are they?"

"Nor have I," said Ralph. "They are like a blessed message from heaven. Listen to what they mean. Canst thou remember them?"

"Surely—do I not remember a hundred songs of which I do not understand a word? Teach me these words daily, and I will learn them. Not as a parrot, Ralph," she added, smiling—"I know the meaning—but with my heart. Yes; she is quiet and happy, and looks only for deliverance when God wills it. I told her of you, and she knows you will deliver her, and all she could send you was this."

It was a lock of her brown glossy hair. "And Anna," continued Sozun, "told me her love went with it. Dost thou love her, then? Once—"

"Once I said she was my sister, and you believed me, Sozun," he replied. "I say it again, and need not swear it."

"I do believe thee; and hadst thou seen them both as they sat together on the bed when I left, and the sun's rays were shining through the little window just before it set—the only time it can shine there, as well I know—when the glory of the light shone around her head like the crown of a houri of Paradise—of the two thou wouldst have chosen my dear mistress. I have told her where thou art, for we are faithful, we three women—one in heart and mind—and of those who have sown in tears, and hope to reap in joy. . . . His destiny? It draweth nigh, Ralph, very nigh. How it is to be accomplished who can tell? I went to the durbar as one of the soldiers with Noor Khan, with my head and face tied up. Had he been a man I would have stayed and kissed his feet. I saw only a thing with rolling bloodshot eyes, supported in his seat by others, slavering, cursing, and drinking. Ah, sir! it was a sore sight, and I could not bear it. Then I asked Nasir to take me at night to him, with my holy vestment on, which all men venerate, for they are my grave-clothes, but he refused. 'Dost thou again wish to be as thou used to be?' he said. 'Hath he not sworn to carry thee off? and would he respect these garments for a moment? Tell Noor Khan to beware! If he were dead, he thinks he dare attack thy people, or they would not care for thee, and he could once more buy thee for money; but no one cares to harm the old man, and Allah protects thee!' All this, and more, he told me. Ah, Ralph! it is hideous altogether — and this is one whom I have caressed and loved—ay, whom I love still, and, if it would save him, would give my life for. It were better we were all gone hence. My countrymen, the Abdallees, they say, are advancing from Delhi, and whether we go to meet them or remain here to receive them, is all that has to be decided. I heard that the army is assembling on the river to meet your people; but he dare not trust mine, and what will he do without them? Now we have spoken long, and thou art weary; and I have not seen the wounds, nor seen thee walk, O dear brother! and they tell me thou art strong."

"Stronger indeed, Sozun—look;" and he rose up. "I can walk as well as ever, and my leg healed at once after the cloth came out of the wound. My arm is weak and numb yet, but they rub it daily, and it is getting strong. I shall soon be well again—quite well. Why should I not go to Mr. Watts, at the Factory? I can ride—"

"Art thou weary of us, Ralph?" she said, bursting into tears. "But forgive me; when they think it right to send thee, Sozun will not weep—no, not a tear. What must be done, must be done—and thou wilt not forget me—never?"

Ralph Smithson never said a truer word, I think, than when, a few days afterwards, he held her to his heart, for he would not be denied this, and, kissing her fervently on the forehead, told her he could not forget, nor even repay her affection, so strange, so true, and so disinterested.

"It is not the last time," she said, almost gaily. "Something tells me that we shall meet again, and then it will be the last time. Go in peace now, and the blessing of the Lord and His Prophet, and of Jesus and His holy Mother, be upon thee and thine."

A few days' travel by night, escorted by a party of the faithful fellows who had so long tended him, brought Ralph Smithson to the Factory at Cossim Bazar; and as his servants announced to Mr. Watts the arrival of an English gentleman—for Ralph had put on his English clothes under a tree as he neared his destination—that worthy individual threw on a dressing-gown, and hurried out to receive him. "Some one Mr. Clive has sent, no doubt," he said to himself. "He would not trust to letters. Who can it be?" And I think that Mr. Watts hardly believed the evidence of his senses when Ralph Smithson advanced towards him and said—

"Have you forgotten me, Mr. Watts? I am one you used to know—Ralph Smithson."

"Mr. Smithson!—God bless my soul, Ralph Smithson in life!

We have mourned you dead, sir, long since. Where have you been all this time, without a word to any of us? Ah! this will be joyful news to Mr. Clive—very joyful indeed!—for he hath not been himself since you left. Come, rest yourself. I have much to hear, I think, and of strange interest; and who are these?"

"The good fellows to whom, under Providence, I owe my life and recovery from some desperate wounds, sir. And I shall need to draw upon you, for they must not go away empty-handed."

"As much as you please, sir. It will be paid right joyfully. Let me but order them what they require, and I will rejoin you directly. Go in and lie down. Even now I see you are limping."

"My leg is stiff riding a long march," said Ralph, "but it will soon recover. I am quite well now, and my wounds healed."

Well, indeed! for he looked strong and rosy as ever, but he was thin and gaunt, and disguised by a bushy beard; and as he lay down on the comfortable sofa in Mr. Watts' sitting-room, he felt a sense of quiet security to which he had long been a stranger, and from his heart thanked God for it.

"And you have heard no news, Mr. Smithson? nothing of what your friend Mr. Clive hath been doing? Strange that even native reports should not have reached you!" said Mr. Watts, as he returned.

"None," replied Ralph. "We have been at a distance, and the people I was with were only interested by the Nawab's doings. I suppose Mr. Clive is at Calcutta?"

"Ah, yes! I know," said Mr. Watts quickly, "the Nawab suspects these Rohillas, and has kept them out of the way; but I think we are sure of Noor Khan among the rest."

"How do you mean, Mr. Watts?"

"Well, it is a long story, but one you must hear as soon as you are rested. Come in, put on some light clothes, and go to sleep; when you wake I will tell you all, for we are on the eve of a strange crisis, Mr. Smithson; but I will spare you now. Here is a cup of tea for you, of which you will be the better, I am sure."

It was refreshing indeed; and when the sweet sleep which fell upon him, almost as his head touched the pillow, was ended, "he arose," as Mr. Watts said when he saw him again, "a new man."

And in the evening—when the Rohillas had been dismissed with a letter of true thanks to Noor Khan—which, inspired by the occasion, Mr. Watts' moonshee wrote in the choicest Persian—a loving message to Sozun, and their waistbands full of rupees, and they had all kissed Ralph's hands, and embraced him after their homely but affectionate manner—Mr. Watts told Ralph Smithson the story of the English progress after the affair before Calcutta and the Nawab's retreat.

"We could not trust the Nawab," he said, "as you very well know, Mr. Smithson; but danger seemed imminent, and Mr. Clive thought us too weak then to bring on a general action, which, indeed, the Admiral strongly urged him to fight; but Mr. Clive could see farther than the Admiral, and he was right, though some blamed him. No matter, sir: we made a treaty with Suraj-oo-Doulah; and as he promised compensation to the gentlemen of the Factory, and even an improvement on our old position, Mr. Drake and the others were quite satisfied. But Mr. Clive was not, sir—no, by Jove! nothing would satisfy him but routing the French out of Bengal; and he hath recently taken their Factory, sir—taken it gloriously. The gallant old Admiral took up the ships, and though the land forces had done most part of the work, the army and the navy between them finished the matter, and on the 23d of April, sir, the dear old flag was flying on Monsieur Crapaud's flagstaff!"

"This takes away my breath, Mr. Watts. What a glorious thing to do! Oh that I had been with him!"

"I have no doubt Mr. Clive will be sorry that you were not, Mr. Smithson, and there's no helping that now; but listen, there is much more to tell you. The people have long been discontented with this Nawab, and they wish for peace and quiet, which he will never give them. They desire to put him aside and set up another: we desire it too, sir, for we are as weary of all this uncertainty as they are, and there is no safety here but in that course. I myself am in no small danger from day to day. At one time I am flattered and praised, and the English are all in all. Then, sir, I am insulted and reproached, and threatened to be impaled. But I am not in that miscreant's power, Mr. Smithson, and if my life be of any use to my country, God, sir, will take care of it, as I humbly trust. One day the Nawab writes to the Emperor that he has destroyed the Feringis; another, messengers go on to M. Bussy, who is in the Circars, to urge him to come on, and M. Law is with the Nawab, and urges this as a last chance for his country's superiority over us.

"But it won't do, sir—it won't do," he continued, after having taken breath; "we have him fast, sir, for his troops are discontented, the bankers are discontented, his very eunuchs are discontented, and his poor wife, who hath many friends, is groaning in a dungeon. So we have determined, all of us, to raise Meer Jaffier, who married his sister, and is one of the Royal house, to the royal seat, and we only wait Mr. Clive's movement to effect it. Of ourselves, you see, we could do nothing; but, with the army and the people on our side, we can, under God's help, assist them and ourselves at the same time, and attain a greater position than ever we had before. Our costly expenses and our losses will be paid, and there will be treasure enough to reward the army and the navy amply."

"And when is this to be, Mr. Watts? Surely you are not safe—I had better remain with you?"

"Oh, I can take good care of myself," was the stout reply; "and my native friends, Juggut Seit and many others, will get me away when the time comes. No, sir, the Colonel will want you more than me; and I must send you off—this very night, too—if possible. You must take the despatches I have for him, and tell him to hurry on. He will be at Cutwah, I am sure, if he have not advanced. Meer Jaffier was to meet him there, but I fear he dare not take the plunge. It is we—it is Mr. Clive, sir, God bless him!—that must show the way. All I fear is, that Omichund—you remember him, Mr. Smithson—may betray us at last, as he hath often threatened, and would do to-morrow if he could get as much from the Nawab as he expects from us; but I think," he added, with a wink, "that Mr. Clive has satisfied him, though the deed he holds will prove to be so much waste paper. The old fox; he would serve us a scurvy trick, sir, if he could, and we can only check his rascality. 'Tis as pretty a game of chess, sir, as ever was played, and one that will be famous in history, I think; but Omichund risks too much, Mr. Smithson, for he knows that if he did cheat Mr. Clive he would be hung up as high as Haman. I am ready to start at a moment's notice: all the treasure and valuables have been sent on: but you must precede me and make the best of your way. I have promised the boatmen five hundred rupees if they take you safely, and they'll do it. Now, I pray you, excuse me while I make up Mr. Clive's packets. By midnight you shall start, and in a few days you will be safe among our people. The Nawab's army is assembling at Plassey; but it's no use, Mr. Smithson—they won't fight as they did at Calcutta, and Mr. Clive will thrash them easily. Now, sir, you must take care of yourself. I will not be long."

Mr. Watts was as good as his word. After a pleasant evening, in which he heard details of all the varying intrigues, and the moves and counter moves, as Mr. Watts called them, on the political chess-board, Ralph Smithson was conducted to the boat which was ready for his reception. He found that a native servant, abundance of supplies, and a comfortable bed, had been provided for him; and, bidding his host farewell, was soon bounding over the wavelets of the broad river, before a hot but freshening breeze.

CHAPTER LIV.

THE EVE OF PLASSEY.

I MUST pass over the happy meeting with Mr. Clive and many an old friend—it can be imagined perhaps better than described; and the joy of Cassim as he once more beheld his master's bronzed and bearded face was boundless. It is not easy to portray emotions which, at the same moment, have varied effects upon so many different people. Strange to relate, Ralph Smithson's appearance was, after all, no sudden surprise, for Mr. Watts had arrived in camp a few hours before him. On the morning of the night on which Ralph left his hospitable host, Mr. Watts found he could no longer remain at the Factory. The Nawab, suspicious and evil-minded, had suspected treachery, and was determined to revenge himself on one, at least, of the supposed authors of it. Dark hints had fallen from Omichund. Meer Jaffier, the commander of his army, had attended the durbar that night with a stronger escort than was consistent with etiquette, and Juggut Seit the banker was reserved, if not uncivil. The Nawab drank hard, but the stronger liquor he took seemed to have no effect upon him, except to aggravate his savage humour; and he had sworn a frantic oath, that in the morning he would see one Feringi, whom he hated, writhing in agony, impaled upon a stake in the market-place, and had given orders for Mr. Watts to be brought before him manacled. I might write of this frightful scene, but I refuse to defile these pages with a record of horrible oaths and curses, and fierce despair; or of drunken raving in which the mutilated Derwesh, with a host of tortured victims, seemed to surround the miserable wretch and mock him with fearful cries. None of his attendants ever forgot the scene; nor how, without one friend left to him, Suraj-oo-Doulah cried frantically for the lost Sozun—flung his turban on the ground—and shrieked for her to come to him. But Mr. Watts, as we know, had many friends; and the order given regarding him passed in a whisper from one to another till it reached the Seit, who, apprehending real danger, sent down his best boat to the Factory with a crew on whom he could depend, and urged Mr. Watts to fly; and as the day broke that good gentleman was safe, speeding before the wind which had carried on Ralph Smithson only a few hours before. Where or how they passed each other they never knew, but when Mr. Watts reached the camp safely, he soon told the tale he had heard to the wondering ears of his countrymen; and it was only a few hours afterwards that Ralph himself appeared, and was received with cheers and welcomes which made ample amends for all his sufferings. This was on the 14th of

June; and on the 20th—that sad anniversary—I think that one very grateful and now humble heart sent up many an earnest prayer and thanksgiving to Him who, through all waywardness and trial, had brought him so far on his life's journey in safety, as he remembered the horrible prison of Calcutta, and those who had died there a year ago.

How different was it now! The missing ships had reached Calcutta, which had been left strong enough to meet any possible attack. The fleet was there, and the brave old Admiral who had shortly before written to the Nawab, "that he would raise such a flame upon the Ganges as all its waters should not quench." A flame indeed! a gallant army, three thousand devoted hearts, was marching up the river bank in array, such as the people there had never seen before, and a fleet of boats kept them company. There was no delay now. Mr. Clive saw what was in his power, and hastened to do it; and yet, when on the 21st he had reached a point at which he must cross the great river, and fight that battle on which the fate not only of Bengal but of all India depended for the future, Ralph Smithson, as many another, wondered perhaps at a temporary indecision, which has become a record in the memorable history of that campaign; and when Mr. Clive re-entered his tent, flung himself on his couch, and told his young friend how he had voted at the council of war, a feeling of bitter disappointment came over the young man, and he turned away to hide his tears.

"We cannot fail, sir—we cannot fail," he cried. "Oh, Mr. Clive, if you had heard only what I have heard from the people themselves, you would not—you could not hesitate. God is with us, sir, and for the honour of England, I, humble as I am, beseech you to go on. If Robert Clive turned back now, what would they say in England? Better, sir, that you had not done so much, than fail now, at your greatest need, to do more."

"I cannot answer you now, Ralph," he replied, sadly—"not now. Leave me to myself for a while. In this matter no one must share what I now feel. Dear to me as you are, I must be alone."

Ralph Smithson left him, and went out of the tent. It was pitched on a high bank of the noble stream, and he sat down beneath a tree growing there, and looked over to the opposite shore with wistful eyes. "May he be firm and resolute!" he cried from his heart; "may there be no deed of shame for posterity to record!" Behind him was the camp alive with merry noise and bustle; the arms were piled before the white tents, the bayonets sparkling in the sun, and the men lounging carelessly about, or gathered into groups singing—the sturdy Telingas, the active, hardy Mahrattas, so far from their dear western mountains, looking over the sacred river which it had been their envied fate to see. How many a tale of it would be told amidst the rocky crags and deep jungles of Maharashtra, when the gallant Bombay Sepoys should return! Bengal had no native army then, and it was with men as foreign to the spot they were on, as those from dear old England, that the work was to be done.

There had been a storm a few days before, and in crashing peals of thunder, and torrents of rain, the south-west monsoon had opened. Now, the sky was mottled with fleecy clouds, which sailed northwards before the soft west wind; the fierce heat had passed away, and over the grassy plain the new herbage was already springing up, clothing it in a tender and vivid green. The river was calm and still, flowing with its silent majestic current, and groups of bathers were plashing in the sacred water, or praying in adoration of its holiness. Beyond was a fair level country, palm-trees and mango groves, with fields of corn and rice, mingled with the deep green of the indigo; and villages of brown thatched huts, and here and there the white pinnacle of a Hindu temple, or the dome of a Mahomedan mosque, nestled among the giant trees, showed the abodes of men. Boats flitted to and fro, with heavy sails set, or, with the low musical chant of rowers, sped down the stream more rapidly. There was no sign of resistance beyond. With his glass, Ralph Smithson could see files of women passing to and from the river with heavy water-jars, and the ploughs and oxen of the farmers busy in the moistened fields. Sometimes the faint lowing of cattle, or the fainter echo of a call from one man to another, reached his ear; but for all he could see to the contrary, the presence of the English host seemed to be unnoticed and uncared for. I think he had fallen into a dreamy state—reviewing old times and scenes perhaps, with the sough of Melcepeth woods, and the low murmur of Coquet, sounding in his memory. It might be such a day as this 21st of June at the dear old castle, and Constance and Grover and his beloved uncle walking on the terrace, perhaps thinking and talking of him: should he ever see them again?

"What! musing, Ralph Darnell?"—Mr. Clive always called him Darnell when they were alone—"of home, I'll warrant. Ah, boy! this is a bigger stream than old Coquet, and I will give thee a penny for thy thoughts."

The tone was merry and confident, and Ralph, who had not heard his Colonel's approach, rose at once and looked into his eyes. How well he knew, and rejoiced to see, the old expression of confidence and defiance mingled. How well he remembered it when they separated before the fight at Calcutta. "Thank God!" he cried; "it is as I hoped, and you are once more yourself."

"Yes, Ralph, we shall be over there to-morrow, please the Lord!" he replied, pointing to the shore beyond; "and then those fellows at Plassey may look to themselves. Why did I doubt? And yet it is better as it is; better I should do in a calm spirit what we have to do, than in a hasty mood which hath often—too often—led me into error and danger, precipitate this inevitable crisis. Listen, Ralph! For years past this crisis hath been shaping itself in my mind, and ever present. I have felt myself urged on, impelled by an irresistible force. It seems to me as if I had often hung back, refused to obey its commands, and yet, after a struggle, made a bolder leap than ever. You are quick-witted, and have heard some of my—my—ravings, perhaps, Ralph, you thought them; but did you see beyond them?"

"I knew you would have the French beaten out of Bengal, and would not rest till it was done," said Smithson, bluntly; "and you did not hesitate about that."

"Yes, I did," returned Clive, quickly. "Had I followed up the Nawab on the 4th of February, he would have left me his guns and fled. Had I attacked the French then, we should have beaten them as we did afterwards; and yet I drivelled with that d—d Calcutta Council; but I am free of that now, my boy. Listen, Ralph! do you know why?"

"I cannot conceive, sir—it was not like you."

"Ah! so there is one that believed in me. Listen! To no mortal have I breathed what I am going to tell you now. It may savour of folly, of bombast, of raving madness; but, by God! who will do it, it is true. Why did I hesitate? Because, Ralph, this movement cannot stop here. Once our territorial power begins, it must grow. State after state, prince after prince, must disappear before us—before the might of England and her civilising power. To-morrow these native hosts will fly. I shall march on to take possession of a kingdom worth millions of treasure; and I, Robert Clive, the son of a poor lawyer of Market-Drayton, shall give it away to another, to be used for my country's good. Dare he who will receive it refuse to do what I dictate? Impossible. Therefore he is but our Viceroy, to be fashioned and directed as we please. Why, Ralph, 'tis a bigger kingdom than England, and will be as rich; and what I begin is but the beginning of the end. Others more daring than I, and more fortunate, will follow me, and our flag shall not only fly from side to side of India, but these people will be our subjects. Yes—I too have heard of the prophecy which they told thee of, and I believe it. For a hundred years? Nay, that will be but a speck in the long glorious future. I am no parson, Ralph, as thou knowest well, and should be a bad hand at preaching from a text, and this is the only one I have ever tried to preach from"—and he touched his sword—"but can we circumscribe the power of the Most High? I believe, Ralph"—and he took off his hat reverently—"that I, Robert Clive, am one humble instrument, to whose hand is committed the beginning of the end, and who can say when that may be? That's what came into my mind when I drivelled and temporised with the Calcutta Council and the Nawab—that's what I was thinking when I recorded my opinion to-day that we should not fight; and when I bade you go away just now, it was to think whether it were not a delusion of the foul fiend—and faith I believe it was! The council of war wouldn't fight, but Robert Clive will, and, with God's help, gain a glorious victory. Listen to the cheers now! I did but tell Mr. Walsh to go and say I had changed my mind, and we should cross at daylight—and hark! the news has spread, and listen—hurrah for King George! Let Mister Bussy look to himself. We shall have money enough to equip armies, and we will rout him out of the Circars, and stop his d—d plotting and contriving. I told them at the India House I would do all this—I must do it. But one might as well have talked to their money bags. Nor could I knock a spark of enthusiasm into that stately uncle of thine; but he shall hear of Plassey, sir—of Plassey!—and if that doesn't stir his heart within him, by Jove! I'll give him up. Come! we are wasting time. Get ye away to Kilpatrick; I will go to Coote and the 39th myself. Tell him to get every boat moored to-night, and be ready to cross at dawn. But, Ralph, I'll not hear of your coming on with us; you are weak, and have had enough of punishment."

"Oh, Colonel! Oh, Mr. Clive! you would not order me to stay! indeed, sir, I am strong—quite strong now. This last week and good cheer hath set me up. I never was heartier, nor have I a pain or ache anywhere."

"You can't use your arm yet, my boy; and it would be hard for a Darnell to keep out of the fray."

"Can't I, sir? Look here!"—and, stooping down, he seized a heavy dead branch that lay there, and whirled it about his head, so that it whistled in the air.

"Nay," said the Colonel, laughing, "if that's your weakness, I say no more. Come, in Heaven's name, and may it keep us safe."

I think no nobler picture, or one of more interesting historic truth, could be painted than the passage of the joyous English force over the Ganges the next morning; when, as the sun rose, hot and brilliant, before them out of the early mist, its light rested upon the red uniforms and glittering bayonets, the sparkling river, the crowds of strangely-shaped native boats, and the rich, lovely country around. As boatload after boatload put off—first the English soldiers, with ringing, hearty cheers; then the Sepoys, with their Hindoo cries of "Jey Gunga Mata! Clive Sahib Bahadur ke jey!"—Victory to Mother Ganges! Victory to the brave Mr. Clive!—and the hoarse "Deen! Deen! Sabit Jung Bahadur ka futteh!" of the Mussulmans, commingling, formed a scene of exciting exultation, such as no one present ever saw again, or ever forgot. Why, in our national palace of Westminster, is not this glorious scene fitly commemorated? Is there one in the annals of our country which has been followed by more momentous results to ourselves and to the millions we now govern?

By four o'clock the army had crossed, and the troops were formed in column. It was eighteen miles to Plassey, and it was one in the morning of the 23d June when they arrived before it, and rested under a grove, which formed, as it were, a fortified position, because of the high earthen mound which the original planter of the orchard had raised up as a boundary; and when pickets were thrown out, the wearied men lay down to rest.

Almost within cannon-shot was the fortified camp of the enemy. Had there been resolution enough then to have attacked the English, weary as they were when they arrived, perhaps the result might have been very different; but no one moved. The shrill horns and drums played during the night, and the torches borne by bodies of men traversing the camp, the neighing of horses, and trumpetings and roars of elephants, came fresh and clear on the night wind, and the bright smoke hung over all, as it had done at Calcutta.

Ralph Smithson could not rest. He had spread a native blanket for Clive, who lay down and slept profoundly; and to while away the time he took Cassim with him, and went to a picket, which, having a field-picce, and a few sailors to guard it, overlooked a good deal of the enemy's camp. The officer in command, wrapped in a cloak, was asleep; but several of the men were awake, and double sentries, pacing, with the usual roll of sailors, up and down before them. In reply to their challenge, "Mr. Smithson!" and the parole was sufficient.

"Mr. Smithson!" cried one of the sentries, advancing; "ye'll no' forget Drrever, surr, an' the Black Hole? Ye savit him, ye ken, surr, under the Lorrd. Bide a wee, surr, yon. A'll be relieved directly, an' a'd just like to speak a word wi' your honour."

"I am glad to hear your voice again, Drever," said Ralph. "I'm not going away. You must not speak while you are on sentry."

"A' kens that, surr," was the reply. And the men resumed their walk.

Presently they were relieved, and Drever came and lay down near Ralph.

"How strange it is that we have never met, Drever, since that night."

"Ou ay, surr; but it wuz the Lorrd's will, ye ken, that sent ye till me agin—jist the Lorrd's will. When a' got doon till the ships, a' took a bad fever, Mr. Smithson, like yersel', an' a' wuz in the hospital when ye went to Madras. Then when ye comed back a'd volunteered into the *Kent*, surr; a' wuz not comfortable aboord the merchantman, an' they rated me A.B., surr, an' sae a've missed ye. A' struve sair, surr, to get ashore wi' the men on the thurrd o' February bit they wudna take me. I was vary weak, surr, still, an' the best went. An' often a'd think of comin' and speakin' till ye, surr, and tellin' ye ma thanks, surr, for a' ye did that nicht; but the Lorrd heerd what I had to say aboot a' that an' the puir leddy, surr. Did ye hear o' her, when ye was wounded amang the blacks?"

"I hope we shall recover her, Drever. It would be strange if we all met at Calcutta to talk over that night."

"Eh, surr, but it 'id be the Lorrd's mercy. But a' sha'n't sey it, surr—a've gotten my message, a' think; and it's just that a' wanted to tell ye of."

"Nonsense!" said Ralph; "you're tired. Lie down and sleep, and you wont think of this."

"It's no' that a'm feered o' deith, surr; for, like yersel', and mair nor yersel', a've been face to face wi' him too often," he replied with a sad smile, "an' a'm quite willing, if it's to be. Bit, all the same, Mr. Smithson, a' never felt sae face to face wi' deith, an' sae near it for sure, surr, as a' did when a' comed up here this nicht. A' tou'd Jack there the same, and he laughed at mey, and sed a' wuz an auld fule—and sae a' is, Mr. Smithson; but ye won't laugh at mey."

Smithson had heard of such presentiments, and the sailor's persistence and calmness had something strange and awful in it. "No, Drever, I won't laugh at you, but we are all in the Lord's hands. Do you remember what the man cried out in the prison? I have not forgotten it."

"Nor I, Mr. Smithson; that text has been wi' me nicht and day. A' can't read, surr, bit the parson on board minded it, and towd me it wuz a' richt. An' a'll nae trubble ye, surr, mair noo; but ance before, a' axed ye aboot sendin' ma things to ma people—they're in Berwick, surr; an' there'll be some prize-money, they say, comin' till uz, an' a'thegither there'll be some guineas for a sister a' have there, or her children maybe. Her name's Mary, and she wuz marreyed upon a man—John Darling, they ca'ad him, surr, an' he's weel kenn'd in thae parts; an' there's what's been aboot my neck, surr, this mony a year, that'll gae wi' a', surr."

"Some love-token, I daresay," thought Ralph. "Well, Drever, I'll do all you wish, if needs be; but don't be downcast. Go to sleep."

"Na, na, surr; a'm nae feered, surr—only reddy; and sae gudenicht, Mr. Smithson; a'm tired, an' a'll sleep, maybe. Ye'd better rest yersel'." Smithson saw him lie down, and in a few moments he was snoring loudly.

For a time Ralph sat and watched, but there was no sign of movement in the enemy's camp, and at last he lay down. Presently sleep came heavily upon him, nor did he wake till the first cannon-shot fired on the 23d crashed through a tree above him, and the battle of Plassey had begun.

CHAPTER LV.

THE BATTLE AND THE SECRET.

But the excellent position taken up by the little army was proof against cannon-shot; and, to say the truth, whether by design or from unskilfulness, most of the cannon-balls sang over it harmlessly, or at best crashed among the tops of the thick mango-trees. Below them, soldiers, sailors, and sepoys rested in the shade, ate their cold salt junk and biscuit, or parched pease or rice and sugar; and now, entirely recovered from their fatigue, burned for the order to advance against the enemy as ardently as they had on the plain of Calcutta; but they were held in hand wisely till the time should come.

On the other side, the Nawab had arisen at his usual hour, and performed his morning prayer, with those assembled outside his tent. He was haggard, and had slept little. The night before had been passed till after midnight in the old drunken orgies, and the mimes and buffoons cried lustily for largesse, as they again represented the tragedy of the Black Hole, the windows and the scenes and contrivances for which had been brought on an elephant from the palace. This was a public representation; for hundreds of officers and men had sat with him in the tent open to the camp, and witnessed the sight. "No more of this foolery," he had said to those about him; "when we take them all to-morrow, we will set stakes in a row, and impale Sabit Jung, and Watts, Kilpatrick, and Coote, and all the Feringi heroes upon them, and see some real amusement, and then we will blow them away from guns, and have peace in the land." I think from what they saw that night in the camp, of hideous profligacy, buffoonery, and cruelty mingled, the French gentlemen present were ashamed of their protector and ally, and had a mind to give themselves up to a generous enemy—it might be their turn next.

When the guns opened on the English camp, after the morning prayer, the Nawab had mounted an elephant, and seemed to wish to lead on his army. He had said he would; but he had missed a word in his prayer—he had not had the evil eye taken off him—the royal astrologer was not to be found—and so he hung back. It was not strange that he did not see the Moulvee who daily expounded the stars, nor the Brahmin Josee, of Plassey, who had been summoned to the astrological council. They had compared notes the day before, and dared not tell the Nawab that nothing lucky appeared for him, but much the contrary. Nor dared they tell him of that curious astrological combination in which men believed till the 23d June 1857, and which has had no small effect upon what was to happen in the interim. Nor could the Nawab see his face in the jar of oil that was brought him—it was thick and cloudy. I think, therefore, when these combinations of gloomy foreboding occurred, that, in spite of the messages which came up every moment of hundreds of Feringis being slain by the cannon, which continued to thunder away for some hours, Suraj-oo-Doulah was not content.

"Bring me their heads!" he would cry aloud—"a thousand rupees, a shieldful of rupees for every head! An estate for life to him who kills Clive!"

At that time Mr. Clive was taking another quiet sleep in a hunting pavilion in the grove, for he was in no hurry to advance, and was not attacked. He well knew the Nawab's custom of sleep at noon, and he and Ralph Smithson and Mr. Coote had concocted a pretty plan of dashing out on the enemy's camp as soon as it was quiet, and so routing it. One gentleman who, thinking he had found a rare opportunity to charge, began an attack of his own, was recalled, and roughly enough reprimanded. Perhaps Mr. Clive was waiting to be joined by Meer Jaffier ere he advanced; and large bodies of horse, which were careering about, with which that nobleman was known to be, were objects of suspicion all the morning. Some had even charged, but the black cavalry, as the men called them, went to the right-about pretty sharply, and fled away when a few rounds of shot and grape fell among them, and some officers fell, and some score of saddles were emptied. Ralph Smithson saw no Rohillas: Sozun therefore was not there. Every moment, as he, with others, looked over the bank, he expected to see a rush of his old blue-coated friends, or to hear the quick monotonous beat of their kettledrum, with their terrible war-cry, as they threw themselves recklessly against the position. But they never appeared; and, except a few stray shots, there was at noon the old strange silence, and Suraj-oo-Doulah slept.

Then in his turn, Mr. Clive arose refreshed, and repairing to the bank, gave a few orders, which were at once carried out. As he used to say afterwards, "he sent his first compliments to his friends the Messieurs," some forty of whom were posted with guns on a knoll; but it does not appear by the record that these gentlemen had much stomach for close acquaintance with bayonets and boarding-pikes, and so cried for quarter, which was given; and as a similar party of men had been sent to an angle of the native camp, which was incontinently stormed, and they entered the entrenchment with the soldiers whom they had driven back, a general flight began, and was vigorously maintained.

Then Colonel Clive led out his main body, and charged up, shouting for King George, and "if there had been a doubt in any of the fellows' minds," as he would say, "by George! sir, they made 'em up so sharp, that though we followed 'em six miles, and killed what we could, they had the heels of us, and we got all their forty pieces of cannon, and their stores, and hackeries, and tents, and gun-bullocks. In short, sir, we were set up altogether, without paying a penny for any of it, and, by God's mercy, lost but few men after all."

Presently, too, a message came from Meer Jaffier—whom, not very well knowing friends from foes, they had not allowed to approach—that he would wait upon the "Colonel Sahib" in the evening if he might; and a gracious answer having been accorded thereto, our brave Colonel and the other gentlemen did what they could to stay plundering and to rout the enemy. Does it not, however, seem wonderful, that when that small host appeared on the bank, some at least of the thirty-five thousand foot, and fifteen thousand horse, every man of which was as good as his own sepoys, did not turn on Mr. Clive, and try to save their honour?—or that a few horsemen did not rally about their Prince, and bear him away with a show of deliberation and respect? Had he not pampered them all, and bestowed ample largesse upon them? Had they not vaunted of the heads they would bring him?—and yet there was not one who went nigh him!

Not one! As the Nawab, dismounting from the elephant, went into his tent, there was nothing to show of the victory he heard of—not even one white-faced prisoner! "The Nawab is sleeping!—Khamôsh!—silence!" was passed through the camp. Did he think Clive would wait while he slept? He ate a slight meal and lay down, but he could not sleep. Juma was once more there, kneeling beside him, kneading his master's legs and arms, while another rubbed his feet.

"All is strangely quiet," said the Nawab. "Even the English are not firing. Have they fled?"

"My lord's enemies dare not fire while he sleeps. It was the same when Calcutta was taken. They respected my Prince's rest, as they do now," was the reply. "Inshalla! my lord will see a pile of heads before evening"—and the "Please God" was echoed by all present.

The Nawab sighed as he turned wearily. After all, he was too anxious to sleep, or, if he dozed at all, it was fitfully; starting up at every distant shot, and shivering as if at some inward fear so greatly, that Juma threw a shawl over him, hot as it was, and saw him drag it over his head and cower down beneath its folds. Even that did not spare what was to follow. Suddenly there broke forth a spattering fire of matchlocks, and two guns were fired in quick succession; then came sound of a heavy volley fired at once—another, and another, followed by a ringing cheer. He knew the sound of old, and it struck chill at his heart, as it has at the hearts of many another before and since in that land. Again he started up, and as he sat there with open mouth and staring eyes, one rushed into the tent, which it had been death otherwise to approach, and cried, in a voice of terror—

"Fly, O Prince!—the Feringis are upon us! Save thyself!—not a man stands, and there is treachery!—treachery! Fly, ere they are upon the tent!"

"He would kill me!—Clive would impale me!" cried the wretched being. "Save me, Juma!—Sidi—Sadoc—where are ye?"

All had abandoned him already. Twisting a scarf hastily round his head, and a shawl round his waist, Suraj-oo-Doulah fled out into the camp. A camel-rider, who had arrived with a message from the palace, was just about to mount. He saw his Prince, and stood aside respectfully. "Take the camel," he said, putting the nose-rope into his hand; "he is fast and sure; he will go at speed, and my lord might carry a cup of water in his hand without spilling a drop. Quick!—the Feringis are yonder. Look!"

There was no need to look. Suraj-oo-Doulah threw himself upon the beast, settled his feet in the stirrups as it rose heavily, and in a moment sped away faster than a horse could gallop.

"Please, sir, said a sailor, advancing with a bloody cutlass in his hand, touching his cap, "I think you're Mr. Smithson, as Drever was speaking to last night at the picket, aren't you, sir?"

"Yes, I am Mr. Smithson. What do you want?—be quick, and don't stop me now. Can't Drever wait?"

"Please, sir, don't hurry on. He's badly hit in the breast, and we've laid him under a bush yonder. He's asking for you, and says you promised him. I don't think, sir, he'll live more nor a few minutes, so I made bold to stop and ax your honour; and if you'd only come to the poor chap, sir, it'd be a comfort to him—its something on his mind, sir—and I'm his comrade, Mr. Smithson; but it's you he wants. He won't tell me what it is. Stay by him till I fetch the doctor. Maybe I shouldn't hear—"

Ralph Smithson had turned when the sailor had accosted him, and heard the rest of his speech as a sort of accompaniment, as he walked in the direction pointed out. He was much shocked by the news, and the old sailor's request came instantly to his mind. There was no doubt of the truth. The white pinched face, the blue lips, and scarcely a stain of blood on the shirt, told an unmistakable tale of death, not far off.

"Drever, my poor fellow!" said Ralph, kneeling down by him, "I am sorry to see you thus."

The dying man opened his eyes faintly, and grasped the young man's hand.

"Ay, surr; a' tou'd ye sae—last nicht the Lord was nigh me, an' a' sed, a' sed, O ma Lord! a'm reddy to come, ye ken; an' a'm goin', surr—goin' noo; a' was sure it wud be sae, and a' tou'd Jack here. Dinna greet, Jack, ma lad, ye'll ha'e to come ane day yersel', an' a' wish ye then as weel as a'am noo. Deed, surr, an' a'm in no pain—only fleein' awey, an' the bluid's chokin' me; but a'll tell ye a' a' ken o' this here, an' ye'll mind it, surr, for the Darnells' sake; them's gran' folk in ma ain dear country, surr—the Barrnit, Surr Geoffrey, an' a' surr. Will ye gi'e me some water, Jack?"

Darnells! The name rang in the ear of the listener like the sound of a great trumpet. What did the man lying there know about the Darnells? was that thing, hanging at the man's heart, dabbled with his blood—"Drink, Drever!" he cried eagerly, holding his flask to the mouth of the dying man—"drink, for God's sake! I am a Darnell—I am Ralph Darnell."

"Ay, it's gude stuff, surr, sure, an' it's givin' me mair strength. Lift me up a wee, surr. What did ye say? Some one sed Darnell!" he cried, wildly; "wha sed that?"

"I said it, Drever—look at me."

Ralph's eyes were brimming with tears, and his nostril and lip were quivering in the agitation which possessed him.

"Eh, surr! a' mind noo. A' thocht sae wanst afore, when we was amang the deid; but I went off into a dwa'm, surr, an' it passed away. Was Henry Darnell yer faither?"

"He was—he was!" cried the young man, eagerly. "Oh, if you know— O God! give him but life to tell me!"

"A'll tell ye a' I know, surr; but a'm bad, surr—just bad, an' it's a sair tale—the Lord help me to tell it. We wuz at Warkworth, ye ken; it's mony a year syne, surr, noo—nae matter—an' Mister Henry, he sezs to me ane fine summer day—'Drever,' sezs he, 'we'll tak' the lassie a braw sail the day'—that's Miss Grracie, ye ken, surr—Grracie Smithson they caa'd her; an' she cam' on boord the lugger, surr—bonnie and beautiful she wuz; an' we sailed awey, an' they landed at a place nigh till Lamberton Pike, an' went ashore, an' cam' back, they sed, man and wife. Bit the lassie, surr," he continued after a pause, "frretted sair, Mr. Smithson, an' sed she'd been marryet by no parson, surr, an' nae God's words had been prayed ower hurr, and she flyted an' worried sair, and sat on the deck a' nicht; an' it was a braw, warm, summer nicht—a' mind that weel—an' nae wind. An' in the morn', we wuz nigh the Farn Islands. Did ye iver see the Farn? Eh my! bit she grreeted sair, surr. An' she sez, 'Henry, my darlin', is there no church nigh? There's Bamborough, will ye no gang till it, an' will ye no tak' your Gracie?' An' Mister Henry, surr, he put aboot the boat and tried hard, but the tide was running strong agin hurr, an' we couldna mak' way, surr, an' a' pit the helm up, an' we ran in to a place they ca' North Sunderland; a few bit cabins there wuz there; and they got a light cart frae ane Rrobert Arrmstrrong—a wild chap he wuz—an' Mister Henry, surr, said they'd gae away to a place they ca' Luckur—a wee bit churchie there is there, an' a' mind it weel—an' a' seed them nae mair till the evenin'; and when they cam' back, the light o' luve was in hurr bonnie een, and she showed me the paper. Eh, surr! bit a'm goin' fast; can ye no gi'e mey a drap mair?"

Ralph Smithson's hand was trembling violently as he put the flask once more to the man's mouth, and poured in the wine, which could hardly be swallowed now.

"It's no much mair, surr, as a' has to say," continued Drever, now very feebly. "'We'll go over the water, Gracie,' sez Mister Henry; an' we sailed away strraight for Holland, an' they lived there a year maybe, and a bairn was borrn, and the mither flyted sair for hame: an' Mister Henry an' she went back, an' left it wi' Smithson, for they couldna live wi' him, an' sae they left Warkworth. An' when we got nigh back, a terrible squall took uz—we had aal sail set—an' the lugger, surr, she went over on her side afore we could loose the sheets, an' a' I seed, surr, was the sweet bonnie face at the companion, an' the wee silk bag in her hand, an' she cryin' oot; an' God help me! but a' niver has lost that white face since; whiles it comes up till me, an' I hear the sair cry; bit the waves drownded it, an' I niver seed hurr nae mair—nae mair.

"A' wuz a fine lad to swim, Mr. Smithson, an' a' soon got oot o' the swirrl, and lookit aboot mey, an' a' seed a wee little rreid bag floatin'—a' had seed it afore, surr; for when she'd think naebody'd be lookin', she'd tak it oot an' kiss it, an' pit it away at hurr heart agin—an' a' made a grab at it, an' caught it, an' a' minded to tak' it to auld Smithson or the puir auld mither; bit a' niver got there, surr, niver mair—niver mair! A' wuz pressed aboord a Dutch Indiaman, an' sent to the Injies, and sae years ha'e past an' it's—it's —in the bag, surr, aboot mey neck—"

"Darnell!" he cried, after a choking pause—"Darnell! Ye sed ye wuz a Darnell! Will ye gi'e what's here to—to—the barrnit? Lorrd save me! are ye the child? Eh! bit that's Mister Harry's ain face. Mister—Harry—" and the sufferer fell back as a torrent of blood gushed from his mouth.

Ralph Smithson could not speak; he held up the fainting head, and saw the dim eyes were fast glazing in death, and he bent down his ear to catch the last dying words.

"The man . . . in the prison . . . surr, the man, he said—he said . . . 'He that goeth on his' . . . a' dinna mind it noo; would ye . . ."

"'He that goeth on his way weeping, and beareth good seed, shall doubtless come again with joy,'" said Ralph devoutly, with a trembling voice.

"Ay—wi' joy, wi' joy; but there's anither—anither—'Them that . . .'"

"'They that sow in tears shall reap in joy.'"

"Ay, that's it . . . that's it: whar are ye, surr—nigh mey? that's it! an' a' thank . . . a' thank . . . the Lorrd!"

It was the last feeble effort, and, with a few slight struggles, the head soon after sank back on Ralph's shoulder, into its last awful sleep. When he looked round he was alone, and the tumult of the fight passing on into the far distance; but the bag, which had lain so long at the poor sailor's heart, was in his hand; what would it reveal? Reverently he closed the eyes of the dead, and, kneeling there by the body, thanked God for a spirit gone to its rest in peace, and prayed for help to guide him in the dim future.

"I am afraid, Mr. Smithson, I'm too late. Ah, I see he's gone, poor fellow," said a naval surgeon who came up with the sailor. "I could have done nothing."

CHAPTER LVI.

PURSUIT AND ESCAPE.

"*I certify that Henry Darnell and Grace Smithson were married by me this day.*

"JEREMIAH JOHNSTON, *Clerk.*

"LUCKER, *14th July* 1734."

This was what met Ralph Smithson's eyes as he watched, with a beating heart, Mr. Clive open the bag of which he had so strangely become possessed. Poor Drever had truly kept it safely. There had been a cover of canvas smeared with pitch sewn over it, and this again was protected by oilskin. As both were removed, the little red bag came out, stained with salt water, but fresh in colour: the same red bag which his poor mother had taken from her heart and held in her hand at the cabin door when the lugger was sinking under her, and she was seen "nae mair." Ralph had sought Mr. Clive directly, but it was not till they returned to the tent in camp late in the evening, that the precious packet could be opened. Ralph had no friend but this one to whom he could trust his secret, if indeed this disclosed any, and till the cover was removed, perhaps Mr. Clive might have doubted that he had to see anything important. When, however, Ralph had withdrawn the silk bag from its cover, and strove with trembling fingers, and eyes blinded with tears, to untie the knot in the cord which was drawn tightly over the mouth—

the Colonel, I think, forgot the great victory he had gained, and felt his eyes prick as if tears were coming into them.

"Let me try, Ralph," he said kindly, "I'm cooler than you. There, that's loose: ah! another bag—and sewn up too!"

A little white satin bag, and the word "Henry" marked on it with red silk in neat sampler-stitch. The white satin was yellow with age, and stained with the colour of the rep silk; but the letters were as clear as the day they had been worked.

Very carefully and minutely did Mr. Clive cut the stitches which had closed the mouth of the bag, and drew from it a paper, yellow also, and stained, and with the ink run and blurred by the salt water, but still quite legible; and as he opened it out, smoothing it gently on the table with his hand, he read what I have written at the beginning of this chapter.

"Thank God!" cried Ralph, with a great sigh of relief, as he heard the words—I think he dared not look at them yet. "Oh, sir, my poor mother *was* married! Thank God! and I'm not—I'm not—"

"And you're heir of Melcepeth, Ralph, and so God bless you! Why, 'tis a romance! you and that poor fellow— 'Gad! I must drink your health, by Jove!" And so he did, pouring out half a tumbler of old Madeira and draining it off.

Was it true—was this paper ever true, or was it only another of the hideous delusions and mockeries of his life? I do not think the young man's feelings could assume any definite form, as, taking the paper Mr. Clive handed to him, he in turn read that simple record. "Is it true?" he said aloud, dreamily, passing his hand across his eyes.

"True, Ralph! of course it's true; there's the parson's signature—and a bold rough hand it is; simply writ enough, too, by Jove! by some Puritan parson. Jeremiah! why it smells of a snuffle, by Gad! After all, what does a man want more than that I, M., took thee, N.; and faith I believe that my wife has gotten no more proof of me. But stay, this must be certified, and we must not delay about that; who knows who might not say thou hadst invented it? Faith! any d—d lawyer might say what he pleased—get me some paper;" and Mr. Clive wrote in his neat, clear hand—

"*I, Robert Clive, Colonel, do hereby certify that the marriage certificate of Henry Darnell and Grace Smithson, signed Jeremiah Johnston, Clerk, was found in a bag upon the body of John Drever, A.B., of his Majesty's ship* Kent, *killed this day in action at Plassey, in Bengal, as witness my hand this twenty-third day of June* 1757."

"There, Ralph, I think that will satisfy the cunningest pettifogger in London, and I'll get Walsh to witness it—he needn't know what it's about. Now put up those things, for there's no saying who may come in; and don't be a goose, Ralph—why, thou'rt shaking as if thou hadst an ague fit—here, drink this"—and in truth the generous wine did good service.

"I'll replace all just as they were," he said, as he looked reverently upon the precious relics, "and I won't open them till—till—"

"Till you get to Roger Darnell again, and take steps to have the certificate proved at Lucker—Lucker! where is it?"

"Oh, I know it well, sir—a little bit of a church not far from Bamborough."

"And the sooner you get there the better. By George! you're just the fellow to take home the despatches, and we'll give you a provisional commission as captain as soon as possible—no one has earned reward better; and I won't have the responsibility of keeping you a day longer than I can help. Mind you don't lose that thing."

"Indeed I won't, sir—I'll keep it about my neck just as it is, till I can show it to my uncle; and oh, sir, if you will only let me go! if I hadn't got this I would never have left you."

"I am sure you wouldn't, Ralph—but hush! here is Mr. Walsh. Please to sign this as witness that it is my hand," said the Colonel to that gentleman—"it is not necessary you should know the contents—'tis a private matter of my own."

When he had signed the paper, Mr. Walsh said, "Somebody had better go on to the Factory and the city, sir; Meer Jaffier tells me he will send some horsemen on whom he can depend; and indeed, sir, 'tis only the having to receive the offerings of the army that delays him."

"I think you had better go yourself, Walsh—and here is Smithson, who will perhaps go with you—it'll do you good," he whispered, "and you may save that poor creature."

Perhaps it was only the agitation caused by what we know to have happened, which had left Ralph Smithson's faculties in a state of utter confusion and amazement, in which hopes, fears, prayers, and memories were strangely confused—which had caused him to forget, for those few hours, the fate of her in whom he was so deeply interested; and with the victory, the first thought had been how she could be saved. Would he be permitted to go on, in advance? and thus the offer of his friend was gratefully accepted.

"Make your preparations, then," said the Colonel, "and start as soon as you can; you had best ride by night, and come to me for last orders;" and the young men, who had already contracted a strong intimacy, left the tent joyfully together, and were soon ready. Their native servants could accompany them mounted, the last orders to have the treasury protected were given, and before Meer Jaffier and his cortege had arrived in camp, the heavy escort he had sent, led by the two friends and a guide from Plassey, were already some miles on their journey.

. . . .

When the miserable Suraj-oo-Doulah fled from his tent as Colonel Clive was storming through his camp, he had no companion. The camel-rider who had given his good beast to his master, tried to catch another to follow him, but in vain; and among the crowd of fugitives who fled by the road track, over fields, and dispersed among the surrounding villages, the Nawab found no companion, and desired none. Whom could he trust now? It were better to conceal himself; if he were discovered and seized, he well knew his fate, and shuddered at the prospect of what it would be. If he could only escape to Lucknow, to Delhi, to M. Bussy in the Circars—he might enlist partisans, and try the fortune of war; but were his brother-in-law to seize him, not even his mother could save him. "Would he were dead!—would he had never been born!" the good old Begum used to cry, as she heard of new instances of cruelty and profligacy; "what miserable fate is mine that my womb bore him!" and all these wailings were repeated to him, and he had many a time cursed her by whom they had been uttered.

No, he dared not go to her, nor could she protect him if he did. He dared not trust a eunuch or a servant—not one. His wife! Ah! she would mock him and exult over his fall; it was her turn now. The Englishwoman! Let her go; he had no anger against one so helpless. Her people would protect her. So, in the desolation of his ride that night—now stumbling through muddy rivulets, now wandering in the fields to avoid stragglers, now trusting to the instinct of his beast, which, unguided, pressed on the beaten track—the only being he remembered in whom he could trust was Sozun. She it was alone of all who could help him to escape; but she was gone far away, he believed. He had not heard of her for months past, and she was little likely to come nigh him now. He could only measure the thoughts of others by his own. Had he an enemy in his power, would he not crush him? Could he secure Clive, or Meer Jaffier, or the Seit, would they be alive an hour?

I do not think these were pleasant thoughts to the young man in his wild ride from Plassey to Moorshedabad that night; but he could not shake them off, and before morning broke the weary beast knelt down in the courtyard of the palace, and the Nawab, dismounting, let him go. He was himself utterly wearied; his limbs throbbed and ached at the unwonted exertion of that night's ride, in which nothing but the certainty of instant death, should he be taken, had sustained him. Oh that he could rest! There was no one at the guard-room except an old woman, who swept it daily, and he saw her crouching over a fire in the corner; but he avoided her and went in. Once, as a servant passed before him, he sat down, and huddled upon the ground lest he should be observed; then again rising, he went towards the eunuch's guard-room, where there was a light burning, and, raising himself on his tiptoes, looked through the arabesque tracery of the window. At first the guard-room appeared empty; but as the lamp flared up before a breath of wind, he saw Nasir sitting upon the floor, his head bent upon his knees in his usual attitude of watching, and drawing his dagger, he entered. Nasir was slight and feeble—from him at least there was no treachery to be feared. The man heard the step, rose, and took up the naked sword which lay before him, and perhaps would have struck, but his master's cry, "It is I, Nasir!—do not strike," stayed the uplifted weapon.

"It is I," he continued—"save me! I am alone and helpless," and the Nawab sank on the ground.

Perhaps for an instant, as the weapon was again raised, memories of wrongs and insults endured, rushed through the man's heart, and urged a blow for which a new Nawab would give ample reward; but with them came the feeling of devotion to one who, wayward as he was, had at least spared his life at Calcutta, and he flung down the weapon, and tried to raise his master. "She is here," he said; "and I am watching her—Sozun, the fakeerni, is here."

Sozun! There was safety in the very name, and the wretched man heard it with a cry of joy.

She was sitting at the window, we may remember, looking into the black void of gloom before her—for there were heavy clouds and no light—not, as before, decked in gorgeous raiment and jewels; but in the humble grave-clothes she always wore now, and the strings of heavy beads about her neck, out of which she had loosed one, which was passing rapidly through her fingers. No one had heard yet of the result of the fight for certain, though rumours had arrived late in the afternoon. Juggut Seit had not been improvident. As the English drums were beating through the camp at Plassey, a carrier-pigeon had been thrown up from the camp bazaar, and had reached the city before evening, whereupon the great banker had only set additional guards, and closed his house more completely; but faint rumours—how come no one could tell—began to be breathed about, and the guards about the palace, except those over the Treasury, went their way one by one and hid themselves till it should be known what master they were to serve. It was about this time that the boat which had brought Sozun from the Rohilla camp above the city rowed under the palace, and, bidding the men wait her orders, she went on into its courts. No one noticed her or stopped her, and of all the hosts of servants she found but Nasir, and bade him watch, and he had done so, as his master found him, without stirring.

Sozun feared the worst. For some days past the event had hardly been doubtful. Noor Khan and her countrymen were indifferent as to the issue. They could at least again travel westwards, and, mercenaries as they were by profession, obtain service. If Suraj-oo-Doulah were defeated, and the English desired them to stay, they had at least a friend in Ralph Smithson. When she saw the desolation of the palace, her first care was for the Begum, and to the wondering ears of the lonely women she told the tale of desertion and coming evil. The door of the underground apartments was not shut, and the women might have walked forth unimpeded; but they did not stir. They dared not encounter the risk, and so stayed on; but I can imagine how Julia Wharton grew pale and flushed by turns, and how with beating hearts the two women sat together all that night listening to every sound, and from time to time sent Anna as far as she dared to go to gain intelligence.

"You will not see me again, mother," Sozun had said to the Begum, "till I have placed him safe beyond his enemies, if indeed he come at all. If not, I will not leave you again; I will share your fate."

So they had watched all that night, where thousands of voices were wont to take up the hackneyed cry of adulation, "May long life and wealth increase!" till the Nawab came in stealthily like a thief, and cried out in a faltering voice—"Sozun, O Sozun! I die—I die! Do thou protect me, else they will kill me. Even now they follow. Listen!" and so threw himself down beside her, utterly exhausted.

Sozun did not hesitate; there was no time for rest, for food, for collecting money or jewels, except some which were in a casket in the room; or for dallying with the grim fate which she knew pursued him. "Come," she cried, seizing his hand—"come, else it will be too late, and I cannot save thee. Come—Food! Is food better than life? Rest! Will not sleep lead thee to the stake, or to be dragged at the elephant's foot? Come! No—not thou, Nasir; stay with them. If the Feringis come, take them to her, and say I sent thee. Guard the place with thy life. Come!" she cried, frantically, placing her head upon the Nawab's feet as he pleaded for rest. "Listen to the shouts—they have the news in the Bazar."

Between them they dragged the almost unconscious man to his feet, and hurried him down the private stair, along the court, and to the window above the boat which Sozun had left moored at the river bank. "Are ye ready?" she cried to the men.

"Ready," they answered. "We waited but for thee; but it will blow hard—can ye not stay?"

Stay! and the shouting became wilder! "Push off," she cried, as she helped the Prince down from the window and lead him on board, where, staggering into the little cabin, he flung himself upon the carpets she had provided, and groaned aloud. Then she spread a blanket over him and retreated to the prow of the vessel, watching the white foam dash from its sides, as with its broad sail set it sped on before the fresh west wind towards the great main branch of the Ganges.

CHAPTER LVII.

DESTINY.

As the night passed—little, indeed, had remained of it—the boat sped on; and as the waves curled before the prow falling off in sheets of foam, still Sozun sat and watched. Occasionally she heard the querulous cry of the Nawab as he called her name, begged for a softer place to rest on, or for food. What wish of his had ever been ungratified? What luxury ever denied him, or become impossible of attainment? Here dry bread would have been delicious. She did not, however, trust him alone, and would not go to him.

Day broke, and the waves curled higher and higher, as the boat rolled before the freshening gale. There was a sense of freedom in the position of the girl, as she sat on the high prow watching the porpoises chasing each other round and round the vessel, and plunging into the foam it cast aside, and a consciousness of daring which infused a new spirit into her heart. If she could only take him away in safety, far far beyond his bitter enemies, she would have done her duty. If, Ya-Allah Kureem! if only that, then no matter what followed herself—some cell of a fakeer, or a tree, or an old tomb by the river bank; or her lute and the charity of men wandering to visit holy shrines, and so pass on to her own land and be forgotten, and there forget the fierce excitement of her life.

Another querulous cry from her companion could not be resisted, and she went to him. Ah! what a face she saw—so broken, so haggard, so wan, with bloodshot eyes and uncombed hair, cowering beneath the coarse black blanket one of the boatmen had thrown over him. "Get to shore," he moaned, piteously; "O Sozun, I die!—what matter if they kill me!"

"Silence," she said, in a whisper; "I dare not come near thee—silence, else they may hear. I cannot trust them. The boat rolls, can we get to the shore?" she asked of the steersman.

"If you please, lady; but it is a fine wind, and we could get very far if you did not stop," was the reply.

"My lord is ill," she replied. "Is not that a fakeer's habitation?"

"It is," said the man, with a reverential gesture; "a holy man, whom we all worship, lives there. He tells us of fair winds and blesses the boats; and all we give him he spends in charity. Yes, we can bear up and go there;" and so, bracing up the sail, the boat heeled over to the wind and reached the shore quickly.

There was a small hut there, built of reeds and thatched with rice-straw, by the side of which were a few rude water-jars. Beside the hut rose a huge banian-tree—one of those glorious monarchs over which the revolutions of ages have passed, marking only the growth of its giant proportions. Its gaunt white arms, flung abroad to the sky, groaned and creaked as the long pendant roots swung to and fro, quivering in the rising gale, and its foliage rustled with a hoarse murmur. As the prow of the boat touched the shore, a gaunt figure, stooping low, emerged from the hut, naked, except a cloth wrapped round his loins, and a tattered black blanket thrown hastily about his shoulders. The man seemed a living skeleton, wasted by illness or perpetual vigils—one of those fearful objects which, in the guise of religious devotees, are sometimes seen and never forgotten.

The figure advanced to the boat and cried with a harsh hollow voice, "What do women here? Begone, daughter!—you have a fair wind—begone, and touch me not!"

"Bawa!" cried one of the boatmen, throwiug him a rope, "be merciful—there is one ill in the cabin, and we will rest but for an hour: fasten the rope—be quick!"

"He took the rope and tied the end to a bush as Sozun sprang on shore, and the boat swung round in calmer water. "Only for a while, father," she said, as she bent down and kissed his feet—"only for a while, and we will go on again when it is calmer."

"Who art thou," he cried, "with so fair a face, that weareth the grave-clothes of God's chosen? Come, in His name!"

"What thou seest," she said, meekly—"one who desires to live and die in a place like this. I am hungry—wilt thou give me to eat?"

"And who is with thee? A man, they said?"

"A helpless man," she said, "who is ill and faint with hunger."

"Wait!" said the fakeer; "the meal is out, and 'tis time I went to the village for more. Can he not go thither?"

"It is far," she said, "and we will wait. He could not walk so far—he is weak."

"Wait, then," he replied—"the gale is rising; bring him to the hut—he can rest there;" and, taking up a staff and wallet which lay on the ground, he strode away across the fields.

"Sozun, Sozun," cried the Nawab, "take me out of this place! it reels under me, and I am giddy and faint."

What should she do? If any one saw him he might be known,

and would be lost; but again, as she hesitated, the despairing cry came from the boat, and she saw him striving on hands and knees to crawl out of the wretched cabin through which the chill gale was blowing in fiercer gusts every moment, mingling with the hoarse cries of the boatmen busy fastening another rope to the bank.

"Help him!" she exclaimed, descending to the boat; and two of the men, taking him up, carried him to her.

"Thou art cold," she said, "but there are the blankets, and the old man said we might shelter thee within. Come, he has gone for food, and we must wait."

There was a rude bed in the hut. The boatmen brought up a carpet and covering, and the miserable Nawab lay down and sank beneath it, cowering at the blast, which whistled through the reed walls of the poor dwelling. "Do not leave me, Sozun," he said piteously; "whom have I now but thee?"

"I will not leave thee," she replied, drawing the blanket more closely about him. "He will return soon with food—sleep, we are safe here;" and she sat there by him silently. How long, she did not know. Time is slow in passing in any great need; but he seemed to sleep—that was enough.

Suddenly the door of the hut was darkened, and the gaunt figure stooped and entered. "I have brought food, daughter," he cried, "ready to be eaten. Let him sit up and eat."

As the hoarse tones of the old man's voice reached the ear of the Nawab, Sozun saw him cower more deeply under the covering above him, trembling violently. In another moment, as if it had stifled him, he threw it aside and sat up with a face in which horror and fear were frightfully combined. "The Derwesh!" he shrieked. "Oh save me!—Oh save me! Mercy, mercy!"

"Dohai Feringi!" cried the Derwesh, at once seizing the shivering man with an iron grasp. "Dohai Feringi! Suraj-oo-Doulah! dost thou remember this?" and he tore down his matted hair, which spread itself over his gaunt shoulders. "Dost thou remember these?" and raising his hair alternately on both sides, he showed the white cicatrices of his mutilation. "Dost thou remember the durbar and the Derwesh? I am he!"

The Nawab struggled to free himself, but what was his power to resist those lean, nervous fingers, clutching his throat?

"Kaffir!" cried the Derwesh between his closed teeth, "be still, else I will strangle thee. Allah hath given thee into my hand, and will do justice! Thy days of iniquity are full, and thou shalt die; but not by my hand. "Ho! without! who are there?" he cried to several men, who, attracted to the spot by the arrival of the boat, were talking to the boatmen. "Come in quickly, and bind him—bind him fast!"

As he spoke, several men crowded in, and in an instant Suraj-oo-Doulah was bound tightly with a turban, and lay on the bed as if dead.

"You have killed him!" cried Sozun, who had vainly endeavoured to wrest away the hands of the Derwesh. "Oh, spare him! let him go if he be alive—in the name of the Most Merciful."

"Peace!" cried the Derwesh, "oh shameless! Thou in the garb of holy saints, to be in his company! Bind her, friends; she is one of his wantons. Let them die together!"

"We have bound him fast," cried one of the sturdy villagers—"fast enough. Who is he, Bawa?"

"Who is he? The tyrant; he who hath robbed ye of your sisters—who hath ground ye to poverty by his extortions—whom the Feringis pursue, and for whom ye will receive plenteous reward at the city."

"The Nawab!" cried the men, starting back with amazement.

"Ay, the Nawab, friends—look at him! Very different is he now from when these ears were laid before him in his power of evil. Look at him—do ye doubt? Away with him—away with him! Take him up—I will accompany ye to the durbar; the Feringis will do me justice. Dohai Feringi!"

"Away with them! We will do your bidding, Baba," cried a burly fellow, taking up the Nawab as he would a child, and passing out. "Bring on the woman, some of ye."

"I will not run away—I will follow him," said Sozun, sobbing piteously. "I am but a weak woman. Loose my arms, for they hurt me sorely."

"Well, it's no matter about a woman, said one of the men, good-naturedly, loosing her bonds. "Come with us, quick! see, they are already far off." And when they went out of the hut she saw the men bearing the almost lifeless body of the Nawab across the fields to the village, and the Derwesh striding before them flinging his arms into the air, while the wild cry of "Dohai Feringi! justice, O Feringi!" came fitfully through the roar of the wind in the tree above her.

"It is his fate," she said, "but I will not desert him. Lead on," and she followed with a heavy heart, weeping.

About the same time that morning, Ralph Smithson and his companion reached the city. They had ridden all night, and as the day broke, the fresh air and rising breeze had refreshed them, and the horses they rode stepped out at a brisk pace. "We shall soon be there," said the leader of the escort, "and my lords can do as they please then; they are our protectors, and we are ready to serve our master's friends faithfully." It caused both the young men to marvel much, as they conversed together, how men they believed enemies yesterday, could be so soon changed into devoted servants; but the Jemadar of horse was no deceiver. The gentlemen had been committed to his care; the English were their deliverers from much tyranny and disquiet; and as the cavalcade passed along, grey-bearded men met them at villages, offered flowers and milk, and bowed before them as conquerors.

As to Ralph Smithson, I should fail utterly were I to attempt to depict his feelings that day. All the uncertainty which had hung over him hitherto had passed away as in a dream, and was already fading before the glorious reality which had dawned upon him. Once more he could take his place among his own people: and his thoughts painted rapidly bright pictures of the joy of his uncles, of dear Constance's and Grover's sweet congratulations, and of his grandfather's joy and comfort in his declining years. Ah, it was almost too much to believe true. Then to rescue Julia Wharton from her wretched condition would be an act of mercy and happiness fitting for such a day, when not a cloud rested upon him.

"The first thing we have to do is to see after the Treasury, Mr. Smithson; you will remember the colonel's orders? These fellows appear very faithful, and we will put them there as a guard. I only hope we may be in time to prevent plundering. What do you think, Jemadar Sahib? is the Treasury safe?"

"My lord need not fear," said the man. "You see we have passed no one, and no one has gone before us; all our people will collect round the new Nawab at once, and there is no fear. The guard over the Treasury is one of hereditary soldiers, who only know the head of the state and their own duties. If Suraj-oo-Doulah were to ask them for ten rupees to-day, he would not get it. But you will soon see; there is the city. Look! there are the minarets, and the Nawab's palace."

"Will the Nawab, Suraj-oo-Doulah, be there?" asked Ralph Smithson. "If so, he may oppose our entrance, and we must take him if we can."

"Suraj-oo-Doulah will be mad if he has tarried there," said the man; "and if even he be there, no one will resist. I know Nasir, the eunuch; he will let you in. But there are women there," continued the man, doubtingly—"they should be honourably treated."

"Their honour is our own—they are our sisters and mothers," said Mr. Walsh. "Is it not so, Smithson? Tell him so."

"They are indeed," was the reply. "Fear not, sir; we have no war against women: but there is one there who must come away."

"Ah! yes," replied the man—"one of your own people, sir. I had been afraid to mention her; and we have all pitied her sad fate. I thank God she will be among ye once more."

And thus conversing, the time and distance were soon passed; and the friends and their escort—traversing the streets of the city with some difficulty through the crowds of joyous people, who welcomed them with shouts, and threw over them garlands of flowers—drew rein in the outer court of the palace. No one was there; and the native officer, dismounting with them, went on to the eunuch's guard-room, and, calling to him by name, Nasir answered the summons, and came out.

"She told me to wait here, and take you to her," said the man, humbly; "I am ready to obey my lord's orders, if you are he who should come."

"She! Who?"

"Sozun, the Affghan girl," he replied; "she was here at night, but she left with the Nawab when he fled."

"I can't go with you, Smithson," said Mr. Walsh; "I must see after the Treasury at once. It is close by they say; you will find me there."

"Lead on," said Ralph to the eunuch, as his companion left him; and I may be believed when I write that his heart was beating very wildly.

Since the Nawab had left the palace for Plassey, the two women in the chambers underground had taken little rest. Different feelings agitated each; both might be freed, and yet how differently! So long as the Nawab lived and was in power, both were hopeless, and the dreary days of the hot weather, without employment, without change, had been passed wearily by Julia Wharton. The Begum's occupation of embroidery was taken up by her, and this was helped out by chess, and whatever else could be resorted to to pass time; but after all those were weary days—very weary; and yet she thanked God it was not as it had used to be, when treasures were laid at her feet only to be spurned—a hideous time, over the remembrance of which many a shudder passed. It was strange, however, how the women grew to each other by a common misfortune, and affecting, too, to see the little indulgences the Begum denied herself, so that her companion might be happy; or if she ailed aught, how lovingly she was tended by her. If Julia could have learned more of her beautiful companion's language, their intercourse would have led to more active sympathy; but Anna had after all to be the general interpreter, and I fear her rendering of the graceful, courtly Hindee of the Begum on the one hand, and the vigorous English of the Englishwoman on the other, did not help either much.

What would the issue be?—would her countrymen be victorious? I believe Julia Wharton never doubted that for a moment; and when they heard that the English were at last at Plassey, her joy was unbounded. "You will see my people—my brave, beautiful people," she said, "and will love them; and when Sozun came so strangely and told Julia how Ralph Smithson had been saved by her, had gone to Clive, and was with him—how, as she thought, he would surely come and deliver her himself, as she should tell Nasir he would—I am sure the poor soul was wellnigh distraught at the joy which seemed so near, and yet might be so cruelly blighted. That night the women slept not; they sat with their arms twined round each other on their carpet scarcely speaking a word, and sending Anna as often as they dared for news; but none came. There seemed a strange stillness in the palace, for which they could not account, till Sozun appeared once more and told them every one had left, and that she dared only remain till daylight, and so they only grew the more and more anxious.

Then Nasir came again and said the Nawab had been defeated, and the English were following him. He had arrived and gone away in Sozun's boat, and the thankfulness of both those hearts was poured forth in prayer. What might not the tyrant have done had any fit of rage possessed him? But we know, though they did not then, that he was already sunk too low for that; and Nasir again left them, and said he would watch outside till morning—and they were once more alone.

Day broke, and its dull light came slowly through the grated windows of the vault; still no one visited them, not even Nasir. Should he fail after all, and leave them like the others? Julia could not rest. Every morning for hours she had paced that chamber, and now her movements were rapid and capricious. She drew the bed to the wall, mounted on it, and tried to look out: but all she could see or hear was the grey sky, with clouds hurrying over it, and the murmur of the trees; and again she descended, sat down, rose, listened, and held her hand to her heart to still its beating. The Nawab was defeated, and the English were following—that at least she understood. Oh, there was no doubt they would come!

"You should be patient, sister," said the Begum. "If it is the will of God, they will come. Sit down and rest."

Rest!—impossible. She would soon hear a bugle-call—the dear old drums and fifes playing a merry English tune, and the cheers of the men as they marched through the town. Rest! When the cries began in earnest, the roar of the people greeting her friends penetrated that chamber! How could she rest? Then came a dull tramp of horse, and sounds of native welcomes, of troops calling to each other in the court, and confused murmurs.

"It must be Meer Jaffier," cried the Begum, with exultation; "and I shall go to my mother. My mother!—to see her with these weary eyes—O Beneficent!"

Presently, as they listened, they heard steps descending the stair. There were two sounds; one, the habitual shuffle of Nasir, which they knew so well, the other, the strong tread of a heavy nailed boot. Julia tried to spring to the door, but she could not; she felt sick and faint from excitement, and crouched down. Then the door opened, and Nasir said, "They are here, my lord;" and a tall figure advanced, holding out its hands in the gloom, but did not speak.

"Ralph!—Ralph Smithson!" cried Julia, rising and throwing herself on his neck. "My saviour!—my—"

She could say no more. He felt her panting against him and trying to swallow, and he held her to his heart more closely.

"Julia, you are saved!—saved!" he cried. "Let us thank God for this." And they knelt down together.

"And this is she of whom Sozun told me?" he said, as they arose. "Lady, I thank thee for all thy kindness to her; but for thee she had died."

"Nay, but not me, sir. Thank Him who hath watched over us both."

The voice was inexpressibly sweet and low, and as Ralph Smithson's eyes grew more accustomed to the light, it was difficult for him to remove them from a face in which so much beauty, resignation, and tenderness were combined.

"Come," he said, "not here—not here, would I see you. Come up into the blessed light of day, both of you. There is no reserve before me lady. Am I not her brother?" And they followed him.

CHAPTER LVIII.

THE NAWAB'S LAST MARCH.

"I AM not fit to look on; you must loathe me, Ralph," said Julia Wharton, as they reached the light, open apartment to which the eunuch led them, and she turned away from him with a gesture of despair. "May God pardon me, for I was very helpless. Can I be forgiven?"

She was pale from long confinement, but perhaps more beautiful than ever; and the strange Mahomedan costume in which she was dressed, increased, if possible, the peculiar charm of her features, while it displayed her graceful figure to the greatest advantage. Her health, strange to say, had been good; and except in the delicate pallor of her face, there were no traces of the weary life she had passed. Once before, he remembered to have seen the same expression on her features, when, in her terror and jealousy, she had thrown herself on her knees before him, and besought him to aid her.

"Forgiven, Julia?" he replied. "Ah, yes! there is no bound to forgiveness prayed for and entreated as you have besought in your misery and need. And He hath heard your cry. See! I never expected to meet you again, but you are here, and have a happy life, I trust, before you."

"Oh, no, no, no!" she sobbed; "never, never--never again. All I trust is, that one so polluted may be allowed to hide away in some quiet nook of England, and be forgotten."

"Have you any friends—any relations?"

"Yes," she said; "but I could not expect them to receive me. Oh! not now, Ralph. I sometimes used to pray for death, and she yonder, my more than sister, used to rebuke me, and say my words were evil. She used to tell me to submit to my fate, and bear it patiently, because it was God's will; and if bright days came I should be grateful, and if misery, still He was great and merciful. O Ralph! I, a Christian woman, have had more blessed teaching from her than I ever had from my own people. I did not know, till I began to understand her, that her faith rested upon our common Father's mercy and pity like our own; and I fear, while I could not express my own thoughts, that my poor servant's attempts to convey them were little better. Can you thank the Begum for me? Have you enough knowledge of her language?"

I believe that Ralph did his best. He had at least acquired a fluent tongue if not a learned one, and in this respect his temporary seclusion among the Rohillas had been of incalculable advantage to him. As he had used to speak with Sozun, so he could speak with the lady before him; and I think, after the first shyness had been broken, that he even became eloquent as he detailed Julia's gratitude, and assured her of Colonel Clive's, and the thanks of all his countrymen, for her affectionate care.

"Noor-ool-Nissa!"—"A light of beauty" indeed. Scarcely eighteen perhaps, fair in face, and with a lithe gracefulness of figure, the lady before him was more lovely than he could have believed a native of India to be. There was no colour in her face, which resulted, perhaps, from her long residence in a darkened room; but in its rich creamy tints her skin was like ivory, and her dark-grey eyes, long eyelashes, and sweet mouth left nothing to be desired. Sozun was beautiful, but her wild excitable features had no charm like these, which had been despised and thrown aside ere their full beauty had been developed.

"No, no—no more," she said, as a faint blush spread itself over her cheek and forehead at Ralph's passionate encomiums; "my lord's estimation of my poor services is too great, and she has cheered me in our loneliness as much as—as— No matter, sir —may she be as happy among her people as I shall be among mine. I have many loving kinsfolk, and my husband's dear mother will protect me till, perhaps—his heart may be softened. Of all this, sir, you will be the author, and till her death—Noor-ool-Nissa will be grateful. Every night a lamp will be lighted in your name, and before it she will pray for your prosperity and my sister's. Ah, sir! how can I part with her?"

"Not yet—not yet," cried Julia in her broken tongue; "till I leave this, I will not go from you. O Ralph! is she not beautiful!"

Julia had crept beside the lady, and thrown her white arms around her. The Begum's cheek rested upon one which was about her neck, and she seemed to nestle there, while tears, though she smiled and patted Julia's face, were fast falling from her eyes.

"To be free," she said—"to see the heavenly sky once more, to breathe the air, to hear men's voices, to look over the broad river and the open country, to see the trees and flowers!—ah, sister! these seem to me like scenes in the garden of Paradise, where the houris dwell for ever ministering to the just, who rise in the judgment and pass into bliss; and are we, so long buried in a living grave, and, under God, raised thence by him, your brother, ever to forget what he hath done? I am no flatterer, sir; but through these weary months, since she was sent to me, I have heard of that night of horror in Calcutta, and prayed I might see him who had saved her. Enough for me that this hath been granted, and that I can go into my seclusion with the memory of the face of one so brave and constant lying at my heart."

I think Ralph Smithson would willingly have lingered in that sweet company, but there was much to be done which he could not neglect. By this time some of the women-servants had returned to the palace; a suite of rooms in the private apartments was hastily fitted up, and for the present Julia and the Begum would remain together, till the necessary arrangements could be completed for both. Of the Nawab there was no news; and it was not possible they could experience trouble on his account.

Ralph found that Mr. Watts had followed them, and was already taking charge of the Treasury. He was well known in the city, and confidence was at once established. The revolution was in fact complete; and the presence of a few British officers prevented those scenes of licence, bloodshed, and revenge which would otherwise have ensued. Did they ever forget the superb breakfast which the head steward of the Nawab's kitchen set before them in solemn exercise of his office, and which their servants seemed weary of carrying in? or did they ever eat a meal with heartier appetite than in that pleasant garden pavilion by the river? And when Colonel Clive followed two days later, marching up leisurely with the troops, and entered the city in triumph, with the horns, pipes, gongs, and drums of native music sounding, and the dear English drums and fifes and bugles rising clear above all the din, and playing many a merry old-fashioned tune—when the people hung about him, covering him with wreaths of jessamine flowers and shouting "Victory!"—when he saw the exceeding richness of the city, the beauty of the buildings, and the evident joy of the people of all classes—he, too, thought that what he had been fighting for was no longer a doubtful myth, but a noble, heart-stirring reality. He walked through vaults full of gold and silver coin; treasure-chests were opened before him, and the torchlight flashed from caskets of precious diamonds and pearls; while piles of gorgeous shawls, fabrics of cloths of gold and silver, were more than could be counted. Had he chosen to take all, he might have done so; and in after times, when in England his countrymen accused him of venality and rapacity, he bade them remember these scenes, and wonder—as he did himself—at his moderation.

Need I pause to describe ceremonials? I think not. How Meer Jaffier refused to seat himself on the royal seat till Mr. Clive took him by the hand and led him there—how the great banker Juggut Seit entertained the English officers, and troops of dancers and singers performed before them; and even the old mummers, who now enacted the battle of Plassey, and showed how their former patron the Nawab ran away, and the victorious English followed. Or how the banker Omichund came to ask for his percentage on the plunder, and showed a white deed of promise on the part of Mr. Clive and other great contracting parties, and was told it was false, and he was to have nothing: when, as the chronicle has it, "his face became livid with rage, and he went home raving, and so remained till he died." I think if I told all this I might weary you, my patient reader, who hath kept company with me so long. I have purposely not led you into that maze of political intrigue in which Mr. Clive, as it seemed just to him then, met stratagem by stratagem, deceit by deceit, and thought all justifiable against combinations which, professing truth, he knew to be hollow and treacherous. Our countrymen in India have since learned better morality; and that, among all Asiatic people, an open, honest, direct course is not only the surest, but the only one which their subtle minds cannot comprehend or oppose, and which of itself defeats all crooked designs.

I have naught to do with Mr. Clive's justification; and I cannot comprehend how so noble a mind or so brave a man should have feared this one viper which chance had cast in his path. I say I have nothing to do with these State matters; they are far beyond the humble capacity of this tale, and have been writ in imperishable history long ago. I only hope there is enough of interest remaining in my own peculiar people, and to them I must return; in particular, to the miserable wretch who had been a prince, and whom, abject and terror-stricken after his capture, feeling that hope was already dead—we left with the rough villagers of ——poor, being borne across their corn-fields, with the old Derwesh striding before him, shrieking "Dohai Feringi! Dohai Feringi!" till he was hoarse.

Perhaps if the village elders, when he was brought to them, and in his abject terror besought their compassion, had had their own way, I think, timorous as they were, and weighing the chances of the Nawab's escape from his pitiless adversaries and restoration to his late power, they would have released him. Had this been done, he might have found his way to his friend Monsieur Law, who, with some Frenchmen and native soldiers of an ally, was marching down the Ganges bank to make a diversion against Mr. Clive; but this was not fated to be. One had mounted guard over the Nawab who could not be defied, and would not be cajoled—whose worst passions of revenge had rendered him alike deaf to entreaty and to greed of gain. Once only did the elders plead for the wretch before them.

"Listen to him, O Seyn!" said one of the village council, who was a rich Mahomedan farmer, to the Derwesh. "He promises a mosque; he will endow it with lands. He will build it where thy hut is, and there shall be a serai for weary travellers to rest in. He will make thee chief of the charity, and thou shalt dispense his bounty, and find a resting-place for thy life. He will make thee wealthy. He will make thee amends for—"

"Perish his gold!" cried the old man, fiercely interrupting the speaker. "Let the earth hide it, as it will hide him soon, who is a shame to God's creatures. Was he charitable when, as God's agent on earth, he sat on the seat of judgment? Was he kind to the aged, helpless Derwesh whom he invited to his court? Was he merciful? As he did, so let be unto him. Dohai Feringi! Dohai Feringi! Let the English do justice on him—not I. Let them be judges between us, not ye who fear him. Have ye known what I suffered? Never yet have I told ye. Look! I had ears once, and he took them. I say," and his voice rose to a scream as he unwound his matted hair, "I had ears! Look ye—are there any now? Blood for blood! Hath not the Holy Prophet said it? Away with him! Dohai Feringi! away with him! Away with him and his wanton to death!"

"Brothers—friends—pity. Be merciful to me—your Prince!" cried the Nawab. "Be merciful to me and let me go. Let me go! Who dare refuse me?—me and mine! Would ye do murder on one who has never harmed ye? Would ye listen to the raving of a mad fanatic? Would ye slay your master? Would ye give him up to his enemies? See, there are jewels. She has them; take them, they are precious. Oh, sirs! by your mothers, by your children, do not this wrong. Let me go! Oh, mothers! by your sons —I too have a mother—let me go to her!"

He was appealing, with piteous cries and gestures, now to the men and now to the women, and not without effect. Many of the latter broke into the hysterical sobbing common to the lower orders of women everywhere, who, forgetting facts, grow excited under such appeals to their sympathy. "He has a mother," some said; "why should he die? The Feringis will hang him. He must die if he be given to them." Perhaps if there had been delay, there would have been reaction in his favour, and it seemed that the issue lay on a moment. The Derwesh saw the danger, and sprang to the Nawab's side, snatched a dagger from the waistband of one of the village guards, and held it to the Nawab's heart.

"I will strike," he said, "if ye hesitate. I swear by God, I will strike! He shall not escape me. He or I!—Beware!"

"Hold him! Take the knife from him!" cried many of the women and some of the men, with a strange clamour; and one burly fellow advanced as if he would essay to do so.

"I said beware!" cried the Derwesh, drawing up his tall gaunt form, about which the long matted locks of hair, before tied round his head, were streaming. "I said beware! If you stir," he continued to the man who had stepped forward, "not only shall he die, but my blood will be on your heads, and on your children's—on your mothers', and on your wives'. My spirit will haunt you! Wherever you go my blood shall cry out against you! In your fields, in your houses, by your beds, ye shall hear the old man's cry —Dohai Feringi!—shrieking in the storm blast and in the thunder; and ye will remember ye denied him the Feringi's justice. Beware! my blood is upon you!" and as he spoke he drew the knife sharply across his breast, and the blood streamed out over his naked body.

Then women shrieked and wept, and beat their breasts; and the men prostrated themselves, Moslim and Hindu alike, before the terrible fanatic. "Curse us not," they cried; "take him away. As ye list with him; but spare us and our children, and let not thy blood be on us and ours."

The Derwesh made no reply; he only pointed to the wound he had inflicted upon himself; and while he held down Suraj-oo-Doulah with one hand, raised the other as if to stab him. "Away with him! away with him!" rose a shout in which there seemed no dissent. No one heard the piteous cries of the wretch who, trembling and gasping at the imminent thought of death, was grovelling at the old man's feet, clasping his knees, and being spurned away like a dog.

"Coward!" he cried; "if thou art to die, bear thy fate like a man. She, thy wanton there, would have more courage. Swear to me," he continued to some of the young men of the village, who had brought up a rude bed-litter, "that ye will guard him safely, and with your lives. Swear on my blood!"

"We swear!" cried fifty hoarse voices, but there was little need now; there was no chance of check to the new excitement. "Away with him!" was the shout from old and young. "Take him to the Feringi; take him to Meer Jaffier."

"I was burned by his orders," cried one hag; "for they said I was a witch. Look at the marks. The hot iron seared me in the market-place, and the smoke of my flesh went up as a witness against him. I cursed him, and see what he has come to."

"Let him go to death!" screamed another woman, who rushed forward with frantic gestures; "did he not seize two of my daughters, and destroy them in the zenana? Where are they? Where are my children—my jewels—my darlings? What hast thou done with them? Oh, friends, ask him what became of them. Ha! ha! ha!" she laughed wildly, "he took them to be his wantons, and they are dead—Dohai Feringi!"

"Dohai Feringi!" echoed the Derwesh; "thou shalt have justice, mother. Come with me and see it—come and see him die, as I shall!"

The litter had come up, borne by four stout fellows—a rude bedstead with bamboos tied to the corners, and a strong pole to carry it by. There was a rough, unkempt pony for the Derwesh, another for Sozun; and without further parley the Nawab, bound as he was, was taken up and put upon the litter. Some one flung over him a tattered blanket, which partly covered him as he lay groaning and shivering with fear. There was no hope now—none. He must go to death. All his own people would be relentless; but Clive might—might have mercy. Mercy? and the memory of the agonies of the English prison at his heart, and the horrible deaths of his murdered countrymen to avenge! Mercy from him? No—there was no mercy anywhere now. The men who ran by the side of his litter jeered and mocked him with grotesque salaams; and, as he implored them to loosen his arms, taunted him with the tortures he had inflicted upon many a victim, and let him lie.

A mad procession! Ere one village had been passed, they heard at the next that the Nawab was coming. The Nawab's "Suwari," as it was called in mockery—the Nawab's retinue! What a retinue it was for one who, a few days before, had ridden to Plassey on an elephant with housings of velvet and cloth-of-gold, surrounded by the pomp of royalty and the gorgeous military display of an Eastern army! Before all, riding a gaunt horse, which some had substituted for the pony, naked, except his waist-cloth, with his matted hair streaming over his face and down his back—the blood still oozing from the wound he had inflicted on himself, and for which he seemed to have no concern—rode the old Derwesh, brandishing his bright steel trident, and shouting in his shrill harsh voice, "Dohai Feringi! Come and see, O ye faithful, the justice of the Nazarenes! Come!—delay not!—a tyrant and his wanton going to death! Come and see!—come and see—a 'coward die!' Dohai Feringi!"

Near where he had resided, the old man was known and venerated; but, as the strange travellers passed on, it seemed that the excitement only grew the stronger. No tarrying for meat or drink—no tarrying for change of bearers. Men jostled each other for the privilege of putting their shoulders under the pole of the litter, and the few village guards had swelled to hundreds, and were increasing. Men left their ploughs and looms, their shops and trades, and hastily snatching up the household sword and shield, or spear and matchlock, still hurried on, and joined the hoarse cry, "Dohai Feringi! Dohai Feringi!"

As to Suraj-oo-Doulah himself, I hardly think I can be expected to say much of him. Men in his position, with a certain and horrible death staring them in the face, may think upon it, if they be brave and self-reliant. If not, they are numb with terror. They cannot realise what is to come. The faculty of thought for any definite purpose is dead; and though the body lives, a corpse might as well be spoken to as a living creature in such a plight. Such was the Nawab in his last march. When there was a trifling delay at any village, Sozun would sometimes go to him, try to rouse him, take him a cup of water or milk, or a cake of bread, which some charitable housewife had offered her in the name of God and the Prophet. He who had been pampered in luxury loathed the coarse food offered to him. Water was his only cry, and he drank it greedily. He seemed to understand nothing. He could only complain that his bonds hurt him; that it was cold, and he shivered; or that the sun burned him: and he flung himself about violently on his rude bed, or, raising himself up, implored, in accents of abject entreaty, those nearest to him to despatch him—to release him—"he would go away—he would harm no one—he would never return. By their children—by their mothers—for the love of Allah—let his life be spared. What had he done? Was there no pity?"

Who pitied him? No one, except the poor Affghan girl, hurried along with him to the same death, as she believed, which awaited him, and that would be welcome to her. She had done her duty; and sinner as she was, could remember and repeat the holy English words which Ralph Smithson had taught her. So the night passed. There was no staying to rest or to sleep. The wild procession hurried on by the glare of torchlight, waking whole villages from their slumbers, and passing them like a hideous nightmare—a rabble rout of demons, as it were—polluting the peaceful night with shouts and execrations.

As they neared the capital next day, the crowd which followed the litter, marched with it or preceded it, increased mightily. As before, men fought with each other as to who should be its bearers, and those who carried it were from time to time jostled out of their places to make room for others. The litter heaved and surged among them; but they went on with wild rushes which increased in speed—a torrent of men and women, howling, shrieking, screaming with frantic laughter—which, if by night it was indistinct and horrible, had now grown into a grotesque but dreadful reality. As the old Derwesh still shouted his cry of "Dohai Feringi!" he was answered by ringing yells of "Feringi ke jey! Victory to the English! Clive Sahib ke Futteh! Victory to Clive! Victory to Meer Jaffier! Death to the Nawab!" mingled with the shrill hootings of boys, and the screams of withered hags, who, running till they were out of breath, spat at the wretched creature as he lay writhing and cowering under his blanket, beat their withered breasts, and howled the death-wail in his ears. I only wonder that, coward as the man was, he lived through the horror of his last dreadful march, or reached Moorshedabad at all; but he did reach it.

CHAPTER LIX.

HOMEWARDS.

Meer Jaffier had arrived, and the city was busy. The streets were choked with people from the country; dealers had spread out their wares, and singers and buffoons were perambulating the streets singing ballads of Clive and the battle of Plassey, and good-humour prevailed. Clive might arrive that evening, and householders were setting out earthen cups on the terraces and balustrades of their houses, and filling them with oil for the illumination. Flower-sellers were stringing garlands of jessamine, and sweetmeat-venders were hawking parched rice or pease for hungry sightseers. Suddenly there arose a wild cry, as it were of shouts from the outskirts of the town. Some said the Nawab had returned with an army, and fled away; others thought Clive had come: and before any one had time to reflect, the strange procession passed by like a whirlwind, led by the Derwesh, cantering on in front on his tall bony horse, shouting, "Clear the way—clear the way! Dohai

Feringi!" and tossing his arms wildly into the air. Hard on his heels followed the mob of village folk, some armed to the teeth, some with long bamboos, clubs with heavy iron rings, or stout quarter-staves, encircling the litter, and the pony which carried Sozun, led now at a rapid trot. "To the palace—to the palace—to Meer Jaffier!" was now the cry. No one dare oppose this torrent; but what was that in the midst of it? None knew then; and when it had gone by, those who remained were told that the Nawab, Suraj-oo-Doulah, was gone before them to his death.

"To the palace! to the palace! Dohai Feringi!" was heard by Ralph Smithson and Mr. Watts as they stood in the court, and asked vainly for explanation. A few moments afterwards, the Derwesh trotted into the gate, standing up in his stirrups, and whirling his steel trident above his head, while his cry never ceased and was followed by the rabble who bore the Nawab.

"Are you Clive?" asked the breathless Derwesh, whose mouth was dry and parched, his lips speckled with foam, and his eyes glowing red and fierce from among his matted locks. "Are you Clive?" he asked of each, as his eye glanced from the one to the other. "I have brought the Nawab, and I demand justice—justice from the English!" The man was fearful to look upon, and both shrank back involuntarily.

"I am not Clive, I am Mr. Watts; what justice can I do for thee?"

"For this," cried the Derwesh, lifting his hair from his ears, and showing the white scars of his mutilation. "Justice for this! Can he disfigure a servant of the Most High God and live? Kill him!"

"I cannot kill him, Bawa Sahib," said Mr. Watts, gravely; but I will see to his safety. Let Meer Jaffier deal with him."

And that wretch, crouching on the bed which had been set down, rocking himself to and fro, bowing down his head, for he was still pinioned, crying, "O Mr. Watts! O Mr. Watts!—save me—save me! they will kill me: take all my money—all my jewels, and let me go! O Mr. Watts, by your mother, by Jesus of Nazareth and His mother Mary—" that was the Nawab! that Suraj-oo-Doulah! Bah! he was a sickening sight; and Ralph Smithson, who had been fascinated for a moment, turned away his head and spat out his disgust. Some guards had come from the gate, and Mr. Watts was giving orders to them.

"Sahib, Sahib, this is another—kill her!" cried a burly villager armed to the teeth, dragging along a weary pony covered with sweat, on which a woman was seated. "Shall I dash out her brains?' and he whirled his iron-bound club round his finger and thumb, causing it to whistle through the air, as he plucked away the scarf with which Sozun had tied up her face with the other.

"Sozun!" cried Ralph, pushing away the man and a crowd of others, "why art thou here?"

"O brother, God hath again sent thee to me," she said, stretching out her arms to him; "I tried to save him, but it was not to be."

"Come," he replied, and he led away the pony out of the wondering people, "Julia and the Begum are safe: they will tend thee—come;" and they passed on into an inner court, no one following them. A few more moments, and the girl was at rest in loving arms.

The villagers followed them with staring eyes, till they were lost to view. "She is one of the Feringis," said the man who, a moment before, would have dashed out her brains with his club. "Did ye not see how white she was?"

"Ah, yes," said another, "there was a story that a Feringi woman had been brought from Calcutta, and that is she! we ought to get a reward for her. Come and ask."

"Not I," said the first speaker; "who knows but she might have us blown away from guns? I shall go home. Come away, these Feringis are devils if provoked—come, let us follow the Derwesh and the Nawab."

We need not follow them to the last dread scene of all, which was not long delayed. The Derwesh never left his captive; and when that afternoon the dread messengers of death came to the miserable man and did their office, he stood by, and recited the prayers for the dying. They said of him afterwards, that he dipped his fingers in the warm blood of his enemy, and put them to his ears; bound up his matted hair over them, and afterwards the weird figure of the old man disappeared from the city, and was never more seen.

When the Begum was removed from the palace to the house of her husband's mother—the dear old lady, whose interest in the English is matter of history—she took Sozun with her. Strong as the girl had been, the fearful trial and fatigue of the Nawab's last march, as the people called it in mockery, had broken her down, and long rest and care were needful. When Julia Wharton had to depart—and that event was not long delayed—I question which of the three women was in the bitterest grief. Had she desired it, the Nawab's mother would have given her a free home for life, free to come and go after the manner of her people; but it is needless to say this could not be: there were yet ties in England, and in India that one horrible memory which would haunt her all her life.

Before Julia Wharton left the city, Ralph Smithson had engaged her passage to England. She was now very rich, for under the success of Mr. Wharton's speculations, and the full compensation for all public and private losses, which was paid by the new Nawab, the settlement upon her was largely increased; and I think had she chosen to stay in Calcutta, what she had undergone would have proved no obstacle to honourable proposals. On one point, however, she was uniformly silent. She never spoke of her English antecedents, nor did Ralph Smithson attempt to discover them, or lead her to speak of them; whatever they might be, was a mystery which were better, perhaps, left at rest. Her desire to leave India was genuine, and Ralph could gather that it was in England only that she looked for any chance of happiness in her future life.

The *Valiant* was lying at Calcutta, and Captain Scrafton offered his best cabin to Mrs. Wharton when she reached the Factory; but Ralph had written to him that he was coming down with despatches for England, and, full or empty, the good ship was to sail with them —and when the captain showed this letter to Mrs. Wharton, she gratefully declined the cabin, and took one in another ship on the point of sailing. When Ralph arrived a few days later, he found she had gone, and a letter explained the motive in a way which we can perhaps understand. It contained also another packet which, Julia wrote, was not to be opened till he himself was at sea, and "she trusted to his honour for this."

There were other letters too awaiting him from his old correspondents; and I have to make a few extracts from Mr. Roger Darnell's, because they concern the course of this history; but there was none from Sybil, nor from Mistress Grover.

"Of your investments," wrote Mr. Darnell, "I have nought but good news to give you; and Mr. Sanders will satisfy you more particularly on this point by the accounts-current and bills of sale. For the present, and till we hear of the result of Mr. Clive's expedition, I consider it most advisable to keep the proceeds in hand, for which you will receive the customary interest. I have no fear but that Mr. Clive will exact compensation for all losses, and secure our interests for the future.

"And now, dear Ralph, I have news to give which will cause you much concern. Poor Mrs. Morton, of whose illness I advised you, died soon after I wrote, and her daughter and the old servant left their house and disappeared. I regret to say I have been quite unable to trace them: and though the annuity which her mother enjoyed died out with her, yet your instructions had provided amply for her support, and I need hardly say that my own desires would have led me to make a suitable settlement upon her. But I am quite hopeless about the poor girl. I only trust she hath retired to some quiet place in the North, or may have married; but to the last she utterly rejected Mr. Forster, and the thought sometimes crosses my mind, that it may have been to escape from his pertinacity that she hath hid herself away. I trust, however, to hear of her after all, and if so, I will not fail to write directly.

"Your beautiful cousin Constance will, I hear, make a very happy and suitable match. The eldest son of the Earl of Whinborough, Viscount Granton, saw her at an assize ball at Newcastle, and is now an accepted suitor. He is come of age, hath a fine independent property, and we are all bound to rejoice at Constance's prospects. We hear he is very handsome, hath a kindly disposition, is none of your town rakes, and, in short, all is at last as it should be for her and your uncle, who is beside himself with joy, and hath written me several mad letters. Peed tells me he is drawing up the settlements, so I suppose they will soon be married.

"Your own affairs, my dear boy, are still as uncertain as ever. We have no success in our inquiries. The people who keep Lamberton Pike are changed, and no trace even of that marriage is discoverable. Why did not your father avow it? Scotch marriage as it was, most likely it would have been legal there, and we could have managed the rest. But as the homely saying is, 'It's no use crying after spilt milk,' and I think you will have seen that the affair is hopeless now, and will have learned to bear your lot with fortitude, and with that complete trust in God which hath hitherto sustained you in all those dreadful perils of which you have written.

"Have you been able to trace poor Mrs. Wharton? or have you any knowledge of who she was? Her property is now *very* considerable, perhaps £50,000 or *more;* what to do with it we do not know, and there is money for his children besides. Alas! alas! it is altogether a miserable story.

"Your old friend and crony, Mr. Elliot, is at last in the King's Bench, and being in distress, and helped by some friends, I have made bold to send him fifty pounds on your account, which you will not grudge. He was in nowise cognisant of, or concerned in, *that* affair, and in spite of extravagance, is a gentleman. I don't think you can now feel any grudge against him on the score of Constance, so if I may give him another fifty, or even a hundred, I shall be glad."

Constance engaged! Sybil Morton gone! Alas! I think this letter was but cold comfort to Ralph, as he read it with a swelling heart. Of Constance, for a long time past, he had given up all hope. It would have been absurd to entertain any; but I should be wrong if I did not suppose, nay, feel very sure, that the sweet image of Sybil Morton, whom absence had even made more dear, was lying deeper and dearer in his heart. His only comfort was, that he was going home, where his rights would at least be established, and he would search England through to find her. Why had not Mr. Darnell traced her from the old house? Why had his own letter of warning miscarried?—but it was too late now. Wilson at least would be sure to know of her—or Selwyn? So when the worthy Don Gomez, and many other friends, bade him a cheerful adieu on the quarterdeck of the *Valiant*, and the merry song of the sailors heaving the anchor rang in his ears, his spirit rose again from its depression higher and higher, as the good ship once more bounded onwards to dear England, and the fruition of his hopes.

"Give this letter to your worthy uncle, Ralph," said Mr. Clive, as he had bade him farewell (it was that dated 4th July 1757, which is seen in Mr. Darnell's picture). "I have writ him all he will care to know about our affairs; and though he and I don't exactly agree in all matters, I think he will allow that this hath been a glorious victory. Tell them all, Ralph, that I think, work, and live only for the glory of England, and that this victory is but a step to a dominion at which the world shall marvel hereafter—the thin end of the wedge, which I will drive as far as I can, and which others will drive home. Tell them all this, if my motives are questioned, as they will be; but I fear no ill consequences, Ralph. My own heart, under God, who rules all, tells me it is for the best; and though the end may be stayed, it cannot alter. What will India be in a hundred years, ay, and in a hundred years after that? I think I can see; but people would call Robert Clive mad were he to tell it. Farewell, my dear boy! When you are successful, believe me, no friend you ever had or will have will rejoice more sincerely than I shall; and if England is dull, come to me again, baronet-elect as you may be—for there is honour, glory, ay, and wealth too, if you desire it, to be won in Robert Clive's company."

END OF PART FOURTH.

PART FIFTH.

PART FIFTH.

CHAPTER LX.

WHAT MRS. WHARTON WROTE.

"OFTEN as I have longed to do so, I have never dared to tell you, Ralph Smithson, what I have been, and why I came to India. I had no business to trouble you with a sad history. I had no right to draw you into any confidence. I have fancied—often fancied—while you lived with us, that you had some secret of your own; for, as well as I can remember, not one word of your family ever escaped you; and that kind of reserve, except for some reason, is not usual in a foreign land. If you had made a confidant of me, I should infallibly have made one of you; but it is better as it is—far better. There was one of whom I should have made one if he had lived; but for reasons that you know well, Ralph, there was a veil between us till the last few hours of a life which, if it had been continued, would have been a source of grateful happiness and love to me.

"But it is very different now. I need your council and assistance: and one who, at the risk of his own life, protected mine through that fearful night, and who hurried on through an enemy's country from Plassey to save me, will not refuse it. I purposely declined to sail in the *Valiant* with you because I would not have my sad history trouble you more than the knowledge of it will cause you. I could not have borne to discuss it with you; and after what is past, I am better alone—alone for many months—to live out what I have undergone, if that be possible, ere I meet my people again. Our good friends in Calcutta might not, perhaps, have spared us either; and after all, you will reach home before me, for the *Valiant* will sail faster than we shall.

"How often, as I have looked at you when you little suspected me, have I thought I had seen you before, somewhere that I could not remember—a faint vision, an illusion of remembrance, which seemed to belong to a different world—a different state of existence, untraceable and unreal. Ah! often have I yearned to test it by the question which I put now: Do you remember George Elliot? were you ever his friend?

"But I dare not, for had you acknowledged you knew him, I could not have concealed the rest, and I was then a married woman, sworn to love another. I shall not know for many months how this question can be answered: but, as I think upon it, my thought becomes stronger that you were sometimes one of his companions, and yet—I may be dreaming.

"George Elliot! If you know him, you will allow how fascinating he was—how rare a combination of manly beauty and grace he possessed. If you do not know him, you may believe me now, and acknowledge hereafter that I was right. I loved George Elliot; I love him still. In my first days of marriage—in the horrible prison—in— No matter; I have never ceased to love him, except for that brief time when I grew into confidence and happiness with my husband, which, if it had continued, would have established an erring, wayward, passionate mind on a firm basis, that would have resisted temptation. Since I have been free, I know not whether it be right or wrong, but my heart has gone back to its old place; and had I died in that horrible palace by myself, my last wishes, that I had written in my prayer-book, would have told you, had you ever received it, what message should be delivered to him, and you would have known, as you do now, that I loved him.

"My real name was Hyde, and I am of a good family; but my father died soon after my mother, and left us, two sisters and a brother, to the care of his brother, my uncle Charles. Ah! what a life it was. My uncle had a passion for the theatre, and neglected his business sadly. Finally he took to the stage as a profession; and, if he is alive, is now an actor with Mr. Garrick. We—my sister and I—were left to pick up what education we could, and my uncle's great ambition was that we should become actresses. He had us taught singing by an Italian master, and perhaps I should have succeeded. Richard, my brother, went to America as a ensign in the army, and soon died there, and so we were left to our uncle's mercy.

"It was a fearful life. He was seldom quite sober latterly, and ill-treated us as far as coarse abuse and evil society could carry him; while again he was at times tender and affectionate, desiring only our settlement in life,—a strange inconsistency, in which cruelty—brutality I should rather call it—prevailed. My sister Isabella was a proud, haughty, selfish girl, who could ill brook this treatment, and when our uncle was playing at York, was courted by, and engaged to, a rich farmer and grazier with whom she became acquainted, and married him, in spite of my uncle, for she was of age.

"We went to Newcastle, and it was there I first saw George Elliot. He was a young squire, with an ample fortune, and he was admitted behind the scenes as a privileged person. He noticed me, followed me, and got introduced to my uncle. He renewed the acquaintance in London, and visited us, as did many other gallants, on an honourable footing. I grew to love George Elliot; to me he was tender and respectful always. I often used to think, God forgive me! that my uncle was ready to sell me to the highest bidder, and I clung to George, not as a brother, but as to the only thing I had left, to love or protect me. He knew all my trials, all my danger, and came to know them better as time passed. Oh, how I loved him!

"There was another man who pursued me with fearful persistence; a man of the city, a merchant, middle-aged, profligate and wealthy. I hated him. His hideous person, his mind, his wealth, were equally horrible. They were not so, however, to my uncle, to whom a large sum was offered for his consent. I need not weary you with a recital of how my uncle pleaded, stormed, raved, and was alike unsuccessful—or how I told George Elliot that I had resisted, and intended to resist. I believe I was mad—I believed when the time came that I could no longer avert the misery with which I was threatened—that I could trust myself to George's honour, and be safe. Else why was he so true, so respectful to me? I had not a friend to whom I could resort. Mrs. Woffington or Mrs. Clive would but have laughed at me. I alone trusted George; and for good or evil I could think of him only, night and day.

"Night and day! Oh, Mr. Smithson, I pray you may never be so tempted. Men are strong, and bear: or, if they fall, the world cares nothing; it is not grieved—only God. Ah! I thought not of Him then,—never. I only saw my own misery. I only believed in George Elliot; to all else I was blind and deaf. He saw my misery, which he shared; but he dared not marry me openly. He proposed a private elopement, and, trusting in him, I consented. We were to go to the border and be married—in what manner I knew not, nor cared, so that he were mine, and I was delivered from the dreadful fate with which I was threatened.

"I do not know how, I never learned: and all that followed, as to where my uncle got intelligence of what had happened, is even now a strange, dull, confusion in my mind. We left London one night, while he was playing at the theatre with Mr. Garrick, and I trusted myself to George. I am sure he would not have deceived me, but we were pursued. The chase broke down near Barnet, and as we sat there uncertain what to do, my uncle and some of his friends came up on horseback. There was a scuffle, a clashing of swords, and I fainted. When I recovered George was gone, a chaise was ready, and I was taken back and locked up. I never saw him again. Whether he was wounded or not I could never ascertain. I had no friend—not one.

"My uncle was furious. The man who had persecuted me no longer appeared; that chance was lost, and I was reproached with vile conduct of which I was innocent. Plead how I would, my uncle could never be persuaded but that I had been living a dishonourable life, and of that I should have no more. He had a cousin in Calcutta, who was married, and as soon as a passage could be provided in a ship about to sail, I was sent to him. Nothing of my story was known. My uncle wrote that he found it impossible to provide for me, and from my youth and beauty the theatre was not a place for me, nor actresses and actors fit companions for an orphan girl. They believed this, and were kind to me, and so I lived with them till Mr. Wharton proposed for me, and I accepted him. Before you arrived, Mr. and Mrs. Lawrence left Calcutta with their children; and with them I am sure of a home. Of my sister I have had no news whatever. She has taken her own road in life, and, selfish as she always was, has followed it. I daresay she believed that I had become vile, and was glad I had been sent away.

"This is all my story, Ralph. Simple enough to tell, but containing within it more misery than I can write, or you would care to read. I repeat, somewhere or other, in George Elliot's company, I remember to have seen you. This cannot be a dream, though, if I am wrong, you will think it one. If it be not a dream, and you know him—I may never meet him, for the hideous past has placed a gulf between us—but you may be able to tell him that in all her trial Julia Hyde never forgot him.

"And now I have written this, I am minded to destroy it. Why, indeed, should I have written it at all? Only, as I have said, for my strange thought about you, which as time passed did but grow stronger. When you took me out of that dark vault into the light of day, and I saw you after that long sad absence, I could hardly restrain my emotion. But forgive me, Ralph—forgive a weak woman, so tried as I have been, and for the future so hopeless. It is a relief to me to have told you all, and to no one on earth but you has it ever been revealed."

CHAPTER LXI.

SYBIL MORTON'S HISTORY.

My readers know already, from Mr. Roger Darnell's letter, that Mrs. Morton had died, and that Sybil could not be traced. That letter had been written on Christmas Eve 1756, like a preceding one that we may remember of the previous year, and there had been intermediate letters, for Mr. Roger Darnell wrote regularly every quarter to his nephew; but as none of these documents contain anything relevant to the course of this history, and are for the most part of a mercantile character, interspersed with some political reflections, I have not thought it necessary to allude to them. Mr. Darnell did not ordinarily trouble himself with family gossip, and it was only on rare occasions that he entered into such topics as I have recorded. I have always thought it strange that Ralph himself did not write oftener to Sybil, his dear true friend, as he loved to think her still; but at the young man's heart lay no real exciting effect of love. He could not have leaped from the violent ardour of his adoration of Constance, into a similar condition of mind for Sybil. That he loved her with a brotherly affection we know; and from the effect of his last visit to her, we may have thought that a deeper feeling had already begun. I think not, however. The young man's behaviour on that occasion was but the overflow of a wounded heart, guilty too, and ashamed; and, touched by a sympathy which could not be mistaken, no wonder that he could not control himself. When he reflected afterwards upon Sybil, I think he felt conscious that she might, probably would, come to know what had happened: and, if so, she would not write to him, and he did not feel disposed to persist in a correspondence which, as his letter had not been answered, might be unwelcome, particularly to Mrs. Morton. For all this, the image of the loving beautiful girl would often rise in his heart, and live there; and when he heard that Forster was rejected, I can fancy that he made a shrewd guess at the cause, and there was time enough for future consideration.

On the other side, there had been no doubt perhaps, but much grief. Sybil and Mrs. Morton never knew the exact truth; but women will talk, and in one of her visits to Mr. Sanders's sisters, Mrs. Morton had been told in a mysterious manner by the youngest, with whom she interchanged pleasant confidences, that "something had occurred to render Mr. Ralph's longer continuance in the office impossible, and he had been sent to the Factory in Calcutta." It was an unpleasant subject to Mr. Darnell, and Miss Sanders exacted a promise from the old lady not to repeat what she had told her. "It's all for the best, my dear, you know," she said, "and he'll make a fortune very soon; but he couldn't stay here, and indeed, ma'am, you know he was a wild lad;" and Mrs. Morton could not deny that, having, as we know, had more proofs of it than the good Miss Sanders was aware of.

To India! This then was the separation at which Ralph had more than hinted when he left Sybil, and said he should work out his own way in life. "He might have told me," she thought. "Could he not trust *me?*" We know, however, what had happened, and how he could *not* tell her; and so I am, perhaps, right in my conjecture as to why he only once wrote to her. Can we believe in that tone of arrogance in Ralph's mind which said, "I am sure she will never forget me;" and how, leaving her to the future contingencies of years and circumstances, he felt happy when he heard that Forster was refused, and grieved when she had disappeared?

Ah, poor Sybil! What a life it had been of sorrow, struggle, and hope, these months of trial and grief! If she had had Ralph by her, all these last declining days of her dear mother would have been endurable in his strength and sympathy. Gradually Mrs. Morton had drooped and died. She had no particular ailment; and all the doctor could say was, that her strength was to be kept up; and poor old Nanny's brains were racked in vain for savoury jellies, nice broths, and beef-tea. But all was of no use—she grew weaker and weaker, and so died.

Mr. Forster was not long in finding out that Ralph was gone. Mr. Wilson, who acted as scout, told him that Mr. Darnell had traced what had happened as far as Ralph was concerned, and sent him away. There was no reason to suppose he would ever return, and there was certainly no suspicion excited as to who were concerned —none at least in his own direction. There was no search even; and I am not sure, when Ralph's disappearance and Sir Geoffrey's wound were coupled together, that, after a time, the gossips of London did not shrug their shoulders and say, the Darnells were a violent family at all times, and there must have been a family quarrel. So Mr. Forster, when his wound was healed, and Mr. Selwyn, appeared in the gay world once more, and followed their usual avocations independently, or as it might happen.

Of George Elliot's pleasant company they were deprived by one of His Majesty's officers, with a certain paper in his hand, which need not be specified, who requested his company till payment should be arranged of a sum recorded; and as Mr. Elliot was, as he expressed it, "run dry," and had not even the means of being squeezed—often successful in a sponging-house—left in him, he had gone into winter quarters, which were unusually hard bound, in His Gracious Majesty's Fleet, and was not likely to emerge from thence for some time to come.

So there being no one in the way, Mr. Forster recommenced his suit for Sybil, and I have no doubt that much of his intercourse with her and her mother was for a long time of a very respectful character, and by that he had secured Mrs. Morton's interest, and also Nanny's. Many a crown had he judiciously adminstered to the faithful old woman. Many a time had Nanny and her mistress discussed the matter: and Nanny's opinion, "that he was jest a weel-faurred canny gentleman, wi' a sweet voice, and blythe for Miss Sybil," met favour in the old lady's heart. More than favour, indeed, when Mr. Forster made a formal proposal, and was accepted so far as Mrs. Morton and Nanny were concerned; and when Mrs. Morton found herself fast declining—"It would so satisfy me, my darling Sybil," she would say, "I should feel such a load taken from my heart, if I knew before I died that you were safe for your world's life. This annuity dies with me—and oh, Sybil! the world's a drear place for one so fair as thou art, and so helpless."

So it was already, so it would be in future, but for one dim ray which sparkled afar off amidst the gloom of distance—Ralph would not desert her, her mother would live, and she could not love Forster.

Why not? He was, as Nanny called him, "jest a gran' man, wi' nane of yer hobbledehoy fancies and wild dooin's like Mister Rraafe. Wasna Rraafe her ain bairn, an' she had tou'd him sae mony a time till his face, an' 'ud tell him agin; bit he was no a body to marry a fine lassie like Miss Sybil, wha'd need somebody to pit her up, and keep her up; and wha better than a true Forster?"

But even this did not prevail, nor Forster's tender manner, for he could be tender—nor his grace, for he could be graceful—nor his accomplishments, for he had these; and during long residence in foreign courts had become a far more accomplished musician and scholar than his absent friend. It is hard to say why Sybil, who sang with him to please her mother, who read Dante and Boccaccio with him to improve her accent, who habitually spoke French with him, for her mother preferred that language to her own in familiar conversation—it is hard, I say, to account for the obduracy he had to encounter, for the positive terror with which Sybil received the slightest advance to love, and her earnest entreaties that they might be friends—friends only for her mother's sake.

We know why all this was; how the true, faithful, loving heart, growing stronger and more faithful under trial and absence, clung to Ralph Darnell's memory with a steadfast but sad persistence. Then the news of the Black Hole came, and Mrs. Morton died. It so happened that there were but a few days between the two—a crisis of misery which it was hard to bear up against. There was no sign of Ralph's safety. For many months afterwards it was indifferently known in England who had died and who were saved, and even had Sybil seen the name of Ralph Smithson among those who survived, it is not possible that she could have recognised it. I believe also that Mr. Forster thought him dead. He and Mr. Selwyn often visited George Elliot in the Fleet, and Wilson came there also, who volunteered to get news; and what he did get from Mr. Peed and Mr. Sanders, to whom he ventured to apply, confirmed suspicion. They had no news of Ralph. Mr. Wharton was dead, and it was but too probable that Ralph Darnell had also perished, either in the fighting or in what followed.

When Mr. Forster heard this as truth which could not be doubted, and laid it before Sybil herself, praying to be accepted—not then, presently: that he would watch over her till she pleased to end his suspense—that he would not urge her as to time, only if she would obey her dear mother's last wishes, breathed to her, to Nanny, and to himself, and consent, he would be satisfied. Surely he might hope? I think, after her earnest, piteous refusal, her pleading to be left in peace, that the man's mind then turned to its old savage humour, and he swore what he could not have fairly, he would have as best he might get it.

Perhaps he let drop some hints of this to Nanny; perhaps her instinct had led her to fear a man who, as her "bonnie lambie" had become more helpless, had changed in manner, and hinted at exacting as a right, what he had once pleaded for as a favour. Perhaps it was the evident fact that, as the annuity had ceased, they must work for their bread; they must give up the house: that, or all combined, may have induced them to do what they did. It is true, Mr. Darnell, who had attended Mrs. Morton's funeral, and defrayed all its expenses, insisted on paying a quarter's pension in advance; promised Mrs. Darnell should visit Sybil; had also promised help in future; and would have given it very cheerfully—but Mrs. Roger never made her appearance.

Thank God! she had done with Ralph Darnell for ever; and "there is not the *slightest* occasion, my dear," as she said to Lady Warrington, "for *me* to interfere for that young person, who has been educated for a governess, and is *quite* well able to shift for herself." So Mrs. Roger was one of those who passed by on the other side, when this poor bleeding heart was lying night after night trembling, praying, and crying, "O Ralph! Ralph! only one word from you, my darling—only one word, and I would go to you, were it to the world's end if you live, or would die where you have died," and might have been kept from harm by a motherly heart, and power to protect her, if— But I have no right to sit in judgment; and Mrs. Roger was the best judge, "whether," as she said, "a young person, who had kept company with a character like Ralph Darnell, and was even supposed to love him, was fit company for *her* daughters!"

Why did not Sybil write to Constance? Was she still hurt and jealous? There was one who would, as a dear, dear sister, have welcomed her, and Mistress Grover would have been more than a second mother. No, only to escape now, and hide herself away till he came; and it was one day after Forster had called to plead again, with the old effect and result, and as he went out had said something to Nanny which she "dare not repeat," she continued—"Ay, they had better gang, and maybe Mistress Janet Rrobson had rooms she ken'd of, whar douce north-country lawyer folk cam' to be nigh the Innes of Court; an' they couldna keep the hoose, and were frighted to be alane in't o' nichts, and Forster wad niver find 'em oot—niver; an' they'd plenty of money for a year and mair; an' a' the stuff in the house wad sell for a gude bit siller, and maybe Janet Rrobson 'ud tak it a' at a fair valiation, an' they'd be weel there; an' it was jist a quiet neuk"—that Sybil's eyes and face lighted up as if by inspiration, and she put her hand to the dear old woman's mouth and stopped it, and cried, "O Nanny, darling, now—now—come now. Don't stay a moment. Oh, he may come again! and—and—and—oh, come!"

So they locked up the house, and went to Mistress Robson, who lived in Queen Street, by Lincoln's Inn Fields, in a coach; and the kind north-country woman, who had braved many a male lodger in her time, and was well to do in her calling, took the beautiful sobbing girl to her heart, and patted her wet face as it lay on her shoulder, and bade her "fear nane, for she had the best of kind north folk livin' with her, an' she could depen' on all o' them." Thenceforth Sybil never returned to the old house by the river: for Mistress Robson and Nanny got away the best of the furniture, and set out two rooms with it, and sold what was not wanted, so that a good sum was added to what was already in store. Then they felt secure, and found the house quiet and well-ordered; and Nanny soon saw the bright old "licht blinkin' in her dear bonnie childie's eyes again," and the old occupations renewed. Nor was there any want: for Sybil's work gained high prices, and she could never finish enough of the lovely embroidery which was ordered by Mr. Price and other fashionable men mercers, for whom she worked.

We can conceive, however, that Mr. Forster was by no means satisfied with this arrangement. When he went next to the old house by the river, he found it shut, and bills in the window, advertising that it was to be let. No doubt he stormed at the door, and looked up in vain at the closed shutters, till a woman put her head out of a window near, and told him they were gone who had lived there—gone many days. "No, she knew nothing of them, nor did the butcher, or baker, or the waterman, know anything either." They had gone, that was all, "and the beautiful kind young lady was sore missed."

Sore missed truly, and apparently without hope. From that time, John Forster's life was not an enviable one. His gloomy, revengeful character bade defiance to all gentler thoughts; he would have been kind and honest with Sybil, had she been but reasonable. Oh the misery of life without her! the dread thoughts of revenge at her desertion, which took possession of him day and night, urging him on to violence—to death even—himself or her, or both, he cared not. I am in no humour to follow these; nor his curses and wild despair. Such a companion as Mr. Selwyn was not likely to put better thoughts into his mind; and even he was shocked by what he saw daily and hourly—a deeper sinking into the mire and slough of hateful jealousy, and a brooding over its misery, such as he could not comprehend.

"Gad," he said, one evening after Forster, vainly trying to drown his thoughts in wine, broke out into execrations at Sybil's perfidy, "this will never do, Forster; thou'lt die, man. If thou must have the wench, take her in the devil's name, and have done with her."

Take her! Yes, that was what Mr. Forster had long made up his mind to do; but how to find her? Even Wilson, who knew everything, had failed utterly to trace the fugitives, and had given up the task.

How often had dear old Nanny laid injunctions upon her "bonnie bairnie" never to go out by herself; never to risk the streets alone. But one day, a bright cold morning in November, an urgent message came from Mr. Price, that a certain satin waistcoat for my Lord March was wanted that day, and was to be sent. It was ready. Nanny was out, was going to Covent Garden, she had said; and when she would return was uncertain. Mr. Price's messenger could not return to the shop—he had other errands to do. "Master he'll be very glad to see you, Miss," he said, "and perhaps you'll take it yourself? It is but a step to the Strand."

Why should she not go? No one would notice her; she would be back directly; and so, tying a thick black veil over her hat, and putting on a long warm shawl, she tied up the parcel carefully and went her way. No one noticed her; she reached Mr. Price's safely, and having received his thanks for the beauty of the work, a handsome payment, and material for more embroidery, she hastened back by the road she had come, and reached home, as she felt, unobserved; refreshed and inspirited too by her brisk walk, of which she told Nanny with saucy triumph.

But she had scarcely left the tailor's a moment, when Mr. Selwyn and Mr. Forster, who were sauntering up the Strand, attracted by the beauty of the gay flowers which seemed to sparkle on the white satin lying on the counter, turned into the shop: and by Forster the work was instantly recognised. He knew the pattern—he had helped Sybil to draw it; and a flush of grim joy entered his heart. "I have her now," he thought,—"she cannot escape me."

"A beautiful bit of work that, gentlemen, isn't it?" said the bland tailor, taking it up and holding it to the light; "no such other in London. My Lord March will cut a pretty figure with it on the Mall to-morrow."

"Gad! I'd like such a thing myself, Price," said Mr. Selwyn; "could you get me one?" Mr. Selwyn would have worn my Lord March's old clothes if he could have got them.

"Certainly, sir," replied the obsequious mercer—"certainly; but it's costly, sir—costly."

"Oh, damn the cost! I'll pay you beforehand if you like. Who did it?—How much d'ye want?" cries Selwyn in a breath.

"A young lady, Mr. Selwyn; you can't get things like that from common people. A young *lady*, sir, whom I have known a long time, who works for me. Twenty guineas, sir, is the price, and cheap too."

"By Jove! a lot of money; now, if you'll give me her address, I'll give you the coin," and he shook a heavy purse in the air. "If not, I'll be d—d if I do. Ain't I right, John."

"Quite right," was the husky reply, for in truth Mr. Forster's heart was beating wildly enough.

Mr. Price hesitated, but the chink of the gold was too much for him. He had a bill to settle, and gentlemen were not free of money just then. "Well, sir, I'll tell you, but she's none of *your* sort," he said, with a wink. "And I'll depend on your honour, sir, not to molest her; but if you *could* recommend her, Mr. Selwyn, she'd be thankful. Let me see; Simkins," he cried to a young man writing up account-books within, "what's Miss Morton's address?"

"No. 14 Little Queen Street," replied the man, looking up for an instant, and then going on with his work.

I think if he had known what the weight of those words were, they had never been spoken; but they were precious to the ears that heard them.

"Well, it's a bargain," said Mr. Selwyn, "here's the coin—all honourable, you know, with a lady—and get the work done as soon as you can; there's a good fellow! Come, Jack!"

"Phe-e-ew!" whistled Mr. Selwyn; "now tell me, Jack, art thou not fit to go on thy knees before me? Hadst thou ever a friend so cunning of device as I? To the devil with all thy megrims. Thou shalt have the wench. Chaise and four, posters, and all the relays on the old road warned and ready. By Jove, but thou'rt a lucky dog! But listen, Jack; I'll have all honest, and it's on condition it is so I'll help thee; no other, upon my soul and honour, and that's flat. Wilt thou give me this promise—wilt thou swear it?"

"Upon my honour, Selwyn—upon my honour! I need not to swear."

"No, no occasion, Jack. I'm satisfied, when once thou hast given a promise, thou'lt never fail, as I know in that d—d Darnell business. Now how will it be? Gretna Green of course—Scotch marriage. I take this woman to be my wife—good as any parson patter—a few tears, then smiles; and, by Gad! thou'rt the happiest man in England, and George Selwyn the next, thinking of thee!"

How these confederates watched No. 14 Little Queen Street, how the place was beset, how Nanny's hours of going out were noted, and how one evening, later in the winter, a man came to the door, said he had a special message from Mr. Price, and it was to be delivered to none but Miss Morton herself—need hardly be told more clearly, were I to write a volume to describe what was done: but as Sybil came there, wondering what was wanted, and was dragged out of the street door, a shawl thrown over her head, and a chaise with four horses dashed up at the same moment, and she was forcibly put into it—she fainted with the shock, and recovered—only to find Forster sitting beside her, and the carriage proceeding at full speed.

There was no triumph or disrespect in his voice, nor in the words he spoke. "You have forced me, Sybil, to do this," he said—"I could not live without you. I will guard you now to my life's end, faithfully and truly, but I cannot go back."

Such events could not happen in these days with A 40 or E 29 looking round every corner. There were no day policemen then in London: and the watchmen would not come on duty for several hours. When she was decoyed out, there was hardly any one in the street. "What's that?" cried a woman passing. "Poor thing! What are they doing to her?"

"It's only a couple going to Gretna Green to be married," said Mr. Selwyn. "Good luck to them! that's all; she is a spunky lass to go, isn't she?"

"Yes, sir," said the woman, dropping a curtsy when she saw Mr. Selwyn's laced coat; "that she is, and I wish her good luck, as you do."

No one else had noticed what had happened. Mrs. Robson was out with Nanny, and they had stayed with a friend for "a cup of tea." No one knew the rooms were empty, and the precious treasure away. Ah, poor Nanny! how to her life's end she bewailed that "cup of tea," I need hardly tell; and, for the present, when they got home, the women raved inconsolably.

The relays were sure: not at inns or in towns, but by roadsides and field-gates known to Mr. Forster. Many such a journey had he taken in "the cause," which should defy detection. On the box sat a confident who watched Sybil if Forster were absent; and in obscure villages, or lonely wayside alehouses, they got refreshments. When they reached their destination, Forster went through the ceremony, gave a liberal bribe to the functionary, took the certificate, and, by Scotch border law, Sybil was his. Then the chaise turned from the main road, along dreary moorlands; and, as evening fell, it stopped at a lonely peel or border castle; lights appeared in the windows, and an elderly woman, attended by other servants, met the carriage respectfully.

"Ye're welcome home, Mister John," she said, "an' you too, mem. Eh! but she's a bonnie lady, surr!"

"I'm not his wife! I'm not his wife!" Sybil shrieked wildly; they were almost the first words she had spoken. "Oh save me, if you have any pity!"

"What nonsense, Sybil!" he cried, taking her in his arms, and carrying her into the house unresistingly. "For your own sake, my darling," he continued soothingly, "for your honour, for mine, do not resist your fate; dear old Nanny will be here in a few days, and till she comes you must be patient."

Nor did Forster molest her. Bad as I believe the man to have been, he had for this one helpless being an affection which resisted the evil pleadings of his heart. He seldom saw her but at meals, and his housekeeper, Mrs. Armstrong, entertained Sybil with stories of the old Forsters and the rough border country. In regard to Nanny Keene, Forster was as good as his word; she arrived in a few days, and took possession of her "ain sweet childie," with a thankful heart that Sybil was safe, "an' for guid or ill," she said, when she had heard all, "like a' the world, for sorrow and joy, ma sweetie, a' believe ye're his wife afore God an' man, an' a' the lawyers in Scotland couldna free him frae you, nor ye frae him; and it wuz yer ain dear mither's wish, ye ken weel, so ye'll no gang agen it nae mair."

But even the special pleading of the dear old servant could not satisfy Sybil; she felt outraged, stunned, helpless, and hopeless. To whom could she appeal? We know there was none; and when, to satisfy her conscience, Mr. Forster proposed they should be married by special licence, she felt as if his respect for her had proved his truth, and in her despair she consented.

CHAPTER LXII.

ROGER DARNELL AND COMPANY—DECEMBER 15, 1757.

We are in the old office once more, and see little change as we look about us. The grand old pictures hang on the walls in all the glory of their mellowing colours, and those generations of Darnells seem to look down more lovingly on their descendant as time passes, and more earnestly than ever give him their approval as he looks up at them. Roger Darnell is scarcely changed in the two years which have passed over him: his figure is the same—the fresh florid colour, the scarlet nostril, the keen eye, and the full ruddy lip, are none of them faded, nor have his habits altered. As on the first occasion that we saw him, he has changed his wig and his shoes, set out his papers, and is sitting before the warm fire toasting his handsome legs, and every now and then holding out his hands to the blaze and rubbing them gently. But he does not set to work: and all that pile of correspondence which Mr. Sanders has placed there must wait. I think he must be anxious, for every now and then he raises his head and turns his ear to the door as if to listen, then pulls out his watch, and after a hurried glance puts it back again into his fob, and falls to rubbing his calves and warming his hands once more. "It's past eleven," he said, "and the boat ought to have been up by this time; Gad, I wonder what he'll be like after all that has happened;" and so he waited, thinking over many things that had fallen out in two years—on the wealth he had accumulated, on his fortunate speculations with Ralph's investments, on Mr. Wharton and his concerns; on his daughter, perhaps, on Constance's marriage with Viscount Granton; and on poor Sybil's disappearance. "Ah! that will vex him—the boy was so fond of her, and perhaps I was to blame in letting such a creature out of my sight," he murmured to himself; "who'd ha' thought of her making off in that queer fashion? Well, well, it can't be helped, and he'll find her if he wants her. I'd rather, however, it was Dolly's chance, for he's a fine fellow, and they'll make a hero of him, by George! they will, and he'll deserve it. I wonder if he'll be up to-day, though I don't think he'll spare horse-flesh if he's in the humour I take him to be. I wouldn't—I can't settle to anything, Sanders," he said, as that good gentleman opened the door, and looked in with a letter in his hand. "Don't bring me business, for goodness' sake."

"It's only from Brown & Marshall, sir, about that saltpetre, and it can wait. I think we had as well sell, Mr. Darnell."

"Oh yes, sell, Sanders, by all means. By Jove! I've never told you, and, faith! I hardly know whether I'm on my head or my heels."

"Why, what's the matter, Mr. Darnell?"

"The matter! why, there's the *Valiant* in the Downs, and Ralph on board with Mr. Clive's private despatches—and he may be here any minute. Read his note. I got it this morning early from Portsmouth."

"God bless the boy!" cried Mr. Sanders, exultingly, as he read a hurried note from Ralph. "Why, it takes my breath away to hear this."

"So it did mine, sir, and my brains too, I think, else you should have heard it long before. What's that? By George! it's Ralph," and he rushed to the window to see a chaise and four, with the horses steaming in the frosty air, stop at the hall door, and a tall figure wrapped in a cloak alight from it, shaking hands with the porter violently. "It's him!—it's Ralph!" cried Mr. Darnell, and before he could get back to his chair, a strong hurried step traversed the office—the door was thrown open—and with a cry of "O my dear uncle!" Ralph was in the arms wide-stretched to receive him.

I am sure neither of them could speak for some moments, and Ralph's hand, slid round his uncle, met a hearty loving grasp from Mr. Sanders; and so they stood together, silently and with grateful hearts, and honest tears in their eyes.

"Let's have a look at thee," said Mr. Darnell, as he held Ralph from him. "Why, God bless me! how thou'rt grown and improved! India has made a man of thee—hasn't it, Sanders? Another good hug, Ralph, and I shall believe I have thee, at last," and the embrace was closer than before.

"At last, dear uncle!" said Ralph, with a great joyous sob—"at last, and I thank God!"

"So do I, my boy," returned Mr. Darnell, blowing his nose sonorously and wiping his eyes—"so do I."

"I could not rest, uncle," said Ralph, "after I wrote a hurried note by a boatman. You got it?

"'Faith, it was the first thing that was put into my hand this morning, Ralph; and, as I told Sanders, I've no notion how I got here or what I did, but I suspect my lady thought I was crazed; and here thou art, my boy, and I'm so happy!—oh! so happy, Ralph. Sit down, sit down, Mr. Sanders. Stay, here's a guinea apiece for the postboys—give it them, Sanders, to drink Ralph's health."

"They've got enough already, uncle. I haven't spared money, with these papers in my pocket, I assure you."

"I choose to give it, Ralph," said his uncle, with his own peremptory humour, "and it's naught to thee. Come, boy, sit down. God bless me! how shall I ever contain what I have to hear? What's the news, lad; and how's Mr. Clive?"

"We have won a great victory, sir, and you'll read Mr. Clive's account of it yourself. That horrible miscreant, the Nawab, didn't fight much, and Mr. Clive beat him at Plassey, and another Nawab's set up, and the old one's dead; and, by Jove! sir, Mr. Clive's Nawab of Bengal, and can do as he pleases. That's my news, sir—isn't it glorious? We're home first, after all, and Scrafton's been carrying on till he's not a spar left, and beaten everything, and run clean through the French cruisers and all."

"Of course he would, Ralph—of course; and we shall have the Tower guns firing such a salute before evening as London hath not heard for many a day. Oh that glorious fellow!"

"Mr. Clive, sir?—ay he is glorious, and nothing can stop him now," cried Ralph, exultingly. "Why, sir, he's beaten Monsieur Crapaud out of Bengal, clean; and he wont stop their neither!"

"Mr. Ralph may be hungry, sir, and I've ordered some luncheon up-stairs. Won't you come?" said Mr. Sanders.

"Ay, lad, let's drink thy health. Champagne, Sanders!—nothing less for his Majesty's messenger. By George! he ought to knight thee, Ralph. Come along," and he put his arm round the young man and drew him on lovingly, and proudly too, as they passed through the office, the clerks crowding about their old companion, wondering at his erect military bearing, and offering their hands. No old grudges or jealousies now. Ralph greeted them all kindly and heartily, and so the gentlemen passed up stairs. There the dear old ladies kissed him, and put him on their best sofa, and they all stood round him; and if tears stood in their eyes, I can't, for one, blame them for their fond emotion.

And by the time lunch was finished, and the party had drained honest bumpers of the glorious old wine to Ralph's health and to Mr. Clive's, and were in a state of joy such as I cannot pretend to describe, Mr. Darnell's coach had come, and Ralph had to change his travelling suit for better garments in which to visit the Minister; and when he returned, dressed as became him for the occasion, there was a shout from the gentlemen, and so many flattering speeches from the dear old ladies, at his handsome appearance, that Ralph's cheeks burned again, as well they might. So also, as they went down-stairs, they found the old hall full—clerks, porters, warehousemen, were all assembled; and Mr. Sanders having told all of the news, and how Ralph had fought through the battles in Bengal, there was set up such a cheer—such cheers, I believe, as the old place had never heard before.

"Remember, dear uncle," said Ralph in some embarrassment, as they had nearly reached the Secretary of State's office, "that I am not Ralph Darnell now, but Captain Smithson, mentioned in these despatches, and you must be careful of that."

I think this simple speech was a sore stab to the worthy merchant, who could not speak for some minutes. "Ah, yes—I remember it all now, Ralph," he said at length. "Thou hadst best tell thine own story; I should but mar it, and we will talk over old times presently."

And very modestly and clearly was the whole story given to the celebrated man who heard it, and with a strange thrill too, as he looked upon one who had survived the horrible Black Hole, and who had borne his part with honour in Plassey's victory.

"I shall lay these important despatches before his Majesty at once, sir," he said, "and take his commands in regard to you. Where am I to find you?"

"With me, sir," replied Mr. Darnell; "my nephew knows no other home while he is in England.

"You are fortunate, Mr. Darnell, to possess such a relation. I can but glance over these documents, but I perceive that Captain Smithson's name is mentioned in the highest terms; and you must excuse me if I leave you, for I cannot delay this glorious news, at once so wonderful and so unexpected. You will hear the Tower guns presently."

"I see," said his uncle, as they returned to the City, "there is nothing for it but to let you be Ralph Smithson to the officials for the present; but among ourselves, I never shall know or use any name but your own."

"And if I could take it with honour," cried Ralph, "I wouldn't allow the other to exist for a day. Nay, I am on fire, sir, to prove —to prove—"

"To prove what, Ralph?" exclaimed his uncle, eagerly bending forward. "My dear boy, what?" and Ralph could see how Mr. Darnell was trembling.

"To prove I am Ralph Darnell, your dear brother's son, and that my—my mother was—was—married."

This came out with a great gulp; and Mr. Darnell listened to his nephew with such amazement that he could not speak.

"Married!" he cried at length, slapping his thigh violently. "Thou'rt not dreaming?"

"No, sir," returned Ralph, "it's no dream, I thought it was one once; but it's all here"—and he opened the ruffles of his shirt to show the little bag round his neck—"and I've never parted with it; and Colonel Clive's certificate, given on Plassey battle-field, is along with it. I'll—I'll—open it, sir."

"No, no, Ralph—not here; wait—wait till we get home. Lord, if it be true—if it be true! who can fathom Thy mysteries?" and as he took off his hat reverently, Ralph could see his uncle's lips moving in prayer, and the tears welling up in his misty eyes. And so they drove to the mansion in Bloomsbury Square; and as the door was thrown open, his aunt and his cousins met the returned prodigal according to their own peculiar fashions. I believe Mrs. Roger so far relaxed that, though she looked away, she held up her cheek for a kiss, such as should be received by one like her, and I'm quite sure that Ralph's heart did not prompt more; nor indeed more to his elder cousin, who shrank back from the handsome young soldier wearing his gracious Majesty's uniform. But it was quite a different matter with Dolly, who, with tears streaming from her eyes, could not contain herself, and fell upon his neck sobbing, and perhaps got more than one kiss, as did her younger sisters who hung about Ralph as the whole party marched up stairs.

"We've a good deal to say to each other, Anne," said Mr. Darnell to his wife as he was dressing, "and I would like to have it out alone as soon as may be after dinner. Well, what do you think of your scampish nephew now?"

"He's improved, certainly," replied the lady, bridling; "but I'm quite sure he's as forward as ever; the way he kissed Dorothy was—"

"By Jove! and he might kiss her to the end of his days," cries her husband. "As to you and your daughter, I'll be d—d if I know how he kissed you at all; I wouldn't have touched either of you, I'll be—"

"You need not swear, Mr. Darnell; what you are pleased to say is quite affronting enough without an oath. I say the young man's improved, as far as outward appearance goes; but as to his heart—if the Lord's grace—"

"Well, be as civil as you can, Anne—that's all. I don't suppose he will give you much trouble."

"Is he to stay here, Mr. Darnell? because—because—"

"Because what?" cried her husband, turning round sharply, with the ends of his cravat in his hand.

"Oh, nothing," says the lady, not admiring her lord's eyes. "Only I hope he'll conform to our habits and—"

"He'll do as he likes, madam. By George! a poor fellow, who's been twice wounded in action, and has escaped massacre—hideous massacre, ma'am—to be—to be— Damme, ma'am, he shall do as he likes." And Mrs. Darnell thought once more that discretion was the better part of valour, and was silent.

Perhaps neither Mr. Darnell nor Ralph had much appetite for dinner. Had they not eaten a capital lunch? We know what was lying at both their hearts, and how slowly dinner must have passed. So when Grimes had left, Mrs. Darnell made a formal curtsy to Ralph, and said to her flock, "Come, my dears," and rose; and Ralph whispered to Dolly, who was fit to cry, "I'll tell you all about India by-and-by;" and they went away, and the men were alone.

"I thought she'd never go, Ralph," said his uncle. "But come, don't keep me in suspense; I'm sick with this excitement. And he filled a large glass with Burgundy, drank it off, and pushed the bottle to Ralph.

"No, thank you, sir; I'd rather be cool." And, taking the bag from his neck, he proceeded deliberately to cut open the covers one by one. Perhaps his hand did not tremble so much as it did when, in Plassey grove, only a few months ago, Colonel Clive unripped what he could not hold; but I am by no means sure that it was steady.

"This is the last, uncle; don't be impatient," he said, sadly. "Look! here's my father's name embroidered over the silk—HENRY."

"Quick—quick, lad!" cried Mr Darnell, almost gasping, as he leaned over the table. "I see—I see! but the paper—the paper!"

"Look! uncle, they are both here."

We know what he saw, or ought to have seen; but even that strong Darnell—the man who dealt with vast combinations of worldly transactions, mercantile and political, without a change of muscle—seemed to be at once helpless as a child; and his hand, holding the two papers, dropped heavily on the table.

"Uncle—dear uncle!" cried Ralph starting up; "you are not ill?"

"No, boy, not ill—not ill; but that paper brings back many a bitter thought. So—I am better now," and he took up the papers one by one, and read them.

"Is it true, uncle? Is it true?" gasped Ralph, for his uncle's face had not moved a muscle.

"Who can say?" he said, with a great sigh—"who can say?" and was silent again, staring blankly across the room.

"Oh, uncle!" cried Ralph, "you don't think it's true—I am sure you don't; and I'll tear it up, and no one'll know but you and me; and I'll go back to India, and you will forget all about it. Give it me."

"Who can say?" said Mr. Darnell, absently, in a hoarse whisper; "and there's Constance married, and all to be undone. God! Is this true?"

"Uncle—uncle, you did not tell me that, you didn't indeed," cried Ralph. "Oh, give it me! What's the use of a fellow like me coming home to trouble you all? I'll tear it up now before you, and I'll never, *never* say one word about it to any one—upon my honour. You kept my secret before, and you'll keep this. Sooner than hurt Constance, I'd—"

"Tear it, Ralph! for shame! What put that into thy brain?" cried his uncle, recovering. "Tear it!—God help me! but you shall have such right as man's justice can give. No—it was but for a moment, boy, that I was confused. I, Roger Darnell, with God's help, will see you in your just place; nor would Constance, nor your uncle Geoffrey, for a moment—*for a moment*, think of disputing your right. But they can't make you Sir Ralph Darnell of Melcepeth. It's the law only can do that, and I'll not sleep till I begin it;" and he got up and rang the bell. "The coach round directly," he said to the servant; and filling another glass as the man shut the door,
I drink to thy truth, Ralph, and to thy right, and may God help it!

We will go to Peed now—I know where to find him. Come, for a cup of tea, and keep thine own counsel. Tell the girls about the Black Hole, if you like—anything to pass the time; but if I were you, I'd rather face Suraj-oo-Doulah's cavalry than those women. Hark! there are the guns—hurrah!'

But Ralph was steady, and bore himself well in the drawing-room. The enthusiasm with which his uncle had thrown himself into the matter, and his prompt decision, dissipated the fear which had gathered about him, and his wondering audience heard what we know of with tears and shudderings. Even Mrs. Darnell relented, and cried too; and admitted to herself that the young man's heart seemed to be touched—as indeed it was, and very deeply. At home among them all again—familiar streets, faces, sounds, with honour and distinction awaiting him, and but two years had passed—could it be otherwise than touched?

I need not go over the same subject again with Mr. Peed. That worthy gentleman's ruffles were as white, his hands as spotless, his snuff-box as full, as ever. It seemed only yesterday that Ralph had seen him, as he went into the parlour in Lombard Street—as he heard the will read. Perhaps Mr. Peed suspected how it had been lost; but when Ralph came in His Majesty's uniform to Queen Square with Mr. Darnell, as an apparition, and he knew how the glorious news for which the Tower guns had fired had been brought—he looked upon Mr. Ralph Darnell in a very different light from the *nullius filius* of whom he had had legal experience. Mr. Peed was alone, drinking his claret and eating his walnuts, as the gentlemen entered; and they were not long, you may be sure, in coming to the point. Despite of his professional etiquette, the production of the certificate staggered the worthy little man. "He had never—no, not in all his experience—heard of such a case. Only to think of how it was found! But, sir, Colonel Clive was right; but for his attestation, the paper would have been open to the gravest suspicion—legally, of course, sir," and he bowed to Ralph. "I don't see how we could have proceeded. Now, sir, this must be proved, and I would recommend instant action. No delay at all, sir; we must set to work at once."

"Certainly, Peed; there can be no delay," said Mr. Darnell; "and that's why I've come to you out of hours."

"I'm never 'out of hours' to a client, Mr. Darnell," said the lawyer, brushing away his snuff—"never; midnight would have been just the same. Curious enough, too, Wilson's in the house, getting up some papers. He's just dined with me.—Wilson!" he cried, rising and putting his head into another door which he opened, "come here. When can you leave London?"

"Now, sir, if you like; I've my coat in the hall. Your servant

Mr. Darnell. My God!" he exclaimed, starting back, "it's not Ralph Darnell?"

"The same, Mr. Wilson," said Ralph, advancing; "and glad to see you again."

"Now I understand," said Wilson; "and I was right after all."

"As you always are, Wilson. Now listen; you have to go with Mr.—Captain—Darnell here, to prove this certificate of marriage. He knows the place, and you must make an extract from the church register, and have it witnessed; that register must be found sir."

"Of course, Mr. Peed, I see what's to be done. Mr. Darnell and I will arrange it, if he'll give me a seat home."

"Go at once," said Mr. Peed; "Jenkins will finish the papers."

And so the three gentlemen returned to Bloomsbury Square.

"And I may quite depend upon you, Mr. Wilson, in this matter?" said Mr. Darnell.

"You trusted me in a more delicate one once before, sir," said Mr. Wilson, with a sly look, "and were not deceived."

"You! God bless me! how?" cried Mr. Darnell.

"Wait a moment and you shall see," was the reply, and he went into the hall. While the two sat wondering what he could mean, a figure with a white beard, a slouched hat, and a long coat, entered limping.

"How mosh per shent, Mishter Darnil? How mosh per shent?" it said, with a strong Jewish accent.

"Ah, my friend, I know you now!" cried Mr. Darnell, laughing heartily; "as you were true in that matter, so be in this, and your reward will be greater."

"What matter, uncle?" cried Ralph.

"Nothing to you now," was the reply; and when Mr. Wilson had departed, and they found the ladies had gone to bed, Mr. Darnell yawned wearily. "Enough for to-day, Ralph," he said; "come to bed."

We may believe it had been a trying day to both, and now that the excitement was past, Ralph was very weary. I think if Mrs. Darnell could have looked in at the door as Ralph knelt down beside his bed before he went to sleep, and heard what he murmured to One who is ever listening, even she might have owned that his heart was touched, and grateful too.

CHAPTER LXIII.

ON THE TRACK.

I DO not think I need to follow minutely the details of the few days in London which intervened between Ralph's arrival and the day of his departure for the north. Every hour seemed an age to the young man: but there were councils at the India House to be attended: there were visits to His Majesty's Secretary of State, and official business to be transacted at the Privy Council Board: and there was also an audience of His Majesty to be gone through, wherein Ralph was not, to be sure, knighted, but all was said to Captain Smithson of a complimentary character that could be desired, and a promise graciously given that the provisional rank conferred by Colonel Clive and the Council at Calcutta should be confirmed. I am not at all sure, however, that the Council in Leadenhall Street were prepared for what some of them, even already, were pleased to term the effects of Mr. Clive's personal ambition and greed of gain; nor were their minds at all able to grasp the probable contingencies of his policy. They refused to look upon the transactions with Omichund and Meer Jaffier as honourable or creditable; and as these opinions spread abroad, a great many persons adopted them, and thus a hot reception was being prepared for Mr. Clive whenever he might return, and when, among others, the mild Mr. Cowper was to write about him in bitter words of satire like these—

'A despot big with power obtained by wealth,
And that obtained by rapine and by stealth;
With Asiatic vices stored thy mind
But left their virtues and thine own behind,
And having tracked thy soul, brought home the fee
To tempt the poor to sell himself to thee!'

Well, those things had to follow; and for the present we have no connection with them whatever. We only know that Ralph could see little to dim his hero's lustre, and wherever he went, or was called upon for an opinion (he was ever too modest to venture one himself), he spoke with an enthusiasm which was infectious, and a conviction which, even from one so young, carried great weight, that heretofore there had been no general in India like Clive; no one with any true political comprehension, no one who, with the decision and firmness necessary, could have carried the British interests through a crisis which, if not met in the spirit it had been met in, would have proved, instead of a splendid triumph, a national degradation. I repeat, I have nothing to do with the public opinion of the time; history has faithfully given all those events, and posterity has judged, and will judge, as it thinks fit, in regard to them.

But I know that Ralph chafed at the delay. He had a mind to have gone to see Elliot, but the *Renown*, in which was Mrs. Wharton, had not arrived, and perhaps for himself Mr. Elliot had no particular interest; but he sent him a bill for a hundred pounds, and begged his acceptance of it in memory of old times, and I am sure George Elliot was too glad to think the good-natured donor had not forgotten him, to quarrel about receiving his assistance as a loan, as Ralph wrote, if he would not take it as a gift.

In truth, Ralph was a rich man; his investments had had lucky sales; he had lived a quiet life in Calcutta, and his share of the proceeds at Moorshedabad, besides a large donation for special services which the Council voted him, altogether swelled his amount in the books to a heavy sum. Mr. Sanders insisted upon giving in an exact account of the stewardship of Roger Darnell and Company, and the balance was a very different one to what we can remember on a former occasion when we looked into the books, for a total of £19,827, 3s. 4½d., which Mr. Sanders displayed in triumph, was indeed satisfactory.

"I don't let it lie here in deposit, Ralph," he said, "but invest it in Company's stock, which gives 12½ per cent. per year; and till you return to India, there's no occasion to disturb it."

I have said all this, because, between Mr. Roger Darnell's earnest pleadings that he would at least eat a Christmas dinner with them, and his engagements, there was no resource but to stay over the 25th. Perhaps that Christmas dinner was not a very merry one; but it was with a bright anticipation of success, of fervent hope that his future position might be established, that he took his seat in the York stage-coach on the next morning—Mr. Wilson being opposite to him; and the lumbering vehicle pursued its slow but steady journey. What could Mr. Darnell say but God bless him! as he bade him farewell? As to the women, none of them knew why Ralph was going northwards, except only to see his uncle and Constance; but Dolly's soft blue eyes told tales, I fear, more plainly than Ralph was prepared for; and on her account, if no other, perhaps the young man was glad to leave the mansion in Bloomsbury Square, which, in spite of his uncle and Dorothy, chilled him by its unbending formality.

So at last York was passed, and Newcastle, and at Alnwick they had but three stages to Belford, where Ralph, who knew the country, proposed they should put up. There was a good, quiet inn there, and they would be comfortable. Mr. Wilson could make allowance for the variable humour of his companion, which now reached a condition of impatience or of wild excitement, and was again depressed. Into the object of the journey, Wilson absolutely refused to enter, as also into answers to inquiries after old friends. Forster, he said, had disappeared; so had Selwyn; and indeed he himself had much withdrawn from gay life, and was too glad he had been able to do so, to risk aught in it again. Mr. Peed had given him a small share in the business, and he had no lack of clients on his own account.

As they passed the bridge at Felton, and the sound of the brawling Coquet, now a deep brown and speckled with white foam, came to them, and Ralph looked up the river with misty eyes, to where the rich woods of Melcepeth covered the banks, and the white smoke rose from the chimneys of the dear old castle high into the calm frosty air—Mr. Wilson guessed what that place might be, for his companion could not speak. There were too many sweet and bitter memories mingling together to attempt vent for them in words, and he did the best he could to divert the attention of the other passengers from his companion's emotion. Nor had they far to travel now: Alnwick was passed, and with the evening sun sparkling from the Hall windows, and the vane over the tall church-spire, and clothing the heavy woods about it with a mellow glory, the pretty little town of Belford was reached.

It was too late that afternoon to do more than inform the clergyman of Lucker of their proposed visit next day. Mr. Wilson wrote on the part of Peed, Peed, & Brisbane, and Mr. Clerk would understand that the registers were required for a legal inquiry. This note was sent by a boy on the inn pony to Bamborough, where Mr. Clerk, the clergyman, lived, and returned with a reply that he would be ready in Lucker Church at eleven the following day, glad to afford any information in his power. Mr. Wilson that night slept in perfect unconsciousness, which the long day's jolting and confinement, and a tumbler of stiff brandy-punch, had helped to bring about; but if his appearance was to be taken as proof, I do not think Ralph had had like good fortune. When he came down to breakfast, he was pale, and seemed as weary as when he reached Belford the day before. He had scarcely, indeed, slept a wink; and we know enough of his nervous cast of mind to believe, that what no physical danger or responsibility could at all affect him in, had in the present instance affected him very differently. He must be legitimate, or the contrary; that was a broad fact staring him in the face, never absent for a moment from his mind, and insupportable now the crisis had come so near. I think Ralph could have quarrelled with Mr. Wilson for the breakfast he ate, which the north-country landlord had served up with a profusion unknown to London innkeepers. Every mouthful seemed but to prolong instead of reduce the capability of consumption: and when Ralph could stay no longer, he went out, and walked about before the inn door, where he was joined by the landlord.

"Will ye be wantin' onythin', Captain?" asked the host. "Ye've eaten bit a puir breekfest, surr. Tired, perhaps? Eh my! bit it's a lang wey till London."

"I'll be better presently, when I've had a walk, thank you," said Ralph, wishing to get rid of him.

"Ay, surr, the lad's reddy to gang wi' ye. Ye'll jist go on straicht afore ye, till ye come till a lane on yer left hand, that'll tak ye by Mr. Forster's of Adderstone: an' if ye follow that, ye'll be seyn at Luckur, surr; an', comin' back, ye may like to see Twizell Dean, surr—that's Mister Selby's, ye ken. It's a fine place."

"Do you remember a clergyman of the name of Johnston there—at Lucker, some years ago?" asked Ralph abruptly, in a tone intended to be indifferent, but which trembled more than he could disguise.

"Jonsin, surr, Jonsin? Na, a' canna sey that a' dey. Stop, a'll ax ma missis, surr; there's naebody like wimen furr mindin' places an' times. If a' sez to ma wife, What dey wuz it as we went till—"

"Please ask her," said Ralph, with a slight gesture of impatience.

"Jane! come here till the Captain. Hey's axed mey if a Mr. Jonsin wuz ever parson o' Luckur Church, an' a' canna remember jist—"

"Jonstin?" cried the woman, dropping a smart curtsy to the well-dressed young man as she came forward; "na, there never wuz no parsin at Luckur caa'd that. There's been Steward, an' Cooke, an' Furlong, an' now there's Clerk; but niver no Johnstin, surr. It's a poor place that Luckur, Captain, an' they's glad to get oot on't, them as comes. Na, there niver wuz none Jonsin, surr—niver that a' mind, an' a'm better nor forty year old, an' niver wuz oot o' they parts. A' wuz borrn at Warenford, an' that's nigher Luckur than Belford, surr."

"It must have been some stranger, I daresay; but we'll soon see," thought Ralph. "I thought you were never coming, Wilson; let's be off. I can't wait—really I can't;" and they strode away together, the frosty earth crackling under their boots.

"That lad's no richt, Rrichard," said the landlady to her lord, as they watched the two figures. "That'll be some lawyer wark, an' nae gude comin' o't. There's that in that laddie's braw een that a'd no care to sey in ma lad's. Eh my! bit there's mair trubble in the warld nor we ken o'; an' the Lord be merciful!"

"Amen!" said the man. "He's a fine lad that, tho', and meybe a'd dee na harrm if a'd tak the spring-cart doon to Luckur, and see for them eggs they promised at the 'Hoose;' an' they'd ha' some at Adderstone tey, mebbe."

"Let 'em get on," said the woman. "It's a guid thocht, an' ye'll jist ask Janet Arrmstrong about the hams she was t' gie us, and them sides o' bakin."

"A' rycht," he replied, going to the stables. "A' mind."

Lucker Church—a poor little place then, and not much improved now—stands on a knoll above the road, with no pretension to appearance inside or out. A comfortable modern parsonage in the Elizabethan style, is a great contrast to the church itself, which has only a certain antiquity to recommend it. It is near the centre of the small hamlet, close to the bank of the Warren, a brook which, having dashed foaming down Twizell Dean from the moors above, follows a quiet course through fields and meadows to the sea. In summer time, when the fine ash-trees by the stream are clothed with rich foliage, and the brook runs on with a gentle hum and murmur, and the gurgling splash of the trout can be heard under the alders, Lucker has a certain quiet, rustic beauty, and such, no doubt, it had that day when Henry Darnell and Grace Smithson drove up in the light cart, and— Wait, O reader! I have no long suspense for you now.

The landlord's directions had been perfectly explicit. Mr. Wilson and Ralph reached the blacksmith's shop at the corner of the lane, where it turned off from the highroad—it is still there—and, dismissing the lad to his destination of Warenford, they went on past Adderstone gates, and as they dipped the brow of an undulation in the ground, the little hamlet of Lucker was before them. How well Ralph remembered it! How many a lovely trout had he not caught in the little river, when his uncle, Sir Geoffrey, long ago, used to pay an annual visit to the Forsters of Adderstone!

The men had hardly spoken since they left Belford, and the pace at which Ralph walked was not an easy one for the London clerk to keep up with; but he did his best.

"I often wonder what's become of Forster," said Mr. Wilson. "I can't trace him. Forster of Adderstone—do they belong to him?"

"The names are different," said Ralph, "But come on—come on. You'll see Lucker directly. Now I remember every foot of the way—come." I think he could have run, so intense was his motion, as he hurried on faster than ever. "See! there it is—and the old church—and the great farm-house in the trees—come!"

It was not far, and as they neared the church they saw Mr. Clerk, the clergyman, with another person, standing on the knoll by the belfry, and hats were taken off and courteous salutes exchanged. Mr. Wilson was spokesman, and they proceeded in to the little vestry. Cold and chill as the church was, it struck heavily to the heart of Ralph Darnell as he looked round the bare walls and homely pews of the place. He shivered as he entered, and took off his hat reverently.

"I am an agent—clerk—of Peed, Peed, & Brisbane, of London," said Mr. Wilson, by way of opening.

"So I see, sir, by the note you wrote me yesterday. What can I do for you?" asked Mr. Clerk, civilly.

"We wish to prove a certificate of marriage, of which this is a copy," said Mr. Wilson, handing him a paper. "We can show the original if necessary."

Mr. Clerk took the copy. "I know the names," he said, "specified in this paper—Henry Darnell and Grace Smithson. I have heard of them; but this I do not know—Jeremiah Johnston. There never was an incumbent here of that name. But stay, some one else may have officiated. A private marriage, perhaps, by licence."

"If so, it would be registered," said Mr. Wilson, decidedly,

"Of course—of course, sir; and here are the books, and the date is—?"

"The 14th of July 1734," replied Mr. Wilson precisely.

"Very good; now we shall see. 1720 to 1750—this is the book. Not many registers, you see, sir, in our little church, but what there are have been carefully set down."

"Ay, surr," observed the clerk, "nae doot o' that. Johnstin!" he continued to himself, biting his nails—"Johnstin! A' mind no minister—no, nor curate o' that name in these parts."

"Silence!" cried Ralph, grinding the iron heel of his boot on the floor. "Don't interrupt us!" and the man hung back timorously.

"1730—31—32—33—34," continued the clergyman, turning over the pages. "Ah! we have it now, January, February—no entries. March, April, May, June, July. Now, sir, this is the page. John Reed and Mary White, 9th; James Robson and Jane Darling, 16th. No, sir, it's not here. There is no such marriage in the register. There must be some mistake—perhaps in the copy. Have you the original? Can you let me see it?"

Mr. Wilson turned to Ralph, who, with trembling hands, was tearing at his shirt-ruffles, and at the bag. Who was to open it now?

"Give it me, sir," said Mr. Wilson in a whisper. "For God's sake, don't tremble so—he'll suspect. Wait a moment, Mr. Clerk. This has been kept with much care, as you see, but you shall have it directly. Hold these, Captain Smithson," and he handed the covers one by one to Ralph, as he opened them with his penknife. How well we know them now, and the last with HENRY sewn upon it!

"Here, sir, compare the two. You'll see there's no error in the draft," said Mr. Wilson.

"A' kno's that writin'," exclaimed the clerk, who had craned forward. "A' kno's . . . in a moment, surr," and he darted out of the vestry.

"It's no use, Mr. Wilson," said the clergyman, with a deep sigh, as he examined the stained and blurred document with profound interest—"no use. I wonder such a paper ever deceived any one. It's in the last degree informal, and there are no witnesses. I hope you're not personally interested in this, but only as a matter of business. You, as a lawyer, sir, can have but one opinion. Well, Richard, what's this?" he continued, as the clerk returned.

"It's his writin', surr. Ye'll mind the letters, surr. Look!" and he handed several old copybooks to the clergyman. "Them's mine, surr, whin I was bein' teached to write, an' that's his writin', the villain!"

There was no question: that of the copyhooks and the certificate tallied exactly.

"Whose?" cried Ralph, in a hollow, wretched voice. "Speak, man! before God, in the house of God, speak the truth!"

"John Armstrong's," said the man, "an' a'll sweer till it afore the altar, the villain—"

"Villain!" cried the clergyman. "What do you know of him?"

"He kept a little school here, Mr. Clerk, when I wuz a lad, and some o' uz went till it. There's mony a ane aboot Luckur as can speak to that writin' besides mey. Villain! yes, surr—smuggler, robber, Jacobite—what ye like! Wasn't he out in the '45, an' hanged an' a'? Not even his black lies aboot Surr Geoffrey Darnell could save him. Stop, surr, there's ma mither—she'd likely kno' aboot this black bizness, a'm thinkin'. He lived there, in that hoose hard by the church, surr, did Armstrong. But stop—ma mither'll remembir, I daresay, better nor mey—"

"Look to your friend," said the clergyman, kindly, to Mr. Wilson. "This scene appears to agitate him."

Never in his life, accustomed to deathbed scenes, where poor possessors of world's riches were vainly trying to gasp out a few intelligible words as to their disposal—never with criminals, vainly struggling against overwhelming evidence—had John Wilson seen such a face as that. "Some wine, sir, if you wouldn't see him die. Quick! Mr. Darnell!—Ralph! Oh, don't take on so! Drink this."

There was sacramental wine in a cupboard, and Mr. Clerk hastily poured some into one of the cups and held it out, and Ralph drank it mechanically. "One of the tried of the Lord," he murmured. "May it strengthen him body and soul, O merciful Father!"

"I cannot bear it, Wilson," said the poor fellow, gasping; "yet I will hear the worst to the end. Let the woman speak when she comes."

"A' mind it weel, gentlemen," said the old dame, when she had seated herself, and a sip of the wine had been given her; "weel—rycht weel. We wuz a' oot in the hayfields, an' naebody here but Armstrong, the schulemester. We heerd, lang after it wuz, that a man an' a womin had gane intill the church wi' him, an' wuz married by him: an' a' remember as weel as if it wuz yesterday, that Armstrong, when we a' com'd hame, wuz tellin' Jeremy Simpson—he wuz the clerk then—that he'd had a deal o' trouble to find the key, an' a gentleman an' lady had com'd jest to see the church, and gon'd awey. There's plenty mair, surr, that kno's o' this bit mey; bit a'm tellin' the truth, surr; an' they said it wuz that wild Harry Darnell an'—"

"Before God! is it the truth, woman?" cried Ralph, with a quivering face, and interrupting her.

"Before the Lord, an' before the holy breed an' wine that I've drunk, I'm tellin' nae lee, gentlemen!" she answered solemnly.

"There's no—"

"Stop!" said the woman, interrupting Mr. Wilson. "It wuz sed after mony a day, them folk had come from Lamberton to North Sunderland in a boat, an' sae come here. Maybe ye'd heer o' them at Lamberton Pike, maybe—"

"Let us go—come away, Wilson—come," said Ralph, huskily.

"If this treachery—for treachery it has been—relates to you, sir," said the clergyman, laying his hand tenderly on Ralph's arm, "I can but offer you my sympathy—that of a poor servant of the Lord who has had his trials too. Try, sir, to bear this heavy wound calmly, and as a Christian man should in his life's warfare; for what saith the holy Psalmist?—'He that goeth on his way weeping, and beareth good seed, shall doubtless come again with joy.'"

Why of all others should he have chosen that text?—who could say?

"Amen!" said Ralph, solemnly. "Before that altar my dear mother knelt, believing one true who knelt by her, but who was false—and a ruffian read God's words over her. I will but kiss the place, sir, alone—it is holy to me," and he went out of the room into the church. They saw him reverently kneel down on the altar steps and pray: then after a while he rose and came to them again, calmer, but with a stern expression on his face, which John Wilson had never seen before.

"I am ready," he said—"let us go. I know the worst now, and it matters little for the future."

"And these?" asked Mr. Wilson.

"They are precious relics of her," he said—"of her who was true—not of him who was false—and they shall lie at my heart till I die;" and he folded them up and put them away as they had been since Plassey, and went out.

"What a noble fellow!" whispered Mr. Clerk, wiping his eyes—"a true soldier of the Lord. I think this is not his first trial."

"He has had some bitter experiences," returned Mr. Wilson. "He was in the Black Hole of Calcutta, and has fought with Mr. Clive."

"And there is no hope in this matter?"

"None," said Mr. Wilson, as they followed Ralph,—"none whatever. No legal firm in England could lay this case before counsel. No, sir, it's a sad business; but there's no hope, and we thank you all the same for your courtesy. Don't we, Captain Smithson?" and Ralph bowed.

"I thought you said—I thought he was a Darnell," whispered the clergyman.

"Not now, I think, nor henceforth, sir," was Mr. Wilson's reply, "or I'm much mistaken."

It was well the landlord had driven down his cart to Lucker. "He would walk home," he said, and gave the reins to Mr. Wilson. I do not think Ralph could have walked back, but he would leave no stone unturned that gave the slightest chance of success. They took a chaise to Berwick and Lamberton, but we need not follow them, for they sought for proof in vain. If the marriage before God's altar was false, what hope was there that one at a turnpike gate would be truer? Who remembered the hasty marriages of twenty-two years ago, or kept registers of half of them? It was enough to most who came there to "tak' a loup ower Lamberton Pike." Some old torn greasy registers were shown; but the pike-keeper of Henry Darnell and Grace Smithson's time had been changed, and was dead long ago. Ralph found some of Drever's family in Berwick, and told them how he had died, and what money was coming to them; but the rest was all a blank; and on the third day Ralph and Mr. Wilson abandoned further search, and returned to Belford. As Ralph wrote the details to his uncle Roger with a heavy heart, and Mr. Wilson made his official report to his principal, there was at least this assurance to Ralph, that the secret was known only to those few, and they would be faithful.

CHAPTER LXIV.

CRAIG PEEL.

As long as any excitement of search or chance of discovering witnesses—even of the Scotch marriage if there had been one—remained, Ralph had borne up bravely, and with far greater mental resolution than

Mr. Wilson had expected. That gentleman was too well experienced in the ordinary actions and emotions of the human mind to expect that Ralph would not suffer some revulsion of the strain to which he had been subjected since his arrival in England; and all the stories he remembered of illnesses at lonely inns, and the possible prospect of having to nurse a patient with brain fever for many days, combined to induce very unpleasant forebodings. I feel certain that Mr. Wilson had some such dread at his heart when, on the morning after their return from Berwick, Ralph pushed away his plate at the breakfast table, and leaning back in his chair, looking hot and feverish, sat covering his face with his hands, and when the cloth had been removed, laid his head on the table wearily, and in the bitterness of his spirit, groaned aloud—"Oh that I had never left India! Oh that I had never come home!"

"For shame, Mr. Darnell!" said Wilson, sharply enough; "you have done your duty, and could not possibly have done more. If you had sent this paper to your uncle, or to Mr. Peed, and we had written what you yourself have heard and seen, how you would have blamed yourself for not coming home! With what a bed of thorns would you not have provided yourself!—regrets, suspicions of us, fancies that we had neglected this or that, and a thousand such morbid ideas. Bless me! if you are so cast down, now that you have seen with your own eyes and heard with your own ears, what would you have been there? and who'd have pitied you? So I say, for shame, Mr. Darnell, that those kind words of Mr. Clerk's—"

"Captain Smithson for the future!" cried Ralph, rising suddenly, and turning to Mr. Wilson with flashing eyes.

"By all means, Captain Smithson," replied Wilson, coolly. "By Jove! there's some sense in that. It's as that you have to live your life—not as Ralph Darnell; and if you'll only think, as you did yesterday when we gave up at Berwick, you will not turn your back on the world because your father—"

"Let him answer to God himself for what he did," cried the young man. "I only remember my mother's faith and trust—"

"And imitate them, my dear fellow," continued his companion. "I'm not used to preaching, goodness knows; but what I heard yesterday seemed to fall nearer my heart than any sermon *I* ever heard, and I shall not forget it. If, out of all this trouble, joy comes to you in the end, you'll have the satisfaction of having worked for it—earned it; and to my fancy that's better than all the baronetcies that ever were inherited. You don't think that now; but you will think it, and remember that John Wilson told you so. Now, what are we to do? I don't like to leave you alone, and yet Peed will be anxious, and you have to go to Melcepeth."

"Are you here, Mr. Henry?" asked a brisk voice, followed by a florid, good-natured looking face, which peeped into the parlour. "Beg your pardon, gentlemen," he continued; "but I thought the landlord was here, and I want him."

"Won't you sit down, sir?" said Mr. Wilson, rising and pushing a chair to the stranger, at the same time ringing the bell. "I daresay Mr. Henry will come back directly. Tell your master he's wanted," he added to the servant who presented herself.

"Master's jeest gane doon the toon," said the girl, curtsying; "but I'll let him knaa', Mr. Embleton, ye're wantin' him. Is't ony thing varra particular, surr? A'll rrin mysel'."

"Yes, Janey, my lass; tell him there's a messenger over from Mr. Forster's of Craig Peel, and Mrs. Forster's taken ill, and I've to ride as fast as I can, and I want his mare. Tell him to come as fast as ever he can," he bawled after her, as she ran out.

"I'm the doctor here, gentlemen," he continued, "and have sharp summonses at times. I'm only glad this wasn't at night. Forster might as well have sent to Gibson at Wooler; but she won't trust anybody but me, it seems. Poor thing! poor thing! I fear it'll go hard with her."

"Mr. Forster?" said Wilson, looking hard at Ralph—"I knew a Mr. Forster once in London, and have lost sight of him this year past. We heard he had settled down for good in the north, with a wife. What is the name of his place?"

"Craig Peel," said the surgeon—"an old border castle, about twenty miles off."

"Craig Peel!—that was Forster's place. I've heard him often mention it," cried Ralph, with sudden amazement. "We were to have gone there if—if—no matter. And Mrs. Forster, sir, may I—may I ask if you know her? Is she a fair girl, hardly eighteen yet, with—"

"She is *very* beautiful, sir. I can almost excuse Forster for running away with her," replied the doctor.

"He used to be in London a good deal?" asked Wilson.

"Always," returned Mr. Embleton, "until this marriage. Since then he has stayed at home pretty regularly?"

"It's the same," cried Ralph. "Is he a friend of yours?"

"Not of mine," returned the doctor, coldly. I don't think Mr. Forster has any friends; none hereabouts, certainly. He is too Jacobite for us, gentlemen. I fancy we had enough of that in the '45; but people say Mr. Forster is as active an agent as ever, and I can't say he's liked for it. But his wife, sir, is an angel—poor thing! poor thing!"

"Do you know who she was?" asked Ralph, with a trembling voice. "I think—that is, I—"

"Oh, yes, her old servant, Nanny Keene, told me all about her.

She was a daughter of Morton's of Birdhope, poor fellow, who suffered. Sybil Morton, she was—"

"She was a dear friend of mine. I knew her from childhood," said Ralph, with much emotion. "Have you any objection to my accompanying you? I should be so thankful if you would let me."

"None whatever," said the surgeon; "but if what the man says is true, I fear you won't see her; as it is, the child may be born before I get there. Now, Henry, the mare. Sharp! that's a good fellow; and this gentleman will ride with me—you can give him the chesnut."

"And I also, if you can mount me well," said Wilson, as the landlord went out to order the horses. "How curious, Ralph—how very strange, isn't it?"

"This is some mystery that we shall soon learn," he replied. "I was repining and fretting only just now, and see what has followed. O Sybil, my darling, if I but meet you again!"

If there had been one thing more than another which could have diverted the thoughts of his own misery, and taught Ralph submission, it was the sudden knowledge which had reached him so strangely in regard to Sybil Morton. This, then, was the solution of Mr. Darnell's mystery, which had also defied his own scrutiny in London, a search which he had intended to resume. Now it was all clear. But was hers a real marriage, or was it a tale of treachery like that he had unravelled? I think he ground his teeth at the thought, as he again addressed Mr. Embleton:—

"You said, sir, Miss Morton was married? You see, sir, I have been abroad for the last two years, and have not heard, and that must be my apology for asking the question. Mrs. Morton, I knew, was dead."

"Oh, yes," replied the doctor, "she's married fast enough. They were married by licence in Wooler Church, and I was present. As you knew Miss Morton, I may tell you that she did not admire the Scotch marriage; and indeed that's how I came to know her, for Forster sent for me when she was so distracted. Hysteria of the worst kind had set in, and if old Nanny hadn't helped me—you know Nanny, of course: she's a character—I should have made but a poor hand of the case. She did more than I, and honest marriage did the rest."

"Thank God it was so!" said Ralph.

"Well," returned the doctor, curtly. "I don't know that there's much to be thankful for, after all; but you'll see for yourself, Mr.—a—a—"

"Captain Smithson, sir, at your service," said Ralph, taking off his hat.

"God bless me! Captain Smithson, who brought home Mr. Clive's despatches?"

"The same, sir, at your service."

"An honour I little expected," said the doctor, making a profound bow and offering his hand. "We must not wait now, and I will tell you what I know of this matter as we ride along. A painful subject in some respects—very, very painful. But if the child lives, she may be more reconciled; it may be a bond of union between them, and the poor thing will have it to care for."

They mounted in the inn-yard, and, led by Mr. Embleton, soon reached the brow of the ridge above Belford, and took the direction of Jedburgh. As the valley of the Till opened before them, it was truly a dreary prospect. Then, vast tracts of moorlands were unenclosed, the roads over them being little better than footpaths. To the west, Cheviot was crowned with snow, and looked ghastly white against the deep grey of the sky. Between were the woods of Chillingham, and farmhouses and hamlets dotted here and there over the sad-coloured landscape. Away to the south, waves over waves of moorland, brown heather and snow-patches alternating, with the woods of Twizell Dean and Adderstone intermingled between them and the lowland cultivation. Eastward the eye followed the sea-line to the noble Castle of Bamborough, standing up grandly from its basalt foundation, and thence to Holy Island and the rugged, iron-bound coast of Tantallon, till in the far distance northwards, Berwick Law loomed mistily in the haze. In summer a glorious panorama indeed; in winter hardly less beautiful, but of a wild character which saddens more than exalts.

"And that's Wooler Church, where Miss Morton was married," said Mr. Embleton—"you see the spire. We shall not go by it, but keep to the right, across the moors."

"He—Mr. Forster, has been kind to her, I hope?" said Ralph, as he pressed to the doctor's side.

"Yes—after his fashion—very. I believe he adores her, but I often think more after the fashion of a wild beast—like a bull of Chillingham Park, ready to fly at any one—than a Christian gentlemen. Good God!" he exclaimed, suddenly, "what would he be if she died!" and so dashing his spurs into his horse's flanks, rode on at the utmost speed the ground would allow of, without speaking more than words of caution in their progress.

I do not think Captain Smithson's thoughts were in a very collected state during the ride. Physically it was most enjoyable—the rapid pace; the clear, calm, frosty air, served to dispel much of his gloom; but there were old memories of Sybil which troubled him, and as to her present condition there was much uncertainty. Mr. Embleton was not explicit. "If the child lived, it might be a bond of union between them," he hoped. Of the rest he could judge pretty clearly. Sybil had been abducted, had well nigh died, and had submitted to marriage. No—she could not have loved Forster—yet he had been true; and another, with one who loved him, false—false as hell! he to whom he owed his life—false. I think the turn his reflections had taken would have led him again into the moody frame of mind on which Wilson had rallied him, when, as they descended the brow of a small eminence, Mr. Embleton pointed to an object before them—"By Jove! they're watching for us; don't you see there's some one on the tower waving a flag? Quick, gentlemen! follow me," he cried, and he urged his smoking horse down the path and galloped on.

On a knoll, a spur of the moorland, round the end of which a small streamlet wound, sparkling in the sun, stood a tall grey building, with a peaked roof of red tiles, crowned by a stack of chimneys, the smoke of which went straight up into the still air. It consisted of several storeys, and the walls were pierced with small windows, from the glass of which the sun's rays were reflected with bright gleams. Round the foot of the building were, as they appeared, outworks, covered in as dwelling-places, or perhaps stables, and a gate, as if for defence, closed the whole. At two corners of the upper storey were projecting round turrets, from one of the windows of which the white flag which had caught the doctor's eye was being waved without intermission. A few straggling fir-trees stood near the gate, and there seemed to be a spot like a garden near them. All else was brown moorland around; but in the valley below, there were a few small cottages, and enclosed fields belonging to them. In his life, Captain Smithson had never beheld any scene more dreary or desolate, and he rode on with a strange, sad foreboding. As they reached the entrance-gate Mr. Embleton threw himself from his horse, which was caught by a boy, and, giving his own to another as he dismounted, the young man followed him.

"How is she? how is she?" cried Mr. Embleton; "where's Mrs. Forster?"

"A'm feered ye're too late, doctor," said an elderly woman, who was sobbing, and wiping her eyes with her apron. "Couldna ye ha'e cum' sooner, surr?"

"God bless me!" he replied, "no! I've ridden at speed nearly. I wasn't a quarter of an hour at Belford before I started. Where is she?—where is Mrs. Forster?"

"Puir leddy! Oh, the puir wee lambie!" cried the woman. "A' couldn't bear it, surr, an' a' cam' oot. She was cryin' for ane Rraafe Darnell, surr; and the mester, surr, he was jist rroutin' an' swearin'."

"D—n him!" cried the doctor fiercely; "let me go on!" and Ralph and he entered the door of the castle together. There was a small low hall, and a stair leading up from it to the storeys above. Mr. Embleton did not hesitate. Throwing his heavy cloak to the ground, as did Ralph, he darted up two steps at a bound. "What, Nanny," he cried, "what's all this? How is she?—Don't be a fool!"

"Ma God!" cried the woman, holding out her hands in a paroxysm of terror, "it's him! it's Master Rraafe cum frae the deid till her! Dinna ye sey him?—theer, theer—ahint ye!" and she sank down on the stone stair bereft of sense.

"Hold her up, Captain Smithson; she's just an 'auld fule.' Who's Master Ralph? Keep her quiet till I get in—the old jade!"

It was impossible; Ralph only waited till he had raised the dear old form from the stair, kissed her face, and said, "I'm Ralph, Nanny dear; don't you know me? Where is she—Sybil?"

"Then the Lorrd's sent ye till her in her deith, that denied ye till her when she was livin'," replied Nanny, in amazement which she could not repress. "Oh, ma bairnie! there's a sair sight for ye yon. Na, na, she'll niver see ye mair—niver mair. Come and sey.'

It was but a few steps more, and he reached a corridor into which several rooms opened. One was ajar, and, preceded by Nanny, who led him in, he entered. Mr. Embleton was feeling a hand stretched out over the counterpane, then the throat and breast, of a figure lying there in death, and shaking his head. There was no doubt of it—the pale, pinched face, the glazed eyes, the drooped jaw, the sweet calm repose before him, was Death. "O Sybil! O my darling!" was all he could utter, as he bowed his head over what remained of Sybil Morton.

"She's gone! poor thing! poor thing!" said Mr. Embleton, wiping his eyes; "but I could not have saved her."

"Who spoke? who said, my darling? who's that? Ralph Daruell?" cried Mr. Forster, advancing from the end of the room with hurried steps; "what brings you here?—what insult is this, sir, to intrude unbidden into a death-chamber—begone!"

Ralph could only point to the sweet face before him—he could not speak.

"Begone, sir!" cried the wretched man; "she raved of you—she loved you! Look at her; the memory of you killed her. Begone, I say; leave her to me—you've no right to her."

"Be quiet, Mr. Forster," said the doctor, advancing. "Be quiet before her! before the dead! Peace, sir, it is a holy presence."

"It is hell!" cried the man, throwing himself on Ralph Darnell fiercely, and striking him heavily on the face. "If you're a man, come out and answer that! If you're a coward, I'll kill you where you stand!" And he drew a sword he had snatched from a corner.

I believe Ralph was very reckless then, and in a dangerous humour. The presence of the dead—of that sweet Sybil lying there in her holy death—rather increased than subdued the fierce passion which rose within him at the sudden and unexpected assault. We must remember that gentlemen wore swords by their sides then, and used them freely on slighter provocation than a blow.

"Come, sir," he cried, as the doctor was vainly endeavouring to hold the infuriated Mr. Forster's arm; "may God do the right between us! I will not avoid you!"

"Gentlemen! Horrible! This is horrible, Mr. Forster! in your own house, with your dead wife lying here. Stop, in God's name!"

But he might as well have spoken to the air. The two men were hurrying down the stair into the courtyard, and he followed them, crying out. Mr. Wilson was still waiting there.

"See, it's all fair, Wilson," said Ralph, unsheathing his sword. "He has struck me, and it's his doing, not mine. Look!" and he hastily wiped some blood from his lips.

"Can't we stay this—some other time, Mr. Forster?" said Wilson, stopping him.

"You!" was the reply; "another devil come to torment me. Begone! let me at him! Hold off, or, by ——, I will stab you!"

But Mr. Wilson was a powerful man, and he and the doctor wrenched Mr. Forster's sword from his hand, and held him panting and foaming at the mouth, cursing furiously; while Nanny Keene, with her arms round Ralph, was crying out to her master, "Ye shall na' kill him, ye fausse reivin' loon! ye shall na' kill ma bairnie that the Lorrd's gi'en mey. Haud him fast, surrs!—Wha's yon? Eh, look!"

"In the King's name," said a grave-looking person none had observed, who, with several stout fellows, well armed, entered the gate —"in the King's name, I arrest you, John Forster, on a charge of highway robbery and murder. Give him to me, gentlemen; I'm well known to you, Mr. Embleton, and here's the warrant."

Forster seemed sobered in an instant as he held out his hands mechanically for the handcuffs to be put upon him. "My wife's dead, Mr. Reed," he said—"just dead; have you no pity?"

"Deed! then, Mr. Forster, I'm sorry to hear it—vara sorry, sir; but this is nane o' my doin', an' the law maun ha'e its coorse; a' can do nothin' o' mysel', an' it's no bailish matter, ye ken vara weel, doctor."

"If you'll take bail, Reed, I'll give you anything you like," said Mr. Embleton.

"And I, sir, cried Ralph, "I bear him no ill-will; Forster, let me be bail for you—anything, Mr. Reed, one, five thousand pounds, sir, if you require it."

"Impossible," said the constable, shaking his head; "this is not the only charge, I fear, against Mr. Forster, there's treason tae—and I must do my duty, gentlemen."

"Then may God help me," said the miserable man, bowing his head; "it's just—it's just, though I did no murder. I'll make no resistance, Reed—I am ready. Only, if you'd let me have one look at her—one look, the last. O Mr. Darnell! O Ralph! can you forgive me? I thank God I did not kill you, unprepared as you are; yet I had nearly done it. May I see her, Mr. Reed?"

The constable was a feeling man in spite of his calling; he was wiping his eyes with the back of his hand. "Ay, surr, but we canna be lang, ye ken; we're to get to Wooler afore evenin', an' a' must be wi' ye. Come two of ye," he said to his men, "wi' Mister Forster," and they took him in; none cared to follow; let him say what he had to say before the pure saint lying there, and be gone. He was not long away, and they stood together silently in the courtyard till he returned.

"I kissed her," he said, calmly. "I kissed her child, and it lives; that is enough. Do not leave her, Mr. Darnell, now, till—till—you know what I mean—in Wooler Churchyard, where her people lie; she always said that. . . . Will you take her child, sir? I have no one—no, not one living, to whom I could trust it—only you and Nanny. There is only this old ruin," he continued, looking up, "and what you see about it, left, of all we had—we Forsters; but there's enough in the house for all expenses, if . . . you will do this, Darnell, for me? I—I have no friends."

"I will, Forster," said Ralph: "before God and these gentlemen present, I will do my duty to her and to the child, if He spares it."

"And will you forgive me, Ralph? One who must soon die begs this. I have done you grievous evil in my life—can you forget it? Yes, she forgave me too."

"I forgive you freely, as I hope to be forgiven," replied Ralph, giving his hand frankly. "O Mr. Forster, you should not have thoughts of the past; it is the future that must concern you."

"I know that, sir, and I thank you. Come, Mr. Reed, we lose time," and they went out of the gate; a led horse was waiting, on which he was helped, and a rough cloak thrown over him; and, guarded by the men, with heavy carbines across their saddles, the little party went on.

"O ma bairnie, ma own sweet laddie, what's sent ye this gate the day?" said Nanny, with streaming eyes. "O hinnie, an' she strruve sair for ye, an' niver forgetted ye—an' telled me. . . . O ma darlin', if I wuz to talk to ye for tin year a'd niver tell ye a'! Come till her, our ain wee pet, that's at rest frrae that wicked man wi'—the Lorrd. Come awey and see the childie—the wee bit bairrnie that God's sent ye. Eh! bit it's a bonnie thing! come away!"

"We must stay here to-night, Mr. Wilson," said the doctor; "it's too late to tempt the moors; there's plenty of stables for the horses, and the housekeeper will give us what she has to eat. So, John Forster! murder and highway robbery and treason—that's all, is it?"

"Not the first, I fear," said Mr. Wilson; "there were queer stories about him when he disappeared from London."

"Ay, when he carried off Sybil Morton," returned the doctor; "did you know him then?"

"A little, sir—like other men one meets about town, that's all; but I always suspected him."

"So did I, Mr. Wilson, and not a little either;" and they went on conversing, till the housekeeper came and said, "the parlour wuz reddy, and wadna they tak' some dinner; it wuz jist hamely, but she hadna' expeckit gran' folk."

And all this time Ralph was sitting by the dead, and Nanny had put the infant into his arms, and was telling him how it was born; how the poor mother—met by Forster after one of his mysterious absences—had been pushed rudely away, and cursed; how she had been taken ill, and the child was born; how she had suddenly begun to sink, and died with Ralph's name upon her lips—a sad tale, O reader, told with streaming eyes and many a bitter sob. Let us pass it by; all that avails nothing now. But still the child slept quietly, and Ralph looked from the living to the dead, in the hope that she died in, and which, wonderingly but humbly, he believed now; for again and again, from that dread night of the 20th June 1756, through all Plassey, and Lucker Church—the solemn, beautiful verse we know seemed to follow him with a holy sound, as if sung by angels.

So he stayed at Craig Peel with Wilson, and the good doctor went to Wooler about the funeral, and in a few days a humble hearse, such as was used in the country, came to the Peel, and many followed it on horseback to the churchyard, where what it bore was laid at rest. Only one word was graven on the headstone—"Sybil" —and no date; that was enough to mark the place for the few who cared to know where the beautiful girl lay in her eternal rest.

The child throve, and it was a new tie to life for Nanny. The Peel was given up to the sheriff, with what money there was—a large sum—in the house. Ralph would not use it, and Nanny from the first said, "Dinna touch it, Mister Rraafe; it's no canny—it's jist blood-money, ye ken; and the shirraa 'll pit it intill the sey if he likes, and mair the better."

Mr. and Mrs. Henry gave hospitable shelter to the little party when it arrived at Belford, and Nanny and Mrs. Forster's baby became at once objects of the highest wonder and interest to the good people there. "They had nivir seen the likes o' the bairn—jest like a wee cherub it wuz;" and even the doctor's good wife wondered at its beauty, and declared it to be certain to live.

"Surely she will have it—keep it for me, my dear darling Grover," thought Ralph, "now she has lost Constance; but I won't take it to Melcepeth till I see her," he said confidentially to Nanny; "Mrs. Henry must take care of ye."

"Ay, that a' will, Captin, wi' a' my heart," said Mrs. Henry, who rejoiced in the arrangement. "They'll be safe wi' uz till ye send for them, an' Rrichard 'll tak' them till ye."

CHAPTER LXV.

MELCEPETH ONCE MORE.

A RIDE of twenty-five or thirty miles was a small matter in days when gentlemen who travelled were accustomed to do much of their journeys on horseback. Mr. Henry's announcement that he "couldna git places in the stage at Belford for some days" was welcome news to the gentlemen, who much preferred riding; and they had been able to send on their portmanteaus to Felton on the Coquet, from whence any light cart could take them to Melcepeth Castle. So far all was pleasant enough, and the weather was glorious—bright, clear days, with a heavy rime at night, which hung on the grass and the hedges, and sparkled in countless spangles in the sun—enough frost to keep the road dry and hard, and yet not more than the sun could thaw sufficiently for the horses to travel swiftly and pleasantly. "Good-bye, doctor; good-bye, Mr. Henry!" "An' a' wish ye a pleasant ride, gentlemen" —and they were gone; and old Nannie, with the "wee bit bairnie" in her arms, and a buxom young woman standing by her, was looking out of the window, and trying to raise the child to look at the receding figures.

"Ye canna sey him, ma lambie; but the Lorrd 'll mak' thee the joy of his puir young life yet, an' ye'll bey a braw laddie yersel', ma preshus, an' like yer ain puir mammie;" and she buried her face in the child's breast to hide the tears that would come.

"Eh, mem, bit ye shudna greet," said the young nurse; "it's no canny, Mistress Keene. Ye'll seyn sey him agin, nivir fear. An' the castle's jest a gran' place. A' seyd it ance; for John Harbottle, hey's the butler, mem, an' hey's ma mither's furrst cozin, ye ken."

But we have no concern with this pleasant nursery gossip. The two men have put their horses into a round trot, and were speeding fast on their way. They pass the blacksmith's shop at the corner of the lane leading to Adderstone, down which Ralph looks with a sort of shiver passing through him; then they pass Twizell gates, and look up the Dean and its hanging woods, and Mr. Selby's old-fashioned snug manor-house then standing; and they splash through the brook at Warenford, and mount the hill at a good pace—and so forward. I do not think Ralph was a very communicative companion that day, and Mr. Wilson did not interrupt his thoughts. How would his dear old uncle receive him, and Constance, and dearest Grover—and his grandfather? How often had he been tempted to go south at once, and bid them farewell from London; and how often had not a better thought come into his mind that that would be a cowardly thing to do? Was he not forgiven?—had not he written to his uncle as he arrived in London, and that letter had been forwarded with one from himself by Mr. Roger Darnell. Posts were not rapid in those days; but he knew he would be looked for—and so he was.

Perhaps I need hardly go back so far as the day when that letter reached Sir Geoffrey, or tell how it was received. Such retrospects are useless matters when one has to press on one's way. "I cannot tell when I shall arrive, and there will be no more time to write, dear Grover," Ralph had said in his note to her; "only prepare my uncle and Constance for my coming. I humbly hope they may be kind and have forgiven the past; but if *not*, I shall go to my grandfather after I have seen them. I write this, of course, in strict confidence."

"Kind?—forgiven? Oh, Ralph, to doubt it!" said Mistress Grover as, retreating to her own parlour, she read the letter which she durst not open at the breakfast table, and was there joined by Constance, who knew what it was. I think if the two women, as with their heads close together they read this letter, writ in the strong manly hand of their young soldier, cried over it, with hearts full of old memories—and yet not so old after all—they did so with thankful hearts that their prodigal was come back. As to the old baronet, I can't pretend to describe his condition. The Viscount, his son-in-law, gave him up entirely; and if he had not been a fine, generous young fellow, might have fallen jealous of Ralph; for what with the baronet's fidgets—his sending down to Felton two or three times a day to see if luggage had not arrived, and Constance and Grover's fussiness about the "Blue Room," and the bed, and fires, and airing of sheets—the said room being now at full stove-heat, the feather beds close to the fire, and the blankets hung to toast upon stands: "It's for the captain frae Injy," says the housemaid to her helpmate, as she turned the pillows by the fire, "an' the mistress an' my leddy seys as they'll nivir be het enough; sae ye'll pit on mair coal, Mary, an' plenty: and if it gits low, a'll jist pull yer lugs, ye skeert daft huzzie ye—a' wull."

But though the stove-heat continued at its highest, and Harbottle looked wistfully at the goodly row of bottles which stood in the *garde-vins* below the sideboard, and declared to Mistress Darling, the housekeeper, that it "wuz jest a shame to move them bottles of port out o' the warrm säadust, it wuz;" and the baronet fumed and fidgeted, and Mistress Grover and Constance were silent and anxious; and the Viscount, finding no good of any one, as he said, spent his days in the woods shooting woodcocks, and beat the fields for partridges, and the moor for grouse, and accumulated more game than Melcepeth Castle could possibly eat in a month—I say all these notwithstanding, Ralph did not come: and we know why. I think he might, perhaps, have written a line from Belford; but he did not then wish his errand to be known. If he had succeeded, he would have taken the papers to his uncle and laid them before him; when he failed, he could not tell his uncle of his brother's treachery—that brother who, in spite of all differences, was loved in death. So he did not write, and all in Melcepeth were grieved and anxious at the delay, not of many days, as we know, but days seem growing interminable when they are such as these.

Yes, the luggage was at the village inn, and Ralph was alone. As Mr. Wilson had passed through Alnwick, he found he could get on by the stage direct to London, and he judged, rightly perhaps, that he should be *de trop* at Melcepeth; so he bade Ralph good-bye, and waited for the coach, while Ralph rode on.

Did any one ever quite make up their mind what they should say at meeting beloved ones after absence? I daresay many have tried to do so, and succeeded as badly as Ralph did, and I can fancy that the more he thought, and the nearer he got to Melcepeth, the more confused was his brain; and the speeches, and matter of them, had become as blurred and confused as his sight was misty, when the roar of the river, the sigh of the woods, the old cooings of the cushats, and cawings of the rooks, blended together in music he had never forgotten—no, not even when he was fighting for water at the bars of the Black Hole, and Julia Wharton was clinging to his knees.

The park gates were shut: but as he rang, a well-known figure came to open them, and dropped a respectful curtsy—as to a stranger. Ralph asked after the family.

"Yes, surr, ma leddy's at hame," she said, "an' the barr'nitt. Ye'll gae streyt on, surr; ye canna miss the wey."

Miss the way!—no, not now.

"Janet," said Ralph, bending down from his horse as the woman turned the gate—"Janet, hoo's a' wi' ye? Ye ha'e forgotten mey, a'm thinkin'."

His old accent had come back on him irresistibly since he had returned to his own country, and he often used it instinctively.

"Masturr Rraafe! Oh, ma bairn! Oh, ma bairnie!" and she

flung her arms round the young man and kissed his bronzed cheeks and ruddy lips, while her fingers wandered about his neck, his hair, his hands—and she could not speak.

"Yes, Janet, your ain bairnie." She had been his nurse, and was married to the gamekeeper. "Yer ain, ain childie, that's never—"

"Mine—mine! bit a'll no keep ye, hinnie—awa' wi' ye, and come back by-an'-by. Yer uncle's been twice here the day, an' he'd ha'e gotten a fit o' the goot if ye hadna come—awa' wi' ye."

What followed? I do not think Ralph could ever tell, when he found himself in the old castle hall, fast locked in his uncle's arms, and trying to slip down to his feet to kneel there; and Grover and Constance hanging over him, and a noble-looking, manly young fellow looking on from behind with a pleasant smile, and the Baronet crying out—"God bless the boy! how he's improved! Welcome, Ralph!—welcome home!" His uncle Roger's welcome had been a loving one too, as we know, but not like this. It was not one to his home, and if there was a place in the world which he could call home, this was it.

"And what have I done to be excluded?" cried the young Viscount, coming forward to the group.

"My husband, Ralph," said Constance, blushing to the roots of her hair, and the two men's hands were locked in a hearty grasp.

What more, dear reader, can I make intelligible to you of this happy reunion, where all sorrow, danger, trial, misery, were for the present merged into quiet happiness? I think meetings are oftener sadder than partings. In the one there is hope to be fulfilled, which often fails; in the other, hope has been too often fulfilled, and there remains no more to look to. But it was not so in this case. We remember Ralph's last partings with those he most loved—his last sight of that group under the hedge, with the footman holding a dim lantern over them, and when the white face of his uncle, and the broad stream of blood over his shirt and waistcoat, scared him away. Now? Why, his uncle was not a day older, in appearance, nor Grover. But Constance? Well, she sat soon after, in the summer, to Mr. Reynolds, and I have already told you of her picture; but in all his life Ralph had never seen a more lovely combination of grace and power than Constance Viscountess Granton, nor indeed had many others.

So he rested at Melcepeth, and grew into his old home once more. What cared he for London in comparison? And Mr. Smithson came to him, and heard all. The old man was not disappointed; he had made up his mind to the truth long ago; but when the precious relics of the dead were taken to him, at Warkworth, by his grandson, he placed them in the chair where his wife had died, which was never used, and knelt down before it, and in his broken voice told both mother and child to look on "what he'd gotten, and he knaa'd a' noo, an' it was gude in His sight: an' he wuz reddy to cum till 'em when the Lorrd had dun' wi' him on errth;" then he rose calm and clear in his mind, and heard all his grandson had done, and his plans for the future, and thought them good.

Did the Baronet and Grover think them good?

Not at first; as they were gradually spoken to Sir Geoffrey, he moaned at the prospect. "My own boy, no matter what he is, if he can't be my heir, he can be my child. I've no child now, and Conny will go, and then"—and so the old man moaned and wept. Or at times a spark of the old fire would come out. "He didn't care a —— for Colonel Clive! Why should his boy go to that infernal country? Hadn't he money enough for all of them? he hadn't expenses now, and he'd even given up the harriers. Constance didn't want the estate, and what was the good of it unless the baronetcy went with it?"

And to all this Constance added her entreaties personally, and through her husband, between whom and Ralph a brotherly kindness had sprung up. I think the young man envied Ralph the honourable scars he could show, and grew fearfully excited by Ralph's glowing descriptions of the gorgeous East, the ambition of those who strove there for dominion, and the fearful ordeals he had passed through. He did not wonder at Ralph's determination, and in the end convinced Constance he was right. How could he settle in England? Not as a Darnell of Melcepeth. Whom could he marry? Not one his equal in what ought to have been his birth. Ah, yes, it is a vexed question: and if we are more tolerant of it now, or careless, than our great-great-grandfathers were, we cannot but feel that Ralph was right. Nor was it many days before Sybil Morton's child was sent for and held close to the hearts of Mrs. Grover and Constance. Ralph told its sad history to his uncle, and there was never a doubt on the subject of his adoption. Dear Grover! she took the infant to her heart, and the boy grew there; grew, and flourished, and twined round it. Such as Ralph had been, was this little helpless creature, but with no mystery to clog its steps in life; and as to Nanny, I do not think there ever ruled in her peculiar kingdom, which was a suite of three rooms at the end of the south wing, a more loving but despotic empress than she was.

Going? Yes, he must go; but he was in no hurry, and the preparation for another long severance was very gradual. Ralph had no concealments; he had made up his mind, and he kept that resolution constantly before them all. What could he do in England? In India there was future service for his country; a noble leader, and a crowd of struggling princes and peoples, among whom he might have his portion of usefulness. I say, as he spoke of all this with a generous enthusiasm, and an eloquence which none of his hearers could withstand, they grew to know what India was; and why, in comparison with the tame prospect of an English country life, or the daily cares of a merchant's office, the splendour of that land, and the free exercise of an honourable ambition, could not be withstood.

I do not think at this present that Ralph Darnell had a care. Mrs. Wharton had arrived, and had written to him. Her relatives had received her kindly, and she found her fortune far more considerable than she had supposed. She wrote in painful distress at the prospect of being discovered by George Elliot. What could she say to him? How explain her life? Perhaps he had forgotten her, and so on. Ah! it was a flimsy covering enough for a poor aching heart, which, however tried, had never been false to its first love; and when Ralph showed the letter to Grover—he daren't tell Constance—that good motherly soul asked why they should not be happy? and Ralph would not err in telling her where George Elliot was. "I daresay he's a different man now," she said, "after a year of the Fleet;" and indeed he was. "Why shouldn't they have their chance in life by and-by? they're both old enough to know their own minds." So Ralph thought too, when he wrote to Julia that George was in the Fleet, and that Mr. Braithwaite, a respectable attorney of Morpeth, who knew his property, said it was not irredeemable.

As long as winter lasted, there were grouse and woodcock to shoot; and as the spring opened, buds, and flowers, and leaves, and primroses clothed the banks of beautiful Coquet. The fresh sea salmon came up, and the two friends killed many a one, and many a lusty trout together. Then Constance had to go awhile to her new home, and the baronet and Mistress Grover were to go too; but there was no fear for the little Ralph, who throve, and chuckled, and crowed as his foster-mother gave him into Ralph's arms, and bade him bless him ere he went forth to his life's work, as she said again and again that she'd never leave him; and years proved that devotion which had never yet failed.

Why should I linger at the dear old place, with all its memories clinging to me? One glorious day in June, when the river was sparkling, and the soft warm sunlight was playing over the rich woods and waving meadows, and the old music of the birds, mingling with the murmur of the stream, was soothing every rebellious thought and softening all regret, the little procession of coaches started from the hall-door, and went on its way. Come with it, O my patient reader! and bear with me to the end. Why should I tell you of farewells which would cause pain, when hope, with a grave but benign aspect, beckons us on?

CHAPTER LXVI.

OUTWARD BOUND.

Ralph had written to his uncle Roger soon after he arrived at Melcepeth. He only allowed Mr. Wilson time to arrive in London, and submit his professional report to Mr. Peed, before he wrote an elaborate letter confirming all that Mr. Wilson had recorded, and Ralph knew his uncle would have perused that report before his letter could reach. I think he had found it on the whole easier to speak to his uncle Geoffrey, who had had no hope, and to whom the discovery of the false certificate was, after all, only a confirmation of what he expected, than to write to Mr. Roger Darnell on a subject which had raised greater hopes than that gentleman chose to acknowledge to his nephew. "At last," he had thought, "there would be one Darnell to succeed both; and for the present Ralph would not refuse a partnership in the house. Yes, he should be managing partner; and he and Sanders should do as they liked with the India business, which they both understood much better than he. Then, when, in the course of nature, Geoffrey died, and he followed, there would be one to represent the old family both as baronet and merchant, and Ralph would have made enough to increase the dignity of the baronetcy very largely. If Ralph liked Dolly, he should have her;" but I think Mr. Darnell had old-fashioned doubts about the advisability of cousinly marriages, and doubts too as to whether his nephew cared enough about her to offer his hand. This, however, was a point of minor importance altogether. His girls were assured of handsome settlements, and would be sure to marry well whenever their time came. Till Mr. Wilson's return, therefore, I am afraid the great merchant indulged, after an unusual fashion to so practical a mind, in building castles in the air; and when Mr. Peed, by his professional declaration, tumbled them ruthlessly about his ears, and poor Ralph's melancholy letter followed to complete the ruin—Mr. Roger Darnell fell into a state of depression and anxiety of which in his life heretofore he had had no experience. To whom could he turn for consolation? Not to his wife, where he should have met it had she been other than she was. If she did not positively rejoice, she at least comforted herself in the opinion that for all that had happened she for one was thankful. She had had no hope of any such results as Mr. Darnell had chosen to anticipate. The antecedents of Mr. Henry Darnell had quite forbidden such in her mind. But I need not follow this; it cannot in the least degree alter or modify what existed, and to which her husband had to submit.

But there was still one point to which the merchant clung even more closely. If his nephew could not be the baronet, and in his turn head of the family, he could at least be head of the house when he himself was gone. He had had enough of business; he could and would retire in his favour; if not at once, at least when Ralph should settle down to the work, and take his place in the parlour. Yes, all this could be arranged; and Mr. Peed was called into council in private, and received instructions as to the drawing up of a certain deed of partnership which was to decide the point. I say, after having done this, and perused the rough draft of that settlement, a feeling of contentment again possessed Mr. Darnell. If it were not all that he had desired, he must be thankful he was able to make it what it was, and so he put the draft among his private papers, and having written such consolation to Ralph as he could find words to express, he anxiously waited his arrival from Granton Towers, where Ralph had gone.

That was altogether a different place from Melcepeth. The Right Honourable the Earl of Whinborough was condescending, and, in the main, meant to be kind; but he was not Sir Geoffrey nor Mr. Roger. Ralph's history was known, and we know pretty well what that signified. The young Viscount was pained at the reserve with which his mother and sisters treated the young man, and poor Constance was much distressed; but what could they do? As to Sir Geoffrey, he was altogether out of place; he longed to be back at Melcepeth with Grover and the baby, in whose development he took the greatest interest. He knew no one. The Midland squires who came to the stately entertainments at the Towers were not of his sort at all. He could not follow Midlandshire politics, nor local allusions or interests. In his own country he was a leading character, and every one had deference to his age and local experience. Here, who cared for the old Northumbrian baronet among the crowds of dukes, and lords, and their ladies, who came? He was not sorry he had come, for he saw his beautiful Constance receiving, ay, exacting, the homage due to her. And he rejoiced at that, and the affection of the fine young fellow to whom she was united; but that was all. He had at least fulfilled his promise to Constance that he'd stand by her till she took her place among the grandees; and there was not the least occasion for him to stay a moment longer than the period of one month, which he had promised. Then all were to break up. Constance and her husband were to go to their own beautiful seat in Herefordshire, nigh to the Welsh mountains. Sir Geoffrey would return to Melcepeth after he had seen them settled at Graydon Court, and might certainly pay an occasional visit there, but that to the Towers was the first and the last.

A month more—could Ralph wait? "O Ralph, you'll stay over that time, and come with us, won't you? And we'll be so quiet and happy at Graydon. Richard says it's not unlike Melcepeth, and there's plenty of fishing: and you can do just as you like when all this ceremony is over."

Such was Constance's appeal to her cousin. He had been all she could have desired. She had often felt the poor fellow's eyes were following her with a grave, sad aspect; but from the first he had been so considerate, so affectionate, so guarded in all that he had said and done, that the apprehension with which she had regarded his coming to Melcepeth had passed away, and he was to her only that dear dear brother she had wished him to be. I do not mean to say that Ralph had not had his struggle about going there, and for a while about staying; and I should not pretend, knowing his disposition, that he had not to fight a good fight against past remembrances, which *would* come up. But he had won the victory: and Mistress Grover, who had been very anxious on the subject, had rejoiced on her knees in her chamber, that strength had come where there had been weakness, and that Ralph was safe.

If Richard Viscount Granton had been anything but what he was, I don't know that Ralph's conquest of himself would have been so easy; but in him there was nothing left to be desired. He had won Constance's love and given his own without reservation. There was perfect confidence and harmony between them, and as Ralph lived on at Melcepeth, resigning himself to this conviction, telling Grover of it in his own quiet fashion, and believing in it more and more every day, he grew to rejoice that his darling cousin had been raised to her proper standing in the world; and now that he knew what he was in reality, he shuddered at what, had she submitted to his love in London, would now be her position. Ah yes, through all that, hard as he had thought it, rebellious as his heart had been, he could now see and feel how he had been guided—how she, motherless girl as she was, had been shielded.

"No, Conny, dear," he replied to her entreaties, "it's no use, the parting must come sooner or later, and it had better be at once. I could not leave you at Melcepeth: but this is a half-way house, and I have no part in it. I know all you would say and do; but going with you and Richard and my uncle to Graydon, would be but the old thing over again, and I could not bear it—indeed I could not. Let me go to my work: the *Valiant* is to sail soon, and I shall be happy with Scrafton; and, if it please God, I will come back to you all by-and-by;" and she felt, as her husband told her also, that Ralph was right, and when he had stayed a week at the Towers, he left them.

I have no occasion to tell of the arguments between Mr. Roger and Ralph which ensued after he returned to London, nor of the manner in which Mr. Darnell felt the ground slip from under him;

and how he was driven from position to position by his now unselfish nephew. As whom could Ralph become head of the house? Officially, and in India, he was Captain Smithson. He could not, and would not, take the name of Darnell, to which he had no legitimate right. He could not take the position to which he was invited; but as Ralph Smithson he had won some distinction, and might, he thought, win more. Mr. Sanders thought so too: he for one, could enter into Ralph's feelings and see the necessity of his determination. It was an honourable one—it was a glorious thing—to work out one's own lot in life, and never to flinch from it till it was fulfilled. Ralph had never had better health in his life than when he was in India, and he had not the excuse, which Mr. Sanders was obliged to admit, that he could not live there.

In the face of these facts, what would be the use of going over Mr. Darnell's ground again and again, O my reader? I could make neither one side nor the other plainer if I did. I don't mean to say that if Ralph had established his mother's marriage he would not have entered into one or other of his uncle's views; but as it was, he felt England was no place for him—this feeling was growing upon him stronger and stronger every day. Letters which followed him from Mr. Clive, from young Warren Hastings, now agent at Moorshedabad, showed him what was to be done, and that men were wanted to the work. There was a letter from Mr. Clive, too, to Roger Darnell, in which he wrote, "that, since Plassey, he had often thought over that certificate, and the more he thought the more suspicion came into his mind: and if there was any doubt about Ralph's position, *he ought not to keep him in a false one;* that he would be no true friend if he did, but only one seeking a selfish indulgence of a morbid affection. He himself felt certain of Ralph's advancement, and he was sure that would be hereafter a far greater source of comfort to his friend than anything short of the Baronetcy of Melcepeth."

In fine, and greatly influenced by Mr. Clive's letter, of which there was much more than I care to transcribe, Roger Darnell gave in with as good a grace as he could; and when he had been driven from his last position—they were in the office parlour then—Mr. Darnell took the draft deed of partnership from his desk and said,—

"Well, then, as there's no use in this, Ralph, and I agree with thee now, hard as it's been to think thee right, I'd better tear it up;" and he was about to do so.

"Stay, dear uncle," said Ralph, "you may do a great good with that if you will: and, if you'll not be angry, I'll mention what's been in my mind for many a day."

"Well, Ralph," replied Mr. Darnell, still holding the paper in his hands, as if to tear it—"Well?"

"The place for the name is vacant, sir, and if you'll write John Sanders instead of Ralph Darnell, you'll do justice to a worthy man and to yourself."

"John Sanders," repeated Mr. Darnell, reflecting; but he did not tear the paper—"John Sanders. Yes, Ralph—next to you, him; but this draft will not suit him exactly. Let us see whether we can make it do so," and he turned to his desk, opened, spread it before him, and they read it over, I think, happily and contentedly. "Now," said Mr. Darnell, "do you take it to Peed, and get it drafted as fast as possible."

When he was with that astute gentleman, Ralph gave some other instructions about his own property. There was £20,000 now invested in India stock; and of this he settled half on Sybil's child, making Mr. Wilson one of the trustees, and Mr. Sanders the other; and he added sundry codicils to his will, in regard to Grover and Nanny, which we need not particularise, seeing that they had afterwards to be considerably modified; but as far as he could, all was made clear for the present, and entirely met with Mr. Peed's approval.

I have not mentioned Julia Wharton; but during this last visit to London, Ralph had called on her, and found her happily situated with her cousins, who lived in a pleasant house near Kensington—an old property of the Hydes. Her uncle was dead. Her sister was still in Yorkshire, near Malton, and had invited her to come; but for the present she had declined, and was happy where she was. She saw no one, and the Hydes excused her when they had company. "I cannot forget the past, dear Ralph," she said, as he asked her concerning her life; "they do not know of it from me, but it is known that one woman was taken away, and how can I conceal it? But they are very kind, and I am, after all, happier here than I should be with my sister. And only to think that you knew George Elliot! I was sure that I had seen you with him when you used to come behind the scenes at the —— Theatre." No, she had had no communication with him; how could she? She would not dare to have it known by him that she lived at all. "And when you go out, you must try and persuade the Begum to send home the children; she will trust them with me, and they will be a great solace and comfort to me." So they chatted on.

But Ralph, as he thought before, could see through this poor girl's heart. She was grown very beautiful; all her old English beauty had come back to her, and more too, for the calm, pensive expression of her face was a charm in itself. Why should she not marry George? and were his affairs so utterly irretrievable? Well, he would find out. Wilson, perhaps, could see clearer than he could. And they went to the Fleet together.

We need not go there with them, perhaps; but it can be understood how George Elliot wondered and was affected at what Ralph proposed when he came to know the truth. The sum for which Mr. Elliot had been arrested was not more than £2000, and though no one would pay this, the rest of his creditors were by no means opposed to entering into an arrangement for the payment of larger sums. So Mr. Peed took the affair in hand, and in communication with Mr. Braithwaite, of Morpeth, got to the bottom of the whole matter. Ralph insisted upon advancing the £2000 necessary for George's release on the security of the Wooler estate; and Mr. Elliot consented that the whole property should be put under trustees, receiving £400 per annum only, till his debts should be paid. And all this being settled, Ralph and Mr. Wilson took him to his old house by the river, whereof he obtained two rooms, sufficient for his purpose; and at a little supper he gave, as a sort of thank-offering to Ralph, very different from one that we have not forgotten, they talked over old times—only three years, after all, but they had grown to be old times, nevertheless; and perhaps the best news they had to discuss was, that Mr. Forster's life had been spared, but that he was to be transported to His Majesty's plantations in Virginia for the term of his natural life. I do not mean to make a saint out of a sinner all at once, nor indeed was George Elliot ever a saint in the ordinary acceptation of the word; but he had had enough of debt, and misery in the Fleet, to make him careful, and I question, knowing exactly what he had, whether the tradesmen and money-lenders would have trusted him at all again. So afterwards he began to lead a steady life, and got himself entered in the Temple to study the law: and perhaps a letter Ralph wrote, and gave to Wilson to deliver after he had sailed, might have a great effect on his life.

Then there were a few days, a very few days only, of preparation, and England began to grow dim in Ralph's sight, and his spirit to go before him to his future home. There was nothing that he remembered or could think on that he left undone, not even a visit to the Golden Cock, and pretty presents to the landlord and his wife, and to Mistress Baker and old Dickiwig, and his merry sweethearts in the bar, one of whom was married, and the other likely to follow her example. I say nothing was left undone, because he strove to render his departure as complete as possible ere he severed the last bonds which then bound him to England. The day the *Valiant* was to sail, he bade his cousins and Mrs. Darnell farewell. I do not think there was much regret exhibited, except by poor little Dolly, who was inconsolable for many days afterwards, and who treasured up a little locket, with Ralph's hair in it, to the latest day of her life. Mr. Darnell had gone before him to the office, where the deeds were to be executed, and where Ralph was to eat his last meal in England up-stairs, and waited his arrival there. Mr. Peed had come, and Mr. Wilson and Captain Scrafton, and they would drink Ralph's health and success to him by-and-by; but when Ralph's deeds of settlement were signed and witnessed, Mr. Darnell took up the other, and somewhat nervously, perhaps, at first, though his voice grew stronger as he spoke—told them all of the devotion of one who, through many years of labour and anxiety, and at the sacrifice of much personal aggrandisement, had helped to raise the house of Roger Darnell & Company to its present greatness; and that he should be wanting in the commonest gratitude if he did not acknowledge services which he could never repay. And when Mr. Darnell put into John Sanders's hand the deed of partnership we know of, and asked him to sign it, and all present, with hearty cheers, stretched out their hands to grasp one which was trembling a good deal, I think that scene presented, in its love and harmony, a very happy contrast to one which we can remember to have occurred there three years ago, but which was now fading out of all their memories. What strong, bold signatures those were to that deed, both of principals and witnesses! how manly and true were John Sanders's acknowledgments! how tearful and grateful were the dear old ladies' eyes! how heartily were the toasts drunk up-stairs in foaming goblets of champagne! and how satisfied at last was Roger Darnell that he had done right when, lawless as the act had been, he had sent his nephew to Calcutta!

"One toast more, dear friends," he said, "for Captain Scrafton presses, and tide will not stay even for the *Valiant*. Fill your glasses: I drink to the health of Captain Ralph Smithson, and may God bless him, and enable him to work out a more glorious career than he would have had in this old office! I have wrestled sorely with him, because of my great love: but he has overcome me, and I believe he is right, because another hand, mightier than mine, leads him on. So, I say again, God bless him! and I pray only that I may see him once more ere I die. Three cheers, gentlemen—hip, hip, hurrah!"

. . . .

Once again the faint low shore of Bengal, the black temples of Juggunath, the slender palms and the fringe of jungle-trees, rise out of the ocean, the pilot-sloop displays her signal and is answered, and news is interchanged between eager questioners and listeners as the pilot comes on board. Is Mr. Clive at Calcutta? "Yes, but he's just going up country with the army on the Nawab's business, and only waiting for the *Valiant's* despatches."

"The fast boat is waiting for you at Injellie, Captain Smithson, and she'll beat the *Valiant* by several days, perhaps, as the current is so strong."

And it was as the pilot said; the boat was there, and a kind note from Colonel Clive, to whom the news of all we know had been written from Melcepeth.

"I grieve and I rejoice at the same time," Clive wrote, "but I shall not distress you by my regrets—on the contrary, congratulate you heartily on your manly resolve. I am just going to take the army up to the Nawab's help, against whom some conspiracies have been set on foot, which must be broken up; I will tell you all about these when we meet. Pray hasten on, for I am anxiously looking for the letters you are bringing, and I can't move till I have them. You shall have your old work to do on my staff, and we will see for something better presently.

"*P.S.*—By-the-bye, you will not have forgotten the Affghan girl whom you rescued from the mob at Moorshedabad the day the Nawab was brought in? Well, she is here, and daily comes to ask when you are to arrive. She's monstrous handsome, and it's well, perhaps, Mrs. Clive is not here, or I might be suspected; but I'll swear she's in love with you, and she's close as wax about something — I daresay you'll find her here when you come to my quarters, and 'faith I'll keep her if I get your signal."

Sozun again! what could she want? it must be she—there was no other rescued. The Begum would be with her people at Moorshedabad; and about the Affghan fakeerin the colonel had been before facetious. "Pull, dandees, pull!" and the twelve stout rowers stretch to their oars heartily, for any amount of sheep to eat, and baksheesh, were promised them: Even now the old Hindi tongue is again becoming familiar: the Manjee of the boat is an old acquaintance, and is amusing the Captain Sahib with Calcutta stories, telling him the Don was well, and one of his daughters married. "And there is an Affghan fakeerin, sahib, asking after you every day at the Ghât, and she wanted to come down with me, but I wouldn't let her."

A night on the river, calm and cool: and the glorious stars sparkle in a clear dewy air—as the boat speeds on with fresh relays of rowers. Ralph Smithson sleeps refreshingly on the soft couch spread for him, without a care or regret on his mind. "Lord, lead me where Thou wilt: do with me as Thou wilt: only use me to do Thy work here, and strengthen me to do it." Such, in some sort, had been his prayer as he lay down: such was his prayer as he awoke, when, in the grey morning light, the tall masts of the English ships were appearing on the river banks, and as the sun rose, the old fort, the white houses about it, the town and the ships, glowed in its bright beams.

CHAPTER LXVII.

OLD FRIENDS.

WHAT a pleasant breakfast table that was the morning Ralph Smithson arrived! Colonel Clive, with his keen eyes and expressive features, Mr. Watts, young Warren Hastings, who had come down from Moorshedabad about the Nawab's troubles, and himself, talking over events at home—the political parties in the Direction, the temper of the Ministry, and such London gossip as occurred to them. When one has been many years absent, and a friend comes who has been among old familiar scenes, what flood-gates of memory are not loosed, and how pleasant it is to hear of old matters, of improvements, of alterations, of increase of streets and houses, of friends, of—of—everything in fact that one remembers. There is an odour of home about a man newly arrived in India which cannot be mistaken. His clothes are fresh and new, and well fitted to him: he has lost some of the old free-and-easy manner, perhaps, and possibly some local conventional slang; he may not all at once put his legs on the table and call for his hookah, as it was then, or cheroot, as it is now; in short, he is again a new arrival, and is not expected to fall into old ways all of a sudden. So Ralph Smithson looks much more spruce than his companions; his laced velvet coat is one of Mr. Price's best: his cravat and ruffles of Valenciennes: his breeches of fine kerseymere, and his tight gaiters, sit on as handsome legs as you would wish to see. There is no heat on this 12th of November 1757; the air feels like a pleasant summer day, and full uniform is by no means unbearable. Ralph Smithson has evidently much improved; Mr. Clive thinks him as handsome a young fellow as he ever saw, and says lightly he wonders he has not brought out a wife. Hadn't Mr. Roger Darnell a pretty daughter with lots of money? "By George! you won't have such a chance here Mr. Da—" he had nearly said Darnell, but checked himself in time—"Captain Smithson, I mean."

Mr. Clive is right. Ralph Smithson is a very different-looking person to the gaunt young man who had come down to Madras: who had reappeared in rags, pale and wasted, before the battle of Plassey: or who had sate with a scared, white face at the table in the tent there, and looked for the contents of the bag which was still about his neck. The change of climate, the sea voyage, but, above all, the absence of care, have done their work. He is vastly improved; and there is a face before Mr. Clive which, unmistakable now in its Darnell character, has a light and buoyant expression, with calm determination in the clear blue eye, and harder and firmer lines about the resolute chin and mouth than used to be there. If the figure were good before, it seems better now—better knit and more flesh upon it than there was a year ago; while in the clustering brown hair falling in heavy curls about the neck—in the white, broad forehead and the florid Darnell complexion, there is manly beauty enough to set any spinsters there may be in Calcutta casting sly glances at him this evening on the Mall, by the river side, or at the dance to which the Colonel has invited all the "Station," in honour of his guest's arrival.

Ralph Smithson has only been a few hours on shore, but he seems to feel as if he had never been absent. Cassim, his servant, has taken possession of the valise which he brought up, and has laid out all his things. He has hired several other servants suitable to his master's quality; and as breakfast is over, Ralph finds his old hookah set down behind him, and the silver mouthpiece slid into his hand from behind the arm-chair. What a breakfast it had been! Prawn curries, chicken curries, delicious fish, rice like snow, and fruit of all kinds. Well, the best things must have an end. Mr. Watts and Mr. Hastings had business in the fort, and Ralph said he would join them soon, and look over the old place, and see the Don and some of his former companions; and when they were gone, and for the first and only time it was ever mentioned between them, Colonel Clive asked, and the young man told, the result at Lucker Church, and his own free determination. He told, in short, what I have been telling since we left Calcutta last, and concealed nothing: and beyond a slight question now and then, Colonel Clive asked nothing, and listened with a rapt attention to the strange, though not unlooked-for tale.

"Could I have done otherwise, sir?" asked Ralph when he had finished. "I could not stay in England as one of them. They were all kind, and what I am, made no difference to my uncles, or Constance, or Mrs. Grover; but when I went to the Towers I saw the difference plainly enough; and when I returned to Bloomsbury Square, my aunt was barely civil—and I felt the reason. God knows, I love them all, sir, as dearly as ever; but they can do without me, and I won't disgrace them, nor repay all their love by remaining, bastard as I am, among them. It's the truth, sir, and I don't mince matters to myself. I only know my darling mother was true in life and true in death; but I won't carry my father's name if I can help it."

"And you are right, Darn—Smithson," cried the Colonel, slapping the table—"right, my boy! I hadn't the heart, that night at Plassey, to tell you I didn't think the certificate worth tuppence, or that it had no witnesses, and wasn't in the same form as my own which my wife keeps—and it's well I didn't; for if I had, there would have been no voyage home, and no good resolution in your heart: always a hankering after that baronetcy, which would have made you either a morbid dreamer, or turned you into a profligate. Enough—for the first time and the last, this subject is mentioned between us; and you know my opinion, if your uncle received the letter I wrote to him about you."

"He did, sir; and I owe to you, I believe, his final decision. You will find a good deal about me, I think, in this letter I have brought you."

"And there will be no turning back, Ralph?"

"None, sir, now; I have no tie, not one, to England, but that infant, and it is already provided for. I am ready to do anything; and wherever there is hard work, in the field or in Cucherry, I pray you to send me. I have not forgotten the language; I find I can talk as well as ever: and I shall imitate Hastings's example and study Persian as fast as I can; and that's all I can say, except—Don't keep me idle."

"Well, I'll settle something about you at the Council to-day," said the Colonel, "and I have but an hour or so to look over all these papers—so I'll leave you here; and as I've caught sight of your Affghan friend several times sitting under the trees, I'd better get out of your way." And he left the room.

"The Affghan fakeerni," said Cassim, "is here, and seems very impatient. Will my lord see her?"

"Certainly," said his master; "bring her in."

"Here, sir? she said she must speak to you in private."

"So she shall; we shall not be interrupted if you will tell the attendants to admit no one."

What could she want? News of Julia? Perhaps some misfortune of her own to tell. And he got up and paced the room rapidly. How many thoughts were thronging into his mind—how many would her presence recall. What had become of his old friends the Rohillas and their gallant chief? As he turned, the transparent bamboo blind which hung outside the door was lifted up, and one said, "He is there—enter;" and a figure advanced to meet him, timidly at first, then with a quivering face hurrying on with outstretched arms, and so sinking down on the ground at his feet with a great sob, and clinging to his knees.

"Sozun!" he said, trying to raise her—"Sozun, dost thou forget me? I am Ralph—Ralph Smithson; not changed, am I?"

"Yes, it is thee," she said, faintly—"I did not know thee at first. Yes, it is thee;" and she rose, and passed her hands over his fair face and soft hair, and over his hands and his dress, and walked round him and felt him all over again, and kissed his hands—then knelt down and put her head on his feet, and remained there weeping. "Do not touch me," she cried; "let me weep—it is good for me. Hast thou forgotten the verse? I have not—day and night, day and night it has been in my memory; and I have prayed Allah to let me see thy dear face once more, and he has heard me. Know thee! Ay—am I not Sozun, and thou my brother? All this is dazzling"—and she pointed to his rich dress—"and unlike the old blue tunic and trousers; but these are thine own eyes and fair face—the most beautiful woman ever looked on."

"Ah, thou must not turn flatterer, Sozun," said Ralph, smiling—"this is not like thyself of old."

"Not for myself—nor for me," she replied eagerly, but blushing deeply. "I am a servant of God, and all love is dead; but for her—for her; dost thou not remember?—hast thou forgotten Noor-ool-Nissa? Thou art not married.

"I am not married," he replied.

"Thank God!" she continued, eagerly; "that was what I feared, and that some beautiful maiden of England would have won you from her. Listen: you left me with her, and the Nawab's mother was kind, and kept me till I was strong and well. She said, 'Be my daughter and stay with me; I am old and feeble now, and thou must not leave me.' She wanted me to come within the screen for my life; but I, a vowed servant of the Lord, vowed to do His work for the poor and sick, I—could not. I have been free all my life—free to go, to come, to live in sin, and now to live to God. I could not stay within; life was dead to me, and all the petty cares and troubles of the zenana hateful to me. So I came away, and have sought thee. Why, Ralph?—because of her. Day after day, night after night, we sat together and spoke of you. I told her all of our sweet time after you were wounded. I told her all. I told her I loved you with a strange love, and I could worship you. Oh, I told her all; more than I dare tell you. Then she thought you would marry Julia, for she was so beautiful; but I said, 'There is one more beautiful than Julia, and he will love her.' O Ralph Smithson, you will love her, for she loves you, and she is so beautiful; and I've come all the way here on foot, or as I could, begging in the name of the Prophet, waiting for news of you; for they told me you would come, and—"

"But," said Ralph, interrupting this eager torrent of speech—"but—"

"I won't have any but in this matter," she continued, with a touch of her old impetuous manner. "It is to be. You can no more resist your destiny, Ralph Smithson, than I can. Look how a hand that you cannot resist has followed you, and sent me, and led you hither: and you and I sit here and talk of her. Oh, my queen, my fairy, my life! Come to her, Ralph; she said she would love you; she confessed to me she would. My oath on it! You will be happy with her, and will bless me all your days. What can I do for you but this? What life can I give for that poor one which you saved twice, and which can but give you another far more precious? Do you doubt? come to Mr. Wharton's lady to-night—she wants to see you, and she will tell you. Come—now—are you busy? Let me go on before. I live with her. She is another sister to me. Wild as I am, she gives me shelter, and bears with me. Come—nay, no excuses; come as you are. I love to see you in your grand English clothes, and the children are crying for you—come!"

"I will come," he replied—"go on; I will be with you presently."

How beautiful she was as she stood before him, raising her arm in the air as she cried 'Come!' A green scarf wrapped around her head, a loose green muslin tunic, and drawers which barely showed her tiny feet, and a green shawl thrown over all; her face glowing, her full grey eye dilated and flashing with the enthusiasm of her thoughts and her message, and a smile of triumph on her lips; browner, hardier-looking than when we remember her first in her luxury; happier too, in spite of her vow of poverty and hardship to come. "Ah! I have no jewels now, Ralph," she said—"none but these poor beads, and they lie on my heart with peace such as strings of pearls and gems never brought me. No dress but these, my grave-clothes; but I am happy—very happy, now thou art come, and I can take thee to her; after that, when the Lord wills, I may die. Come, we lose time," and she passed out.

Noor-ool-Nissa! was she forgotten? I do not think so. When Julia Wharton had her last talk with Ralph Smithson, she had said —"Oh, if she were one of us, and you married her, you would be happy—would she were!" Oftener, at Melcepeth, when he went alone and lay down under one of the noble chestnuts, and looked on the ever-changing surface of the brawling stream, there would come up clear and fresh to his mind the picture of the beautiful girl he had seen in the palace, who had been Julia's protectress and companion in their lonely prison, so calm, so sweet, so plaintive as it were, was her beauty. It seems to me that however long courtships may be, however the end may be crossed or delayed, that it is the one first impression, wherever and however it is given or received, which rules whatever follows. It was an image which Ralph Smithson desired to shut out at first, but which would not be denied. At home, on the voyage out, the nearer he came to India—should he ever see it again? what had become of her? did she remember him? were thoughts which continually recurred with an almost irresistible power to draw him on.

"Pshaw!" he cried, as he sat long upon the sofa after Sozun had left him. "They would never give her to me; her people are princes, and it would be an insult to them to ask for her; and if I did ask, all our folks would laugh at me, and say I was a fool. . . . and yet—"

And yet—and yet, he followed Sozun to the Begum's, as they called her, and the children received him with shouts of joy, hanging about his neck, climbing upon his knees, and tormenting him for stories about England and King George, which he had much ado to invent. Perhaps we may guess also at another subject of discussion in which the women had the best of the argument, and so the time passed till he could stay no longer. That day, I fear, the Don, and the old friends in the counting-house of the Fort, were forgotten.

CHAPTER LXVIII.

MARRIED.

I do not argue for it or against it—I do not say whether it were right or wrong, advisable or inadvisable—I only accept as a fact that, in those early days of Indian life of Englishmen—Englishmen in power and high station—there were many marriages like those of Ralph Smithson's, which grew out of circumstances like his perhaps, or other—what matter? They were, and they were often happy. There were no Englishwomen to marry; men who went home might bring out a wife, and there were some who, like Colonel Clive, met with ladies in India with whom they could make happy alliances; but in 1757 these were few indeed. I have before my memory a beautiful picture by Zoffany, painted long after, in which an English gentleman, in the red uniform coat and laced and frilled costume of the day, is sitting on a low couch in an Eastern room, and a fair, beautiful woman, in a simple native dress of plain white muslin, is looking up to him from the ground where she is sitting with a look of loving truth and quiet happiness, exquisitely depicted, which made a great impression upon me. Many years have passed since then; but the picture, in all its rich detail, is as vividly before me as are the portraits of the Darnells at Granton Towers. It was, perhaps, that of Ralph Smithson and his wife, Noor-ool-Nissa; and I am inclined to think so, because of the attendants with gold and silver sticks in waiting in the verandah beyond, and a moonshee or secretary behind them, who is reading out a long Persian document. Such a scene could only belong to a person of as high diplomatic rank as that which Ralph Smithson reached, and the picture represents a man under forty years of age, which coincides with the date of Zoffany's visit to India.

I say, then, such things were, and this was one of them.

Colonel Clive marched with his army from Calcutta on the 16th November 1757, and Captain Smithson accompanied him, Mr. Warren Hastings having gone to his post at Moorshedabad by express "dawk" to carry out some instructions. I do not think that in the long consultations which occurred at the house of Mr. Wharton's lady there was any difficulty suggested which was not overcome. Insult! It would be an honour. Princes! were not the English princes, to whom Meer Jaffier owed not only his kingdom but his very existence—would not a marriage with his house be a tie between them? Long ago, the dear old Begum at Moorshedabad had said to Noor-ool-Nissa, when Sozun spoke rapturously of the young Englishman, and declared that none but he was fitted for her young mistress, "Oh, that it could be, daughter! Why shouldst thou pine out thy life alone? What can we do for thee? Who among our people could now marry thee? He would be true and faithful till thou art dead—ay, till the judgment. They are all true, the English—not like us, false and treacherous." If they were not all true, the grand old lady believed from her heart they were, for her husband, Ali Verdy Khan, had thought so, and to its close this belief was part of her life.

So in many a winning form those Noor-ool-Nissa most loved in life brought the subject forward day after day, month after month: and in the quiet seclusion of their hareem, the tales Sozun could tell were listened to with increased and increasing interest. It was true the old Begum often despaired, and that the gentle heart of her daughter-in-law, clinging to a hope she dared hardly define, was often mournful and sad. But the hope did not die: and we can conceive how easily, undisturbed and unaffected by other influences, it was not only maintained but increased. I think we all worship the ideal more than the real. Is it any wonder, then, that what she remembered was the more tenderly cherished?

I suppose Sozun felt that she had conquered, for she suddenly disappeared; and before the English force reached Moorshedabad, she broke suddenly into the old Begum's apartments, with a wild joyous cry of, "O mother! O sister! he is come, and I have seen him. He will be here with the army—O my Peri, make ready for him, for he loves thee!"

There were no long preparations, and there could be no courtship. When Ralph Smithson had paid a visit to the dear old Begum, who sat behind a screen and welcomed him with true affection; when he had made a formal proposal for Noor-ool-Nissa, and heard his acceptance spoken in low faltering tones by her, seated as she was by the old lady; when this was ratified by the Begum, who conveyed the Nawab's consent, already gained through Mr. Watts; when the usual formalities of sugar-candy and spices, of a dress of honour, and other gifts had been interchanged—he went to Mr. Clive and explained to him what he was going to do. Perhaps Mr. Clive was not quite satisfied at first: "I'd rather you'd chosen an English girl, Ralph, as I have done," he said; "but after all, this is honest and above board, and, considering all things, I think, were I you, I'd do the same. You at least know what she is, and there's no disgrace in marrying a native lady of rank, with a handsome dowry to boot."

There was no looking back either: for we all know what had preceded this event, and what had become of the only two women by whom the young man's heart had been touched. He had deliberately cut away all the bonds which might have connected him with England. He had cast his lot with the English progress in India; and this would be a new tie to the people whom he was growing to love. Above all, there was something so strange in the wild Affghan girl's persistence that he would return, when there was, as he had thought, little chance of their ever meeting again—that, as he reflected upon it, I can believe that a tinge of superstitious feeling may have arisen within him which was not without its effect. All he begged for was that there might be no parade or ceremony; and in a marriage of this kind native customs do not prescribe any. A few near relatives were assembled; and on his own part, Ralph took Mr. Warren Hastings as a witness to the contract and marriage. Ralph did not understand the four chapters of the Koran which were read to him, nor the articles of belief; but when the "Nika" was to be read, and a small white hand was put out from behind the screen, he grasped it with a hearty, honest clasp, and repeated, after the Kazee, "that he took Noor-ool-Nissa to be his wife with all his heart and soul; and that through joy and sorrow, sickness and health, he would protect and cherish her as long as he had life." Then the prayer and blessing followed, "that mutual love might reign between them as that of Adam and Eve, Abraham and Sarah." and many congratulations and blessings were echoed from all around, which perhaps need not be enumerated, and the guests departed. Then the screen was drawn up by Sozun, who was within; and raising Noor-ool-Nissa, she led her gently forward and put her hand into her husband's.

"Be true and faithful, O my sister!" she said, "as he will be. Never leave him. If he be sick, tend him; if he be wounded, let no one help him but thee. As the Lord hath heard my prayer for this happy day, so He will hear it for that true love which will never die between ye—and thus may the blessing of the poor servant of God rest upon ye both for ever. Ameen and ameen!" Then Sozun hastily bent down and touched their feet, and as Ralph drew his wife to him, and her head sank upon his shoulder, the Affghan girl turned to leave them. At the doorway she cast one last hurried, tearful look upon them, and fled away—where, they could never discover. All they knew was, that she had joined a company of her people going to their homes; and Ralph and his wife loved to think of her as one who—Magdalen as she was—had been accepted to work out a life of penitence.

Shall I tell how Ralph Smithson took his place among the working men of that period, where he served, and what he did? I think the histories which have been written of the time would tell the story better, and that, too, of his friend and patron, Robert Clive: so I forbear. But this I know, that wherever there was work to be done, whether in the field or in native durbars, Ralph Smithson was ever a true and valuable agent and commander. When Monsieur Bussy had to be driven out of the Circars, and the French power extinguished—when Sir Eyre Coote fought the battle of Buxar—when Colonel Clive was organising a government of Bengal, and step by step laying the foundation of the English power which now rules there—Ralph Smithson's mind was ever one on which he could rely for calm counsel, and that advocacy of native rights which his countrymen were slow to recognise, and which had to grow up through a rough experience. He saw his friend return to Bengal as a peer of England; he saw him rise superior to the detraction which the fierce party spirit of the time evoked; and when the mutinous combinations of the civil and military services had to be quelled—when laws and regulations had to be framed and put into execution—Lord Clive had many stedfast friends to help him, but none, though there were more brilliant men among them, more trusted than Ralph Smithson. I say, therefore, let history tell what was done in that brief period from 1757 to 1767, when, early in the latter year, Lord Clive left the scene of his greatness for ever—not I. How over all India the political power of England had been not only recognised but established; how ambassadors came from distant princes to Clive, beseeching alliance and protection; how over those provinces where Englishmen had been traders on sufferance, and where a crowd of them had perished miserably in a dungeon, they now ruled supreme, feared and yet respected; and how trade and general prosperity, with security, were advancing beyond belief. I say again, history tells all this wondrous tale for those who choose to read it; and those who do so will find the truth far more interesting and romantic than any fiction that I could write for them.

They often wrote from England to Ralph Smithson — Roger Darnell, Mrs. Grover, Constance, and sometimes George Elliot and Mr. Wilson, by turns; and he heard all he cared to know of what was passing. As he had anticipated, and hoped, the past was forgotten between George Elliot and Mrs. Wharton; and iu the complete redemption of Mr. Elliot's property, Mrs. Wharton found a more useful and pleasant investment for her large fortune than she had ever dared to anticipate. When Colonel Clive went first to England, he pressed his young friend to return with him: but this was declined, as we can well imagine it would be. When, as Lord Clive, he returned home for good, his friend was alike immovable: and Clive knew that he was happier there doing his duty, than living a life which, at the best, must be one of comparative obscurity and inaction. Noor-ool-Nissa lived secluded, except to her husband's intimate friends; but with Clive there was no reserve. He could speak to her very indifferently, to be sure, in her own language, but he grew to love her—and he took away with him many memorials of her which she perhaps little suspected—an odd slipper, a handkerchief, and the like—which he would show to friends in England as relics of the dearest and most beautiful native lady he had ever seen. "He did not wonder Smithson had married her," he used to tell them. "What more could an English wife have been to him?"

Perhaps, indeed, not so much of comfort in those rough times in India, which, except at the Presidencies, as they began to be called presently, were little fitted for the conventional requirements and social habits of English ladies accustomed to gay lives, and little tolerant, either by habit or education, for the self-reliant monotony of out-stations. We know how few Englishwomen went to India unmarried in those days, and those there could not have been very attractive either as to manners, education, or connection. So the longer he lived, the better Ralph Smithson was satisfied that he had done right. I do not think the simple, trusting, affectionate character of the man altered with time: but, on the contrary, increased in strength. His heart had yearned for something to love, and had found it. We know why he could not look back upon his past experiences with any future hope, except of that sisterly love from Constance, which never changed throughout his life. Who, of his own rank in life, would have accepted him in England?—for he was in spirit still a Darnell of Melcepeth. His cousin Dolly, perhaps, might have followed his fortunes: but her mother's opinions had undergone no change, and she herself had no attractions for him. "What could I have done with her here?" he would ask of himself, as he underwent many a privation and discomfort, which showed little of Indian luxury. "She'd have borne it for a while, and then been off to England, sick or well," he thought, "and left me to take care of myself, and send her money, like the rest of 'em."

I say, then, for all these reasons, Ralph Smithson had no misgivings or regrets. He was very happy, after his own quiet fashion, with the woman he had chosen. I have never claimed for him any high standard of intellectual attainment; such was not very common in 1757 even in England, and in India still rarer. What powers he possessed led him more into eastern than western literature, and on this ground his wife could help him very materially. She had been well educated after the fashion of her people. She read Persian authors easily, and was not unacquainted with Arabic; and thus their tastes and occupations blended pleasantly. Those who first began to study Oriental languages in Bengal, went deeper into them than men do now, and their works gained for them credit, and fame too. There was more, it was thought, to be gained from the stores of knowledge locked up in them than has since been discovered; but that did not affect the enthusiasm of the first explorers, and among them our friend was a zealous partisan. Gradually, too, a knowledge of native character, Hindu and Mahomedan, was opening out; of manners and customs which have now lost the charm and freshness of first acquaintance, and to the comprehension of which his wife's experience was a sure key. As a busy diplomatist —an active, hearty sportsman—and, after his fashion, a profound student, I can very well imagine Ralph Smithson to have been full of occupation; and whether in the busy duties of the field, or the pleasant quiet life at home, the ardent sympathy, the practical companionship, of his wife, were ever present; and gradually, indeed, a higher standard of love and respect arose than perhaps he had at first contemplated.

And his wife! Perhaps I ought not to have shut her out so entirely from the observation as has been the case for reasons that will be apparent. What could I have told of her in that constant seclusion, except that she was patient and submissive, bearing her lot with the calm reliance of her faith? Julia Wharton had proved her, Sozun had proved her, and both were women whose sufferings had excited her pity, though arising from causes in which wrong had been done to herself. Such a woman, lovely, too, as she was in person, could not change to him, Ralph had thought, and he was right. The originally loving, beneficent nature had its power increased by the comparatively free life which opened upon Noor-ool-Nissa; the perceptions of her intellect were enlarged and purified; and when she compared the steady affection, the high moral principle, and the active mind of her husband, with what she knew of the sloth, the sensuality, and immorality of her countrymen—she felt herself raised to the one the more entirely, as she comprehended and contrasted it with the other.

Oh what love she bore him! she could never tell it; but he felt and acknowledged it as a gentle ever-pervading presence, never importunate, never exacting, humble even to him; and yet how confident—defiant of all else—how triumphant in its knowledge and belief of his faith and truth!

If I say such men as Clive respected and loved her among her husband's countrymen, it will not be deemed strange that among her own people she should have attained a like respect and honour. Some sneered at first, and possibly to the last. The offspring of a noble house to ally herself with a Feringi—was degradation; and the wives of men of her own rank sometimes looked down upon her, or affected to patronise her. But Noor-ool-Nissa took her own place and maintained it. She went into camp, into actual war with her husband, none the less that noble ladies sneered or wondered at what she did. She refused to become the channel of representations to her husband, or to exert the private influence she was supposed to possess; but her practical charities never ceased: they were a stream full of benevolence, and to her the poor went without apprehension. To apply to the Begum Sahib in any distress, was to find unfailing comfort and relief from high to low. "She is our mother," the people would say lovingly of her; and they had many a familiar name for her in their houses, and many a song was written in her honour by local poets, and sung at festivals; and, as the poor ground their flour at the quern in early morning for the day's bread, and sang merrily as the mill went round, "the mother's" name was oftener on their lips than any other.

The mother's! Ah! if she could have kept what was once sent her, her daily prayer would have been answered, but that was not to be. One girl, beautiful as a lily, blossomed for a while and died; none followed, and thus Noor-ool-Nissa's life grew more and more into her husband's as time passed. I mean no profanity when I compare it with that beautiful womanly character of Ruth, which combines so purely the simplicity, the energy, and the devotion of love—better not told here, perhaps, because consisting of an aggregate of years and events which made up her life.

So twenty years passed—twenty years of war, of peace, and unceasing labour in both, without change and without rest. Rank had come, and wealth more than Ralph Smithson needed, but the light of his life left him—the light of trust and faith which had illumined and cheered all the dark places of his heart with a mellow lustre, went out—and left him—lonely, very lonely. That place could not be filled—he did not wish to fill it; and his ties to India were fast breaking. He believed he had done what he could, and to say the truth he belonged to the past more than to the present. Clive had come, had gone, and was dead. English power had grown, and was fast overspreading the land; but there were events in progress of which he did not, and could not, approve. To the natives an almost reign of terror had begun, which made them fly to the protection of one of their oldest and ablest advocates with a confidence which General Smithson could not refuse. Remonstrances, private or public, produced no effect, and were perhaps ill-received; the younger generation of rulers and strivers thought themselves wiser than the old, and heeded no cautions. So sick at heart, he perceived plainly that he had lived out his time; he had done what he could, and must give way to others; above all, the one precious bond which had tied him to India was broken. It was time to go, and he set his house in order to depart. He could look to many a loving heart in England ready to receive and welcome him, and so far as letters could serve, he had, as I have recorded, kept up a constant communication with those we know of. All seemed to be sweet and fresh there, and he could look forward with many happy anticipations of the rest and peace which he needed.

Not long before he left the station, there came to him one day an Affghan soldier, who said a holy woman, who lived at Jellalabad, and who was held in high reverence there, had given him a letter, which she said would insure him a reward for safe delivery, and untying his turban, he presented an envelope, upon which Ralph Smithson looked with a strange interest. The superscription was correct; but within there was no letter, or address, or signature, and for a few moments he was puzzled by the words written there, as it seemed from the spelling, in an unknown tongue; but the mist cleared up, and to Ralph they were plain enough. I need hardly record them again; I think, perhaps, they may not be quite forgotten by any reader of this history. Below there was a line: "I am well. Do not forget me: I have not forgotten,"—and that was all. It read like his dismissal—the last cry of truth and hope, coming to him over the interval of many years.

CHAPTER LXIX.

CONCLUSION.

After twenty years! How few return after such an unbroken absence and find all the old loved ones to welcome them! But for Ralph Smithson there were many; both his uncles were living—aged, of course, but hale and in possession of all their faculties. At eighty-eight the grand figure of the venerable Sir Geoffrey Darnell was a sight to see, as he stood upon the terrace at Melcepeth, with a hale old lady beside him, and a handsome, active youth showing him the finest salmon which had been caught in Coquet that season, just below the castle in the kelpie's pool, where one Mistress Constance Darnell once distinguished herself. I think we can guess who they are.

"And he's coming home for good and aye now, Ralph," says the baronet, cheerily; "and we'll all be happy again: and he'll help thee with the fish, my lad. To think of the boy being Sir Ralph Smithson too, Grover! mind that—*Sir* Ralph."

They were all to meet there to welcome the General, who had but stayed in London to receive the knighthood he had been promised in India, and which he had richly earned. Was there ever a happier party met at the old castle? I think not. Why, Constance Countess of Whinborough's children are a merry party of themselves, and some of them grown up nearly into men and women; and there are others younger, who ride on General Smithson's back as he crawls about the floor, making an elephant of himself, with a row of noisy urchins astride on his back driving him, as he has taught them, with Hindostani cries of "Mul, chul," and other adjurations; and doing many more foolish things than I care to record, after all his Indian wisdom and pomp. And a great coachful of happy Elliot faces has come from Wooler Hall; and a buxom matronly woman with them, who, never heeding her husband, straightway throws herself into General Smithson's arms, and cries and sobs there as impetuously as she did once at Moorshedabad, but with far different thoughts at her heart; and kisses his face all over—"and I don't care a bit," she exclaims to her husband, who is grasping the hand held out to him behind—"not one bit for you, sir—for he's the dearest and truest friend I ever had in all my life, and I love him—Oh, how I love him!"

So I am quite sure, dear reader, that you feel already how happy they all are, and I need not tell you more about them; or how rejoiced the General has been to see Sybil Morton's son grown up to such future promise, and so like what his dear mother used to be. If the two grand old brothers grieve that their nephew is not what they hoped and prayed he might be, they have many thanks to render for bountiful mercies which have been dispensed to them all with a full hand. Uncle Roger has been consulting with the Earl whether, for special services, the baronetcy could not devolve upon the General after all under the name of Darnell, and the Earl is quite sure that his friend Mr. Pitt will make no objection, and the thing can be done—and so they sound the General upon the subject: but he will not hear of it, for there is still the bar sinister between him and the Darnells for ever; and very reluctantly, they give the matter up.

Then the women took counsel together—Constance and dear old Grover and Mrs. Elliot—and decided that Sir Ralph must marry. Why! was he not in the very prime of his life, and one of the very handsomest men in England? India hadn't made him a bit brown, or yellow, or sallow; nor old-fashioned, nor pompous, nor anything nasty, like other nabobs. Ralph Forster was in no want of his money either; Peed and Mr. Sanders between them, had nursed his father's property and managed his affairs right well, and he was fast rising in the great house of Roger Darnell & Company. Who was there to inherit the wealth Ralph had brought home? and so forth. And one day, the Countess being selected as the most impressive spokeswoman, she went after him to the river, and found him lying under the old chestnut-tree alone—it was too hot to fish—with his creel beside him and his rod idle upon the grass; and she sat down by him as she used to do in old times, and after a while told him what they thought. But none of them had anticipated the effect it had upon him, and it was certain that from that day forward the subject was mentioned no more. It is ever a painful thing to see a strong man weep; but, as Constance told her message and pressed him to acquiesce, or at least to give them some hope, she saw her cousin's broad chest heave, and a burst of passionate weeping follow, for which she was ill prepared.

"No, no, Conny dear," he said, when he had grown calmer, though his voice was still choked with heavy sobs; "if you love me, never mention this again—never any of you. Will you promise me this? For eighteen years—a little—soft—face—rested here—here on my breast, and nestled close to my heart—in such quiet love—as I thank God to have been permitted to enjoy on earth; and, Conny—she—she—died here peacefully—sleeping her life away.—Could—could I—"

"Oh! no, no! Ralph, my own dear cousin, forgive me!" she cried, sobbing too. "The first time and the last, and never again will we mention this;" nor did they.

All that we remember were not there: some had already gone to their rest. Mr. Smithson and John Sanders, his eldest sister, and dear old Nanny Keene were all gone on before. Miss Sanders no longer lived in the old rooms in Lombard Street; they were too large and desolate, and some friends had given her quiet apartments in their house at Clapham. Ralph Forster, who is a clever young fellow, and has already attained Mr. Sanders' old place in the office, has chambers there; so Roger Darnell & Company still exist in name, and in deed too, for the grand old merchant still comes every day in his coach to sign cheques and papers, and the time-honoured firm will continue as long as he lives. Mrs. Darnell is dead, but her daughters all married before she was called away, and in their various conditions of life were well settled. Sir Geoffrey pressed his nephew to reside near him, and to purchase an estate by Melcepeth, which was in the market; but Sir Ralph, though he passed as much of his time as he could with his uncle, found that he could still be useful to India, and after some few changes, settled down in a pleasant old-fashioned mansion near Kensington, and lived there.

. . . .

Another twenty years is past. How many have dropped away into the eternal tide which sweeps majestically on! Sir Ralph Smithson has laid his uncles to rest. Miss Sanders is gone. Melcepeth is dismantled, for it had grown too rickety to repair, and the old woodwork was quite rotten. Constance and her noble husband live at the Towers, and Sir Ralph often goes to them, as he does every year to shoot grouse on Cheviot with Mr. George Elliot. Many of the children in both families are married; so is Ralph Forster, and from uncle, Sir Ralph is promoted to the dignity of "grandfather," which he enjoys immensely, and is not yet beyond the effort of making himself into an occasional elephant: and there is many a reunion gathering at the dear old place at Kensington, when the families come to town. An old lady, still brisk and strong, but with the whitest hair, and softest downy cheeks that ever were seen, lives with him, and keeps his house for him, and it is one of the most hospitable of the neighbourhood, a place where no gloom is ever known to dwell. Her name is Grover—do you remember her?

There charity is dispensed without ostentation, but with a most liberal hand. There statesmen, both of England and India, soldiers, authors, poets, artists, merchants, and great lawyers, mingle with the proudest nobility of the land, on the same common ground of strong intellect, and are proud to call Sir Ralph Smithson their friend. Again and again he has been solicited to take a government in India, and I think he might have succeeded Mr. Warren Hastings as Governor-General, if he would, but the honour was declined. His public life had ended, not his private life of useful and benevolent occupation; and at the India House his presence is ever welcome. Sir Ralph is become a Director of the East India Company: and at its Council he fights the cause of the native people, whom he still loves. He has no belief in the stability of native princes as independent powers, nor has he any good opinion of them; but he will not have them interfered with, so long as they keep their faith, and when they fail in that, and are conquered, he will not regret them. He has larger views of an English future in India than is perhaps relished by his coadjutors, and he believes that in years to come the spread of the mighty power which Clive founded will be as irresistible as it is beneficent. Apparently Sir Ralph has good health, and yet—and yet— Mistress Grover is often more anxious than she cares to acknowledge about spasms which come on suddenly, and which the "drops" do not always alleviate.

The house is handsome and commodious, and the General has his own suite of apartments, in which he can be private when he pleases. He is seldom without guests, old Indian friends, Whinborough or

Wooler children, or London acquaintances, who are grown to be numerous. None, however, intrude upon the General when he says after breakfast—"Grover, I'm going to my room;" or, "I've letters to write—don't let me be disturbed," and so his time is his own. There are two apartments leading from his study, one of which used to be the dressing-room of the suite, and is where Sir Ralph sleeps on a small camp-bed which he brought from India. The other is a large bedroom, and into this no one has ever been permitted to enter. It is known to the servants as "master's own room," and is looked upon with a sort of awe. When Mrs. Grover one day said to him, "Really General, you *must* allow the maids to clean out that room; it *must* be inches deep in dust by this time," she had received so sharp a rebuff for what he chose to call her "infernal curiosity," that she never dared mention the subject again; and if she dared not, assuredly no one else could.

In this room several chests had been deposited when the house was occupied; and a peculiar safety-lock kept on the door, the key of which hung around the General's neck, together with a small bag like an amulet. These matters seemed mysterious at first, but by degrees all had grown accustomed to them. Housemaids came and went, and nothing was ever altered. They knew that the General opened the mysterious room door sometimes, drew up the blinds, and opened the windows; and he occasionally asked for a brush, and himself brushed the carpet, and dusted the bed-hangings. Once, too, the housemaid heard him through the floor praying aloud; and when she told this in the kitchen in confidence, the room became more sacred than ever in the eyes of the household, and "Master always says his prayers there," was quite enough to keep it so.

Prayers! how many had ascended from that bedside! How many had been heard already and graciously answered, he knew who prayed there, and the All-Merciful who heard and granted them.

One morning—"I really will go to the doctor, Grover, and get something, if this pain lasts till to-morrow." "There now, I've promised you, so don't fidget," he said at breakfast; "I've just a few letters to write, and then we'll walk over to Ralph's; so get through your housekeeping, old woman, and I'm sure a good walk is all I want."

And the General got up, strolled into the garden, upon which the breakfast-room opened, cut a handful of roses carefully, and went up-stairs to his study. For some time they heard him moving about, and they knew that he had gone into the bedroom; but no one noticed what was of almost daily occurrence. Then Mistress Grover came down-stairs, put on her gloves, went into the garden, pulled some flowers, and returned, but he had not come. "Go and see whether Sir Ralph is ready, James," she said to the servant who answered the bell; "tell him I'm waiting for him."

The man went, knocked at the study, got no answer; called out his message, and knocked again and again; but all was still He grew anxious, opened the door, and saw no one: but the key was in the door of the bedroom, which was ajar, and with habitual respect, he called out as he approached it, "If you please, Sir Ralph, Mistress Grover's waiting for you." Still there was no reply. Was it fancy, or a passing breath of wind? but the servant thought he heard a faint sigh, which was not repeated, and, unable to restrain himself any longer, threw open the door. Then a strange sight met his eyes—one at which the simple fellow stood awe-struck, and trembling.

A faint odour, as if of Eastern perfumes and spices, pervaded the room. On the bed lay a still female figure, dressed in gorgeous apparel of cloths of gold and silver, and the finest Indian muslin, and a few fresh roses were strewn about it and placed near the face. A gleam of sunshine, resting upon the bed, flashed back from the glittering stuffs and jewels which were on the wrists, arms, and neck of what lay there, with a strange, unearthly lustre—a mockery of the pale, wax-like face above them, lying in its calm sleep of Death. Beside the bed, the tall figure of the General leaned over it motionless. One arm was thrown round what rested there, the other hand still grasped some fresh roses; and his head, with the sunlight playing amidst his soft white hair, rested upon that arm, close to the heart which in life had beat only for him. There was a bright, sweet smile upon his still ruddy lips, and the dim, glazed eyes were turned to the face near them; but he was quite dead—and the sound the servant had heard was the last sigh of Ralph Darnell.

They were buried together privately, as the last words recorded by him requested. They must have been written under a presentiment of death, just before he went to her; for the pen lay beside the paper on his table, and the ink in it was not dry. I may copy the last few words of this memorandum, now yellow and faded, though written in his bold, strong hand—without a tremor.

"I come, O sweet spirit! surely soon now—soon, dear Lord! I am ready, quite ready, even now. Once more I write—

"'He that goeth his way weeping, and beareth good seed, shall doubtless come again with joy.' Joy! Oh, what joy and peace! Mother—Wife!"

There was no more. As he had written these last words, he had taken up the roses, gone into the room, strewn some over her, and there died—died peacefully.

Fade out, O dim memories of early trial, of early error, and yet—of much earthly happiness! Fade out and die with him, in a peaceful calm and trust like his. I believe that many of our earlier Indian servants had their sore trials, and that out of them grew that devotion to India and its people which only ceased with life. By such men was the power of England established there; and as a glorious company, peace and honour be to their memories! Since they lived, three generations have passed away. Mightier battles than Plassey have been fought and won, and its anniversary of a hundred years, as was clearly foretold, brought with it misery and suffering such as we still hear and think of with a shudder, and fervently pray may never return. But English might and fortitude prevailed, and still prevail, to be used, as we may hope and trust, to fulfil the inscrutable purposes of Him by whose aid they are continued—in a splendour of power and usefulness before which all others that have passed away are becoming dim and faded.

THE END.